A THRONE
OF BONES

CASTALIA HOUSE

ARTS OF DARK AND LIGHT

BOOK ONE

A THRONE OF BONES

VOX DAY

CASTALIA HOUSE

A Throne of Bones

Vox Day

Published by Castalia House
Kouvola, Finland
www.castaliahouse.com

Cover by Kirk DouPounce

To Spacebunny, whom I love truly, madly, and deeply.

ACKNOWLEDGEMENTS

Thanks to Jeff, for his courageous vision and baseless confidence. 494 days of madness! Jamsco, for his keen and Christian eye. JartStar, for his excellent map and his encouragement. Markku, for his inimitable attention to detail. The kids, for their patience and understanding when Daddy is writing. And no, you can't read it, not yet. Kirk DouPonce, for yet another spectacular cover. The Dread Ilk of Vox Popoli, for their enthusiasm. And my mentor, the Original Cyberpunk, for finally convincing me to focus on the story, not the subtext.

Ecclesiastes 9:9

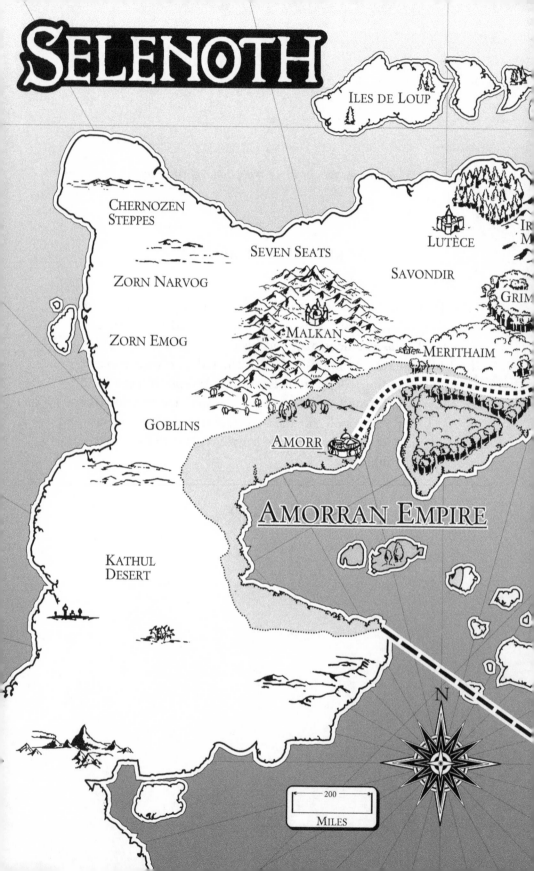

RAKNARBORG

HAGAHORN

USKILUHK

ZOTH
OMMOG

UMMAT-MOR

ELEBRION

KURS-MAGOG   GOG

KIR DONAS

Amorr & Allied Cities

1. Amorr
2. Marruvium
3. Aeternum
4. Caelignus
5. Larinum
6. Silarea
7. Telinus
8. Salventum
9. Galabrus
10. Quinqueterra
11. Trivicum
12. Tarquinia
13. Vallyria

Amorran Provinces

20. Illyris Baara
21. Cynothicum
22. Thaparus
23. Epra
24. Mindoros
25. Sablema
26. Thursia
27. Mirbonensis
28. Andriscedon
29. Terracondus
30. Orontis
31. Ptolus Triticus
32. Bithnya
33. Avarus
34. Gorignia

AMORRAN EMPIRE

PROLOGUE

WHO are you?"

Ahenobarbus stared at the faded painting in the gilded frame mounted on the wall in front of him. The flickering candles cast an eerie glow upon the scene: Six armed men stood over the fallen body of a seventh man, from whose face Ahenobarbus, or as others reverently called him, His Sanctified Holiness Charity IV, couldn't take his eyes. The victim was nude, and though there were six assassins in the painting, the body bore seven wounds. Someone had struck twice.

"Why did they kill you?"

The painting was entitled *Decessus Inmortuus*, "The Death of the Undying." It had once been considered a masterpiece. Then it had spent decades deep underground in the storage vaults. His Sanctified Holiness was now standing before it in an insignificant room occasionally used for receptions by minor functionaries deep in the bowels of the sanctal palace. The painting had recently been moved here from the storage areas, but this wasn't exactly an honored location.

The bright colors and the flat, unnatural perspective were typical of the artist: Mariattus, the great Nardine. Only the face of the stabbed man was facing toward the viewer. The six assassins were all in profile. It was almost as if Mariattus had intended to draw particular attention to the face.

Ahenobarbus reached out an arthritic finger and lightly traced the outline of the fallen man's jaw. "And how can it be that you are not dead?"

There was a soft, respectful knock on the door behind him.

"Enter."

Through the door came Giovannus Falconius Valens. Even dressed as a simple monk, as he was now, Valens could never be mistaken for anything but a noble prince of the Church. He was a tall, handsome man with a demeanor that most perceived as arrogant, though as his sometime confessor, Ahenobarbus knew better. But Valens was the very man whom Ahenobarbus required now.

"Holiness." Valens kneeled and kissed the sacred ring of office that adorned his right hand. "How may I be of service to you in this... unusual setting? I was surprised when Father Hortensius said you wanted me in the vaults. I half expected to find you knee deep in dust and relics. Are you well? I saw Gennarus Vestinae led the evening mass."

"I am as well as any man with twelve years more than his allotted four score and ten may hope to be, my son." Ahenobarbus led him to the painting. "What I require of you at the present is your eyes. I suspect they are keener than my own. This picture here. When you look at the man who has been struck down by the others, what do you see?"

Valens frowned, and his eyebrows momentarily rose. No doubt he found the request puzzling. But the obedient habits of a lifetime reasserted themselves, and he turned his attention toward the painting. For a moment, there was silence, and then it was broken by a sudden intake of breath.

"By the Virgin!" he exclaimed softly.

"So, you see it too," Ahenobarbus said. It was not a question.

"I do, Holiness."

"And what do you make of the resemblance to Laris Sebastius?"

"I... I could not say. A coincidence, mayhap? Perhaps even a descendant?" Valens took a candle and used it to peer more closely at the victim's face. "The likeness is uncanny, especially when the limitations of Mariattus's primitive technique are taken into account."

Ahenobarbus smiled. "Of course you would recognize the brush. How does a poor monk come to know so much of art and culture?"

Valens shrugged slightly. "I fancy myself an ascetic aesthete, Your Holiness."

"Have you seen this painting before?"

"I have not previously had the privilege," Valens said. "The style and theme is readily apparent, of course, as Pisanus describes it in his catalogue of the ancients. It could not be anyone but Mariattus. That peculiar shade of orange—you see it there—he habitually used it in the place of yellow, and it is unmistakable."

Valens set the candle down. "If I may hazard a guess, I should venture to say this is *Excessum Inmortuus*. No, I fear my memory fails me. *Decessus Inmortuus*. Painted sometime around the year 185 Provitiatus for a noble of the Severan house. It came into the possession of the Church after the fall of Andronis and the establishment of the Republic. I did not know it had been removed from the vaults. Had I known, I would have come to see it sooner. It is a joy to behold."

"You have a prodigious talent, my son."

"Mariattus had a prodigious talent. I am merely blessed to appreciate his skill."

"Even so."

"We are but as the Immaculate has made us, Holiness."

"Aptly put. And yet, if this is not a coincidence, if this is not a trick of the familial bloodlines, then we must ask what this is that the Immaculate has made here? Long life is not sinful in itself, of course. Indeed, there are elves who were old when this was first painted. But this is no elf. Can it be there are truly men still living among us who live five hundred years or more?"

"I should not have imagined so, Holiness. And yet, we know from the Inviolate Word that the First Men were said to live as many as two thousand years. It has always been assumed that the great decline in the lifespan of Man was a result of the departure of the Lesser Gods from Tellus Demittus, but the proposed connection between the two events has never been more than circumstantial. Oxonus emphasized that the Inviolate itself is mute on the matter."

"It is conceivable, then. Difficult to credit, unlikely, and yet conceivable even so." Ahenobarbus turned his eyes back to the painting and the disturbingly familiar face of the fallen man. "We must know more of this, Valens, and we must know it soon. Preparations for the investitures have already begun, but we cannot permit them to proceed when we are not even sure we are dealing with a mortal man or not. To welcome our elder brothers within the bosom of Holy Mother Church was one thing, but to permit one who may be unsouled to advance higher in the hierarchy would be unthinkable!"

"Without doubt, Holiness. But the candidates will not begin their fasts for another three days. The ceremony could be postponed."

"If necessary, we shall do so. Speak to no one of this. Tomorrow we shall order an inquisition into each of the candidates. That should suffice to allay any suspicions that our attention has been drawn to a particular individual. You will be assigned to the candidate of interest. The inquisition will spark a few rumors, which is to be regretted. But even that may prove beneficial. Even the most outlandish whispers will appear far more credible than our true concern."

Valens bowed deeply. "You honor me with your confidence, Sanctified Father. If there is aught amiss, rest assured I shall uncover it."

"Three days, Valens. We must take a decision in three days. In the meantime, we shall arrange for a reasonable excuse for delay, in the event one is required."

"A propitious timeframe, Holiness." Valens smiled faintly. "The Immaculate shattered the Gates of Hell in three days. I shall pray that the secrets of the *Inmortuus* will reveal themselves with similar alacrity."

"We shall do likewise, my son." Ahenobarbus extended his hand.

Valens knelt again to kiss it. "Your blessing, Holiness?"

"*Beatus homo qui invenit sapientiam.*" He lightly sketched three lines on the younger man's forehead, and his finger left a trail of white light glowing briefly behind where it had touched. "*In hoc signo vinces, in nomine Puri, in nomine Immaculati, in nomine Domini.*"

Valens, his eyes closed, waited until the light faded from his skin. Then he rose gracefully from his knees, bowed again, turned, and walked quickly out of the room. He closed the door silently behind him.

Ahenobarbus, who very rarely felt either sanctified or holy, picked up the candle Valens had used, and he held it closer to the painting, peering closely at the rough texture of the brushwork. He had heard that artists often incorporated hidden meanings into their works. Was there any significance to the seven wounds or the six killers? To the fact that only one face could be seen? And then there was the title of the work— "Death of the Undying"—was that not a sign of some import? There were so many questions.

He wondered what would happen if he ordered the palace guards to bring the bishop concerned down to this room to confront his painted doppelganger from the distant past. A crude stratagem, perhaps even a dangerous one, but it might be that a direct approach would be the simplest path to the answers required.

No. There was always time for that later if more subtle means of inquiry failed.

He looked at the painting one last time. It occurred to him that if Valens could learn who the six were, or who or what they were supposed to represent, that might eventually lead him to their victim, be he dead or alive these five centuries past. He reminded himself to tell Valens that on the morrow.

"Who are you?" he asked the man in the painting again. "And if indeed they killed you, did you remain in the grave?"

Priests, bishops, and even princes of the Church hastened to get out of Valens's way as he followed the cerulengus hurrying through the palace in his full episcopal vestments. Valens himself was followed by no fewer than twenty-one Curian guards, each ceremonially clad in gleaming white-lacquered armor and red cloaks. Cries of astonishment and alarm trailed in their wake, but the elderly cerulengus did not so much as slow his stride for any man, regardless of his rank.

Valens heard the whispers as they passed.

"What is happening?" he heard a grey-haired archbishop whisper to a Jamite priest as he walked past them. "Has someone been arrested?"

The little priest was shaking his head, his eyes wide with astonishment. But Valens couldn't tell if the priest's look was from ignorance, from the sight of armed men marching through the Sanctal Palace with grim purpose, or simply from the fact that the Archbishop of Lanobus had deigned to speak to him.

They approached the bedchamber suite that belonged to His Holiness. Both sets of doors were open, so the cerulengus entered the bedchamber without knocking, as did Valens. The remainder of his entourage took up positions outside the doors, in case anyone thought to disturb this most holy of tasks.

The Sanctified Father was lying on his bed, still wearing his nightrobe, with the rich velvet covers of his bedding drawn up to his chest. He was being attended by two Ospedalers. The older monk was the first to notice their entry and quickly dropped to one knee. His companion quickly followed suit. Four princes of the Church watched over the Ospedalers, one positioned at each of the bed's four corners. Valens took note of them— Baccius Antonius, Paulus Masella, Ildebrando Ortognan, and Mamercus Severus Furius—as the cerulengus turned his attention to the Ospedaler who was the senior medicus.

"You have listened?"

"Yes, Eminence. His heart is still."

"You have attempted the mirror?"

"Yes, Eminence. His breath is still."

"You have seen no sign of anything untoward?"

"No, Eminence. His flesh is unmarred. His scent is clean." The cerulengus nodded, and when he did not ask another question, the two Ospedalers filed solemnly from the bedchamber to join the soldiers and the growing body of ecclesiasticals standing just outside the second set of doors.

Valens watched, bearing witness on behalf of the Sacred College, as the cerulengus approached the motionless figure of His Holiness, leaned over him, and withdrew a small iron hammer from the dark blue leather bag tied to the sash around his waist. It was engraved with the insignia of House Flavius, a bear and a wolf rampant. The cerulengus reached out, placed it over the Sanctiff's forehead, and gently tapped the hammer against the white skin stretched out like a papyrus over the elderly man's skull.

"Quintus Flavius Ahenobarbus," he whispered softly. There was a hush in the room. No one moved. No one breathed, least of all His Sanctified Holiness Charity IV. The cerulengus tapped again with the hammer. "Quintus Flavius Ahenobarbus," the cerulengus repeated, a little more loudly this time. Again, there was silence in the room. Again, the Sanctiff failed to respond.

The third time, the cerulengus barely touched the iron to the Sanctiff's forehead. "Quintus Flavius Ahenobarbus," he called in a commanding voice. Even so, no answer was forthcoming. The elderly celestine slipped the hammer back into its bag, placed his right hand upon the Sanctiff's chest, and took the man's right hand in his left.

"*In paradisum deducant te Angeli. In tuo adventu suscipiant te Martyres, et perducant te in civitatem sanctam. Chorus Angelorum te suscipiat, et æternam habeas requiem.*"

Valens gritted his teeth as the cerulengus removed the sanctal ring from the lifeless hand and turned toward him and Masella. He could feel a burning pressure behind his eyes, but he was determined not to weep for the Sanctified Father, not yet.

He looked away and saw that, outside the suite, several of the soldiers were weeping in silence, tears streaking down their faces and spilling onto their white breastplates. Others wore faces of stone, clenching their jaws and looking off into distant horizons as the cerulengus cleared his throat and pronounced the ritual words that forty-three of his predecessors had spoken before him.

"The Sanctiff is dead! Let the penitentiaries be summoned. Let the Sacred College be convened. Let the world be told. The Most Holy and Sanctified Father has gone to the glory that is his certain and well-merited reward!"

CORVUS

SEXTUS Valerius Corvus stood on the crest of a small hill that commanded the surrounding terrain. He watched thousands of men under his command rapidly building the wooden equivalent of a small city on top of a slightly higher hill to the south. Four riders stood beside him, both as his messengers and his guards. He intended to keep the army here for at least three days, which should give his outriders enough time to determine whether or not the Chalonu and Insobru tribes were coming to the aid of the goblin tribes with whom they'd already been skirmishing for weeks.

The men were getting the castra assembled quickly, he noticed with approval. The square shape of the defensive ditch was already discernible, and the first trees were being dragged from the nearby woods as the sound of axes beat a familiar rhythm. Then again, there were few things more motivating than the realization that twenty thousand shrieking goblins could fall upon your arse at any moment, without warning. Everyone slept better with the knowledge that there was a deep ditch and a tall wooden palisade standing between his tent and an enemy that would as soon rape you and eat you as kill you.

Corvus frowned as he saw a pair of riders exit the woods, galloping hard. They were scouts from the Second Knights, if he recalled the patrol schedule correctly. The two men were briefly stopped by the guards already stationed at what would soon be the Porta Principalis, then rode toward the command tent that had already been set up near the middle of the camp.

Corvus smiled grimly as they dismounted and began gesticulating at the guards standing outside it. Unless he missed his guess, the two scouts had finally located the army of the allied tribes he was seeking. With any luck, he would be able to bring them to battle soon, preferably on the morrow. If the goblin army had been found, the only real questions that remained were how many tribes comprised it and where he would meet them.

"Go to the camp and tell the legate and Tribune Valerius to come here at once," he ordered one of his guards. "Armed and armored."

"At once, General." The knight saluted and started to mount his horse, then hesitated and turned back. "Ah, which Tribune Valerius do you want, General? Fortex or Clericus?"

"Marcus," Corvus answered with a smile. "Son, not nephew." He wasn't keen on the name the men had given his son. But it was much better that Marcus was nicknamed Clericus—priest—than actually sworn to holy vows.

"At once, General!" The man rode off down the hill at such speed that for a moment, Corvus feared his horse would stumble and its rider break his neck.

They were so young, these knights, and so desperate to impress everyone around them, especially the command staff. They would be difficult to keep in check when they met the enemy, which, if he read the two scouts' actions correctly, would be sooner rather than later.

It would be a relief to finally bring the wretched goblin tribes to battle after one long autumn march after another. The sun was growing shorter each day, and lately the morning dew was frost as often as not. He glanced at the rapidly lengthening shadows on the slope below him. If he couldn't bring the goblins to grips soon, he would have to march his legions back to imperial lands and decide where he was going to winter them.

Sudden motion from outside the camp disturbed his internal debate over where he might station the three legions under his command at the end of the campaign. Four horses were riding toward him. He could not help smiling at the sight of the crested tribune's helm among them. Marcus. How easily the helmet could have been a bishop's mitre!

Beside his son rode the commander of the legion, Marcus Saturnius. Saturnius was a short man, given to softness rather than actual plumpness, and beneath the round, pleasant face of a well-fed butcher lay concealed a keenly tactical mind. The legate fought his battles like a butcher too, moving his cohorts in decisive slashes through the enemy formations, consistently carving a bloody and devastating path through their midst. This goblin campaign was their eighth together, and just as Corvus had learned to place implicit trust in his legate's tactical instincts, so Saturnius was content to follow Corvus's strategic lead.

Though they shared a name, his son had little in common with his subordinate. Marcus Valerius was a true Valerian—he was more than a head taller than the legate. And where Saturnius was round-faced and cheerful, Marcus appeared reserved, even haughty. The men might call him Clericus, but Corvus was certain that one day his son would merit a more warlike cognomen.

"How many are they?" Corvus called as the four riders approached the summit and reined in their horses. He could see from their slightly disheveled armor that Saturnius had wisely brought both newly returned scouts with him, although the two men were both mounted now on fresh horses.

"Eighteen thousand foot and two thousand wolves," Saturnius answered, confirming his assumption. "Only two tribes. And, judging by the state of the two encampments, the Vakhuyu have been there for several days, perhaps even a week. The Chalonu look to have arrived last night. They're both about five leagues due west."

"No sign of the Insobru?"

"None at all. Looks like Proculus will win his bet."

Corvus wasn't terribly surprised. He had fought the Insobru twice before, and both times the goblins had panicked and routed at the first legionary charge. They were a cowardly tribe, even by goblin standards, and they took their cue from their yellow-livered chieftain. He wasn't the only one who had fought them before. Proculus, Legio XVII's senior centurion of the second cohort, had done so as well.

"He usually does," Corvus nodded. He turned to the two scouts. "Were you seen?"

Both men shook their heads.

One of the two, a stout man with a long—and recent—red scratch across his left cheek, sat up in his saddle. "Not as such, General. After we caught scent o' their fires, we dismounted. We couldn't get too close even on foot, but we found a hill in the woods nearby so we could see almost everything. The two tribes was camped separate, and you could see the Vakhuyi'd been there for a while, because it stunk something fierce."

"So, did you cut yourself shaving, then?" Corvus asked pointedly.

"Well, I was just going to say that when we was riding back about a league, we run into a foot patrol. We killed all three o' them, but one nearly got my eye with his pigsticker. They didn't scream or nothing, and we drug the bodies back into the woods afore we came back, so I doubt they has any idea the legion is about."

"I think they was Chaloni," the other scout added. He looked alarmingly young to Corvus, even younger than his son. Corvus couldn't recall the boy's name precisely, but he thought it might be Faberus. "The patrol we killed, I mean. The others, the Vakhuyi, has always been out in fours, not threes. And there was something different about the way their hair was tied—it was kind o' twisted."

Corvus nodded approvingly at the detail in the younger scout's observations. He suspected Faberus, if that was indeed the lad's name, would have been the one to smell the campfires first. He cast about for the older scout's name. Was it Lacunus? No, that wasn't it. Labeculus.

"Very well done, both of you. Now Labeculus, back to camp if you please and straight to the medicus. Get that scratch cleaned at once. I'm not saying you're pretty now, but you'll be a damn sight less pretty if the rot sets in and they have to cut off half your face. Those gobbos don't keep their spears clean, and I'm sure Faberus will be able to lead us back to them. Tell your decurion that Third Squadron is to receive double rations of meat and wine tonight."

Labeculus looked as if he wanted to protest being left behind, but he acknowledged the order with a sharp salute and a crisp bow. "At once, General. Thank you, General."

As the wounded scout turned his horse back toward the camp, his young companion gaped, seemingly astonished that Corvus knew their names.

Corvus was amused, and he hoped Marcus was paying attention. It might be the oldest trick in the commander's bag, but calling a soldier by name was still the most effective way to begin forging those intimate bands of iron that distinguished a disciplined fighting force from an armed mob.

He turned toward his son, who was sitting on his horse, his expression neutral, quite properly pretending to not have noticed that his commanding officer had said or done anything at all. "Well, Tribune Valerius, as it seems our scouts have located the enemy, it now falls to us to decide precisely where we shall meet him. I assume you are prepared to assist the legate and me in this task?"

"Yes, sir, General. I am prepared, sir."

Corvus smiled at his son's steadfast refusal to meet his eyes. He was adhering firmly to junior officer etiquette, and appeared to be staring intently at something over Corvus's left shoulder. "At your ease, Tribune Clericus. Marcus, you're coming with me in your filial capacity, not because Saturnius has any need of his most junior tribune to help him determine what would be the most advantageous terrain."

"With all due respect, General," Saturnius said, "Valerius Clericus is not my most junior tribune. That would be Trebonius."

"Is that so? Well, be that as it may, it appears we find ourselves on the eve of Legio XVII's first proper battle, and I am naturally concerned about the readiness of the right wing, which will be under the command of Fortex, seconded by you, Marcus. That is enough to strike terror into any man's heart, even if not the enemy's, if he had known the two of you as boys. And since the shadows are not so long that we cannot ride ten leagues before sunset, I thought it might be useful for you to put some of that reading you've been doing in practice."

"I am at the stragister's command, sir." Marcus nodded impassively, but he couldn't quite hide a faint smile of delight cracking his formal reserve. "Thank you, General."

"What a touching display of paternal affection," Saturnius snorted derisively at their formality. He turned to the scout. "Faberus, what do you think of this formality between father and son?"

The young man squirmed in his saddle. "I wouldn't presume to have no opinion, Legate."

Saturnius guffawed. "Well said, lad! All right then, Corvus, let's be on our way and see if we can find a place suited to kill some goblins. Tribune Clericus, until we return to the camp, you will address the stragister militum as 'Father.' That is an order, Tribune!"

"Yes, sir. Understood, sir."

"Patricians!" The little legate laughed. "Heads of wood and hearts of ice. It's a wonder the Houses Martial didn't die off centuries ago. Faberus, go round up four knights and meet us at the bottom of the hill. There must be some reasonable ground lying between us and them."

The sun had reddened like blood, as if an omen for the morrow, when Marcus Saturnius finally pronounced his satisfaction with the ground that lay before him. Corvus breathed a sigh of relief. It was the third location presented by the young scout, but it was easily the most to Saturnius's liking. An open meadow spread out from the woods and culminated in a large hill that was higher on one side, lending itself to an oblique line of battle. The knights were already off their mounts and dicing with Marcus and Faberus while Corvus and Saturnius stood together in the middle of the field, looking up at the hill.

Corvus frowned. "We're farther south than I'd like."

"I know," Saturnius said, patting his horse's nose after tying its reins to a bush. "But the goblin army's natural line of march will push them southward. No goblin wants to cross deep water, and that stream about a league to the north will turn them here. There being no roads out here, they will naturally gravitate toward the open field—here—rather than through those forests we passed earlier. Too much brush." The legate pointed. "I'll position cohorts one, six, and eight, there, there, and there."

Corvus nodded in approval. Those three were the XVII's best cohorts, although since the entire legion was greener than a spring apple, he couldn't put as much faith in them as he would have in another, more experienced legion.

The three sides of the meadow around them were lined with crimson and gold, festooned with leaves fallen from the trees. Their horses grazed placidly on the browning autumn grass, unperturbed by the talk of the violence to come.

Corvus picked up a golden leaf and twisted it in his hand. It seemed almost a travesty to stand in the midst of all this natural beauty for the express purpose of slaughtering hundreds, more likely thousands, of God's creatures. He hoped the scholars of the Church were correct about the goblins being without souls, even if he had doubts that they were outright creatures of pure evil. It would make tomorrow's slaughter easier on his mind.

Not that it mattered. For better or for worse, he was a soldier, and slaughter was his true vocation. And right now, turning the young men of Legio XVII into one vast killing machine was his most sacred responsibility.

"We can establish the bulk of the mules and scorpios on the heights there," Saturnius said, "behind the second cohort on what will be the right wing. Put the cavalry on the left flank, up against the forest there, and another cohort behind them to deal with any infiltration from the trees. We'll have room for five cohorts across the front, so we'll keep two in reserve and leave one to guard the camp."

Corvus shook his head and overruled him. "No. Don't put all the horse on the left wing, I only want eight squadrons of the First Knights there. We'll put the Second Knights in front of the artillery, and we'll stand with the remaining eight behind the center. The incline is gentle there, but it's enough to provide sight of the whole field, and that will free up an additional cohort. We won't be quite as high, but if we put our staff on the hill, we'll lose sight of the right flank because of how the treeline curves."

He chewed the inside of his cheek, thinking hard. "It's going to be a little tight for the men with that many goblins in their faces. We'll need enough space to rotate the men on the front lines, so we'll keep the extra cohort in reserve."

"I like the additional reserve, but why split the cavalry?" Saturnius asked. "They may have seven wolves to every horse, but their riders aren't disciplined enough to bring their numbers to bear. And I doubt they'll stand for more than two charges."

"Because I want to keep them out of it if I can."

"By 'them' I sincerely hope you are speaking of their cavalry and not our own," Saturnius said carefully. He was very pointedly not looking at Marcus.

A surge of anger flashed through Corvus, which he restrained with some difficulty. He couldn't deny the thought of keeping Marcus and Fortex out of harm's way had crossed his mind several times during the afternoon, but that wasn't his primary motivation for stationing the cavalry on the heights. Of course, Saturnius couldn't know that and Corvus was certain that his old friend intended no insult. He took a deep breath to calm himself before explaining his reasoning.

"Saturnius, recall that we'll have at least two full squadrons detached to serve as messengers and so forth, here and at the camp. That leaves three hundred knights between the two wings, and if whoever is commanding the other side sees only three hundred lined up against two thousand on our left flank, he'll be tempted to engage immediately. The goblin commander will probably suspect he can't break through our knights, given their armor, but he'll have to try. We'd probably see three or four waves of them before he gives up. We'd lose dozens of horses to the wolves, perhaps a squadron or two of knights, and for what? To hold our ground? To pin down their cavalry?

"On the other hand, we can't simply keep our horse in reserve, because those damn wolves kick up such a hellish ruckus that infantry as green as ours will be pissing themselves if we throw them out there without support." He pointed at the hill. "If we hold the right with a full wing, and mix the rest of the horse in with a cohort on the left, they'll be forced to split their wolves. Same odds, of course, but a thousand wolves isn't going to inspire any foolhardy charges when they're facing a mixed force on the one flank and a bloody steep slope on the other."

"And if they don't split them?"

"Then we hit their flank, and they hit ours. Who do you think breaks first, our foot or theirs?"

Saturnius shrugged by way of concession. They both knew there wasn't any doubt as to whose infantry would stand against the other's cavalry and whose would run. "All right. So we take their wolves out of the equation, most likely without loss to either side, and let the infantry slug it out. Yes, I take your point. We'll split the horse. However, the ballistae should be in the center. They can't loose over the horses and down the slope. The onagers can stay there if you want, though. And I have one more suggestion."

"We might as well put half the onagers behind the left wing," Corvus said. "It really doesn't matter where they are since they can hammer the rear from either side. But what else are you thinking?"

"The Balerans. We didn't have enough men to fill up the complement for the ninth cohort, so I swore in some auxiliaries from Legio XXV after their contract expired. They're trained as proper infantry now, but they still have their slings."

"I do recall. I wasn't enthusiastic about them. How many did you swear in?"

"Mmmm, around two centuries."

"Two hundred Balerans?" Corvus nearly swallowed his tongue. "Dammit, man, I thought you were talking about ten or twelve of them! 'A few good men with experience,' you said. I thought, well, we could take on a few provincials so long as they're veterans."

"They've had the same training now that every other legionary has—and considerably more combat experience besides. My concern is that if the goblin cavalry isn't going to come to us, eventually one of their captains might get the bright idea to bring ours to them since they've got the numbers. Maybe it will be artillery, maybe a shaman or two, or maybe some of those piss-poor bastards that are supposed to pass for archers.

"My thought is that if we second twenty or thirty Balerans to both wings, that should be enough to keep them from peppering the cavalry and inciting some hotheaded decurion—or tribune—into doing something rash that will get his whole wing cut off and killed. And speaking of somebody doing something rash, I'm going to order the knights to refuse all challenges. Win or lose, if we're trying to keep the cavalry out of it, single combats are asking for trouble either way."

Corvus nodded. Inspiring the men to glorious deeds of solitary heroism was the very last thing they would need against the more numerous but inferior enemy. There were times when tactical brilliance and battlefield heroics were needed, but tomorrow's battle—assuming the enemy stirred from its camp—should be a relatively straightforward affair. Freeze their cavalry in place, funnel their lightly armored foot against the heavy infantry holding the center, then slaughter them until they break and attempt to withdraw.

Only then would he unleash his knights, who would sweep aside the wolfriders trying to screen the enemy retreat, who would kill and kill and kill until nightfall. The infantry might be green, but more than a few of its centurions were veterans with decades in the ranks. He wouldn't want to test them against the mountain orcs of Zoth Ommog yet, but against goblins, they would hold.

The only real question in his mind was if the goblin commander had sufficient control of his forces to attempt an orderly retreat or if the chieftains would simply flee and leave their desperate troops to rout as best they could. Most likely the latter, he guessed, especially given that two rival tribes were involved.

A thought struck him. "It occurs to me that if we want to keep their cavalry sitting, the ballistarii should be instructed to leave them alone."

Saturnius agreed. "I will see that Cassabus understands and instructs his men accordingly. Now, if you will excuse me, Corvus, I'm going to take Faberus and the guards to see how we can best encourage the gobbos to join us here for our little gathering tomorrow. Do you want your boy?"

Corvus appreciated his old friend's perceptiveness. "Yes, but don't be long about it. It would be best if we got back to camp before sundown."

The legate nodded and mounted his horse then rode toward the far side of the field where the others were crouched on their haunches and gathered in a circle. He extricated Marcus from the game and sent him riding back to Corvus.

Corvus nodded at his son, who dismounted and regarded him quizzically. Corvus smiled and smacked him hard enough on his steel-armored shoulder to rock the boy sideways. How tall his son had grown, and what an unmitigated pleasure it was to see him in the attire that was good and proper for a son of House Valerius!

"Have you any thoughts about tomorrow, Tribune?"

"I do, lots of them." His son finally stopped hiding behind the junior officer's mask and shook his head ruefully. "Very little of which likely has anything to do with what you and Marcus Saturnius were discussing. But I assume you're taking an approach that is relatively similar to the one Flaminius used against the Trinatine orcs. I hope it will work out as well for us."

"So all that scholarly training has served you after all!" Corvus smiled again, pleased to learn that the boy was taking his service seriously. "Have you got a copy of Moridides in that little library of yours? I think you might find his *Taktikon* of interest."

"No, I heard it was worth reading, but the centurions kept us so busy that I never got around to having one copied."

"Saturnius has one. I'll see that he sends it to you. In fact, you can probably keep it, I doubt he's ever unrolled it, much less read it."

"Really? Never? And he's had it how long?" He shook his head. "Thank you, Father, but I will copy it myself and return it to him. I find I recall the material better if I write it down."

"You're not a scribe anymore, you know. But listen to me, Marcus. You have to understand that reading is not the only way for a man to learn. Nothing you've ever read, nothing any man's hand has ever written, will prepare you for what you're going to see, and hear, and feel tomorrow."

Corvus stared out across the meadow toward the direction from which the goblins would come, remembering his first battle. The waiting. That was what he remembered most. The waiting. And then the fear. He must have lapsed into silence, because his son cleared his throat.

Corvus looked seriously at Marcus. "It's beyond our limits to envision. The terror that grips your belly when you first catch sight of the foe in all his numbers. The horror of seeing your comrade's face split open by an axe. The fierce pride in your men when they stand fast and turn back the enemy. The relief that weakens your knees when you suddenly realize it's all over… I can tell you these things, but until tomorrow, they'll only be words. Battle isn't words. It is sounds and sights and smells, and some of them are more terrible than you can imagine."

Especially the smells. He grimaced. Every time, he thought he would be ready for them. And every time, he was wrong.

Marcus nodded, equally grave. "I think you're essentially describing the distinction between the form and the substance of knowledge. In this case, the true knowledge of battle isn't the abstract form one constructs from the descriptions of others after the fact, but that which can only be obtained through the varied phenomena experienced within it."

Corvus stared at his son, nonplussed. "For the love of all that's clean and holy, please tell me you don't talk to your knights like that."

"No, Father. In the course of my admittedly brief career, I have learned their two preferred subjects of discussion are the women they have known in the past and the women they anticipate knowing in the future."

Marcus laughed. "When they're not gambling, that is. Their interest in philosophy is best described as *de minimis.*"

"Yes, you're not the first to observe that the interests of the Amorran soldiery tend to be limited and focused primarily on the distaff." Corvus suddenly had a very vivid picture of what the look on the first decurion's face would be if Marcus were to offer a few of his more esoteric observations, complete with citations, in company with his orders. He laughed.

It was at times like these, when this young man spoke at such heights, that Corvus found himself wondering if it were somehow possible that Romilia had been less than perfectly faithful to him. He had been away on campaign a great deal in the first years of their marriage, after all, and she was a highly sought-after beauty. On the other hand, he couldn't think of a single suitor of hers possessed of a mind inclined toward his son's scholarly predilections either.

"Very well, Tribune, shall we not acquaint ourselves with the true knowledge of the hill upon which you and your cousin will be commanding the right flank? It is one thing to envisage the abstract form of its degree of incline, and another to experience exactly how difficult it would be for a thousand screaming goblins on wolfback hell-bent on ripping out your throat to ride up it."

Marcus didn't answer, but he did look ever so slightly pale. It seemed that even scholarly young philosophers could be moved to emotion by contemplating the abstract form of violent death in battle. Corvus chuckled and strode toward the gentle incline that marked the beginning of the hill.

Before too long, both of them were standing at the summit, breathing hard.

Corvus stretched out his arm to encompass the breadth of the field visible from their vantage point.

"Do you see that tree there?" He pointed to a tall maple on the southern edge of the field with bright yellow leaves that had not yet begun to fall. Its colors stood out clearly against the browns and reds of its neighbors on three sides. The ground between it and them stretched nearly a third of the way to the field's western end. "If the scouts are right, that's about where their last rank will be."

Marcus didn't answer. He was still breathing heavily but faster and louder than before. Corvus moved closer to his son and put his arm around his crimson-cloaked shoulders. Slowly, surely, the young man's breathing slowed until he relaxed with a deep sigh.

"It's different when your mind sees the clear picture, isn't it? Don't worry, though. You will be afraid, Marcus. Of course you will. It's not only normal, it's necessary. A man who faces battle without fear isn't brave—he's little more than an animal who neither knows nor cares if he lives or dies. And a young man with your imagination, well, I expect that in some ways, you may even find the real thing to be less dreadful than whatever nightmare you've concocted inside your head.

"It's a test of your manhood, but it is a test I know you will pass. You are a true Valerian, and no man bearing the Valerius name has ever failed the test of battle. Even when the battle went badly. In four hundred years we Valerians have been defeated, we have retreated, and we have died where we stood, but not a single one has ever shown himself a coward. You will not be the first."

"What's it like?" Marcus asked in a voice barely more than a whisper. "In Elebrion, when the false priests attacked the embassy, everything happened so fast. I didn't even have time to be afraid. I simply reacted and did what I had to do. And on patrol, in all the skirmishes we've fought, we always defeated them so easily that it seemed more like hunting than warfare. But here, seeing the field and taking in the scale of what will come, it's almost beyond comprehension!"

Corvus laughed. "That's the advantage Marcus Saturnius has over you and me. He has absolutely no imagination. He doesn't see the individual men that make up the centuries and he isn't impressed by the magnitude of the numbers involved. To him, it's nothing more than a problem of basic geometry, and he goes about solving it without being distracted by the overall picture. That's why he's a better tactician than me. Of course, that's also why I'm a better strategist than he is. Strategy requires imagination. Tactics take focus.

"As for what it's like… it's not real. I mean, war is real, of course, but it truly doesn't feel real. There is so much happening on every side around you that it often seems as if you're standing outside your body. You can see and hear everything, but it doesn't really feel as if any of it has anything to do with you."

Marcus kicked at the turf at his feet. "That sounds strange. I don't know what I was expecting you would say, but it certainly wasn't that."

"I don't know how else to describe it. My first campaign was under Falconius Carnifex during the Fifth Tribute War. At times during the first two battles against the Eprani, it was as if I wasn't even there. I remember that both times I felt… detached. Yes, detached—that describes it.

"I remember seeing a spear strike the man standing next to me. It hit him just above the breastplate. He staggered back and fell to his knees, as you can probably imagine, and all I could think about at the time was how strange the expression on his face was just as he collapsed to the ground. I stood there, staring at him lying on the blood-stained grass, and I didn't pay attention to anything else until the centurion slapped me."

"The centurion?" Marcus asked incredulously. "He hit you?"

"Oh, yes. Carnifex didn't believe in coddling his tribunes. He threw us right into the front lines from the start, although at least we were usually assigned to the veteran cohorts. He went through tribunes the way a messenger goes through horses. But if you survived him, you knew you had the respect of the infantry. They considered you one of them, a proper legionary, not a knight or a patrician."

"I can't imagine the Houses appreciated his method of instruction."

Corvus snorted and shook his head. Every tribune lost meant a noble house lost a potential heir. "No, they most certainly did not. That was why his cousin, Falconius Bardus, was commanding the legion in my second campaign. One of the Caerans drowned Carnifex in the baths when he returned to Amorr over the winter. Titus Caerus was one of the tribunes

killed in the lines during the second battle against the Eprani when the
sixth cohort was overrun, and it was his father who killed Carnifex."

His son wasn't listening. He was pointing toward the far end of the
field instead. "Look, they're coming back." Sure enough, Saturnius and
the five riders accompanying him were cantering across the prospective
battlefield toward them.

"Come around this way. They'll untether our horses and meet us as
they ride up the center." Corvus whistled at Saturnius and pointed to the
horses; the legate waved back in response.

A little less nimble at his age than his athletic son, he was several steps
behind Marcus as they ran and occasionally slid down the gentler incline
on the southern side of the hill.

"Did you see anyone chasing them?" Marcus called back to him.

"No, nothing. There can't be any wolves too close behind, or they'd
be riding harder."

Once they reached the area where Corvus intended to establish the
legion's center and station the first cohort, they came to a stop, since the
others had already reached the horses and were pulling out the spikes that
prevented them from roaming. Corvus had never felt more alive. He
laughed and once more put his arm around his son. God in Heaven, but
the boy was as tall as he was!

"It may be hard tomorrow, but I'm so glad you're here, Marcus. I
know as a boy you must have wondered where your father was all those
years. This is where I've been all along—waiting for you to join me. This
is what we are, this is who we are, this is what we were made for!"

His son looked over at him. There was a half-smile on his lips. "It's
strange. As children, we're told we must love our fathers. We're told we
must respect them. But I hardly knew mine."

Corvus nodded, unperturbed. He knew that, in some ways, Magnus
was more the boy's father than he was. He certainly could take little credit
for what a fine example of patrician youth Marcus had become. He'd given
the boy his height perhaps, but he bore the unmistakable signs of Romilia's

beauty and Magnus's upbringing. And only God knew where he'd gotten his mind.

"But now that I'm one of your soldiers," his son continued, "I can see why your men love their general as they do. I was afraid when I was standing up there, imagining the terrible scope of it all for the first time. Truly seeing it. But after talking to you, I'm not afraid anymore. So, maybe this is where I was always supposed to be."

"Ha! If you can still say that after tomorrow, boy, perhaps I'll believe you." Corvus teased his son, but he felt a powerful warmth spreading out through his body from the core of his heart. "What ho, Saturnius!" he called as the legate rode toward him, leading his horse. Faberus led Marcus's mount.

"We'd better be moving along, Corvus," Saturnius said. "We caught sight of a large patrol out roving, about twenty wolves. They'll be on our scent soon, if they're not already. I don't know if we'll even have to bother sending out a few squadrons to draw them here tomorrow, although we'd better plan to deploy by sunrise if we don't want to risk them stealing a march on us." Corvus leaped astride his horse and took the reins.

One of the knights shouted. "They're coming!"

There was a rustling motion at the far end of the field, as if the trees themselves were shaking. Then wolves began to boil out of the forest like long grey wasps coming out of a hole in the ground. They were lean and low to the ground, and their scrawny, long-limbed riders looked almost like green spiders clinging to their crudely saddled backs.

But as fast as the wolves could lope along the ground, their legs weren't even a third as long as those of the horses the men were riding. The goblins had no chance of catching the Amorran riders in the five leagues that now separated them from the camp. And it wasn't as if the wolfriders were likely to make a serious attempt at chasing them anyway, since they couldn't possibly know that the patrol they'd encountered happened to include three of the legion's command staff.

"Will you really retreat in the face of the enemy, General?" Saturnius dared him.

Corvus peered at the goblin riders. They would win. The seven of them could likely drive off the twenty or so wolfriders, but not without loss. And they had neither shields nor lances with them. The thought of engaging was ever so slightly tempting, but to take such a risk would be monumentally stupid. Romilia would have his ears if she ever heard of it, and more than that if Marcus got so much as a scratch.

"Retreat?" Corvus shouted back. "Never! Let us advance—speedily—in the direction of the camp!" He kicked his horse forward into a gallop.

He glanced over at his son, who was thundering along not far behind him, hoping that this unexpected sight of the enemy had not unmanned him in any way. He was delighted to see that Marcus had thrown back his head and was laughing at something one of the knights had said, as fey and unconcerned in the face of the foe as any of their legendary forefathers.

Behind them, the sun's rays were deepening from oranges and reds into scarlets and purples. Before it would rise again, Corvus knew, the seven of them would be back atop that hill overlooking the field, but in the company of nearly six thousand armed men.

A large black crow flew overhead as they rode, and Corvus smiled up at his namesake.

"Come back tomorrow, little brother," he shouted at the crow. "Come back tomorrow, and I shall feed you well!"

MARCUS

THE ragged lines of the goblin army below stretched out to the south as far as Marcus could see. The evil sound of their drums boomed rhythmically without cease, as if they were the heartbeat of a single giant beast.

Over the drumming—and between curses directed alternately at the legion's scouts, its artillery, and its suppliers—Marcus heard the first decurion telling his reguntur that the army they were facing was somewhere between twenty and thirty thousand strong. Marcus tried to find some relief in the grizzled old cavalryman's apparent lack of concern at the legion being outnumbered five to one and focused on his assigned task of counting the number of wolfriders on the enemy's right wing.

The enemy lines were only about one hundred paces away from the legion's front line, but the drums, the shrieks of the crudely armed warriors, the growling and howling and whining of their wolves, and the occasional shouting of the men behind him made it surprisingly hard to keep track of the number. The fact that the goblins were not arrayed in tidy, disciplined lines, but in loose mobs in constant movement rendered it more of an exercise in estimation than an actual count.

It was considerable comfort to be up on the hill and on the left flank, above and well away from that teeming mass of inhumanity. He glanced back toward the center, behind the reserves, and saw the legionary standard. He couldn't see his father, but he knew Corvus was down there somewhere. He did recognize Saturnius, though, stout and portly in his armor, waving his arms as he shouted at someone. He grinned, glad that he wasn't the object of the legate's ire.

The goblins had arrayed themselves much as his father had predicted they would, although there seemed to be rather more wolves lined up on the flank facing Marcus and the Second Knights than on the other side of the battlefield.

"How many wolves, Tribune?" Julianus demanded.

"I make seven hundred, perhaps seven hundred twenty, Decurion."

"Lucius and me both count eight hundred. Remember, it's better to err on the side of too many than too few. Still, that's not bad."

Not bad that only three hundred knights held the right flank against eight hundred enemy wolfriders? It wasn't exactly a state he would be inclined to describe as good, either. But he held his tongue. The decurion was not a man known to appreciate wit at the best of times, and this did not seem to be a wise moment to try his temper.

As if in response to the wolves snarling below them, Marcus's stomach growled. He had done his best to choke down some bread and cheese when they'd been awakened before sunrise and ordered to take their position on the northernmost hill, but he'd had little appetite.

It wasn't that this morning would be the first time he'd ever seen combat. On his journey to the elven royal city of Elebrion with the Church embassy last year, he'd been attacked by an ulfin, a grotesque wolflike creature, although he hadn't even managed to draw his sword and had only survived the attack thanks to the alertness of his dwarven servant, Lodi. Since the campaign began, he'd ridden on more patrols than he could count and had gotten into five skirmishes. He'd even killed his first goblin three weeks ago—two of them, in fact, when the patrol he was leading encountered a small band of raiders. But today marked his first actual battle.

He had known that war wasn't likely to be as glorious as the chronicles recorded, but as his father had predicted, his senses were reeling in shock from the impact of the experience. The sights, the sounds, the scale of it all… it was simply too much for his senses to take in at once. His heart was pounding, his palms were moist, and his mouth was dry. He hadn't been this frightened since the night he'd found himself soaring through the night sky over the towers of Elebrion, dangling like a giant mouse caught up in the talons of Caitlys Shadowsong's warhawk.

And today's fighting hadn't even begun.

The sound of thundering hoofbeats suddenly stopping nearby jarred him from his thoughts. "Pissed yourself yet, cousin?"

Marcus looked up. Gaius Valerius Fortex, the tribune commanding the Second Knights and his elder by three years, towered over him from the back of his big black warhorse, Incitatus. His cousin's pale green eyes glittered with amusement. "I imagine that right about now you're wishing you'd taken that bishopric Magnus offered you!"

I was holding out for an archbishop's hat, Marcus tried to reply, but the words stuck in his throat.

"I'll take it, if the tribune's got no use for it," Julianus said, making Fortex and some of the nearby riders laugh.

"How pretty you would look in a red cassock and mitre, Julianus! And with that bull's voice of yours, the priests could give their bells a rest. They'll just tell you when to bawl out matins and vigils." Fortex swatted the decurion on the shoulder and turned back toward his cousin. "Don't worry, Marcus. You'll live to see your little elf girl again. Yonder pack is a big one, but they'll run as soon as we charge them. Those wolves look fearsome enough, but their bark is worse than their bite. Count yourself bloody fortunate we didn't have to break out the pigstickers."

Marcus nodded and attempted to grin but his mouth didn't seem to work properly. Everyone around him was cheerful, almost jocular. Even the decurion had an uncharacteristic smile on his face. They all seemed to be eagerly looking forward to the incipient clash of arms. Were they all mad? Didn't they realize they might die here today? He hadn't lost control of his bladder yet, thank Immaculatus, but his mouth was dry, and he was finding it hard to swallow.

Fortex was right. The very last thing he wanted to try at the moment was to ride down the hill wielding one of the giant oaken lances that were used to penetrate the thick hide of a warboar. One slip at just the wrong moment, and a rider would catapult himself right out of the saddle.

"Courage of the vine, cousin," Fortex suggested, handing a half-empty flask down to him. "Remember, an officer has to keep his throat well-wetted throughout the day. You can't expect anyone to hear an order when your voice is cracking."

Marcus nodded and squeezed a dark red stream into his mouth. He winced at the sour taste, but it did relieve the dryness. "Thanks." He handed the flask to Julianus, then pointed at the enemy lines. "What are they doing down there?"

Below them, a group of goblins on foot was beginning to emerge from the mass of wolfriders. Each carried little curved objects that looked much too small to be proper bows, but it wasn't until they stopped about twenty paces from the base of the hill and began to withdraw equally small shafts from the quivers slung on their backs that he realized that was precisely what they were supposed to be. His cousin and the decurion were quicker on the uptake. Fortex had already kicked his horse and galloped away from the front.

Meanwhile Julianus was waving his free hand and bellowing orders. The decurion did not, however, drop the wine flask. He used it to point out the approaching archers.

"Slingers, front and center!" His voice was loud enough to drown out the goblin drums, which, up close, was nearly deafening. "Knights, shields ready!"

Marcus fumbled for his shield, a wedge-shaped piece of wood covered with a thin plate of blackened steel with his name, tumae, and legion engraved. He took two steps to the left to stand in front of his horse, as he'd been drilled, slipped the shield on his left arm, then held it before him. He'd already learned in the early skirmishes of the campaign that the goblin bows had little range, and he also knew their archers would have time to loose only a few shafts before the Amorran slingers would force them to retreat.

Without thinking about it, he began to count the goblin archers. There were thirty-six of them in all, at a distance of around sixty paces. He was relieved to see they were raising their bows high, to shoot for the cavalry, rather than aiming them directly at him and the others at the fore of the Amorran line.

The goblins loosed their first volley.

"Shields up!" Julianus roared. "Shields up, dammit!"

Marcus raised his shield, and a moment later, he heard a loud clattering sound behind him as the arrows began falling on the upraised shields of the knights, followed by the terrible, gut-wrenching shriek of a wounded horse screaming. While their riders' shields guarded their vulnerable eyes and their saddles protected their backs, the horses' naked haunches were still exposed to the falling arrows.

A few moments passed, and his arm began to ache, but another round of clattering rain quickly quenched any desire to lower his shield. Fortunately, the two dozen Balerans seconded to them by the ninth cohort arrived, and he lowered his shield as the air resounded with a series of whip-like cracks. With the ease of long-practiced experts, the elite slingers hurled their tiny missiles at the archers below.

Two goblins collapsed immediately, followed by a third, who fell clutching a shattered knee. The remaining goblins managed to loose one more haphazard volley, in which most of the shafts fell well short of the Amorran lines. Then another hail of stones drove them back to the safety of their own lines. They left seven of their number on the ground behind, presumably dead.

To Marcus's far left down the front lines of the army there was a hissing sound, followed by a thunderous report. He turned his head. An evil-looking purple haze was rising from the midst of the infantry cohorts positioned on their south flank.

"What is that?" he asked the decurion.

"Battle shaman," Julianus replied with disdain. "Not much of one, by the looks of it. A damned stupid one too. He should have saved those spells for the assault, used them to blast a hole in our line for their spearmen to enter. The scorpios and mules will put an end to that nonsense soon enough."

"Pity we don't have any Michaelines," Marcus mused regretfully.

"We don't need them. Goblin magic is nothing. Watch and see."

Two more purple explosions erupted somewhere in between the seventh and eight centuries before the shaman's position was spotted by the artillerymen. Marcus could tell the goblin had been seen because a dozen or more of the legion's onagers loosed in quick succession. The last rock was hurled high into the air before the first one had even landed. Two of the scorpios also sent their huge bolts sailing into the mass of goblins in the same vicinity.

He couldn't see if any of them actually hit their intended target, but the massive projectiles must have at least put a fright into the shaman, as no more magical attacks followed.

Time passed, and the sun rose higher. Based on its height, Marcus guessed it was about an hour before noon. The air was heating up, and the last patches of frost had vanished some time ago. The steam was no longer rising from the horses, and he was beginning to feel the first sense of perspiration under his arms.

The cohorts chanted, the goblins shrieked, and the wolves howled. Finally, after another shaman caused a great purple cloud to explode high over everyone's heads, the goblin infantry moved forward to engage its Amorran counterpart. Then the air was filled with the clashing of metal on metal and the cries of the combatants. But that was all to Marcus's left.

He glanced back to the standard, and this time he saw the yellow plume of his father's helmet bobbing amidst a group of centurions' helms, though he couldn't see what Corvus was doing. Somehow, seeing it helped ease the tension in his guts a little.

The wolfriders before Marcus were still doing nothing more than mill about, snapping and snarling to little purpose. From time to time a goblin would ride out from the lines, gesticulating and screaming at Marcus's men, but to no avail.

"What are they doing?" he asked the decurion.

"They're trying to draw us off the hill," Julianus answered. "They don't dare to come up to meet us for fear we'll charge them while they're climbing the slope. The archers didn't bring us down to them, so now they're trying insults."

"It might work better if we could understand anything they were saying."

"Or if we gave a damn what they thought of us." Julianus grinned and pointed to movement at the front of the wolfriders' lines. "No one said they were clever. Look, they're going to try the archers again. *Slings,* get your useless Baleran arses up here!"

Once more, the goblin archers advanced and loosed a pair of volleys, to little effect. Once more, the legion's slingers rained stones down upon them before they could manage a third volley. Once more, the goblin archers fled in disarray, leaving more of their fallen behind them. It was rather like a ritual dance, Marcus observed, albeit a deadly one. Like Sisyphus and his rock, if the rock kept rolling over the condemned man.

Marcus heard Julianus muttering curses again, only this time the decurion's ire was directed at the goblins rather than any of the legion's various functionaries. He looked at Julianus and was puzzled—until he noticed the black shaft that transfixed the muscular underside of the man's left arm.

It was pure bad luck; the arrow had narrowly missed the brass greaves that protected his forearms and had punctured one of the leather straps that held the armor in place. But seemingly oblivious to the pain, Julianus was pointing to an injured goblin who was slowly crawling back toward its fellows.

"Can you hit that, Corander?" Julianus demanded of the tall Baleran who led the slingers.

"Can you hit the ground when you shit, sir?" the slinger snorted, withdrawing a stone from his pouch. He twirled it in his fingers. Its shape was oblong, and it had been ground to a snub point on either end. "Ten crowns says I will."

"All right, but you can't just hit the damn thing, you got to kill it. Ten says you don't."

"Done." The slinger whirled the long leather once, twice, three, four times over his head, then released the stone.

A moment later, a small red flower bloomed from the back of the crawling goblin's skull, and it slumped to the ground, unmoving. A roar went up from the watching cavalrymen, both a salute to the Baleran's deadly skill and a heartfelt expression of relief. They might have to stand here all afternoon sweating under the increasingly hot rays of the sun, but at least they would not have to endure goblin arrows, as well.

"Double or nothing for the big one on the black wolf," Julianus said.

"I'll leave him for you, decurion," the Baleran replied, smiling. "That pelt would look well on your shoulders. But I'll want my ten crowns later, so try not to get yourself killed today."

"Lucky bastard," the decurion growled at the slinger's back. But then his lips curled slightly, and the men around him cheered raucously.

Marcus suddenly suspected that Julianus had made the bet in order to distract them from his wound. Although Legio XVII was well-salted with veteran officers like Julianus and his fellow decurions, it was still a new and untested legion, and most of the knights in the Second were as green as Marcus was.

"Decurion, your arm." Lucius, the reguntur, reached over and grabbed Julianus's wrist. Blood was flowing down to the older man's elbow in three narrow rivulets and dripping down to stain the grass near his feet. "You had better get that removed and cleaned. God knows what sort of swamp shit was smeared on the arrowhead."

Julianus glared at both Lucius and Marcus, then looked back at the goblin cavalry's lines. Despite the infantry battle raging to the south, the wolfriders still showed no signs of budging. Reluctantly, he shrugged. "Well, it seems they've got no belly to come at us today. Don't either of you think of being a hero and going after them. You heard the legate's orders: We hold the flank and hold the hill. You do not attack unless they actually start riding up the hill. All of them, not just one or two mad buggers. Are you clear on that, Tribune Valerius?"

"Absolutely clear, Decurion." One of the first things that had been drilled into him since the day he'd pledged the legion was that there were only three penalties for disobeying battle orders: flogging, degradation, and death. Officers had a little more leeway, by necessity, but only insofar as the situation demanded it.

"Do you understand, Reguntur Dardanus?"

"Understood, Decurion! The Second holds its ground unless attacked in force, Decurion!"

"I'll be back as soon as I can find Sedarius or one of his assistants. Belike you'll all have naught to do but pick your arses anyhow."

Marcus fervently hoped so, but he thumped his chest and nodded again as the decurion mounted his horse and rode off in search of someone who could safely remove the arrow for him. He glanced at the goblin lines. Were the drums louder? Were they beginning to move forward? Not now, of all times, surely! A trickle of sweat ran down from his hair into his eyes.

"Too tedious for old Julianus, sir?" asked the rider on his right, a young knight by the name of Servius Commius.

"I am given to understand our good decurion finds moving his own bowels to be more exciting than watching those wolves squatting and shitting all day," Marcus told him. "But I don't imagine it should take more than an hour or three for the novelty to wear off."

Commius, Dardanus, and the other men around him laughed harder than his feeble joke merited, but at least they didn't seem to notice that he was very nearly nervous enough about the decurion's absence to imitate the wolves himself. Still keeping half an eye out for the return of the goblin archers, he turned with the others to watch the battle raging to the south.

The goblins were pressing hard against the principes of the three co-horts holding the center but making absolutely no headway. Their stone-tipped clubs and wooden spears shattered against the steel of the Amorran armor, and their own leather armor offered little protection against the swords that flickered out like silver snakes' tongues from between the imposing wall of shields.

Marcus saw two goblins hurl a third warrior over the first line of troops, its arms and legs flailing wildly, but a quick-thinking hastatus brought the aerial assault to an end by intercepting the goblin with the sharp end of his spiculum. A roar went up from the hastati and the triarii alike as the legionnaire triumphantly raised and lowered the impaled goblin as if it were a gruesome standard.

Goblins died by the dozen, but the drums continued to boom without ceasing, and no sooner had one rabid green-skinned warrior fallen than another leaped to take his place.

The fourth hour was barely half gone when a horn sounded and the hastati let out a roar even louder than before. The horn was echoed by horns throughout the centuries, and almost as one, each of the sixty mules and scorpios were released, targeted at a wide area that, from Marcus's perspective, looked perilously close to the Amorran lines. The goblin assault buckled in disarray as the massive boulders bounced and crushed as many as ten goblins each, while one well-aimed bolt slashed a visible line that ran nearly to the rear of the massed goblins.

As the enemy reeled from the massed artillery assault, a third horn blew, and the tired principes in the five lead cohorts smoothly exchanged places with the fresh hastati. The energy of the replacements appeared to sap the spirits of the green-skinned warriors, and for the first time, the goblin line fell away from the wall of shields against which it had been pressing for nearly an hour.

The rapid pounding of hooves announced the return of Gaius Valerius Fortex, who cut a dashing figure with his long blue commander's cloak flowing behind him. He was wearing his helm now, a silvered construc-tion with a blue horsehair plume and a beaked mask that was meant to represent the Valerian crow. He also held a cavalry lance about half the width of a pigsticker, and his shield was slung on Incitatus's side.

"They're on the verge of breaking," Fortex announced breathlessly. "If we can only scatter these gutless wolves before us, we can hit their main body on the left flank and send them all running. Can't you feel it! This is the moment of truth!"

As Fortex pointed at the wolfriders below, the warrior on the big black wolf rode out from the lines. Unlike most of the infantry, he bore a curved sabre, and his armor looked as if it was made of iron or perhaps even painted steel. He wore a human skull in the place of a helm. As the knights looked on from above, he pointed his sword directly at Fortex and shouted something unintelligible. Jerking back on the reins, the goblin made the giant wolf rear back and emit a bone-chilling howl before it fell back to all fours.

"He's challenging me," Fortex said, incredulous. "Single combat. Can you believe that?"

"Don't do it, Gaius," Marcus urged, forgetting that he was not speaking to his cousin, but his commanding officer. Even behind the masked helm, he recognized the unmistakable anger flashing in his cousin's eyes; Gaius Valerius had always been hot-tempered and regarded a dare as a personal insult to his courage and his honor.

Even Dardanus saw it. "Sir, our orders are to hold the hill until they attack! No single combat, they said."

"Damn our orders! They're going to break. I know it. This is the moment!"

"Gaius, you can't!"

"Shut up, Marcus. What the hell do you know about war? It's your first bloody battle. This is the right time. I can feel it. We have to strike now." His cousin looked around. "Where's Julianus?"

"He took an arrow in the arm, had to get it bandaged. But Gaius–"

"How long... no, there's no time. We can rout them right here if we hit them hard enough. Marcus, you're the tribune—you have the command in my absence. Lucius Dardanus, you second him. If he kills me, you simply hold the hill as before. But if I kill him and they look like running, then you sound the charge. Everything clear? That's an order!"

"But Gaius!"

"I said that's an order, Tribune!" his cousin roared.

"Sir," Marcus and the regentur answered in instant unison, thumping their blackened steel breastplates. He and Fortex might both be tribunes, but his cousin outranked him, and as his superior officer, his orders could not be ignored.

"Saturnius said–"

"I know what Saturnius said! And I know it's your first bloody battle too! Now shut up. The Knights are yours."

Marcus watched in despair as Fortex reared his horse violently and raised his lance in acceptance of the challenge, provoking an enthusiastic cheer from the nearby knights. *Almighty God, You watch over children and fools, so please save my idiot cousin from himself.* Marcus saw the goblin below raise his sword in a salute, then urge his wolf forward to a position about thirty paces from the bottom of the hill.

Fortex reached back and unslung his shield from his saddle, slipped it on his arm, then raised his lance one more time. His gesture was greeted by even louder cheers, as the word had spread and the entire Second Knights now appeared to be aware of the imminent duel between the two mounted commanders.

"Fortex, Fortex, Fortex!" The knights began to chant as Fortex kicked the big black warhorse forward and plunged down the hill toward the waiting wolfrider. The chant rose to a wordless roar as the horse and rider closed with the mounted goblin.

The wolf crouched and sprang to the side at the last possible moment. There were cries of disappointment as the Amorran's lance barely missed the wolfrider's armored shoulder.

Being quicker and lower to the ground, the wolf was the first to recover and attack, springing toward the horse's hind legs and snapping at them in an attempt to hamstring them. But before its flashing jaws met tender horseflesh, Fortex twisted his upper body, lifted the heavy lance in his right arm, and somehow managed to hurl it right into the wolf's left shoulder.

The giant wolf howled as the lance penetrated its body and pinned it to the ground. It flipped up into what looked like an awkward, one-legged headstand, throwing its rider. Then the lance snapped, and the wolf collapsed, convulsing, onto its back. The goblin somersaulted through the air, past the horse's rump, and slammed hard into the ground.

There was a triumphant shout from the Amorran lines, and the chant began anew.

"Fortex, Fortex! Amorr, Amorr!" Marcus couldn't help joining in. The men had even drawn their swords and were beating them on their shields in time with the chant. On Marcus's left stood a draconarius pumping his signal horn aloft in victory.

In response to the cheer, Fortex unsheathed his sword and caused Incitatus to rear again. His stunned foe had pushed itself to its feet unsteadily, but both its sword and shield were lying on the ground well out of its reach.

Fortex urged his horse forward in a gallop, drew back his arm, and struck the head off the helpless goblin commander in a single powerful stroke. The skull helmet flew off with the force of the blow, and for a moment it looked as if his cousin had slain a two-headed monster.

A terrified wail arose from the watching goblins that drowned out the victorious shouts of the Amorrans, and it grew even louder when Fortex leaned over to spear the severed head on the end of his longsword and raised it over his head like a pagan hero of old.

He may have shouted something, but if he did, no one heard it, as the deafening roar from the Second Knights that answered his gesture drowned out the wailing wolfriders as well as the sounds of the battle raging to the south. Marcus joined the knights around him in raising his lance and returning what he thought was a salute.

Caught up in the excitement of the victory, the draconarius standing beside Marcus half-sounded the horn he was already holding to his lips. It came out more like an aborted fart than a proper signal, but it was enough to cause about twelve or thirteen knights—already mounted and stirred to the edge of violence—to urge their horses forward and begin making their way down the steep incline.

"They're going forward!" cried Dardanus. "What do we do? Clericus, what do we do?"

"Sound it," Marcus shouted at the standard bearer, who was frozen in fear, shocked by what he had inadvertently done. "Sound it again! We can't call them back—just sound the advance!" He leaped into the saddle. "What's done is done! Gaius killed the brute, so let's pray they look like running." He raised his fist. "*Fortex!*"

"*Fortex!*" Most of the Second's knights were already mounted now, and they echoed his cry, their lances stabbing at the sky.

"Amorr!"

"*Amorr!*"

The draconarius sounded the horn, properly this time. Its deep booming resonated powerfully over the tumultuous clangor of the battle and was echoed by the roars of the bloodthirsty Amorran cavalry.

Marcus rose in his stirrups, raised his lance, and pointed it toward the foe below. The terror was gone, and in its place was only fury and the desire to drench the field in oceans of goblin blood.

"Advance!"

THE CROWS

A large black crow, one of hundreds eagerly anticipating the evening's feast to come, rode the winds high overhead. As the black mass below began to pour down the hill in ever-growing numbers, small rivulets began to leak away from the vast grey pool that awaited its onslaught at the bottom. The little rivulets grew to a stream, and then a flood, until the pool began to flow like a river before the first black tendrils even reached out to touch grey.

The crow emitted an excited "caw" to its brothers. Tonight they would gorge themselves on wolfsmeat and glut themselves on goblinflesh.

CORVUS

THE ebb and flow of battle always seemed to follow a similar pattern, Corvus thought as he watched the ragged ranks of the goblin army march into what he intended to be the field of slaughter.

A less experienced commander might be impressed by the huge quantity of armed troops as they moved, apparently inexorably, across the very meadow over which he'd ridden the day before. There were an awful lot of them, between four and five to every man of his, but the numbers were almost unimportant once a critical mass was achieved.

It was surprising how little actual killing occurred while the outcome of the battle was still in doubt, when the two front lines crashed into each other and sword met with sword. No, most of the bloodshed would take place after one side broke, its will shattered by the iron resolve of the enemy, and what had moments before been an army dissolved into a fleeing crowd of frightened individuals.

That was the moment for which every general worth his salt planned, anticipated, and feared. It was the moment in which every decision, every purchase, every piece of equipment, every hour of weapons drill and unit maneuver, was thrown into the cauldron of Fate and the bitch-goddess stirred up her bloody witch's brew, seasoned it according to her whim, and served it to you. You had no choice but to swallow it.

He was determined that his would not be the side that broke.

At the moment when he caught sight of the sleek sinuous forms of the wolves slinking through the tall grass below, it was too late to regret splitting his two cavalry wings. It was too late to wonder if he should have stationed more of the artillery on the heights to his right instead of behind him in the center. It was too late to consider if he should have positioned the second and fifth cohorts on either side of the first cohort instead of the fourth and sixth.

That was the worst part of being a general. Everyone else in the legion, from the tribunes to the lowliest legionary, believed you were in command. Only you knew you weren't. In truth, you were little more than a helpless observer, watching as the events you'd earlier put in motion played themselves out without much in the way of guidance from you or respect for your intentions. It wasn't what he did in the heat of battle, but what he had done to prepare for it, that mattered.

And yet, he was entirely confident that it would be the goblin commander who would be drinking Fortune's bitter draught tonight. Legio XVII might be green, but they damn sure had stouter hearts than goblins, who, despite the beating drums that urged them forward, continued to slow their march as they came closer to the Amorran lines.

The goblin advance slowed, then slowed some more, and finally came to a complete halt about fifty paces from the ground where the first cohort stood, steadfast, flanked on either side by the fourth and sixth cohorts. The drums stopped.

Corvus heard the primus pilus shout, a loud cry that was echoed by five hundred voices chanting in response. The centuries in the neighboring cohorts began to pick it up as well. A thousand voices chanted a single word, then slammed the butt of their spears twice on the ground, then repeated it again. Then two thousand voices, then three thousand.

"Legion!" *Thump-thump.* "Legion!"

Men stomped their feet, clapped their hands, slammed their gauntleted fists into their steel breastplates. The very hill upon which Corvus stood seemed to shake with the echoes, but not as much as the goblins. Their front ranks were visibly quivering with fear.

"Legion!" *Thump-thump.* "Legion!"

It sounded as if his men were summoning some ancient demon of war—no, an army of demons—from the bowels of the earth.

"Legion!" *Thump-thump.* "Legion!"

Corvus nodded slowly, pleased. No one, least of all the enemy ranks lined up against them, would imagine these were men who had never seen battle before. Saturnius's centurions had done their work well.

He glanced to the left. As expected, the goblin commander had divided his wolves between the two flanks, and their right wing looked no more eager to rush forward into the teeth of the infantry fortifying the thin line of horse than their foot was to come to grips with the cohorts in the center. On the right, he saw a desultory exchange of missiles was taking place, but it was nothing to cause him any concern for the safety of the two young tribunes he had stationed atop the hill there.

But if the goblin masses were intimidated, their commander was not. His response was spectacular, if not particularly effective. A strange humming filled the air, gradually swelling until the Amorran chanting began to break up as the legionaries wondered what it was. Then, with the sound of a thunderclap, purple fire arched from the goblin rear over their lines and exploded in the midst of the first cohort. He saw men fly into the air, heard other men scream, burned by the shaman's fire. The goblin drums began to thunder again.

"Ballistarii!" Saturnius turned around and screamed at the optio who commanded the artillery. "Cassabus, find me that devil-spawned bugger and flatten him now!"

Corvus squinted and attempted to see where the shaman might be, but he shrugged and gave it up after a moment. The sharpest eyes in the legion were assigned to the artillery squads, and if they couldn't spot the goblin, his aging eyes certainly wouldn't be up to the task either.

Saturnius's face turned redder with each of the two subsequent magical blasts, both of which ripped small holes in the Amorran ranks. But despite their alarming effects on the morale of the troops forced to stand there helplessly enduring the magical barrage, Corvus knew the shaman wasn't doing them any significant harm.

"They have him, legate!" Cassabus called down to an irate Saturnius. "First cohort, loose!"

There was a loud thrumming sound and the shriek of much-abused wood as the supports absorbed the force of heavy slings slamming down, one after the other.

Ten huge rocks sailed over the heads of the Amorran infantry—and the greater part of the goblin infantry as well. All crashed down into a remarkably small area and left little more than smears of green ruin behind them as they bounced and tumbled to an eventual halt well behind the enemy's rear.

"Well done, Cassabus," Corvus shouted to the optio. "Commend your men!"

He doubted the man could hear him over the creaking of the onagers as the ballistarii rewound their huge coils, but Cassabus saw Corvus was shouting at him, and the optio raised his fist triumphantly.

"That'll do for the bastard," Saturnius said with satisfaction, his complexion gradually returning to something more resembling its customary color. "And it should give any of his little bastard friends second thoughts about throwing that devil's fire about willy-nilly."

"Who needs Michaelines when you've got mules?" Corvus laughed at the sour expression on the legate's face. No matter how well things were going, Saturnius was always foul-tempered throughout the course of a battle.

"At least we've got a few lads who can hit the broad side of a barn," Saturnius said. "But I don't know what those bloody scorpios thought they were trying to hit."

Corvus looked behind them, momentarily confused. Sure enough, two of the scorpio squads were reloading their giant crossbows. He hadn't even realized they had loosed their bolts.

A horn sounded, and a great purple cloud appeared out of nowhere before exploding harmlessly well over the heads of the first cohort.

It was a signal, not an attack. The goblin lines began to move forward again. There was a piercing scream, followed by another, and soon all the wretched breeds were running, shrieking like the souls of the damned as they rushed madly toward the black shields of the waiting legion. Finally, the battle would be truly joined.

Corvus glanced at Marcus Saturnius, who was scowling furiously. How many times had they witnessed this together, Corvus thought. It was always the same. It didn't matter if you were fighting men or goblins, elves or orcs. All the sights and sounds and strategies and tactics were eventually reduced to this: two lines coming together into one.

Without any signal from either of them, as if the onrushing goblins had crossed some invisible line, a roar went up from the centurions, and a murderous flock of flying serpents leaped into the air from the first two Amorran ranks as the centuries hurled their spears.

The goblins fought with courage, but man-for-man they were much weaker than the legionaries. Their weapons were seldom able to pierce the Amorran armor, and their own armor couldn't withstand the forged steel of the legionary blades and spearheads. And whereas a wounded goblin was prone to be crushed under the feet of his comrades as they pressed forward, a wounded legionary was quickly extracted by the men behind him and assisted, or carried if need be, to the medici positioned to the left of the reserve cohorts.

Corvus saw Saturnius looking pensive as the pressing goblins fell back momentarily following an extraordinary, but ultimately futile, effort that had seen several men in the front ranks fall, including a centurion from the sixth cohort, at the cost of more than one hundred goblins. Saturnius whispered thoughtfully to himself, then abruptly turned and said something to his draconarius, who blew four rapid notes in a signal that was acknowledged in ragged succession by the centuries fighting below.

After the last horn sounded, the ballistarii launched their missiles en masse just over the helmets of their own troops and into the enemy's front lines. The three embattled cohorts used the resulting disarray among the goblins to rotate their first three lines of troops back and exchange them with the three lines that had been waiting, more or less patiently, for their own turn at the bloody mill.

"Nicely done," Corvus complimented his subordinate. "They might have been on the parade ground."

"They'd damn well better have gotten it right," Saturnius growled. "I didn't spend four months standing over them making them practice every day, rain or shine, for my own health. And those two centuries from the bloody sixth still tried to go right instead of left! I'll have their centurions' guts to lace my sandals tomorrow."

Corvus smiled. Things were going well indeed if Saturnius was cursing his troops instead of the enemy. And unless he missed his guess, the century that bumbled its withdrawal had lost its centurion only moments before. Considering that this was their first battle and they had just lost their officer, the century from the sixth were doing well to have merely muffed a rotation. That was the ultimate tribute any unit could pay its commander, to maintain its discipline even in his absence.

Another hour or two, perhaps three more rotations, and the goblins would wear themselves out. Due to their observable lack of discipline and reluctance to come to grips, Corvus suspected the goblin cavalry would be the first to withdraw. They would use their superior speed to run away rather than screen the infantry's retreat as they should. Then the rear ranks of the infantry would begin to melt away, until the front ones, realizing they were being abandoned, would take fright, throw down their arms, and try to flee.

And then the slaughter would begin. Lightly armored as they were, the goblin foot would easily outpace the cohorts, but they would be cut down from behind by the fresh lances and long swords of the cavalry riding in from the flanks. It was a pity about the woods being so near, as the trees would prevent the cavalry from continuing the killing until night fell, but he guessed they would be able to cut down at least two thousand across the full length of the field.

The left flank was still quiet, but the right was suddenly in an uproar over something. The cavalry were shouting and waving their spears in the air. Some had even mounted their horses, but Corvus couldn't see what the excitement was about.

"*Castita merda!*" Saturnius swore. He sounded genuinely distressed. "Oh, you stupid, stupid, *sopio!*"

Corvus had to step sideways to see around the crest of Aulus Crescentius's helm, which was blocking his view. What he saw filled him with horror.

At the base of the hill, alone and facing the entire goblin left flank, was a mounted tribune, resplendent in a blue captain's cloak. He held his sword, or perhaps it was a mace, aloft, and behind him lay sprawled the dead bodies of a large, dark-furred wolf and its rider. The Amorran cavalry he commanded was chanting his name.

"Fortex! Fortex! Fortex!"

By all the gods, Gaius Valerius, what have you done?

He exchanged a look with Saturnius. The legate's face was nearly as ashen as it had been suffused with scarlet before. Around them, the officers of the legion's command staff fell entirely silent. They too had seen the tribune's triumph.

"I'm sorry, Sextus Valerius," Saturnius said. His old friend came closer to him and placed a hand upon his shoulder. "I can't tell you how sorry I am."

Corvus nodded, maintaining his composure even though the urge to ride down the hill himself and throttle his vainglorious fool of a nephew was so strong it made his hands shake. As a horn sounded from his right flank and the knights of the Second began to advance down the hill, he deliberately turned his back on them and returned his attention to the infantry still fighting hard below.

What would happen would happen. It was all in God's hands. There was simply nothing he could do about it now.

FORTEX

THE exultation of the kill faded, and Fortex knew a moment's stark terror after he raised aloft the wolfrider's severed head.

Only a bare handful of knights responded to his signal. No trumpet sounded, no advance ensued, all he could hear were the bestial shrieks of the goblins and the howls of the wolves not fifty paces behind him.

It was his helm, he realized too late. With the silvered steel covering most of his mouth, no one could possibly have heard his cry from the summit of the hill! And if the damned gobbos charged now, he'd have no hope of escape. Even a horse as fast and powerful as Incitatus would not be able to climb a hill that steep without being pulled down from behind.

"Dammit, Marcus!" he cursed his cousin's cowardice. Then he remembered he had ordered Marcus to hold his ground until the goblins broke. Did they look like running?

He wheeled Incitatus around to face the enemy and was deeply disappointed to see that they did not. If anything, they were howling and shrieking even louder than before. This close, the sound was almost deafening, a palpable wave that washed over him like a river smashing against a solitary rock.

He was, he knew, a dead man. At this range, their bloody archers could hardly miss, and even their pathetic little wooden bows could generate enough force to punch a shaft right through his breastplate. He glanced at the severed head weighing down his sword, which was now streaked with dark green ichor. The dead goblin didn't have any answers for him, and the gaping mouth hanging loosely open made it look about as stupid as Fortex was feeling. It was also making his sword feel distressingly heavy.

Well, if nothing else, he'd killed the big bastard. For a moment there, when the monster wolf had turned on him with such unexpected speed, he'd thought it was going to chew off his arse! With no time to think, he'd simply reacted. So there was that. If Fortex had to die in battle, then at least they would say he did it in bloody style! Anyhow, a warrior's death was better than an ambusher's arrow through the throat or shitting your life out in the latrines.

He slipped his useless shield off his left arm and slung it on the saddle, switched hands, then grabbed the goblin's hair and tugged it off the end of his sword. Or rather, he tried to tug it off. Bloody hells, it was really stuck on there! He gritted his teeth and pulled again. Finally it came off with a grotesquely unappetizing sucking sound.

"Do you want this?" he shouted at the shrieking, unhearing goblins. "Do you want it back? Then take it and be damned, you swamp-stinking, frog-humping, demon-spawned buggers!"

He rose in his stirrups and hurled their dead commander's head at them as if it was a firepot.

To his surprise, the wolfriders in its path cringed as if it terrified them. They shied away from the grotesque missile as it struck the ground before them and bounced harmlessly through their lines. Fortex returned his sword to his right hand and kicked Incitatus forward, hoping to kill at least two or three more of the little monsters before they brought him down. And then, from behind him, he heard the most beautiful sound he had ever heard in his life. First one horn, then a second, and finally the third, each sounding the advance!

Why, Marcus Valerius, you magnificent disobedient puppy! Perhaps, he considered happily, his cousin wasn't entirely the bloodless ninny he seemed.

Glancing back, he saw the entire cavalry wing was beginning to descend the hill and the first small group of knights, led by the second decurion of the fourth squadron, Gavrus, had already reached the bottom and was galloping madly toward him with their lances lowered.

"What took you so long?" he shouted at the decurion as he came within earshot.

"You didn't say you wanted company, Tribune!" Gavrus pulled up his horse and raised his lance when he reached Fortex's side. "We thought you was going to beat them all by your own self!"

"I'm a generous man, Gavrus. I wouldn't deny you your share."

He looked past his small half-squadron of reinforcements at the majestic sight of the entire cavalry wing picking up speed as they approached the level plain. The thunder of eight hundred hooves made the ground shake, and he wasn't the slightest bit surprised to turn and see the goblins in the front line beginning to back away. The twelve knights with him looked far more wolfish than the beasts on which the enemy rode.

"Well, men," Fortex said, "there are at least twelve of us against, what, seven hundred? I like those odds, don't you?" He didn't wait for a response, but instead raised his sword and urged Incitatus forward. Behind him, the decurion shouted "Fortex!" and the cry was echoed by the others.

Three wolfriders leaped toward him, their beasts snarling. But they were the brave exceptions as the goblin cavalry crumbled before the black wave of the approaching Amorran onslaught.

Incitatus reared up and smashed the skull of the wolf on his left with an iron-shod hoof, and Fortex slashed the head off a spear that jabbed up at him on his right. Incitatus leaped forward again as Fortex brought his sword up and around in time to sever the left arm of the third wolfrider, and then he was past the combatants and in hot pursuit of their companions.

While the wolves were fleet of foot and their riders were less than half the weight of an armored human knight, they couldn't hope to outrun an Amorran battle steed, much less one the size and breeding of Incitatus. Fortex cut down one, two, three goblins before any of them had even realized he was upon them, and Incitatus simply galloped right over a fourth, trampling wolf and rider alike. The wolf yelped like a beaten puppy as it rolled to its feet and fled, but its rider was silent, reduced to little more than a battered mass of shapeless green gore. The big horse stumbled momentarily but soon regained his stride, allowing Fortex to kill two more goblins in quick succession.

After a few more minutes of effortless slaughter, he pulled Incitatus up and saw that the fastest-riding knights were already flying past him. Their lances were expertly spearing goblins by the dozens as they rode down the shorter-legged wolves from behind. As their lances splintered or were lodged in the bodies of their foes, they dropped them and switched to the sword. A few of the riderless wolves caught up in the chaos of battle snapped and slashed at the horses' legs, but the knights were alert to their presence, and no few wolves were impaled as well.

Here and there a horse went down, more often brought down by the uneven ground over which they galloped than by the spears or teeth of the enemy. But such falls were seldom fatal to either horse or rider, and overall, their casualties were so light as to be almost nonexistent. Fortex grinned as he saw the red standard of the Second Knights snapping smartly above the heads of a small group of approaching riders. The draconarius held the flag proudly aloft in both hands, defended on one side by a decurion of the third squadron and by his cousin on the other. A riderless wolf standing over the corpse of his rider snarled as they rode past, and Marcus adroitly leaned over as if he were at the tilt and drove his lance right through the wolf's open jaws. The lance snapped with a loud crack as the wolf collapsed, its skull pierced fore and aft, and Fortex had to laugh as his cousin threw the remains of the now-useless weapon at the dying animal in apparent disgust.

"You should have saved that for spitting goblins, Marcus! Leave the wolves alone, they don't have much fight in them without their riders."

Marcus shrugged indifferently, but Fortex thought he looked a little greenish. "How far do you want to chase them?"

"To the ends of the earth!" Fortex laughed again. He felt like a veritable god of war. How glorious it was to ride over a battlefield covered by the broken, bleeding bodies of the foe! "No, we can't afford to let the men extend themselves much further and risk getting cut off. We'll give them their head for a little longer, then call them back to reform. You may recall, after all, the entire point of this little exercise was to relieve the center."

"With the cavalry screen gone, we can hit their infantry from behind," Marcus noted. "That should do for them."

"Your timing may be impeccable, Marcus, but there is more to winning battles than simply killing the enemy. If we hit their infantry from behind, we'll trap them between us and our infantry. With no way out, that will put even more pressure on our cohorts in the center, at least until we kill them all." Fortex laughed at the expression of chagrin on his cousin's face. "Never corner a rat if you can avoid it. We'll hit the buggers on the flank and give them room to run. That will trigger the rout and put them in a position where the First Knights can ride them down even easier than we did the wolves on our side."

Fortex sighed and reached out to clap Marcus on his armored shoulder. "I won't say it doesn't pain me to let Sulpicius and his boys in on the action, but that will make things considerably easier on the infantry, and they've had a long morning. And they've still got their lances, whereas we don't. Now, why don't we see if we can kill ourselves a few more goblins before we sound the recall?"

Two hours later, the sun was past its zenith and the contested ground belonged to the legion. It had taken longer than Fortex had expected for the decurions to recall their battle-maddened riders and assemble them into a reasonable formation, but nevertheless, the Second Knights still managed to arrive in time to take the unsuspecting enemy infantry in the left flank with a devastating charge that was accompanied by a chorus of cheers from the watching Amorran centuries.

Fortex was deeply grateful to whatever optio was commanding the ballistarii, because as soon as his draconarius had sounded the horn to signal the shift from skirmish to a wedge, two groups of twenty onagers unexpectedly hurled their massive missiles into the left side of the goblin line, preventing it from turning in formation to defend against Fortex's charge.

The artillery barrage made all the difference. Instead of trying to force their horses into three rows of braced enemy spears, however hastily and haphazardly assembled, his knights found themselves crashing against a broken, bleeding line, with huge gaps torn in it. The goblin infantry hadn't run before contact like their cavalry had, but stunned and in disarray, they were even more helpless than the fleeing wolfriders against the shock of the Amorran cavalry charge.

A centurion approached him. It was Caius Proculus, the senior centurion of the second cohort. "Well met, Tribune."

Fortex grinned and extended his hand, but the centurion gripped his forearm as if he were a fellow legionary, not an officer. "Most kind of you to leave us a few goblins, Centurion," Fortex replied, well-pleased by the implicit compliment. "I thought surely you'd have eaten them all by the time we got here."

"They say you knights all have arses like plums and livers like sheep, but I say you can stand with the hastati any time, Tribune."

Fortex was delighted, but he hid it with a contemptuous snort. "Proculus, the fact that I'm foolish enough to do your bloody work for you doesn't mean I'm dumb enough to walk when I can ride. Tell you what, though, you buy yourself a mule when we get back to Berdicum, and I'll make you a decurion."

The centurion barked with laughter and saluted. "By the bones, Tribune, don't tempt me! I just may take you up on that! God and Amorr, sir!"

Fortex returned the centurion's salute with his own, then urged Incitatus to follow the rest of the Second Knights, who were trotting leisurely toward what looked to be the general direction of the camp. He was desperately hungry, and now that the rush of battle fury had faded, the disgusting smell of the goblin blood in which he had all but bathed was beginning to make him feel faint.

He mused upon the centurion's salute as they rode. God and Amorr? He didn't see that the Immaculate had had much to do with the charnel house of this battlefield. When he looked down at the stinking blood and gore splattered across his arm, chest, and leg, it was, in fact, hard to imagine anything less immaculate.

He wasn't even sure what Amorr had to do with it either, come to think of it. Had there ever been a goblin tribe known to march on the great city? Marcus would know, he supposed. But, to be honest, he couldn't care less. Victory in battle was its own reward, and a man no more needed to justify war than he needed to justify wine.

The camp was in sight when he saw a tribune and a centurion riding toward him. It was Crescentius, the laticlavius, easily recognizable by the broad white strip at the bottom of his red tribune's cape. He didn't know the centurion's name, although he seemed to recall the man was with the seventh cohort.

They were probably coming to fetch him on behalf of the legate, Fortex concluded. He wasn't surprised that Saturnius would want to honor him in some way, although the infantry hadn't been in nearly enough danger to justify anything like the grass crown. Wouldn't that have been something, though! Magnus would have been fair to burst with pride.

Caught up in his idle daydreaming, Fortex nearly fell off Incitatus at the first words out of Crescentius's mouth. They were, in fact, very close to the last thing he could have possibly imagined under the circumstances.

"Gaius Valerius Fortex, you will accompany us now. Give the centurion your sword. I have orders in the name of Marcus Saturnius, legate of the legion, to place you under arrest."

SEVERA

THE autumn sun was unseasonably hot as it beat down on the forty thousand people sitting or standing on the stone rows of the great arena. Fortunately, the slaves had brought some thick white cloth with them and, with the use of some wooden posts, had arranged it to provide shade for Severa and the others seated in the box. Below them, a pair of female fighters in leather armor were jabbing their spears at a nearly naked male goblin armed with only a dagger, but the uneven battle held little interest for her. She was thinking about one of the attractions to come later in the day, and her stomach was tight with dread and anticipation.

Her father and three brothers were seated in front of her, to her left. As one of the women nearly managed to skewer the green-skinned inhuman with a clumsy jab, her father leaned over and said something to her oldest brother, Regulus, who threw back his head and laughed. Her mother, being more than a little squeamish, wasn't there. She was at home with Severa's younger sister, Severilla, who was too young for the bloody violence on display.

But not Severa. What was more, she had been permitted to bring her friends Caera and Falconilla with her, both of whom were tremendously excited to be seen by everyone sitting in the princeps's box.

"Those creatures are so disgusting," Falconilla commented, staring at the goblin with an incredulous expression on her face. "Can you imagine how they must smell? Where do they find them anyway?"

Severa's brother Tertius, only a year older than her, leaned back to reply. "Considering that House Valerius has three legions marching through their lands right now, I imagine there will soon be a surfeit of them in the markets. Would you like one, my lady Falconius?"

Falconilla didn't deign to provide Tertius with a verbal response but merely turned up her nose at him. Tertius laughed and turned his attention back to the amateurish battle.

The goblin was nearly as tall as the shorter woman but much skinnier, and its legs and arms were disproportionately long by human standards. Its skin was a light green color with hints of yellow here and there, and a faint dusting of dark green hair covered its chest and lower belly. Whatever passed for its goblinhood was mercifully concealed by a dirty cloth that may have once been white. The goblin's face was a mask of bestial desperation. It bared sharp and yellowed teeth at the women as it once again managed to duck a spear thrust at its chest. The women seemed to be a little slower than the goblin, and their failure to coordinate their attacks made it easy for the greenskin to evade them. But despite its long arms and greater speed, the short length of the crude dagger with which it had been provided made it difficult for the goblin to get past the iron spearheads without taking a high risk of being impaled.

"Whatever did those poor women do to find themselves thrown in the arena?" Caera asked Severa.

"Who knows," she answered. "Maybe they're slaves no one wanted."

"Do you think so?" Caera sounded surprised. "The taller one is pretty enough to be a bodyslave."

"What of it?" Falconilla asked dismissively. "That filthy goblin is pretty enough to be an Andronican lady-in-waiting."

"Or the wife of a Valerian," Severa said, laughing. "Maybe that's why House Valerius sent their legions north—it's the only way they can find anyone to marry their sons and daughters!"

There was a scream below, and the three girls in the box looked down. The goblin had managed to slash one woman's left arm, leaving a deep wound running nearly the length of her upper arm. The woman grimly held onto her spear with both hands even though the blood was running down her forearm and dripping onto the sand, but her next pathetic attempt at thrusting the spear at the goblin revealed that she'd been badly hurt.

"She poisoned her husband," Tertius said unexpectedly.

"What?"

"That woman." He pointed down at the woman who'd just been wounded. "She's a Lucanian who poisoned her husband. The other one is an adulteress who went to a witch to kill her unborn child after she fell pregnant. I don't know where she's from, but she looks Epran. They're not warriors or slaves. They're damnatii."

"Really?" Falconilla was staring at Severa's brother in amazement. "How do you know that?"

"I sent Marsupor to talk with one of the trainers at the stable. It's rather stupid to wager on combats if you know nothing of the combatants involved, don't you think?" He picked up a wooden tablet from his lap and waved it dismissively. "The libellus bills this travesty before us as a battle to the death between two Cynothi warrior women and a goblin blademaster of the savage western tribes. But I very much doubt either of those women has ever held a spear or even been north of Amorr. So I bet on the goblin."

"Do you always do that? Have your slave ask around the stables?" Severa attempted to sound curious rather than terrified.

"I wish I dared." Tertius sighed ruefully. "No, only when there is cause to think something's amiss. Such as, for example, the idea that there are any Cynothi captives of either sex to be had. If you recall, the Cynothii defeated Legio XIV a few months ago, so I imagine it is rather more likely there are Amorrans fighting for the amusement of the crowds in Cynothicum than any of their warrior women are fighting here for us."

"To say nothing of the fact that their women are no more inclined to take to the battlefield than our own," added their father, shaking his smoothly shaven head in disapproval. "They may be rebels and provincials, but they're hardly barbarians."

An air of anticipation swept over the crowd, and her father returned his attention to the sands. The two women appeared to have finally understood the need to coordinate their attacks. The taller woman, the adulteress, took a more aggressive stance and was calling out instructions to the wounded poisoner as she circled to her right and attempted to drive the goblin toward the spear of the other woman with a series of quick, conservative jabs.

The goblin also seemed to realize its danger, and it glanced back and forth between the two women, as if trying to decide which one it should attack first.

It decided quickly and bared its stained, triangular teeth. It leaped toward the wounded woman and with its free hand slapped away her feeble attempt to thrust her spear at its face.

She screamed and stumbled backward, dropping the spear and covering her face with her hands.

The crowd roared, and the goblin pounced. But it reached for the spear instead of stabbing the defenseless woman. It was seemingly unaware of the second woman rushing toward it from behind, her pretty face a mask of desperate determination.

Severa heard Tertius groan. Even she could see there was no way the goblin could pick up the spear and turn around before the charging woman plunged her spear into it. But it didn't try. Whether it heard the sound of footsteps on the sand or its move toward the spear was never more than a feint, no one would ever know. Regardless, the goblin stopped, twisted its upper body, and hurled the dagger right into the woman's face with all of the force in its long, wiry arm.

A gasp filled the arena. The shock of being struck by the knife sent the woman staggering off-balance to her right, and she dropped her own spear and instinctively raised her hands to her face. The goblin's dagger fell harmlessly to the ground beside her.

The crowd roared, a wordless cry of fear and anticipation, until it realized that the woman had been struck by only the hard wooden handle and not the blade.

But even if the blow wasn't serious, it gave the goblin enough time to pick up the second spear, raise it overhead, and plunge it once, twice, three times into the chest, throat, and abdomen of the disarmed and screaming murderess. The woman's screams subsided into the chokes and coughs of the mortally wounded, and the goblin pulled the spear from her body and turned to stalk the remaining woman.

Her right cheek was red from where the handle had hit her, but she was otherwise unharmed. She bent to retrieve her spear. But the other woman's fall had clearly sapped her courage, and her steps became tentative, and she was forced onto the defensive.

With every thrust and jab of the goblin's bloody spear, the woman's determination gradually transformed into wide-eyed terror. She was soon reduced to little more than parrying its attacks. It wasn't long before droplets of the other woman's blood from the spear's head sprinkled her face like freckles.

"I'd rather be executed," Severa heard Caera say in a low voice.

"What's that?"

"Look at that poor woman. It's awful. If I ever did anything deserving of a death sentence, I'd rather they simply strangled me or threw me from the Rock than go through that kind of hell. I don't care what she did— look at her. No one should ever be that terrified!"

As if to emphasize her words, the goblin let out a ghastly, inhuman shriek, and the woman lost control of her bladder. The goblin sprang upon her, first beating her spear aside with its own and then releasing it in order to grasp her throat with both its dexterous, long-fingered hands. It squeezed with all of its wiry strength, snarling and snapping at her purpling face as if it was some sort of giant, green hairless cat.

The woman, unable to pull its hands from her throat, gave up and cast desperately about for the knife, which was near her right side. Her fingers scrabbled blindly over the sand. At last she came across it.

But it was already too late. Before her fingers could curl around the handle, they suddenly straightened and went rigid, and she began to convulse in her dying straits. Finally, her hands relaxed, lifeless, as her spirit left her abused body behind, off to face its own judgment.

Tertius rose to his feet and raised a fist in triumph, but the crowd's reaction to the goblin's victory was less enthusiastic. Perhaps many of them had bet heavily upon the women. Perhaps they simply found the sight of two human women slain by a goblin displeasing. By whatever cause, its mood abruptly became ugly.

The crowd jeered as a pair of men wearing the colors of the Green stable, armed with clubs and whips, walked out to escort the victor back into the bowels of the arena. The goblin was no sooner divested of its crude weaponry than six slaves ran out—two pairs to drag the dead women's bodies from the floor of the arena, and the remaining pair to follow them with rakes and eliminate the furrows in the sand left by the bodies.

The musicians struck up a jaunty tune, and a shaven dwarf walked out and began juggling small skulls to pass the time until the next match.

Caera looked at Severa with tears in her eyes. "It's so cruel. How can you stand it?"

"Everyone dies sooner or later." Falconilla was in high spirits. Her eyes were bright and her cheeks were flushed. She, at least, was thoroughly enjoying herself. "What difference does it make if a woman gets strangled in the prison cells or in the arena? It's the same either way."

Severa stared at a bloody patch of sand. "I wonder what happened to the witch."

"What witch?" Falconilla asked.

"The one the adulteress went to to get rid of her baby. What happened to her?"

"Oh. I don't know. Who cares? Bring her here and we'll find out what happens to her."

Severa looked away. As was often the case on her visits to the games, she found herself more interested in the varied reactions of the people around her to the violence than in the violence itself. The combat was exciting, to be sure, and it stirred her blood. But there was also an element of pagan, even ritual, brutality to the spectacle that she found unsettling.

It felt almost as if they had witnessed a human sacrifice, although one to the greedy hunger of the crowd instead of a god. She did not find it hard to understand why more gentle souls, like Caera, had no taste for it.

"Do you want to leave?" she asked her friend. "I want to see Clusius fight, but then after that I'll take you home. We don't need to stay all day if you don't want to."

Caera pursed her lips, then nodded. "When does Clusius fight?"

"Tertius, who is Clusius fighting today, and when will it come?"

Her brother consulted the libellus. "The dimachaerus Silicus Clusius of the Blues is scheduled for the fourth bout. He's facing Caladas the Thraex, of the Reds. It should be a decent match. They're both unbeaten. Clusius has seven wins and two draws, and Caladas has nine wins and three draws. Two blades are flashy, and Clusius certainly knows how to use them, but I like Caladas here." The look he gave Severa's friend was not without compassion. "Caera, there's only one more match involving a damnatius today, and it's after the Clusius match, so it's quite possible you needn't fear seeing anyone else killed before you go."

Caera smiled. "What odds will you give me on Clusius, Tertius?"

"What is your fascination with him, little sister? I thought it was Caladas who all the young widows are panting for."

"I'm not a widow, am I? Anyhow, it's none of your business. What odds will you give?"

Tertius frowned and looked up at the makeshift shade that protected them from the cloudless blue sky. "Two to one, so long as you keep it under a thousand sesterces."

As if she had a thousand sesterces, Severa thought, annoyed. Of the four of them old enough to count, Tertius was the only one who ever had any money of his own. "Fifty, but you have to give me three to one." She didn't actually have the money, but she knew her mother would give it to her in the unlikely event that she lost.

"Fifty at three to one it is." Tertius took up the bronze stylus attached to the libellus and made a note in the wax covering it. "Falconilla, Caera, you are both witnesses."

None of them was particularly interested in the next bout, which was a venatio featuring five wolves being set against a bear. The venator in charge of the bout had the devil's own time getting the wolves to pay more attention to the bear than to his own assistants, and not until the bear had raked its claws across the face of one curious wolf did they show any interest in it. The crowd was openly hissing its contempt by the time the small pack managed to bring the half-starved bear down. The venator himself finally had to put the wounded beast out of its misery, as well as one of the wolves with a broken shoulder.

The next event went over rather better, as it was a comedic hunt in which a dwarf and a goblin, both dressed in orc-style armor, were mounted on large pigs, given lances, and set to hunting hundreds of rabbits that were carried into the arena in ten large cages then released on the sands.

"Ser Borgulus the Bunnyslayer versus Ser Snotshafter Rabbitsbane," read Tertius, smiling and shaking his head. " 'The winning knight shall be he who spears the most rabbits in the time of one glass. He and his stablemates shall dine on rabbit stew tonight. The loser shall face a savage warboar in a subsequent match.' I suppose that should suffice to give the buggers incentive."

Laughter echoed off the stone seats of the arena. The crowd, so recently displeased, appeared to have forgiven the master of games for the previous debacle. Especially since the pigs, lashed by the venator's assistants, squealed and dashed madly into the mass of rabbits. The rodents scattered in what looked, from Severa's perspective, like a furry explosion, dashing in literally every direction.

The goblin, which she presumed was the one designated Rabbitsbane, appeared to have a more instinctive grasp of riding, as it was leaning to its right and attempting to spear the rabbits as it rode through the scurrying mass of them. It actually managed to impale one on its first pass, although the pig it rode was even more successful, as the mottled brute left three trampled behind it in its porcine wake.

"Ten on the goblin, ten on the goblin!" cried Falconilla, leaping out of her chair.

"Done!" called Regulus over his shoulder.

On the other side of their father, Tertius was shaking his head and laughing, though he didn't seem taken by the absurd spectacle before them so much as by the excitement of the others.

Ser Borgulus the Bunnyslayer, meanwhile, was having trouble merely staying upright on the back of his black mount, despite the ropes that bound him to the rude saddle. The dwarf fought to keep his balance, nearly dropping his lance, and failed to make even one attempt to spear a rabbit on his pig's first wild charge, although one was crushed to red ruin underneath the cloven hooves of the beast. However, as the pig calmed down from its whip-inspired frenzy, the dwarf managed to get it under control and begin attempting to live up to his false name.

While the goblin was riding its pig as if it were a real war boar and attacking the rabbits one at a time in succession like a lancer, the dwarf simply aimed his mount directly at the largest gatherings of the little creatures and tried to trample them. He even reversed his grip on the spear and held it just above the spearhead, using the long shaft as a club that sent rabbits flying as he rode past. Soon he had equaled, then surpassed, the goblin's total. The crowd shouted out the current count each time another rabbit fell to one of the hunters or its mount.

"No! No! No!" shouted Falconilla, stricken at the sight of the dwarf's unexpected rabbit-killing prowess. The anguish in her voice made even Caera laugh out loud, as everyone in the Severan box, as well as the rest of the arena, had risen to their feet and were chanting the body count with every rabbit speared, swatted, or trampled. "It doesn't count! It doesn't count! Look, that one got up and ran away after he whacked it!"

The goblin, seeing the dwarf's tactic was more effective, tried to imitate it, but soon discovered that its long, slender arms were not as strong as the dwarf's much thicker limbs, and were therefore too weak to deliver a sufficiently deadly blow with the butt end of the lance. Even when it managed to strike a rabbit cleanly, the force only sent the animal tumbling across the sand before it regained its feet and hopped away unharmed.

After a few such failed attempts, the Rabbitsbane switched back to using its lance properly, but now it had no hope of regaining its earlier lead.

The dwarf had now truly mastered his weapon, and in addition to swinging at the rabbits, he was also crushing them with savage, downward thrusts, as if angrily sounding the depth of a river. By the time the master of games held up his hand and caused the trumpeters to blow the call for the hunt's end, the count was thirty-five to eighteen in favor of Ser Borgulus, who in the eyes of the crowd had truly merited the name of Bunnyslayer.

The dwarf cast his lance aside and slumped in his ersatz saddle as the crowd rejoiced in his triumph. The goblin looked for a moment as if it was going to charge the venator's assistants as they approached it, whips in hand. But when one of them aimed a large crossbow at its chest, the greenskin relented and followed the dwarf's example. But as the dwarf exited through the gate that led to the Green stables staging area, he raised one meaty fist in triumphant salute to the crowd, which went wild in response.

"Borgulus, Borgulus, ave Borgulus," thundered the chant, punctuated with rollicking laughter. The master of games took a theatrical bow as a small army of slaves ran out, some of them with leashed dogs, to collect the dead rabbits and chase the living ones back into cages that were being wheeled back out upon the arena floor.

Falconilla, her face a portrait in bitterness, folded her arms and complained that she'd seen at least three rabbits that shouldn't have counted for the dwarf's total, until Regulus pointed out that even without the three, she would still owe him the ten sesterces. Unsurprisingly, it turned out that Falconilla didn't have so much as a single coin of any type on her person, so it was agreed that the debt would be collected later. Severa had absolutely no doubt that her friend would manage to forget about it unless Regulus elected to press her on it.

Finally, when the slaves finished their work and the sands were once more free of debris, the moment for which she'd been waiting arrived. The summa rudis entered, flanked by his two assistants, after which the

master of the games announced the two combatants. The crowd replied
with thunderous cheers.

Severa held her breath as Silicus Clusius stalked out into the center of
the arena like a young lion, bearing his daggers as if he were a demigod
and they were lightning bolts. His smooth, muscular arms were unscarred,
testifying to his courage as well as his skill. And when he turned to salute
the crowd in the direction she was sitting, her heart skipped a beat. For
there, wrapped around his upraised right wrist, was the strip of red she
had been hoping to see, the strip of red silk that she'd torn from one of
her gowns three nights ago and sent him as a token of her love.

Severa stared at the beautiful gladiator in silence as the crowd roared
its affection for him. They loved him even though they knew nothing of
him. How little they knew his heart! She, and she alone, knew of the
sweet lover inside the fearless killer. She alone had read the gentle poetry
in which he spilled out the unspoken longings of his secret heart to her.
She sighed, her eyes drinking in the perfection of his warrior's body, her
hands itching to caress the powerful expanse of his chest.

She could have stared at him forever, but the strange sensation that
someone was watching her gradually worked its way into her consciousness. Then she started. Someone *was* staring at her, it was her father. His
dark, penetrating eyes seemed to bore their way inside her, making her
feel as if he could read the treacherous intentions that the sight of that silk
token had now burned into her soul. She felt like the mouse ensorcelled
by the cobra, and she waited for the fatal strike, for the deadly words that
would expose her in front of everyone.

But they never came. Her father's hooded gaze unexpectedly released
her, and he turned back to the arena, where Caladas the Thraex, Clusius's opponent, was standing with his arms spread wide, basking in the
adulation of the crowd.

Severa sank into her seat, her legs weak with relief, and began to pray.
Surely God would not be so cruel as to let Clusius perish today, in front of
her very eyes! Surely He would be kind! She prayed as she had not since
she was a child: fervently, sincerely, and emotionally.

As she pleaded for the favor of Heaven on behalf of her beloved, she heard the first ringing clash of metal upon metal.

LODI

THE wind howled down from the north, cruel and cold. The sun was nowhere to be found, hidden behind a thick mass of grey clouds piled one upon the other like stones. Lodi was tired, frozen nearly stiff, and desperately wishing he was just about anywhere else than sitting with his legs dangling over the lip of a shallow cave sitting halfway up the barren, nameless mountainside.

It was the seventh day since he and his young companion had last seen the black dragon emerge from its rocky lair. It had been inside there so long that Lodi was beginning to wonder if Thorald might have somehow imagined its return. Bored, he rolled the rope attached to the iron pike affixed to the cave floor behind him back and forth over his thigh.

Actually, the mountain probably did have a name, but it wasn't likely to be one that Lodi or any other dwarf could pronounce easily. They were so far into the northern mountains that, for all he knew, they were in troll country now. He shuddered. Dodging orcs was one thing, as when push came to shove, one could always kill them. But as a survivor of the seven-year siege of Iron Mountain by the great troll king, Guldur Goblinsbane, he knew better than most how much killing a troll required.

Not for the first time, Lodi regretted taking this job. But when he'd been sitting in front of the massive hearth in the king of the Underdeep's private chamber with a well-brewed ale in one hand and fried cavesnake in the other, recovering a stolen item from a dragon's hoard had seemed like an almost trivial task. Especially when compared with the risks he'd previously survived tracking down fellow dwarves taken by Man slavers.

That was then. This was now.

"How much longer are we going to wait here?" Thorald asked. The lad wasn't complaining, not exactly, but at only fifty-six, he was still subject to the habitual impatience of youth. "I've read dragons can sleep for years without needing to feed, and we've only got enough grub for another five days if we don't get to hunting."

Lodi raised an eyebrow. "How does dragon stew grab you?"

"You can't be serious!"

"No, lad, I'm not," Lodi admitted. "I wonder if they're even edible? Seems to me it wouldn't be no safer to roast a beast as makes poison in its gut than to eat a spindelskivling mushroom. But there's no fear that brute won't come out soon. It's only the big monsters, the old magic ones, that don't have to eat for decades. A young drake like our Aslaughyrna, he's still growing, so he'll be feeling the pinch in his lizard belly soon. Today or tomorrow is what I think."

"I hope you're right." Thorald leaned back against his pack and took a bite out of a stone-dusted biscuit that was virtually indistinguishable from the rocks that were scattered all about these high-peaked mountains. He offered one to Lodi. Lodi refused it.

"Keep an eye out for our friend," he ordered, then leaned back and closed his eyes. If it weren't for the north wind howling over the barren mountain face, he could almost imagine he was safely underground. It didn't take long before he was dreaming of gold and of a warm darkness enveloping him safely.

Lodi woke with a sudden start. It was growing dark outside, and someone was shaking him and whispering.

"What is it?"

"Keep it down! I think he might be coming out. I heard rumbling sounds and a sort of coughing, hissing noise coming from below."

Lodi nodded and rolled over, then crept on his belly to the lip of the little cave. Even in the cloud-enshrouded darkness, he could see the mouth of the lair some distance below them.

Thorald wriggled up next to him. He was holding a loaded crossbow in his right hand.

"Put that thing away," Lodi whispered, rolling his eyes at the young dwarf.

They waited patiently, side-by-side, long enough to cause Lodi's left hand to fall asleep. They were at last rewarded with the sight of a black, triangular head the size of a warhorse, with large, forward-facing eyes emerging, snake-like, from the mouth of the cave.

Two long spikes protruded backward from both sides of the monster's jaw, giving it the appearance of a massive arrowhead. Its sinuous, muscular neck followed, then its low-slung, elongated body with its wings tightly folded over its back and sides. It was armored in black, overlapping scales mottled with dark purple blotches. A ridge like a downed sail ran from its shoulders to the tip of its tail. Sticking out from underneath its jaw, on either side, were two swellings that Lodi supposed contained the drake's lethal venom. They were tight now, rather than flaccid, so he assumed this was not the ideal time to attract the beast's attention.

But the drake showed no sign it knew they were there. It leaped from the protruding lip of the cave mouth in a single, leonine bound, then spread its broad, bat-like wings to catch the updraft from the hills that overlooked the valley far below. Its wings were lighter on their underside, as was its belly, making it easier to see from below.

Lodi watched until the drake was merely a speck in the distance. The steady stroke of its wings suggested that it intended to cover a significant amount of ground. He sat up and tugged on the rope to make sure it was still firmly secured before tying its end around his waist. He grabbed his empty pack, slipped the strap for his hand axe over his head, and handed the loose rope near the pike to Thorald.

"Keep a sharp eye on the horizon," Lodi said. "If you see anything in the distance, anything at all, bang three times on the rock with a hammer.

Bang three times twice if you're sure it's coming back. A false alarm is better than none. And mind the rope, you may have to pull me up in a hurry."

"I'd rather come with you. I've never seen a dragon's hoard, except for that empty one we found before."

Lodi nodded. He understood. No true dwarf wouldn't long for even a momentary glimpse of such treasure. The very words "dragon's hoard" were magical enough to stir the gold fever in any dwarf's veins.

"If there's time," Lodi promised. "But we need a lookout, and you'll be safer up here." He patted his young companion on the shoulder, then withdrew a vial of moonflower extract from his belt pouch and smeared the acrid oil on his palms and the bottom of his boots. It was supposed to mask the scent of dwarf, although Lodi wasn't sure what good that would do when the beast could simply follow the moonflower scent straight to him. But if it could conceal his trail, it would be well worth the three silvers he'd paid for it.

Thus prepared, he reached out and began to clamber around the side of the mountain in the direction of the cave mouth. The mountainside was neither sheer nor smooth, which made for fairly easy going. As he worked his way across, he kept a watchful eye out for the easiest way down to the dragon's den. He saw a largish projection above the lip, so he ended up climbing sideways until he was directly above the cave mouth. He looped the rope around the jutting rock and used it as a crude hanging belay to rapidly descend to the floor of the cave's mouth. After untying the rope from about his waist, he quickly drove a spike with the flat hammer back of his axe into the cave wall to hold it fast, then waved to Thorald to let him know everything was proceeding according to plan.

He withdrew a glowstone from his belt pouch and smacked it against the cave wall to light it. The stones lasted no more than a few hours, but if he was still in here by the time the stone's light gave out, darkness would likely be the least of his troubles.

The cave was deep and wide but shorter than he'd expected. Although its walls were at least somewhat protected from the wind, they were as barren as the mountainside outside. As he walked slowly into the depths of the cave, Lodi noted that the stone floor was not only scored by the drake's claws but pitted as well. Its venom was potent enough to burn through rock, he surmised. One large stain, just above the level of his head, was still smoking slightly as it ate its way deeper into the stone. He wondered if it might be the result of the coughing Thorald had mentioned earlier.

If only beasts like this could be tamed, what a tremendous metal etching tool their venom would make. But how one would even go about trying to domesticate such a monster was more than he could imagine. He saw a skeleton, and then another, but rather fewer than he'd expected. The drake either made a habit of eating elsewhere or periodically removed its victims from its residence. Lodi counted only five, three that looked like deer and two that had belonged to thick-boned beings about half-again the height of a dwarf. Based on their broad, thick skulls, he assumed them to have been a species of Orc rather than Goblin or Man. He very much hoped to avoid giving the monster the opportunity to add Dwarf to its gruesome collection.

Underneath the scent of death and decay, Lodi detected something else—the aroma of something much sweeter and enthralling.

He turned a broad, gentle corner and he came upon the cavern containing the dragon's hoard.

His heart beat at a gallop, and the blood fairly sang in his veins at the sight. Gold, silver, and bejeweled objects that the drake had collected over the years lay heaped in a pile at the center of the cavern, which would've been completely dark had it not been for the glowstone.

On second glance, the hoard was smaller than he'd initially thought. In fact, it was downright minuscule in comparison with the hoards of legend. It was little more than a pathetic pile of coins, helms, goblets, and weapons little more than three times Lodi's size. Still, there was more than enough lying there for the taking to stir the gold fever within him.

There is no time for this, he told himself severely, even as his hands itched to caress the lovely objects, several of which appeared to be relics of ages long past. Perhaps one day he could return here with enough dwarves to kill the drake. But in the meantime, he had best concentrate on finding the king's bloody shield and escaping before the black monster returned.

All the legends he'd heard were quite clear on the notion of the beasts being acutely aware of the disposition of their inventories, so he resisted the urge to start shoveling some of the smaller treasures into his pouch. But he did give in to the temptation to pocket two small gold coins that were lying under a horned silver helmet. Surely the dragon wouldn't notice that, at least not until he and Thorald were long gone!

He spotted the edge of a gilded shield with the tell-tale signs of dwarven etching along its perimeter. He was just beginning to ease it carefully out from the pile when he sensed, rather than heard, three sharp metallic sounds. *Tink-tink-tink.*

Then it repeated. *Tink-tink-tink.*

Damnation and deepgas! He was out of time.

He pulled the shield free, heedless of the consequences. The little pile spilled over as he ran the glowstone over the shield face, recognizing the platinum sigil that confirmed it had once belonged to the former lord of Iron Mountain. Its ancient leather strap was decayed, but a tug proved it was still sturdy, so he slung it over his shoulder and began to run in the direction of the cave mouth, slipping the glowstone back into the pouch as he sprinted toward the faint grey light that indicated the way out.

He stood at the cave entrance and grasped the rope. That was when he heard the screams. It wasn't the drake's screech. It was something—or, rather, someone—screaming unintelligibly in pain and stark terror.

There was no time to pull the piton from the rock, Lodi realized. He would just have to hope that the moonflower oil would prevent the drake from tracking them.

He gripped the rope firmly in his hands and began to pull himself up, hand over hand, toward Thorald and the little cave in which they'd been encamped. Breathing hard, he had almost reached the top of the cliff when he saw the huge, dark bulk of the drake soaring over the entrance with a shrieking, struggling dwarf-sized body in its claws.

THEUDERIC

THE five royal mages stood in a conventional pentacle pattern, but a much larger one than Theuderic had ever seen. This was necessary because the object of their working was also much larger than usual. It was a giant red dragon. A dragon that slumbered unconcerned in the midst of all the arcane activity.

The spell had been ready for more than ten days, but they'd had to wait until the dragon fell asleep to begin their preparations. If fortune was on their side—and numerous prayers had been said and auguries had been cast to assure it would be—the dragon would not awake until he was safely under the control of the haut mage, who was casting the dangerous spell.

Despite Theuderic's confidence in the superlative skill of the haut magicien, he was still very glad to be watching the grand experiment unfold from the safety of a distance of many leagues. Awareness of the mage's abilities was one thing—confidence in them was something entirely different. He was observing the preparations through l'Académie's largest crystal ball, in the company of eleven other battlemages, three or four immortels, and an elven princess.

She leaned her head against his shoulder, her blond locks spilling over his sleeve.

"How glad I am you decided not to take part in this madness," Lithriel Everbright whispered into his ear. She was the first elf to visit l'Académie since its establishment. Theuderic had brought her here in order to teach his fellow académiciens the spell used by the elvish sorcerers to tame and control their giant warhawks.

He very much hoped she would never find out that he was also the individual responsible for the capture and enslavement that had left her too abused and ashamed to return to her people. But there was very little risk of the truth ever surfacing, as he had killed very nearly everyone who knew the truth of the situation.

The chamber was a comfortable one. The king spared few expenses in support of his royal battlemages. The crystal ball, about the size of a catapult boulder, was set up in the center of the chamber, and five couches were arrayed in a pentagon around it so that all the académiciens were afforded a good view of the events taking place many leagues away. There wasn't quite enough room on the couches for everyone, but most of the younger battlemages were too excited by the experiment to sit down anyhow.

"Well," Theuderic replied, stroking her slender arm and shoulder, "you were very persuasive. And, of course, the fact that I couldn't manage to master that accursed spell of yours may have played a role."

Lithriel giggled. "But it's so simple! I did not know to laugh or to cry when you finally gave up on the poor hawk and tried to cast it on the sparrow."

"I'm a battlemage, not an enchanter! Walls of flame, bolts of lightning, dark and ominous clouds of crippling fear… that's what I do. If you want to tame an animal, hire an animal tamer! Anyhow, you appear to have forgotten that it worked on the sparrow."

"Forget? How could I forget? What elven maiden is not impressed with her hero's warsparrow? It was a sad day for us all when the buzzard took him."

"Meurtrier was a brave little bird, but he didn't stand a chance against that monster."

"To speak of monsters, that is a very big bird indeed." She pointed at the slumbering dragon. "I have my doubts about your high mage's ability to tame him. Anyway, I still fail to see why you think a spell created for birds could possibly work on a dragon. They may both have wings, but can you not see dragons have six limbs to the bird's four? To say nothing of their intelligence. Our warhawks have been bred for intelligence for millennia, but even though my Eveanor understood my commands, he could not speak, and neither did he reason."

Laurent, one of the younger battlemages, overheard them and joined their conversation. "As strange as it seems, Lady Everbright, the bird and the dragon share a common ancestor. Maupertuis, who I myself consider to be the greatest of the immortels this academy has ever known, explained most convincingly in his writings how birds, lizards, and dragons all came into being from natural processes and from a single origin. One might go so far as to say that, in a certain viraisonique sense, a bird is merely a lizard that is capable of flight, or that a dragon is nothing more than an extremely large bird capable of speech."

"One might go so far? Even to say that a lizard is a flightless bird?" Theuderic said with a smile. "So, is the peacock more truly a colorful crocodile, or shall we say that a crocodile is nothing more than an ill-tempered peacock?"

"Neither is true," Laurent said. "It is merely that chance produced by an innumerable multitude of individuals, and a small portion of this multitude found themselves constructed in such a manner that the parts of the animal were able to satisfy its needs. However, it was far more commonly the case that the parts were not harmoniously arranged and there was neither fitness nor order. Of these latter examples, all have perished. Just as animals lacking a mouth could not live, those lacking reproductive organs could neither breed nor perpetuate themselves. The animals we see today are but the smallest part of what blind fortune has produced, and they all stem from a common source."

Lithriel threw back her head and emitted a piercing peal of laughter. "Oh, how beautifully you put your nonsense," she told the mage.

"Nonsense?" Laurent said. Theuderic was glad the boy was so young, otherwise he might have expired from apoplexy. His face was as red as a beet. "It's not nonsense at all!"

"Of course it is, you silly child," Lithriel said. She was eighty-six years old, and she naturally considered young men in their twenties to be children, as elves of that age truly were. But since her appearance was that of a very tall, very slender eighteen-year-old girl, her contemptuous treatment of the prideful young mages seldom went over well. "Were you there?"

"Well, no, of course not! It was long ago!"

"Was this imaginative gentleman, this seigneur Maupertuis—was he there?"

"No, but–"

"Was any Man there at all?"

"No, but that's the whole point of the common ancestry!" Laurent was speaking rapidly now, attempting to forestall another question. It didn't work. Lithriel simply leaned forward and placed one long, slender finger across the young mage's lips. His eyes widened and he blushed, but his mouth stayed closed and he held his tongue.

"I was not there either. But my people were, and I have read the records of those times. Neither man nor orc nor goblin existed in those days. There were trolls, of course, for they are a very ancient race, even older than the elves. But the dragons did not come about by chance, as your beloved Maupertuis thinks. They were created by the people who came before. I think in your tongue you would call them the ascendants. They were great masters of magic. They had skills far beyond your Académie or even our own Collegium Occludum. It was ascendants upon whom the Witchkings patterned themselves, and it was their attempt to become ascendants themselves that drove them to madness and fell deeds."

"Will you three shut up?" someone snarled at them.

Theuderic whirled around to snarl back at the voice, until he realized it was one of the immortels who had spoken.

"Yes, of course. My apologies, seigneur."

Lithriel elbowed him, and he could see she was stifling a laugh. He didn't quite understand why, but the older and more crotchety a mage was, the more amusing she found him. He was relatively certain that it had something to do with elvish longevity, but precisely what she found so funny about the old men was still a mystery to him.

"Seigneur de Segraise is beginning the spell," someone whispered.

In the crystal, Theuderic could see that the haut magicien was beginning to move his arms. He appeared to be speaking as well. Sound did not project through the crystal, so it wasn't entirely clear if he was actually chanting the incantation or not, but the general consensus in the room was that he had begun.

The five other mages at the location far away didn't appear to be doing anything. Their job was simply to maintain the circle in which de Segraise and the dragon were bound. If things went very badly awry, only de Segraise, and not the other mages, would come to harm. At least, that was the theory.

Theuderic was of the opinion that five royal battlemages would be far more usefully occupied riding the borders in the west or hunting reavers in the north than serving as living candles in de Segraise's pentacle, but no one had inquired as to his thoughts on the matter. And he knew very well what hopes the King, and perhaps more importantly, the Red Prince, were placing in this outrageous experiment.

"This will be the difficult part," Lithriel told him as the small shape of the mage in the crystal lifted both his arms, threw back his head, and shouted. "The rest was all foundation. Now he has to take the forces he drew from earth and sky and apply them to the beast's mind."

"Uh, oh," someone said.

The dragon moved. Its wings, folded across its broad horny-spined back, twitched like a horse's skin shedding flies. Then it lifted its massive head and turned to stare de Segraise in the face with great yellow eyes that looked more like a cat's than those of a snake or a reptile.

"No, no," someone else said, "I think he's got it under his control now."

"I wouldn't be too sure about that." Theuderic didn't like the way the huge creature was staring at de Segraise, and he really didn't like what the increasingly rapid motions of the haut magicien's arms implied. It was hard to be sure, as he couldn't easily make out his facial expressions, but it looked very much as if de Segraise was panicking and either trying to cast another spell or recast the one that he'd just used.

"I wish we could hear what he's saying," Laurent complained.

Then the entire room, Theuderic included, emitted one great collective gasp of horror. For in the crystal, the dragon lunged forward without warning. With one mighty snap, it seized the upper half of de Segraise in its fearsome jaws and tore him in two. His legs fell to the ground in the pool of blood that suddenly surrounded them. Lithriel clapped her hands and shrieked with laughter.

"You see, Sieur Laurent? Dragons aren't birds! I told you it wasn't going to work!"

"Lady Everbright!" One of the immortels started to protest her hilarity, but events in the crystal were demanding everyone else's attention.

After swallowing half its would-be tormentor, the dragon nosed at the bloody remains then attempted to take flight. But the magic circle was also a dome, and the beast couldn't force its way through the invisible walls that surrounded it above it and on every side. De Segraise might be dead, but the pentacle he'd constructed was an extraordinarily powerful one, with lines connecting each of the five mages standing inside a sorcerous circle made from his own blood to each of the others.

"The circle—it's holding!" The dragon threw back its head, roaring in frustration, anger, or perhaps even pain, and then tried again, only to be flung back to the ground. The earth appeared to tremble with the impact, and Theuderic fancied he could feel it. But either the earth shaking or the sheer effort of maintaining the dome was troubling the mages of the circle, as two of them swayed and nearly stumbled.

"Don't break the circle, you fools," one of the younger mages shouted.

"Easy to say," an immortel snapped. "Those lads are strong ones. Absorbing that much force will drain you straight off if you're not careful. Now what is the cursed beast doing?"

The red dragon turned slowly around inside its magical cage, stopping to angrily glare at each of the five mages in turn, as if committing them to memory. Each met the beast's fearsome gaze without betraying too much alarm, although the legs of the man standing at what from their perspective was the upper left of the pentacle were shaking.

"What on Earth do they expect to do with it now?" Theuderic wondered aloud. "They can't keep it in there forever, not so long as they're holding the circle up themselves."

"It will be tricky indeed," the immortel who'd earlier hushed him commented. The room quickly fell silent. "Narcisse was prepared for this possibility. We discussed it last week before he left for the mountains. He'll have told them to have candles ready, I assume very large candles made of some particularly potent fat. Dragon fat would be best, but I doubt they have any of that. In which case he might have elected to use human fat, or now that I think of it, dwarven fat would be even better."

Theuderic glanced at Lithriel. She was staring at the old sorcerer and looking vaguely disgusted, although whether it was the idea of the candles made from human fat or just the mere mention of dwarves, he couldn't tell.

In the crystal, he saw each of the five mages withdraw a large candle from a satchel slung beneath his robes. They were huge, nearly as wide as they were tall, and Theuderic guessed that they would last for hours, if not days. And if they were sufficient to keep the magical shield intact, they would burn long enough to give the mages time to vacate the vicinity— probably in five different directions—before the furious dragon could escape.

The watchers at l'Académie held their breath as the mage at the point of the pentacle touched his finger to the candle wick, lighting it with a simple spell, then leaned down to place it in the precise center of the bloody circle in which he'd been standing. He adroitly stepped out of the circle without marring it. The mages around Theuderic applauded, and one or two of the younger ones actually let out a cheer.

"Does it matter if they go widdershins or not?" one of them asked.

"Widdershins?" The elderly immortel scoffed. "What are you, a hedge witch? No, it makes no difference if they proceed with the needles or contraire. It's a simple matter of placing the candle and leaving the circle intact."

As they spoke, it became apparent that they were not going according to a counter-clockwise sequence. The mage to the first mage's left followed his example, lit the candle, and stepped out of the circle without incident.

The dragon continued to sit motionless, watching them, and it was impossible to tell if the beast had any understanding of what the five men were doing. But Theuderic didn't like the way its eyes seemed to be focused on the mage who was exiting the circle, although it was entirely possible that this was nothing more than movement drawing its attention.

Another round of applause filled the room when the third mage successfully extricated himself as well. He must have been aware of the crystal, because he smiled and waved directly at them once he was safely out of the spell.

The fourth mage had just lit his candle when the dragon struck. It leaped directly at him, spreading both its wings and its jaws. Although no sound could be heard through the crystal, the flames that erupted from the dragon's mouth were terrifying even from afar. Theuderic, his arm around Lithriel, felt her start with alarm. The mage was also startled at the violent onslaught of the massive creature, and despite being protected by the safety of the magic field, he inadvertently stumbled backward out of his blood circle, still holding the lighted candle in both hands.

"No!" screamed several of the mages.

"Oh, the poor fool," Theuderic murmured to himself. He groaned and shook his head. Next to him, he could feel Lithriel's shoulders shaking, and even without looking he was certain it wasn't because she was crying.

With the pentacle broken, the magic shield abruptly vanished, and the clumsy mage was immediately engulfed in the deadly fire of the dragon-flames. Extending its wings, the dragon threw back its head, presumably roaring in triumph at its newfound freedom, then took to the skies. For a moment, Theuderic dared to hope it would fly harmlessly off to its lair.

But his hopes were dashed when a huge shadow appeared in the crystal, rapidly closing in on one of the fleeing mages.

"Is that Tycelin?" one of the mages cried in dismay.

It was. But Tycelin was not helpless, and in his courage showed himself to be a true royal battlemage. Staying calm despite his imminent peril and somehow sensing the dragon's descent, he whirled around and hurled a pair of thunderbolts that struck the beast in the face, not far from its eyes, causing it to veer away from him and retreat higher into the sky.

"At least he has the sense to try *le coup de foudre* instead of *l'enflammer,*" Theuderic commented to no one in particular. Fire spells would be of little use against a beast that breathed it.

The dragon circled around again, and this time when the mage hurled another pair of thunderbolts, it closed its eyes and ducked its massive head. The bolts crackled and sparked impressively as they struck against the horned skull but didn't even slow the dragon as it bore down upon brave Tycelin. The young mage disappeared in a hellish blast of fire that melted the flesh from his bones. When the flames died down, there was nothing to be seen but charred rocks and something scattered across them that might have been a widely dispersed collection of blackened bones.

The fleeing mages were gone from the picture, as was the dragon.

"I can't see anything," someone complained.

Then the view from the crystal abruptly shifted to a vantage point from up in the sky, although Theuderic didn't see which of the immortels was controlling the spell. The tiny shapes of the mages were now visible, as well as the much larger shape of the angry monster that stalked them.

It didn't take long for the dragon to hunt down the three remaining survivors. The landscape was too broken and stony for the men to run, but even if it had been flat prairie, there was no way they could possibly have hoped to escape the murderous wrath of the vengeful beast.

The third mage did not resist. He kneeled in what looked like prayer as the dragon fell upon him, but his divine implorings availed him little— the great dagger-like teeth closed over him. A moment later there was no sign of him except for the dark blood trickling down over the lighter red scales of the beast's chin. The fourth mage's death was by far the worst to watch, as he was seized in one huge clawed foot and shredded into bloody tatters by the repeated application of the other foot as the beast soared into the sky.

Only one mage left. Theuderic hoped he might have somehow escaped. The cries of horror and dismay voiced by the watching mages were interrupted by high-pitched peals of elven laughter. Lithriel was no longer shaking in silence, but was now laughing openly. Her slanted eyes were glistening with tears, and she was shaking almost uncontrollably. The other mages were beginning to look at her with disbelief and even a little disgust. It was one thing to hear of the famous cruelty of the elves, but it was something else entirely to witness it as your colleagues, brothers-in-arms, and in some cases, friends, were torn to shreds by a dragon.

"Stop it," Theuderic hissed at her. "You may not care about these men, but their friends and colleagues have just watched them die. So for the love of all that's clean and holy, hold your tongue!"

"I… I'm sorry," she gasped. "His face, it was just so f-f-funny!"

Theuderic put his head in his hands, abandoning the attempt to talk sense into her. He wasn't sure it mattered anyhow. The elfess had been a tremendous help to Narcisse in trying to adapt the spell, but given the spectacular failure it now appeared to be, she would also make for the ideal scapegoat.

She elbowed him. "Theudros, darling, do you know how to break the link to the crystal?" Her voice was suddenly under control again, and a worried note in her voice made him feel tense.

"I know the basic idea behind it, but I've never even tried the spell. It's an advanced one and requires some very expensive materials, if I understand correctly. Only the immortels make use of them."

She frowned at him. "So, you don't. But do you see that the last of your little mages is standing in front of the crystal there? He seems to be shouting at it."

Theuderic noticed. The view had shifted again and was now focused directly on the one mage who was still alive. Theuderic recognized him.

His name was Charles-Francois, he was from a noble family in the Seven Seats, and he was about to die. Behind and above him, the shape of the onrushing dragon rapidly grew larger.

"The sound doesn't come through the crystal. The light does," Lithriel said. "Do you know if anything else comes with it?"

Already annoyed with her, Theuderic almost dismissed her seemingly cryptic and untimely question with a *mot sarcastique* when its significance struck him like a thunderbolt. He realized, to his horror, that heat tended to be rather more closely akin to light than to sound. "Seigneur Gabrien," he called to the oldest académicien present. "Break the link to the crystal now! You must break the link!"

"Why must we do that? It's a terrible sight, but there is still much to be learned. If you have a weak stomach for such things, Sieur Theuderic, I advise you to look away." The old man shook his head and leaned toward seigneur Josce-Robinet. "Are all the young ones so tender these days? In my day, they were made of sterner stuff."

"The heat from the dragon's flames," Theuderic said desperately, seeing the dragon looming behind Charles-Francois's head. "It may come through the link!"

The old master of magic looked vaguely surprised. "The heat? Oh, yes, the flames. Do you know, I hadn't considered that."

Theuderic had heard enough. "Everyone, get down and shield yourselves!" He grabbed Lithriel and rolled off the divan with her. As soon as she was safely beneath him, he summoned his strongest shield, one that had saved him from many an arrow or sword thrust, to cover them both.

It belatedly occurred to him that a shield with a stronger Water component might be better suited to defeat the heat, but his instincts were faster than his reason, and anyway, it was already too late now.

For, as he looked over his shoulder, he saw old Gabrien kneeling in front of the great crystal, his aged hands reaching out for it as he sought to dispel the arcane link that connected the two attuned crystals. Then there was a blinding but silent burst of pure white light so bright that Theuderic was forced to look away.

But he could still hear. He heard the old sorcerer's scream as the terrible heat from the dragon's fiery assault was transmitted through the magical connection. Theuderic could feel the sudden heat flaring against his shield as a sort of psychic pressure, but it was less than he had feared, and it lasted for less than a ten-count.

As suddenly as it appeared, the heat vanished, although from where he lay, it was impossible to know if that was because the link had been severed, the crystal on the far side had been destroyed, or if the dragon were simply preparing another blast. He released his shield and rolled off Lithriel. To his horror, he saw Gabrien covered with flames and thrashing madly at his robes as he burned. Smaller fires were burning on various paintings, chairs, and two of the couches.

Fortunately, he also saw that all the young battlemages had proven worthy of their training and reacted with alacrity in raising their own shields, as had the three other immortels. Everyone with the exception of Gabrien appeared to be unharmed. With a gesture, Theuderic extinguished the flames and wrinkled his nose at the scent of burned flesh mixed with smoke. But the old immortel's screams continued.

A quick-thinking mage with black hair cast a *soporifique* spell on the badly burned sorcerer, who immediately slumped into blessed silence. But it was clear from a glance that the extent of his burns was too severe for the man to survive. Standing directly in front of the crystal, now cracked and smoking, Gabrien had taken the full extent of a blast that had been hot enough to spark fires on the far side of the chamber more than forty feet away.

Theuderic helped Lithriel to her feet and was relieved to see that at least the old man's death hadn't struck her as amusing. And he doubted that her previous amusement would be held against her, not now that her astute perceptions had saved them all from Gabrien's fate.

"Are you well?" he asked.

She nodded, but her eyes went quickly to the motionless body of the burned man, and she inhaled sharply. It appeared that even to the elvish sense of humor, death by dragonfire, when seen up close, was more hideous than hilarious.

Theuderic looked at Josce-Robinet, one of the three surviving immortels, and shook his head. The old sorcerer nodded, sighed, and kneeled down next to his unconscious colleague and placed a hand to his chest. "*De la cendre à la cendre*," he said with a distinct note of irony in his voice. "The peace of *l'Immaculé* upon you, Gabrien de la Poterrie." He rose and brushed the charred ash from his hands.

Theuderic sighed too. He hadn't much liked the cranky old immortel, but he mourned for the loss of arcane knowledge the man's death represented. He had been one of the most respected immortels in the academy, and combined with the death of Narcisse, who had arguably been its foremost experimentalist, it was clear that l'Académie had suffered a grievous blow today.

And that was before taking into account His Royal Majesty's fury at the loss of five of his precious battlemages. The King's Own had not suffered such losses in a single day since the Duc d'Carouge had lost most of his army to a rampaging orc horde nearly fifty years ago. But although the duc's defeat had cost the king nine battlemages, today's debacle had added two immortels to the account.

And even though the mad idea of taming dragons had not been Theuderic's, but rather had been the brainchild of the late Narcisse de Segraise and the Red Prince, it was not outside the realm of possibility that he might be held responsible. He was the one who had obtained the failed elvish spell that had been attempted today, after all. Such disastrous failure demanded a scapegoat, and since de Segraise was no longer in the running, and since the Red Prince was above all such recriminations, who else did that leave to face the wrath of the high council? Perhaps it was time to see about returning the Lady Everbright to her people.

He felt like laughing, felt like imitating Lithriel's behavior. What an utter disaster! And yet, could it truly have ended any other way? How arrogant, how foolish they had been, to think that their learning and their art would suffice to bend the most powerful, most ancient, most magical beings in all Selenoth to their will!

He looked up and saw that Laurent was staring at him. The young mage looked as dazed as if he, and not the dragon, had been the one struck by lightning. It was a good thing the lad had scholarly instincts, because it was readily apparent that he wasn't cut out for the violent vagaries of warfare. Laurent was destined for the academy, not the battlefield, if only he could survive long enough to claim a seat there.

"Remember," Theuderic said to his younger colleague, "there is a gold coin in every coffin." He clapped the young académicien on the shoulder and pointed to the smoking wreck of the cracked crystal. "Now that Narcisse and Gabrien are gone, that's two more chairs L'Académie must fill. At this rate, I daresay you'll find yourself an immortel by summer."

THE SACRED COLLEGE

T HE princes of the Church gathered. Some wore black, their reddened eyes and somber miens indicating their depth of grief over the loss of the Sanctified Father. They knew their loss was Heaven's gain, of course, for if ever a soul had labored long and hard for the Kingdom of God, if ever a man had run the good race and fought the good fight, it was the Sanctiff Charity IV.

Others were clad in their most elaborate vestments. And though they kept their expressions carefully guarded and appropriate to the solemn occasion, there was no mistaking the meaningful glances that were exchanged between one celestine and another in response to a greeting, a word, or even a simple nod.

The naming of the next Sanctiff was the holy burden of the Sacred College, but few would be so innocent as to deny that worldly ambition lurked in some of the hearts of the thirty-three men sworn to the service of God and Holy Mother Church. Some of them had been waiting a lifetime for this moment, had devoted their entire lives to ensuring that they would one day be here, in this humble wooden chapel that had been erected overnight by an army of priestly laborers, on such a day.

Here they would meet in conclave, thrice daily, until all were unanimously agreed upon a new Sanctified Father, who, by tradition, would be chosen from one in their midst. The process could take months. Once, following the untimely death of Righteous III, the bitter rivalry between Valerius Deprecatus and Severus Exigo had prevented anyone from being elevated to the Throne of the Apostles for eighteen months—until Exigo

finally died of old age and Deprecatus triumphantly claimed his place as
the 37th Sanctiff of Amorr. He was a man of great energy, as befitted a
Valerian, and many historians considered it a pity that the conclave that
preceded his reign had outlasted it by nearly a year.

The cerulengus rose wearily from his unpainted wooden throne at the
right hand of the empty one painted white to symbolize the sacred bones
of the *Sedes Ossus*. Of the thirty-three men present, only he could not be
the man chosen to succeed Charity IV. As cerulengus, it was his role to
secure the transition, not play the central role in it.

"We meet in sadness, but also in joy, my brothers," he said. "Let
us put aside all thoughts of ourselves, of our individual concerns, and
our personal allegiances, and praise God that the Sanctified Father is safe
in the bosom of the Immaculate, beyond every pain and every sorrow,
encompassed in light and glory."

"Heavenly Father, we praise You," the celestines murmured.

"Let us thank the Immaculate, who intercedes for fallen Man, who
died the death of a sinner though He himself was sinless, and who even
now stands advocate for the Sanctified Father before the throne of the
Almighty God."

"Immaculate Son, we thank You."

The cerulengus cleared his throat, which had started to crack a bit
upon the word *advocate*. He looked around the room, from one celestine
to the next, before proceeding.

"And let us beseech the Sacred Fire to descend upon us and grant us
prudence, that we may choose wisely and well."

"Sacred Fire, we beseech You."

The cerulengus stood there for a moment longer, unmoving, his head
bowed and his hands uplifted in silent prayer. But what more he asked
of God, only he and the Almighty knew. Then he looked closely at a
nondescript man of middling height, who was seated slouched upon his
throne in a manner that bordered on insouciance given the solemnity of
the occasion, before returning to his own chair.

He knew, as nearly everyone of any import in Amorr knew, that His Eminence Gnaeus Attilius Bulbus expected to succeed to the Ivory Throne, as he had spent ten years and a considerable fortune amassing the support of many of the celestines present in the chapel.

The cerulengus also knew that this conclave was as much a political event as a religious one. Bulbus's expectations were not due to any exceptional piousness or scholastic brilliance but to his support among the majority of the Houses Martial. His chief supporters in the conclave were Severus Furius and Falconius Tigradae, behind whom stood all the weight of House Severus and House Falconius. One of the two would most likely become the next cerulengus. Tigradae, he assumed. Furius was an adept politician, but his heart wasn't truly in it the way the Falconian's was.

But Bulbus would not be anointed unopposed. The cerulengus amused himself by watching the expression on Bulbus's rosy-cheeked face and seeing how it flushed as His Eminence Sextus Aemilianus Damasus stood and delivered a speech of no little length in copious praise of the virtues of another candidate, Carvilius Noctua, who was the author of a popular text on virtue and was known to have considerable support among the plebian classes, being one of the few non-patricians to currently wear the sky-blue robes.

Bulbus's face grew darker as two more celestines, and then a third, rose to speak in favor of Noctua's considerable personal virtues. Finally, he could take no more, and he glanced briefly at Furius, who was sitting almost opposite to him on the other side of the little chapel.

Furius coughed delicately, which act inspired His Eminence Giovannus Falconius Valens, one of the younger celestines, to stand up and speak eloquently of the need for a Sacred Father who would command the respect of the great men of the Senate as well as that of the virtuous and humble.

Valens was a young man of surprising substance, the cerulengus thought approvingly, even as he was amused by the transparency of the Falconian's support for Bulbus.

The cerulengus smiled. It was ever thus. One might be tempted to despair at the sight of the princes of the Church all but pawing the ground and bellowing bullish challenges, even if they did so in a refined and discreet manner, but was this not Man as God had created him?

It had been no different forty-four years ago, when the youngest celestine in the conclave had stood to speak in favor of the worthy Quintus Flavius Ahenobarbus, an ambitious cleric with a temper as fiery as his beard.

Man proposes, but God disposes. Only now that Ahenobarbus was in his sarcophagus, and he himself was stumbling toward the end of his own race, did he understand the extraordinary depths of that humble truth.

Whether it was petty ambition, kingly lusts, or towering self-righteousness, God always found a way to make use of even the most unlikely tool. That, the cerulengus thought as Valens took his seat and was replaced by another of Bulbus's known supporters, Gennarus Vestinae, was what so few of the men sitting here in this conclave understood.

They were under the impression they were elevating a man to a mighty office, but in truth, they were only offering up, as a sacrifice to the ineffable will of the Almighty, a broken vessel.

SEVERA

SHE waited as long as she could after the day's end, lying on her side feigning sleep in the unlikely event her mother came to check on her. Severilla had fallen asleep long before, and Severa lay in the darkness, listening to her little sister breathe slowly and evenly, wondering that she had ever been so young and innocent. Finally, when the sounds of loud reverie died down and the last of her father's clients departed, she leaned over, kissed Severilla on the cheek, and slipped silently from the bed.

She spent hora after hora agonizing over which dress to wear, finally settling on a dark blue one that not only made her breasts look a little larger, but would also help conceal her in the darkness. She drew it over her head, then kneeled down and fumbled about for her new sandals but did not put them on yet.

It sounded as if her brothers and a few of their friends were still drinking in the triclinium maius, but by now, they would be so drunk that she could probably walk right past them without any of them realizing it was her. It was the household slaves she had to fear. She'd already arranged for Verapora, her personal slave, to bribe the four night guards who would be at the gate. It had cost her a necklace and two earrings, but it was well worth it, and she was sure her mother would never notice their absence since she never wore them anyway.

She knocked once, softly, at her door, and the answering knock from outside came instantly in return. Taking a deep breath, she opened it and, in the very dim light from the candles downstairs, saw Verapora, already

cloaked in dark grey. Verapora handed her a similar cloak, which Severa
put on. She carefully closed the door without making any sound. She ran
her hands through her hair and pulled it sideways, tucking the curly mass
of it underneath the neckline so the hood would cover her face and stay
comfortably on her head.

"No, don't put up your hood yet, my lady," Verapora whispered. "Not
until we're past the gate."

She was right, Severa realized as they walked hand-in-hand down the
hallway that led to the stairs. If they were caught bare-faced, her father
would punish her tomorrow, and Verapora would likely be whipped. But
if they were spotted while their faces were covered, they could be easily
mistaken for thieves or assassins, and one or both of them could end up
on the wrong end of a spear or crossbow bolt. She closed her eyes. With
her free hand she clutched the icon she wore around her neck, and called
upon Saint Raphaelus, the patron saint of lovers, to intercede for her.

The saint must have heard her, for they encountered no one in the
halls or on the stairs, and Verapora was able to slip the bolt from the front
door without the least bit of trouble. Her slave had arranged with one
of the kitchen slaves to check it at the prima hora, and to reopen it in
the event it was bolted again during their absence. But since few of the
slaves and none of the guards were permitted to use the front door, she was
confident it would remain unbolted in the interim. They stepped through
and into the night.

The air was cool, and Severa found it almost intoxicating, so excited
was she at the prospect of meeting her lover at last. God had been kind,
and Clusius had survived his bout with Caladas with little more than a
deep scratch across the outside of his left arm. More than a few gamblers,
including her brother, had been disgusted that the much-anticipated
match had ended in a draw.

But for Severa, the sight of that red token had meant more to her than
a hundred victories, because it meant that tonight, the beautiful young
gladiator would be waiting for her at the statue of Andronicus Geminus,
as she had instructed in her letter. The thought of seeing him, up close

and in person, of feeling his mouth against hers, made her shiver right down to the base of her spine.

"Put your hood up now," Verapora instructed as they approached the gate, a tall geometric construction of thick iron bars lit by a pair of torches that flickered in the fittings fixed in the stuccoed wall. Verapora left her own hood down, however, so that, as far as the guards would know, the two of them were simply young slaves of the household, slipping off into the city at night to meet their lovers.

Severa wondered how many times her slave had done that very thing before, as Verapora was only four years older than her and yet Severa knew the young woman had taken at least two lovers, one of whom was not a Severan slave. The guards certainly didn't seem surprised to see Verapora in the middle of the night, and one of them even offered a wry invitation to Verapora that made Severa blush under her hood.

The well-oiled gate opened, and the two girls walked through it without hesitation. Severa felt a moment's pang of fear as it clanged softly shut behind them, but the sight of the hundreds of flames lighting the city night below her restored her courage. She felt no fear of the dark— tonight, the darkness was her shield and her friend. Even counting the long walk down the Quinctiline, she would still have at least three, maybe four, candles worth of time with the beautiful warrior before she had to return again. There would be time enough for love.

They had just begun walking down the brick path that led to the city when two lamps suddenly flared, first to her left, then to her right. The sudden burst of light blinded her for a moment, so it seemed almost that the four men who now stood in her way had risen out of the earth itself.

The two lampbearers were young and strong, and wearing undrawn swords at their belts. But the figures who put the sudden fear of God into her were the unarmed pair of bald men standing between them— one short and stout, the other tall and slender. The shorter man was Delmatipor, the majordomus of House Severus. And the taller one was Aulus Severus Patronus.

Her father.

"It's late for an evening stroll into the city, daughter. Take off that hood and let me see your face."

Silently, she complied, and somehow she found the strength to meet his eyes. But as he stared at her in the lamplight, his face expressionless, she saw neither anger nor disappointment. His eyes were too opaque to read.

In the sparse light of the torch, she saw that they had very nearly reached the point where the bricked path began to slope sharply down toward the city. There were wooden benches on either side. It sent chills through her blood to imagine her father waiting there in the darkness for her, steeped in his anger and disappointment in her.

Severa started to say something, but her father raised his hand in warning, and she was quick to subside.

"Now is not the time, Severa. Master Delmatipor, you will escort my daughter to her room and place a guard at her door. We shall depart for Samnia in the morning. Himcrius, Apidamus, take the slave and have her flogged. Nine strokes. And tomorrow, Delmatipor, you will sell her to a whorehouse and donate whatever pittance you happen to get for her to Saint Stridonius and the orphans."

Verapora gasped.

Delmatipor saluted. "As you say, my lord."

Severa clutched at her father's hands in disbelief. "Father, no! You can't do that to her!"

He looked at her as if she was nothing more than street filth in his path. But his hands were gentle, even when he forcibly removed hers from his own. "Count yourself fortunate that I love you so dearly, daughter. Were matters otherwise, you'd find yourself standing on the block alongside her in the morning."

FJOTRA

WHO could build such a city?

Fjotra was in a half-dreaming state somewhere between awe and wonder. She followed her brother up the hard stone road gawking about herself.

Her father and older brothers, red-handed reavers all, had told her about the great stone cities across the Small Sea to the south, but she'd never imagined anything so astonishing as what she now saw on every side.

The royal city of Lutèce was filled with massive buildings, many of which were larger than some villages she knew. The inhabitants lived in strange rectangular castles made of white stone. Yet the dwellings bore inexplicable holes in the sides that rendered them entirely useless for defense. And she saw more wealth in the time it took to walk from the entry gate to the great fountain in the center of the city than she had previously believed existed in all the world.

Even the very ground upon which she walked was a marvel. The road was neither the dirt of which all the roads in the north consisted, nor was it the gravel over which she'd walked many leagues once they'd crossed the sea. It consisted of a series of strangely regular stones that had been carefully placed in a pattern that rendered the surface smooth and very nearly flat. Such a road would never turn into a bog of mud when it rained or when the snows melted in the spring. But how could thousands, no, tens of thousands, of stones be laid so carefully and for such distances?

It must have taken many men generations to make! And how had they made the stones so uniformly flat?

She couldn't understand how anyone could hope to find anything here in this vast unfamiliar sprawl. Brynjolf pointed out strange markings that apparently served to identify each building, but they all looked essentially the same to Fjotra, and it seemed that Brynjolf could make no more sense of them than she could. They were searching for the castle where the Comtesse de Domdidier was said to reside, but with whole rows of the strange castles extending for as far as the eye could see on either side of the road, how could they hope to find it?

She noticed two green-liveried guards standing in front of a closed iron gate of the strange castle she and Brynjolf were passing. They appeared to be torn between staring at her and gawking at her brother. She felt self-conscious and aware of their impoverished appearance, so she pulled her stained cloak more closely about herself.

Brynjolf, a powerful young man who stood more than a head taller than the larger of the two guards, stopped and placed his hand on his sword hilt before turning to address the men.

"Where do the Comtesse Domdidier be?"

The two Lutèceans looked at each other in apparent surprise, as though they found it unbelievable that Brynjolf spoke Savondese.

"The two of you are looking for the comtesse?"

"Yes, I be Brynjolf Skulison. This be my sister. We come many leagues to see the great lady."

"You're Dalarn, you are," the taller guard said. "What business could a pair of ragged young reavers possibly have with the Comtesse de Domdidier?"

Fjotra grabbed Brynjolf's arm. She could feel his tensed muscles. He was not accustomed to being questioned by mere huscarles. She squeezed hard, but he took a deep breath and drew himself up. She kept squeezing until he finally glanced at her and, irritated, shrugged his arm out of her grasp.

"What was that for?" he snapped in Dalarnsk.

"Don't be causing trouble, Bryn. Hold your tongue and be gentle," she replied in the same language.

He grimaced at her, but for now he was keeping his temper under control, and that was all that mattered. He reached into the leather bag he wore slung over his shoulder and produced a yellow scroll with a broken seal. "I be told to give this if anyone ask."

The taller guard took it from him, unrolled it, and showed it to the other guard, who whistled softly, then nodded at Bryn in a more respectful manner.

"Do you see that jaunstone manor at the top of the hill there, on the right side?" The first guard pointed at a building about two hundred paces away. His companion rolled up the scroll and handed it back to Brynjolf.

Fjotra thought she saw the building the guard was pointing at. It was a larger castle than most in the vicinity, although not so large as some they had seen in the heart of the city. Two very tall trees that were shaped almost like thick green masts stood at what looked like might be the gate to the comtesse's residence. Its walls were made of yellow stone rather than the veined white rock from which most of the other castles had been built. Square red ornaments hung on either side of the big holes in the walls, giving it a bright and festive appearance.

"I do see it. I thank you, sirs," her brother said.

Both men laughed. "We're no sirs, boy," the taller guard said. "But give our regards to the comtesse, will you?"

"The honor be to me," Brynjolf said solemnly, and he did his best to bow in the way her father's man had taught them was common for nobles in the south.

One of the guards appeared to turn red in unexpected pleasure of the compliment, and the other one experienced a sudden coughing fit, but they both bowed deeply to him in return.

It seemed as if Hrolfstan had known what he was doing when he'd instructed them on how they should behave in Lutèce. These Savoners were indeed a refined people, much dedicated to their strange and ritualistic etiquette.

But then, unexpectedly, one of the guards blew her a kiss. Fjotra, not knowing what the proper response would be, could only manage to blush. Fortunately, Brynjolf had already turned toward the comtesse's castle or he might well have forgotten himself and cleaved the offender's skull in two.

The walk uphill was arduous after what had already been a day spent on their feet. Fjotra found herself starting to sweat under the hot Southern sun. She clung to her brother's arm and wished, not for the first time, that they had stolen some horses after beaching the longboat. It would have taken precious days from their travel and saved her feet the blisters that now turned every step into a momentary kiss of fire. But Hrolfstan had been firm, they were here as pleadants, not reavers, and they dared not risk any acts of theft or violence aimed at the very people from whom they hoped to obtain assistance.

The comtesse's castle was protected by a short, decorative wall outside it, but it had no gate, which made Brynjolf snort in disbelief, and it stood farther back from the stone road than it had looked when viewed from below.

The grounds surrounding the building seemed false, as if the trees and bushes had been fashioned by some skilled artificer rather than grown from the ground, and a little path made of red stones that matched the color of the square ornaments, which she could now see were carved and painted wood, led to a fountain that stood between them and the two large doors of the front entrance. The leaping waters created a rainbow of light that shimmered and danced in the mist, and Fjotra, amazed by the leaping colors, clapped her hands with delight.

"It's just some kind of water magic," Brynjolf said, seeing that she had fallen behind. "Come now, we had better hope she is to home. I don't know what we shall do if she is not here."

"Or if she will not receive us." Fjotra had been worrying about that since before they'd climbed aboard the snekkja to begin crossing the Small Sea. Why should a high-ranking Savoner noblewoman be willing to aid them, or even speak to them? What little they had to offer was unlikely to be of much interest to a southern woman who lived in a castle of yellow stone. What possible use would she have for raiding ships, swords, and fighting men?

"She will receive us," Brynjolf said grimly. "I promise you that, sister. The Comte has been true to his word, and his letter has seen us through every obstacle. It will not fail us now."

They rounded the fountain and came upon the comtesse's guards. Bryn had to give up his sword to them, but then the men immediately recognized the stamp on the letter and escorted them through the broad red doors of the magnificent dwelling.

Fjotra's eyes fell upon a huge, high-ceilinged entry, which was chiefly decorated with the golden light that came in through the gaps in the walls. She caught her breath at the magnificence of it. Inlaid into the white stone floor was an image of the comtesse's arms in blue and black and gold. She attempted to touch the edge of it with her battered sandal. But somehow her foot passed through it.

Brynjolf laughed at her. "Turn around, Fjo. Do you see how that window matches the pattern? It's a colored glass, and it is cleverly placed so that when the sun shines through it, it creates the image on the floor."

"How wonderful!" Fjotra breathed. "Is that what the holes in the walls are called?"

"Windows?" Her brother laughed. "They're not holes. Well, I suppose they are, really, but they're covered with a hard glass you can see through. It is the same thing they use to make the goblets they drink from here."

"They're beautiful. Why don't we put *windows* like this in our castles?"

"The glass is easily broken. Much too easily. It would leave them indefensible. We make our enemies break through our walls. We do not dig the holes for them! These people are too soft. Lutèce probably hasn't seen a battle since Sigfrid Gold-mouth raided it with his three hundred ships."

Fjotra nodded, disappointed. How lovely it would be to have more light inside the grim towers of Raknarborg. What meager shafts were permitted entry by the arrow slits were pathetic compared to this. Her eyes were drawn from the window to the sight of a beautiful woman with long red hair descending the broad, carpeted staircase from the landing above. This must be Comtesse de Domdidier, she thought. The woman wore a simple and unadorned blue gown, but it shimmered like the mist above the fountain, and the two gold bracelets she wore on her wrists looked substantial enough to gild a dozen breastplates.

She looked younger than her twenty-six years. This, despite the fact that she had been widowed two summers past when the previous Duc d'Aubonne had fallen in battle against an army of marauding orcs. Some said the comtesse was a paramour of the king. Others whispered that she was the secret mistress of his unmarried heir, the Red Prince.

The comtesse carried herself with the lazy certainty of a lioness, and while her dress covered most of her body, it left most of her white breasts exposed. And yet she was no dull-eyed whore, her gaze was clear and appeared to take in everything in an instant. The comtesse reached the bottom of the stairs, and their eyes met. Fjotra found herself quickly looking aside. The intense curiosity in the other woman's green eyes was more than she could bear, and for some strange reason, she felt a sudden impulse to cry.

"You have travelled far." The woman's voice was a little lower than Fjotra would have guessed from her youthful appearance, but it was warm and sounded almost friendly. "And it is a warm day for a long walk. May I offer you refreshment? Come this way, and we shall sit down."

"I thank you," Brynjolf said in Savoner. Fjotra only nodded.

They followed the comtesse into a large, bright room with strange, fat-looking chairs with pretty patterns covering them. Fjotra suspiciously prodded the plump seat with her finger. It was very soft to the touch. She looked up and saw the comtesse smiling at her.

"You may sit down upon it safely, my dear. It is merely a cushion. You will find it comfortable, I think."

Fjotra sat down. But the chair seemed of a mind to swallow her whole. She nearly leaped to her feet again. The comtesse laughed, and Fjotra blushed furiously. But the comtesse's laughter was not unkind, so Fjotra tried to settle herself upon it again. She looked over at Brynjolf. He was scowling, although she didn't know if it was out of embarrassment at her ignorant behavior or disapproval of the soft comforts of Savoner civilization.

The Comtesse sat on one of the overstuffed chairs that faced Fjotra. It was marked all over with pretty green flowers that were the very shade of the comtesse's eyes, and Fjotra wondered if that was a coincidence or not. "Do tell me your names," she said. "The Viscomte's letter merely said that you had come from across the sea. The Sea Nordique, I assume. You are northerners, are you not?"

"I am Brynjolf, son of Skuli," her brother said. "She is my sister, Fjotra Skulisdattir."

"My, what a reaversome name," the comtesse favored her with a half-smile. "Do you know, it occurs to me the Viscomte is not much interested in etiquette, so he has not informed you that here in Lutèce, one customarily addresses a noble as 'my lord' or 'my lady.' However, I invite you to call me 'Comtesse' as a mark of my particular favor. Now, Brynjolf, am I correct in assuming that your father—Skuli, did you say?—is a gentleman of some importance in the Iles de Loup?"

Brynjolf looked as puzzled as Fjotra felt. "Illdalupe?"

"The Wolf Isles, I think you would say it."

"Skuli is not gentle man, Comtesse. He is great warrior and king over the Fifteen Clans!"

"Is that so," the comtesse sat back and raised her eyebrows. "Fifteen, you say? My goodness."

"All fifteen," Brynjolf assured her proudly. Fjotra noted that he didn't see fit to mention that eleven of the fifteen were now gone.

"Why, I dare say that makes you a prince of reavers, does it not? And you, Fjotra, are therefore a princess. I cannot tell you how delighted I am that you should honor my humble abode with your royal presence!"

Fjotra had the vague impression that the comtesse was laughing at them, and certainly the older woman's eyes showed an amount of amuse-

ment, but she didn't appear to be mocking them in a malicious manner. Fortunately, Brynjolf was too taken with her flaming hair and half-
exposed bosom to notice, or he might have taken offense. Fjotra was not
inclined to do so either, since Hrolfstan had told them the comtesse would
be their best hope. So, she simply smiled, a little uncertainly, not wanting
to say anything that might cause offense.

Two servants entered bearing a tray upon which were the most beautiful painted cups that Fjotra had ever seen. They had little blue birds
painted on them, birds that were feeding upon a rose-petaled flower.

She took a cup with a nod of thanks and sipped at the cold liquid
inside. It was sweet, sweeter even than mead, but with a strange taste of
sour curds to it as well. But she liked it very much indeed, and she drained
the cup with her second try at it.

"You have never tasted lemons before," the comtesse surmised as she
indicated that the servant should pour Fjotra another cupful. "Or sugar,
I suppose."

Fjotra shook her head.

"I see you understand me, Fayo… Fjotra. Do you speak?"

"A little," Fjotra replied shyly. "I not know lots the words. Brynjolf,
he speak good Savone."

"He is more intelligible than one might have expected, at any rate."
The comtesse looked more closely at her brother. "I will say you are a
handsome lad. Are they all made so large across the sea?"

"Gudruk the Mighty, he be one head higher than me," Brynjolf
replied. "Many Dalarn be big, be the best warriors. Skuli be not so big as
me, but he greatest warrior of all!"

The comtesse sighed. "One can only imagine. Well, my dear prince
and princess reaver, now that we have all been refreshed, perhaps you
might enlighten me as to why my darling Saint-Agliè believed it was so
vital for the two of you to honor me with the privilege of a visit. Not
that I object, you understand. I confess, my interest is partially piqued
due to the fact that our dear viscomte's interests appear to be growing ever
more esoteric. Some might even say erratic. I do hope he isn't going mad.

Yesterday it was Wagrans, today it is reavers, what will tomorrow bring? Dwarves? Mountain trolls?"

Brynjolf exchanged a significant look with Fjotra. He clearly had no more idea what the comtesse was talking about than she did. About all she could gather was that it had something to do with the viscomte who had given them the magic letter. They had argued all the way to Lutèce over the best way to present their case to the comtesse, but despite the many hours of discussing the matter, they had never come to a firm decision.

Fjotra made up her mind and glared defiantly at her brother.

"There is evil. Big evil come. It kill… all. It come to here, to Savone."

The comtesse's green eyes narrowed, but she did not appear to be either shocked or skeptical. She merely pursed her lips and looked to Brynjolf for further explanation.

"The *loup-garou*, you say, comtesse. Or *loup-diable*? We say aalvarg, they be beast they walk like Man."

"Ah, you refer to the ulfin, of course," the comtesse nodded. "Yes, I know whereof you speak. An army of ulfin invaded the north coast many, many years ago, with rather less success than your forefathers have enjoyed over the centuries. The Duc de Montreve, whose daughter married my late husband's great-grandfather, smashed them at the Battle of Crociers. They say more than ten thousand ulfin were killed that day, so many that afterward, the duc gave all of his knights and men-at-arms three wolf pelts each." The comtesse smiled, a little wolfishly. "No ulfin has been seen in Savondir since that time, and I don't believe they ever dared to cross the Nordique to trouble us again."

"No, they take our islands first."

"You are saying that the ulfin are attacking your people? That the reavers are themselves reaved?" She smiled and shook her head. "You must understand that the news will not be mourned in Savondir. Of course, it does explain why our northern shore has been relatively unmolested in recent years."

"No, Comtesse," Brynjolf said, shaking his head somberly. "I say the aalvarg defeat my peoples. Only Raknarborg stands. When it fall, they kill the Dalarn. All mans, all womans, all childs. And then they cross the seas to come here, to kill your people. To kill Savone... Savonne."

Fjotra closed her eyes. She could vividly recall the terror of their desperate retreat from their village of Garn to the last remaining fortress in Ulvøen.

"Are you well, Fjotra?" The comtesse was leaning over and holding her hand. "For a moment, I thought you might faint."

"You help, lady. You need help." Fjotra took the comtesse's delicate hands in her own and implored her. "You need know. If Dalarn no can come to Savone, we all die!"

The Comtesse de Domdidier looked from Brynjolf, to Fjotra, then back again. Then she nodded and smiled brightly. "Well, we certainly can't have that now, can we, my dears?"

"You help us?"

"I will ensure you receive an audience with the king. The assistance you seek can only come from him. I can promise you nothing in my own right. I am merely a woman. I have no armies, I cannot use a sword, and I fear even my household guard has been chosen with more concern for aesthetics than martial valor. Nor can I give you permission to settle reavers on my lands. For one thing, my comté is too small, and for another, it has no access to the sea."

"But the viscomte say with you we must talk above all!" Brynjolf protested. "You say you can give no help?"

The comtesse laughed and tucked her wayward hair behind her left ear. "I said nothing of the kind, my dear prince of reavers. I am merely telling you that my weapons are not the sort you are likely to know, or perhaps even understand. Nor are the battles you are unwittingly asking me to wage on your behalf any less vicious for all that they are bloodless. Well, not entirely bloodless, I suppose. On occasion one can admittedly find the judicious use of the duel to be of some utility."

Fjotra had no idea what the Savonnean woman was trying to tell them. "I no know."

"No, my lovely girl, you most certainly do not." She squeezed Fjotra's hand, then patted it. "But you must understand this, my pets. We have two weeks. The Duchesse de Méridiony is giving a ball, and His Majesty is going to be there. So is the Red Prince, which may actually be more important. Naturally, I shall be there as well. I will bring you in the guise of one of my guards, Brynjolf. And you, lovely Fjotra, shall be my lady-in-waiting. How fortunate that the two of you are suitably handsome, which I doubt escaped the viscomte's eye. And then, we shall arrange what we can arrange.

"But you must understand two things. Not everyone in Savonne will be as well-disposed toward you and your people as the viscomte and me. You reavers have harried our coasts and rivers for five hundred years and for some, the bitterness runs deep."

"Some hate us, we know," Brynjolf admitted. "But if you make them see danger to all Savoners, not just Dalarn, they need help!"

"Oh, I shall certainly be sure everyone who matters understands the danger, never fear," the comtesse said, her green eyes sparkling with an emotion that Fjotra could not read. But the smile she gave them this time was more fox than wolf. "Indeed, I imagine I shall have little difficulty in convincing certain grand personages to see something rather more important, which is to say, the opportunity this presents."

MARCUS

THE ride from the battlefield to the legionary camp was not a long one, only about five leagues. But after the long hours of tedium and terror had climaxed in a furious orgy of violence, it was exhausting, which made it feel more as if it were twenty leagues.

Marcus pitied the poor infantry, who had not only borne the brunt of the savage combat throughout the day, but who were now forced to march back to camp under their own power. On most days, Marcus and his fellow riders bristled at the way their horseless fellows taunted them as being lazy and effete, but today he found that he didn't mind the occasional jibes from the infantry they rode past.

Their victory had been as complete and as glorious and as devoid of personal injury as any virgin soldier could hope his first battle to be. What he wouldn't have given for Caitlys to see it—what a view she would have had soaring high over the battlefield on her hawk!

Fortex had not only been correct about the goblins being on the verge of running, but his timing had been absolutely magnificent. After driving the wolfriders from the field and killing more than one hundred of them in the process, the Second Knights had wheeled left and smashed into the goblin infantry, pinning them between the crashing charges of the cavalry and the inflexible line of the infantry's steel shields.

The decurions estimated that more than twelve thousand goblins had been slain, pierced by swords and pila, crushed by stones, impaled by bolts, trampled by hooves and speared by lances. The Second lost only five dead—one to an arrow, two had fallen off their horses and been trampled in the initial charge, and two more had fallen to maddened wolves fighting on in the absence of their riders. Another fifteen had been wounded, including the decurion, Julianus, but only the two who suffered broken legs were seriously injured.

For the knights, the most dangerous part of the battle had not been fighting the enemy, but simply riding down the steep incline of the hill on which they'd been positioned.

It would have been a famous victory even without his cousin's single combat with the goblin cavalry commander, which was already approaching mythic proportions. The legend of Fortex's Duel was growing throughout the legion. Marcus had already heard a version of the tale from a man in the fourth cohort in which the skull-helmed goblin killed by his cousin was transformed into a fearsome mountain orc, and the big black wolf upon which it had ridden into a bear.

Finally, the familiar wooden walls of the legion's camp came within view. They were more easily seen now than would normally have been the case, as the massive field of tents and wagons belonging to the female camp followers and the many small merchants who lived an itinerant life following the soldiers around was missing. The legion's camp was usually a lively place akin to a moderately-sized, albeit movable city, but because the XVIIth was more than ten days' march from the nearest town or legionary fort, the general had ordered everything and everyone that was not essential to battle left behind at Berdicum. Most notably, the small army of women who lived off the lusts of the soldiery in one way or another.

A few foolish traders attempted to follow the legion when they'd marched out of the fortified town, but the burning of their wares on the first night, followed by a public flogging of the vendors, had been sufficient to prevent anyone else from imitating them.

The sentries on guard at the gate of the Via Praetoria saluted Marcus as he entered the camp. He was surprised to see Julianus, his arm neatly bandaged, standing near them. The decurion's face was grim. He didn't seem to be at all inclined to celebrate the day's victory. He waved Marcus over.

"Come with me, Tribune Valerius. Take his horse to the stables, Jeron. What's your lad's name?"

"Ask for Deccus," Marcus told the rider as he dismounted and handed the reins of the horse to him. "Is something wrong, Decurion?"

"Why did you let him to ride out to meet the goblin, Clericus? He was your cousin! You couldn't stop him?"

"Are you talking about Fortex?" Marcus had to walk faster to keep up with the bigger man.

"Do you have any other cousins here?"

"Of course I tried to stop him! I told him to ignore the gobbo's challenge and to remember your orders, and I kept telling him that until he told me to shut up! You know Fortex. Since when does he listen to me? He isn't in trouble, is he?"

The decurion shook his head and spat. "Worry about your own arse, Clericus. The men say it was you, not Fortex, who gave the order to advance, when we all knew damn well our orders were to stay on that hill. What in the seven dirty hells were you thinking? How hard was it to do what I damned well told you and just hold your filthy ground?"

"How could I? He ordered me to hold the legion until they looked like breaking, then ride in after him. What was I supposed to do? Anyhow, you saw what happened. He was right."

The decurion shrugged and didn't press him further. Marcus wondered how much trouble he was in. He had caused the Second Knights to disobey its orders, he couldn't deny that. But he'd only done so in obedience to an order given by the Knights' commander. But would Saturnius see it that way? For that matter, would his father? Of the two generals, he had the sneaking suspicion that the legate would be more inclined to be merciful than the stragister.

They walked past the rows of butterfly tents belonging to the officers, including the tent Marcus shared with Gaius Marcius. But instead of turning right at the Forum, where those who had been wounded in the early part of the battle were being tended, the Decurion turned left.

Among those being treated, Marcus recognized Quince de Sorrengis, an ornery young legionary who hailed from a small village within the Valerian lands, arguing with the doctor trying to sew his wounded shoulder closed. He would have liked to stop and see how the Valerian liege man was faring, but it was not an option. Julianus didn't so much as glance at the group of wounded soldiers but continued walking toward the large canvas tent in which the standards were kept.

"Decurion, where are we going?"

"The general's quarters," he snapped. "Your father wants to see you."

A number of officers were gathered in the huge open tent that served as the headquarters. They looked quizzically at Marcus and the decurion as the two of them passed by. They arrived at the regal, crimson-dyed leather tent that belonged to the legion's general, Sextus Valerius Corvus, Propraetor, Count of Vallyria, and Senate-appointed Stragister Militum and Dux Ducis Bello for the Senate and People of Amorr's campaign against the Chalonu, Vakhuyu, and Insobru tribes.

The guards saluted both Marcus and Julianus without expression and stood aside to let them enter.

His father was seated in an imposing wooden chair that served as a makeshift throne when it was deemed necessary to cow the enemies of Amorr who were summoned before it. By the looks of it, he was deep in conversation with the legion's general and Caius Proculus, the senior centurion. All three of them were still wearing their battle armor. Proculus's right arm was well stained with blood too dark to be his own. Marcus did his best to avoid looking directly at any of them, but instead focused on the chair.

The crows that had become his father's sigil were carved into towering ears that rose from the back of the chair, while its legs were shaped into large talons to signify the eagles of the legions, one for each that Marcus's father presently commanded. The other two were both many leagues away, and considering the apparent lack of pleasure with which all three officers greeted his entrance, Marcus found himself fervently wishing that he was serving with either of them right now instead of Legio XVII.

"I brought Tribune Valerius here immediately, General," Julianus addressed his father. "I met him at the camp gate, as instructed."

"Thank you, Decurion. I cannot tell you how delighted I am to learn that at least one officer in this legion is capable of following orders. I see you took a wound to your arm?"

Julianus glanced at the white bandage wrapped around his left arm and shrugged. "Just an arrow. It ain't nothing, sir."

"Decurion, were you there when my nephew and my son were overcome with what I can only conclude to have been a moment of sheer madness?"

"No, sir, I'm sorry to say I weren't. After I took that arrow, I thought I'd have the medicus wrap it up since those howlers didn't look like they was in any mood for a fight. Nothing had happened all day. So you might say it were my fault, General."

"Don't be absurd," Marcus Saturnius broke in. "Valerius Fortex is neither green nor a child, and while he may not have as many years of experience as you do, he is your superior officer. As for Valerius Clericus here, this may be his first campaign, but given his scholarly training, he is perfectly capable of understanding an order as simple as the one he received today. You are no more to blame in this than the draconarius or any other knight who was on that hill."

"Yes, sir. Thank you, Legate."

"The disciplinary issue aside, Decurion," Saturnius said, "I must commend you for the performance of your men today. I saw them rout the wolfriders on the enemy right. See that they receive a double wine ration tonight with my compliments."

"Yes, sir. Thank you, sir. General. Proculus." The decurion saluted crisply, bowed, and marched from the tent without once glancing at Marcus. The centurion saluted too and followed suit. After the two officers departed, Corvus leaned back in his chair and folded his hands together. He still looked weary, but for the first time since Marcus had entered the tent, he smiled at his son. He rose stiffly from his chair, then startled Marcus by walking over to him and embracing him. "It has been a long day, but I am pleased to see that you are unscathed, Tribune Valerius. How did you find your first battle?"

"I didn't piss myself," he answered truculently, looking from his father to the legate. "There was a considerable amount of noise. I discovered horses can slip on goblin blood, if there's enough of it splashed about. Oh, and one more thing. Even when the enemy is running away instead of standing his ground, your sword arm gets tired much faster than you would have thought."

He wasn't sure if he'd killed eight or nine goblins today, but he remembered exactly how heavy his sword felt by the time he'd leaned out of his saddle to chop down the last one. He was vaguely surprised he'd managed to hang onto it.

"How very fortunate for you that you were able to learn such lessons so early in your career." Saturnius poured wine from a winesack into three crystal goblets. "After my first battle, the singular lesson learned by most of the men in my century was that neither a shield nor a breastplate will suffice to stop a dwarven battleaxe. Sadly, they were in no position to profit from the lesson afterward."

Marcus winced. "Can I conclude from the fact that you are offering me wine instead of screaming at me that I am not in imminent danger of mortification?"

"Never fear, Marcus Valerius," Saturnius said, glancing at him and chuckling. "Even when we are under the *Modus Austeris*, we are not inclined to punish inexperienced young tribunes every time they make foolish decisions or issue unaccountably stupid orders. If we were to make a habit of it, we would very soon find ourselves without any young tribunes at all."

Marcus was almost embarrassed at the intensity of his relief. Not that he was actually worried that Saturnius would dare to have him flogged or broken, but he was fully aware that he had violated his orders to remain on the hilltop.

"As it stands," Saturnius said, distributing the goblets, "I would not even go so far to say you made the wrong decision, considering the impossible position in which you were placed by your cousin."

Marcus froze, wondering if he was going to be put on the spot and queried about Fortex's actions. But neither Saturnius nor Corvus seemed inclined to ask him further questions about the subject. He breathed a sigh of relief. If he wasn't going to get in trouble over disobeying orders, he couldn't imagine that the hero of the hour was going to, either.

His father, being the senior officer there, gave the toast. "To Amorr, to her Senate and People, and to her most recently victorious general, Marcus Saturnius!" They drank and Marcus was unsurprised to discover that, even deep within enemy territory, the wine served in the general's quarters was a rather better quality than that which was provided to the junior officers.

"Thank you, Sextus Valerius," Saturnius said. "But I should say it is more properly accounted as yet another famous victory for your most noble House."

Corvus snorted. "I can't blame you for not wanting to take any credit for it. Perhaps I should give Polycarpus free rein. I have little doubt that anyone who takes the sort of liberties with the truth that that 'poet' does would soon have this shabby little affair numbered among the most valiant triumphs our scribes have ever recorded."

"Perhaps you should consider doing so." Saturnius laughed. It was an infectious sound, so much so that it drew another half-smile from his father. "I imagine we'll be fortunate if the Senate and People even manage to recall they are presently at war with the goblin tribes. These particular tribes, in any event. No doubt our letters will be the first that half of the Senate has heard of it."

Corvus shook his head, but Marcus wasn't listening anymore. Having escaped the prospect of punishment, he found that the nervousness and fear that had been keeping him going now that the battle was over were sustaining him no longer. He was finding it hard to even pretend to pay attention to the conversation.

At length, his father removed the goblet from his hand. "You're dead on your feet, Marcus. Go now: Wash that goblin blood off you and get some sleep while you can. You'll have an hour, perhaps two, before we summon the general assembly."

Marcus nodded dutifully, saluted both Saturnius and his father as sharply as he could manage, then staggered out of the tent and down the Via Principalis in the direction of his tent. He decided the washing up could wait, but before he took a nap, he was determined to write down his impressions of the battle while they were still fresh in his mind.

He woke to the sound of horns, startled to discover that he was seated. He had fallen asleep at his camp desk in the midst of attempting to record his thoughts about the day's earlier events. He wiped at his left cheek, which was slick with his own saliva, and squinted in the receding light at what he had written.

> *Small-boned and wiry creatures. Skin is green, but ranges from light yellow-green to dark grey-green. Faces sharp-featured and bestial, but not especially reminiscent of any specific animal. Their speech is said to be guttural, but war chants and cries during battle tend to mostly consist of high-pitched shrieking. Could not discern any coherent words. Armor is crude, consisting of either boiled leather reinforced with wood or various bits and pieces of metal or chainmail acquired from men and orcs over time. Do they even have their own metalworkers? ~~Little~~No tactical imagination. Poorly disciplined as units but individually brave in some cases. The suddenness with which they collapsed into a routed mass almost like scaring up a flock of birds. The rear lines*

Marcus desperately wanted to continue writing things down while he could still clearly recall the shape of the battle as well as the foe against whom it had been fought. But as his mind began to emerge from its sleepy fog, he realized that the horns were summoning the entire legion to the forum in the middle of the camp, as his father had told him earlier. Fortunately, except for his arm greaves and his helmet, he was still wearing his armor, so he was able to simply slide his helmet on his head, grab his greaves in one hand, and a moment later, he was on his way down the Via Praetoria.

As he approached the forum, he could see the great mass of the men gathering in orderly formation behind their standards. Four of his fellow five tribunes were already standing on the two sides of the raised wooden platform behind the legate and the laticlavius. He made his way past the rows of legionaries and mounted the stand, still tightening his greaves.

Lucius Volusenus nodded to him in a friendly manner as Marcus, being junior to him, took his place to Volusenus's left. Marcus imitated the others, and stood with his chin upraised and arms behind his back.

Volusenus leaned over and whispered to him. "Have you seen Fortex?"

"No, I lost track of him once we hit their infantry. He's all right, isn't he?"

"I think so. I saw him after the battle. Did he really kill the goblin commander?"

"Yes. It was the commander of the cavalry on their left, though, not the warleader."

"Oh. Still… did you see it?"

"Yes, I was at the front with the draconarius. I saw the whole thing. You would not have believed–"

A trumpeter sounded a triple blast on his horn, and all the men throughout the assembled legion, Marcus included, fell instantly quiet.

Marcus Saturnius stepped forward and put his hands on his hips, nodding as his eyes swept over the thousands of troops.

"I hope you bastards don't think you're going to hear any praise from me for spanking a few greenskins and sending them running. That wasn't a battle today. I don't know if it was even worth calling an exercise!"

The legion roared its approval. Scattered shouts of "Saturnius" could be heard interspersed with the general laughter.

"I've seen Titus Falconius work the first century of the second cohort harder in sword drill than they got worked today. And I noticed the left flank saw even less action than Publius Licinius gets in a whorehouse! I'm going to have to consider replacing the horses of the First Cavalry with some sturdy wooden stools. Their precious soft arses would be more comfortable—and the damned stools would eat less hay."

The legate's barbs weren't actually amusing, Marcus thought, and yet Saturnius barely had to open his mouth before he had legionaries laughing harder than a crowd watching clowns at the theatre. The jokes at the expense of the cavalry wings went down particularly well, but the knights bore it with noble aplomb. Saturnius proceeded to methodically pour false contempt on every group of soldiers in the legion, from the artillery to the surgeons. He poked fun at one century after another, and the men not only endured the mocking criticism he directed at them, they seemed to swell with pride when their unit was singled out, even in this fashion.

Ever since he'd joined the legion, Marcus had wondered about his father's high regard for this vulgar little man, but now he began to see that the legate was a charismatic genius. Saturnius played the mass of soldiers as expertly as a skilled musician handling his instrument. He disguised his flattery of them under a veneer of denigration, and he praised them by belittling their deeds. And, Marcus suddenly realized, by demonstrating his contempt for their victory over a foe that had badly outnumbered them, he was instilling in the men a powerful belief in their own superiority.

The little legate was, Marcus began to realize, an exceedingly dangerous man. Saturnius was a seducer—not of women but of soldiers.

There was movement behind him, and he saw two centurions carrying his father's high-backed chair, placing it on the dais behind Saturnius as the legate stalked back and forth across the stage.

Marcus began to realize that there was an additional purpose to Saturnius's taunting. Thanks to his relentless chaffing, the men were stirred out of what could have easily become a post-battle depression born of exhaustion and repressed fear. Several chants of "Imperator, Saturnius, Imperator" began, but each time, Saturnius waved them off as if they were nothing but a petty irritation. It was masterfully done, and not even the most perennially paranoid Senator could have found anything objectionable or ambitious in the legate's behavior.

And then, with the legion all but eating out of the palm of his hand, Saturnius smoothly effaced himself in favor of Corvus, who was already seated upon his favorite chair. Saturnius went and stood behind the stragister militum's right shoulder, while Honoratus, the primus pilus, stepped forward to stand at his left.

Unlike Saturnius, his father didn't attempt to encourage the men or win them over. He didn't need to. They chanted "Corvus, Corvus" until he raised a hand, and they fell obediently silent.

"Men of the Legion, the People and Senate will soon hear of your victory. Your valor and your discipline has defeated the combined might of the Chalonu, the Vakhuyu, and their allies. Tonight, we shall celebrate their defeat at your hands."

The legionaries cheered lustily.

"Your legate, Marcus Saturnius, has ordered a double-issue of the wine ration to be released to you and your centurions will oversee the distribution."

Another cheer.

"Tomorrow, I intend that you shall recuperate from your labors today while messengers ride out to the chiefs of the Insobru, the Vakhuyu, and the Chalonu, demanding their submission to the People and Senate of Amorr."

The men cheered again. They didn't care in the least about what the goblin chiefs did or did not do, but they understood very well the gift their General was giving them. Tonight, everyone who was not on sentry duty was free to drink himself senseless without fear of having to march out the next morning.

Marcus groaned, and he could hear the other tribunes doing the same. Without a female army of camp followers nearby to distract the men, there would be an ungodly number of fights tonight. He, the other tribunes, the centurions, and the decurions were in for a difficult and possibly sleepless night. He did not relish the thought of having to break up fights between men who had stood bravely in arms together this very morning.

The officers were still quietly grumbling amongst themselves when Corvus called two centurions and several legionaries to the platform to honor them before the legion for the courage they had displayed during the battle. Marcus paid little attention, except to cheer at the appropriate moments. He wondered if Fortex would be honored for his bravery or punished for his recklessness. Probably both, if he knew his father. He wasn't sure which his father treasured more, courage or discipline, and God knew his cousin had as much of the former as he lacked the latter.

But surely the rout of the enemy's left wing would count in Fortex's favor! The legion's center hadn't been in any danger of collapsing under the goblin pressure, but the cavalry charge against the goblin infantry's left flank had broken it much sooner than it would have otherwise and without a doubt saved more than a few lives among the stalwart cohorts stationed in the middle.

The legion cheered for each man singled out for praise, but they were particularly pleased when Gnaeus Sextius Baiulus was presented with a vitis and raised to the rank of centurion.

Baiulus, a short, balding man who looked to be nearing his thirties, shook the vine staff warningly at his former fellows, and the platform trembled with the men's good-natured jeering it provoked.

Marcus was disappointed to see the Baleran slingers who had driven off the archers from the Second Cavalry were not honored, but three ballistarii were presented with medals marked with the image of St. Michael, the patron saint of those who warred against magic. Marcus guessed it was their onager that had killed the goblin's shaman or at least forced it from the battlefield.

Then the proud smile faded from Corvus's gaunt and bearded face. He glanced at Saturnius, who nodded at the tribune laticlavius.

Crescentius turned to his right, toward something Marcus could not see from where he stood, and shouted. "Bring the prisoner forward!"

Marcus gasped as two big centurions, one of whom was Proculus, marched forward—escorting Fortex. They pulled him forward, his hands bound behind his back. Gaius Valerius didn't look the least bit afraid. He looked outraged. For a moment, Marcus even feared that his cousin might spit in his father's face.

The entire legion was shocked into silence. A moment later, the murmurs and whispers began. It was as if a giant swarm of bees had risen from the ground.

"Gaius Valerius Fortex, Tribune of the Legion," Corvus declared loudly enough to be heard over the uneasy rustling of the soldiers, "I charge you with breaking ranks and with disobeying a direct order from the senior legionary officer to stand your ground."

There was a second shocked pause, a little shorter this time, and then the chatter among the troops not only increased but took on an angry tone.

Fortex opened his mouth to interrupt, but Corvus held up a hand.

"After conferring with the legate of the legion and several of the senior decurions, I have decided that you had sufficient reason to set aside your initial orders. Events on the battlefield change rapidly, and orders that make sense before battle is joined may, at times, become less than relevant once the enemy is engaged. The Senate and People expect a tribune to exercise his own judgment in these matters on the basis of his training and experience. In this case, your judgment was correct. It was your decisive action that permitted the Second Knights to break the enemy cavalry and come to the assistance of our center. Therefore, I have determined that the charges of breaking ranks and disobedience will be withdrawn."

Marcus breathed a sigh of relief. A few sporadic and tentative cheers rose from the assembly. He found himself standing a bit taller at the praise given to his unit, and he noticed a half-smile flash across his cousin's face. It rapidly disappeared, as Gaius Valerius assumed the stoic, but confident attitude of one expecting to be praised, which was perhaps why he was unable to hide his reaction to Corvus's next words.

"However, the courage and effectiveness of your action does not mitigate the fact that you disobeyed a direct and personal order given to you before the battle by the senior officer of the legion when you engaged your opposite in single combat. Nor does it alter the fact that you chose to disobey that order at a time when the legion was deep inside enemy territory, in danger, and under extraordinary martial discipline."

The entire legion groaned with dismay, and Fortex looked as if he had been stabbed in the stomach. Marcus saw the blood rush from his cousin's face, and he could see that Fortex knew, from the firm resolution in Corvus's eyes, that his uncle was not inclined to turn a blind eye toward his crime or to let him off easily. Marcus held his breath, seeing how his father stared directly into his cousin's face without blinking as he pronounced his judgment.

"Gaius Valerius Fortex, you are charged with disobeying a direct and standing order from your commanding general during battle. After conferring with the legate and the primus pilus of Legio XVII, as well as the senior decurions, I have determined that you are guilty of the charge. As this offense occurred when the legion was engaged in battle and under *Modus Austeris*, I hereby sentence you to death by beheading."

What? No! Marcus instinctively started forward and opened his mouth to protest, but Volusenus grabbed his arm and dug his fingers painfully into the unarmored inside of Marcus's elbow.

"Control yourself, Valerius!" he hissed into Marcus's ear. "You are an officer of the legion, damn you. Now bloody well act like one!"

Fortex was blinking rapidly, and he was visibly grinding his teeth as he fought to control himself.

Marcus, horrified, desperately wanted to plead with his father for Gaius's life, but he didn't dare so much as take a single step in his direction, not in front of the five thousand men of the legion. You can't do this, Father, he silently screamed. You simply cannot do this! Flog him, break him if you must, even ban him from the legion, but do not kill your own brother's son!

Corvus rose from his chair and leaned down to whisper in Fortex's ear. Marcus was just close enough to hear what his father said over the angry murmuring of the troops below. "They say you are brave, Nephew. I pray you will die as courageously as you fought today. And may the Immaculate be your advocate before the Throne of the Almighty."

Fortex was staring at Corvus as if in shock, as if he simply could not believe what he had heard. But the fear quickly vanished from his face, replaced by a fey and fierce pride.

Protest, Marcus thought desperately. Beg him for mercy!

Instead, his cousin merely stared into Corvus's eyes with a fearless arrogance that was almost contemptuous. "Our House is Amorr," he replied icily. "Tell my father I died as befits an officer of the legion."

Corvus, unmoved, neither blinked nor looked away. "Do so, and I shall." He backed away, placed his hands behind his waist, and nodded to the primus pilus.

The big centurion, Honoratus, stepped out from behind Corvus's chair and approached Gaius, revealing an oversized woodcutter's axe in his left hand. To Marcus's and everyone else's surprise, the first thing he did was thump his chest with his free right hand in a last salute to the condemned. The crash of two or three thousand legionaries following his example echoed throughout the otherwise silent forum.

Marcus glanced at his father and saw a brief spasm of irritation cross his face, but Corvus made no move to intervene or remonstrate with the men. Honoratus asked for the *venia carnifex*, the executioner's absolution.

"I absolve you," Fortex replied, his voice calmer than calm. To Marcus's disbelief, he was smiling. "Now, do me a favor, Gnaeus Junius, and tell me that monster is cursed sharp."

"You'll feel less than that goblin you killed today felt your blade," Honoratus promised. "Heaven or Hell, save us a seat, Fortex."

Honoratus glanced at his two fellow centurions, and they gently turned Fortex sideways, then held his arms so that he did not lose his balance as he kneeled before the primus pilus. Fortex held his head out parallel to the ground and stretched out his neck, presenting the centurion with a clean, pale expanse of skin at which to aim. His eyes were closed and his lips were moving silently. Was it a futile plea for mercy that would not be granted? Was he steeling himself for the inevitable? Or was he, as Marcus hoped, commending his soul to the Immaculate?

When his lips stopped moving, Honoratus looked over at Corvus, who nodded.

Marcus forced himself to watch. The centurion raised the axe high over his head, the muscles in his corded arms bulging with the effort. Then, with deceptive speed, the thick wooden shaft described a blurred downward arc that ended in a loud thunk and a spray of crimson as the well-honed axehead buried itself deep into the wood of the platform.

A loud, collective groan erupted from the legion. Marcus bit his lip to stop the instinctive cry of horror inspired by the sight of his cousin's head rolling off the platform, leaving a gory trail of bloody slime behind it as if it was some sort of obscene giant snail. His cousin's headless corpse vomited forth blood like a giant armored leech with food poisoning just a few paces in front of him. Only the fact that his senses had been gradually inured to such horrors over the course of the campaign permitted him to maintain his composure.

Saturnius strode forward again to address the men, heedless of the blood splashed all about the platform.

"Fortex was a brave man. He was a bold warrior. I admired his courage."

Only a few of the soldiers, some of whom were audibly being sick, murmured in agreement. The execution of a young and heroic officer whose actions had secured their victory today was not going over well with the legion, that much was certain. Marcus didn't blame them. He was feeling more than a little mutinous himself.

"But we are not warriors!" Saturnius shouted without warning. "A warrior is fierce—yes, he is. A warrior is brave. But a 'warrior' fights alone. And he dies alone. We are not warriors! We are *soldiers*, men of the legion. We are *disciplined*. We stand together, and we die together. We follow the *orders* given by our *officers!* And that is why one Amorran soldier is worth a dozen brave 'warriors.' That is why one Amorran legion, *this* Amorran legion, defeated ten times its numbers today!"

There were a few scattered cheers, mostly from the centurions. The angry mood, if not quite gone, was moderately dissipated.

Saturnius demanded more. "Tell me, men of the legion, are you warriors, or are you soldiers?"

"Soldiers!" more than half of the legion roared back.

"I asked you a question, men of the legion: Are you warriors, or are you soldiers?"

"Soldiers!" This time, the entire legion answered him.

Marcus could see Saturnius had them back under his control now. He paced across the platform, and barely anyone, Marcus realized, was still much cognizant of the dead body that lay in front of the legate.

"The third time answers all, men of the legion. Are you warriors, or are you soldiers?"

"*Soldiers!*" the legion thundered. The impromptu chant broke out again. "*Saturnius, Imperator, Saturnius Imperator!*"

The legate raised his hand, and the chanting quickly subsided. "Enough of that. Well, men of the legion, since you have decided you are soldiers, after all, I hereby order you to disperse. Go now. Return to the camp. Eat. Drink. Boast of your brave deeds and the goblins you slew today. But I will remind you of this: When you drink with your brothers, do not forget the shades of your brothers-in-arms who died today."

The legionaries saluted and began to make their way toward the camp and their evening meals.

Marcus watched Saturnius turn to his father. Saturnius asked Corvus something, but his father shook his head and waved the legate off. Marcus wondered if he should go to Corvus too, but something inside him rebelled at the notion. Corvus might be his father, but he was also the Stragister Militum, and the legion's youngest tribune suddenly realized he wanted nothing whatsoever to do with his senior officer at the moment.

Lucius Volusenus clapped Marcus on the back. "We'd better get something to eat before the fights begin. And I don't know about you, but I could use a flagon of wine. I don't suppose we get double rations too, do we?"

Marcus did his best to smile at the other officer. He appreciated how the tribune was trying to distract him. He cleared his throat. "I'd be glad to share one with you, Volusenus."

But as he stepped down from the platform and followed the other tribune toward the camp gates and the Via Praetoria, he couldn't help looking back at his father.

Corvus was seated on his wooden chair, staring impassively off into a distant horizon in the direction of the setting sun. Two soldiers knelt in front of him, removing the bloodstained armor from his nephew's body.

Marcus turned away, shaken to the depths of his soul. He had looked up to his cousin for as long as he could remember. He hadn't been as close to Fortex as he was to Sextus, who was of an age with him. But he had grown up with Fortex and had always envied his confidence and easy smile.

How was it possible that such a fiery spirit could be gone from the world? How was it possible that it could be snuffed out in mere seconds? He could feel the tears begin to fill his eyes. How could his Father have done such a terrible thing? To order the death of ten thousand goblins was one thing, but the execution of his own nephew? It was unthinkable. And then Marcus thought of his uncle, of Magnus, and a chill of pure fear ran down his spine.

Our House is Amorr, Father, yes. But what will happen to Amorr if your iron honor has broken House Valerius in two?

FJOTRA

F JOTRA whirled around in delight. Never had she known that such delicate cloth existed, much less how lightly it would fall about her body. Wearing the dress felt as if she were almost naked, and yet the fabric caressed her skin with a feathery touch that was a joyfully sensual experience.

Amelot, the comtesse's lady-in-waiting, who was supervising her preparations this evening, surveyed her with a critical eye. She was an older woman with the first streaks of grey in her hair, and she did not appear to be entirely pleased with the results.

"I do hope my lady Roheis knows what she is doing tonight. I should have thought she would have you dressed in some sort of barbarian splendor, draped in wolfskins or the like."

Fjotra paid the comtesse's woman no mind. She was too enamoured with the look and feel of the cloth—the "silk"—to be overly concerned with whatever Amelot was saying. "I see look-glass?" she asked hopefully. "I see me?"

For the two weeks since their arrival, the Comtesse de Domdidier had hosted her and Brynjolf in her house, preparing them for this evening's ball. It was the strangest two weeks Fjotra had ever known, and in some ways, the most arduous. Every day, she was awoken early by Maronne, a pretty maiden about her age, and taken for a walk in the gardens behind the house—a structure, she had soon been informed, that was not, in fact, *un château*, but *un manoir*—and given her first language lesson of the day.

During dinner that first evening, the Comtesse had nearly laughed herself to tears when Fjotra had innocently asked her, through Brynjolf, how she could possibly expect to defend her "castle" in the event it was attacked by the inhabitants of one of the many castles nearby. Fjotra had turned bright red, mortified by her ignorance, but upon thinking about it later, she realized it was a useful lesson in the vast difference between life on one side of the White Sea and the other. She would have to think twice about all of her assumptions. And even then, she realized, there was a very good chance she would be wrong.

After that first morning lesson with Maronne, during which they would walk together and the other girl would point out objects and make her repeat the names for them, they would meet for a breakfast that, except for the ornate nature of the preparations, could easily have passed for a feast in Garn. Fresh bread, softer and sweeter than any she'd ever tasted, still hot from the ovens and covered with an astonishing variety of jellies that came in every color of the rainbow, smoked herring, cheese, and golden beer that was lighter and yet more flavorful than any brewed in Ulvøen.

After breakfast came a second language lesson, again with Maronne, followed by dance lessons with Amelot and a man named Henriot. The dances were slow and languid compared with the more strenuous dances to which she was accustomed, but she enjoyed them far more than she did wrestling with the awkward Savonner tongue. Sometimes the comtesse joined them, and Fjotra was amazed by the effortless way she glided about the floor in Henriot's arms. Comtesse Roheis even danced with Brynjolf a few times, but something—probably the close proximity to her beautifully curved figure—proved to be too much of a distraction for her brother, and he regressed badly whenever she was his partner.

After a light repast at midday—usually wine, cheese, and more of the wonderful bread—they were permitted an hour of rest, after which came yet another language lesson. An older servitor by the name of Huguet instructed her, this time in the grammatical rules and conjugations of *Savonnaise*. The comtesse didn't expect them to be fluent, but she made it clear that they had to be capable of engaging in simple conversations by the day of the Duchesse's ball.

The rest of the afternoon was spent practicing the ballad they were to sing if the opportunity presented itself. It was a simple, abbreviated variant of the Arrow King's death song. But with Huguet's help, Brynjolf had adapted the lament and translated it into the southern tongue. It was a tale of the coming of the wolves to the Wolf Isles and the death of the Dalarn people. Fjotra found she had to focus on her singing rather than the words or she would find herself thinking of her burned, abandoned home and start to cry.

> *We were forced to flee*
> *Our land abandoned*
> *Brave bold warriors*
> *Fought through the night*
> *We seemed to carry*
> *Burdens of sorrow*
> *Throughout the dark nights*
> *We fled the hunters*

Amelot brought Fjotra a looking glass, and Fjotra admired herself in it. "Yes," Amelot said with a withering shake of her head, "I suppose this is all new to you, reaver girl. Naturally you must be curious about your appearance. Never fear: That mass of white hair will set off the blue to perfection once we arrange it properly. I am aware you are an illiterate barbarian, but that is no excuse for behaving as if your hair is nothing more than a nest for rats. It's a pity the color of the dress doesn't quite match the blue of your eyes, but it's close enough as to make no difference."

Amelot rang a bell, and a young girl appeared. They exchanged words too rapidly for Fjotra to even try following, and a few minutes later the girl returned with the comtesse herself.

Fjotra bowed to the comtesse, who smiled and air-kissed her cheek before stepping back and looking her over critically as if she was an ornament the comtesse was considering as a decorative addition to the chamber.

"She's lovely, my lady," Amelot said, "but I wonder you don't wish to play up the barbarian aspect. So much more dramatic, don't you think?"

"To be sure, but you fail to grasp my purpose, Amelot darling. There is no chance that either she or her brother could possibly be mistaken for anything other than what they are, even before they open their mouths. My object is not to belabor the obvious but rather to demonstrate that the dread reavers can be tamed, perhaps even civilized with time."

"It will take more than a pair of pretty young reavers dressed in the height of fashion to convince any of the nobles north of the Deinar that they are harmless, much less that they should be succored. It's their lands that the reavers have been pillaging for centuries. They'll want their pretty heads on poles."

The comtesse smiled. Fjotra thought she rather resembled a cat when she did so. "In that case, we are fortunate that His Majesty resides well south of the Deinar River. I don't see how the northern nobles count for much these days. Vevenny can be persuaded. It's in his interest, after all, since he'll be the first to have to fend off the wolves should they cross the sea again. The Viscomte de Verdanne isn't important enough to matter either way. No one will care what he thinks. And the new Duc de Montrove is unlikely to express any opinion at all, seeing as he is still at his mother's breast."

"Do you think Montrove might be an option for them?" Amelot asked. "I imagine its walls need to be rebuilt, or at least repaired, after the Red Prince took the city. And from what I heard about the way his men sacked it, I imagine it may well need to be repopulated too."

Comtesse Roheis waved her hand dismissively. "The rumors were exaggerated. Charles-Phillippe himself assured me there was no serious pillaging. Why, he didn't even have the entire garrison killed, only the officers. I thought it was extraordinarily generous of him to permit the duc's little son to claim his inheritance. He would have been entirely justified to extinguish such a traitorous line. Of course, even a rebel's son is going to create less trouble when he is an infant than any of the other claimants for the duchy were likely to cause. Especially since the child permitted him to name Sieur Charibert as the ducal guardian. The good chevalier will stamp out any treasonous embers still glowing there."

"There is… war in Savonne?" Fjotra wasn't able to completely follow the two women's conversation. They were speaking too quickly for her. But she understood enough to make her worry.

"Never mind, *ma chérie*," the comtesse said quickly. "One of the great… clan leaders, you would say, was foolish enough to rebel against the king, and the king's son put an end to the rebellion. But that was months ago, and you will meet the king *tonight*. You must be sure to smile at him. He likes pretty young girls, and he would be a great ally for your people. Now, we have more important things to discuss, such as what jewelry you are to wear!"

It was dark by the time they were bundled into the comtesse's carriage. The wagon was black and was painted on the side with her totem: an argent beast on a field of alternating blue and yellow stripes. The carriage moved with a strange swaying motion, a little like a snekkja with the waves coming against its side. The seats were comfortable enough, though, being overstuffed pillows similar to the divans in the comtesse's manor, but Fjotra thought she'd prefer the freedom of a horse to being trapped inside a land-boat.

In their own language, Brynjolf, sitting across from Fjotra, said he thought it was strange that the comtesse's totem was a bear, since she was about as unbearlike as it was possible to be. But Fjotra insisted it was a strange southern dog.

The comtesse, looking amused, listened to them debate the issue. Finally, she leaned forward and placed her hand on Brynjolf's arm.

"It is not a bear, nor is it a dog, but a lion, my dears. It is a large and very dangerous beast, similar to a cat in the way that a wolf is akin to a dog. Tonight, you must be aware that you will be surrounded by every sort of dangerous beast. Even lions, in a manner of speaking. So guard your tongues, do not drink too much, and say exactly the words you have been practicing. Do you remember?"

Fjotra and Brynjolf both stared at her, astonished and a little alarmed.

"You speak our tongue?" Fjotra asked.

"A little," the comtesse said with a mysterious smile. Then she shook her head and laughed before switching back to Savonner. "Why do you think you were sent to me, my pets, of all the nobles in Savondir? I spent three years as a lady-in-waiting on the north coast. One of my closest friends there was half-Dalarn. Now, try it again, and try to enunciate each sound."

"I beseech your Majesty," Brynjolf began, with a bow from the waist and a flourish of his arm. His Savonner accent was improving quickly, Fjotra thought, although she thought he looked a little ridiculous in his outlandish clothes and with a silver circlet resting on his head.

The comtesse interrupted him. "You need not repeat it now, my prince. If Henriot hasn't already drilled it into your head, you're not about to perfect it now. I will also remind you of one more thing: Do not wander off with anyone. You especially, Brynjolf. You're different and exotic, and I daresay there may be women there who will turn your head. But you are to stay within sight of me at all times, do you understand?"

Brynjolf nodded. "Yes, Comtesse."

"Of course, my lady," Fjotra said.

The carriage moved along slowly in jerks and halts for what Fjotra guessed was about half a bell before it finally came to a stop in front of a magnificent edifice that was nearly as large as mighty Raknarborg, though without the three towers of the northern fortress. Unlike the comtesse's manoir, this was a proper château, with proper stone walls defended by pike-bearing guardsmen in heavy metal armor. The flames from the torches attached every few paces along the wall seemed to dance off their polished breastplates and cast strange shadows on the cobblestones.

Henriot opened the door and stood aside as Brynjolf stepped down from the interior, then gave Fjotra a hand before assisting the comtesse.

She whispered something in his ear, and he nodded grimly before climbing back into the little land-boat.

There were many other carriages lining the cobble-stoned street outside the walls, some pulling away and others waiting to disgorge their passengers. In the torchlight, the Duchesse's guests were a riot of colors and perfumes, and the whole crowded scene struck Fjotra as a bizarre, beautiful fantasia. Somewhere nearby, she could hear masculine voices singing, accompanied by a stringed instrument of some kind.

A tall man in a black cape smiled at her as they passed. A moment later, an older, overweight woman wearing enough gold to purchase a longboat and crew looked her up and down and then sneered at her. Fjotra was too overwhelmed to be offended. She simply stood there and stared in confusion at the people flowing through the gate on all sides around her. "Come along, Fjotra," she heard a familiar voice call. She looked ahead and saw the comtesse on Brynjolf's arm, beckoning to her.

"I'm sorry, my lady, it's all just so... wonderful!" She stared in awe at the moat that surrounded the château, surmounted by a wooden bridge. She'd never seen anything like it. She'd never even *imagined* anything like it.

"I'm glad you're enjoying the bridge and the crush at the carriages, but I imagine you'll find the ball itself to be even more entertaining." The comtesse took Fjotra's hand to prevent them from being separated again, and together the three of them walked over the wooden bridge that spanned the moat. Below the bridge, floating on the water, there were four little boats, each holding two singers or a singer and a musician playing a wooden instrument that sounded a little like a lyre.

They entered through a gate into a courtyard that was brilliantly lit by torches fixed high up on the walls. The courtyard was immense, larger than the comtesse's entire garden. It was almost like finding the country in the heart of the city: a stony field under a clear and starry sky.

Everyone appeared to know the comtesse, and not a few of her acquaintances, after greeting the comtesse, stared at Brynjolf and her with unmitigated astonishment. However, the comtesse did not see fit to introduce them to anyone yet. She merely nodded pleasantly to the various lords and ladies and exchanged noncommittal pleasantries in lieu of satisfying their obvious curiosity, looking past the newcomers and toward the château. Fjotra wondered if she was looking for the king or for someone else.

Looking up, she saw the wall surrounding the courtyard was thick enough that guards could patrol it high over their heads. One... two... there were six guards in all. They were armed with a strange sort of weapon that she hadn't seen before. She pointed them out to Brynjolf, and he told her they were a special type of bow called a crossbow. The weapons looked deadly, although their strange shape made her wonder how the string was drawn, and she shivered when she realized how easily the men standing atop the wall could turn the courtyard into a butcher's pen full of helpless people. It made her uneasy, and she wished they could go inside the château. It might not actually be any safer, but at least she wouldn't feel so exposed.

Brynjolf felt it too, she could see. He kept his back to the nearest wall, barely took his eyes off the guards, and kept feeling at his side for his nonexistent sword. Given the way he then proceeded to run his right hand over his left wrist, she suspected he might have ignored the comtesse's orders to leave all his weapons at the manoir.

"Ah, there he is," said the comtesse. "Come, both of you. I must introduce you to a friend of mine."

She led them to a tall, lean man with a short, neatly trimmed beard and dauntingly intelligent eyes. When he looked at her, Fjotra had to resist the unconscious urge to shrink away from him. She had grown up among enough killers to recognize one when she saw one. He was accompanied by an even taller woman in a green silk dress with hair as white as Fjotra's own. But it wasn't until she noticed that the woman's ears were pointed that she realized the woman was an elf. She gasped. She had heard tales of elves before, but she never seen one. Truth be known, she hadn't actually believed they were real.

"Magicien Theuderic," the comtesse said, "how good it is to see you! And you, as well, Milady Everbright."

The man called Theuderic kissed the comtesse's hand. He smiled, but Fjotra could see that it never touched his brown eyes. "My lady, you look lovely. How the priests will be ruing their vows tonight."

"I doubt there will be many at the ball tonight, Magicien. May I present Prince Brynjolf d'Ulven and his sister, the Princess Fjotra de Raknarborg?" The comtesse turned to Fjotra and Brynjolf. "Your royal highnesses, this is Magicien Theuderic of l'Académie Royale, and his companion, the Lady Everbright of Merithaim. She is, as you may see, an elf."

Theuderic grinned at her. "Roheis, you are unconscionable! Only you would dare to dress up two Dalarn reavers and pass them off as royalty!" He glanced at the elf and squeezed her hand. "And here I feared *we* would be the talk of the ball."

"They are not true prince and princess?" the elf woman said quizzically. Her accent was strong enough that Fjotra, much to her surprise, could hear it even through the Savonner. Fjotra thought the exotic woman was beautiful despite her unnatural slenderness, perhaps even more beautiful than the comtesse. But she sensed there was something sorrowful behind the elf's green and slanted eyes.

"Their father is what passes for a king in the Iles de Loup. I tend to doubt Skuli Skullcrusher's line compares favorably with the Miridines, much less your own royal lineage, Lady Everbright. But he is the ruler of the Dalarn there. We usually refer to the son and daughter of a ruler as a prince and princess, do we not?"

"*Hjerneskalstyrtsø*," Brynjolf interjected.

The two Savoners and the elf lady looked at him as if he had suddenly sprouted horns.

"I do beg your pardon, your Royal Highness," Theuderic said, pretending to look alarmed. "But I tend to doubt that anyone here, with the possible exception of your sister, understood that dreadful noise."

"I think you would say 'breaks the skulls,'" Brynjolf explained helpfully. "Not crush them. There is a difference, yes?"

"Yes, of course," the comtesse said with an uncharacteristically tight smile. "Skullbreaker. I do stand corrected. Well, from the various tales the dear prince has shared with us concerning his father, his father's father, and his father's father's father, most of which involve the enthusiastic slaughter of more people than even you would consider reasonable, Theuderic, you can rest assured that the Skullbreaker line is as royal as any in the Iles de Loup."

"Then I am indeed honored to make your acquaintance, your royal highnesses," the magicien said gravely. He bowed to Brynjolf, then took Fjotra's hand and kissed it. She couldn't help an involuntary shudder, and his eyes flickered with momentary amusement at her response. He turned back toward the comtesse. "Am I genuinely to assume that you are serious about this northern alliance, Roheis, or is it simply one of your hare-brained schemes to score off the Duchesse?"

"Score off the Duchesse?" The comtesse's laugh was rich with genuine amusement. "My dear sieur, I could not possibly care less about Ysoude one way or the other. They must be introduced to society, and one way or another, I intend to see that they receive an audience before the Haut Conseil, if not His Majesty himself."

Theuderic stared intently into her face for a moment, but the comtesse didn't flinch. She merely smiled provocatively at him. Finally he nodded, turned to Brynjolf, and extended his hand with his palm up. "Give me the blade, reaver prince. The King will be here tonight. You can't be introduced to him in possession of that."

Brynjolf blinked in astonishment. Inadvertently, his hand leaped to his wrist. "How you know I have blade?"

Theuderic sighed. "Your royal highness, I happen to be one of the King's Own. Which is to say I am one of his royal battlemages. Detecting metal hidden about another's person is a simple spell every court mage learns in his first year at l'Académie. You wouldn't have come within fifty feet of His Majesty without one or another of the various counterspells surrounding him setting you on fire. Roheis, didn't you warn them about this?"

"I told him not to bring any weapons," the comtesse said. "I didn't know about any magical wards. How would I know about such things?" She made a displeased face at Brynjolf. "With all due respect to your father's fifteen clans, if you cannot manage to follow my instructions, I will arrange to have Henriot bring you back to the manoir, do you understand? Fjotra, what about you? Do you have any knives about your person?

Fjotra shook her head and surreptitiously kicked Brynjolf before he tried to argue about the command to surrender his weapon. It was no surprise that he was carrying a blade, since the men of her people considered themselves naked without a weapon of some kind. Chagrined, Brynjolf apologized as best his limited vocabulary would permit and slipped the knife out of his sleeve. Theuderic took it from him and adroitly concealed it somewhere in his bright blue finery.

"Will it not make you on fire?" Fjotra asked the magicien. She wasn't sure if she was more embarrassed or furious with her brother. How could Brynjolf be so foolish? If Lady Roheis sent them away now, they might never have another chance to meet the king!

Theuderic smiled. The magicien was handsome enough, but there was something deeply disturbing about him that made her want to shriek and flee from him. He looked at her, at everyone, in a way that put her in mind of a hawk studying at a mouse, deciding if it would be permitted to live or die. "I am one of the King's Own battlemages, Lady. He has nothing to fear from me, and even if I was a traitor, my possession of a small and sharpened earth element would be the very least of his concerns. The wards will not touch me. But since we are speaking of concerns, perhaps you might tell me of this pressing matter that Comtesse Roheis intends the two of you to set before His Majesty."

She glanced at the comtesse. "We ask him that we come here, to Savonne," she told him.

"You mean to Lutèce, the city?"

"No, the lands by the sea. In north."

"Who is we? Yourself and your brother? Your family would like to move here?"

"No, 'we' is... all Dalarn. All that still live."

Theuderic's jaw fell open. He looked from her to the comtesse. "Are you mad, Roheis? You can't seriously expect His Majesty to agree to settle tens of thousands of reavers inside the realm!"

"Tell him about the ulfin, Brynjolf," the comtesse ordered. "They call them 'aalvarg.'"

Brynjolf told him how the aalvarg had driven their people from the two larger islands in the Iles de Loup. The sorcerer folded his arms, but as the story unfolded, his bearded face gradually transformed from a mask of skepticism into one of reluctant interest. Brynjolf's tale ended with the news that the Dalarn were now reduced to less than one-tenth of their former numbers and were all living behind the walls of the great fortress of Raknarborg.

Theuderic shook his head. "I'm truly sorry to hear about the travails of your people, highnesses, but this still strikes me as madness. To create a new demesne... to effectively create a new duchy, actually, is what you're asking the king to contemplate here. From whom would you have him take the land, Roheis? It is a small thing to be generous with someone else's territory, perhaps. My lady, such an act could risk tearing the realm apart."

"Is that anything those of true scarlet blood should fear, sieur?"

Theuderic glared at her, and the comtesse fell silent even though her eyes still flashed defiance. "You don't know what you are asking, Roheis. You push too far, too fast. Do not think you can expect to fully understand the Red Prince's purposes, no matter how close you are. Even less can you understand His Majesty's. You must let your dreams go. Have you learned nothing from the example of Montrove?"

There was the short sound of a fanfare, and the crowd stirred as heads turned toward the entrance to the courtyard. "It sounds as if the Red Prince has arrived," the comtesse said, her voice flat with either irritation or anger.

Unlike the others, Fjotra wasn't looking toward the gate and the crowds awaiting the prince's entrance. She was looking up at the walls. A movement had caught her eye, and she noticed that there seemed to be more guards there now than before. She counted them again quickly and saw that there were now eight of them, all dressed in black to blend in with the shadows, and all armed with crossbows. She turned to Theuderic, knowing he was the only one who might be able to do anything. "My lord mage, who want to kill your prince?"

"Kill the Red Prince?" The magicien laughed. "Depending upon the day of the week, nearly any number of people. He can be difficult. I suppose there are a few surviving rebels left in Montrove who would like to see him dead, given how he killed their duc last year."

She nodded. "They be here. I count eight men on the wall now. Before, only six."

"*Merde!*" the magicien swore, startling both the comtesse and his elf lady with his sudden vehemence. "Can you tell me which two?"

"I think those," Fjotra said, pointing to the only two guards who were walking together. Both were walking slowly but in a direction that would soon bring them to a point above the crush of people near the entry gate, which was presumably gathered around to see the prince's entourage enter the courtyard.

The sorcerer faced them and closed his eyes. Then he turned toward one of the other guards and closed his eyes again. When they snapped open, there was certainty in them. "They are assassins. Both of them. They're carrying far more metal than the other guards. Brynjolf, can you climb the wall?"

Her brother nodded, as Fjotra knew he would. The bricks had enough edge on them that she thought she could probably climb the wall herself, although she would be sorry to ruin her beautiful gown.

"Good, then climb up behind them. Out of sight. Don't attack them right away. Do you understand? Wait until I interfere with their attack. Then just shove them off the walls. I can't imagine both will manage to break their necks in the fall. We'll want one for questioning, preferably both."

The comtesse held both her hands to her chest. "Shouldn't you alert the other guards?"

Theuderic shook his head. "That will cause too much confusion and panic. It might even start a stampede that would prove more deadly than the assassins themselves. Trust me, I can stop their attack." He turned to Brynjolf. "I need you to make sure they don't escape."

Brynjolf nodded eagerly, obviously pleased to be of service in the sort of activity he understood. "I will throw them down to you." He smiled at Fjotra, bowed to the comtesse, and quickly began making his way through the crowd toward the wall.

Fjotra was worried, but mostly because she suspected her brother was eager to do this to impress the comtesse, not for what two unsuspecting southerners might be able to do to him. Her brother had never reaved, but he had been fighting the aalvarg ever since he had been old enough to hold a sword.

It wasn't long before there was a ninth man atop the wall. Fortunately, none of the guards saw Brynjolf climbing up to join them, as it belatedly occurred to her that the guards would have no way of knowing his intentions in scaling the wall. All four of them—Fjotra, the comtesse, Theuderic, and the elf woman—were now watching the walls.

Without any visible sign, the two false guards raised their crossbows to their shoulders. No sooner had they done so than the sorcerer said something unintelligible and gestured with one hand. The two crossbows erupted into white-hot flame. One of the assassins cried out in surprise and dropped his flaming weapon at once. The other, more self-controlled, somehow managed to hold onto it long enough to loose his bolt. It hit something on the other side of the wall with an audible *thwunk*.

Screams erupted. It sounded as if someone had been hit. Fjotra could only hope that the prince was not the victim.

Then Brynjolf struck. He ran up behind the first assassin and shoved the unsuspecting man off the wall. The assassin fell down into the crowded courtyard below, his arms flailing uselessly about. The people screamed. Brynjolf didn't pause even to watch the first man fall. He was already moving toward the second assassin.

But the second man was aware of him now, alerted by the screams, and whirled around to face Brynjolf's approach. One moment, the assassin's hands were empty, and the next, Fjotra saw he had a large, curved dagger in his hand.

Brynjolf fell upon the assassin just as the man lunged at him.

Fjotra saw the dagger plunge into her brother's chest, causing him to stagger backward from the force behind the blow. She screamed.

Brynjolf cried out too, but he was the son of Skuli Skullbreaker, the Reaver Lord of Raknarborg and the last clan chief of the Wolf Isles. With a shout that was more rage than pain, he grabbed the assassin's knife arm with his right hand before the man could withdraw the blade, stepped backward, and smashed his forearm against the other man's locked elbow. The sound of the arm snapping was quickly drowned out by the assassin's disbelieving shriek of agony, which was abruptly silenced by Brynjolf's forehead slamming into his face.

"Don't loose, don't loose!" Theuderic shouted at the guards, two of whom were on one knee and aiming at the two combatants. "In the name of the king, I command you, do not loose! Capture them, you fools—don't kill them!"

The battlemage was pushing through the panicked crowd of nobles and ladies, although Fjotra couldn't tell if he was trying to reach the prince or the first assassin Brynjolf had pushed off the wall. She tried to run toward Brynjolf, but a long-fingered hand gripped her wrist and stopped her.

"Calm yourself, child, there is nothing you can do," the Lady Everbright told her.

Fjotra tried to shake her arm to escape the other woman, but the slender elf was much stronger than she looked. She gave one last futile tug, then gave up, realizing that the elfess was right.

Up on the wall, the remaining assassin was staggering backward, his right arm hanging awkwardly from his side. Brynjolf, the dagger still sticking out of his chest, roared like a true berserker, then stepped forward and kicked the man in the chest, sparking another scream from the crowd below as the assassin plunged backward into their midst.

Only then did her brother withdraw the dagger from his chest. He raised it above his head and shouted in triumph. In the flickering light of the flames, standing high above all the frightened shrieks and cries from below, he looked like a pagan god of war accepting a bloody sacrifice.

"Your pet has sharper teeth than you thought, my lady," Fjotra heard Lady Everbright tell the comtesse.

"What a magnificent young beast he is," the comtesse said, her voice breathy. Then she gasped and Fjotra froze, her heart in her mouth.

Brynjolf, still holding the dagger, collapsed to his knees on the edge of the wall. The two nearest guards on the wall lowered their crossbows and rushed toward her brother, but he slumped slowly to one side, clutching at his wounded chest. Fjotra could do nothing but watch in helpless horror as Brynjolf, unable to catch himself, slipped from the blood-slicked bricks and fell toward the courtyard below.

CORVUS

THE camp was quiet throughout the day as the legionaries were permitted to sleep late and recover from their excesses the night before. The butcher's bill had been light: Only two more soldiers had died of their battle wounds during the night. Bacchus's bill had been a bit higher, as there were twenty-seven soldiers who now faced castigation at the hands of their centurions because of fights and related mayhem. But Corvus knew his officers and was confident they would be laying on the strokes lightly this evening. The hangovers presently being suffered by the men awaiting discipline and hundreds of their fellows were arguably sufficient punishment for them.

Corvus stood in front of the flaming bier that had been constructed near the stables, watching as the flames burned away the last of his nephew's flesh from his blackened bones. He could still see the astonishment on Gaius Valerius's face, the young man's incredulity at the word of his fate. Had he done wrong in sentencing Fortex to die? He didn't see how. The law of the legions was perfectly clear. And yet his conscience condemned him.

The fire was hot, and he was relieved that the disturbingly appetizing smell of cooked meat had mostly dissipated. But soon, he would give orders for the blaze to be extinguished. Corvus did not have the heart to fully cremate the lad. The least he could do was to send Gaius Valerius's bones back to Magnus for a proper funeral with the family.

No reply had arrived yet from the Vakhuyu, but the Chalonu and the Insobru were already indicating their intention to submit. Corvus found he could take little satisfaction in the knowledge that he had now fulfilled fully half of the charge laid upon him by the Senate and People. He kept seeing his nephew's pale, angry face even though it was now nothing more than a charred skull.

He wondered how Magnus would react. Angrily, of course. He had no illusion that his brother would accept the execution of his second-youngest son with any of the stoicism of the old patricians whose standard he now proudly bore in the Senate. In time, though, Corvus knew Magnus would come to see the inevitability of his decision. After all, his brother was a general and had been forced to execute his own soldiers before. Gaius Valerius had possessed potential, there was no denying that. And bravery too. His nephew had more than merited the cognomen Fortex. But if there had been the seeds of greatness in the boy, there were even more that hinted at disaster.

One of his guards approached. "There's a rider from Amorr waiting in your tent, General. Says he has a message for you."

Corvus nodded. He pointed to the fire. "Get that put out and see that my nephew's bones are cleaned and prepared for travel."

"At once, General!"

Corvus turned his back on the flames and returned to his tent in the middle of the camp. He pushed past the hanging leather that served as the tent's doors and saw a small, thin man wearing heavy leather trousers turn toward him as he entered.

Corvus recognized the man at once. He was Clodipor, Magnus's most reliable messenger. For a moment, he felt unaccountably alarmed, almost frightened. Surely it wasn't possible that Magnus already knew about his son's death! No, of course not, it wasn't possible. The news probably hadn't even reached Berdicum yet.

"It's good to see you again, Clodipor," Corvus lied. "I assume you bear the latest from Magnus? Is there anything of interest happening in Amorr?"

Clodipor's pock-marked face lit up at being recognized. "It is an honor to see you again, Lord Corvus. Or I suppose I should say 'Lord Stragister Corvus,' sir."

"You may suppose whatever you like, but Corvus will do. This is a legionary camp, not a ballroom." He took the sealed scroll that Clodipor was offering him.

The wax upon which the familiar Valerian seal was stamped was still intact, so Corvus broke it in half and began to unroll what was a rather lengthier message than he was expecting. He was relieved to see it was written in the familiar hand of Dompor, the more relaxed of Magnus's two slave-scholars. Lazapor, by contrast, fancied himself more of a scholar-in-residence and permanent guest than secretarial slave. But even Lazapor's hand was better than Magnus's own writing, which was virtually illegible. Corvus glanced up and belatedly realized that Clodipor was still waiting on him. "Guard!" he called.

One of the legionaries stationed outside his tent entered immediately. "General?"

"Take this man, see that he is fed and that his horse is given priority with the grooms. They'll be busy, but don't let them put you off." He beckoned the guard closer and whispered into his ear. "Stay by his side at all times, and be bloody well sure he does not speak to anyone else or hear about what happened to my nephew. He will be leaving within the hour. Do you understand?"

"Perfectly, General!" The guard saluted and turned to Clodipor. "Sir, if you will come with me?"

"Lord Magister, will you have a return message for me?"

"Most certainly. One for Magnus, one for my wife, and one for the Senate. Come back after you've eaten. You'll be able to make Berdicum well before sundown."

"As you command, my lord."

Magnus's man bowed low and was escorted by the guard from the command tent.

Corvus closed his eyes and breathed a sigh of relief—at least the man hadn't asked to see Fortex or deliver a letter to him. He began reading.

To Sex. Valerius Corvus, Dux Ducis (in Gorignia, somewhere near Berdicum, I presume)

Amorr (September)

My dear brother, if I chose to send letters as short as yours usually are, I should easily beat you and be much the more regular in writing. But, in fact, as it is only one more item in an immense and inconceivable amount of business, I will allow no letter to reach you from me without its containing some definite sketch of events in the Senate and the reactions arising from them. And in writing to you, as a lover of your city and your nation, my first subject will naturally be the state of the Republic; as our House is the next great object of your loyalty, I will also write about myself and our kin, and tell you what I think you will not be indisposed to know.

Well then, in public affairs, for the moment the chief subject of interest is the sudden and untimely death of the Sanctiff. It has been five days thus far, and five votes, but as yet we have no new Sanctified Father. Balbus and Noctua are said to be the two leading candidates, but obviously neither has a majority of the electors yet. I should prefer Noctua, but since neither he nor Balbus has ever shown any interest in interfering with the Senate, I cannot see that this is of any great relevance to our House. Do be sure to let our Clericus know—I suppose it was inevitable, wasn't it?—as I believe he developed a personal attachment to the Sanctiff on the basis of his embassy experience.

Corvus laid the letter down on his desk. The Sanctiff was dead? How could that be? His Holiness was the only Sanctiff that Corvus could remember. Reading of his death—and it was so like his brother to only mention it in passing, as if the succession politics were the relevant aspect—was rather like reading that God had died.

How would he break the news to the legions? He would have to order a special mass tomorrow. The men would expect no less, and besides, the late Sanctified Father had merited it. For many of them, as for Corvus, the devout old man had been the living embodiment of their connection to the Almighty. He wiped at his eyes, which somehow had gone a little blurry, and returned to the letter.

> *The other matter of much discussion and rather more import to you is the disturbance in Cynothicus. The Consul Aquilae took Legio XIV to quell it after the uprising there, but he recently fought a losing battle and was slain by the Cynothii. Now the entire province is undoubtedly in arms and making raids upon Moenica and Rapulum. The senate has decreed that a consul suffectus shall be named to replace L. Andronicus Caudinus, that a levy for a new legion should be held, that all exemptions from service should be suspended, and that two legates with full powers should be sent to visit the neighboring provinces and ensure that they do not join the rebels. The legates are Q. Martellus Durus, L. Favronius, and the new Consul Suffectus Aquilae is—a case of "to whom much is given"—one Sex. Valerius Corvus, of the most highly regarded House in Amorr!*

What? Corvus had to re-read the last line three times before its import hit home. He was to replace Caudinus? He was to be—in fact, he already was—the new consul of the legions? For a moment, fierce exultation filled his soul.

That was replaced a moment later by the devastating realization that the truculent goblin tribes were no longer his concern. He could no longer focus his attention on a single campaign and a single foe but was from this moment personally responsible for all of Amorr's wars, especially the one against the rebel provincials in Cynothicus. Then he laughed to himself. How pleased Romilia would be. And it could have been worse. At least the Sacred College wasn't going to name him Sanctiff Suffectus too.

> *And while on this subject I cannot omit mentioning that, when among the consulars my name was the first to come up in the ballot, a full*

meeting of the senate declared with one voice that I must be kept in the city. The same happened to Patronus after me; we two are to be kept at home as pledges of the safety of the Republic whilst you secure the safety of the Empire's provinces as you have already secured its borders by your recent exploits in Gorignia. Why should I go seeking additional plaudits abroad when I get these compliments at home?

So, my dear brother, you are hereby charged by the Senate and People to return at once to appear before the Senate and receive your new commission from your consular colleagues. The city legion is to be at your disposal, along with the three Valerian legions, and you are to transfer your present commission as Stragister Militum to the legate of your choice. I imagine you will name Saturnius, although I know you would prefer to have him at your side when you march on Cynothicus. And not that it should factor into your decision, but I suggest our two young tribunes will be safer facing the tribes than the Cynothii now that the latter have tasted Amorran blood.

Corvus winced. The goblins might be safer for Marcus. For Fortex, it was already too late to matter.

Now, as to the state of affairs in the city, which is as follows. The citizenship law is being vehemently pushed by the tribune Fulvius, with the support of Patronus and several respected members of House Severus, but it has nothing popular about it within the Senate except its chief supporter.

From this law I, with the full assent of a public meeting, proposed to omit all clauses which adversely affected the rights of the current citizenry. I proposed to except from its operation all voting for the offices of the cursus honorum and the tribunate, as had once been the case for the plebians in the consulship of P. Genucius, G. Crescentius and L. Calpurnius. I proposed to confine the offices of magistri militum, legati, and the military tribunes to those who actually held lands within the bounds of the current Republic. I also proposed to limit the citizenship of the provinces to what was essentially equivalences of tax and legal protection.

There was only one section in the bill that I did not propose to omit, namely, that the provincial citizenship should be granted on the basis of a payment equal to the amount expected to be paid in land tax over the next five years. But to this whole citizenship scheme the senate was opposed, suspecting that some novel power for Patronus was aimed at. The Severan, indeed, had set his heart on getting the law passed. But the debate on the matter was interrupted by the war, as you can surely understand, and has cooled off for the present.

As for your two colleagues in the consulship, Torquatus has been an exceedingly good Consul Civitas and is well-regarded in the Senate. He is much attached to me. Your other colleague, M. Fulvius Paetinus, whom I don't believe you know, is a fool and has no idea what to do with the Provinces, especially now that they are aflame.

This is all my public news, unless you regard as touching on public affairs the fact that a certain Herennius, a tribune, and a Severan on his mother's side—a fellow as unprincipled as he is needy—has now begun making frequent proposals for transferring Severus Regulus to the plebs; he is vetoed by many of his colleagues. It is more Severan intrigue, though to what purpose I cannot imagine. That is really, I think, all the public news.

Do not fail to hasten back to Amorr upon receipt of this letter. Three legions will be sufficient to discipline the Cynothii in the spring. But if the revolt spreads, I fear we shall soon find ourselves in want.

I look to see you soon. Greet our noble tribunes for me!

M. V. Magnus

At Amorr

Corvus stared at the letter in his hand. It was almost too much to take in at once. He was still aggrieved about the Sanctiff's death, of course, but

Consul! Of the Legions! It was a height he had never seriously expected to attain. He was four years too late to have made consul in his year. But unlike Magnus, politics had always been a means rather than an end to Corvus. Although he had dutifully walked the cursus honorum as tribune, quaestor, and praetor in the past, placing his name before the Comitia Centuriata and asking the people to make him their king for a year was not something he had ever seriously contemplated doing. And yet, the consulship was now thrust upon him, unasked!

But it was not a gift without cost. He knew why the Senate had chosen him, when six months ago there would have been twenty names ahead of his own: They were afraid of the Cynothii, and rightly so.

Caudinus was a competent commander, and Legio XIV was the better of the two Andronican legions, to the extent that the retired legionaries of Legio XII, now settled to a well-deserved retirement on their Senate-granted farms three years ago, could still be counted. If he recalled correctly, the Cynothii were a fierce race who relied heavily upon their mounted infantry. But mounted infantry were lightly armored, by definition. The little horses they rode couldn't bear the weight of a properly armored man. So how could they have beaten one of Amorr's more experienced legions? How could they have not only beaten it, but beaten it so badly that its legate and staff had fallen?

Was it possible that Caudinus had not been slain in battle proper but in an ambush of sorts? Perhaps the loss of the legate had led to the loss of the legion, rather than the other way around. He wished Magnus would have seen fit to provide more detail on his predecessor's death.

He withdrew a clean sheet of vellum from his dwindling supply and dipped his pen in the ink. He would write not to Magnus but to Titus Manlius Torquatus, his new consular colleague.

To T. Manlius Torquatus, Consul Civitas (at Amorr)

Gorignia (October)

Forgive my soldierly brevity, respected colleague, and provide me with the answers to the following questions at the earliest opportunity.

How badly was Legio XIV beaten? Must know total casualties and present location.

How did Caudinus die? Battle, ambush, or assassination?

How quickly does Favronius believe he can raise the new legion? Where will it be raised?

Please arrange to send four spies to Moenica and Rapulum. We must know if either of them intend to join the Cynothii in their revolt.

I shall leave for Amorr tomorrow. Do not trouble to send a letter in response to this, as I expect to arrive no more than three or four days subsequent to this missive. I would prefer to receive your responses in person.

Sex. Valerius Corvus, Consul Suffectus Aquilae

Corvus was certain Lucius Favronius would be the legate assigned the task of raising and training the new legion. Durus would be expected to command the city legion upon its arrival because his family, the Martellans, were not one of the Thirteen Houses Martial that had led the rebellion against Amorr's last king, and they did not possess either the required wealth or imperium to raise their own armies.

What he had not informed Torquatus in the letter, but what he needed to decide right now, was who would command the Valerian legion he had been ordered to take to Cynothicus. If things stood differently, he would certainly have done as Magnus anticipated, assigned Marcus Saturnius to replace him as stragister militum, and brought one of the other two legions back with him.

But with Fortex dead, there were other factors he now needed to take into account. There was no way he dared to face Magnus without having Saturnius present; the legate had been the one to give the order that his nephew had so fatally ignored, and fully concurred with the deadly sentence of *carnifico*.

But if he brought Saturnius with him to Cynothicus, that meant that he would have to bring Legio XVII along as well unless he ordered two of the legions to exchange legates. And that, he knew, would never do. The greater part of the men's confidence stemmed from their unique relationship with their commander and their subsequent trust in his decisions. Transfers tended to signify a serious loss of confidence, in either the officer leaving the unit or in the new man joining it. Morale would deteriorate over the winter, and in two legions facing battle in the spring, that was the last thing Corvus was willing to risk.

Then a thought occurred to him: With their most aggressive tribes defeated, the goblins were unlikely to engage in further incursions for months, perhaps even years. There was little benefit to leaving two legions here when they could winter more comfortably in Vallyrium, recruit and restock, and prepare more fully for the spring campaign in Cynothicus. The Senate would not be inclined to question his judgment, not when word of it arrived in company with the news of the submission of the goblin chieftains.

Even so, he had to decide between the two other legates. He made up his mind, reached out for the letter to Torquatus, and added one more sentence to it, being careful not to smear the drying ink.

I have appointed T. Didius Scato, the present legate of Legio VII, to replace me as Stragister Militum in Gorignia, to be confirmed in this command by the Senate.

So, it was done. Marcus Saturnius and Legio XVII would march to Cynothicus to keep the rebels pinned there over the winter, while the Legio Civitas would follow him to Amorr, then return for the spring campaign. Scato and L. Gerontius would bring the VII and XV Legions to winter quarters in Vallyrium, then join the campaign in Cynothicus as well.

The downside was that the XVII was the newest and least experienced of the three House legions, but balancing that was the fact that Saturnius was his best general. Also, despite its inexperience, the legion had performed admirably well against the goblin tribes, not only in yesterday's battle but in the numerous skirmishes that had preceded it. The deciding factor, in his mind, was that Legio XVII had twice the cavalry of the other two Valerian legions, as he had correctly anticipated its need to chase off band after band of wolfriders when he'd raised the legion last spring. The three hundred extra knights of the legion's second cavalry wing would likely prove equally useful in harrying the Cynothii's highly mobile mounted infantry.

The only problem was that one of those knights would be his son.... He shook his head. It was the right decision. He couldn't think like a father, he had to think like a general—no, like a consul!

How to explain any of this to Magnus? It would have been much easier if there was any way he could hope to do it in a letter, but now that he was ordered back to Amorr, he had no choice but to deliver the dreadful news himself. You did what you had to do, he told himself for what must have been the twentieth time. But what if Magnus somehow got word of his son's death before Corvus reached Amorr? He wrestled with his options, until finally, he settled upon a compromise. He pulled out a new sheet of vellum.

To M. Valerius Magnus, Senator (at Amorr)

I have received your letter from your slave, Clodipor, and I assure you that I shall make all haste to return to Amorr and be at your side. What an honor to our House that we two should both serve the Republic as consuls! How proud our father would have been to know of this! I am well-pleased to hear of the respect the Senate has shown for you, as well, for surely Amorr shall never fall so long as Magnus guards its walls. I have decided that I shall require M. Saturnius to spearhead the campaign against the Cynothii, and we shall ride to Amorr in all haste, departing tomorrow at first light.

Sadly, my dear brother, it falls to me to inform you that your son, G. Valerius Fortex, tribune of Legio XVII, is no longer with us. He is now at peace in the mighty bosom of the Inviolate. He died following yesterday's battle with the Chalonu, Insobru, and Vakhuyu tribes, in which he acquitted himself with extraordinary bravery, having slain one of the enemy's cavalry commanders on the battlefield. He died well, without fear, and fully confessed in the holy name of the Most Immaculate. It grieves me to be the bearer of such evil tidings to you and Julia, but if I may offer a small consolation, I have arranged for his bones to be returned to you so they may be laid in the family crypt with all the ceremony that befits a true son of Amorr and House Valerius.

Be strong, brother, and do not let this misfortune weigh too heavily upon your great spirit. Fortex, for he was well-named, is not the first Valerian to die for our beloved city nor will he be the last. Our House is Amorr!

I will see you soon. Look to my arrival three days after this letter.

Sex. Valerius Corvus at Gorignia (October)

Corvus leaned back in his chair, flexed his half-cramped hand, and sighed. The letter might be more delicately worded, but that did not matter. There were no words that could alter the dreadful truth of the content it contained, although at least it spared his brother the knowledge of the exact nature of his son's death until Corvus could explain the situation to him.

That left one more letter to write, and for the first time that day, Corvus felt himself smile. It seemed there was no disaster so evil, no burden so heavy, that it did not come with something to lighten the heart. He reached into the coin purse that was slung at his waist and withdrew the largest object in it. He stared at it for a moment, running his thumb over the embossed lines that he knew by heart as much as by sight or feel.

It was a medallion, one that he had ordered carved and stamped before his first campaign as the legate of Legio IV. He and Romilia had been married for only three years at the time; she was newly pregnant with Corvinus and still at the height of her famous beauty. He raised the medal to his lips and kissed her brow, her cheek, and finally, the tip of her aristocratic nose. Even in profile, there was no mistaking her for anything but a daughter, wife, and mother of patricians. The pearl of House Romilius, one poet had named her. Thank God she will be there, he thought as he traced the lines of her face, bright and blurred with years of wear, for I cannot hope to endure the wrathful grief of Magnus without her. And how proud of his consulship she would be! He smiled and withdrew a third sheet of vellum.

To Romilia at Amorr

Best of women, best of wives, to you I write news that I hope will salve and gladden your heart. First, be informed that our son, the tribune, has distinguished himself in his first battle with both his courage and his good sense. Never have I been more proud, or more terrified, than when I watched him lead half our cavalry in a headlong charge against the foe. It was all I could do to resist the paternal desire to send our reserves after him and ride to his side myself. But his judgment was sound, the enemy fled before his knights, and our victory was complete.

I will now confess you were correct, and my fears that his ecclesiastical training had rendered him too soft or effete were misplaced. He will never be the soldier's soldier that Servius is, but he may well make a superlative general one day. That being said, the name that I mentioned in one of my previous letters, Clericus, appears to have stuck with him. But he wears it well, as the men say it with affection and not mockery.

Well, my other happy news is that I am coming to you, and indeed, I expect to be with you within one week of your receiving this. I am sure you already know the Senate has done me the profound honor of naming me Consul in consequence of Caudinus's fall. I am ordered to come and receive my commission from that august body at once. Marcus will not ride with me, but he too should be able to visit you over the course of the winter. I am told you have a certain

influence with his commanding officer. Perhaps, if you are sufficiently
persuasive, you will be able to convince that mighty eminence to grant
your son leave. In the meantime, as you await me, I should like you
to look for a larger domus that we can purchase upon my return.

I must also tell you some less happy news. Our nephew, Gaius Valerius
Fortex, did not survive the day of battle, and I fear my brother will
be most displeased when he sees me next. I have already written to
Magnus, so you need not serve as the messenger of evil tidings. Only
pray for my nephew's soul and offer all due condolence to Magnus and
Julia. I shall tell you more upon my arrival.

Be well, my heart, for I am coming to you with all the speed an
earthbound crow can muster.

Sex. Valerius Corvus, Consul Suffectus Aquilae at Gorignia

He quickly scribbled a fourth note to Didius Scato, informing the
legate of his immediate promotion to stragister militum and ordering him
to see to the withdrawal to Vallyrium of both his legion and Legio XV. The
other three letters had dried sufficiently by the time he completed the last
one, so one by one he rolled them up, carefully dripped a measure of red
wax upon each one, and pressed his seal down upon the wax before it
hardened.

"Guard!" he called. One quickly entered, shorter and darker-skinned
than the last. "Go find the rider who left with Sebelon a little while ago.
He's probably in the Forum eating. If he's not there, try the stables. Bring
these three letters to him, and tell the stablemaster to give him his choice
of horse from the cursors. He can finish his meal, but he should leave as
soon as he's done. See him off, don't let him speak with anyone, and don't
answer any of his questions. Then find Saturnius and tell him to get his
hairy arse over here at once."

The guard took the letters but stopped before saluting. "Does the
rider have a name, General?"

"Ah, yes, of course. He's called Clodipor, one of my brother's slaves. He'll be with Sebelon. Find one, and you'll find the other."

"Yes, General. And that fourth letter?"

"Is still drying. I will send it by another messenger."

The guard saluted and departed.

Corvus sighed and slumped back in his high-backed chair. By the time the guard came back with Marcus Saturnius, the letter to Titus Didius would be dry, and he'd have one of the legion's cursors bring it to his camp. But there was so much to do, so many decisions to make if he was to depart with the sun's rising.

He pressed his hand to his eyes and rubbed at them. He was exhausted, not in his body, but in his spirit. The burden of command, some called it, and he could feel it pressing on him as if it was an actual weight. And the worst of it was that there was no one with whom he could share it.

He picked up Magnus's letter again. "*The new Consul Suffectus Aquilae is one Sextus Valerius Corvus,*" he read aloud. He laughed in disbelief. Corvus, Consul? Who would have thought it? Were men mad, that they *sought* these public honors and offices even as the ones they already held weighed them down? Was it pride or vanity that drove them? He did not exclude himself: If he had never thought to put his own name forward, it was only because he knew he had few clients and no following of any substance.

That no longer mattered. The Senate had spoken its will, for good or ill. He slipped his wife's medal back into his coin purse and rose to his feet. He was the Consul of the Legions, and all the armed might of Amorr had been entrusted to his mortal hands. There was ever so much to do, and yet there was only one proper way to begin.

He bowed his head, closed his eyes, and held up his open palms toward the heavens. "Almighty Father, I beg You to forgive me for what I have done in the name of justice and honor. Lord, grant my nephew eternal solace in Your arms. Protect my son in my absence, my Lord. Be there to guard him and guide him when I am not. And, King of Kings, Lord of Lords, I beg You to grant me courage and grant me strength, but most of all, God, grant me wisdom! You have broken the gates of Hell and shattered the chains of Death, so in the name of Your Immaculate Son I ask You, do not let me fail Your people!"

LETTER

To Lady Caitlys Shadowsong (at Elebrion)

From Marcus Valerius at Berdicum (Aprilis)

Greetings to my Lady Shadowsong. I have received two of your letters from the hand of Philotimus, which filled me with delight. As to your anxiety for my personal safety, I am grateful for the concern you have expressed, and I must hasten to assure you that you need have no fears for me. We have recently engaged in battle an enemy that consisted of three, or possibly four, goblin tribes, and our single legion put them to flight with little difficulty. I imagine it will amuse you, who have surely seen many battles over the years, but I am pleased to have survived my first without disgracing myself. I must not mislead you, we of the cavalry merely stood and watched the enemy for most of the day while they occupied themselves with our infantry. When finally we rode at them, they fled before us with the greatest alacrity.

You ask me what I have done about the books I had begun to write prior to the present campaign. Even here in the wilds, I have not been idle and am not being idle now, but I have frequently changed the whole plan and arrangement of the work. I fear it is rather like a mirage in the desert, which I am told recedes in the distance even as one rides toward it. The more I learn of the long history of your ancient race, the more I find myself cognizant of the errors and misapprehensions I have already committed to parchment. Perhaps I should acquire a palimpsest, upon which I may write and rewrite a single page, over and over again, like Sisyphus laboriously rolling his rock up that accursed hill!

But no, I jest. I will send you the first book as it presently stands, for I fancy it will convince you that I have not abandoned my task. How I shed tears upon reading of the fall of Lannonia! I trust I do not misconceive your intention in sending that account to me; I take your warning, and I shall not overstep the proper limits by which our relations must naturally be bound, according to the wisdom of the Immaculate.

I am extremely gratified by the affection of that great soul who still insists upon remaining nameless and am much indebted to you for my knowledge of it. The wisdom which he holds out to me though your letters is something I treasure more than any honours or glory, and I look forward to the continuation of his guidance. Indeed, I am much in need of it. I ask that you would consult with him, for I find myself troubled by my present duties as a soldier in the service of the Senate and People of Amorr.

You will recall that, when I rode to Elebrion the first time we met, there was still some question with regards to the controversial notion that your people possessed souls that were naturally united to them. Thankfully, His Sanctified Holiness was moved to decide that the immortal nature of the Aelvi was, in fact, an aspect of the Creator's original design—don't laugh, my dear pagan, for I can hear your amusement even as I write these letters—and now there is nary a man in the legion who would admit to ever having believed otherwise.

And yet, could a similar argument not be put forth on behalf of those we fought so recently? True, there is a vast gulf between the crude barbarism of the Goblin tribes and the noble civilization of your ancient race. But now that I have seen with my own eyes that a Goblin may exhibit courage or cowardice in much the same manner as a Man or Elf, I find myself wondering if there is not the possibility that Goblins too possess their share, however small, of the Immortal Fire.

Then again, when I consider some of their more abhorrent culinary customs (I suspect you know whereof I write), to say nothing of their filthy marital practices, I am tempted to conclude that it would be much better if this were not the case, for if so, it would appear they have all damned and twice-damned themselves.

As to your coming to me, as you say you will if I wish it, I should ask you to remain where you are. While we have at present returned to Berdicum, I do not yet know if we shall again be ordered to march into Solum Goblinensis, in which case the camp followers will not be permitted to accompany us, if we shall establish new permanent camps, in which case they will, or if we shall return to Amorr. I shouldn't think there is much likelihood of the latter, but I have heard rumours that prevent me from dismissing the possibility entirely. Stay, I beg you, at least until I can tell you where I am likely to be. I know you can travel much faster on the mighty wings of Vengirasse than the legion can march, but I am uneasy about exposing you to the eyes of our sentries without warning.

And, as I have previously written, you must promise not to make any use, any use at all, of your sorcery before I can permit you to visit me. Until I have your most solemn and binding word on the matter, I shall have to go to you when my duties allow, if we are to see each other once more.

Take care of your health, and assure yourself that nothing is or has ever been dearer to me than you are. Good-bye, my dear Lady Shadowsong, whom I seem to see before my eyes, and so find myself ensorcelled once more.

Good-bye!

Marcus Valerius

MARCUS

THE march from goblin territory, which had taken Legio XVII weeks and across three provinces, had been cold and tedious. Nevertheless, the campaign against the rebel Cynothii was already considerably more enjoyable than the one now concluded, Marcus decided as he sat at Saturnius's desk in the legate's office and reviewed the duty assignments for the third cohort.

For one thing, now that they were lodged in a proper castra, the legion didn't need to dig the trenches, cut down the trees, and build the legionary fort every single evening. Although after spending more than a month in the goblin lands, Legio XVII could practically do the routine in their sleep, with each legionary having become expert at the specific task to which he was assigned, it was still an arduous process. Marcus was far from the only man relieved they would not need to do it again for the duration of the winter.

The return to the more or less civilized lands of the provinces meant they had been able to simply march from one legionary fort to the next. Sometimes there were even baths, and the severe discipline that claimed his cousin's life had been relaxed.

Instead of riding ahead of the column scouting and seeking out ambushes, Marcus found that his primary responsibility involved dragging his riders out of an outlandish collection of whorehouses, pubs, and drinking establishments before they managed to kill anyone or get killed themselves. One knight from the sixth cohort had been stabbed to death in a fight over a pockmarked woman whom Marcus privately thought looked less appealing than the average goblin. And three legionaries from the eighth cohort had been arrested after beating two villagers to death in a drunken brawl.

They would have been hanged before nightfall had he and Julianus not rounded up twenty knights and descended upon the local magistrate to lay claim to them this morning. The thought of having freed three obviously guilty men from justice bothered him, even after the decurion and a centurion from the eighth had beaten all three to within an inch of their lives. But the rescue had been popular with the infantry, and even the more hard-bitten centurions were inclined to show Marcus a modicum of respect now.

It was strange, because while they clearly approved his laxness, they also seemed to consider his father's decision to execute his cousin to be the epitome of admirable leadership. Before, they had spoken of the General in terms of affection, but now it was with a sense of awe. They were also fiercely proud of Corvus's appointment as consul. They saw his elevation to the consulship as reflecting on them well as a legion.

And, he supposed, it rather did. What only that spring had been an unruly collection of six thousand raw recruits wearing bright red wool and black iron had been gradually transformed into something that grumbled, creaked, swore, drank, and in all other ways much more closely approximated the disciplined killing machine that was known as an Amorran legion.

The legion had transformed him as well, Marcus imagined. Whereas it had once been almost impossible to imagine driving his sword into the flesh of another living being, by the time of the battle with the goblin tribes, his training had made the action automatic. And whereas he had initially been reluctant to kill anything, it had been easy to overcome that reluctance once it became clear that the enemy was trying very hard to kill him.

Indeed, the incident with the magistrate had made him realize that he had been only one sudden hand movement away from ordering his men to slaughter five men whose only crime had been to arrest two murderers and attempt to bring them to justice.

Though the men and the other tribunes still called him Clericus, he now found it hard to believe that he had ever thought he might be fit for the Church. He was no longer a scholar, and still less was he a man of God. He had become a man of blood like his father and his father's father. He tried to keep up with his writing in the evenings, but often it was easier to join Lucius Volusenus, Gaius Trebonius and the other tribunes not on duty, to share the day's wine ration with them and spend the evening telling stories, jokes, and lies.

One night, too well fortified with wine, he'd even accompanied Aemelius Petrus to a whorehouse in Caprotae. But thoughts of what Caitlys might think of that had ultimately deterred him in a way that thoughts of soiling his body and soul did not. He spent an indecisive, tortured hour drinking with the madame and two of her least attractive girls, then had had to listen to Aemelius for most of the ride back to the legionary fort rhapsodizing about size of his whore's large white breasts and how they'd spilled over his hands.

How big were Caitlys's breasts? He couldn't recall. He suddenly wasn't sure that he had ever even noticed if she had them or not. Of course she did—she must! Elfesses did have breasts, didn't they? But when he thought of her, all he saw was her perfectly sculpted face, her inhumanly high cheekbones, and the bright intensity of her emerald eyes.

It was madness, he knew, to be so utterly obsessed with the thought of an elf maiden. And not merely a maiden but an outright sorceress, one whom the Michaelines would kill and the Church would burn on sight. And yet, there seemed to be nothing he could do about it.

There was no shortage of women in the sizeable army of camp follow-ers that straggled along behind the legion as it marched, and there were girls pretty enough to draw appreciative remarks from the legionaries in almost every village, town, or city they rode through on their way toward Cynothicus. But none of them, no matter how attractive, could possibly compete with Caitlys Shadowsong. In comparison to the elven princess, they were a herd of indistinguishable, thick-waisted, stump-legged cows.

He heard a noise outside the door, and a moment later, Gaius Trebonius entered.

"The legate has finally deigned to rejoin us," he announced a little breathlessly. "And with him arrived some news that I expect will be of no little interest to you, Clericus."

"Out with it, if you already know it."

"Your father didn't arrive with the legate because he isn't coming this fall. He's going to stay in Amorr to contest the election."

"He's declared for consul, then?" Marcus wasn't entirely surprised. He was also a little relieved that he wouldn't have to face his father anytime soon, since he still wasn't sure how he felt about Fortex's execution. What had seemed so horrific and excessive at the time seemed a little more reasonable now that he had a better understanding of how difficult it was to keep the men in any reasonable semblance of order even when they were only marching from one point to another. He was beginning to understand the importance of discipline to the legion, but the execution still struck him as an unnecessary evil. "Who opposes him?"

"They say one of the Falconians was already running, but I don't remember which one. And one of the more vocal auctores has declared as well. He wouldn't matter, except that it's said Severus Patronus is backing him."

"He would."

"Well, you can't expect him to take the thought of another Valerian consul lightly."

Marcus shrugged. "The Senate wouldn't have appointed Corvus as Consul Suffectus if they didn't intend for him to lead the fight against the Cynothii. That doesn't mean the People will follow their lead when it's time for the vote, but I can't imagine they'll turn down a Valerian with a province on the boil."

"Especially not when the alternative is a filthy Severan puppet." Trebonius smiled. "I suppose you know he declared for the Eagles."

"What else?" Marcus stood. "I'm filthy from the ride this morning, and you look as if you haven't bathed for weeks. What do you say we visit the baths and get cleaned up while you tell me about anything interesting that doesn't involve my family in any way."

It took them an hour to get permission to leave the fort, obtain a new horse for Trebonius, and canter the four leagues to Gallidromum, which was a moderately sized town of around fifteen thousand inhabitants about a two day's march from the provincial border with Cynothicus. Fortunately for them, whatever sympathies the townspeople might have had for the nearby rebellion had completely vanished with the arrival of the legion last week, and both the officers and men of the legion had been given the run of the town when off duty.

As they rode, Trebonius brought Marcus up to date on the latest events in Amorr, which included news that the college of electors was still locked in an electoral standoff between the two rival cardinals vying for the sacred chair. In the arena, the Reds had claimed an unexpected victory in the last great gladiatorial event of the season. And it seemed that one of Gaius Maecenas's freemen, a Larini named Guiberto, had scored a triumph in the theatre with a popular comedy that poked fun at three haplessly rural Utruccans, a Caeligni, a Silarian, and a Vallyrian, each of whom happened to arrive in Amorr on the same day.

The baths were larger and of better quality than Marcus would have dared to expect so far from Amorr. The pillars were made of granite rather than marble, and the tilework was crude and childlike in comparison with the art that decorated the Amorran baths. But, having been constructed over three natural hot thermal springs, they were a draw for invalids and tourists alike. They weren't what one would call crowded by Amorran standards, but they were considerably more popular than any of the baths he had seen in the provinces before.

They tied up their horses, which as branded legionary mounts were about as likely to be stolen as the legionary fort itself, and entered the complex. Entrance cost one denarius apiece, which struck Marcus as exorbitant, so he paid the balneator for Trebonius as well.

"You don't need to do that," Trebonius protested, fumbling at his near-empty purse.

"I invited you. And besides, you know perfectly well that you're practically a pauper. You can pay for our clothes if you want."

"Practically?" Trebonius's laugh was hollow. "One centurion's medal has more silver in it than I have in the aquilifer's chest. I wouldn't be surprised if Castorius has more money than half the patricians in the Senate!"

In the apodyterium, they stripped off their armor and weaponry, as well as their underlying tunics and small clothes.

Trebonius gave the bearded capsarius two quadrans to watch their possessions, and two more to polish their mud-spattered armor. "If you steal anything, we'll have your head," Trebonius warned him.

The slave only grinned and shook his head. Bath slaves were notorious for absconding with the personal items they were supposed to watch, but few were stupid enough to vanish with a legionary's possessions. The clothing was too easily identified, and it was not the sort of crime that, if caught, a man could commit twice.

Being already chilled from their ride and the cool wintry air, they didn't linger in the frigidarium, but merely jumped in the water and clambered quickly out, prompting complaints from a group of men they'd inadvertently splashed.

Next they moved to the tepidarium, which was large, but the mosaics on the floor were crude, and Marcus found the yellow walls to be overly bright. It did not appear that the good citizens of Gallidromum went in much for contemplation. It was not the sort of place that invited it, and they were the only ones there besides the slaves armed with pots of oil. They sat on the wooden benches, amusing each other by pointing out the incompetence of the art. As they were being oiled by the unctores, Trebonius drew his attention to one particularly comical section of the mosaics, wherein what was apparently supposed to be a fearsome minotaur more closely resembled an emaciated dog with horns.

The oiling didn't take long, and soon they entered the caldarium, which Marcus was pleased to see was not overly crowded. The air was heavy with steam and the scent of minerals. The thermal springs produced water that was every bit as hot as the furnaces of the great Amorran baths. Perhaps even a bit hotter, Marcus thought happily as he closed his eyes and enjoyed the sensation of the warmth penetrating all the way through to his very bones.

There was no sound except for a few murmured voices, some soft splashes, and the occasional hiss as a slave poured cold water from the labrum over someone's head. No more cold. No more riding. No more mud. No more shouting and being shouted at. It was more than peaceful—it was glorious.

"You lads are legion, aren't you?"

Someone speaking Utruccan with the atrocious northern accent heard in these parts intruded upon his blissful reverie. Marcus refused to open his eyes. Perhaps the wretch would take the hint and go away.

"Hey, I knows an Amorran when I sees one. You can't mistake those noses, that's what I says. Even without your armor and all, I knows you."

No, he would not. Oh, by the Undefiled Mother. Marcus wished he had his sword with him. Or better yet, a centurion armed with a vine staff and a bad mood.

Grudgingly, he opened his eyes.

He saw about what he expected in the only now mentioned dim light of the caldarium. The voice belonged to a middle-aged provincial man, balding, no doubt possessed of an expanding paunch below the waterline, and betraying the all-too-familiar avaricious gleam of the trader in his eye. Marcus sighed. While the rest of Selenoth rightly dreaded the Amorran legions and the death and devastation that so often followed in their wake, merchants everywhere seemed to view them as huge herds of milk cows, where the milk was all but free for the taking.

"With all due respect, sir, my colleague and I have no need for food, equipment, wine, jewelry, female companionship, or anything else you, or anyone you know, is likely to have for sale. We merely seek to worship in blessed silence at this holy altar of cleanliness. As you are no doubt a God-fearing man yourself, I bid you respect our devotions."

Trebonius snorted. Unfortunately, the provincial took neither offense nor the hint. Instead, he laughed, as if he and Marcus were old friends given to jesting with each other. Marcus, in response, wondered if Julianus would come to his rescue if he gave in to his impulse to strangle the annoying old man.

"Aye, I'm a merchant, laddie, but I won't tries to sell you nothing. I gots nothing to sell! I solds it all to a bunch of your lot not two weeks ago in Saenott."

Saenott? Where was Saenott? It couldn't be too terribly far from here if the merchant had been there only two weeks before. But what legionaries could he have sold anything to, if the nearest legion was in Clusium? He sat up and turned to face the merchant.

"Do you mean Cynothicus?"

"Aye, that's what you lot calls the province. Allus gots to be sticking an extra syllable or two on there, you Amorrans."

"I suppose we do. So, you were selling to Amorrans in Cynothicus? Were they traders, these Amorrans?"

The man laughed again. "Traders? No, when I said you lot, I meant soldiers. You know, legion boys like you two lads."

"Of course, of course," Marcus nodded affably, mainly to keep the man from noticing his suddenly intense interest. "What were you selling?"

"Had two carts of good Cortonan wine. They took it all, they did. Got me a good price for it too! The victucustos said they was short on meat, so now I'm looking for a likely herd of cows or pigs. I figures there must be some farmers about that wouldn't mind saving on the winter feed if they haven't butchered yet."

"That sounds like a good plan," Marcus said approvingly. "The victu-custos... what legion was he with?"

The merchant shrugged. "I don't know. A legion is a legion, right?"

"More or less," Marcus agreed, disappointed. "But they were in Cynothicus proper?"

"Hey, now I remembers something." A triumphant smile lit up the balding man's face. "They had these lightning things all over the place. A symbol, like. Do you know what I mean?"

Marcus looked at Trebonius and could see from the expression on his face that he had been listening too. Trebonius nodded slowly. Yes, they knew exactly what he meant. But what they did not know was why Legio III, also known as *Fulgetra*, would be in Cynothicus. And Marcus had the distinct impression that it might have something to do with the fact that Legio III was one of the two legions belonging to House Severus and controlled by one Aulus Severus Patronus, his uncle's chief rival in the Senate and the head of the auctores faction.

"Back to the fort?" Trebonius asked. He too was suspicious.

Marcus nodded. Then he turned back to the merchant. "What is your name, man?"

"Why, Clautus of Medonis," he answered, surprised.

"Well, Clautus of Medonis," Marcus told him as he reluctantly pushed himself out of the steaming water, "if ever you bring your wares to any of the Valerian legions, I guarantee you will get a very good price for them."

FJOTRA

FJOTRA was not the first to reach Brynjolf's side. The mage was already there, kneeling beside him, as was a big man with a thick, black mustache and a commanding presence. Without thinking, she tried to push past him, which occasioned a collective gasp of dismay from the people around her.

"Fjotra!" barked the comtesse from behind her in a manner that made it perfectly clear that she had made a dreadful mistake.

But Fjotra didn't care, she was too worried about her brother. He was conscious and groaning, and Theuderic was having some trouble preventing him from pushing himself up to a sitting position.

"Lie back, you bloody fool—you might have broke something!" the large man told him. "Now hold still so we can get a closer look at that dagger wound. You're lucky you didn't land on your head, the way you fell!"

Despite his large hands and bluff manner, the man was surprisingly gentle as he cut away the finery that surrounded the assassin's blade and examined the wound. Even so, Brynjolf winced as the man produced a red silk cloth out of his clothing and pressed the cloth tightly against the wound.

"Bleed on this all you like, boy," the man said lightly and his remark was greeted by rather more amusement than Fjotra would have thought possible. He handed the dagger to the mage. "What do you say, Theuderic?"

"I'd say he's lucky the bastard missed the heart and lungs." The mage sat back on his heels and examined the knife. "No poison either. But I'll bet there is on the bolts they were carrying. They were planning to shoot you, not stab you."

"Will he live?" Fjotra interjected. "Please, sieur, will he die?"

"Not from this. I've had worse myself." The big man glanced up at her, initially disinterested, then did a double-take. "Who the hell are you?"

"It's the boy's sister," the mage answered before Fjotra could say anything. "They're reaver royalty, of a sort. Your comtesse's new pets."

"Damned useful pets," the man said, staring at her. His dark eyes seemed to devour her. "I can see why she was keeping them to herself."

"If I'd known Brynjolf would save your life, I might have contemplated leaving him at home, your royal highness," the comtesse said in tones so icy that Fjotra looked at her in alarm. But it was hard to tell if Roheis's green eyes were more amused or satisfied, so Fjotra concluded she didn't actually mean what she seemed to be implying. "Prince Brynjolf, Princess Fjotra, allow me to introduce to you his Royal Highness Charles-Phillippe, the Red Prince, Duc de Lutèce, the recent victor of the Siege of Montrove, and the likely target of the two assassins you just threw off the walls, Brynjolf."

Fjotra gasped. She'd knocked the prince aside? She stood and tried to curtsy as she'd been trained.

Brynjolf laughed then grimaced and gestured with his right hand. "Please no offense if I not bow, Royal Highness?"

"I suspect my dignity will survive the insult, Prince Brynjolf. May I say it is indeed a pleasure to meet you both, particularly in light of the circumstances. Speaking of which…" He rose to his feet and bellowed to his guards. "Fouquat, tell me you got at least one of them alive!"

"We got both, Your Highness. One of them is busted up pretty bad, I don't think he'll make it. The other just has a broken leg."

The Red Prince nodded in satisfaction and looked down at Brynjolf. "Well done, reaver prince! It looks as if I'm in your debt." He ordered the assassins taken to the royal palace and Brynjolf taken into the Duc's residence, born on a litter carried by his own bodyguard.

As Fjotra and the others followed Brynjolf through the gawking crowds and into the high-arched entry to the ducal manoir, Roheis whispered into her ear.

"Your brother is in no shape for what we'd planned. You're going to have to do this yourself. Can you do it?"

Fjotra winced. She'd forgotten entirely about their planned performance that evening. The thought of doing it alone in front of all these southerners frightened her nearly as much as seeing her brother fall from the wall. But if her brother could risk his life for this audience, she could risk public humiliation.

She nodded as grimly as a warrior ready to enter his last battle.

"I can, my lady. I must."

They settled Brynjolf in a bedchamber that befitted his supposedly princely status, and his wounds were being attended by two priests. The priests themselves were assisted by three young nuns attractive enough to draw a wry comment from the Red Prince as they were ushered from the room.

The comtesse assured Fjotra that her brother was in the very best of hands. It seemed the priests were from a medicinal order that were well regarded throughout the kingdom. No sooner had they left Brynjolf's chamber than the prince took his leave of them, as his attendants were flocking around him, bearing urgent messages from one noble or another. But he was gracious enough to kiss Fjotra's hand, a gesture that made her feel very funny indeed. And not merely because the coarse hairs of his mustache tickled either.

"Very gallant, our prince," Theuderic said to the comtesse as he sipped from a glass from which a disconcerting blue smoke was emanating.

"Yes, it's remarkable how a fresh young face inspires him to new heights of courtesy," the comtesse answered.

Fjotra couldn't tell if the comtesse were irritated or not. If the prince were her lover, she certainly would have been furious that he had made advances with Fjotra. But things were so different here in the south that she had no idea what to think. The prince wasn't exactly what she would call handsome, as his face was red and fleshy, his hair was thick and black, and his teeth were big and yellow. And yet, he was not an easy man to ignore. Or forget.

"Shall I lean on him for a royal audience tonight?"

"You still want to do that?" Theuderic glanced at Fjotra. "Is she up to it without the brother?"

"They're not jongleurs, Theuderic. Yes, it would have been better with them both. But look at her: She'll suffice to hold the king's attention."

The mage laughed. "She held the prince's, anyhow."

Fjotra tried not to laugh, herself, as the comtesse's artfully placed elbow nearly made the mage spill his glass.

It didn't take Theuderic long to come to a decision. "Very well. It will have to be soon after the dancing begins. Neither the king nor queen will stay long past the first five dances. She is leaving for Châlaons to take the waters tomorrow. But not too soon, or you will play to an angry audience. So, let us enter now and pay our respects to the Duchesse, and then we shall see what we can do."

The sorcerer went off to speak with the ball's hostess, as the large hall resounded with the sounds of the string quartet. The comtesse was speaking with the elfess, too rapidly for her to easily follow, so Fjotra watched as people danced. Although only a few couples were on the floor yet, their effortless motions made her entirely certain that she would not dance this evening. The comtesse had been kind enough to see that she'd been given lessons in the most popular dances, but Fjotra knew that she was just familiar enough with them to ensure that she would look clumsy rather than ignorant.

The music changed twice, as did the dances, before Fjotra spotted the tall sorcerer making his way back toward them. It was clear from the resigned expression on his bearded face that the Duchesse de Méridiony had given her consent to an additional musical performance.

The comtesse smiled up at Theuderic as he rejoined them and offered him a goblet of sparkling wine. "Thank you, my dear magus. How did you persuade the lady?"

Theuderic laughed and arched an eyebrow at his elven mistress. "I lied. I told her that you, my lady, wished to sing a song of ancient Merithaim. Naturally, she couldn't resist, since not even His Majesty has ever been able to boast of an elven bard in Lutèce."

A slow, amused smile gradually spread across the elf lady's face. "You are incorrigible, my lord. But I suppose it is better that you amuse yourself with lies than with murders."

"The night is yet young." He raised his glass to his lover. "I wouldn't count out the possibility, seeing as we've already had one assassination attempt—and considering the looks that some of the Duchesse's guests are directing at Roheis's young reaver friend here." He directed their attention to one large, broad-shouldered man who looked distinctly out of place in the effeminate clothing that most of the Savonner men were wearing, whose hate-filled stare was making Fjotra feel increasingly uncomfortable.

Theuderic looked at Fjotra. "I do hope neither you nor your brother have ever been reaving along the coast. Because if you have, I fear you may find the program for the evening's entertainment has been changed again. I'm told it is very difficult to sing when your tongue has been ripped from your mouth with steel and fire."

"Never, Sieur Theuderic," Fjotra assured him. "They choose Brynjolf and me to come here because we are children of Skuli, but also because we never reave. I have killed no one, and my brother is a sea virgin." She bit her lip, instantly regretting the disclosure of her brother's secret. "Please, don't say him I tell you this."

The comtesse smiled wryly. "If I understand things correctly, by Dalarn standards, that means Brynjolf is essentially considered a mincing, limp-wristed fop until he proves otherwise by raping and pillaging his way across our northern coast. Which I find a little ironic given that it has been all my servants could do to keep the boy from gutting Henriot every time Henriot tells him he's placed a foot wrong while waltzing."

"And here I was so looking forward to serving as a Dalarn dance instructor," Theuderic said, nodding to Fjotra. "Never fear, little reaver. We shall not disclose his shame."

She flushed at the intensity of his gaze and looked away. Was he not with the beautiful elfess? Why would he stare at her in such a way?

"I say, Roheis," Theuderic said to the comtesse, "the prince appears to be coming this way."

They all began to rise, but the heir to the throne raised his hand and stopped them. "Stay, sit, please. I am determined that we shall start this evening afresh. How beautiful you look tonight, sweet Roheis. My lady comtesse, will you not honor your future sovereign with a dance?"

"Your Royal Highness, I should be most honored," Roheis breathed.

Fjotra couldn't help but notice that, as the prince assisted the comtesse stand up from her chair, his hand slid across her silk-covered bottom and gave it a firm squeeze. So was the comtesse truly his mistress, after all? It seemed likely. Lady Roheis tended to rise closer to noon than daybreak, and Fjotra had seldom seen her around the manoir after dark.

She and Brynjolf had argued over the lovely widow's chastity on several occasions. Her brother, being more than half in love with her, insisted that she was as chaste as she was kind. Fjotra found the comtesse to be charming and generous, but she found it implausible that any woman as effortlessly seductive as Roheis could possibly be producing the effect she had on men without serious intent behind it.

Theuderic leaned toward Fjotra. "There, Princess Fjotra, is His Royal Majesty, the King of Savondir," murmured the sorcerer as he leaned toward her.

Fjotra nodded and resisted the urge to recoil from the man as she looked for the first time at the man who held the fate of her people in his hand.

She was not surprised to see that Louis-Charles de Mirid, the four-teenth of his Name, was a big man. She had already met his son. But she was surprised to see how fat he was. His grey-shot beard barely served to conceal the fat sprawl of his neck, and not even the silk elegantly draped over his swollen torso could disguise a massive expanse of belly. He was nearly three times the width of his slender queen.

After seeing the two of them side by side, Fjotra could understand why Queen Ingoberg was leaving the capital to take the restorative waters. She had no experience in such matters, not yet, but she imagined the king's lovemaking would bear a distinct similarity to being crushed in the arms of a bear. The sight inspired her to firmly resolve that, no matter what the future might bring, she would never marry a fat man.

But there was strength to the king too and a surprisingly athletic grace. He stepped out onto the floor alone then bowed to his queen, and she rose from her seat and came to him with a smile when he extended his hand. Perhaps, Fjotra considered, however implausible it might be, she actually loved her grotesque bear.

Both the king's movements and the long white scar above his left eye made it apparent that he had once been a warrior, like his son appeared to be. He led the queen well and smiled easily, which made the thought of speaking to him a little less frightening. She raised her glass to her lips, and realized to her dismay that it was already empty. She had been drinking faster than she'd realized.

Once the king and queen were on the floor, the nobles and courtiers in attendance hastened to join them. In a matter of moments, the tables were all but emptied of everyone under the age of forty, with only a few exceptions such as herself. The floor was transformed into a glorious mass of whirling colors, and a hundred rival perfumes battled it out for supremacy in the air. Fjotra found herself transfixed by the elegance of the movements and the graceful way the dancers moved around each other, as effortlessly as two blademasters crossing swords.

When the dance wound down, the king and queen returned to their seats at the front of the room, and the Red Prince returned the comtesse to the table where Fjotra was sitting. As he did so, he glanced at Fjotra and winked at her.

He knows, she realized with a jolt of excitement. He wants to help us!

Maybe none of the help she'd been providing was actually the comtesse's doing. Could it be the prince who was behind her generosity and support? But why? She didn't know much about Savonner royalty, but somehow, she found it hard to imagine that such a vain and self-centered people would be overly concerned about the fate of a centuries-old enemy, except to celebrate their demise. And yet, as the comtesse whispered some last-minute instructions into her ear, she was almost certain the prince was watching over them with an approving, even a possessive, air.

To her surprise, Theuderic rose and strode to the center of the floor, not far from the king's table. "Lords and ladies, your Royal Highness, and Your Royal Majesties, I am sure you all know our beloved Duchesse is a kind and generous hostess."

The sorcerer inclined his head in the direction of the duchesse. She was a woman of an age similar to the queen, but rather more stout and practically draped in gold and emeralds. She smiled patiently as her generosity was noisily saluted by the guests, particularly the men who had spent most of the first hour drinking rather than dancing.

"And she is also one of the greatest Savondese patrons of the musical arts, which is why it is my very great pleasure to present to you, on the Duchesse's behalf, a royal singer from the Iles de Loup, the Princess de Raknarborg and daughter of the Dalarn High King, Skuli Skullsmasher."

For a moment, Fjotra was almost glad Brynjolf wasn't at her side. He surely would have tried to correct the sorcerer. Then she saw the duchesse staring at her, her brow wrinkled with suspicion. For a moment Fjotra feared she was about to make a scene and protest that Fjotra was not the promised elven singer, but instead the noblewoman settled for directing a furious glare at Theuderic. The bearded magicien, unsurprisingly, appeared unperturbed.

Fjotra rose as gracefully as she could manage and did her best to pretend that the eyes of half the nobility of Savonne were not upon her. Whispers erupted, and there were even some who pointed at her, but no one dared to openly object. She walked toward the mage, as instructed, bowed to the duchesse, then turned to face the king and queen and bowed even deeper.

"I am Fjotra de Raknarborg, the Last Princess of the Iles de Loup," she said loudly and clearly. "Tonight, I sing for you of the death of the Fifteen Clans and the triumph of the wolves."

THEUDERIC

HE could tell that the prince was irritated, although he wasn't certain why. Charles-Phillippe, the Red Prince, future King of Savondir and Fifteenth of his Name, was a man of action, and as such, he was naturally impatient. As the heir to the throne, he faced few, very few, situations that demanded patience from him. But the Haut Conseil could do what even the fortified walls of Montrove could not, and force him to stew impotently outside closed doors.

If he dared, Theuderic would have smiled. The Red Prince paced angrily about the hall, scorning the chairs that had been provided for their comfort, glaring at the doors as if he were waiting for a battleram to arrive. Had his father ever been like this? It was hard to imagine. His Majesty was a strong man, and underneath all his fat there was no shortage of muscle, but whereas the Red Prince was all fire and vigor, his father was stone and stolid earth.

It had been hard enough for the prince to convince his father that a duc's rebellion called for a violent response, so they both knew there was little chance that he could persuade the king to embark upon a more ambitious venture. But the drama with the Dalarns at the ball would at least permit him to broach the subject with the king's councilors in the hopes that they would support his case when he brought it before his father.

"Blasted flock of withered old hens," the prince groused. "If that damned archbishop so much as rattles his neck wattles at me, I swear

I'll strangle him like the turkey he was born to be. Don't you think he looks like a turkey?"

Theuderic was not a religious man, nor did he shrink from many things up to and including murder, but openly comparing the Archvêque du Royaume to a barnyard fowl in the heart of the palace was taking things a bit far for his liking. "I do wish you would have spared that assassin. We can't be certain they were from Montrove."

"Of course we can. You know perfectly well they were. He confessed didn't he?"

"Under torture!" Theuderic shook his head. "A man will confess to raping the queen if he's being tortured. Hells bells, Charles, a man will confess to *being* the queen if he's pressed hard enough."

"Well, if they weren't Montrovian, they were bloody well hired by Montrovians. I've half a mind to go back there, dash the new duc's brains out, and install someone halfway reliable to oversee the duchy."

"You don't think Sieur Charibert is reliable?"

"Not reliable enough or there wouldn't be blasted nightstalkers sneaking about trying to kill me, would there? Anyhow, you'll be glad to know the Dalarn boy is going to live. Roheis finally managed to drag him out of the Duchesse's clutches. She said the lad was so well tended by his little nurses that she practically had to lay siege to his room before she could bring him back to her manoir."

"I find it hard to blame the lad."

"Aye. But he won't win back his islands from his bed."

"I thought you intended to do it for him."

"You heard his sister's song. Damn near brought a tear to my eye, it did. Of course, how do we know what is real and what is poet's license? We both know there is only one way to find out." The Red Prince laughed. "They're certainly optimistic about the idea we'll let bygones be bygones, aren't they? Either they're stupid or they're truly as desperate as they claim. But who are we to turn down supplicants in need? Don't you think the sister is a lovely young thing? Of course, she needs a bit of feeding and filling out to become interesting."

"No doubt the Lady Roheis can teach her some interestingly bad habits."

"A man can only dream."

The doors to the council chamber began to open. A small man in an expensive, silver threaded tunic poked his head out, rather like a mouse looking out of its hole to see if any cats are lurking about. It was the King's Chancelier, François du Moulin, who was arguably the least important member of the Haut Conseil, though far from its least intelligent. And, as Theuderic knew, easily its most ruthless.

The little man bowed.

"Your royal highness, the King's High Council is grateful for your attendance upon it today. And you as well, Sieur Theuderic."

Theuderic bowed even more deeply in order to greet the chancelier as befitted his high station—and the fact that he had seen the unassuming little man order the deaths of men with no more hesitation than an ordinary man brushed away a fly.

The Red Prince, on the other hand, practically ignored du Moulin as he pushed past him. "What have they been nattering on about for the last hour, François? Didn't you know I was waiting outside?"

"It would be more appropriate for the king to tell you himself," the chancelier replied, nonplussed.

"My father is here?" Theuderic was amused to hear what appeared to be a mild note of alarm in the Red Prince's voice.

"He is indeed!" His Royal Majesty's big bass voice echoed off the dark wood-paneled walls.

The Chambre de la Conseil was a much smaller and less imposing room than Theuderic had expected, but then, the king's councilors had been meeting here for more than 150 years, and the realm was significantly larger and more prosperous now than it was back then. The table was a sturdy oak specimen with ornately carved legs, but it was not overly formal, while the chairs were a mismatched collection betraying signs of hailing from at least three different ages of fashion. Seated in those chairs

were the four most influential men in the kingdom, as the king himself
had risen from his chair to greet his son.

Without the least care for his dignity before the others, he embraced
the prince with the fierce emotion of a mother bear.

"Charles, my dear Charles, I was beside myself when I heard it was
those cursed Montrovians behind the attack on you. I vow I was of a mind
to order Sieur Charibert to take off the head of the new one, before your
mother talked me out of it."

"I trust His Royal Majesty would have thought better of it in his own
time," said Pierre-Gaston Bonpensier. The querulous old Archvêque du
Royaume was stroking the long flaps of excess flesh that hung down from
his chin with one hand. "The duc is still at his mother's breast and a most
unlikely participant in the crime. One hardly wishes history to saddle one
with a reputation as a child-killer. To say nothing of one's duty as a true
and immaculate king who rules by God's grace."

"You can trust His Royal Majesty will personally strangle every child
in Montrove with his own hands if that is what is needed to teach those
rebels who is their rightful, God-given king," the king said, making fists
with both his hands. They were meaty enough to pass for an ogre's.
"Immaculéan forgiveness does not extend to lèse majesté, Bonpensier, so
you can reserve the homily for your next mass."

"I can't tell you how relieved I am that it proved unnecessary," the
prince said. "However, speaking of Montrove and its rebels, I should like
to know how it is that an assassination attempt on the heir to the throne
appears to be of less urgency than whatever this council has been contemplating since the fifth hour?" Charles-Phillippe attempted to present
the question in a light and carefree manner, but he was clearly irritated at
having been forced to wait outside.

"As difficult as it may be for you to imagine, I fear there are weightier
events afoot, your royal highness," said Theuderic's master. Jacque-Rene
D'Arseille was the grandmagicien of *l'Académie des Sage-Arts*. He was
perfectly bald, elegantly attired in a black robe with scarlet slashes, and
lethally intelligent. "Around the time you were occupied with obtain-

ing confessions from your would-be killers, a church rider arrived from Amorr. It appears the Sanctified Father passed to his well-merited eternal reward last month. The college of electors has been summoned to select his successor."

"Ah," the prince nodded, somewhat mollified. "What a pity we merit no princes of the church, despite the Sanctal-scot we have so faithfully contributed to its coffers. How much did we send last year?"

"Three hundred pounds of silver, your royal highness," answered the Chancelier promptly. He had returned to his seat between the Archvêque and de Beaumille, the Haut Connétable of the realm. "Three hundred and three, if indeed I recall correctly. We anticipate collecting a similar amount this year, perhaps as much as three hundred twelve."

"We could maintain two legions with that much money, two royal legions. I imagine that would be rather useful in discouraging the ambitions of certain overly ambitious nobles, Father."

"To be sure," concurred the grandmagicien. "And it is the conclusion of this council that the influence of the crown is not what it should be, given the impact of decisions taken in Amorr that not infrequently lead to undesirable consequences in this realm. Decisions in which we not only have no voice, but of which we are often completely unaware until events have overtaken us."

"I still cannot believe that oaf of a Sanctiff granted the ensoulment of the elves!" The Bishop de Châlaons was even fatter than the king but nearly a head shorter. He had a keen mind, though, and it was said that he was certain to succeed Bonpensier as the Archvêque du Royaume. "Thank God he is at rest, bless his sanctified soul, before he managed to do the same for the dwarves."

"Or, God forbid, the orcs," D'Arseille said wryly, prompting a loud burst of laughter from the king.

"Do you intend to withhold the scot then, Father?"

"Withhold the scot?" The king laughed again. "Don't be an ass, Charles. We seek closer relations with the Ivory Throne, not a break with it! You're a fine general, son, but you still think like a general, all tactics and strategies for right now, today. A king is not like other men. He must think about tomorrow, next week, next year, and beyond! What we are attempting to plant here is a seed that will not flower in my time, or even in your time, but perhaps in your grandson's time."

"We have in mind a small embassy to the Sanctal Palace. Small, but influential. Our objective will be to strengthen our position within the Church, which at present is nearly nonexistent." The bishop looked to the archevêque. "Sadly, at present, none of the current celestines in office have any ties to the crown. Since de Callix passed on to his reward five years ago, Savondir has not been able to boast a single prince of the church, whereas ten would barely suffice to properly reflect the king's influence throughout the civilized lands. But we have reason to believe that one of the king's subjects will soon be bestowed with the honor."

"Good Lord, they're not going to select you, Bonpensier, are they?" The Red Prince seemed to notice, belatedly, that he'd perhaps spoken in a way that was less than perfectly judicious. "That is to say, we should of course miss your valuable counsel!"

The archevêque smiled coldly. "No, your royal highness, they are not going to elevate me to the Sacred College."

"Pity, that. I understand the winters are rather more bearable down south."

"Indubitably."

"Anyhow, I'm sure a celestine or two would be an ornament to the realm and all, but I suppose three kings can achieve a great deal with the use of two legions over the course of three reigns." The Red Prince seemed to think he had made an effective point, and Theuderic rather considered that he had, but they were both rapidly disabused of the notion.

"That is because you only think of conquest! The battle and its aftermath. Ha!" The king pounded the table, and it shook under the impact. "Where would we be today if the second of our name thought as you do? Or the fifth? For every generation of conquest, there must be three, or four, or even five devoted to consolidation of the gains made!"

"Consolidation?" Theuderic almost laughed out loud at the expression of dismay and disbelief on the prince's ruddy face. His superior, D'Arseille, knew no such restraint, and his mirth earned an irritated glance from the king. "Where is the glory in that?"

"I realize this may come as a surprise to your royal highness, but it is the opinion of this council, and I daresay the entire realm, that there is a larger objective to your future reign than the mere maximization of your personal glory."

"Enough, D'Arseille!" snapped the Bishop de Châlaons. "Your Royal Highness, you need not fear your reign is likely to enjoy a period of the sort of peace and prosperity that your youth and energy appear to find so distasteful. Indeed, we already appear to be rapidly approaching a sword age of the sort that inevitably requires men of your talents and disposition. And, as such, it is the belief of this council that you will be admirably well suited for the times."

"Even so, a king must learn to distinguish the important from the merely urgent." The Maréchal de Savonne, Lord Antoine de Beaumille, spoke for the first time. He was a tall, distinguished man with thick white hair and an aristocratic face that was marred by a white scar that cut diagonally across the left side of his face. "Montrove, the Iles de Loup, the inevitable peasant uprising here and there, the next rebellious noble, these are all urgent matters one must face. But even as you address them, your royal highness, the good of the realm demands that you also consider the distant future. It will be upon you sooner than you imagine."

He directed a significant look toward the grandmagicien, who acknowledged the maréchal with an ironic smile. Looking around at the others, Theuderic suddenly realized that the entire Haut Conseil was well aware of l'Académie's grand project. Indeed, it was not impossible that they knew rather more about it than he did, despite his direct involvement in it.

"You mentioned the Iles de Loup," the prince told the maréchal. "It was concerning that very matter that I wished to speak to the council."

"Of course." De Beaumille's manner was so relaxed that it was easy for Theuderic to forget this was a man whom even the prince himself must salute and obey. "I have no doubt you wish to request the ships required to transport the royal army, flush with its victory over the late Duc de Montrove, across the White Sea."

If the prince was annoyed at being anticipated so easily, he showed no sign of it. "I do indeed, my lord maréchal."

"And how many ships do you think you require?"

"As many are needed to transport eight thousand men and their mounts."

"But you will not be transporting eight thousand men. I will give you two thousand and the ships to carry them. And that is all."

Instead of attempting to argue with de Beaumille, the prince turned to his father and raised his hands in protest. "What is the sense of only taking two thousand men to the Iles de Loup? That's not enough to conquer them! It's not enough to do much more than reinforce that fortress they call Ragnarborg, and for all we know it may not even be enough to guarantee holding it for more than a few months. I can't be expected to make any headway against an island full of ulfin with only two thousand men, even if they're all cavalry!"

"Nor are you expected to, Charles. We have our councilors for a reason. Listen to Antoine, then tell me if you still want to plead your case. I assure you, I will listen to it."

One of the things Theuderic most respected about the prince, despite his impatience, was that he knew when to fight and when to retreat. He nodded to his father and bowed respectfully toward de Beaumille. "My Lord Maréchal, I should be grateful for your instruction."

"The honor is mine, your royal highness. Now, I invite you to consider the question of why the Duc de Montrove considered himself able to revolt against the crown this year, setting aside the fact that events subsequently demonstrated the foolishness involved in doing so."

"Why he was able... do you mean to ask why he revolted or why he had the means? He had the means because he was the ruler of a large and wealthy duchy, which mistakenly led him to believe he had sufficient manpower to fend off the royal army. As for why, I suppose it was because he's an arrogant bastard like damn near every other bloody noble in the realm."

"He had the means ten years ago. He loved the House of Mirid in no greater measure ten years ago than he did this spring. So why revolt now?"

The prince looked at Theuderic. Theuderic shrugged. He couldn't think of anything specific that could have triggered the duc's ill-fated rebellion either.

"Do you recall the last serious Dalarn raid within our borders?" de Beaumille asked.

"It was seven, no, eight years ago," the prince answered slowly. Then he smiled, exposing his big yellow teeth. "Ah, I see. The Duc de Montrove was the Warden of the North Coast. Since the reavers were uncharacteristically quiet for the last few years, he was able to use the warden's subsidy to build up his army instead of spending them on ships, scouts, and forts."

"And what does that suggest about the Dalarn?"

"They're desperate and hard-pressed. But we already knew that!"

"Yes, we did. But that's not the significant conclusion. What the failure of the reavers to reave suggests to me is that they are not only desperate, but they have lost control of the sea as well. And the only thing I can imagine that would cause the reavers who have harried our coasts for centuries to lose control of the sea is that the wolf-creatures have built themselves an effective navy."

"Ugh," the king groaned. "Although I suppose we should have considered the possibility. After all, they managed to get across the sea somehow when they invaded us during my grandfather's reign."

"I think you're overestimating their capabilities, my lord maréchal." The grandmagicien waved his hand, a little languidly, over his goblet of wine. "I don't think we can safely conclude the ulfin have done anything more than provide themselves with ships that sail faster than the Dalarn ships do. The Dalarn don't fight ship to ship, so there's no reason to assume that the Witchbreed do either. The reason they've forced the reavers to port could be as simple as the fact that the wolf demons are physically stronger and can therefore row faster than the reavers do. Or, it could be that the wolves haven't taken to sea at all, merely that the reavers are too busy trying to stay alive to put any effort into raiding our coast."

The prince nodded and put up his hand in royal submission. "My lords, I take your points. There is a great deal we do not know about the current state of the Dalarn clans or the degree to which the ulfin are presently ruling the Iles de Loup. Obviously it behooves us to learn more before we contemplate our next action, which is why you are only providing me with two thousand men, Maréchal, as that will be enough to fend off any small attacks without tempting me to launch an offensive."

"It is, of course, highly unusual that the heir to the throne should be permitted to lead such a perilous reconnaissance," the archevêque said sourly.

"I have three more sons, each more capable than the last," the king said with a hearty laugh.

That was not entirely true, as Theuderic knew well. There were four royal princes, but of the four, only the Red Prince was truly fitted for kingship.

"How many mages can I have?" the prince asked, giving Theuderic a sideways glance.

"You may have two," his father replied. "I can't imagine you'll require any more than that, as there are no records of the wolf-creatures showing any capacity for battle magic, or any other kind of magic, for that matter. However, you may not take the magus here, as I have other uses for his particular talents."

Charles-Phillippe glanced at him quizzically.

Theuderic shrugged. He hadn't been given any intimation of the conseil's intentions. He was merely pleased to discover that the Académie debacle looked unlikely to redound upon his head.

"It is my honor to serve His Royal Majesty according to his will," he said smoothly, bowing toward the king as he repeated the salient part of the vow he'd sworn upon the completion of his training.

"Do spare us your false humility, de Merovech," said the grandmagicien, all but rolling his eyes. "The reason you are here is because the Lord Archvêque has requested you to serve as this conseil's eyes and ears in the embassy to Amorr. Since the Amorrans take nearly as much exception to the esoteric arts as the lords of the Golden Circle do, and because you managed to penetrate the walls of Malkan without being discovered, it is my considered belief that you are the most likely candidate to survive a trip to that unenlightened city."

Theuderic nodded. The grandmagicien was almost surely right, in his considered opinion. And since the southerners didn't permit any magic at all in their empire, whereas the Malkanians simply refused to permit foreign mages to enter, not getting himself in trouble would be nothing more than a simple matter of not using his magic. Of course, events often had a way of putting one's self-discipline to the test. But for every magical solution, there were usually several alternatives that even the most benighted did not find intrinsically objectionable.

"May I ask the conseil about my purpose?" He addressed the archevêque, but his eyes were on the maréchal.

"Ostensibly, you will be the captain of the military escort for the embassy accompanying the scot, utilizing your secular title." To his surprise, it was de Beaumille who answered him. "The King has already granted the dispensation until your return. Given the amount of silver being transported, it is entirely credible to have a retinue of a size appropriate to your rank. However, both of the senior clerics will answer to you as head of the delegation, because, God and the Sanctified Father willing, both will be remaining in Amorr as newly appointed princes of the Church."

"Will we be traveling by sea?"

The connétable looked at the king and the grandmagicien in confusion before spreading his hands. "Why would you go by sea?"

"Because otherwise, we will have to travel through Malkan, and it is my understanding that there is a death sentence on my head there."

"You were there under the guise of an impoverished mercenary captain, de Merovech." The grandmagicien dismissed his concerns. "In the extremely unlikely event anyone notices any similarity between the royal ambassador to the Sanctified Father and a mercenary who disappeared last summer, you'll have twenty horse and fifty foot to help you convince them otherwise. Is there anyone in particular you deem likely to recognize you, seigneur?"

Theuderic remembered the astonished look on the face of a young Malkanian mage at the moment Theuderic's steel blade had entered his throat. The lad had been so confident in his skills, never imagining that he faced a trained royal battlemage instead of a fugitive wardog. "No, Grandmagicien, I don't believe there is."

"Then it is settled," declared the king. "Though, if you don't mind, seigneur de Thôneaux, do try not to get yourself killed or start a war while you're passing through. I don't suppose there is any chance your elf lady will be willing to stay at l'Académie and assist with the spell-working in your absence?"

"I should say it is impossible, Your Majesty. I believe she will prefer to accompany me on my travels, if she does not wish to return to her people in Merithaim. She does not appear to have any great affection for my colleagues. Nor, I fear, they for her."

There was a flicker of dark amusement in D'Arseille's deep-set eyes, and Theuderic knew the grandmagicien was thinking of the reports of her behavior he'd received after the debacle with the dragon. "I could not concur more with the comte. The Lady Everbright has helped us enormously, but as she has already told us everything she knows and can no longer work spells herself, it would be as ungrateful as it is unnecessary to forcibly retain her if she wishes to depart."

The king pounded the arm of his chair, clearly uninterested in the mundane details. "Very well. In that case, I give her leave to depart with you, if that is indeed her desire, and Magicien, or rather, Comte, I hope you will convey the crown's appreciation for her efforts to her. D'Arseille will give you your instructions tomorrow as well as a royal warrant and credentials, as you will be departing three days from now."

"As you command, your majesty." Theuderic knew a dismissal when he heard one. "My lords. Prince Charles."

The Red Prince caught his eye as he finished bowing and turned to go. "This is just a scouting expedition, Theudo. You can come along when we go back in force."

Theuderic smiled at the prince. He had no doubt Charles-Philippe would do exactly as he intended. In fact, by the time he returned, he wouldn't be terribly surprised to learn that the prince had conquered the isles with only the meager force given him by the maréchal.

SEVERA

S EVERA thought that if she had to listen to one more tale concerning to whom one of the less discerning daughters of the village peasantry was granting the pleasure of her dubious favors, she would demand the flogging of the entire female population of the estate staff. It wasn't that the servants in the city gossiped any less, but at least when she was residing at the domus in Amorr, there were far more interesting rumors to be heard and stories to be told. Her great-grandfather had built what were really rather civilized baths in the nearby village, but Severa increasingly found herself inclined to use the smaller one on the grounds even though it lacked a tepidarium.

It was quiet and isolated, and about all it had in common with the city's great social center was clean water in varying degrees of temperature, but bathing in lonely silence was to be preferred to the endless chatter about who was sleeping with whom. She would have been dreadfully bored too, were it not for her brother's letters, which were delivered faithfully every week by her father's messengers. Their regular arrival every second or third day convinced her that he was up to something, although what that could be she could not imagine. It was not like him to remain at a distance when the Senate was in session, nor to stay in close contact with his clients or anyone else in the city when he had retired to his estate in Salventum.

Aulus Severus Patronus might have reached his fifty-ninth year, but Severa found it impossible to imagine that he finally decided to relinquish his grasp on power in the Senate to his many rivals. Indeed, it was easier to imagine that he would force Death to relinquish its skeletal grasp on him, such was the force of his indomitable will. It was unwise to have crossed him, Severa freely admitted that to herself now, and foolish to think the mere stubbornness of a young woman could hope to conquer the resolve of one who had broken many far stiffer spines than hers.

She sighed, thinking about Silicus Clusius, the extraordinarily handsome young gladiator who had captured her heart from the very first time she'd seen him. His dark, smoldering eyes still held her fast, penetrating her dreams with all the savagely burning intensity he brought to the sands of the arena. She was no less his victim than the luckless men who died before his blade, and she was more of a prize than he could ever have hoped to win.

Alas, after being caught sneaking out to meet him, her tears and her pleading had availed her nothing, and her father had unceremoniously packed her off to the rural countryside in Salventum, the center of House Severus's power for the last seven generations. Calcetus, the traditional family seat, was now deemed to be too close to Amorr to serve as a retreat and Severa had only visited it once as a child. She was desperate to discover what had befallen her beautiful young man since her banishment from the city. She feared the worst and didn't dare asking her father about him again; she had seen coldness in his eyes but never before that awful night had it been directed at her. She shivered at the memory.

None of the family messengers would take her letters to the city, no matter to whom it was addressed or how extravagant a bribe she offered. None of her friends in Amorr even knew where she was, nor did she expect their letters would be delivered to her if any of them happened to guess correctly and address one to her here. Her mother and her sister were here as well, and as for her three brothers, Regulus was too busy serving out his year as quaestor, Aulan was marching through one province or another with the family legions, and while Marcius Severus wrote to her, he dutifully refused to tell her anything that was even remotely related to the arena, much less Clusius. No doubt he did well to obey what was doubtless a direct order from Father, but her brother's meek compliance irked her even so.

But she had to find out about Clusius! Was he well? Had Father harmed him in any way? She winced at the thought of that perfect body striped with the marks of the whip, that godlike face twisted with pain. And all because she loved him and he dared to love her back!

It was so unfair! She would have hardly been the first patrician woman to take a gladiator lover, though admittedly that was usually the act of widows, divorcees, or the sort of scandalous women to whom Amorran society turned a blind eye. And then, none of these abandoned women were the daughter of Aulus Severus Patronus. Father had never spoken to her about her indiscretion, not even hinted by any word or gesture that he even knew she had been in contact with what amounted to a fighting slave. His very silence on the affair alarmed her. What was he hiding from her? She had to know! She simply had to know!

There was only one option left to her. It might be wrong, it was almost surely wrong, but she couldn't think of anything else and she couldn't bear to wait any longer. She rose from the divan on which she had been lying and walked across the room to a little table upon which was set a little silver bell. She picked it up and flicked her wrist; it produced a clear and distinct ring that was audibly different from the bells belonging to the other members of the family.

Eudiss appeared quickly enough that she must have been either waiting in the corridor outside or simply happened to be walking by. "My lady," she said softly as she entered the room, her eyes fixed firmly on the floor.

Eudiss was a tall young woman with dark, reddish skin and black hair that was long and straight, but needed a brushing. More handsome than pretty, she moved with all the lack of grace of a newborn colt, but she was both kind and close-mouthed, two attributes which set her apart from the rest of the estate staff. She was two years older than Severa. Severa had claimed the woman for her own due to her ability to guard her tongue, much to the irritation of the other servant girls who obviously believed Eudiss to be better suited to the kitchens or the cleaning staff.

There was another reason why Severa preferred Eudiss, though. Unlike most of the local Salventians, who were staunch members in good standing with the Church, Eudiss was the daughter of a slave who had been brought to Salventum from Illyris Baara, and she wore three earrings in both her ears. In Amorr, Severa had heard many whispers about women who did not worship the Immaculate, or even God Himself, but secretly worshipped a goddess instead. She had not really credited the stories at the time, since they sounded too far-fetched to be true, but supposedly, three earrings was the symbol of the goddess.

"Close the door," Severa ordered, and the young woman complied. "I have a question for you."

"I will answer it, if I can, my lady."

"You don't worship the Immaculate, do you?"

Eudiss's eyes widened with instant alarm. "No, no, my lady. I am clean! I am pure, like a good Amorran."

"Don't be afraid. I saw your earrings. They signify the Three, don't they? It's okay, I'm not going to tell anyone." Severa walked over to Eudiss and placed her hand on the other woman's shoulder. It was bony and trembling with fear. "You have nothing to fear from me. I need to find a wise woman, a woman who knows the secrets of the moonblood. I imagine there must be a woman like that around here somewhere, in one of the villages."

"Is… is my lady with child?" Eudiss asked nervously.

Severa stepped back and covered her mouth with her hand, shocked. "No, of course not!"

"Oh, I thought… well, there is a woman in the village of Seijiss who knows many things. Many secret things. She is wise, perhaps she is the one you seek?" As she spoke, Eudiss ran her first finger lightly along the line of her left ear, touching each of the three earrings in turn.

One, two, three. Maiden, Mother, Crone. Yes, that was exactly what she sought.

"What is Seijiss? Is it far? Can you take me to there?"

"It is the next village to the east. It's not a long walk."

"Even less if we ride."

"It would be better if we walk. I could take you to where she lives, my lady. But I do not know if she is there today." Eudiss shrugged, her eyes still fixated. "Also, I fear it might not be wise for the daughter of Severus Patronus to be seen visiting her house. It would be the subject of much conversation, here in the house and in the town too. People would... assume things of you. But if you were to give me a token of your desire to speak with her, I am sure she would arrange to meet you in a more discreet manner."

"Yes, of course," Severa agreed reluctantly. There were times when being a patrician's daughter felt like being trapped in a gilded prison. Everything one did or said was an object of interest to someone. Even if they had no legitimate interest in her, it might be a weapon against her father, or someone else in the family. If she had learned anything from her sudden removal to Salventum, it was that she could not be too cautious.

"What sort of token would you recommend? I would have her understand that it is important. Urgent, even."

Eudiss nodded. "If you had need of her services, I would suggest a coin. Silver, not copper. But since you speak of secrets, and wisdom, then I think jewelry would be the better choice."

Severa smiled. Of course. It only made sense. She went to her jewelry box, a yellow-white square said to have been carved from a unicorn's horn, and withdrew two golden hoops, small, but thick. But when she extended her hand to Eudiss and offered them to her, the young woman withdrew in alarm.

"Gold, my lady? If you are not with child, then surely your need is not so dire!"

Severa wanted to slap the woman. My need is more dire than you could ever imagine, you country cow! But she held her tongue and smiled sweetly instead. "Let us say I wish the wise woman to understand that I am very serious about my desire to speak with her."

Eudiss could not take her eyes off the earrings. She had not moved to touch them. "Only one, for now, perhaps. I will tell her that you will present her with the other when you meet."

"Very well. If you are certain that will not offend her."

The servant woman laughed. There was a note of near-hysteria in it. "I promise you, she will not be offended, my lady. Seijiss is a poor village, and although many have need of her, few have much to give her in return."

"Then go," Severa ordered after the woman finally reached out and delicately took one of the little hoops in her long fingers. "Go now, and if anyone stops you, tell them you are on an important errand for the Lady Decia. For my lady mother, mind you, not me. And tell your wise woman she shall have both its match and a silver coin when I speak with her. But before you go, tell me, what is her name?"

"She is called Idemeta, my lady. Idemeta Venfica. I shall return as soon as I can." Eudiss nearly ran from the room.

Idemeta, mused Severa. Idemeta the witch. That sounded promising indeed, although it was a pity she was already so well known in the nearby villages. She would have to create an excuse to see the woman on a regular basis, and one that didn't cause her father, or as was much more likely the case, her mother, to suspect she was stealing off to see another young man.

Three days later, Severa was on her knees, pretending to pray before the shrine of Saint Malachus, the patron saint of Salventum. According to the garrulous sister of the order which was nominally charged with maintaining the shrine, long before the fall of the Andronican kings, long before the imperial conquests of the Sacred Republic that followed, Saint Malachus had been tortured for thirty-nine days and nights by the pagan king of Salventum. On the fortieth day, he had died of his multitude of wounds, but not before inspiring the Salventian king, who was duly impressed by the saint's boundless courage, to cleanse his soul.

As was so often the case in those simpler times, as the king worshipped, so too had his people to worship. Now the Salventians were as reliably immaculate as the Amorrans themselves. Indeed, much more rigidly so, from what little Severa had seen of them thus far.

The paint on the small statue at the shrine was faded and flaking away, but the stone face underneath still revealed a calmly stoic expression. It was a face to inspire bravery, and the thought encouraged her, even if Saint Malachus himself might not look any more favorably on her less-than-immaculate intentions than her mother or her father. But she was determined even so. She bowed her head and prayed—neither to the saint nor his God, but to the mysterious goddess of the three earrings.

Bless me with love and beauty, Maiden. Grant me my heart's desire, Madonna. Teach me your secret wisdom, Crone. And please, please, tell me that he lives. Tell me that he loves me still!

"The sisters say he was one of us in the end."

A voice behind her stirred her from her prayers, which had subsided into a wordless wave of tears and hope and longing. Severa wiped at her eyes and turned her head. Behind her, in the dim light, she saw a small, hooded figure wearing a simple brown robe. Judging by the sound of her voice and the shape of the robe, it was an elderly woman, stooped with age. Could it be Idemeta Venfica?

"The sisters?" she asked, unsure of whether she should ask the old woman if she was Idemeta.

"The sisters." The woman drew back the left side of her hood, and Severa saw that her hair was white and she wore three earrings in her left ear. Severa's heart beat faster when she noticed that the bottom one was the hoop she had given Eudiss two days before. The woman gripped the unpainted stone of the crèche and carefully lowered herself to her knees. She raised her face to the saint and her hood fell back, revealing wrinkled, desiccated features and thin white hair, streaked here and there with grey. Her lips were thin and colorless, her jaw was strong and masculine, but her eyes were unfilmed despite her age.

"The last of his wounds, the one that killed him, was when King Egnacias had him gelded. In some older versions of the tale, the king ordered him used as a woman as well. That is why you will see the cult of Saint Malachus established in places very far from Salventum. He is she, and she is we. Thus the goddess hides us in plain sight, behind the mask of a man of their god."

"This is a shrine to the goddess?" Severa asked, startled.

"This is a shrine to Saint Malachus. Everyone knows that. Perhaps it is something more for those with the eyes to see. But first, the sisters wish to know why the daughter of Severus Patronus seeks out the goddess. Are you not cleansed? Are you not purified by the Immaculate? By what right do you seek access to the secret mysteries?"

It was a question Severa had been considering herself for the last two nights. "The priests tell me I am cleansed, but I do not feel clean. They tell me I am purified, and yet my heart is full of shame. But I am a woman. I claim the secret mysteries by my womanhood."

The old woman shook her head. "It is an answer, but not a sufficient one. Do you bleed?"

"Do I bleed? Of course–" Severa cut herself short. The woman was telling her something. Of course merely being a woman wasn't enough. "I claim the secret mysteries of the goddess by the blood the moons call from me."

The woman nodded and grunted as she pushed herself back to her feet. She nodded stiffly to the statue, then beckoned to Severa. "I have something to show you."

Severa felt a little silly, but she imitated the woman's gesture and bowed before the saint's impassive, particolored face. She followed the old woman as she shuffled down a narrow brick passage that was lit by a single torch flickering in its sconce. It led to a room that was barely better lit than the passageway, an unadorned chamber with a brick floor and crumbling stucco exposing the bricks beneath it. In the middle of the room was a strange bronze contraption, a metal disk supported by a wooden tripod. On its rim, each of the 22 letters of the alphabet were inscribed.

"Can you read?" the woman asked her. Severa nodded. "You have a question for me."

"How did you know?" Severa stared at her, astonished.

The woman only shook her head and made a wheezing noise that Severa didn't immediately recognize as laughter.

"Few come to me without questions. They say you were brought here because you took a lover and were discovered. You want to know if he loves you still?"

"I did not take a lover!" Severa protested, stung by the unfairness of the stigma.

"But you would have, had your family not prevented you, yes?" The woman wheezed and shook her head again. "I have eyes, girl. You may be a maiden yet, but your body betrays you. Those ripe young curves are itching to be taken and conquered, to be mounted and ridden. That is the way of the goddess, and you will fight her in vain. She is stronger than parents, stronger than patricians, stronger even than great men such as Severus Patronus. For the journey to reach its end, every step along the way must be taken in its time. The Maiden must be loved by men before she can become the Mother."

The old woman withdrew a long thread from her bodice and muttered something Severa couldn't understand as she ran her thumb and forefinger along its length. "Give me your ring," she demanded unexpectedly.

Severa reluctantly complied; it took some effort to work the simple gold ring adorned with a single amethyst off her finger.

But the woman didn't pocket the ring or slip it on, as Severa half-expected. Instead, she slipped the thread through the ring and held it suspended over the etched bronze disk.

"Your lover. What was his name?"

"Clusius. Silicus Clusius."

The witch, for Severa was now convinced the old woman had to be Idemeta Venfica, began to chant in a tongue that was not Amorran. It sounded similar. She could almost understand a few words, but it sounded crude and rough. She wondered if it might be the original tongue of the Utruccans and reminded herself to ask Father or one of his scribes about it.

Then she gasped. The ring was swinging, somewhat like a pendulum, but in a pattern that was anything but natural. It leaped from one letter to the next. As she watched, it indicated the letters r and t, then u twice, followed by an s.

It didn't make any sense to her, but the old woman dowsing the letters seemed to understand it. "How?" the old woman hissed. "Tell me how, in the name of the Crone—the goddess requires it!"

The ring moved from letter to letter, beginning with the letter c and spelling out the word cruentes. Severa stifled a cry. She suddenly knew what she had missed at the beginning of the first word. As tears began to run from her eyes, she watched as the last word was spelled. Sands. The answer to the witch's question was *bloody sands* and the first word had been *mortuus*. Dead.

Clusius was dead now, slain on the very sands on which he had triumphed so many times. It could have been an accident, it could have simply been that the beautiful young man who had awoken her heart finally encountered a more deadly opponent. But she doubted it. Her father could have arranged Clusius's murder in a hundred ways. There were a thousand stories about murders in the arena, from poisoned weapons that killed with a scratch to soporific seasonings that slowed a fighter's reactions just enough to make him vulnerable.

She was suddenly angry. Very angry.

The crone could see the rage in her eyes.

"My lady, I am sorry. Do not be angry with me!"

"I am not angry with you," Severa said, staring past the woman, staring past the walls, and seeing nothing but the cold expression on her father's face the night he'd caught her slipping out of the house. "You said the goddess is stronger than men, even men such as my father?"

"She is, my lady. She is indeed."

Severa took a deep, deep breath. With it, she could almost feel the hate and anger penetrating down to the very depths of her soul, burning the last vestiges of her innocence from her.

"Then you must teach me, Idemeta Venfica. You must teach me of the goddess!"

The old woman sat back and looked deeply into her eyes. Then she looked away, as if she did not like what she saw there. "If the goddess calls you, Severa, it is not for me to deny you. But I can only teach you a little, for you will not be here in Salventum for long. You must find a teacher in Amorr."

"There are those who worship the goddess in Amorr?" Severa found it hard to believe. It was forbidden to worship the old gods, forbidden on the pain of death for man, woman, or child.

The old woman smiled, exposing gums that were missing more teeth than remained. "There are those who worship the goddess everywhere, daughter of Severus Patronus. The goddess is older than your city, older than your Sanctiff, older even than your religion. If you wish, I will put the mark on you, and in her time, the goddess will come. But you must be certain, girl, because come she will, whether you later wish it or not."

Severa stared at the old woman, knowing she was standing on the very edge of a precipice, at the brink of a new dawn that could change her life forever. She thought of her father, of her family, of her tall, fierce brothers and her innocent little sister. She could turn and walk away now, and her life would go on as before, the comfortable life of a patrician's daughter, a patrician's wife, a patrician's mother. Then she thought of a beautiful boy and a brilliant smile, and a red token wrapped around his wrist. He was dead now, murdered, and all because she was powerless to resist, helpless, and entirely in the dark about the invisible hand that had struck him down. The invisible hand of her father.

"Let her come, Old Woman," she hissed angrily. "Give me the mark, and let her come!"

CORVUS

T HEY had made excellent time, all things considered, thought Corvus as he and Saturnius approached the bridge over the river that separated the Republic of Amorr from the vast empire over which it ruled. They had left most of the twenty guards who had accompanied them the day before, freeing them to separate and visit their families, which were settled in Vallyrium. The two who lacked families, and the two whose families lived in the city, were following a few lengths behind where they could talk freely without concern for their officers overhearing. Saturnius had initially balked at abandoning most of their honor guard, but he'd withdrawn his objections when Corvus had pointed out that no brigand would attempt to interfere with six armed men wearing legionary cloaks within a day's ride of Amorr.

He was more eager than ever to see Romilia but reluctantly concluded that it was Magnus to whom they must go first. Corvus didn't relish delivering the bones that were presently stowed away on the back of one of their two pack horses. But over the course of their travels he had convinced himself that Magnus would be inclined to receive the news as a proper stoic should. Did he not pride himself on his equanimity? The guards at the bridge tower recognized their rank and saluted as he and Saturnius passed. One of them must have been acquainted with one of the legionaries, as a series of glad cries erupted behind them.

Corvus smiled at the sight of the hustle and bustle of the city life that was so familiar, and yet seemed so foreign after four months in the wilderness of Gorignia. The smells were nearly as strong as the stench of the battlefield from which they'd come, but far more varied and significantly less vile. And some of them were mouth-wateringly delicious.

"I have dreamed about those for months," Saturnius said, eyeing a vendor who was selling garlic-fried songbirds on a stick.

"Go on then, buy as many as you like. Get me one, no two, as well."

"As the consul commands," Saturnius said with a grin. He didn't even bother dickering with the vendor, but simply grabbed a handful, tossed the man a silver coin, and popped one in his mouth as he rejoined Corvus. "Mmmmph, now that is really good! Why can't our cursed cooks manage to feed us decently if these fellows can create such delicacies out of the birds they catch on the street?"

Corvus wrinkled his nose after taking a bite of his bird. It was crunchy, and all he could taste was the potent garlic in which the little bird had apparently been stuffed, rubbed, and fried. "I think you could serve goblin this way and it would taste no different."

"If goblin tasted like this, I'd eat it," Saturnius vowed. "It would certainly simplify the logistical situation."

"My son once told me he read the orcs do just that when they march. They use the goblins as shock troops and provisions alike. Probably just a story, though. They're also said to grow from rocks. Or maybe that's trolls, I don't recall."

"Not a bad idea, actually. Although I don't see either the men or the Church smiling on it." He looked at Corvus appraisingly. "And I can't imagine you'd be good for anything but soup, being as lean and stringy as you are."

They had no sooner turned into the quarter in which both Magnus and Corvus himself resided when Corvus spotted a pair of familiar faces among a group of young men dicing on a corner. One was Marcipor, his son's longtime slave, and the other was a man from Magnus's stables. Both of them looked up at the sound of the iron-shod hooves on the cobblestones, but their reactions were completely different. Marcipor smiled and rose to his feet, but Magnus's stable slave's eyes narrowed and after exchanging a word or two with the young man holding the stakes, he ran off in the direction of Magnus's domus.

Corvus sighed. It wasn't as if he intended to surprise Magnus, but something about the slave's reaction suggested that there might be trouble ahead.

He glanced back. The four guards were only a few lengths behind them. But surely they wouldn't be needed!

"My lord Corvus, welcome back to Amorr," Marcipor said, following his words with a deep and theatrical bow. The slave was a tall, golden lion of a man but about as martial as a kitten. He was deeply attached to Corvus's son, and Corvus found him quite likable in his own right. "Did my master accompany you?"

"I'm afraid not, Marce," Corvus replied. "But thank you, it is good to see a friendly face. Speaking of which, that slave, Magnus's man. He ran off to warn Magnus, I presume, and he did not appear pleased."

It was as if a light switched off. Marcipor's face abruptly grew serious and his voice dropped. "I fear your welcome will be rather chillier at Magnus's manse, my lord. There are rumors abounding, some of which I can scarcely credit! It is said that Gaius Valerius is dead, and not by the hand of the enemy either."

Corvus and Saturnius looked at each other. Had word of the execution gotten back ahead of them somehow? Was it even possible?

"Who says it?" he asked the slave. "Who told you?"

"Sextus," Marcipor replied. Corvus shook his head. Magnus must already know then, for he recalled that the young slave was as close to Marcus's cousin as he was to Marcus himself. Damn that Clodipor. He should have sent the man back at once, empty-handed, no matter how strange it would have seemed under the circumstances.

"Trouble?" Saturnius asked.

"There may be." Corvus reached into one of his saddlebags and withdrew a scroll with a broken Valerian seal. "Marce, run to the Senate, as quickly as you can. Find the primus fascitor and tell him their new Consul Aquilae requires eight fascitors at Magnus's domus at once. At once! Accept no delays, and tell them to run, don't walk. The primus should comply once he learns you're of my household, but give him this letter if he requires additional convincing."

"Consul, Lord Valerius?" The young man stared at him in astonishment. "Congratulations, my lord!"

"Consul Suffectus, it would seem. At any rate, I am entitled to the fascitors, so if you will please fetch them for me now."

"At once, my lord consul!" His son's slave took the scroll, bowed more respectfully than Corvus could ever recall seeing him do before, and ran off toward the heart of the city.

"Fine-looking lad," Saturnius commented. "One of yours?"

"My son's birth-companion. They used to be all but inseparable, but he's always been on close terms with Magnus's son Sextus, as well. Marcus gave him to Sextus when he kissed the eagle. Whatever he's heard, rest assured it has reached Magnus's ears as well."

Saturnius sighed. "Damn that Fortex!" The legate immediately regretted his outburst and made the sign of the tree. "No, no, *requiescat in pace* and let there be mercy upon his soul. But truly, Corvus, how hard is it to not engage in a bloody single combat? Were my orders unclear? Three hundred other knights didn't seem to have any trouble comprehending them."

"Don't waste time thinking about it. Your orders were perfectly clear. The boy was always headstrong to a fault."

"It can be hard to tell the difference. The lad fought like a demon, though, I'll give him that. And I was surprised when he returned to the field that day. Once the Second broke their cavalry and chased them off, I was certain we'd seen the last of him until nightfall. So he had a modicum of discipline."

"Well, we did see the last of him that night," Corvus said grimly. "And therein lies the problem. Are you sure you want to involve yourself in this, old friend? Magnus will make for a bad enemy. I'm family and a senator besides. You don't have the protection of either."

"I'm already involved, General. The dice will fall as they will. Even if I make an enemy of Magnus, Amorr doesn't have so many competent generals that he can justify interfering with my appointments. No one would take him seriously, and he wouldn't risk that. But you don't honestly believe you'll need the fascitors, do you?"

"I'd rather have them and not need them than need them and not have them. You know as well as I do that Magnus is accustomed to having things his way." Corvus took a deep breath as their horses trotted past the curve and the white gates of his elder brother's domus came within view. They were open and unguarded. As they rode past them, Corvus could see Magnus was sitting on the top step of the mansion, leaning back against a marble column. He looked old and unwell, and he was uncharacteristically attired in a torn and wine-stained tunica.

But upon catching sight of Corvus and Saturnius, he rose unsteadily to his feet, and his unshaved face darkened. He was a big man, Magnus, and as he approached, Corvus realized he was glad he had the advantage of being mounted, especially when he saw the size of the empty wineskin that had been concealed behind Magnus before he rose.

"Hail, Nepoticus!" He greeted Corvus with an angry, contempt-filled sneer. "Hail, to the uncle of corpses! How proud you must be to have defeated those unpronounceable goblin tribes, at the cost of a mere tribune? Shall the Senate grant you a triumph? Shall we name you Tribunicus?"

Corvus remained on his horse. "Brother, I mourn with you, and I regret exceedingly what has happened. I rode here immediately to bring you the news myself. Marcus Saturnius came as well, out of respect for both you and Gaius Valerius."

"Never speak his name!" Magnus raged, taking a step closer and jabbing his finger up toward him. "You damnable crow! You say you mourn, but where is my son? Where is my *son!*"

Corvus been prepared for anger, he had been prepared for outrage, he had even contemplated the possibility of violence, but he had not been ready to witness such raw and boundless grief. He had seen his elder brother bury two infant daughters, as well as their own father, without shedding so much as a single tear, and he knew Magnus had sent hundreds, no, thousands, of men to their deaths without a pang of conscience or even a later moment of regret. And yet, the erstwhile stoic had been as unmanned by his son's death as a eunuch by a heated blade.

Filled with pity and grief, Corvus could not find it within himself to meet his brother's anger with anger.

"He is there, brother," he said hoarsely. "On the grey."

Magnus staggered past him, as if unseeing, toward the white horse that bore his son's remains. At a gesture from Saturnius, two of the guards slipped off their mounts and loosened the straps that held the heavy canvas bag tight against the horse's back. Sobbing, he embraced the bag. One of the legionaries reached out to steady him when it looked as if his legs might buckle. He staggered backward with it in his arms, then fell to his knees and unfolded the top. He did not reach in, but merely looked inside, as if to confirm that the bones he could undoubtedly feel through the canvas were really there.

It was a dreadful thing to see. Corvus felt his eyes watering, and he tried to control them, but even though he blinked repeatedly, a single insistent tear burned its way slowly down his left cheek. He didn't look at Saturnius, but he heard the legate clear his throat twice and knew that Saturnius too was having to keep his emotions in check. Neither of them had ever wished this on the late tribune or his father.

Magnus arose with some difficulty, still clutching the charred remains of Gaius Valerius to his breast. Tears streaked his face, but when he looked up at Corvus, what he saw on his brother's face provoked him to fury again. "You would shed tears?" he demanded. "Better you shed blood! I sent you my son, I trusted you with my son, and you bring me back this... this bag of blackened bones? What did you do to him? How did he die?"

"You don't know?" Corvus asked, confused.

"Of course I don't know, you bloody fool! You wrote that he died after the battle in your letter. Clodipor didn't see him or Marcus in the camp. Was he wounded? Did he take ill?"

Oh, dear God, cleanse and purify us now, Corvus thought. This was not good. His brother's derangement was bad enough just knowing that his son was dead. Hearing the actual reason for his death could only make matters worse. Steeling himself as if for a blow, he forced himself to swallow and look his brother directly in his grief-reddened eyes.

"I am sorry, but there is no easy way to tell you this, so I will be direct. He was executed, Magnus."

His brother stared dully at him, so long that Corvus wondered if he needed to repeat himself.

"*What?*" Magnus finally shouted. "He was *executed?* My son was *executed?* At whose command?"

"Mine."

His brother's eyes widened with utter astonishment and, for a moment, Corvus seriously thought Magnus was going to drop his son's bones and attack him. "You *executed* him? You *executed* your own *nephew?* For *what?* You can't expect me to believe he was a coward or that he ran from bloody *goblins!*"

"Fortex was no coward, Magnus," Saturnius said. "He was brave, certainly. One might even say he was too brave. But his orders were clear. The legion was under special discipline, and before the battle I ordered the cavalry to accept no individual challenges. Fortex defied my order and engaged in single combat with the commander of the enemy cavalry. He killed him, and his men scattered the enemy afterward, but the entire legion witnessed his action. Sextus Valerius had no choice. He was honor-bound to issue the sentence."

"Honor? Where is the honor in killing young officers, especially one as courageous and promising as Gaius? Young officers make mistakes, they make stupid decisions, and they give ludicrous orders, but you don't kill them for it! How can they ever learn, if the penalty for every mistake is death? Good lord, Corvus, have you gone mad? You once killed an Avaran in single combat yourself!"

"I'm here to mourn with you, brother, not to argue with you." If you weren't half out of your mind with grief and anger and wine, you'd remember we weren't under austeris at the time and I didn't defy any orders either. And you would know it all perfectly well, since *you* were the one who told me to accept the bastard's challenge. "Magnus, please, I beg you, forgive me. I had no choice in this, no choice at all."

"Spare me your false tears! Of course you had a choice! You were the stragister militum! You could have subjected him to degradation or stripped him of his rank, you could have put him on rations. Or you could have done what you should have done and simply sent him home to me! If you didn't want him on your staff, there are ten other legates who would have been delighted to have a Valerius as their tribune! Blood and bones, you didn't have him stoned or beaten by common legionaries, did you?"

"He was beheaded, Magnus, by the primus pilus, Junius Honoratus. He died well."

"With all the courage that befitted his name," Saturnius added.

Their assurances were not helpful.

"Is that supposed to comfort me?" spat Magnus. "Post-mortem plaudits from the murderers of my son?"

Suddenly, Corvus found that he had had enough. "Brother, your grief maddens you. Gaius Valerius was not murdered! He was guilty, and he admitted his crime openly before the legion. His fate was the same as would have been meted out to any other man in the legion. I did not tell you how he died in order to comfort you or to ease my conscience, but to honor his last wishes. Those were his last words, his last and final request. 'Tell my father I died well.' And so he did."

Their raised voices had attracted attention within the domus. Several of the household slaves had already gathered around the windows, and now the front doors opened slowly. Julia, Magnus's wife, appeared. She had been well past her prime when Corvus had last seen her eighteen months ago, but she had still been an attractive woman, tall, with long black hair fading gracefully into grey. Now she looked like the grand-mother she was, as if her son's death had aged her a decade or more. She was painfully thin, and she leaned on Galerus, the majordomus of Magnus's household in the city, for support.

"Corvus?" she asked, as if bewildered at his presence. "It is good of you to come. Do you bring word of our poor boy? And Magnus, why are you shouting at your brother?" She looked from one to the other, and both of them were reluctant to answer her.

Magnus turned toward her. "Corvus has brought us back our son, my love. He has brought us back his bones."

Julia closed her eyes and clutched at her chest, but she did not otherwise react. Lost in the depths of mourning, she looked to have no more tears left in her. Corvus desperately hoped Magnus would not say anything about the execution, as there was already an ugliness in the air that a woman's hysterics could easily set on fire. Fortunately, he merely stared at Corvus as if daring him to speak.

Instead, Corvus dismounted from his horse.

"Help the ex-consul bring his son's remains into the atrium," he ordered the two soldiers already dismounted.

But Magnus waved them off, instead beckoning his slaves to come and take his burden from him. Four of them came forward, and they handled Gaius Valerius's remains with reverent care. From their stricken faces, it was easy to see the lad had been well-loved throughout the household.

Corvus approached Julia with care, and with half an eye on Magnus. He took her too-thin hands in his and squeezed them gently. "Sister, I am deeply sorry I could not bring your son back safely to you. Gaius Valerius was the bravest officer in the legion, and his men admired him exceedingly."

She nodded hesitantly. "Thank you, Corvus. He was a man, and he took a man's chances. Do not blame yourself."

That was too much for Magnus to bear. "Galerus, take Julia inside," he snapped with barely repressed rage. "My love, see that Gaius's bones are washed and laid out on clean linen cloth. I must speak with my brother about the funeral. And Galerus, see that you find something to occupy these eavesdroppers. If you catch any of them sneaking back and trying to listen, have them flogged. To death."

"Of course, my lord," the majordomus said, his eyes wide with surprise.

"Yes, Magnus." Julia took Galerus's arm and bade farewell to Corvus with a sad half-smile, then followed the slaves bearing her son's bones inside the house.

Magnus watched her go, and as soon as the doors were safely closed behind her, he turned back toward Corvus and fairly spat at him.

"To Hell with your pretense at pity! If I see you at the funeral, I will kill you. I don't give a damn about your imperium, I will strangle you with my own hands. Do you understand me, Corvus?"

"Magnus," Saturnius said, "with all respect for you and your son, you must know that if your brother hadn't taken it upon himself to pronounce the sentence, I would have done so. With no hesitation. We conferred with the senior centurions, as well. It was agreed. To ignore such a blatant violation of discipline on the battlefield could not be done. You know as well as I do that the law of the legion is iron, and there is no mercy in them."

Magnus scoffed. "Who are you, Marcus Saturnius, to speak of the law of the legion to the head of House Valerius? A Valerian has led Amorr's legions since the city still had kings! I was leading three legions against the Avarii when you were but a tribune. Would that I had the foresight to take your damned head! Tell me, Marcus Saturnius Inglorious, who was your father? Who was your father's father's father? Has Amorr fallen so far already? Can this be the city I, my father, and generations of Valerians before him have fought to defend, a city where Amorr's noblest patrician blood is shed by plebian scum?"

Saturnius appeared unruffled. "I have never sought fame or fortune, only victory for Amorr. And it is not noble blood that makes the general, Magnus—it is noble deeds. Amorr knows only one law. There is not one law for the patrician and another for the plebian."

"Our House is Amorr," Magnus shot back. "Surely you have heard that before. Neither you nor any pleb can ever truly understand what it means. Without House Valerius, without the other Houses Insurgus, there is no Amorr."

"No, it is you who have never understood what that means, brother." Corvus shook his head, half in pity, half in contempt. "You have it precisely backward. Other great houses are loyal to the family first, the city second. House Valerius stands apart because we do not distinguish between our interests and the nation's interests. Honor demands, honor *dictates,* that we will be the last to exclude ourselves from the standards we demand of others. Even Gaius Valerius Fortex understood it at the end, and he died a true Valerian's death."

"Honor! You were always so damned concerned about your precious honor! That's all this was, wasn't it? You murdered my Gaius as a sacrifice to your filthy honor!" Magnus spat upon the ground. "That for your honor. It's not even worth my piss, let alone my son!"

Corvus started to reply, but a rhythmic *tromp-tromping* of iron-studded sandals over the cobble-stoned street caught his attention. He looked back and saw the eight fascitors enter through the open gate in two lines of four. They were helmed and armored, and they bore the ceremonial axes indicative of their authority. They marched without hesitation past the horses, wheeled around, and stopped in front of Corvus's horse.

"My lord consul, we are at your service." The fascitors saluted as one, and Corvus nodded to acknowledge them. "I am Caius Vecellius."

Magnus, however, only sneered at their arrival. "I see you feared to face me alone, little brother. Four legionaries, a squad of fascitors, and even a legate to hold your hand while you offer me sanctimonious justifications in defense of your murder."

Corvus didn't bother trying to argue with Magnus. What was the point? After all, it wasn't entirely untrue, and he certainly felt safer now that the fascitors had arrived. But his brother wasn't finished.

"Don't make the mistake of thinking your imperium renders you immune from consequence, Corvus! I made you consul, and I can unmake you just as easily. And as for you, Marcus Saturnius, you had better leave for Cynothicus now if you know what's good for you. I'll find a way to see my son avenged. Just see if I don't!"

"To think I once wondered where Gaius learned his lack of discipline!" Corvus spat back.

His brother struck Corvus across the face with an open hand. Magnus might be over fifty, but he was still a big man, and the force of the blow drove Corvus to one knee.

He tasted blood in his mouth; the unexpected slap had caused one of his canines to puncture his lip.

Slightly dazed, he rose to his feet again to see two of the fascitors had dropped their axes and seized Magnus.

Between them, they forced him to his knees, and Caius Vecellius stepped toward the kneeling man with a lethally impassive expression as he shifted his grip on his axe to hold it in both hands. The two legionaries had drawn their swords, as well.

The fascitor looked to Corvus.

"Do you want this man arrested, my lord consul? In striking you, he has struck the city."

Corvus, his cheek burning, stared into his kneeling brother's eyes. They were still red and filled with madness, but the fury had faded enough for him to see grief and despair behind it. Corvus suspected that his brother half-wanted to be executed for treason, if only to escape his pain. Fascitors had been known to behead men for lesser crimes than the one Magnus had just committed. And for the crime of *vituper-maiestas*, arrest meant summary execution.

He realized he had to leave right now and get the fascitors out of Magnus's presence before what was already an ugly situation spiraled completely out of control. It was bad enough that he had had his nephew beheaded. If he didn't end this farce immediately, he'd find himself saddled with the reputation of a fratricide, as well.

Corvus wiped the blood away from his mouth. "The ex-consul has insulted neither me nor Amorr, Caius Vecellius. He has only just now learned of the manner of his son's death, and he is understandably aggrieved. It would be unjust to hold him responsible for his actions. Release him, and we will leave him and his family to their mourning. Now, I must speak with my consular colleagues, so if you will lead us to the Forum?"

"At once, my lord consul!" Caius Vecellius bowed smartly and returned his axe to his shoulder.

Two of his fellows helped Magnus to his feet, then rejoined the others and began to follow Vecellius toward the gates.

Corvus didn't say anything to Magnus; he remounted in silence and turned his horse around.

Saturnius did likewise, and the two knights also clambered into their saddles and followed them out to the safety of the street.

When he reached the gates, Corvus looked back and saw that Magnus was still standing motionless, watching him, and his eyes burned with an unfraternal hatred that chilled Corvus's soul.

"Well, that went well," Marcus Saturnius said.

"In what way?" Corvus spat, and a red gobbet splattered against the white wall outside the gate, leaving a faint crimson stain behind as it slowly trickled its way down the wall.

"I was listening to the lads earlier," the legate indicated the knights riding behind them. "It was four to one that either you or your brother wouldn't survive that meeting."

"And yet you decided to ride along—out of morbid curiosity?"

Saturnius grinned up at him. "I always bet the chalk, General. But sometimes it helps to keep an eye on your investment."

FJOTRA

FJOTRA found it strange to be standing on the broad deck of a Savoner warship rather than behind the narrow prow of a Dalarn snekkja, like the one on which she'd previously crossed the White Sea.

The Savoner ship, which the sailors called a caraque, was a little shorter, but much wider and taller than even the biggest drekar. It had three sails to the longship's one, and it carried five hundred soldiers in addition to the crew of forty.

It had been slow and awkward in the harbor, wallowing like a whale about to beach, and she'd heard the laughter carried across the water from the hardy crew of the snekkja that had accompanied them in the return to Raknarborg.

But the laughter had quickly stopped once the sails were fully unfurled.

Then it had become obvious that *Le Christophe,* as the ship was called, and her three sister ships were capable of keeping pace with the longship. More than capable, even, especially when the wind wasn't coming from the south. Their multiple sails allowed the caraques to beat against the wind more efficiently than the single fixed sail of the Dalarn ship.

Their pride affronted, her kinsmen had labored manfully at the oars for hours the one day that a westerly wind had prevented their progress, angrily refusing when the Lord Admiral Hurualt asked if they wished one of the Savoner ships to tow them.

That one day aside, the crossing had been a quick and uneventful one, although by the second day, the smell of what was essentially an entire Dalarn village crammed into a single large ship had become something that Fjotra feared she would never be able to wash off or forget.

However, the Red Prince had been kind to her and had even asked her to dine with him and the Lord Admiral on the first evening. The Savoners ate remarkably well even when at sea, as she was astounded at the quality and variety of the foods that were served. She dined on stuffed duck and pigeon eggs washed down with a sweet white wine that bubbled and burned as it went down, all the while knowing that on the longship, the men were eating pickled herring and three-day-old bread washed down with water.

It was early morning when land was first sighted, and they reached the bay over which Raknarborg's three towers cast their shadow before midday. She didn't realize how frightened she had been that the fortress would have fallen in her absence until she saw the towers, intact and unburned, and felt her knees weaken with abject relief.

She wished she could send Brynjolf a message and put his mind at ease, but he had been left behind. Brynjolf had survived both the stabbing wound in his chest as well as the arm that had been broken in his fall from the wall. He had not recovered sufficiently to accompany the Red Prince to Raknarborg, however, which was why it had fallen to Fjotra to serve as the royal Dalarn aide-de-camp to the heir to the Savoner throne. There was the possibility of sending him a message via fire-talking, but the younger of the expedition's two battlemages had told her that, although a fire could be built on a ship, the fire-talking the mages used to speak with each other over long distances did not work across oceans, rivers, or large bodies of water.

Although the issue of fealty had been agreed, and sufficient treasure had been loaded on the four Savoner ships to satisfy the Red Prince that the negotiated payment to the crown would be made, there was still tension between the heir to the throne and Fjotra's father. As one of the few who could speak to both men, and the only one personally acquainted with both, Fjotra was required to serve as their primary translator, with the assiduous assistance of the young battlemage, Patrice. But the two men butted heads from the start.

The main issue of contention was when the evacuation would begin taking place. The three of them were standing on the South Tower, which overlooked the harbor. Her father wanted to load up all of the available ships with women and children and send them south at once, whereas the Red Prince had insisted that the four Savoner ships must remain at Raknarborg in case an urgent retreat across the sea was required.

"I do not wish to accuse this royal princeling of cowardice," Skuli told her in their own tongue as the prince glared uncomprehendingly at him. "But what sort of warrior's first concern is being able to run from the fight?"

"He is no coward, Father," she assured him. "No coward would have come here. He did not have to make our people's battle his own."

"Then remind him of the treasure. Little good it will do him or our new liege lord if it never crosses the sea."

"What does he say?" the prince demanded to know.

"He say he know you are brave, maybe too brave, for you come here." The prince nodded, satisfied. "He say you take treasure to your father with the women and the childrens. Six days, all ships come here."

"I have sixty longships," her father pointed out. "We must keep ten here to guard against the wolfships entering the bay. But fifty can carry fifteen hundred women and children besides their crews. That needs five trips… a month for all of them. With the Savoner ships, we can take forty-five hundreds, which means only two trips and less than a fortnight on the sea."

"That is nine thousand. But you said we have about seven thousand women and children?"

"Seven thousand, three hundred eighty four. Yes, we only need three of the Savoner ships. Tell him that. If he's more concerned about his own skin than his troops, then he'll be satisfied with the one."

Fjotra smiled at the Red Prince, who was no longer glaring at her father, but still looked less than pleased with him. The comtesse had told her that the prince was a man who well appreciated women, and she noticed that despite her youth and uncertain grasp of his tongue, he seemed to be rather easier for her to manage than for any of the men, Savoner or Dalarn. "Your royal highness, my father say he want send 50 longships and three of your big ships tomorrow. Then we stay here twelve, thirteen days."

"Only three caraques? I thought he wanted to send all four. But even three presents a problem. I'm not concerned about myself. I can always keep a longboat crewed and kept ready for the battlemages and me. On the other hand, one could argue that there is considerably less risk to my men if we are only here for two weeks rather than a month while the noncombatants are ferried over. Can you ask him when the last attack was?"

"Eight days ago," Fjotra's father told her.

"So, eight days ago. And you reavers turned them back without any help from us. I don't see why together we shouldn't be able to fend off another attack or two, no matter how many of them there are. Very well, I agree. Three of my ships will assist the transporting. But until their return, one longship and its crew are to be set aside for my personal use."

She translated his suggestion for her father, who agreed to it at once. That issue was much more easily resolved than their difference of opinion over the best way to defend Raknarborg while four thousand children and five hundred of their mothers were sailing to safety on the other side of the sea. Skuli wanted to remain safely ensconced behind the high walls of Raknarborg, whereas the Red Prince was intent on actively sending out patrols night and day in an attempt to gauge the strength of the enemy as well as its current locations.

As a tactic, it wasn't a bad one, except for the fact that the Savoners were completely ignorant about the wild lands surrounding the fortress on three sides and required guides familiar with the local environs if their patrols were going to serve any purpose. But the only available guides didn't speak their language.

The two men argued vociferously, and mostly through her, for nearly two hours before Skuli finally, reluctantly, agreed to provide each day-patrol with two Dalarn guides and each night-patrol with four. With no translators, they would have to communicate as best they could.

Her father didn't approve of the Red Prince's idea of harrying and probing away at the enemy until a direct confrontation could be risked. While he agreed that the Savonders' two thousand mounted and heavily armored men might be able to defeat up to five times their number in battle, his concern was that they didn't know if the wolves had five hundred or twenty thousand warriors in the hills and valleys surrounding Raknarborg. Thus far, no overwhelming assault on the fortress had come, but every day they spied watchers keeping an eye on the main road as well as the lesser paths, and every night the great stone walls echoed with their bestial howls.

The first two days, only day patrols were sent out. The riders went out in groups of twenty, usually accompanied by one of the two mages. No signs of any massing aalvarg armies were found, although the second patrol did manage to ride down and kill three of the wolves caught unaware traversing the road near the bridge that spanned the Goldwater. Along with the return of one of the escorting longships, which had developed a potentially dangerous leak and come back to report that the combined Savoner-Dalarn fleet was safely crossing the sea without incident or catching sight of any wolfships, the three pelts greatly cheered the fortress's mixed garrison. One was presented to the Red Prince, and one to each of the two battlemages.

Fjotra thought Patrice looked rather absurd in his new wolfskin cloak, but the breeze from the sea was cold and damp and he was rarely seen without it. The Red Prince too made a habit of wearing his, as he had sensibly decided to adopt the warmer Dalarn fashions, and if it were not for his olive skin and dark, sensual eyes, he could almost have passed for a reaver himself.

Despite herself, Fjotra found her heart fluttering a little bit each time the prince looked at her with his piercing, hawk-like eyes and called her "princess" or "your royal highness." He was teasing her, she knew, but she didn't mind. And she found, somewhat to her surprise, that she didn't mind having to accompany him everywhere, translating for him. In fact, she began to feel a little bereft when he left her to meet with his captains, exercise his horse, or any other activity that didn't require the Dalarn tongue.

Sometimes, when she found him looming over her, she wished he would simply grab her and... do something. Kiss her, perhaps? She wasn't sure. All she knew was that she was beginning to grow jealous of the comtesse despite her absence, because she had become increasingly certain that the Lady Roheis was the prince's mistress.

On the sixth day, a patrol spotted a sizable force of around five hundred wolves moving toward the fortress. Unsurprisingly, this sparked yet another argument between her father and Prince Karl. Skuli only wanted to keep watch over the enemy force, whereas the Red Prince urged an immediate attack on them before they could be reinforced.

"He says they don't know our numbers and they are accustomed to fighting Dalarn, not armored knights. And he wishes to remind you that your men are taught to fight in raids and to skirmish, but his men are trained in fighting together, as a single piece. No, that's not the word. As a single unit."

"Every man we lose out there is one more man we don't have to defend the walls when the attack comes," Skuli growled.

Fjotra didn't even need to translate that before knowing what the prince's response would be. "Every wolf we kill out there is one more we don't have to defend the walls against," she said before the Savoner had even finished speaking. "And his horse warriors can't use their horses fighting inside the walls."

In the end, it was decided that three hundred Dalarn warriors would engage the aalvarg as they crossed a river that stood between them and Raknarborg, then fall back as if they were routed. There were two large hills that were just visible from the fortress, on the other side of which was a large and open field. Five hundred of the Prince's cavalry would be hidden behind those hills, and they would ambush the wolves, who would be spread out and vulnerable as they pursued the retreating Dalarn.

It was also decided, after both the Prince and his battlemages insisted, that Fjotra would accompany the Savoner riders in order to reduce the chances of any messages being misunderstood. After a brief demonstration of Patrice's ability to cloak her with a concealment spell, her father reluctantly agreed that she would be nearly as safe with the battlemages as she was behind the great black walls of Raknarborg, especially since the Savoners' horses could easily outpace the wolves and there was no way to cut off their line of retreat without it being seen from the fortress.

The next morning was cold and grey. She forced herself to eat a little oatmeal, but her stomach was bound up in uncomfortable knots. If it were not for the knowledge that she would be at Prince Karl's side, she didn't think she would have had the courage to ride out with the Savoner horsemen. But her spirits rose when she saw the knights lined up in their ranks, their polished silver armor brighter than the faint rays of sun that occasionally broke through the mass of clouds above.

She herself wore a leather jerkin borrowed from a small squire whose knight was not in the ambushing force, and she'd even tucked an oversized dagger that would serve her as a sword into her belt. It wouldn't be of much use against the powerful jaws and sharp claws of the wolves, but at least she would have the ability to avoid capture if need be. In fifty years of brutal struggle throughout the islands, no man, woman, or child had ever been known to escape aalvarg imprisonment, and it was widely believed that they devoured their captives rather than enslave them.

"You're very brave to ride with us, Lady Fjotra," Patrice told her as she climbed into the saddle. "But don't you worry, Blais and I will keep you safe. We have very strict orders from the Red Prince that your survival and safe return to the castle is our paramount duty today."

She smiled at him. He was sweet. But she couldn't take her eyes away from the commanding figure of his prince.

The Red Prince sat astride his giant warhorse as if he were a god. His shield was painted red, and he wore a long red plume set jauntily atop his visored helmet. Yellowish teeth flashed at her, and he raised a mailed fist to her in a royal salute before ordering his men to move out.

The Dalarns whose feigned retreat they would cover had departed at sunrise, but since the wolf people usually preferred to fight by night, her father was confident that they could launch a convincing attack on the aalvarg camp before falling back and drawing the enraged wolves onto ground where the Savoners could easily ride them down. It wasn't a perfect plan, he had told her, but it had the advantage of being simple enough that not even the language barrier between their allied forces were likely to pose much of a problem.

They rode slowly in order to spare the horses, so it took them nearly an hour to reach their position. The Dalarn warriors led by Steinthor Strongbow were to begin their attack when the sun reached its zenith. So, after stationing scouts at the top of both hills, the prince allowed everyone to dismount and eat what Fjotra feared for some would be their last meal.

The combination of riding in the company of so many fearsome knights with the careless, confident chatter of Blais and Patrice was enough to keep her fear in check, and so she had little trouble eating the bread and cheese that was distributed to everyone.

Prince Karl, she noticed, broke off pieces of the same bread and helped himself to hunks of the same cheese that his men ate. The way they treated him as he walked among them was strange. It struck her more like the familiar affection a man might have for his older brother than the healthy mix of respect, fear, and awe that was due a chief or warleader.

"He is much-loved in the ranks," Patrice commented as if he had read her thoughts.

"They're not afraid of him the way the clans fear my father," she said. "Is he not a true warrior, then?"

The battlemage laughed in disbelief. "The Red Prince? No, he is most certainly a warrior, and a valorous one at that. Battle is the sport for which he lives. I daresay that if your father had not given in to him, he'd have led us out here even without your men-at-arms. If we're going to fight these ulfin, and it appears we may have to whether we want to fight them or not, then our officers have to engage them in order to learn how they make war. This little battle today, as small as it is, could very well lay the foundation for regaining the entire chain of islands for the king on behalf of your people. I have no doubt the wolves can be deadly. But then, I doubt they have ever seen the thundering fury of a royal cavalry charge. It is truly marvelous to behold!"

"This is what you call a small battle?" She looked around the huge mass of armored knights and their giant steeds, more than twice the size of the horses her people had ridden before the aalvarg had killed and eaten most of them. "Before my father bring together what is left of the tribes, I don't think he ever bring more than one hundred men to war at the same time."

"The king has more than one hundred royal battlemages alone at his disposal, my lady. Blais and I are but two of the younger and less skilled ones. And there are another fifty acolytes of varying abilities, as well as a number of elderly adepts who no longer take the field but are some of the most powerful sorcerers at l'Académie. And, as you can probably imagine, he has ten knights and a hundred men-at-arms for every mage. The scale on which the king makes war is several orders of magnitude greater than is the case with your people—or, we can hope, the wolf-people. Although I doubt that was always the case."

"Why do you say that?" Even though she'd seen the wealth of Savonne and had travelled across nearly half of its extent, Fjotra was still a little shocked at the idea that the Savoner king had so much military might under his command. While it confirmed for her that they had done the right thing in appealing to him, for surely he had the ability to crush the cursed aalvarg if he so desired, she began to realize that subjugation to the throne of Savonne might only mean a slower and more gentle form of extinction for her people.

"That giant black monstrosity of a castle in which your father has been hosting us wasn't built by one hundred men, or by men who feared an attack by a hundred, or even a thousand, men. I imagine it must have been a great redoubt during the time of the Witchkings. Many men fled their cruel rule, and those who crossed the White Sea would have been able to escape them. It's not inconceivable that Raknarborg was built by men who later returned to settle down in Savondir."

"But that would make your people the same as my people!" she protested. "That doesn't make any sense. We don't even speak the same language or look anything alike."

The young battlemage didn't respond to her. He was cocking his head to the side with a strange expression on his face. He glanced at the older mage, who nodded. "Come on, our orders are to climb to the top of that hill there. You're to come with us. But don't crest the summit. Once we get close to the peak, we'll get down on our bellies and crawl. We don't want to expose ourselves and give them the chance to see that we're waiting for them."

She hadn't heard anything herself, but she had no doubt the mages knew what they were doing. Fjotra dutifully began following Patrice after first checking to make sure her horse's reins were securely tied to the rope that was pegged to the ground. If this allied effort went awry and they had to retreat to the castle, she wanted to be sure she had a horse waiting for her.

On that terrible night's flight from Garn, they had all learned the hard way about how fast the aalvarg could move when they were running down their prey. She belatedly realized that her father's men had no chance of reaching the safety of the castle walls on their own. If the ambush were unsuccessful, or if the Red Prince's courage failed him at the sight of hundreds of great ravenous wolves rushing toward him, every single Dalarn warrior would die.

"You had better not abandon them, your Royal Highness," she muttered to herself. "Or I swear by the All-Father's crows that I'll kill you myself."

"What's that?" Patrice looked back at her. He was clambering up the steep hill behind Blais, occasionally using his hands to help him manage the slope. A squad of archers followed the three of them. Another squad was just beginning to climb the other hill. Below them, the knights were putting on their helmets and sliding on their gauntlets, while their men-at-arms prepared their mounting stools.

"Nothing." She winced as the uneven edges of the rock poking through the cold grass made her palms ache. Once, she caught her knee on an exposed stone, and the unexpected jolt of pain nearly took her breath away. But it faded after a brief pause, and after taking a deep breath to gather herself, she continued climbing after the others. It didn't take them too long to reach the crest, but once they had crawled to the top and concealed themselves there, she was surprised to see there was nothing in either the valley below them or the treeline that followed the curve of the river. "Where are they?" she hissed.

"We started climbing when they began their attack," Blais told her without bothering to whisper. "You needn't keep your voice down, my lady, just your head. Ulfin ears may be keen, but they can't hear us from here. We're downwind. And they won't scent us, or the horses either."

The cold from the ground rapidly penetrated her body despite the leather armor she was wearing over a heavy wool tunic that belonged to one of her father's men. She lay there, shivering in silence, for what seemed like an age.

Patrice finally nudged her with his elbow. "There," he said, pointing toward the far end of the valley.

She could just make out some movement at the edge of the treeline. Then Patrice passed his hand in front of her face. She jerked her head back and stared at him, which drew a pleased smirk from him and a chuckle from Blais. She scowled and looked back at the strange circle which floated unsuspended in the air in front of her face. When she moved her face close to it and looked through it, it made the distant trees look much closer. Startled, she jerked her head back, then frowned and looked through it again.

By moving her head slightly and changing the angle, she could see not only the figures of the lightly armored Dalarn men running toward her, with axes in hand and their shields slung on their backs, she could even make out two or three faces that she recognized as young men from her father's retinue.

"How you do that?"

"It's a simple water spell," Patrice told her in an annoyingly condescending tone. "Arrayed properly, it reflects the light and expands the vision. Quite a useful little trick, but entirely harmless."

"Like young Savoner mages?" she snapped, irritated. She was already on edge, knowing that good men were likely to be dying soon right before her eyes, and she had no patience for this poorly timed male tomfoolery. Blais's chuckle turned into an open guffaw. "Lord Patrice, sometimes Dalarn men play knife game before women. They think to impress us but only stab their hands. Maybe even cut off finger. Is no good. You want to impress me? Win the battle. No play water games."

The battlemage wasn't abashed. He grinned at her and shrugged. "I did not mean to show off for you, my lady. I only thought you might like to see better. Sadly, His Royal Highness has not ordered me to win the battle, but perhaps I can hope to be granted an opportunity to impress you if events proceed differently than we anticipate. In any event, my lady, if you don't wish to use the lens, simply pass your hand through it to break the spell. Your hand will get wet, but touching it will not do you the slightest harm."

She didn't favor him with a response, instead she returned her eye to the suspended disk, watching as more of her father's men emerged from the trees. She tried to count them, hoping that too many had not been lost in the attack on the aalvarg encampment, but it was impossible. Still, the fact that there were too many of them for her to count easily struck her as a good sign. The men were running easily too, without any frightened looks backward, and they ran together in loose groups that seemed to indicate that this was an intentional and disciplined retreat rather than a panicked rout.

Fjotra recognized the last group of men as some of her father's most renowned warriors. She saw Steinthor, Glammad, and Asmund Hairy-

Arse. Unlike the others, the rearguard was carrying their shields on their arms. Several appeared to be wounded, and she could see that their axes, in some cases still dripping blood, had been recently used.

She stifled a scream as the man behind Glammad abruptly disappeared. One moment, he had been running alongside the big black-haired warrior and approaching the open ground, and the next, he was gone, pulled violently to the ground by something she couldn't see.

The men preceding them had already turned and formed a shield wall about a hundred paces from the treeline. They walked slowly backward as a unit, awaiting the rush of the still-unseen enemy.

Steinthor, easily recognizable with his long, waist-length blond braid, shouted something. In response, ten of the men at the forest edge suddenly stopped running and whirled around, while the rest of the warriors in the final group sprinted as fast as they could manage, weighed down as they were with their weapons and armor, for the relative safety of the shield wall.

"What do they do?" Fjotra cried out in dismay.

"They can't all reach the others, my lady. Those who stay behind will slow the wolves long enough for the rest of the rearguard to join the main body."

Steinthor had no sooner given the command than the aalvarg burst from the trees like a dark and monstrous river overrunning its banks.

They ran low to the ground, using their long claw-like hands in much the same way she had used them when climbing the hill. They were every bit as dreadful and ugly as she remembered from those terrible days of flight. The ulfin were perhaps one-third man and two-thirds wolf—a demonic abomination with none of man's nobility nor the wolf's canine grace, seemingly created to do nothing but kill and destroy. They were somewhat smaller than they appeared in her nightmares. It was actually hard to tell exactly how tall they were due to the way they ran on all fours, but they were certainly shorter and lighter than the Dalarn men.

Many were unarmed. Those few that carried weapons bore either clubs, rudely sharpened stakes, or, occasionally, a weapon that Fjotra recognized as being of Dalarn origin. Fortunately, for the sake of the men arrayed on the field, she saw none carrying the bows that, however crude, had proven sufficiently lethal at Garn.

Their armor, to the extent they had any, was of equally poor quality. One large beast missing its left eye wore a man's leather breastplate on its back as if it were a saddle.

Poorly armored as they were, they howled like demons as they leaped upon the ten brave men who were sacrificing themselves for the sake of their brothers-in-arms. Six of the monsters fell at the first exchange, their skulls cloven and their breasts shattered by Dalarn axes. But after a moment's hesitation, the grey flood swirled viciously around the small circle of doomed warriors as if they were a few small stones attempting to dam a winter-fed river.

First one man fell, his leg bitten through. Then the next was overpowered by a huge beast that leaped over its fellows and knocked him down, tearing at his throat.

Horrified and sickened, Fjotra lifted her hand to banish the sorcerous lens. But Patrice reached out and stopped her.

"Look away for a little while, if it troubles you," he urged her. "It's dreadful, I know, but so far, everything is going exactly as planned. And you may want to see what comes next."

"Where is your prince?" she demanded. "Why don't he come out to help them?"

"It's too soon," Blais said with a growl. "If he attacks when they're too close to the woods, they'll simply fade back into the trees where our horse can't follow. We have to draw them out, get them entangled with your infantry. The Prince doesn't seek to merely drive them from the field, he wants to smash them utterly."

So did she, Fjotra realized, as she felt impotent fury coursing through her at the sight of the foul beasts that had killed half her friends, slain her mother, destroyed her village, and forced her proud people to submit to the rule of a foreign king. In less than thirty years, the aalvarg had done what neither the Witchkings nor generations of royal Savoners had managed in five centuries: They had defeated the northern tribes and forced them to the very edge of extinction.

But they have not defeated *us,* she reminded herself, for we still stand and fight! And, with the aid of the southerners and by the grace of the gods, one day we will kill them all, every single one, for what they have done to us!

Even so, she did not know if she could have the ruthless patience of the Red Prince who could wait so calmly, watching his allies fight and die. Steeling herself, she looked back through the magical lens and saw to her horror that part of the monstrous pack was tearing at the unmoving bodies of the ten fallen men while the leading line of wolves was now loping toward the Dalarn shield wall.

The warriors there had stopped retreating and were arrayed in a semi-circular fashion with the ends farther back than the center. It was three men deep and about sixty wide, which suggested that about twenty warriors had fallen in the attack and subsequent retreat. Twenty men was a pittance in comparison with how many men, women, and children had died in Garn and the nearby villages alone. And yet the bravery of their heroic deaths made her want to weep for them.

The shield wall was not such easy prey for the wolf-people. Fearsome as they were, they were not fearless, and they shied away from hurling themselves upon it. It was easy to see that they had experience of such formations before.

From the hilltop, the shield wall looked like a single great creature, bristling with spears and axeheads. Despite their greater numbers, the aalvarg facing it seemed reluctant to pay the price in blood required to attack it. They prowled back and forth, snapping at the Dalarn, whom they outnumbered at least two to one, but after one scrawny beast ventured too close to the shield wall and was promptly dispatched by an axeman who bravely darted out from the line, they refused to get any closer.

"Undisciplined cowards," she heard Blais grumble. "Come on, you bastards, get yourselves stuck in now!"

"What's that?" Patrice responded, pointing to a small group of wolf creatures emerging from the forest. "*Sacré bleu*, this could be a problem."

Twelve black-furred aalvarg, bigger and less feral than their grey-furred counterparts, stalked onto the field of battle as if the Dalarn warriors weren't even there. They were escorting two large timber wolves that were nearly three times the size of any Fjotra had seen before, as well as a powerful aalvarg with mottled fur who wore an iron breastplate as well as a longsword in a scabbard.

The warrior wasn't quite as big as his black-furred guards, but his posture was more upright than the others, and he radiated a keen sense of intelligence. But he soon showed himself to be as grotesquely bestial as the rest. As he approached the half-eaten remains of the fallen Dalarn, he sniffed at them, then briefly went down to all fours and contemptuously raised his leg, releasing a large stream of urine over the bodies of the dead men. The aalvarg howled with what sounded like delight.

The dead men's former companions howled too, but in rage.

"*Damné salaud!*" the elder battlemage cursed, expressing Fjotra's own indignation.

"Fascinating," Patrice commented, unmoved by the vulgar spectacle. "They must have a primitive aristocracy of sorts. Perhaps even a priesthood, I shouldn't wonder. I imagine those two wolves he's got with him could be some sort of religious iconology, perhaps even symbols of his authority. Why didn't you say anything about this hierarchy of theirs, Lady Fjotra?"

"I know nothing of this. I never seen it before."

But the young mage's suggestion struck her as a sensible one. The dreadful beasts that she had seen before, against whom her father had been fighting for nearly his entire life, had never shown any signs of a formidable intelligence. Their ships were as primitive as their bows, the sharpened sticks they used as spears, and the rock-studded clubs they used as axes. They had always defeated the Dalarn with their ferocity and their sheer numbers. Perhaps only now, with the broken remnants of Fjotra's people penned into their last redoubt, did their leaders dare to openly show themselves.

With a combination of slaps, snaps, and snarls, the big aalvarg and his bodyguard soon had the huge pack of wolf-people back into a loose form of battle array. One of the giant black-furred monsters claimed the pride of place in the center, while two more assumed positions at the head of the left and right wings.

But their tactics were still simple to the point of nonexistence, as after a series of what sounded like ritualistic barks and howls, the aalvarg commander threw back his head and emitted a long ululating howl that was echoed by his warriors as they lowered themselves to all fours and began to rush forward like the beasts they were.

A few, mostly those armed with scavenged Dalarn weapons, stayed upright as they ran. One forgot that he was carrying an iron-tipped spear, stepped on the butt end of it with his rear leg, and somehow managed to impale his lower jaw.

As Fjotra watched, holding her breath, the speedy grey mass of aalvarg smashed against the round iron shields of the waiting Dalarn warriors like the waves of a tempestuous sea crashing against a rocky island shore.

MARCUS

THE legate of Legio XVII looked less than thrilled to see Marcus entering his command tent. Unlike his tribunes, Marcus Saturnius had clearly not bathed, and if the five piles of parchment and assorted scrolls that littered his table were any guide, he would not be visiting the baths of Gallidromum anytime soon. He looked exhausted and hollow-eyed, and he barely managed to lift a hand in response to Marcus's salute.

"Your father sends his greetings, Clericus. He is well, and I expect you have heard he will be remaining in Amorr for the winter elections. Now, as you can see, I have no time for idle conversation, as it appears that Crescentius has somehow managed to avoid making a single decision of import in my absence."

"Sir," Marcus said, refusing to take the hint and leave.

"Still, I suppose I should be grateful that he managed to get the legion here in one piece without getting waylaid or accidentally starting a war with anyone. It would be a bit much to expect bureaucratic efficiency to accompany command competence."

"Sir," Marcus repeated.

Saturnius stared at him with a mixture of annoyance and resignation. "Very well, Tribune Valerius, what is it?"

"I'm afraid I have bad news for you, sir. I have some reason to suspect there is already another legion in Cynothicus."

Saturnius whipped his head up, but then he made a dismissive gesture. "That's absurd! There isn't another legion within fifty leagues of us,

unless you're talking about the remnants of the XIVth. But they retreated
to Clusium after being thrashed by the Cynothii. The Legio Civitas is
heading for their winter quarters, and the new legion Lucius Favronius
raised will be training through the winter. I don't expect to see Durus
here until the spring."

"Did they ever decide what number to give the new legion?" It wasn't
important, but Marcus was curious.

"Favronius wanted to call it XXIX, but since the Senate provided the
funds for it, mostly out of new provincial taxes, it's been named the Legio
Provincia. They are an imaginative lot, are they not?" Saturnius waved
his hand dismissively. "Why do you think there is another legion in the
vicinity? Did you see it?"

"No, sir," Marcus admitted. "But I spoke to a merchant from Medonis. He took us for soldiers belonging to the legion he'd sold his wares to
the previous week. It was either wine or pigs, I don't recall at the moment.
Trebonius will remember. What struck me as significant was that he'd
come from Cynothicum."

The legate frowned. "I find it hard to imagine a Medonite unable to
identify his customer, particularly one as large as a legion."

"I believe it may be Legio III, legate. The merchant said he saw
twin lightning symbols at the camp." Saturnius's eyes narrowed. As an
officer who had spent his entire career in the Valerian legions, the legate
understood the potential significance of the legionary icon as well as he
did.

"Fulgetra. House Severus."

"So it would appear, sir. I'm not saying that what the Medonite said
was true, sir. But even if we admit the possibility of a strangely elaborate
trap that depended upon men from this legion showing up at the baths
while he was there, the most reasonable explanation is that he was simply
telling us what he saw."

"That isn't completely beyond the realm of possibility. Once we
arrived here, it was only a matter of time before someone went to the

baths in Gallidromum. They're rather well-known in these parts, and you and Trebonius were far from the first to take the waters there."

"I agree. But what would be the purpose of convincing us that another legion was already in Cynothicus? To make us rush to their assistance and get ambushed? And why would anyone assume that a Valerian legion would go to the assistance of a Severan one without a formal request or Senatorial order?"

"They're provincials," Saturnius pointed out. "They wouldn't necessarily know about the various Senatorial factions, much less the historical animosity between the two Houses Martial. For all we know, it's the Cynothii behind this, hoping to draw us onto their ground before Durus arrives with the city legion. This is tremendously interesting information, Clericus, but we must know more before we can expect to proceed in an intelligent manner."

"I concur, sir. Which is why I would like to volunteer to take a squadron in search of this legion and see if we can confirm the truth of what the merchant says."

The legate frowned and shook his head. "The new consul suffectus would have my head, and rightly so, if I permitted any of our officers to take part in a mission so dangerous. And unnecessary. I'll not send you or anyone else into the waiting jaws of the Cynothii, or the Severans for that matter. There are much easier and less risky means of learning the truth of the matter."

"Hiring provincials could be risky. How will you know if they stay bought?"

Saturnius shook his head. "Oh, we'll send a few local spies out to the likely camp locations. I'll just have to send the orders to the men we already have in place in Cynothicus. I'd be surprised if your father hasn't got a few of his own there as well. It's not as if we were ever going to march blind into a rebel province. But what I have in mind is to kill two birds with one stone. I'll give you that squadron, but you're not going to need to ride it into Cynothicus—you're going to use it to catch their spies in our camp."

"You think they have spies inside our legion?" Marcus was appalled. "We're being spied on by our own men?"

Saturnius laughed. "Indubitably. For all that it's been blooded, this is an infant legion, Clericus. It didn't exist two years ago. And I can assure you, no sooner did the other Houses Martial hear that House Valerius was raising a third legion than they sent one or two likely young men to enlist in it. All of the common legionaries are potentially suspect, including those who come from Valerian lands, as are any officers who didn't hail from VII or XV. It's a sensible precaution on the part of the various Houses. I'm sure your father will be sure to place a few men inside the new city legion."

"And you think that if the merchant was telling the truth and it is Fulgetra, any Severan spies in our camp would know about it."

"I should think they must. In the event House Severus is up to something it shouldn't be, their reports won't be going back to Amorr. It would take too long to reach the legion. Someone, at some point, would have gotten them word."

A guard entered the tent. "Legate, the Primus Pilus would speak to you about the rotation of the cohorts with regards to the patrol schedule."

"Send him in." The general glanced ruefully at the mass of paperwork on the table and spread his hands. "I doubt you're susceptible, given your ancestry, but never let anyone convince you that there is any glory to be found in command, Marcus Valerius. It's nothing but paperwork, making decisions for others who should have already made them, then procrastinating in the hopes that the problem will go away. And every once in a great while, your men will fight a battle. If you are fortunate and they happen to win four or five times, you will be celebrated for your military genius. But none of those blasted historians ever sees fit to mention all the damned paperwork."

"Sir," Marcus replied, stifling a smile. If ever he had dreamed of finding immortality in the legions, his first campaign had certainly taught him otherwise. "Have you any orders for me?"

"Select your eight best men from the knights. Men from Vallyrium who can hold their tongues. Hold yourself ready and be sure they are excused from all night duties. I shall have more orders for you later. Dismissed, Tribune."

"Sir, yes, sir," Marcus saluted as the senior centurion entered the tent behind him.

Already he was wondering what sort of orders he would be receiving. But one thing was certain: He had better start finding a way to take a nap in the afternoon if the legate was going to have him riding throughout the night.

It was three days later when he received his orders directly from the legate himself. Marcus was overseeing the seventh cohort going through its sword drill in the forum when Marcus Saturnius strolled by along the Via Decumana. He was alone, and he waved Marcus off before Marcus could order the cohort to attention.

"Never mind, Tribune." He waved to the men, about half of whom had paused in their drill. "Good work, men. Carry on." He turned back to Marcus and dropped his voice considerably. "The seeds are planted. Are your men ready?"

"Yes, sir. Eight from Vallyrium. Good riders all, sir."

"Any with loose tongues."

"Not a one, sir."

"Very good. Take them out on patrol after dinner, but don't return. Ride out two leagues along the road to Gallidromum and watch for riders after dark. Those will be the messengers carrying word from the spies. I doubt there will be more than two."

"Yes, sir. May I post two of my men to watch the camp? Six should be enough to take the rider, and there is the chance that whoever is spying on the legion will not be the messenger."

"True, if there is a messenger, he'd be with the camp followers. And even if we catch him on the road and he's inclined to talk, he may not be able to say who the spy is. Very well, Tribune, use your best judgment, and go with God."

"Yes, sir. Thank you, sir." He saluted formally. Marcus Saturnius acknowledged it with a casual wave of the hand. The legate walked off, looking remarkably unconcerned.

Marcus wondered how Saturnius intended to inspire the spy, if indeed there was one, to action. Well, that wasn't his concern at the moment. It was more important to make sure that no one suspected anything unusual was going on between him and Saturnius. One of the words of advice given to him by his father when he joined the legion came to him: Whenever you find yourself in doubt, shout.

"Put up those swords and get back to it, you miserable slackers," he shouted at a group of the men who had been doing more staring than stabbing, doing his best and deepest-voiced impression of the iron-lunged Proculus. "You'd better be on your knees and thanking God when you say your prayers tonight that I'm not a centurion, because more than a few of you would be feeling the *vitis* across your backs right now if I was! You've embarrassed the entire cohort in front of the bloody legate!"

He smiled to himself as the men of the cohort, chagrined, returned to their drill with a vengeance born of mortification and a furious contempt for young, noble, know-nothing officers. Their curses and grumbles were reassurance that no one had noticed anything out of the norm.

It was impossible to tell the time in the dark, but judging by the stiffness in his legs and the degree to which the autumn cold had penetrated to the depths of his being, Marcus estimated it was at least four hours after nightfall. He'd allowed the men to dismount. At least they were able to move around and stretch their legs a little.

There had been little evening traffic headed for Gallidromum. Marcus was trying to decide if it was more likely that Saturnius's plan to frighten the Severan spies into action had failed or if the Severans were riding across country rather than on the roads. It was more likely, he imagined, that if they were cautious enough to avoid the obvious road, they would try one of the roads that followed a more circuitous route to Cynothicum. It would be faster than riding through unfamiliar countryside by night and a good deal less dangerous too.

Five times they had stopped solitary riders, twice more they had stopped a pair, but none of them were from the legion, showed any alarm at the unexpected sight of Marcus's tribune's helm or his men's legionary armor, or appeared to be carrying messages to anyone.

It was always possible that they had failed to find the damning evidence on those riders, of course, but Marcus felt that even the calmest, most collected spy would show at least some sign of panic at being intercepted by a legionary patrol. Instead, the riders they'd stopped had looked openly relieved, which was not hard to understand given their initial fears that Marcus and his men were a bandit gang.

He allowed a pair of carts to pass unmolested, one carrying a merchant and another a small family of Narretines. Marcus was wondering if he should have stopped them and if perhaps the spy, or the messenger, had been concealed on one of them, but he consoled himself with the thought that at the speed the carts were travelling, the spy would have had to have left the Amorran camp before Marcus and his men had. That could have happened, but there was no reason it was necessarily the case.

It was the tedium that was getting to him, Marcus reminded himself as he stomped his feet and tried to stay warm. The mind tended to wander, and soon one found oneself contemplating absurdities as if they were certainties. He smiled, thinking about the times he'd been out riding at night, either on his family's estates or through the hostile lands of the goblin tribes, and how every shadow had seemed to contain a potential monster or deadly ambush.

Now, he was the danger lurking in the dark, and he wondered if those imaginary threats of the past could possibly have ever felt as tired and uncomfortable and bored as he did now. He would have felt significantly less jumpy if he'd ever stopped to think about it from the situation of those nonexistent foes as they watched him ride by.

As he thought back to the merchant's cart and wondered if a man could have been concealed inside it, his horse suddenly raised its head and looked toward the road. A moment later, Marcus heard the distant drumming sound of hoofbeats. The rhythm was a quick one—whoever was riding was moving fast. And it was only one horse, not two.

"This could be him," he told his men. "Claudius, we'll do it the same as before. Take Orissis and Leporius with you; I want you three on the road now. Draw your blades and don't let him pass. If he tries, grab his reins if you can, hurt him if you need to, but kill him only if you must. We'll come in from behind once you stop him."

Claudius and the other two riders saluted, mounted their horses, and trotted down to the nearby road. They spread themselves apart to block it entirely, and while a determined rider might try passing them if he was willing to take the risk, the chances were good that he would lose his head or an arm in the attempt. The three knights' swords glinted silvery in the light of the three-quarters moon.

As the sound of the approaching hoofbeats grew louder, Marcus signaled for the others to mount, mounted his own horse, and walked it slowly through the tree-shadowed darkness above the road, followed by his remaining two riders. He hoped the unknown rider would simply surrender. He was too tired and cold to be in the mood for activity, let alone bloodshed.

The sound of the approaching horse grew louder, and soon the rider's dark shape became visible upon the road. He was riding fast, but easily, and he did not appear to be wearing armor.

Marcus exhaled. That probably meant he was no false soldier. For some reason, it was a relief to know he would not be forced to confront a traitor to the legion tonight.

The man slowed suddenly when he saw the three cavalrymen blocking his path. He was nearly even with Marcus when he called out to the others.

"Stand aside. I have nothing of value. I am a messenger for Legio XVII en route to Cynothicum!"

"Are you now?" Claudius drawled, unimpressed. "Well, I think you should get down off your horse and put your hands on top of your head."

"You're no highwaymen!" the man accused him, sounding suspicious.

"Can't rightly say we are, friend." Claudius whirled his saber in a circle, causing the moonlight to flash off the highly polished blade.

Marcus took the opportunity of the distraction to draw his sword and ride down onto the road, followed by the two remaining men of his patrol.

"Now," Claudius said, "where did you think you were going?"

The man was edging his horse slowly backward. But, alarmed by either Claudius's demand or the sight of three drawn swords, he jerked on the reins and brought the horse rapidly around—only to find himself facing three more cavalrymen. Marcus almost laughed at the disbelieving look on the man's face.

"Tribune!" he said, with a note of fear in his voice. He might not have recognized the armor the knights were wearing under their cloaks in the darkness, but the shape of Marcus's helm was unmistakable.

"Get off your mount and drop any weapons you might have," Marcus ordered. "If you try to ride for it, I'll gut you and leave you for the wolves."

Thanks to the moonlight, Marcus could see that the man's face wasn't familiar to him. He felt relieved, although he knew an unrecognizable face didn't mean there wasn't a traitor in the legion. All it meant was that he had an accomplice outside the camp, which tended to suggest the situation might be even more serious than he'd thought. One man indicated a spy. Two or more suggested a conspiracy.

The man didn't say anything, but to Marcus's intense satisfaction, he dismounted. Then he gingerly withdrew a long dagger from his belt and tossed it near, but not too close, to Marcus.

"Do any of you know this man?" Marcus asked the others.

Some shook their heads immediately. Two peered more closely at him before deciding they hadn't seen him before either.

"None of us never seen him before," Claudius finally concluded on behalf of his fellows.

"Make sure he doesn't have any more blades on him."

"Why are you stopping me, Tribune?" The man tried to present an innocent pose, even as two of Marcus's men searched him, but he had waited too long and expressed too much irritation for it to be convincing. "I was riding with an urgent message on the legion's business!"

"I have no doubt of that." The question, of course, was on behalf of which legion. Marcus looked the man over. His clothes were of reasonable quality and, while his horse was nothing special, neither was it a worn-out nag. "Whose message were you carrying? It couldn't have been for the legate—he has his own riders. It wasn't any of the tribunes, since we use our own knights as messengers. So, you see, I have to question how vital this message could possibly be if it didn't come from the legate or any of the officers of the legion. Was it a centurion who sent it? Or a decurion, perhaps? Did Proculus decide to make good on a gambling debt for once?"

Seeing that his feeble lie wouldn't work, the man abandoned his attempt to feign innocence. "Well, maybe it wasn't on the legion's actual business, but I was given a message by a legionary. It's true! He said it was important and said I'd be paid well if I arrived in Cynothicum before tomorrow night."

"And the name of this legionary?"

"I didn't ask. He come out and gave it to me at the whore's place, the one where they got the two redheaded twins."

Marcus didn't know it. He glanced at Claudius, who nodded.

"Could be, sir. The Lady Julia's, that's what the madam calls herself. I been there a time or two. No tell if he's lying about the hire, but he sure enough came from the whore's camp."

"Give me the message," Marcus held out his hand to the captive.

He shook his head. "He didn't give it to me to carry. He give it to me to remember."

"Very well, out with it, then." Despite his best efforts, Marcus yawned. The effects of his afternoon nap and the initial rush that had come when they'd intercepted the man were rapidly wearing off, and they still had a long ride back to the camp ahead of them.

"I was told to ride to the legion's camp outside of Cynothicum. The senior tribune there is Appius Mallicus, and I was to tell him that the legate knows. That's all. He said, 'Tell Appius Mallicus the legate knows.'"

"Knows what?" Claudius asked before Marcus could.

"I don't know," the man shrugged. "Just that he knows. That was the whole message."

The men looked puzzled and began suggesting a wide and increasingly improbable range of possible interpretations, but Marcus paid them no mind. He already knew what the message meant. He didn't know who was commanding the Severan legion yet, but he was sure that whoever its legate happened to be would want to be informed as soon as his presence in the rebel province was discovered by the newly arriving legions.

The more important question was, what was the Severan legion doing there? Was the legion there legitimately, on orders from the Senate or one of the consuls? Or was it possible that it was somehow involved with the unexpected defeat of Lucius Andronicus and Legio XIV? Legionary against legionary in battle? That seemed unthinkable. Never in the history of the Republic had one Amorran legion attacked another. And it didn't make any sense either, since the reports of the legion's defeat had reached Amorr weeks ago and no one had suggested that there were any other enemies but the rebellious Cynothii involved.

And for all that he didn't have any problem thinking ill of the Severans, House Severus was as fiercely loyal to Amorr as House Valerius was. He found it impossible to believe that a patrician as proudly Amorran as Severus Patronus could possibly have ordered one of his legions to wage war against another Amorran legion. But the princeps senatus was getting old, and perhaps there were other Severans who might not share his devotion to the city.

Marcus rubbed at his increasingly clouded eyes. One thing was certain: He wasn't going to figure out any answers tonight. Tomorrow, the legion's spy would be caught, both he and the messenger would be questioned by the senior centurions, and then they would have some answers. But now it was time to return to the camp.

He gave orders for the man's arms to be bound and his legs tied together underneath his horse's belly. One of the riders who wasn't securing the man collected the discarded dagger, while Claudius tied a rope that attached his saddle to the captive's.

"What's going to happen to me?" the man asked. He was impressively calm, but even in the moonlight Marcus could see that he was sweating a little despite the cold night air.

"That's up to the legate. But if you're not a spy, you haven't much to fear. There's no law against carrying messages, after all. I'm sure if you help us identify the man who gave it to you, you'll be paid well for your trouble. And you'll even have saved yourself a day's ride."

The man appeared to relax somewhat. "I won't cause you no trouble. My name's Berroga. I don't got nothing against nobody. I just wanted to earn some coin. If I promise to ride back with you, will you untie my hands? You already got me roped to that horse there."

Marcus smiled and shook his head as he urged his horse forward on the road and the others followed suit. "I'm sure you mean well, Berroga, but I prefer to spare you any temptation that might befall you en route. And anyway, I envy you: You're the only one of us who can sleep on the way without worrying about falling off."

The dark, cold ride back to the camp wasn't long, but tired as they were, it felt brutal, and none of the men were in the mood for talking. Marcus tried to think about who the spy in the camp might be, but his brain was barely functioning, and he realized he was mindlessly repeating ten centurions' names in the order of their seniority, much as he had when he was a newly minted tribune. He shook his head and gave it up.

He would simply have to hope that the two men he'd left in the makeshift town had caught, or at least seen, the spy talking to Berroga. What strange names these provincials had! Of course, there was a very good chance the spy had gone unseen, as it wouldn't be a surprise if the two men abandoned their watch and headed for a brothel as soon as Marcus and the others had been out of sight.

He breathed a great sigh of relief as the light from the torches atop the wooden walls of the legionary flickered off the polished metal of the men's armor. He glanced back to ensure that their captive was still with them, safely bound, and nodded with satisfaction to see that he was there. He was just about to call out to the crossbow-armed guards atop the gate when a strange thought occurred to him. Turning around in his saddle, he quickly counted the horses. Eight men had ridden out and eight men had returned. But now, they had a captive.

Claudius noticed his expression as the terrible truth suddenly dawned in his mind. "Sir, what's wrong?"

"Where is Lucius Orissis?"

The knight whirled around, and just as Marcus had done a moment ago, he quickly counted men. "The bastard's gone! He must have dropped behind after we left the road, or we would have heard him."

Berroga threw back his head and laughed. Not even the hard smack of a backhand across his face from the rider next to him was enough to silence him entirely. As he softly chuckled, Marcus and Claudius stared at each other, astonished by realization that they, and with them, the legion, had been betrayed. By tomorrow evening, someone in Fulgetra would know whatever it was that the spies wanted them to know.

THEUDERIC

THEIR entry into Malkan had been much easier than he'd feared. Instead of travelling through the heavily forested wilds this time with only a taciturn native guide for company, he'd been able to ride through the mountain passes without much trouble. The mule-drawn carts containing the silver and their gear occasionally ran into difficulty, but with thirty footmen to push, pull, and otherwise muscle them around the narrow switchbacks, they were able to get through the three passes without losing one.

He wouldn't have wanted to attempt the journey even a month later, when the snows started, though. By the winter fête, the route would be hopelessly impassible. As it was, it took two weeks to reach the circular double walls of Malkan, and while it was cold, rainy, and unpleasant for ten of the fourteen days, he found the two archevêques made for unexpectedly good travel companions.

His one regret was that he was unable to share a tent with the very tall and slender "sister" who made up one third of the female portion of the entourage. The Lady Everbright wasn't fond of being banished to the women's tent, and even less enthusiastic about the uncomfortable religious attire she was being forced to wear, but she usually rode with him and dined with him at the end of the day. And if he were honest with himself, the truth was that they were both too exhausted at the end of the long day's ride to do much more than exchange a chaste kiss in the evening before staggering off to their blankets and sleeping soundly until being woken to the cruel dark skies of their pre-dawn mornings.

Their embassy was, of course, unmolested, as any lurking eyes had no more to do than count the number of swords in the group before deciding to wait for more vulnerable prey.

Having sent a messenger on ahead, they were greeted graciously at the gate just before sundown by two of the city's seven lords. And while the city mages immediately detected his magical abilities, they didn't so much as ask him to refrain from using them. They did, however, insist on disarming the footmen.

Theuderic wondered if anyone had ever found the body of their young colleague he had killed the year before, when he had visited in the guise of Nicolas du Mere, a Montrovian cavalry captain down on his luck. He doubted it, and he wasn't about to ask. He was simply pleased that the king's warrant gave him such easy entry to a place he'd never thought he could visit again. But there was no other way to reach Amorr by land without daring to pass through the Elvenlands, or worse, a long, circuitous journey through a wilds populated only by various orc and goblin tribes.

Malkan no longer derived most of its wealth from sitting in a privileged position on the north-south continental divide, but those ancient transit taxes had provided the original capital from which the great banks and merchant houses that now dominated the Golden Circle had grown.

The Malkanians put them up in a private manor that wasn't far from the brothel where the Lady Everbright had been imprisoned the previous year. The archevêques, however, were invited to stay at the Bishop of Malkan's residence, so Theuderic didn't hesitate to take the opportunity to install his lover in his own bedchamber.

Afterward, he was lying on the bed in a languid post-coital stupor when she stood up, still naked, walked to the window, and looked out over the torchlamps lighting the cobble-stoned streets of the wealthy city.

"Did you kill them all?" she asked him unexpectedly.

He shook his head, not sure he'd heard her aright. "Kill who?"

"You said you were going to kill everyone who made me a whore. Here in Malkan. You promised me."

He sat up and folded his arms over his knees. Backlit by the light of the outside lamps entering the window, her body seemed more slender and alien than usual. Her breasts were too high and a little too far apart to be human, and the paleness of her hair against her white skin made her look almost hairless. Her very lack of sensuality was itself provocative, a seduction by the innocent. But he was not fooled by her maidenly appearance. And even if her sexual experience was slight, it was colored by an experience of life that exceeded his by nearly forty years.

"Not yet."

She was silent for a moment, then turned and looked out the window. She raised a hand and tucked her hair behind one pointed ear. Then she turned back to him. She looked vaguely surprised. "I don't care."

He was getting better at following the strange way her mind leaped from one topic to the next. "Are you saying you don't want me to kill all of them?"

She pursed her lips, which like the rest of her, were pale and thin, making them look almost human. "Maybe just the rich man."

She was talking about Aetias, the owner of the brothel, who had outbid Theuderic for her. But she didn't know anything about that, and Theuderic was determined that she never would. "Alas, I must apologize, my love. I cannot do that."

"You can't?" She frowned. "Or you won't?"

"I would if I could. Sadly, I inquired at the gate and learned that Quadras Aetias died in a quite tragic fall in his mansion. A terrible shame."

Her eyes brightened. "You already killed him for me?"

"Well, I paid someone to do it," he said modestly. She clapped her hands and kissed him enthusiastically, so enthusiastically that Theuderic almost regretted that she had absolved the remainder of her list. "I'm glad that you're willing to spare the others. It's not good to hold onto your hate."

"Why not?"

"Well, you have seen how they call me Comte now, instead of Sieur. Do you understand why?"

"It is your noble title as opposed to your priestly one."

He hesitated, then nodded. Close enough. She didn't seem to grasp the difference between religion and magic, between l'Église and l'Académie. Was it an elven idiosyncrasy, or was it simply her? "More or less. I was born to the title and inherited it, along with the comte of Thôneaux, when my father died eight years ago. Or rather, I would have inherited it, only when I was ten years old, it was discovered I possessed an amount of magical talent. Every boy in the kingdom is tested at that age, and if any significant talent is found, he is claimed by the king and henceforth regarded as the property of the realm."

"They enslaved you?"

"In a sense, although for those of us who show any real talent, it's an affront to slaves to describe us as such. The chains we wear are golden, and for nine out of every ten lads, maybe ninety-nine out of a hundred, it is a key to a much better life than they ever would have known without it."

"And the girls?"

"They are tested too, but not until they are twelve. Those with sufficient talent are claimed and sequestered, and depending upon how strong the talent runs in them, they are required to bear between one and four children to the King's Own."

Her slanted eyes narrowed. "Their chains are not so golden."

"Call them silver, perhaps. I doubt any of them would trade their decadent lives at l'Académie for the peasant drudgery that would otherwise await them. Most of them eventually marry mages, though not always the mages to whom they bear their children. Even nobles have been known to marry vadémagiques."

"That explains why Savondir produces so many mages," she remarked. "Whereas we elves, despite our greater natural endowment, produce so few."

"It also explains how Savondir conquered all of the human kingdoms of the north. Even when two or three kings joined their forces together against the king's knights, what army could hope to stand against twenty, or thirty, or once, even fifty battlemages? Not that they didn't try. Only your people have been able to defeat the royal armies, but that was long ago and who knows what will happen over the course of another twenty generations, when the king has a thousand or more mages at his disposal. Which is, of course, something you may well live to see."

"So you think your Académie will one day defeat the Collegium Occludum?" She smiled. "I doubt that."

"So do I. The Collegium defeated the Witchkings, before whose dark knowledge and power even our immortels are little more than untutored children. I find it hard to believe even ten thousand battlemages would suffice."

She nodded. "There are a few who could shatter the world if they wished. Bessarias. Amitlya. Possibly Galamiras, though I've never quite known what to make of him."

"It's strange to speak with someone who knows such legends personally. I always believed they were more or less myths, until I met you."

"Oh, I don't know them." She shook her head regretfully. "I've never even met Bessarias, although I've seen him occasionally from the sky. He left the Collegium long ago, before I was born. I do know Amitlya, she substituted for one of my teachers once for a few weeks. She's very kind and was much more patient than our teacher ever was. You had only to speak to her to realize that her mind exists on an entirely different plane than ours."

"Probably thinking about sex, I imagine. If I was a virgin for six hundred years, it's all I would ever think about."

She stared at him, absolutely dumbfounded for a moment, then burst into a high, elven peal of laughter. It was always vaguely unnerving to him. Her laughter never sounded entirely sane by human standards, and she had been through a rather difficult time before they'd met. "You haven't been a virgin for years, and it's all you think about now! We just futtered, and I have no doubt you're thinking about it again already!"

"In my defense, my lady, you stand before me in your naked elven splendor while I have spent the last two weeks sharing my tent with a pair of church knights in your stead. I am a man deprived of love, and as the poets say, who can live without love? Even if Sieur Osmont and Sieur Gautier weren't sworn to chastity, they are shockingly hairy, and I fear their perfume is nowhere nearly so delightful as your own, my lady. But we are fortunate that we reached here no later than we did. Another week, and I fear I'd have been contemplating assassinating the archevêques. No one even notices if the head of a royal embassy happens to have a woman in his tent. Or six, for that matter. But bring churchmen along, and I must go without."

"So the return trip should be more pleasant. What a pity we still have leagues to go on this one."

"It will go faster now. The road to the south is Amorran, and while they may have a primitive outlook on magic, there is something to be said in favor of their attitude toward transportation. They build good roads."

"Oh, yes," she nodded, uninterested. "I don't understand what any of this has to do with hate."

He sighed. For all their brilliance and beauty, the elven ability to follow straight lines was limited. "I was just saying that, even though the king took my title from me and made me a slave, I don't hate him. It took a long time, but I truly don't. I've traveled far enough, I've seen enough, to know there are worse kings than Louis-Charles de Mirid. And his son is a good man, maybe even a great one. If I still hated them for what was done to me as a child, I would be blind to that."

She stared at him then shrugged. "If you say so. I will still kill them if I see them. I just don't care enough to have you hunt them down. I'd rather you stay with me."

He smiled and stroked her cheek. "You're very sweet, in a remarkably savage manner."

"We built our cities when men were still living like goblins," she said. But she was smiling. "What will you do when we reach Amorr?"

"For now, what the king has commanded. We won't return north until the spring. If there is to be a campaign against the wolf-people then, Charles-Phillippe will lead it, and he'll want me with him. It may be years before I even have to think about it again. Or it may be never. Only God knows what tomorrow will bring."

His sealed orders made it clear that there was something brewing in Amorr, and his primary mission was to learn what it was before it happened. Bonpensier was no spymaster, but one didn't reach the position of archevêque to the realm without understanding the importance of information, and his contacts in the Church reached much further than either of the networks belonging to the grandmagicien or the chancelier.

"How about you?" he asked her. "What will you do? If you don't wish to stay the winter there, I'll arrange to have you brought safely to Merithaim. Or I'll take you there myself once the archevêques are safely crowned or whatever it is they do to them to make them celestines. They aren't familiar with elves there, and it won't be safe for you to go out without a guard."

"Are you in such a hurry to be rid of me now?" She smiled and waved away his protests. "No, I have no wish to return to my people now. Even though I will be forgiven for the theft of my magic, I will be scorned by some and pitied by the rest. They simply won't want to be reminded that even a great magistress like Amitlya can be robbed of her mighty powers by an unwashed man-rat."

He held his tongue. He still didn't understand the bond between elven virginity and magic, and he suspected it was little more than a tradition akin to l'Académie's preference for keeping talented women as breeding stock instead of training them as battle mages. But she had not reacted well to his previous inquiries on the subject. And if there was one thing he'd learned about elves in the past year, it was that they made absolutely no distinction between their iron-bound traditions and the dictates of nature.

She turned around again, her expression half-hidden in the shadows. "What is a year or even a decade in the life of an elf? As you say, only the gods know what the morrow brings, but there are no gods. If we are fortunate, then tomorrow will be the same as today. I thought my life ended with my magic in that whorehouse, but you showed me there were still pleasures to be found in it. Perhaps there are even things worth living for."

"Yours is a cheerful philosophy, my lady Everbright. How well-named you are!"

"Even where there is no hope, there is always pleasure. We are an old and decadent people, isn't that what your people say?"

"I've heard the thought before. What is it that you find so intriguing about our young and innocent race?"

She loomed over him, as thin as a young girl but taller than most women grown, her hair falling over her shoulders in a ghostly cascade that shined through the shadows. Then she smiled wickedly and pushed him over backward.

"You speak well of the slenderness of elves, Magicien. But since we met, I've come to understand that being slender is not always a virtue."

CORVUS

A rush of mixed emotions filled Corvus's mind as he walked up the familiar streets leading to his domus. There was excitement and anticipation, of course. It had been months since he'd laid eyes on Romilia, and he was almost trembling, so eager was he to see her again. But there was nervousness too. She had probably heard about Fortex's death by now, but did she know of his responsibility for it? He didn't relish the thought of trying to explain it to her.

After facing his brother just this morning, he wasn't sure if he was up to a long interrogation session or spending the evening attempting to explain the harsh realities of legionary justice to a woman so tender-hearted that she would force the cats to release the rats they caught.

He'd been glad for the company of his fascitors earlier today, but they were beginning to feel more like his jailers than an honor guard. At the baths, he'd practically had to order them to wait in the apodyterium. He had the impression that Caius Vecellius and the rest of the squad would have blithely followed him into the caldarium, still wearing their full armor, had he not instructed them otherwise.

Now they were leading him home, and he found himself wondering if they would actually follow him into his bedchamber if he did not tell them otherwise. Then it belatedly occurred to him that perhaps they were waiting for him to release them from their duty. He slowed a little so that he could address Vecellius without the others overhearing.

"Forgive me, Captain, but as you know, I am unfamiliar with my new status. Would you mind telling me the extent of your duties?"

"Why, to accompany you, my lord consul. We are to ensure that the Sacred Republic's dignity is respected and its safety is secured at all times."

"Yes, yes, of course. But I'm afraid the nature of my question is a little more specific. What I mean to say is, don't you ever go off duty? Am I expected to feed the eight of you and put you up for the night?"

Corvus couldn't be certain, but for a moment, it appeared that the faintest of smiles might have briefly threatened the dignity of Amorr. "Yes, my lord, we do go off duty on occasion. Tonight, we will do so once we deliver you to your home. Two of our fellows will stand guard outside your door. I sent a message to the commander when you were at the baths, so they should be in their position already."

"Ah, good. It's not that I should mind giving you all dinner, you understand, it's just that I haven't been home since the legion marched in Aprilis. For all I know, my wife has run off with a young lad from the theatre and the domus is empty."

"In which case, we shall retrieve her for you, my lord." Corvus couldn't tell if Vecellius was joking or not. His face was about as expressive as a marble statue. "If that is the consul's desire."

The neighborhood in which he lived was much less fashionable than his brother's. The houses were perhaps one-third the size, and they were built right next to each other. But it was a livelier place. Children were playing in the streets, and more than once a dog ran up to confront the two lines of armored men, barking madly before making a hasty retreat as the fascitors marched toward them without slowing. Corvus saw an old married couple walking slowly down the street in the opposite direction. He recognized Quintus Sabenus and his wife, who lived a few houses down from him. Risking the dignity of the Republic, he waved to them, and they waved back in a friendly manner without appearing to notice anything odd about the men accompanying him.

The two fascitors Vecellius had mentioned were indeed already standing outside the little wooden gate that marked the limits of his humble property. They looked slightly absurd in their full armor, towering over the two waist-high brick columns upon which the gate rested. But they drew themselves erect and saluted as he approached, every bit as crisply as he had ever seen their fellow fascitors do at the Forum or a Senate session.

"Thank you, Captain." Corvus nodded to Vecellius. "I trust these gentlemen will be able to defend me in case one of those dogs we passed earlier realizes that I am no longer being guarded by your full complement and takes the opportunity to attack?"

"They will, my lord consul. And now that I am off duty, my lord, may I offer my congratulations on your victory over the goblin tribes?"

"Why, thank you, Captain. You may, indeed." Corvus was surprised: For the first time that day, Vecellius actually resembled a human being more than an animated statue.

"My brother was a farmer up north," Vecellius said. "Bloody breeds killed him and his family four summers ago. I don't know if you recall, but that was when the raids got really bad. It's good to see someone has finally given them some of their own back."

Corvus nodded. "My condolences, Caius Vecellius. Perhaps it will ease your heart to know that every farmer who died in the raids was avenged ten times over. I'm afraid it won't do your brother or his family any good, but there won't be any goblin tribes raiding across the border for many years to come."

"That's good to hear indeed, my lord. I only wish I could have been there with you. Adete, consul."

"Adete, Captain."

Corvus was surprised to see no one in the house had seen him approach or had heard the squad of fascitors marching up the street. The foyer was empty, and there was no sign that there was anyone in the domus at all. A flash of irritation crossed his mind. It wasn't as if he'd expected a civic festival to mark his return to Amorr, but he didn't think it was unreasonable to anticipate at least a modicum of welcome in his own home after months of absence. Could it be that she had heard the news about Fortex and was angry with him? Or perhaps she really had taken a lover and left him. He didn't think Romilia had it in her—but then, what betrayed husband ever did?

But betrayal or no, it was simply rude to fail to receive one's lord and master, let alone consul of the whole damned republic, in this way! He'd sent her a messenger from the Forum, so she had to have been aware of his intended return tonight.

Then he heard something in the next room. Mastering his disgruntlement, he strode through the doorway, and his annoyance vanished in a flash.

There, laying on the floor in front of the fire, was his dear old friend, Marsra. The sound he'd heard was the thumping of the aged dog's tail against the floor, stirred into action by the familiar sound of his master's step. His muzzle was almost entirely white now, and his ribs showed on his age-emaciated body. His once-golden eyes had gone rheumy and blue, but the elderly dog nevertheless struggled to rise and welcome him. Corvus could feel tears spring to his eyes as he rushed to his faithful dog's side and embraced him.

"Don't rise on my account, old friend." He kneeled down, curled his dog's head under his chin, and inhaled the familiar scent of his short-haired fur, which had changed little in the fifteen years since Marsra had been a pup. The thump-thumping of the tail didn't cease for a moment as Corvus rocked back and forth, holding the dog's alarmingly thin body in his arms, delighted and surprised to discover he had survived Corvus's latest absence. He hadn't expected the dog to live so long. In fact, he hadn't even expected the poor old beast to survive the previous winter, or the winter before that.

In campaigns past, Marsra accompanied him, running easily alongside his horse even at a canter, ranging back and forth along the line as if he was one of the scouts. But age had slowed him, and for the last five years, Corvus had been forced to leave his loyal companion home with Romilia when he left with the legions.

"How very glad I am to see you, little boy! I can't tell you how much I've missed you."

"If I must come second in your affections, I am glad it is to one who loves you so very dearly."

Corvus smiled. He didn't look up at his wife. He didn't want her to see the tears that were still in his eyes. Instead, he surreptitiously wiped them on the dog's silky-soft ears as he embraced the dog one more time, then kissed him on his slender, streamlined head. "When I left this spring, I had not thought I would see him again. We said our farewells for the last time, I thought."

"He has missed you. For the first two months you were away, every time a horse rode past, his ears would perk up and he would make his way over to the door."

"Once a legionary, always a legionary." Corvus ran his hands over the dog's long ears one more time, then rose to his feet. "Where is everyone?"

Romilia was wearing her hair pulled up and back in a style that reminded him a little of a tribune's crest, and the dark kohl that lined her eyes made them look enormous and white. She was still beautiful, and in the dimming light of the setting sun, she looked barely older than the beautiful young girl he'd married. But her body was no longer slender and sylph-like. It was alluringly lush, rich with curves that pulled the white robe she was wearing deliciously tight across her breasts and hips.

"I sent them all away," she said, smiling mysteriously. Her lips were painted too, he realized. "I wished to reserve to myself, and myself alone, the privilege of being the first to serve Amorr's newest consul upon his return to the city. I have heard that it is a great honor to have a consul attend one's table."

"A very great honor indeed, I should imagine." He took her in his arms and kissed her. She kissed him back and pressed her body against his for a moment. He ran his hands over her buttocks, which were still pleasingly taut, if no longer a mere hands-width across, but when he started to slip them inside her robe, she pushed him away.

"I think not, my lord consul! Surely you must be dreadfully famished after a long day consorting with senators and knights galore! Come into the triclinium, and I will see that you are refreshed."

After many years in the field, Corvus knew an ambush when he found himself in one. He contented himself with one more kiss accompanied by a squeeze of her bottom that produced a noise that sounded suspiciously like a squeal, then obediently released her before following her into the triclinium.

There, he found a table set with flowers, fruits, a pair of goblets, and a flagon of what he presumed was wine.

She picked up the flagon, poured something red into the two goblets, then paused after she returned the flagon to the table.

"Forgive me, my love, but I really must ask. Our son is well?"

"Marcus is with his legion and in good health." Corvus stretched out upon the solitary couch and sighed at the comfortable sensation. He hadn't dined while properly reclining since Bergamum, and even there the couches had been strangely hard. "Or perhaps I should say Clericus, as the men have taken to calling him. I can't say I'm fond of it, as agnomina go. But he seems to regard it as a compliment even if it wasn't necessarily meant that way."

Romilia laughed. "He would, wouldn't he!" She offered him the goblet. "I will ask no more. Not tonight. But you will tell me everything tomorrow, do you understand?"

"I do indeed, beautiful lady." He sniffed at the wine, then tipped back the goblet and took a healthy draught. "Ah! Now that is a distinct improvement on the horrors I've been drinking!"

"It is good, isn't it?" She sipped at her own goblet and licked her lips. "It's from one of Magnus's southern estates. Julia gave me two amphorae to celebrate your consulship."

"Only two? I assume these must be the dregs, then?"

"Of course. A lonely woman gets thirsty after spending the evening being pleasured by her household slaves, one after the other after the other."

Corvus laughed as her eyes sparkled mischievously. "In that case, I'm surprised you managed to save me the one flagon."

"I was saving it for all the gladiators I was expecting tonight. Or was it the dwarven ambassadors? So many come though here in your absence, it is all but impossible to keep them straight." She leaned over him and kissed him on the mouth. Her tongue tasted of wine and honey. "Drink your wine and have some fruit. You'll like the little oranges, they're very sweet."

She walked out, throwing in an extra sashay in the correct assumption that he would be watching. Her hips were a little riper than he'd remembered, but that only made her more attractive as they accentuated the slimness of her waist. It was with some reluctance that he turned back to the table. He discovered that she was right: The little oranges were not only delicious but somehow complemented the flavor of the wine.

The thought of the wine reminded him that it had been a gift from Julia. It was clear, then, that Romilia didn't know anything about their nephew. She must not even know that Fortex was dead. He wondered if he should tell her or not. Probably, he concluded after a moment's thought, but he was loathe to break the lovely spell she was casting. Whether he told her now or in the morning, Fortex would still be dead and Magnus would still be caught up in his grief and fury. And Julia would still look like a shattered, elderly version of the woman she had once been.

That was what haunted him the most, more than the terrible images of his nephew's headless body bathed in its own blood or the contemptuous barbs that his brother had flung his way. It was the hunched, painful way his sister-in-law held herself, as if her sorrow were a cancer eating her from the inside.

No, he was not going to tell Romilia anything tonight, he concluded. If she didn't want to know more about Marcus tonight, then she certainly didn't need to hear about Fortex right away either. When she appeared a few minutes later, bearing a silver tray upon which reposed a small roasted pig wreathed in aromatic steam, he was certain he had made the right decision.

The succulent young pig tasted even better than he imagined it would. It made the beef and pork upon which he'd been subsiding throughout the campaign taste like a half-cooked saddle in comparison. He discovered that he was famished, after all, and when he finally returned the carcass to the tray for the last time, it looked as if the crows had been at it for a week or more.

He dipped his fingers into the bowl of water his wife proffered, then lay back on the coach, very nearly satiated. They had spoken of trivialities only. In fact, she had done most of the talking, bringing him up to date on the various events in the lives of their eldest son, their two daughters, and the seven grandchildren that their three older children had presented them to date. True to her word, she did not ask further questions about their youngest son. Or, thank God, their nephew.

"Is there anything more my lord consul might wish?" Romilia said, suddenly playful.

"The pork was superlative. I think some sweets might not be amiss at this point. You truly don't want to know what the goblin tribes consider dessert."

"What sort of sweets would you prefer?" she asked him, slipping her robe from her shoulders. "I trust you didn't find this sort of dessert while you were off among the goblins."

He smiled and looked over the familiar curves of her body with shameless appreciation. Her stomach was still nearly flat, with the three soft white lines that rose up from beneath her belly that marked her as a mother. And if her breasts were not as buoyant as they had once been, they still filled him with longing.

"Oh, God, I've missed you, my love," he whispered.

"Shhhh." She pressed herself against him for a moment, then pulled away, but only so she could remove his toga, which she did with a wife's practiced deftness. She ran her right hand lightly down his chest and beyond. He groaned as the delicious sensation caused him to lose all awareness of where he was, of who he was, of anything but the warmth of Romilia's touch.

But that was as nothing compared to the pleasure that seemed to swallow him up as they moved together in the wild rhythm of the sweetest dance.

"Yes, oh, yes," she murmured. "There, my love, my lord, my Corvus."

As the spasms subsided, he lay back. She crouched silently on top of him.

Then a throbbing pain in his left shoulder stirred him from his lassitude, and he looked down at her quizzically.

"Did you just bite me?"

She opened one unrepentant eye as a satisfied smile played across her lips. "Isn't that a wife's prerogative?"

Corvus laughed. She had always been as incorrigible as she was uninhibited. It was one of the things he loved about her.

"I shall have to confer with my fascitors in the morning. I fear that, in attacking my body, you have committed a very serious crime, my love. A consul, even a consul suffectus, is the city, insofar as the law as concerned."

"Mmmm, ravished by a whole city? No wonder it was so much better than the gladiators!"

Corvus burst out laughing. Romilia wrinkled her nose with delight, then tried to bite him again. This time, he managed to stop her.

For the first time in his life, Corvus found himself walking toward the Forum surrounded by a small phalanx of clients. He had been greatly startled earlier this morning when his first visitor had arrived, a young plebian senator with ambitions that belied his reputation for extreme conservatism. As more and more senators had arrived at his door, most of them men he'd recognized at once as clients of Magnus, he'd realized that, as Consul Aquilae, even Consul Suffectus, he was no longer seen as a mere adjunct to Magnus, but as a potential power in his own right.

As far as he could tell, the more radical portion of the Senate's conservative faction was looking to him for leadership they had not found in Magnus. The fact that he had none of his brother's vast wealth to bestow upon them did not appear to concern them at all, and after the first few conversations, it had quickly become apparent that it was direction, not favors, they sought from him.

His fascitors had arrived with the rising of the sun, bringing with them the news that the princeps senatus had issued an order for the Senate to meet at the Temple Fides. He had returned to the bedchamber to break the news to Romilia. She had been as proud as she'd been worried. Corvus had been neither, as he was much too busy trying to get a handle on the sudden changes in his station to be overly pleased with himself or concerned with his brother's actions.

It felt strange to be kissing her goodbye already. It felt even stranger to be wearing a clean, sweet-smelling winter wrap made of wool instead of his stained, stinking, leather-and-steel armor. But even if he had to leave his armor behind, there was nothing preventing him from strapping his sword to his side. Others might trust in the axes of the fascitors, but he preferred to rely upon his own devices.

"What do they expect of me?" he said quietly to Carvilius Maximus, an ex-consul who seemed to have appointed himself Corvus's Senatorial advisor, as they approached the sparsely populated forum. A few men, mostly ambitious knights, applauded as they saw the fascitors and realized that the new consul suffectus had come. "I could probably tell you more about the internal politics of the goblin tribes than whatever the Great Houses are sparring over now."

"It's the initial impression that matters. Everyone knows you're fresh from Gorignia and you've barely had time to wash the goblin blood off your hands. They just want to see if you're the man to stand up to Patronus, Ferratus, and the damned auctores."

"What is Patronus up to now? Magnus wrote to me about a citizenship law, but I understood there was little enthusiasm for it."

"That was before that wretch Caudinus got himself killed by the Cynothii. People are nervous. They're frightened, and you know as well as anyone that once people are sufficiently scared, they stop thinking. They'll stampede in any direction, so long as someone spurs them into action.

"Now some of the sheep are bleating about how we have to incorporate the allies into some sort of greater Amorr with the idea of using the increased manpower that will give us to keep a tighter rein on the provinces. Others are baahing about how we should simply let the provinces go, thinking it's too much effort to hold onto them and a larger state will serve as adequate compensation. And Patronus is the shepherd. He quietly goes about his business, collecting one sheep at a time, waiting until he has a large enough flock to trample the few sensible men that remain."

"And we are the sensible men, I presume?"

Maximus laughed at Corvus's skeptical tone.

"Some of us are, I hope. But even the most conservative among us are more sensible than the sheep. I honestly don't know what game Patronus is playing. He keeps pushing for extending and expanding the citizenship, as if calling a Galabrian or a Quinqueterran an Amorran is somehow magically going to transform them into proper Amorrans. He's a hard man to know and a harder one to anticipate. I was his colleague, you know."

"As consul? I didn't know that. Was he City or Provinces? I know you sat the Eagle chair. I was with Turrinus at the time."

"I remember. Gaius Mamilius was my best legate. We could use him now. As to Patronus, he was consul provincae. Do you know, I suppose he must have already started conceiving the outlandish notions he's been trying to push through the Senate around that time."

"Gone native, in a way. What's the law called again?"

"*Lex Ferrata Aucta.* Ferratus is the public sponsor, but Patronus is its true author. Do you have a speech prepared? It would be best if you make one against the law, you know. Now that you've arrived and all three consuls are present, they'll probably press for a vote today. Especially once they see that Magnus isn't here."

"Don't you have a tribune lined up to veto it?"

"Two of them. They're reliable enough when they feel confident of our support, but they're not going to do it if there isn't any serious senatorial opposition. We need you to provide a flag around which that opposition can rally. A solid showing will be enough—we don't need to win."

Corvus sighed. "You'd better go over the details with me then. Will I have the chance to hear what Patronus has to say first?"

"More or less," Maximus laughed. "Patronus won't speak. He doesn't need to. Every word that comes out of Ferratus's mouth will be coming straight from Patronus's tongue. He may as well jam his hand up Lucius Pompilius's backside for all that the puppet act convinces anyone."

Two hours later, Corvus was seated in the aquiline splendor of the Chair of Eagles, with the golden heads of the legionary eagles on the back of his throne rising above his left and right shoulders as if the birds were whispering in his ears. He felt a little self-conscious, sitting before the temple auditorium and the four hundred senators who filled it. He sat to the right of his two consular colleagues, Titus Manlius Torquatus and Marcus Fulvius Paetinus. The latter was seated imperiously on the Chair of Oxes, while the former was so relaxed that he was practically reclining between the two roaring bears heads that stood for the City.

Corvus recalled that earlier conversation with Maximus and reflected that, if the puppet act itself wasn't convincing, Ferratus certainly was. Patronus had not waited long to strike—no sooner had a celestine given the invocation and Corvus had been welcomed by the men who would be his colleagues for the next seven weeks, than one of his clients asked Marcus Fulvius for permission to request a vote on the Lex Ferrata Aucta.

It was a clever move, Corvus realized. As a Valerian and the presumed voice of Magnus, everyone assumed he would be opposed to the new law, as was in fact the case. Of his two fellow consuls, Torquatus was known to harbor some sympathies toward the more traditional factions, even if he wasn't directly involved with any of them, and he would have almost surely suppressed an immediate vote in deference to his new colleague.

But Paetinus possessed little in the way of either principles or brains, and since the proposed law concerned neither the city nor the legions directly, it was one of the few that fell under the jurisdiction of the consul provincae. Unsurprisingly, and as Patronus no doubt anticipated, the pompous little man didn't hesitate to leap at the chance to assert himself. His chest swelled nearly to bursting as he rose from the Ox Throne and looked around the temple chamber before addressing the assembled Senate.

"City fathers," Paetinus said, "the allies of Amorr are among the weightiest responsibilities borne by the members of this august body. Like a father to his children, it is our duty to guide them, to guard them, and if necessary, to chastise them. For four hundred years we have done so, often at great cost in both gold and blood to the Senate and People. But it is a price we have paid willingly, for never has this body or the republic shirked its solemn duty."

The little man raised his chin, waiting for applause that Patronus and his faction were all too willing to provide. Nodding happily, Paetinus continued.

"Now Lucius Pompilius Ferratus suggests that the children of the republic have grown into manhood and are prepared to take their place at our side, with all the rights and responsibilities that entails. He has proposed a law that would expand the borders of this noble republic and grant full Amorran citizenship to the people of the allied cities.

"As consul provincae, I hereby recognize the proposed Lex Ferrata Aucta and ask you, city fathers, to debate the merits and demerits of the proposed law prior to a vote that will take place after the tenth bell sounds. And because it might be deemed improper by some were I to speak on behalf of a proposal that would add so greatly to the influence of my position, or against a proposal that would vastly increase its responsibilities, I shall recuse myself from the discussion and ask Lucius Pompilius, as the law's sponsor, to speak on its behalf."

It was rather a pity that Paetinus hadn't spoken on behalf of the enlargement of the republic, Corvus mused while listening to Ferratus gracefully weave his way through the compliments paid to the Senate that were obligatory for those members seeking to win its favor. Hearing him bumble his way through that argument might well have aided the conservative cause.

The fool saw nothing but the prospect of his own enlargement now that the end of his consular year was approaching, without realizing that provinces that were no longer provinces had no need of an ex-consul to oversee their interests. It seemed that, in politics as well as in battle, men tended to think primarily about the consequences they intended, never stopping to consider the unintended ones.

Ferratus, on the other hand, was so convincing that even a war-hardened cynic found it hard to not be swept up in his grand vision of a Greater Amorr. He made use of Paetinus's analogy about parents and children so deftly that Corvus assumed Ferratus must have fed it to the consul beforehand, pointing out that the increased Amorran reliance upon food, taxes, and even men for the legions from the provinces could be seen as evidence that the erstwhile children were not only capable of standing on their own and supporting themselves, but supporting their revered parent too.

He appealed to their civic pride, to their self-perceptions, and, without being too obvious about it, to their desire for power. More citizens would mean more clients for even the least important senators, and the laws they passed would now reach much farther to the north, the east, and the west. Ever so delicately, Ferratus played upon fears that the senators did not even realize they possessed. He never articulated any concrete threat, but it was there all the same, implicit in his honeyed words. Amorr was outnumbered by its allies and its provinces alike. If the Senate and People did not bind one or the other to them by ties that could not be broken, they would one day find themselves facing the combined might of both, and on that day Amorr would fall.

Amorr had waxed by defeating its rivals and its enemies one after the other, and it would wane rapidly if it was ever forced to fight them in combination. So it must not make the mistake, he said, of allowing them to be unified by their mutual self-identification as outsiders and the rejects of the Republic.

And then he painted a vision of the glorious future for them, a new Golden Age that would never cease to hail the wisdom of the Senate in this, the year of the four consuls, in the year of Torquatus, Paetinus, and Caudinus-Corvus, when Amorr ceased to be a solitary city and was transformed into the most powerful, most numerous nation of Man in all of history. Ferratus spoke of increased trade, of new ports to the east and west, and of legions that would be numbered in the dozens. He all but promised them that they would become as gods, regarded with envy, fear, and awe by the diverse peoples and races of the world.

It was transparent, but the Senate ate it up like pigs at a trough. Corvus could see that radicals and traditionalists alike were enthralled by the spell that had been cast upon them by this tall, eagle-eyed orator who could not only see into the shining future, but help them to see it too.

Were he not seated at the fore of the grand assembly, Corvus would have curled his lip. For, judging by the reaction of the senators, it seemed as if he alone could see through Lucius Pompilius's feeble web of words. They were fine words, to be sure, but that was all they were. And yet, at every lengthy pause, there was applause or shouts of approbation. He looked over at Patronus, where the man was sitting in the middle of his coterie of radicals, looking for all the world like an ascetic monk.

The most powerful man in Amorr's eyes met his, and they were like black diamonds, dispassionate and harder than stone. Patronus showed no sign of satisfaction or even interest in his puppet's preposterous rhetoric. He merely sat and stared at Corvus without blinking.

After decades in the legions, Corvus recognized a killer when he saw one. This was the sort of man who killed quietly in the dark of night, without malice, without hesitation, and most of all, without remorse. He had known of Patronus for many years, had even seen him on several occasions, but never before had he ever felt even the slightest need to pay the man any serious attention. Now he felt a sudden surge of respect for his brother, who had confronted that dark, intimidating stare time after time, never backing down and never giving in no matter how many times he was defeated on this strangest of battlefields.

And yet, seeing his enemy face to face gave Corvus that strange sense of calm that always filled him once he was able to lay eyes upon the actual dispositions of the forces opposing him, when it was too late for more plans or stratagems and all that was left to do was watch and wait for the decisive moment to appear. He had been nervous before, but now he felt almost unnaturally relaxed. Laws and debates and politics might be new to him, but if there was one thing he knew and understood, it was a battlefield.

He smiled.

Patronus, whether he was taken aback by this or his eyes were simply dry, blinked. It was probably nothing, a trivial coincidence, but Corvus decided that he would take it as a sign of weakness and a good omen.

In the meantime, Ferratus concluded with a succinct and memorable slogan that would probably be on the lips of a dozen poets by nightfall. The Senate erupted with enthusiastic applause that echoed throughout the temple, and Corvus imagined that Patronus would have given much for the opportunity to end the debate and see the matter voted upon at once.

"I thank Lucius Pompilius for his most excellent explication of the proposed law," Paetinus said, beaming as if Ferratus's rhetorical triumph somehow reflected well on him. "As consul provincae, I will not be speaking on this matter, and therefore I shall ask my colleagues if they wish to avail themselves of the opportunity to advise this body."

Torquatus, as Corvus knew was his custom, merely lifted his hand to decline. His colleague believed it was beneath the dignity of the presiding consuls to enter directly into the debates, but preferred instead to work behind the scenes while studiously maintaining a loftily objective front when the Senate was in actual session.

"Then perhaps the Consul Aquilae Suffectus will rise?" Paetinus placed ever so faint a stress on the "Suffectus," and from the challenging glint in his eyes, Corvus knew his fellow consul assumed he would follow Torquatus's lead.

Corvus cleared his throat, glanced across the chamber toward Patronus, and smiled again.

"Do you know, Marcus Fulvius, I rather think I will." He didn't wait for Paetinus to respond but rose to his feet and spread his hands before addressing his fellow senators. He took a deep breath and tried to imagine that he was addressing not the great and powerful men of the city but merely a legionary cohort as he had done so many times before.

"If, city fathers, I give you thanks in a very inadequate manner for the regard you have shown to me, and to my brother, and to my House, I entreat you not to attribute it so much to any coldness of my heart, as to the magnitude of the honor which you have done me. I am no orator, neither am I a politician. I am merely a common soldier. And even if I were trained in the rhetorical arts, what eloquence could be so great, what clever turn of language could do justice to the sobering responsibility you have entrusted to me?

"Wherefore, since your authority has summoned me—since the Senate has recalled me to the city I have always loved and served to the full extent of my ability—I will take care never to lose my virtue and loyal attachment to you, who are the conscience, and the voice, and the guiding genius of this great republic and its People."

There was a little polite applause for the uncontroversial sentiments expressed, but it was readily apparent that, although it was his virgin speech, there was little appetite for the usual cliches and conventions in light of the more weighty matters to be discussed.

"It is in accordance with the customs and established usages of our ancestors, that those who, by your will or by the election of the People, have been seated before you, should, the first time an assembly of the Senate is held, take an opportunity of providing a panegyric on their ancestors in order to demonstrate that they are worthy of the rank they now bear. I, however, have no intention of speaking before you of my House, not because they were not such men as you see me also to be, born of their blood, and educated in their principles, but because, as it is rightly said of we Valerians, our House is Amorr.

"However brief my term as consul suffectus shall be, however short the time in which the weight of this responsibility shall be placed upon my shoulders, I will sit before you as a man whose sole concern is for the

Senate and for the People of Amorr. Patricians and plebians alike, your ancestors shall be my ancestors, and you shall all be my House."

There was a little more applause for this, even from the auctores camp. Patronus continued to stare at him, though, like a man with a stick waiting for a snake to strike.

"Not only have you made me consul, though that is of itself a most honorable thing, but you have made me so in such a way as very few men in this city have ever been made consuls before. And though I lament the death of the noble Lucius Andronicus Caudinus that made my appointment possible, a sorrow which I am well aware you all share, I am greatly sensible of the honor that has been shown to me. I think of this eminent and unexpected kindness of yours, O city fathers, as a reward for my courage, and as a source of joy to me, but still more calculated to impress me with care and anxiety. For many and grave thoughts have occupied my mind since the letter arrived in the legionary camp informing me of your desire that I appear before you.

"First, there is anxiety about discharging the duties of the consulship, which is a difficult and important business to all men. Second, there are the strategic concerns about the present military crisis, which as consul aquilae, falls directly to me. And third, there is the weighty matter at hand, concerning which Pompilius Ferratus has spoken with great skill and passion. Now, as I have already said, I am but a soldier. I cannot expect to convince you, city fathers, with any soaring feats of rhetoric, for such things are well beyond my capabilities. Nor can I hope to set your imaginations on fire as Ferratus has done, for I am speaking of the world as it is rather than the world as I would wish it to be."

He saw Patronus lean forward at this. And the Severan was not the only one, for if the assembled senators had listened to one speech, they had listened to a thousand, and they very well knew when a speaker had finished with his prelude and was approaching the salient point.

Corvus smiled. How very like battle this truly was, even down to that vital moment when one side made the vital decision to stand and fight or break and run. But he was a Valerius, and in four hundred years of making war, House Valerius had never run.

"You will indulge and forgive me, city fathers, if I draw upon my experiences as a soldier. War has been my teacher for many years, and the lessons it teaches its students are hard ones not easily forgotten, for they are written not with pen and ink, but in bone and blood. The law that Pompilius Ferratus has proposed, this Lex Ferrata Aucta, brings to mind the construction of something familiar to many senators in this assembly, which is the plan of battle.

"When constructing his plan of battle, the wise general must take into consideration many things, some of which he knows, and some of which he does not. He knows how many troops he has, but he does not know how many troops the enemy possesses. He knows the strengths and weaknesses of his officers, but he cannot know the weather on the day of battle. If he is lucky, perhaps he can choose his ground, but even the most carefully prepared field may still present surprises once the battle is joined.

"City fathers, once more I call to your attention the memory of my predecessor in this office: Lucius Andronicus Caudinus. Caudinus was a veteran of many wars. He was neither inexperienced nor foolhardy. He suppressed no fewer than four provincial rebellions before he was charged by this body to march his legion into Cynothicum.

"I cannot say that I know what his plan was, but I am certain he had one, and I am convinced it was the sort of plan that any experienced commander would prepare prior to going to meet the foe. We can be certain that Caudinus would not have given battle had he not been confident of victory. Indeed, who among us harbored any doubts that Caudinus would return from the north wearing the victor's laurel?"

At this, there was a good deal of murmuring throughout the temple. Even Torquatus was sitting up and paying attention now. There were enough generals, past and present, in the audience that the talk of battle stirred their interest.

"And yet, he failed. Despite all his plans, all his experience, all his good intentions, and all his confidence in his legion, it is clear that he did not foresee some vital factor. So it was that he met with consequences that were very far from his intentions. So it was that he perished, and his legion with him."

An unsettled air filled the Senate, and many of the senators murmured to one other. But Corvus couldn't tell if it they were sharing their agreement with his words or their resentment of them. He might, he began to realize, have made a mistake by choosing as an example a defeat that could be laid at the Senate's feet as its chosen general now lay buried in the cold northern ground of Cynothicum. The Senate did not deny it made mistakes, on occasion, but neither did it enjoy being reminded of them. But there was nothing for it now except to carry on. He would have to hope there were still enough men who valued reason more than rhetoric.

"Like every general, I have known sleepless nights, wondering if I had anticipated everything correctly, if the scouts' reports were accurate, if the estimates they provided me were trustworthy. Not two weeks ago, I stood with my command staff and watched the young men of Legio XVII stand its ground against an army four times its number, an army consisting of two of the fiercest and most warlike goblin tribes ever known to Man, tribes that have ravaged our northwestern borders for decades.

"Some attribute our subsequent victory to the favor of the Most High God. Others attribute it to the military genius of the commander, but I can tell you with certainty that the main reason Legio XVII defeated the united Vakhuyu and Chalonu tribes was the skill and fortitude of two legionary scouts. They spotted the enemy, noted his location, counted his numbers, and defeated an enemy patrol before returning to the legion. Despite being wounded in the process, they provided their general with the precious information he required to lay the foundation for the legion's victory.

"I ask you this: What scouts does Ferratus offer as he asks you to embark on this march into unknown lands? What preparations has he made against the many dangers to the Republic that lay hidden within his proposal, waiting only the inopportune moment to rise and imperil us?

There is nothing, I tell you. He is asking you to walk over a perilous abyss upon a bridge built from nothing but dreams and air!

"Ferratus tells you that the people of the allied cities deserve citizenship. I answer that not one in five thousand has ever served in the legions or served Amorr in any way! Ferratus says the allies have fought loyally for the Republic in her legions. I remind you that, like every legionary under my command, they have fought for gold and land, and they have duly received their just rewards.

"Ferratus tells you that the allies will be grateful. I answer that their children and their children's children will astound your descendants with their ingratitude! Ferratus tells you that Amorr will be enriched by new taxes. I remind you that the allies are already taxed more heavily than the citizenry. And, under the new law, they would be given a voice in their own taxation! Ferratus speaks of a city that will become more than a city, but I warn you of a republic that will no longer be a nation and an empire that will shatter and fall!"

The murmuring of his audience swelled into outright arguing, and the group of men surrounding Patronus no more radiated an air of casual certainty. The great man himself was still expressionless, but Corvus fancied he could see concern hidden behind his apparent nonchalance.

Now was the moment to strike, and strike hard. He could feel it in his bones as clearly as ever he had felt the decisive moment on the battlefield.

"City fathers, as a general, I dare place no trust in a scout who cannot tell me the enemy's numbers or his whereabouts but instead flatters me with the great glory that is sure to come on the morrow when the enemy lies broken and defeated. As a man, I do not buy a piece of property when my agent cannot tell me where it is but only assures me that I shall be the envy of all my neighbors. As an Amorran, I cannot trust a proposal that leaves a thousand questions unanswered but promises me that I shall be admired by posterity.

"And as a Senator—no, I forget myself, as a Consul of the Senate and People of the Sacred Republic of Amorr—I cannot vote for a law that will bring about one hundred unintended consequences for every one that is correctly foreseen.

"You cannot turn a new recruit into a veteran centurion by simply calling him one. You cannot turn an orc into an elf, or a goblin into a dwarf. And not even this august body can transform a Malkanian, a Bithnyan, a Galabrian, or even a Vallyrian into an Amorran by simple decree. We are Amorrans by blood, by tradition, by history, and most of all, by the grace and favor of the Most Holy and Immaculate God.

"And so now I plead with you, I implore you, and I advise you to set your faces against the Lex Ferrata Aucta. This law will not enlarge Amorr but diminish it, perhaps even extinguish it altogether. For twenty years, I have defended the Senate and People against her foes on every side, but I cannot defend this noble assembly against itself. City fathers, instead of my military command, instead of my legions, instead of this consulship and the other badges of honor you have so kindly granted me in reward for my many victories won on your behalf and in your name, I ask nothing of you except that you exercise wisdom and diligence in preserving this sacred republic which you hold so very dear!"

Corvus stepped back and sat again upon the red leather of the consul's chair.

The Senate erupted again. This time, however, it was not the rapturous explosion of enthusiasm that had greeted Pompilius Ferratus's address, but the rancorous sound of a hundred arguments breaking out. It was hard to tell, but judging by Maximus's broad smile, his virgin speech as consul appeared to have accomplished its purpose. Here and there, senators were applauding. But more importantly, he saw that Severus Patronus had risen to his feet and was stalking angrily out of the temple, followed by three or four of his acolytes. He left Ferratus still seated behind him, looking pale and bewildered.

"The princeps is highly displeased, I think," said Torquatus, leaning toward Corvus. "Until you opened your mouth, he knew he had the vote sewn up. Now Ferratus won't even get three hundred. You'd better make sure you have an escort home this evening. Don't linger around the Forum."

"He's that desperate?" Corvus grinned, unconcerned. If the Severan wanted him dead, he'd have to get in line behind one Marcus Valerius Magnus. And it was a little much to expect a soldier newly come from the battlefield to worry about being attacked by a few unarmored street thugs. "Why is this law so important to him?"

"I have no idea," his consular colleague answered. "Vanity, perhaps. He's getting old, and I imagine his desire to leave his mark is growing stronger as his days grow shorter. But he's been spreading the gold around pretty thickly over the last month or two, so he's definitely not going to appreciate you interfering with his plans, whatever they might be."

Corvus mused on Torquatus's words as their other colleague called the senators to speak to the assembly, one-by-one, in the order of their rank. Since the princeps senatus had abandoned the assembly, Marcus Fulvius began to call upon the ex-consuls, followed by the praetors and ex-praetors. A few of the pro-law party attempted to chip away at some of the points Corvus had made. Others, even more ineffectually, tried to revive the glorious vision painted by Ferratus, but their lack of his rhetorical gifts only rendered their efforts all the more grotesque.

And for every senator who rose to speak in favor of Lex Ferrata Aucta, three more stood to speak against it. Some of them simply underlined Corvus's points. Others raised a panoply of new questions and objections, which soon served to make it clear to all and sundry that there were a myriad of details that would have to be addressed before the law, even if passed, could reasonably be implemented by the magistrates.

How would the new citizens be ruled? Would they have their own senates, or would they elect senators to the Senate itself? How many senators would they be permitted? What would happen to their kings and other rulers? Should they all be classified as plebians, or would it be necessary to introduce a new class to distinguish between the original Houses, those who came later, and those who were granted citizenship via the proposed law? The more it was considered, the more it became clear to all and sundry that the Lex Ferrata Aucta was a treacherous and twisted skein indeed.

In the end, it became apparent to everyone, even Fulvius Paetinus, that there would be no need for a vote. Based on those who had spoken out and the general demeanor of those who had not, Corvus estimated that Severus Patronus still held the loyalties of perhaps one-third of the senators, but most of them were either too stunned or too demoralized by the unexpected turn of events to do much more than mouth a few vague platitudes in support of the proposed law. Finally, no one rose to speak. The Senate appeared to have exhausted itself, and silence filled the vast chamber. Fulvius Paetinus glanced over toward Torquatus. Torquatus, in turn, looked to Corvus, who shrugged. When Torquatus nodded, Paetinus wearily pushed himself up from his throne and cleared his voice.

"City fathers, the wisdom of your advice concerning the proposed Lex Ferrata Aucta has been received by your consuls in the spirit it was given. It is in our considered opinion that the tide of this august body is against the measure, and unless Pompilius Ferratus, its sponsor, objects, we shall not hold a vote upon it but shall deem the matter closed. Do you object, Pompilius Ferratus?"

Ferratus was sitting in near isolation, in stark contrast to his position earlier in the day. His face was ashen, and Corvus wondered if it should be Ferratus, not him, who would be in need of an escort tonight. But his voice was clear and strong as he replied to the consul provincae.

"I have no objection, my Lord Consul. I should like to thank the consuls and the members of this Senate for the time they have devoted to contemplating my proposal."

It was well said, Corvus had to admit, especially in light of Patronus's churlish departure. Ferratus would bear watching in the future, indeed, it might be very interesting to learn if the eloquent man had any ideas of his own, or if he was willing to play puppet for other hands than those belonging to House Severus. To win him over to the traditionalists would be very useful indeed. Corvus laughed silently at himself as the celestine who had opened the session now closed it with the traditional benediction. Politics must be dreadfully infectious if he was catching the disease already.

And now it was the turn of the consul aquilae to address the business of the legions. Fortunately that was a simple matter, and moreover, one that greatly pleased him to lay before the Senate. Corvus cleared his throat, rose from the Eagle throne, and smiled.

"City fathers, before we conclude the business of this assembly, I would ask your indulgence in a military matter. One that is dear to my heart. Since, as consul, I can no longer serve as stragister militum for the northern campaign, it is necessary for the Senate and People to name my replacement as the general responsible for the three legions presently operating in Cynothicum and the goblinlands.

"And it gives me great satisfaction to propose to you now the name of Marcus Saturnius, the legate of Legio XVII, the general who defeated the united Vakhuyu and Chalonu tribes with an untested, unblooded legion that he himself trained, and a worthy man in whom I have the utmost confidence…"

As senators began to file out of the temple, Corvus found himself surrounded by twenty or more senators. Maximus was at their fore, congratulating him as if he'd won the field of battle. As, perhaps, he had.

"You were magnificent, Sextus Valerius!" The ex-consul beamed with delight. "I declare, the first thing I found myself thinking when you finished and Patronus was slinking out of the session with his naked rat tail between his legs was that we'd given the name Magnus to the wrong brother!"

"You do me too much credit, Senator." Corvus shook his head and laughed. "One hardly needs a silver tongue to tear down a bad idea. Ferratus had the much harder task, and I don't mind telling you that I despaired when he was rattling on about the Golden Age of Greater

Amorr. He damn near had me convinced until he stopped speaking and the spell wore off."

The senators roared with laughter, half-drunk with their unexpected success, and more than half-drunk upon the wine they had been imbibing throughout the course of the long day. Corvus could feel a sense of the familiar camaraderie he normally felt only when surrounded by his staff officers.

For the first time, he began to feel that winning political battles was no more mysterious, and no more difficult, than winning military ones. It wouldn't be easy, of course, as he would make mistakes, and Severus Patronus promised to be a more cunning and experienced opponent than any general he had faced in the field. Corvus had taken the man by surprise today, but judging from the sight of that cold, calculating stare, he would never turn his flanks so easily again.

"My lords, my friends," Corvus said, "I have been told that there are certain parties who may be displeased with me as a result of their disappointments today. So much so, in fact, that they may even be willing to offer me violence despite my imperium. Therefore, I should like to invite you all to dine at my home this evening, if you would be so kind as to escort me there."

To a man, the senators accepted his invitation with lusty enthusiasm. Even as they did so, the thought that he might have just made a terrible mistake suddenly occurred to Corvus. While Patronus could afford to buy the best assassins money could purchase in Amorr, any would-be killers would have to deal with his bodyguard first. And Corvus very much doubted that the twelve guards, or even an entire century of them, would suffice to save him from the wrath of Romilia were he to appear unannounced with twenty senatorial guests for dinner in tow. In such an event, he imagined, it was very likely that the Church archives would record his consular reign as the shortest on record.

As the senators continued to joke amongst themselves and mock the more absurd arguments their opponents had made, Corvus frantically waved to one of the younger senators who lived only two streets away from him. "Quintus Curius, as you value your life, I implore you to run—run, mark you, not walk—to my house ahead of me and tell my wife to prepare a dinner for twenty, no, thirty."

The younger man, his curly hair still unflecked by grey, grinned at him. "Ave, my lord consul." He departed with alacrity, if not quite as urgently as Corvus would have liked.

Maximus, having overheard the exchange, put his meaty arm around Corvus. "It's hard to come home and find yourself demoted to tribune, is it?"

"It's not that," Corvus replied with a grin. "I was only thinking that if my wife happens to have an encore of last night's, ah, banquet in mind, she will be dreadfully annoyed if I show up for dinner with thirty of my new best friends."

MARCUS

AFTER handing over the captive he'd taken on the road to Cynothicum to a pair of guards and giving them strict orders to keep
him bound, Marcus led his horse to the night grooms and
staggered off in search of his tent. He made his way through the quiet
camp without a torch. There was enough moonlight to see by, and since
the camp was laid out in the exact same fashion as every other legionary
camp, he probably could have done so in pitch darkness. His tent was
the fourth in the row, and he fumbled at his belt as he pushed through
the untied entrance, trying not to make too much noise in order to avoid
waking Gaius Marcius or anyone in the nearby tents.

But he wasn't the only one making noise. He heard a grunt of exertion,
followed by a gasp that was accompanied by a thrashing sound. For a
moment, he thought Gaius Marcius had somehow smuggled a woman
into their tent, until he heard the telltale sound of creaking leather and
caught the acrid scent of a male body that hadn't seen the baths in too
many days. Something was very, very wrong here.

Suddenly wide awake, he drew his gladius and stepped to the right
even as a shadowy mass crashed into the empty canvas cot upon which
he normally slept. He felt something hit his midsection and heard the
scraping sound of metal on metal, but his steel breastplate protected him
from harm.

Without thinking, he turned and thrust his sword hard in the direction of his attacker and felt it punch through leather armor and into the
flesh beneath it.

There was a cry of pain, which quickly subsided as the leather-armored man he'd just wounded stumbled over the now-collapsed cot and scrambled on his hands and knees out through the tent flaps. Marcus leaped over the cot and slashed at the fleeing man, but this time he met only air.

He started to sprint after the man then realized that, with a torch, he could simply follow the trail of blood to where the man, presumably another spy or an assassin, was sleeping. Then it occurred to him that his attacker had been occupied with Gaius Marcius when he entered, and he spun around and ran back to the tent.

"Gaius, wake up," he called softly as he laid his sword down amidst the wreckage of his cot. But there was no response, and when he reached out to shake his tentmate's shoulders, he could feel something warm, sticky, and wet under his left hand. His heart sank, and he forced himself to confirm what he had already guessed.

He shuddered at the feel of the terrible wound under his fingers. The assassin had slashed his fellow tribune's throat. Marcus took a deep breath and forced his imagination to set aside the vision it had conjured of what would almost surely have happened to himself too if Marcus Saturnius had not sent him out to catch the spy tonight.

He reached down to collect his sword then ran outside to raise the alarm. He resisted the urge to shout out and wake everyone. Rousing the camp would only ensure the killer was not found. A dreadful thought occurred to him. If the killer was truly an assassin, then surely the legate would be a more desirable target than his subordinate officers. He ran toward the nearest gate, where the guards would be stationed. He was just about to shout out to them when he stopped.

You're reacting—not thinking. Stop and think about what you know before you walk right into another trap.

He reviewed the facts. Unless the assassin he'd just stabbed in his tent was also the spy, there must be more than one traitor active within the legion. Of course there was more than one. He already knew that, due to Lucius Orissis's disappearance. That message had been focused on Saturnius, and since the assassin was targeting tribunes, there was a good chance Saturnius was already dead. There was only one reason he could imagine for simultaneously killing the legate and the other officers of the legion.

Someone was trying to take control of the entire legion!

Marcus looked over at the torches that indicated the Praetorian gate through which he'd ridden not long before. If the goal was to take control of the legion, the guards on duty there, or at least the guard commander, were almost certainly involved in the plot. Running to them could very likely end in his capture or death. Or, quite possibly, both, the one following the other.

How could this be happening? His mind reeled. It occurred to him that there was always the chance that the assassin had started with the softer targets first. The legate always had at least a pair of guards stationed outside his tent. If there was only one assassin, he would be in no shape to attack the guards after being stabbed in the side or in the guts.

Marcus ran his finger down his gladius. The blood on the blade extended down from the tip for more than a hand's length. Probably not a killing wound—he hadn't driven it deep enough into the man for that. But it was more than a mere scratch and was probably enough to prevent the man from any further assassinations tonight.

He didn't dare walk openly down the Via Praetoria toward the Forum. Even if Saturnius and the other tribunes hadn't been attacked, being discovered with a bloody sword in hand could easily lead to his being blamed for Marcius's murder. He glanced up at the moon and was glad he was still wearing his riding cloak. It was dark red and would cover any untimely gleams from his armor. After quickly crossing the wide street, he flipped up the hood to cover his head and obscure his face, then wiped his sword clean on the edge of his cloak and returned it to its scabbard.

Moving as quietly as the metal and leather of his armor would permit, he made his way through the sea of leather tents that belonged to the first and second cohorts. Once, he tripped over a rope and landed hard on his stomach. He lay there on his stomach, motionless, but no one stirred in the tents on either side of him. He counted to twenty, then started at the sound of a horse whinnying in the stables far in front of him. Relax, he told himself as his heartbeat echoed loudly in his ears. Be calm!

Carefully, stealthily, he pushed himself to his feet and made his way more cautiously past the rows of tents that stood between him and Marcus Saturnius's quarters. It was at the northern end of the Via Principalis, facing the stables, and it lay past the legionary standards, the altar, and the great headquarters tent in which staff meetings were held. He didn't dare approach it from behind, so he decided to stay hidden among the tents on the other side of the north-south street bisecting the camp to see if the guards were still posted outside the legate's tent.

As he crept past the last tent on the corner, hiding in the shadow it cast in the moonlight, he could hear the sound of voices speaking softly in front of him. He lowered himself to his belly and crawled to the very edge of the road, where the grass around the tents met the hard-packed dirt of the Via Principalis. He couldn't make out any words, but he could see two figures standing in front of the tent. It was their voices he had heard talking. Their presence there meant the legate must be safe. He closed his eyes and exhaled with relief, feeling suddenly weak with the release of the near-panic that had held him in its grip since he'd entered his tent.

Still, he had to wake Saturnius and let him know that an assassin was loose in the camp. Marcus started to push himself up again but froze. Something wasn't right. He wasn't sure what it was, but he had the distinct feeling that there was something wrong about the guards.

He couldn't see more than their silhouettes, one taller and broader than the other. The taller guard was wearing a helmet… and the other was not! That was what had bothered him. What guard would stand duty without a helmet?

Then he felt foolish. The taller man turned his head and Marcus could see from the unmistakable shape of the silhouette that it was a centurion's helm. That guard said something to the shorter man, clapped him on the shoulder, then strode toward where Marcus was lying hidden in the darkness.

As he came closer, he moved from shadow into moonlight, and Marcus saw the strong-jawed profile of the primus pilus, Junius Honoratus. As the officer responsible for the first two centuries of the first cohort, his tent would be on the same row as the tent beside which Marcus was lying, but on the other end, just inside the brick walls of the castra.

Marcus was tempted to stand up and call out to Honoratus, but he decided not to. The centurion was a hard and unfriendly man, and he'd never appeared to think much of Marcus. Marcus didn't relish the thought of trying to explain to the man why he had been creeping around the tents of the infantry cohorts, and he doubted he would receive any benefit of the doubt from the battle-scarred centurion.

The primus pilus was carrying something in his hand. Just as he disappeared from view behind the tent to Marcus's left, Marcus saw that it was a gladius. But even in the moonlight, it did not gleam. It was covered with a dark substance that Marcus realized was almost surely blood. Whose blood? Surely not that of the legate! But where were the guards? Marcus looked back at the front of the tent where the other man, the shorter man, had been standing, but he had disappeared. Had he reentered the tent or had he walked toward the tents of the third and fourth cohorts?

He hesitated, trying to decide if he dared to run across the street and enter the tent. But while he was still debating the risks, he saw the shadow of the second man, the shorter man, emerging from the tent. He was breathing hard. Marcus could hear the man puffing and saw him wipe his brow. Then the silhouette bent forward and disappeared from view. But Marcus heard him grunt and heard a scraping sound that continued until the tent flap rustled as it opened briefly before falling closed again. With the closing of the tent flap, the scraping stopped.

Now Marcus had a very good idea where the missing guards were. They had been lying dead at their post outside the general's tent, murdered by their own senior centurion! And the nonchalant manner in which Honoratus's companion was dragging them into the tent meant that Marcus Saturnius must be dead, as well. His heart sank. He was too late.

Now what? He was too tired and frightened to be angry yet at the murder of a man he had known since he was a boy, a man whom he greatly respected. He had to get out of there now. But where could he run? To whom could he turn? He couldn't stay where he was until morning, and for all he knew, one or more of the centurions of the second cohort might even be in on the murderous plot. If the senior centurion of the first cohort was involved, almost anyone else in the legion might be as well.

He could rouse the camp, but doing so in the middle of the night would serve no purpose because the traitors were awake and would be in better position to take advantage of the confusion than anyone else, including him.

A chilling thought struck him: If Saturnius were dead and none of the other tribunes were alive, responsibility for the legion would fall to him.

But while he was certain that all of Legio XVII's fifty-nine centurions couldn't be involved, he had no way of knowing who was, and who was not, loyal to House Valerius.

The decurions!

While the knights were considered to be elite by those outside the legion, within it they were always second-class citizens. It was the infantry that mattered. For one thing, the horse was outnumbered twenty to one by the foot in most legions, and for another, they were considered little more than a small adjunct force, like the artillery and missileers.

While he doubted Proculus would have thrown in with the traitors, he wasn't willing to bet his life on it. He was much more confident that Honoratus and the other leaders of the plot wouldn't have thought it necessary to involve any of the decurions, and he found it impossible to imagine that Julianus, at whose side he had now fought on three occasions, would ever willingly raise a sword against another man of the legion, much less Marcus Saturnius, a man he openly admired.

Marcus didn't dare walk down the broad road to the forum, so he began to make his way toward the other side of the camp through the tents of the second cohort. He knew Julianus shared a tent with three other decurions next to the stables in which the horses of the Second Knights were kept, so he cautiously rose to his feet and began stalking back through the tents the way he'd come before.

He maintained a low profile and stalked cautiously past the rows of canvas that concealed hundreds of sleeping men, listening hard for any sounds that might indicate the conspirators were still active. He had to assume that he hadn't wounded the assassin badly enough to kill him, although it was possible that the blade had punctured a vital organ. It all depended upon where he had struck the man, but it was safe to assume the assassin had survived long enough to warn the others.

Even now, there might be one or more men hunting him throughout the camp. That thought was enough to prevent him from hurrying as he slowly moved through the slumbering camp like an exhausted angel of death.

Finally, as the pungent smell of horses filled his nostrils, he reached the final row of tents. Knowing he was taking his life into his hands, he slashed through the cord tying the entrance closed and slipped inside, being sure to close the tent flaps behind him in case anyone might pass by while he was inside.

It was too dark to see anything distinctly. One of the sleeping men was snoring softly. He wished he had some idea which of the four sleepers was Julianus, but then, he was going to have to convince all four of them in any event.

"Julianus," he whispered softly. "Julianus, wake up. It's Valerius Clericus." The man on his left mumbled something incoherent, but none of the men woke. "Julianus!" he repeated a little louder. "Julianus, it's urgent. Wake up! We have to speak, now!"

He could hear the man on his right finally begin to stir. "Clericus, is that you? What the hell are you doing in here, lad? Or sorry: 'sir.' We're not under attack, are we?"

"Shhhhh, lower your voice," Marcus urged him. "Assassins in the camp. One attacked Gaius Marcius as he slept. He's dead. I think the legate is probably dead too. I saw them dragging off the bodies of the two men posted as his guards."

The cot creaked as Julianus rolled off it and came closer to Marcus. "The general is dead? Are you certain?"

"I'm not certain of anything, except that Marcius and the two guards posted outside the general's tent are dead. The assassin tried to stab me too, but the dagger didn't get through my armor and I managed to stick him in the side before he ran. Not enough to kill him, though, and he got away."

"Dammit," the decurion cursed. "But you did well to scratch him. We shouldn't have much trouble finding him tomorrow unless they sneak him out of the camp tonight. There aren't many wounded in the infirmary. You said the general's guards are dead?"

"It was the primus pilus. I saw the blood on his blade."

"Gnaeus Junius? Hell's poxied whores, Clericus, you think Honoratus killed Marcus Saturnius? Are you absolutely sure it was him?"

"I was almost close enough to stab him myself. I know it was him. But I don't know for certain if Saturnius is dead. I think he is, because whoever was with Honoratus, a shorter man I didn't recognize, was dragging the dead guards inside the tent."

"Sounds like he's done for. But why? Why would they kill the legate?"

"I wasn't in the camp earlier tonight, so I don't know what Marcus Saturnius did to alert them, but he must not have suspected Honoratus's involvement in whatever was happening. I didn't, so why would Saturnius? Honoratus must have been ready to act on short notice, but he didn't know the general had sent me to intercept any messengers riding to the other legion."

"The other legion? What other legion?" Julianus sounded incredulous.

"The Severan one. It's in Cynothicum."

"There's a Severan legion already here? Which one?"

"Fulgetra. I talked to a merchant at the baths in Gallidromum, and he described their sigil to me. I don't know what the Severans are doing there, but I'm sure it's not for our benefit or the City's. I've been thinking about it, and the only thing I can imagine is that the Severans intend to kill all the officers and take control of the legion. The men aren't political, so with the officers dead, they'll probably do what they're told. Even the men from Vallyrium."

"Yes, especially if whoever is behind this is clever enough to keep the politics out of it. They must have been planning this since the legion was formed. But that would mean there must be something serious developing back in Amorr itself."

"Intrigue? I should say it means civil war!" Marcus shook his head. "It must be House Severus, if Fulgetra is involved—but why them? They've always been our rivals in the Senate, but I never thought of them as outright enemies or traitors. But who else could it be? The House Andronicus can hardly be trying to reclaim their old throne after all this time!"

Julianus, not being a patrician, had no ready answer for him. Shocked into silence by the thought that they might have witnessed the first blow in what could be a long and bloody internecine war, the two men sat and stared at the whites of each other's eyes. That was all that could be seen in the darkness. "Why did you come to me?" Julianus asked quietly. "What do you want me to do?"

"I came to you because I think there must be at least one centurion involved besides Honoratus. I didn't think any of the knights or decurions carry enough weight with the infantry to replace the officers." Marcus shrugged. "And to be honest, I tried to imagine you betraying House Valerius and your oath. I just couldn't picture it."

Julianus snorted. "I can't say I love your House so much as all that, Valerian. But you're right. I'd run through any man who'd try to turn me against my own damned legion, new as it may be. The boys are green, but they've been blooded, and I daresay they're as good as any legion in the Empire now."

"So what do we do? I don't think there could be more than a handful of men involved, but I could be wrong. And I'm too tired to think straight."

"The second of the first had the watch tonight. I'd bet on their centurion being involved. I still find it hard to believe Gnaeus Junius would turn against the legion, though. He's the primus bloody pilus!"

"I don't know. Is it any easier to imagine the praefectus doing so, assuming he wasn't responsible himself? After Orissis... I would have sworn we could count on the men from Vallyrium. Now I'm not so sure if anyone can be trusted."

"Orissis—wasn't he one of the men you took on patrol tonight?"

"Yes. After we caught the rider, we were bringing him back to camp. I may have made a mistake: I forced him to divulge his message. Then, during the ride, Orissis disappeared. I have to assume he rode for Cynothicum, in which case he must have been involved. And he's from Vallyrium."

"Don't read too much into that. I know the man. He's a gambler, worse than Proculus. And I know he's in heavy debt, so maybe Honoratus bought him. Or it could even be that he wasn't even involved with the conspirators beforehand. Maybe he just saw his chance and took it. It's not out of character for a gambler to act on impulse."

"I suppose it's possible." Marcus nodded and yawned. And yawned again. He closed his eyes, just for a moment, and the next thing he knew, he was staggering over to the empty cot, leaning heavily on Julianus.

"You've had a rough night, Tribune," the decurion said. He picked up Marcus's sword from the ground. "I better clean this before suspicion falls on you. Get some sleep now, and I'll keep watch until the morning. Just sleep. What's done is done, and you can't raise the dead. There's nothing we can do until sunrise."

Marcus tried to protest, but the sensation of getting off his feet and lying down, even in his armor, simply felt too wonderful to resist. He closed his eyes and the welcome darkness of oblivion claimed him almost immediately.

When Marcus awoke, the sun was high and the decurion's tent was crowded. He felt strangely stiff and heavy, but his head didn't hurt in the least. That seemed almost inexplicable, until he heard himself creaking as he tried to sit up and realized he was still wearing his armor. He looked down and saw a deep scratch nearly as long as his first finger on the left side of the metal covering his abdomen.

The memories of the night before came rushing back to him, and he shuddered. Whoever had left that mark had known how to strike with a blade. If Marcus hadn't been wearing his breastplate, he'd have been gutted.

He looked up and saw a group of five men crowded inside the tent looking at him. Julianus wasn't among them, but Marcus recognized four of them as decurions. They were older than the average knights. Two had grey hair, and two were bald. The man who wasn't a decurion was the optio who commanded the legion's ballistarii and architecti.

"Good to see you're still with us, Valerian," the optio said. Technically, he was outranked by the decurions, but he had seen more time in the legions than any of them, and because he was responsible for men serving in each of the ten cohorts, his influence was considerable. "I'm afraid I can't say the same of your fellow officers. It's too soon to be certain, Tribune, but it would appear that you are now the senior officer of Legio XVII."

"Damn near the only officer, you could say," a decurion added. "The laticlavius and the other tribunes were all killed in their tents."

Marcus nodded calmly and did his best to hide the depth of his dismay. As of yesterday, he had been sixth in the line of command and no one had cared about his comportment. But he knew that if the events of last night meant he was now the senior officer, he was going to have to convince the legion he was worth following.

Beginning with these men.

"I feared as much when I discovered Gaius Marcius had been murdered. How about the praefectus? And the primus pilus?"

The optio laughed. His name was Titus something, Marcus knew, but he simply could not recall the man's nomen. He was usually known as Cassabus. "They must have known better than to try killing the old mule. Honoratus has been stalking all over the camp, trying to find you and the other young tribune, Trebonius, and vowing red vengeance for Marcus Saturnius."

So Trebonius had survived! That was unexpectedly good news. He wondered how his friend had managed it. Had he belatedly taken up whoring? That didn't seem likely, but it hardly mattered now. "What about the praefectus?"

"No one knows. One of my men said he saw Sextus Castorius in the outer camp yesterday evening, but we don't know if he came back or not."

Marcus nodded. "Let's hope he didn't. If the guards at the gate were in on this, we'll probably never find his body. Where is Julianus now?"

"He's sounding out the senior centurions. They're being summoned to help the primus pilus decide how to break the news to the men. There have been rumors sweeping through the camp like wildfire, of course, but each is wilder than the next, and no one knows what to believe, if anything. But everyone knows something is amiss since one of the night guards found a trail of blood through the forum that ended halfway along the Via Decumana."

Marcus frowned and looked down at his breastplate. Could it be the man who'd killed Gaius Marcius and marred the polished surface of his armor? "Did anyone search the nearby tents?"

Cassabus shrugged. "Julianus might have set someone to it. I don't know what he has in mind yet. He wanted us here to keep you safe until he's able to determine who is responsible and what their plans are. We haven't found the man you stabbed last night, but we're looking."

"And your men?" Marcus glanced at the other decurions to include them in the question as well.

"I've got three teams of ballistarii, each with a scorpio assembled and hidden in the stables across the street. Gavrus and Barbatus each have their squadrons there, armed and armored, as well. We won't have any problem dealing with these bastards… if we can figure out who they are."

"Well done," Marcus nodded approvingly as if he actually had a plan of his own in mind. "But what if they don't make their move soon?"

"I should think they'll have to," one of the decurions said. From his heavy beard, well-salted with grey, Marcus assumed it was Barbatus. "It's not enough for them to behead the legion—they'll have to take control of it, or it's no use to them."

"That depends on what their goals are," Marcus said. "If they simply want to neutralize us and keep us out of Cynothicus, it would work for a time…. But that doesn't make sense. We weren't planning to move on the Cynothii until spring, which leaves plenty of time for a new general and staff to arrive from Amorr."

He felt as if he was on the verge of figuring something out, something important, but before the thought could coalesce in his mind, a horn interrupted him by sounding four thunderous blasts. It was the signal for the legion to gather in the forum.

Marcus stood up and fumbled at his side, relieved to discover that Julianus had cleaned his gladius and returned it to his scabbard. He wished he had his tribune's helm. If he was going to take command of the legion, it wouldn't be a bad idea to hide his youthful face. But it was back in his tent, assuming his tent was still standing. When he looked up, he was surprised to see the decurions and the optio all standing at attention, as if waiting for his orders. That was exactly what they were doing, he belatedly realized.

He cleared his throat and did his best to assume a decisive manner. "Cassabus, wait until the men are assembled, then move your scorpios into place pointing straight down the Via Principalis. Don't loose on anyone unless we've badly misjudged this and we're completely outnumbered. They're just there to show we are ready for trouble. Barbatus, I'll want your squadron as an escort. Gavrus, mount your squadron and take a position behind Cassabus. The rest of you, get your men and show up in your usual positions, but every man is to be ready for battle. If we can't end this quickly, it could get very ugly very fast."

"What about insignia?" Gavrus asked. "If it comes to blows, how can we tell who is with us and who is not?"

Marcus winced. He should have thought of that.

"Right. Everyone is to be fully armored. But each man is to leave the greave off his left leg. Some of the other men will be armored, others not, but no one will forget to strap one greave on."

"That will work," Cassabus said approvingly. "By your leave, Tribune?"

"Not yet, Optio. First, I believe we had better pray. If we ever needed it, it's got to be now."

There were grim nods, and several of the decurions exchanged significant glances. But no one objected, and each man unhesitatingly lowered himself to one knee.

Marcus might have felt more self-conscious leading the men in prayer if he weren't terrified of what was going on outside this tent. At least in battle, the enemy stood before you. But now, who could say where to stand and which way to face when no one knew who was the enemy?

"Immaculate Son—hear our prayer. Lord, we are men of war, but we know we are washed in Your most holy blood. We do not fear to face the enemy, but now we find ourselves betrayed by our own comrades. Son of God, You know what this is like. You too have been betrayed. Be with us! We thank You that You stand with us now. Guide us, guard us all, and grant us victory. You are the Alpha and the Omega, You are the Rider on the White Horse, Lord. Show us Your hand, and may Your Father's will be done. Amen."

"Amen." The decurions rose, their faces grim. Perhaps the reminder that the Son of God himself was a decurion of sorts had given them courage and resolve.

The tents nearest the forum were cleared away, and the great mass of the legion had arrayed itself by cohort, century, and squadron as Marcus, wearing a borrowed decurion's helm, approached the rostrum on the western side of the forum.

Julianus, the chief decurion, was already there, standing on the platform with the primus pilus and four other centurions. To Marcus's considerable relief, Gaius Trebonius stood there as well. It was bad enough to have lost his general and his colleagues, but losing the man who had somehow become his closest friend in the legion would have been an even more devastating blow.

He did not see the praefectus, however, which meant he had to assume that the legion's third-in-command had been killed as well.

He could feel the nervous excitement spiraling outward, cohort by cohort, as his knightly guard marched him through the crowd. The thousands of men didn't intimidate him, though, as he was too focused on running through the cognomina of the dozens of centurions, trying to determine which of them might have some family tie or other connection to House Severus. But he couldn't think of a single one. Nor did he think it was likely, as Marcus Saturnius was too cynical and too politically astute to have ever knowingly permitted a Severan, or anyone belonging to one of their satellite families, to hold a position of authority in his legion.

The two centuries closest to the rostrum were the first and second of the first cohort, which meant they were Gnaeus Junius's men. If, as Marcus was increasingly beginning to suspect, the primus pilus was behind the murders, this could be his moment of greatest danger.

His knightly bodyguard, which had initially felt so imposing, now felt far too paltry in light of the dozens of armed men through whom they were making their way. Being infantry, both centuries were more heavily armored than the unmounted knights, and the weight of their numbers was physically palpable.

Were those men there pressing in against Barbatus's men? Was that flash of movement he saw out of the corner of his eye an arm drawing back to throw a knife? It would be so easy to break through the double line of men that protected him, front, back, and sides. They wouldn't even have to attack the guards—a simple surge of movement toward him followed by the lethal jab of a pilum or the silent thrust of a gladius, and he would be mortally wounded before his protectors even knew he'd been attacked.

He felt a trickle of cold sweat run down his left side. A sense of claustrophobia seized him. The noise, the jostling, the smell of leather and cotton, steel and sweat, combined into a fierce assault on his senses. But he breathed in deeply through his nose and kept his eyes firmly focused on the men standing on the platform to whom he was coming closer with every step.

We should have been mounted, he told himself bitterly. That's the reason officers are always mounted, so they can be seen. No one would have dared to strike him down if he were in the full view of the entire legion. He gripped the hilt of his sword tightly then walked toward the imposing silhouette of Honoratus, the primus pilus, who stood on the platform looming over them all like a murderous shadow god.

MEERFIN

EVEN by goblin standards, Meerfin Shistgurble felt life had been unnecessarily cruel to him. It wasn't easy growing up the youngest of nine in a crowded, ramshackle hut woven of reeds that was perched precariously on the edge of a swamp. But he had survived his rough, tumble, and occasionally cannibalistic infancy, and by sheer hard work and determination he raised himself to become a valued, if not necessarily well-respected, member of the Mequanu tribe.

As Third Assistant Frogcatcher to Groonul Poisonspear, the tribe's age-spotted master frog hunter, he owned no less than four of his own tri-pointed frog spears, a half-share in a hut within walking distance of the main creek, two pairs of pantalons, a net made from cured rabbit intestines, and a small collection of the engraved stones used as currency on account with the tribe's Stoneholder, Wobbran Twice-bitten. More than a few young goblines had watched him carrying his spears and a sackful of plump-legged frogs home to the village with something akin to interest in their green and yellow eyes.

Then one rainy spring day, he'd come back to find the reed huts smashed and giving off a dreadful purple-tinged smoke that made one's eyes water, the pretty goblines either missing or sprawled naked and dead on the ground, and nearly half the goblins he knew chained by their necks in a long line attached to the tree that served as the center of the village. No sooner had he turned to run than a massive gauntleted hand caught him by the throat and lifted him from the ground. He fumbled for the knife he used to scale the fish he sometimes caught when the frogs were scarce, but the big orc that held him fast only laughed.

"Stick me wid dat tickler and I'll squoze you stupid head off, gobbo!"

Meerfin reconsidered and left his knife in its sheath. Eventually, there might come a time when he would question that decision, but at that moment, submission seemed massively preferable to being squozed.

At first, his life in the Eighth Goblin Auxiliary Foot marching under the menacing green-and-black banner of Chief Gutripper of Zorn Narvog hadn't been a bad one. His skill with the frogspears translated quite well to the crudely sharpened thin wooden poles the orcs gave to their infantry auxiliaries, winning him a rapid promotion to first sergeant, and his ability to forage for meat of various kinds made him more popular with his unit than he had ever been with his village. He also forged a close friendship with a young forest goblin from the Aeglu tribe, who with his big eyes and soft yellow skin was as pretty as any of the Mequani goblines and shyly admired Meerfin in a way that made him feel nearly as tall as a great orc.

He hadn't known it was possible to be so happy, especially in the army, bossed about by ruthless orcs. But the idyllic journey lasted no longer than it took for Gutripper's army to reach the stony foothills of Hagahorn. There, both game and grain were hard to come by, and it was then, to his horror, that he learned how the orcs managed to travel without any wagons stocked with provisions for when the foraging of the wolfriders wasn't sufficient to feed the army.

His first warning that the auxiliary troops served a dual purpose was one evening, when they were all sitting around the fire and grumbling about the lack of food, and a squad of giant mountain orcs wearing creaking leather armor showed up and announced the arrest of five of his fellow goblin foot for treason. Their conspiracy was news to Meerfin, but like the others, he simply shrugged and assumed the orcs must have a spy in their midst.

There was much hushed whispering that night, and many suspicious glances were cast at the less popular members of the troop, but Meerfin didn't see fit to give the matter any more thought. Instead, he went out into the night and managed to pin a noisy little bird to a tree with a lucky cast of his frogspear, which he plucked, then brought back to the camp and shared raw with Barkmoss in the privacy of what had over the course of the march become their tent.

Three days later, with the infantry reeling under the assault of a merciless sun, the march was halted early in the afternoon. Meerfin took the opportunity to climb the peak to the west in search of rock rats and managed to find two fat ones that were hiding out in the shadow of a large rock. But when he returned, his friend was nowhere to be found. A frightened young goblin in his phalanx said that the orcs had come back and dragged off Barkmoss and another goblin from the troop. Worried, but convinced there was some mistake, Meerfin immediately set off for the orc encampment. Perhaps the traitors had been forced to name others, or perhaps it was a case of mistaken identity.

But a part of him must have suspected the truth, for when he heard the crackling of the fire and smelled the mouth-watering aroma of meat being cooked, his fear knew no bounds. He charged recklessly into the midst of the huge, armored orcs and stared in horror at the sight of his sweet, sensitive friend spitted and roasting over the flames. They hadn't even bothered to take his clothes off but were letting them burn away as his blood hissed and smoked when it fell on the coals. Speechless and sickened, he turned to face the nearest orc, who was grinning as he slowly pushed himself to his feet.

"Lads, we's eating good tonight! Here's anodder and we don't even have to cotch it!"

Meerfin screamed and hurled the frogspear in his hand at the orc's face. His aim was true, and the huge brute bellowed in bestial pain before staggering toward him with one arm outstretched. Meerfin ducked under it, drew his blade, and sank it into the orc's exposed armpit, then withdrew the blade and shoved with all his might. Wounded and off-balance, the orc stumbled into the firepit, reached blindly out, then crashed face-first into the flames clutching the corpse of the spitted goblin in both arms.

As the orc screamed in agony and his fellows roared with cruel laughter, Meerfin fled for the mountains, tears of grief and anguish burning two hot trails down his face.

After waiting three days to be sure the Gutripper's army had moved on, Meerfin traveled south. But he was soon lost in the unfamiliar terrain and somehow managed to wander west instead of east, toward the Man lands.

Two weeks after his unplanned desertion, he was captured by slavers, transported to Amorr, and sold to the Green stables as part of a lot of thirty whip-scarred orcs, half-starved goblins, and a wounded dwarf. He survived his first appearance on the sands of the great arena by pure happenstance, and his second on the strength of his rage when he and eleven goblins equipped with nothing but wooden spears were matched against a pair of armored orcs armed with spiked maces. Eight of his companions died, but in the end, both orcs were lying lifeless on the sands. The stablemaster fed them well that night, but in the morning, he was taken from the goblin compound with his hands and mouth bound and given to a man who promptly popped him into a rough burlap sack and carried him onto a cart.

It didn't travel far, though, before he was taken off the cart and his hands were freed just long enough for his new owners to stretch out his arms and legs and tie them to some sort of posts driven into the ground.

He didn't even struggle. In fact, he couldn't summon up more than a mild curiosity about what would happen next. Whether he died on an orc's spit in the army, upon an orc's spear on the sands, or here on this cold stone didn't matter to him any more than it did to the gods or the rest of an indifferent world. The gag still silenced his mouth, but even if they removed it, he would not have cried out. Who was there to hear? Who was there to care?

As he lay there, candles were lit around him, something wet was sprinkled upon him, and one or two men went about some mysterious business. He heard an amount of the strange and unintelligible language of Man being spoken, and eventually, the meaningless babble lulled him to sleep....

He awoke choking, with the sensation of a foul-tasting liquid filling his mouth. He gagged and tried to spit it out, but someone behind him lifted his head with one hand, and with the other, held his mouth clamped shut. He swallowed convulsively, then gasped for air once his throat was clear.

Around him, the candles suddenly burned high, then extinguished themselves as an evil-smelling smoke wafted upward from the wicks. Then, as he lay there, something inside him seemed to wake up, and he felt himself possessed by a strange sense of well-being, even of strength.

Why am I lying on this floor? What am I doing here? Who am I?

He—no, no longer he, but it—stared with fascination at the strange yellow-green feet with the curled claws that appeared to belong to its body.

What am I?

Looking up, it saw a domed ceiling arching over his head. A temple, it thought. Or to be more specific, a church. Its arms were tied to something, it realized as it tried to sit up. With a snarl, it curled its right arm and tore in half the cloth holding it down, then freed its other arm as well as its legs. Leaping to its feet in a single bound, it looked down at its naked body. It was thin and mostly light green, with yellow highlights upon its belly.

Goblin, it realized, and male. I am goblin?

Then awareness filled it, followed by exultation and a terrible feeling at its core that it dimly recognized as hunger. A wizard had placed it here, had reached a sorcerous hand down into the nether planes, had plucked it forth, and had implanted it in this body of flesh.

I am no goblin, it realized as it searched the feeble, barely sentient mind of the body in which it was imprisoned. *I am not this "Meerfin." I am Vermilignum, and I am free!*

It looked around and saw the remnants of a summoning circle, but the blood was smeared and dry in places. The salt was scattered, and the candles had guttered out. The magick circle could no more hold it than the paltry rags had held the spindly arms of the goblin it possessed.

The demon hurled himself out of the circle, out of this weak and worthless material form that could serve as nothing more useful than the doorway to this plane.

But some invisible, impalpable force held it in place, and instead of soaring free into the world, its body merely dove forward and landed awkwardly amidst the blood and salt. What was this? It tried again, and again, but all it succeeded in doing was causing the body in which it was trapped to jerk and hop about in an unnatural manner.

Exultation was replaced by rage. Who had done this to it? It ransacked the goblin's mind, destroying everything it touched in its haste and fury, seeking to find the useful memories.

Finally, it found something relevant. A hand. Red robes. A man's voice speaking the words of the binding spell. Then fear seized it as it recognized the spell and realized the implications. The spell drew its strength from the goblin's blood, which was why it could not break the binding from inside the goblin's body. In fact, every attempt to break the binding would only weaken the body, possibly even kill it. And, to its utter horror, it realized that the nature of the spell was such that death of the goblin's body would not free it, but would rather dissolve it little by little, as it would still be bound to all the various components of the body as that mortal vessel slowly rotted away into nothing.

Power! What it needed was more power, enough blood to break through the spell and free it from this diabolical trap of mortality! What enemy had done this to it?

Furious and frightened, it turned its thoughts away from such pointless avenues and toward what the goblin senses were telling it. The scent of men filled its nostrils, an ideal source of blood and more than enough to suit its needs!

Sniffing and scrabbling on all fours, it followed the scent down the hall and into a large chapel in which five or six men in blue robes were talking with one another. Or rather, they were arguing, it realized from the angry tones of the voices. They were priests of some god or another, it seemed. It could have understood them had it wished, but it had no interest in the men, only in their blood that might free it and the flesh that might sate its ravenous mortal body.

Quietly, quietly, it stalked them, unseen in the long shadows of the torches in the center of the room. Closer, and closer, it crept, until it was nearly in range to spring.

"What's that!" one of the robed men shouted, pointing at it.

That one was the first to die—with the goblin's short, sharp teeth in his throat. It snarled and growled as it tore at him. Then it leaped at the next man, who stood there transfixed with sheer terror.

A third man simply collapsed, clutching at his chest, while the fourth tried to banish it, shouting banishments and exorcisms that did no more to free it from the goblin body than its own efforts had.

The fifth man, a hairless one, was fleeing as fast as his aged and decrepit legs would allow. It threw a candelabra at him, causing him to fall. Then it scampered over and smashed his bald head with the bronze device as if it were an egg.

The sixth man, the last, did not flee, but stood before it without any visible signs of panic, although it could smell the acrid scent of his fear.

"You are no goblin," the priest said calmly. "Tell me how you are called, spirit, in the name of Our Immaculate Savior!"

"Vermilignum," it told him. "Can you free me?"

"I don't know. But I can pray for you, and for the poor beast whose body you possess."

"This is no possession!" it hissed in anguish. "If you cannot free me, all I need from you is your blood!"

The priest nodded slowly. "Then take it, if you must. And may the Most High have mercy on whatever passes for your soul."

It struck. The priest fell to the floor, and it fed upon him, filling its ravenous maw with the sweet taste of Man flesh.

Thus fortified, it began to consider how it might banish the spell. It hadn't been summoned often, but often enough that it could picture how the summoning spells were structured. Presumably a reversal might be used to banish it. Even a return to the nether realm and its harsh master would be preferable to the slow dissolution it fancied it could already feel. But that was nonsense. The goblin might be dying as the binding slowly drained its life from it, but it was not dead yet.

It painted the floor with blood, both the circle and the reverse of every evocation it could remember. Then it gathered up the remains of the candles and placed them in a pentacle. A taste showed they were made from goblin fat. With a curse it lit them and then lay down in the midst of the crimson circle and began reciting the most likely invocation backward.

Nothing happened. It tried a second spell, then a third, and finally, in frustration, tried to hurl itself out of the goblin body by a sheer effort of its demonic will. A cold wind filled the death-desecrated chapel, and the candle flames vanished, but it was still imprisoned in a body that was rapidly weakening now as a result of its efforts to escape. It looked around the chapel, desperately trying to think of another way.

Then it saw the answer in a small fountain on the other side of the chapel. Holy water! Surely that should suffice to break the connection! It rushed over to the fountain and plunged its head into the much-feared liquid, bracing itself for the inevitable burning to come.

But there was nothing! It thrashed about in bewilderment for a second, then slowly lifted its face from the water. Either through its summoning and binding or its own deadly actions, the chapel had been desecrated. The water was now simply water.

There would be holy water elsewhere, but even if it could be found, it might be hard to reach. Running water wouldn't be as strong, but at least it was available. There was a river running through the city to the sea. There was always one somewhere in the middle of a city this size. Once it saw a bridge, it knew the river would be easy to find. But even as it made its decision, the goblin body shuddered with convulsions that made it hard to stay upright. The body was weakening too fast under the burden of the binding. It didn't have much time.

Shrieking with frustration and despair, it returned to the corpses, wrestled a blue robe off the body of the murdered priests and slipped it over its own head. The robe was too long, but would have to do if it didn't want to attract deadly attention in the streets of the city of men. Bunching the priest's robe up over the goblin's thick and bony knees, Vermilignum ran out of the chapel and into the darkness.

SEVERA

THE letter was sealed with red wax and bore the stamp of House Severus. It was with genuine delight that Severa began reading it for the first time.

It was with disbelief and dawning horror that she began reading it for the second time.

By the time she had finished reading it a third time, her horror and disbelief had given way to a fury unlike anything she had experienced before. It was one thing to suspect evil of those nearest and dearest to you, but it was something else altogether to see it confirmed in ink, written in a familiar and trusted hand.

My dear sister,

I trust this finds you and the others well. I must apologize for not having written you previously, but I am confident you will forgive me, for none know so well as I do your gentle nature. Do not harbor a grudge against me, little sister, for as you have no doubt guessed already, my failure to write you was no wish of my own, but rather a command from that authority which brooks no disobedience.

All Amorr mourns your absence. I only exaggerate slightly. The poet Gnaeus Rabirius (I refer to the young man of the knightly class, not the Senator, of course), was heard to declare that the departure of the three women of House Severus from the city was like the three stars of Kandaon's Belt disappearing from the night sky. Nor is he alone in his sentiments.

But you must be strong now, sister, for now I must tell you something that I fear shall wound your tender heart. Even prior to your sudden departure, I was not unaware that you may have held a regard for a certain young hero of the arena, one which our father would not approve. I do not condemn or condone your feelings, for as it is written in the Ars Amatoria, "We are always eager for forbidden things, and yearn for what is denied us, like the sick man who longs for water because his doctor forbids him to drink it." I have always had the utmost confidence in you, sweet sister, and I am confident that you are well-armored in virtue. If ever there was a woman capable of withstanding the soft whispers of her treacherous heart, it is you, my dear Severa.

I only tell you this so you will know that I understand your sentiments and that I grieve with you at the fall of Silicus Clusius of the Blue. He fought with courage and with skill, and I am confident that he would have been granted Missus had the wound dealt him by the trident of the great retiarius, Montanus, not proven mortal. The brave manner in which he departed this world has been much remarked in the days following the games, as upon seeing Clusius had received his death, the crowd first applauded the victor for his victory before applauding the defeated for the nobility of his defeat. Still on his feet, Clusius saluted the crowd with his sword before falling stricken to the sands. The victorious Montanus rushed to his side and was even seen to dash tears from his eyes. I was there, and I can tell you it was most affecting.

Indeed, the fall of Clusius has been the talk of the city. I regret that I cannot recall the man's name, but last night I hosted several of my friends to dinner, including Quintus Falconius, whom you may recall has long been an admirer of yours, and a libation was made in honor of the bout. I thought it was rather well phrased. "In the West and in the East the name of Clusius shall be known to posterity, and because of Clusius, the name of Montanus shall live on." Montanus was already a champion, of course, but he may well find himself presented with the wooden sword at the end of the season thanks to the noble death of Silicus Clusius.

That is all my news, sister mine, and I beg you to write to me soon and assure me that all is well with Father, Mother, and little Severilla. If you are not permitted to return until after the harvest festival, then I shall come to you.

Your affectionate brother,

M. Severus Tertius

Half-blind with tears that were more rage than sorrow, Severa stormed out of her room and down the marble stairs toward the courtyard, the last place she had heard her father's voice since he'd returned from the city the day before. He was not there, but she saw her younger sister playing with a kitten in the shade of a wide-branched tree.

"Have you seen Father?" she demanded.

"What's wrong, Severa?" Severilla was only twelve years old and entirely absorbed with her cats. She showed signs of one day boasting their mother's famous beauty, and her eyes were large and dreamy, betraying a tranquil nature that was decidedly uncharacteristic of the women of House Severus. Or, for that matter, the men.

"Everything!" Severa snapped. "And it's all Father's fault!"

The kitten batted at a leaf that was falling, then pounced upon it once it reached the ground, and her sister erupted into peals of laughter. "What are you doing, silly kitty-kit-kit? Do you think it's a bird?"

"Severilla, do you know where Father is?" Severa demanded from behind gritted teeth. Sometimes, it took all of her willpower not to slap the dreaminess right out of her sister's eyes. Or strangle one of her wretched cats. "I really need to speak with him."

"Oh, he's in the library with one of the scribes. Maybe some of the barbarians too." Severilla giggled. "Feronia jumped up on the table and knocked over one of the ink pots. Her front paws were all black from the ink, and she made the cutest little kitty prints all over the parchment!

I thought Father was going to be ever so furious with her, but he just laughed and said I should call her Feronia Scriptoria! Isn't that funny?"

"You're funny," said Severa, her rage abating momentarily because of the smile that adorned her sister's pretty face. It was so charming it was almost contagious. She leaned over and kissed Severilla on the nose. "Be sure her paws are clean before you bring her back into the house."

"I shall!" her sister promised cheerfully, before racing off in pursuit of the wayward kitten. "Come back here, you naughty baby!"

Severa laughed and shook her head. Seeing her sister chasing her cat reminded her that it was not all that long ago when the estate's kittens and puppies were her foremost concerns in life. She looked back over her shoulder at the courtyard as she reached the top of the steps that led to the front door. There was a tranquil beauty here that she had been too young and restless to perceive at the time, but she could remember how happy she was here when she was Severilla's age, running through the fields and orchards, living each day as it came and never thinking about tomorrow. She could still appreciate the natural beauty now, but it no longer touched her soul. She simply had to return to the stinking, sinful, man-made splendor of Amorr, and in order to do that, she first had to confront her father. Her ruthless and murderous father.

She found him in the library still, dictating a letter to one of his small army of scribes. Upon seeing her enter the room, he stopped his dictation, and with a single gesture sent the elderly man scuttling unceremoniously from the room. She did not trust her voice, so she did not speak. Instead, she simply placed the letter on the table the scribe had left behind him.

He picked it up. Aulus Severus was a tall, spare man, and his white eyebrows were the only hair that remained on his head. He was not entirely bald, but every morning one of his bodyslaves shaved the stubble from the rear quarter of his scalp as well as his face. His face was large and bony, with the deep-set eyes of an ascetic or a monk sworn to one of the more rigid orders. His expression was calm, in direct contrast to most of his family. He was famous for seldom losing his temper or raising his voice. On the other hand, he was seldom seen to smile, except occasionally at his daughters. His skin was unblemished by the sun, as befitted a man who was at his best in the Senate or the scriptorium.

Not a spot of color showed on his cheeks as he glanced at the letter in her hand and nodded.

"I was aware Tertius was writing to you. I assume he is well."

"Did you think I wouldn't find out, Father?" Severa was so angry that she found it hard to decide where to start with him. "Did you really think someone wouldn't tell me!"

"I might ask you that very same question, my dear." He looked directly at her.

Despite her fury, she discovered to her chagrin that she could not bear to meet his serenely icy gaze. It was like trying to outstare a statue. She looked away.

"I assume you are referring to the death of the young gladiator from the Blue stable."

"Clusius!" she shouted. "His name was Silicus Clusius. He was brave and he was beautiful and I loved him! I loved him, Father! And you had him killed! I know it, and you'll never convince me otherwise even if you swear on the Tree of the Immaculate himself!"

"Why would I deny it?" Her father looked genuinely mystified. "Of course I had the poor lad killed. What else did you expect?"

Severa simply stared at him, mute with shock and astonishment. She had imagined and re-imagined this conversation over and over again in her head after reading Tertius's letter, but never had she pictured it proceeding in this fashion. She had not imagined that he would freely admit to killing the young man she had loved without showing any more remorse than a cat killing a songbird.

"What did I expect? I don't know! I suppose I expected you would be angry with me. I expected you would be disappointed in me! I can't even say I was surprised when you interfered and swept me away from my life and my friends and my family in the city. But I never expected that my own father could ever sink so low as to murder a man his daughter loved!"

Her father didn't react angrily to her words; he didn't even look the slightest bit sorrowful. He merely sighed, as if she was just another tedious client, and ran his hand over his bald head.

"Oh, I am sorry, Father—am I boring you? Do you order so many murders each day that you find it tiresome to be called to account for one too minor to recall?" She stared at him challengingly, and this time, she did not look away.

Nor did he, until finally the faintest whisper of a smile seemed to touch his lips.

"You are a very beautiful young woman, Severa. You have your mother's beauty and her passion too. I have no doubt you think you are a woman grown now, ready for love. But you are as untamed and as innocent of the ways of the world as your little sister's cats."

He tapped the letter and shook his head. "I hoped it would not be necessary to talk to you about your behavior. I hoped you would understand the error of your ways and the senseless danger into which you placed yourself, and the harm you could have done to our House. But most of all, I wished to spare you pain."

"To spare me pain!" Severa shouted at him. "You killed a brave and beautiful man, the man I loved, and you're going to tell me you murdered him to spare me pain? I don't even... I can't..." She ended with a wordless shriek, too angry and indignant to even think of what she wanted to say. She clutched at her hair, then buried her face in her hands. It was too obscene for words! It was abhorrent! It was grotesque!

"Severa," her father said softly.

She felt his hand caress her shoulder, and she blindly slapped it away.

"Don't touch me!"

"Severa, my dear, I'm truly sorry."

She raised her tear-stained face to look up at him and shook her head.

"No, you're not. You just did what you always do: You went ahead and did whatever you wanted to, because you can always pretend that you didn't do it for you, you did it for the family, or the House, or the City, or the Senate. It's always for someone else. But somehow whatever you do is always just what you want! My poor Clusius got in the way of your plans for me, so of course he had to die. They might all call you Patronus because everyone in the Senate bows down before you, but you don't fool me, Father. You're every bit as selfish and self-serving as Bibulus or Sarmentus or any of those parasites at Virro's table you despise. You just hide it better!"

To her surprise, he didn't even blink at her angry words. He didn't raise his head, flare his nostrils, or betray any other sign of irritation with her. For the first time since she'd finished reading the letter, she began to wonder if perhaps she had missed something important. Anger, she was ready for. Defensiveness, she could handle. But this unconcerned and disdainful calm unsettled her.

"Very well." Her father sighed. "My dear, you leave me no choice. Am I correct in assuming you kept the gladiator's letters to you?"

Severa hesitated. She sensed a trap closing in on her, but for the life of her, she couldn't figure out what it might be. Father already knew she had been exchanging letters with Clusius. And she knew that, except in her dreams, she hadn't ever so much as kissed those full, enticing lips, much less run her hands over that magnificent, chiseled body. She decided to tell the truth.

"I have them."

"And did you never stop to ask yourself where a young fighting man— a slave—would have learned to read, much less to write with such a neat hand? A Thursian slave, no less."

Severa froze. It felt as if an icy hand had suddenly gripped her heart. She forced herself to swallow.

Her father continued, still speaking in an uncharacteristically soft voice. "You could not have been expected to recognize any of the allusions in his letters, of course. They come from a compendium of verse not fit for a young woman, and as such, they were not included in your education. But surely you have at least heard of the *Amores*, the *Ars Amatoria*, and the *Dilectiloquium*. If I were to read them to you now, I can assure you that you would recognize certain delicate turns of phrase, certain flowery expressions, all carefully selected to feed the fires of passion in a young woman's heart."

"You're saying Clusius didn't write his letters to me?"

No, that was impossible! She had seen him blow kisses to her, caught her breath as he winked at her. He had even worn the scrap of silk she sent him as a talisman of love and good luck on his arm! She had seen it with her own two eyes. How could he have done that if he hadn't truly been corresponding with her? "I don't believe you. You're lying! I know you are!"

Her father reached behind him and withdrew a slender scroll from the wooden case behind him. "I am not lying to you, Severa. It is only that there is more to this situation than you imagine. Things are not always as simple as they seem. Read this."

The letter was only a few lines long, addressed in a shockingly crude hand to one of her father's scribes. She read it in an instant, her hand over her mouth.

To D. Aulapor, in the household of A. Severus Patronus

The slave named Silicus Clusius can't no more read nor write than me. We got no fighter in the stables who can do neither. M. Ladrus is writing this down for me, same as he does for everyone in the Blues.

M. Ladrus for Pullus Mucro

Weaponsmaster

Stabulum Hibernum

Underneath the name the wolfshead insignia of the Blues was stamped, across which a large X had been scrawled.

Severa handed the scroll back to her father. She suddenly felt very hollow, very tired, and she could not bring herself to meet his eyes again. It wasn't merely that Clusius couldn't have written his letters, the crudeness of the gladiatorial scribe's writing made it obvious that her erstwhile lover couldn't have even dictated them.

"Why?" she asked dully. "I don't understand. He knew me. He looked at me. He even wore my token the last time I saw him fight, one that I sent him myself."

Her father nodded. Now she understood why he had been so calm and patient with her, why he hadn't asked her any questions or angrily confronted her about her secret lover after whisking her away from the city. He had known the truth all along. She was still a virgin, which was his only real concern. Her secret love affair was nothing more than a dream, a puppet show she had mistaken for the real world. The love between her and her beautiful gladiator had never truly existed at all, except in her imagination.

"You were deceived, my dear. I'm not sure of the intentions of those who wrote you those letters and used the young lad. That night when you ran away... they may have been planning to take you and hold you for ransom, either for monetary gain or to neutralize me concerning an important matter in the Senate. They may have thought to weaken the House in the eyes of the public by making my daughter the butt of an infamous scandal about which the whole city would talk for weeks, if not months. Or perhaps they simply intended to kill you as a warning because they were not able to strike directly at me."

Severa gasped, horrified by the deadly vista of evil to which he had opened her eyes. Never for one moment had she entertained the notion that the beautiful young gladiator might not be genuinely enamored of her, or that she could be putting herself, or House Severus itself, in any danger.

"I didn't know," she told him defensively.

"Yes, I am aware of that. You were foolish and disobedient, Severa, but it was not entirely your fault. I knew very nearly from the start, and yet I permitted it to continue nevertheless. Aulapor told me that you were writing to an inappropriate young man, and he gave me a copy of one of the letters from the youth in question. It was immediately apparent to both of us that no unlettered gladiator could possibly have written it.

That was why I gave you your head. I was hoping to discover who was attempting to use you to strike at the House."

"To strike at you, you mean. So you used me!" She pushed herself away from him. "You knew it was a lie, and you didn't tell me!"

"You would not have been half so convincing had you known you were not actually writing to the young man. Your mother even noticed the change in your behavior. She approached me about it before you even sent him that scrap of silk."

"But you could have told me something!"

He reached out and grasped her shoulders. "Listen to me, Severa. You know I am the first man in the Senate. Aside from the Sanctiff, I may be the most powerful man in the City. Now that the Sanctiff is gone and no new one is yet in his place, that makes me the most powerful man in all the Empire. Do you know the saying, 'With great power comes great responsibility'?"

She nodded reluctantly.

"Well, hatred and envy and danger also come with responsibility. Amorr is a great city riven by powerful factions. A man can smile at you in the Senate in the morning and plot your death in the evening. The Houses Martial wage a secret war amongst themselves that has lasted for centuries, with the right to rule Amorr as the prize. Now, I have a vision for Amorr, one that will sustain it and assure its greatness for another four hundred years. But there are those who oppose that vision and will stop at nothing to prevent it."

"But what senator would oppose that? Those disloyal to the city?"

"No, and therein lies the problem. My enemies believe the city will remain great simply because it is already great, that the key to success in the future lies in repeating what was done in the past. Nothing could be further from the truth! My enemies are Andronicus, Cassianus, and Valerius, all great Houses, but they are blind, obedient slaves to the rigid traditions of the past. None of them are willing to recognize that Amorr needs to transform itself before it is overwhelmed by the growing power of the allied cities. They distinguish between the City and the Empire, and in doing so they fail to realize that the two must eventually become one. They possess all the strengths and virtues of the Old Amorrans but fail to recognize that the world has changed. Their strengths are now weaknesses, and their virtue has become vice. It is their very loyalty to the City, admirable as that may be, that now threatens its long-term survival."

Severa frowned. "Why does this have anything to do with me?"

"It has everything to do with all of us, Severa. With me, with you, with your children, and with your children's children! Either the city will admit the allies to full citizenship or they will find common purpose with the provinces and one day swallow us whole. One or the other will happen. It is inevitable. There are too many provincials and too few Amorrans. If we cannot find a way to make them Amorrans, then they will destroy Amorr.

"When I was consul of the legions, I led five legions into Cynothicum. Five years later, Andronicus Caudinus became consul of the legions, and his first order of business was to march a legion into Cynothicum. When Regulus and Aulan are consuls, I don't want them to be marching the same legions into the same provinces trying to suppress the same rebellions. Because one day, our legions are going to be defeated, and the next, there will be provincial armies marching on Amorr."

"That will never happen!" Severa scoffed.

"It can and it will, if I don't act to stop it. And that's only the provinces, my dear. God forbid our allies ever turn against us and join them. And yet, men such as Andronicus Aquila and Valerius Magnus turn up their noble patrician noses and refuse to acknowledge the men of the allied cities as our equals or permit them their place in the Empire they so desire. And, I would say, the place they deserve."

Severa folded her arms and thought. Her anger had faded. Now she felt mostly sad and perhaps a little frightened. Father had used her, but he wasn't the only one. She was just a tool, a weapon, something for men to use as they fought with one another for power. Without the goddess, she was nothing, and she would never be anything. But regardless, there was one thing she had to know.

"I understand why you saw my… saw my foolishness as a chance to expose your enemy, Father. But I still don't understand why Clusius had to die. If none of his letters were real, then why did you have him killed? He'd never done any harm to me, or to you, or even to the honor of the House!"

"Our enemies," he corrected her. "The boy was already as good as dead, Severa. He'd been in contact with those who were using him. He might not have known much about them, but he surely knew something, or he couldn't have recognized you or worn your token. I have little doubt they would have killed him the moment you were in their hands, or as soon as they realized I knew about the affair, simply because he might have led me to them.

"So you can see, they couldn't afford to allow him to be put to the question. The boy was nothing to me, but since you cared for him, I arranged for him to fight Montanus. He never had a chance, not against such a great champion, but it was a death of which the poets are singing, a far better death than he probably imagined for himself. And the young man played his own part in that, he died like a man worthy of your regard. I honor him for it. Nor am I alone. Montanus will never forget that he owes his freedom to Clusius's courage."

Severa didn't know what to say. It was too much to absorb all at once. She had come here prepared to rage at her father, but the discovery that Clusius had never written to her, had never been in love with her, and may well not have even known who she was was more than she could comprehend right away. And the idea that Father might have been merciful, perhaps even generous, in ensuring him a fast and glorious death in the arena rather than an ignominious one somewhere in the bowels of the city was too much for her. She put her hands over her face and began to cry.

Her father put his arms around her and patted her back, as she remembered him doing when she was still small enough to curl up on his lap.

She sobbed into his chest, not sure exactly for what, or for whom, she was crying. Was she crying for that poor beautiful young man who had proudly bled out his life on the sands before a roaring crowd? Was she crying for herself and the way she had been deceived?

No, she realized, as the burning flow of tears finally began to subside and her chest ceased to heave so uncontrollably. What she was mourning was the loss of her innocence.

She dried her eyes with her hands and pushed her hair back from her face. She called upon the goddess to give her strength. Everything was backward, upside down. But she knew that there was only one way to freedom, and that was to put on the mask of repentance. And so, for the first time in her life, she consciously looked into her father's eyes and lied.

"I've been a child, Father. A stupid and selfish one. I admit it. But I'm a woman now, so I know I can't continue behaving like that. And I won't ever do anything that will endanger you or House Severus like that again, I promise you."

"I know," he said. "You have a good heart, Severa. But a good heart and good intentions are not always enough. When we are deceived, even the best of our intentions can go terribly awry. And you are too young and too inexperienced to see through the words and actions of others to their motivations below."

"How can I learn?"

"Time and observation. There is no substitute. It's a skill most never learn, one that most never even know exists, but keep your eyes open and eventually the patterns will begin to present themselves."

She nodded, not entirely sure she understood what he meant, but knowing that he expected humble agreement.

"Now, your mother and I have been discussing this, and we have decided that the best way to ensure that you don't find yourself in similar entanglements is for you to marry. I suspect we should have married you last year to that Crescentius. He's running for curule aedile this year and is certain to win."

"To marry? But I don't know if I want to marry! To whom?" Goddess, to be forced to marry now… that would ruin all her plans.

"That is the question, isn't it?" Her father smiled. "You needn't look so stricken. You're not a prize sow to be auctioned off to the highest bidder."

"Will you promise me this one thing?" She took his hands and held his gaze. "I know you've had many provincials and nobles from the allied cities visiting you over the summer. You don't intend to marry me to any of them, do you?"

"There have been offers, of course. You wouldn't like to be a queen? The high prince of Epra has two sons, including his heir, for whom he would like to find Amorran wives. Severan wives."

"No, absolutely not! It would be an insult, Father, not just to me, but to you and our House. Will you not promise that I shall only marry an Amorran, a patrician from a good consular line?"

"Come, Severa, you know I cannot bind myself in such a manner. Who can predict what fate will dictate? But I can assure you, the Houses with whom I am considering an alliance will not shame you. Does not your husband reflect on me, and on our House? Even if you will not trust my words or my intentions, I should think you could safely place your trust in my pride!"

He smiled at her, and she laughed then embraced him. He was right. If there was one thing in which she could trust, it was his towering pride.

"But father, will you see me in a nunnery? For surely there is no man in Amorr or anywhere else who could hope to meet such an exacting standard."

"I shall endeavor to humble myself a little, for the sake of your happiness, my dear. Now, as delightful as it is to have this all out in the open at last, I do have a tremendous amount of letters to dictate before we return to the city."

"We're going back to Amorr? Soon?"

"Yes, I intend for us to depart for Amorr the day after tomorrow. So naturally you needed to be apprised of the true situation prior to our return. Tertius's letter seemed to be the kindest way."

"We're all going back to the city?" she exclaimed, delighted. "I can go back too?"

"I have reason to believe it is now safe. And there is much to do, even more than you can imagine. This may be the most significant year Amorr has known since the last Andronican king was dethroned. And as much as my heart longs to stay here, I cannot control the Senate from Salventum. I am like a fish out of water so long as I am here."

Severa was barely listening, so delighted was she at the prospect of returning home and escaping the dull tedium of the countryside. She felt a slight pang at not being able to learn more about the goddess from the old woman at the shrine of St. Malachus, but not only would there be other servants of the goddess who would be able to teach in Amorr, it would be much easier for her to slip away and visit the shrine in the city. She hugged her father, this time in genuine delight, and ran out of the library, looking for Eudiss so that she could begin her preparations for the journey back to the city.

But when she reached her room, a thought suddenly struck her: Her father believed it was safe to return to their domus in the city. So what had he done that now allowed him to conclude they were safe when they had been in danger only a few weeks before? She shuddered. It was not only the hidden goddess who harbored dark secrets. And she was not certain which frightened her more: the mysterious secrets of St. Malachus or the lethal ones of House Severus.

CORVUS

AFTER sending his majordomus outside with a sack of silver coins and strict instructions not to permit any client calls, Corvus had hopes for a quiet morning with his wife.

But his hopes were soon dashed, as Romilia did not easily take his news that their nephew had been executed. Whether it was out of concern for the dignity of House Valerius or the reputation of their late son, Magnus and Julia were permitting most of Amorr to assume that Gaius Valerius had fallen in battle. Corvus would have preferred to let Romilia continue to believe that too, and he'd been putting off telling her otherwise for days, but he knew that any day she might receive a letter from Marcus or take it into her head to visit her sister-in-law. So he finally told her the truth after they had broken their fast, and any hopes that he'd had that she would see the matter his way rapidly vanished when he made the mistake of mentioning that Marcus had been present at the execution as well.

"You forced him to see his own cousin beheaded?"

"Of course I did. He's a tribune, after all. The entire legion was there." Corvus did his best to put the awful event in perspective, but he only succeeded in managing to make things worse. "My love, it was after the battle. It's not as if he hadn't seen a hundred other men die that day, to say nothing of the thousands of goblins that were slain. And considering the way the boys led that cavalry charge, I daresay he probably killed ten or more himself."

She stared at him, aghast. "Sextus Valerius, are you mad? First you tell me that you killed your own nephew, then you're going to justify forcing our son watch the execution by telling me that you've turned him into the same sort of inhuman killer you've become?"

We kill humans too, he almost said, barely managing to stop himself from digging his grave any deeper.

"He's an officer in the legion, Romilia. He's not a priest anymore. He's a soldier now. Killing is what we do. It's what he does. You know that."

"But you don't kill your own family!" she shouted at him. "How could you do this to Magnus? To Julia? Or to Marcus—you know how sensitive he is. He'll be dwelling on it for the rest of his life! Or even to yourself!"

"Look, I didn't kill Fortex. I only gave the order." He stressed the last word, only to realize, even as he said it, how pathetically unconvincing it sounded.

"Do you really think that excuses you in the slightest!"

"Of course not. Now wait a moment, woman. In what dirty stinking Hell do you think I am looking to be excused of anything?" He could feel his voice rising, but at this point he didn't care anymore. He got to his feet and pointed at her. "Who are you, woman, to question a legate concerning the discipline of his legions? To question a stragister militum? Listen, not one man in the five thousand questioned Fortex's guilt. Not one spoke to defend him! We were in battle, and they all saw what he did with their own eyes. Gaius Valerius himself didn't dare to protest his sentence, nor did your son!

"And if I hadn't passed the judgment, Saturnius would have done exactly the same. He was intending to. He offered to. He begged me to let him do it, because it was his order that had placed his legion under *modus austeris*. He tried to take the responsibility off my shoulders. But the burden was mine! It was mine, and it will always be mine, and the idiot boy's blood is on my hands, no one else's! So don't you ever try to tell me that I tried to evade responsibility for it! I knew what I was doing, and I accepted the blame because it needed to be done. Do you understand me?"

Her reaction astonished him. Instead of screaming back at him, or striking him, as he half-expected, she reached out tenderly to touch his cheek.

"Corvus, you're crying."

"No, I'm not," he denied stoutly. He wasn't either: A single tear didn't amount to crying.

She touched her tongue to her finger and smiled sadly. "Yes, my love, I'm rather afraid you are. Tell me this, Corvus: Are you sure it was absolutely necessary to… to do what you did? Wasn't there anything you could have done to punish him in some other way?"

He met her eyes and shook his head. "No, I had no choice. The law of the legions is simple and clear. It has to be, so that everyone in the ranks can understand it. The infantry is not filled with poets and lawyers who reflect on the meaning of things. To break it would have been to dishonor my name, my rank, my House, the legion, and even Gaius Valerius Fortex himself. The damned young fool wasn't worth it. And that's assuming Saturnius and the senior centurions would have even accepted my order to spare him. I suppose they probably would have. I've earned some leeway, after all. But they'd never trust me completely again."

"And is it so important for them to trust you? What if it had been Marcus, Corvus? Would you have done the same if it had been Marcus instead of Gaius who broke, what did you call it, the laws of the legion?"

He stared at her silently for a moment.

She looked away and shook her head. "You would, wouldn't you? You would murder your own son for the sake of your precious honor." Her face was suddenly a mask of contempt. "Don't you see how small and pathetic that makes you?"

It was no use. Trying to explain the harsh necessities of warfare to a woman was like trying to mount a cavalry charge against a city wall. It wasn't so much that it was a futile act and doomed to failure, it was more that one didn't even have the wherewithal to imagine the smallest possibility of success. And yet he tried.

"Romilia, wife, as much as I love you dearly, you must understand that your opinion of me bears absolutely no weight whatsoever on how I command fifteen thousand men in battle, when every single one of those lives rest completely in my hands. If I make a mistake, they die. If I don't do anything, they die. If I conceive a brilliant strategy that brings victory, they still die—only fewer of them do then.

"No one is safe—not the ranks, not the centurions, not the tribunes, and not even the generals. Look at Caudinus, he may have been consul and general, but the Cynothii slaughtered him all the same. He made a mistake somewhere along the way, and he died for it, and two thousand brave men died with him. Because of him. In the legions, everyone is liable to the same fate and subject to the same discipline. There is no pass for gross insubordination on the field of battle just because your uncle or your father happens to be the commander."

She shook her head in denial. "I just can't believe you are willing to sit there and tell me you would execute your own son! I wouldn't have believed that you could possibly have given the order to kill Gaius if you hadn't told me yourself."

"But that would never happen in a million years! For God's sake, Romilia, Marcus is so damned punctilious he wouldn't think of disobeying Saturnius's most veiled suggestions, let alone a direct order. He keeps a diary of his patrols that looks like a bloody quartermaster's report. He's not a pig-headed fool who thinks he's a hero out of legend like his idiot cousin!

"Do you know what Fortex did that got himself killed? Do you even know? He abandoned his position, he abandoned the men he was supposed to be commanding, just so he could engage the commander of the enemy cavalry in a duel! And the damned fool did it when Saturnius had given every knight in the cavalry a direct order not to issue or accept any challenges. It would have been bad enough for any rider from the ranks to pull a stupid stunt like that, but for the tribune commanding the right wing? It was sheer madness!"

"I don't care," Romilia said stubbornly. "Maybe duty demanded it. Maybe honor demanded it, if he was caught up with honor like you are. But I still think you should have found a way to save him. He was your brother's son!"

"Do you now?" Corvus slammed his open palm against the wall. She stepped back, surprised by his sudden fury. "Very well, do you know what your precious grandfather did when two cohorts ran during the war against the Great Orc, Romilia? He decimated them. He murdered, as you say, one man in every ten in both cohorts. At five centuries per cohort, that means he ordered the death of more than one hundred of his own men. Do you really believe those one hundred men didn't have mothers, didn't have fathers, didn't have uncles and aunts and cousins too? He didn't give them a quick, clean death by beheading either: He had them beaten to death by their comrades. Was he pathetic and small like me?"

"I don't believe you," she said, but he could see the uncertainty in her eyes. "He would never have done anything so cruel."

"I was there, Romilia! I was a junior tribune on my first campaign, just like Marcus is now. I saw them run, I saw your grandfather pronounce his judgment, and I saw them beaten into bloody, lifeless pulp by the fists of their fellows. It may have been cruel, but he was absolutely right to order it, because I can tell you that there were three or four other cohorts damn near to running themselves, and if they had, the Great Orc's war boars would have trampled us all into the mud and eaten our bodies afterward. And the only reason they didn't run is because our centurions were screaming at them, shouting at them, whipping them, and above all, promising that running might save them from the orcs, but it wouldn't save them from the wrath of your grandfather!"

Romilia didn't answer. Nor did she look at him. She just stared at her hands, until the tears running down her face began to drip from her chin and onto her folded hands. "I suppose you're right. It's just so awful," she finally said. "It's so cruel. I don't know how you can stand it. And I wish you hadn't permitted Marcus to follow in your footsteps."

As it always had before, he found his anger washed away by her tears. He stepped forward to cradle her head in his left arm, and he dried her cheeks with the back of his right hand. "The world is cruel, my dear. You have a soft and merciful heart, and I am glad of that, but we live in a fallen world, and there is no room for mercy in the legions. That is why I give thanks, almost every night, that the Almighty is merciful as well as just. If man's justice is colder and harder than steel, I fear to even imagine what divine justice would be like."

She bit her lip and shook her head. "This must just be killing Julia."

"She looked like an old woman when I saw her two days ago. Magnus hadn't told her the whole story then, but she must know by now. He's more than half-mad with grief himself."

"You saw them already?"

"The first thing I did upon arriving here was to deliver Fortex's bones to them. Saturnius came with me to pay his respects."

"Did Magnus know the truth? About Fortex's death?"

"I told him, fortunately before Julia arrived. It was ugly. I didn't expect him to thank me, but my idiot brother actually struck me. Can you believe that? In front of my fascitors, no less."

"Oh, no," she gasped, alarmed. "You didn't have him arrested, did you?"

"Of course not! Do you think me mad? That wouldn't have been justice—it would have been pure sadism. He was out of his mind with grief. I ordered them to forget it ever happened."

She put her arms around his waist and pressed her head against his chest.

He could feel her shaking as she cried. He would have liked to have said something to comfort her but, considering how his previous attempts had gone, decided to simply hold his tongue. A few moments later, she dried her eyes on his tunic and pushed back from him.

"Never mind what I say when I'm angry with you, Corvus. You're a good man, you are. I know you would have saved Gaius Valerius if it was possible. I don't understand these things. I don't even want to think about them. But someone has to, and I'm glad it's someone like you rather than the likes of Patronus or Centho."

"Damned by faint praise indeed." He stroked her hair. "I'm sorry. It's going to be hard on you, I know. Don't blame Julia if she doesn't want to see you or speak to you for some time. The wound is still raw, and it isn't going to heal anytime soon, if ever."

"Poor Sextus. He looked up to Fortex so. I hope this won't cause too much of a rift between him and Marcus when Marcus returns home."

"I don't think you'll have to worry about that anytime soon," Corvus told her. "I don't like the reports I'm hearing from the provinces. If we don't put down the Cynothii quickly next spring, I wouldn't be surprised if the rebellion spreads to two or three more provinces by mid-summer. I've even heard that there are some unpleasant rumblings among some of the allies, and that would be a real nightmare."

Corvus heard a polite cough behind him and turned around. Nicenus stood in the doorway with Torquatus at his side. The majordomus looked a little embarrassed, but he could hardly be expected to have denied entry to the ruler of the city.

"My lord consul, my lady, I apologize for disturbing you, but the Consul Civitas assured me it was urgent."

"Of course, Nicenus," Corvus assured him as he stepped adroitly away from his wife. "Good morning, Titus Manlius. This is an unexpected honor. What is it?"

Torquatus entered. He was neither tall nor short, and his close-cropped hair had mostly receded, but he carried such an air of unconscious power that he seemed to fill the room. His features were thick and rounded, and this morning, they were weighed down with obvious worry.

"I'm sorry for the intrusion, Lady Valeria, but there has been murder, concerning which I very much need to consult with your husband."

"Think nothing of it, my lord Manlius," she assured him. "But since when is murder a matter for the consuls? Isn't there a quaestor available?"

Torquatus glanced at Corvus, then grimly shook his head. "This is no matter for quaestors, Lady Valeria. Six princes of the Church were murdered while in conclave at the Sanctal Palace last night. Including, I am deeply distressed to report, both of the leading candidates to replace the Sanctified Father."

"There is something exceedingly troubling about this," Torquatus commented as the two men took in the full extent of the gory devastation that surrounded them in the chapel. "I've seen murders, and I've seen the aftermath of some reasonably hard-fought battles, but I can't say I've ever seen anything like this before. And certainly never anywhere near here!"

The two consuls were surrounded by a small army of fascitors as well as guards from both the Manlian and Valerian households and a squad of armored Michaeline priests. Six Sanctal guards stood watch at the door. They could hardly have been safer were they ensconced in the heart of a stone-walled castra, surrounded by two legions.

And yet Corvus felt a cold frisson of terror run up his spine as he looked at the dead bodies of the once-powerful churchmen sprawled in a variety of impossible poses around the high-ceilinged chamber. Two had their throats torn out, and three had been disemboweled as if by the claws of an enormous feline. Their flesh looked as if it had been torn by teeth that were pointed, though not necessarily sharp. It was a tableau out of a mad butcher's Hell.

"No man did this." Torquatus turned to a pair of gold-cloaked Michaelines, who were examining a large pool of blood that appeared to have been forcibly liberated from the body of Carvilius Noctua, the less likely of the two main contestants for the Ivory Throne. "A demon—or demons—wouldn't you say?"

The warrior priest, whose scarred face made Corvus think the man had probably seen as many battles as he had himself, shook his head. "I would not. There is no indication of any demonic activity here, my lord consul. Not in the material sense, at any rate. The wounds may not be consistent with conventional bladed weaponry, but neither is there any of the spiritual pollution that a demon capable of manifesting physically and wreaking such havoc would leave behind."

"You're sure of that, are you?" Torquatus demanded.

"As sure as my lord consul is confident that these men were neither struck down by arrows nor run through with swords. However, there is something more. Look here. These smears of blood look convincingly ritualistic. They're complicated, and there is an amount of detail to the patterns. To the uneducated eye, they would appear to be indicative of something esoteric at work. But they're almost entirely without meaning."

"How can you possibly know that?" Corvus's colleague demanded. "You Michaelines aren't magicians. By the blood of Unctios, how would you know it's not some sort of occult inscription used for a demonic summoning or something?"

The priest blinked slowly and did not respond right away, clearly unimpressed by Torquatus's consular status. "Our training is comprehensive, my lord consul. In order to counteract the various magicks of our enemies in the field, it is necessary for us to be familiar with them. The fact that we refuse to soil our souls with the practice of their dark arts should not be taken as ignorance of them."

"Then what are you suggesting, sir?" Corvus broke in before Torquatus could further annoy the Michaeline.

"It is not a suggestion, my lord consul. At this point, it is at most only a suspicion. My thought is that it is no secret to anyone that this republic brooks no traffic in the esoteric arts. Therefore, it is reasonable to suppose that whoever did this would have believed that the quaestors investigating the murders would think these false symbols are real. They can't have anticipated that the consuls would be involved or turn to our order for assistance. Nor would they necessarily have known the full extent of our knowledge of the occult."

"A false trail, then," Corvus nodded. It made an amount of sense. Whoever did this couldn't have thought it would go uninvestigated, so an amount of misdirection would be wise. "Orcs, do you think? Or kobolds."

The Michaeline smiled approvingly. "You are on the right track, Lord Consul Valerius, but I should guess neither. You've fought orcs before, I believe, so I draw your attention to the observation that none of these men has been vivisected."

"Not orcs, then." The priest was right, Corvus realized. Orcs, especially those eschewing the use of conventional arms, had often been known to rip a man's limbs off his body. But each of the dead men were more or less whole. Also, when he looked more closely at the body of the nearest celestine, he could see that the teeth marks on his face and chest were much too close together to have been left behind by the jaws of an orc. And now that he was on that train of thought, he could also see that the wounds were also much too small to have been inflicted by an orc's massive tusks. "Not kobolds either?"

"No, my lord consul. Kobold teeth are small and somewhat needle-like. These marks were left by teeth that were thicker and more jagged. See how the edges of the wounds are torn and crushed rather than slashed?"

"Goblins," Torquatus interjected. "Nasty creatures indeed. But how would a pack of goblins get into the palace? Or into Amorr, for that matter? It's not as if they're permitted residence here."

"You have it, my lord consul. I am confident it was goblins. But I see you are not one for the games. The Greens always keep quite a few of them in their stables, mostly as minor attractions between the major bouts. I saw some in the arena just a few months ago myself—they were pitted against dwarves. The poor creatures didn't last long, but I should think two or three would have been more than a match for a few unarmed old men."

"That's as may be, but even if the priest here is correct, who is to say that there wasn't some sorcery involved in disguising them?" Torquatus asked. "It's not as if one could simply march a pack of goblins through the streets and into the palace without attracting attention." He looked around the room in disgust. "And in any event, I'm not convinced there wasn't something seriously amiss here. I can't imagine evil has penetrated so deeply into the Church hierarchy that this many celestines were involved in some filthy practice. Could it be that there was a secret coven active within the Conclave and what we're seeing here is the consequence of some black magick gone awry? Evil ever delights in feeding upon evil."

"We can search the city for goblins, beginning with the stables," Corvus suggested. "But how do you propose determining if there was sorcery at work here if the Michaelines don't see it?"

Torquatus snorted bitterly. "I suppose it would be easier if over the years we hadn't executed everyone likely to know anything about it. There must be a few secret practitioners hidden away somewhere in the city, though. There always are. We can have the quaestors make inquiries, and I'm sure the Michaelines must have a few inquisitors who would be helpful."

"No, that's not necessary," Corvus told his colleague as a thought occurred to him. "We don't need to dig for any hidden mages, not when there are two highly skilled sorcerers who practice their arts openly. They don't practice them here, of course, but they will almost certainly have the knowledge we need. And if they don't, I can't think who would."

"Sorcerers, here in Amorr?" Torquatus looked at him as if he'd lost his mind. "What are you talking about?"

"Take some men with you to the elven ambassador's residence." Corvus had already turned to Caius Vecellius. "Give the ambassador our regards, and inform him his presence is requested at the Sanctal Palace by the Consul Civitas and the Consul Aquilae. Escort him here and answer his questions, but don't tell him about the murders. Just tell him we have urgent need of his esoteric expertise and ask that he come without delay."

The captain of his fascitors saluted, divided his squad with two simple gestures, and departed hastily with five men at his heels.

Corvus looked at Torquatus and shrugged. "The ambassador is surely of noble elven blood, and from what my son tells me, most of Elebrion's aristocracy are far more learned in their various witcheries than any human could hope to be."

"This is a dirty business, Corvus. I don't like it. Involving elves in a Church affair? The Church is already going to be in a state with this many celestines dead in the middle of a conclave!"

"No more do I, my friend. No more do I. But as we're told they have souls too, I can't see any harm in it or that it's any more sinful than asking a ruffian about how a knife was used."

"It is already going to be bad enough when word leaks out. People are waiting for a new Sanctiff. They're going to think the worst when they find out half the electors are dead. And if anyone discovers elves are involved somehow, they're bound to get it wrong. They might even think the elves were responsible!"

"Then it will be up to us to make sure they know that is not the case. We can handle the people." Corvus indicated the dead bodies surrounding them. "I shouldn't think what's left of the Sacred College will be in any state to object either. Now let's go outside. It will take Vecellius some time to fetch the elf, and this place stinks like a charnel house."

FJOTRA

THE grey fury of the aalvarg pack crashed into the Dalarn shield wall. All the howls and shrieks, to say nothing of the clash of metal on metal below them, carried easily to Fjotra's vantage point high above the battlefield. How downright deafening it must be to be caught in the middle of such chaos! She thanked her stars that she was only witnessing the furious violence safely from a distance.

Claws and teeth tore at exposed flesh, but more often than not, they failed to pierce the iron shields and boiled leather armor of the northmen. Whereas the tough shaggy fur of the aalvarg was not nearly tough enough to protect them from the heavy axe blades that severed limbs and split skulls and breastbones alike with equal ease.

"I'm not sure your father's men even need our knights," Blais, the elder battlemage, commented with satisfaction as the big black creature that had led the attack was staggered by an artfully swung shield that smashed against its right knee from the side, followed by an axe head burying itself into its opposite hip.

The beast shrieked and lunged at its tormentor, but received the bottom half of the shield in its jaws for its trouble. A second Dalarn warrior stepped forward and put the howling aalvarg out of its misery with a spear thrust that pierced its throat.

The fall of their leader was too much for the undisciplined beasts. Demoralized, they fell back from the shield wall in some disarray. They left behind nearly thirty dead and wounded, and about a dozen men slipped from behind the safety of the shields to finish off the latter. It was a brutal business, and for a moment, Fjotra felt her stomach beginning to roil, but the memory of Garn's fallen sustained her.

There were only three Dalarn down upon the ground, and at least one of them was crawling slowly toward the rear of the line, his right side a mass of blood. Two of his companions lifted him and began carrying him back toward the hills that hid the Savoners.

The aalvarg leader and his guards, or perhaps they were his officers, stopped the retreat of the creatures by means of a series of barks, blows, and bites.

"If the big one is going to simply keep smashing them against that shield wall, these things are less intelligent than I'd imagined," Patrice observed.

Blais didn't reply. The elder mage was too busy studying something on the field below them. "Do you notice anything strange about those two wolves the leader has near him? I mean, the real wolves?"

"They appear to be better trained than his troops," his younger colleague replied with a wry smile.

"I'm not sure they're even animals. There is something strange about them. I can feel some sort of aura radiating out from them, and it's getting stronger. It's almost as if there is some sorcery surrounding their bodies, or it may even be contained within them."

"An illusion, perhaps, or some sort of enchantment?"

"If it is an illusion, it's too strong for me to see through it. But in that case, the aura isn't anywhere nearly as powerful as it would have to be."

"Do you think they might be the leader's familiars? He could be drawing some sort of power from them."

As the two mages discussed the wolves, Fjotra observed them closely. The older man was right to be suspicious. There was something very strange about them.

Their predatory eyes were clearly more intelligent than those of the wolves that she'd so often seen lurking around the evening fires. They were unusually calm and showed no signs of agitation even though they were very nearly in the midst of all the extraordinary sights, sounds, and smells of a violent battle. And then, when the two animals exchanged a glance with one another, she knew.

"Those are no animals, my lord mages. Those are *sigskifting*."

"They're what?" Patrice asked incredulously.

"Sigskifting. It mean they change their skin when they want. I hear those things before, but I do not believe them. The Wolves and the Moon—it is stories for children. But those two, I think they are not true wolves."

Patrice shook his head, but more in disbelief than denial. "That's not possible. Masks and illusions are one thing, but to materially change one's corporeal being…. I can't think how one would even begin to go about it."

Fjotra looked back at the aalvarg. As the commander's black guards shoved and snapped their milling ranks back into a semblance of rudimentary order, the two big wolves moved in a perfectly coordinated manner behind them, stopping to urinate on the ground every few seconds. They appeared to be making a pattern of sorts, but it was complicated, and she was unable to make any sense of it. But their movements confirmed for her that, whatever they were, they were more than mere animals.

"Look at that," she pointed as the two giant beasts squatted again to release a splash of urine. "Do beasts do that?"

"Amazing," Patrice breathed. "It's clearly some form of ritual. If it's a spell, I'd imagine it must be based on an earth magic. Blais, do you realize we may be witnessing the first known example of ritual urine magic?"

For the love of the Thunderer, did the foolish man ever stop babbling? Fjotra wanted to strangle him. It was obvious that whatever the two sigskiftings were doing wasn't likely to be harmless to the men standing in the shield wall. The Dalarn were too few to attack the waiting aalvarg, who still outnumbered them two-to-one. They had no choice but to stand their ground and wait until whatever evil magic the skinchangers were preparing was ready. And, of course, the Savoner warriors couldn't possibly have any idea what was in store for them, never having fought the beasts before.

"Can you not stop those?" she asked the two mages. "What you wait for?"

"I would think we probably could, but we're under strict orders not to reveal ourselves." The older battlemage shook his head. "The ulfin don't even know we have battle magic, since your people don't. It would be most unwise to show our hand this early. Unless we can be certain to wipe them out completely, we do not dare."

"If it is bad magic, many Dalarn will die!"

"Don't you think we can signal the prince now, Blais?" Patrice pointed to the mass of aalvarg. "I'd say it's more important to kill the two whatever she called them, the wolf-mages, than a hundred of the regular sort. If nothing else, a cavalry charge by a few hundred horse should distract them nicely and interfere with any spellcasting."

"Yes, that's true, I suppose. But I'd quite like to see whatever it is they're preparing. Right now, we have no idea what their capabilities are. This won't give us a ceiling, but at least it will provide us with a conceptual floor of sorts."

Fjotra was aghast. She didn't understand what they were discussing, but one thing was clear: They were willing to let her people die in order to satisfy their damnable curiosity about wolf magic. She reached out and grabbed the front of the silvered breastplate that Patrice was wearing over his blue robes.

"If you no sound horn now, I jump up and scream!"

The two Savonders looked at each other, then at her.

She glared back at them, undaunted. They might be masters of terrible magics and capable of turning her into a fox or boiling the very blood inside her, but she knew they wouldn't dare, not so long as she had the favor of their king's son and heir. Or as long as they were planning to stay within the high-walled safety of her father's great fortress. Of course, they could simply bind her mouth, either with rags or by magic, but threatening to scream and alert the enemy was about her only option.

"We've already learned a considerable amount," Patrice admitted. "And we really should save as many of those northmen as we can. God knows the Reaver King needs every man he's got, and every one we save today means one less man-at-arms we've got to bring from across the sea when the king decides to add the isles to the realm."

Blais glanced down at the pattern that the two wolves had nearly finished marking on the ground. He sighed, but at last he shrugged and reached for the horn tied to his belt. "I suppose we have our orders." He adroitly untied the leather thongs, raised his horn to his lips, and blew three sharp blasts. The heads of the aalvarg jerked up in almost perfect unison as the signal echoed across the battlefield below, followed by a loud cheer from the Dalarn shield wall.

The two wolf-mages, however, paid it no heed. Their complicated pattern completed, they appeared to be snarling and growling, although at such a distance it was impossible for Fjotra to see exactly what they were doing. She wished for another water lens. The steam rising from the pattern in the ground abruptly flared red, and the assembled aalvarg began to howl, loud enough to drown out the cheers of the Dalarn warriors as well as the rumbling sound of the Savonders who were beginning to ride out behind and below her.

"Did you feel that?" Patrice asked Blais, sounding worried. The older battlemage nodded.

"Let it be. Whatever it is, we're not to interfere further unless the prince is in danger. We don't want them to know we have magic too."

"What is it?" Fjotra pulled at Patrice's sleeve.

"The spell. Whatever power those two mages summoned with their piss magic is being released now. Blais and I can feel it, but we don't know what it is. We could try to break it up, but if we did, their mages might learn about us, and we can't have that."

But when the two companies of cavalry entered the field, they discovered the nature of the aalvarg spell. The mass of aalvarg began frothing at the mouth and snarling uncontrollably. Fjotra recognized it immediately—even in monstrous beasts, it was impossible to mistake the signs of a berserker. Only instead of five or ten battle-crazed warriors tearing off their clothes and biting at their shields, there were nearly three hundred wolf monsters going mad with rage!

The two mages recognized it too.

"Well, it must be a new experience for your friends to see the berserkers on the other side for a change," Patrice commented. His tone was cool, but his eyebrows had nearly climbed to his hairline.

"Why you say that?" Fjotra was confused. There were often berserkers on both sides when the tribes fought, which, prior to the coming of the wolf demons, had not been uncommon.

The gleaming sight of the two massive groups of horsemen cantering toward them was enough to nearly sober the maddened aalvarg. But their magical courage soon returned, and despite the furious efforts of the aalvarg commander and his officers to arrange them into some sort of defensive position that would allow them to face both cavalry forces at the same time, first one aalvarg broke away from the pack and charged at the shield wall, then another. Soon they were followed by a third, then a fourth, and before long nearly all the monsters were baying and charging recklessly back toward the Dalarn warriors.

It was a terrible sight to see that maddened grey flood rushing at what looked like a painfully inadequate dam, but even though the front two lines of the wall staggered as the crazed wolf-beasts leaped fearlessly upon their shields and impaled themselves on spears, they did not break and run.

A grey flood of wolf flesh surged toward the shield wall, which now looked tragically weak. Like a storm wave crashing upon rocks the crazed wolf-beasts leapt savagely upon the shields.

The front two lines in the shield wall staggered but held, and scores of aalvarg squealed, impaled on spears. The warriors shouted and steadied and kept their shields raised.

"Perfect!" Blais exulted. "Those furry bastards finally stuck themselves in, precisely as we'd hoped. And here comes the prince, precisely in time to hammer them against the anvil."

The Red Prince looked a brave and formidable sight in his crimson armor. The powerful black horse upon which he rode was nearly as magnificent as the prince himself, and behind him rode a burly man-at-arms who sat his horse with all the grace of a sack of flour. But the man's arms were thicker than Fjotra's thighs, and he held a staff upon which the prince's unadorned red flag proudly sailed beneath another flag bearing the royal crest. Behind them rode two hundred armored horse, the bulk of the Savonder force, looking calm and lethal.

A horn blew once, and the armored riders lowered their lances in unison. It blew again, and the riders picked up speed but held formation. One giant arrowhead of riders aimed at the aalvarg right, the other aimed at the opposite flank.

The riders on the left struck their target just moments before the riders on the right. A tremendous cacophony of shrieking metal, crunching bones, and horseflesh slamming hard against wolfish muscle. Aalvarg died by the scores almost immediately, and panic erupted in the middle of their ranks.

Some of the beasts tore at each other with their claws and jaws even as their companions closer to the edges fought desperately and died—some spitted on the ends of the knights' long lances, others having their skulls crushed by the heavy warhammers wielded by the stronger knights.

Inspired by their reinforcements, the Dalarn in the shield wall began to sing as they fought to straighten out and stabilize their line. Their deep voices provided a haunting accompaniment to the high-pitched howls and screams of the wounded and dying aalvarg.

Many warriors didn't even use their weapons but simply pressed their shoulders against their companions on either side and, using their shields alone, manfully shoved back the wolves snapping and clawing at their faces.

Too berserk to pay any attention to their leader or even bother to defend themselves, the aalvarg were surrounded on three sides and slaughtered as fast as the Savonders could cut them down or trample them.

"They've got to get those mages," Patrice shouted to Blais.

"But how will they know to do that?" Blais responded. "If the Red Prince or one of the other captains even notices them at all, they'll think they're just animals like we did."

But if the Red Prince didn't notice the two wolf-mages, he most certainly had his eyes on the aalvarg leader, who was still standing toward the rear, his disbelief at the overwhelming devastation being wreaked in a matter of moments by the heavy human cavalry palpable even on his lupine face.

Fjotra watched as Prince Karl, having lost his lance, smashed his mailed fist into the jaws of a scrawny, undersized beast that snapped at him, then drew his sword and brought it down in a vicious sweeping motion, causing a fountain of dark red blood to erupt from the throat of another aalvarg. He raised the dripping blade high above his head in what was either a salute or a threat directed at the enemy leader, then spurred his horse toward the aalvarg.

The big horse launched itself forward, and the Red Prince brought his sword around in a powerful side-stroke.

But the aalvarg leader wasn't there. Fjotra watched, astounded, as the aalvarg abruptly transformed himself into a giant mottle-furred wolf, just in time for the prince's sword to slash through the air a hands-breadth above its head, where its chest had been but a moment before. The transformation happened without warning, in a flash as quick as any lightning.

"Did you see that!" Patrice cried out in awe.

Neither Blais nor Fjotra replied, both struck dumb by the incredible sight.

The force of his missed swing nearly caused the prince to lose his balance, and his unsteady seat was made still more precarious by the jaws of the wolf as it slashed at his horse's right leg as it passed by.

But the prince's steed was trained for war, and the prince himself was an excellent rider, even in his heavy armor, and he managed to stay in the saddle to bring his horse around for a second pass. The aalvarg leader had no intention of fighting to the death. The big wolf broke and ran toward the forest with the two mage-wolves on either side of him. When it reached the edge of the trees, it lifted its head and howled. There were four or five answering howls, and five more dark-furred wolves extricated themselves from the melee and began to flee after the three *sigskiftings*.

Four of them managed to evade the cavalry that was milling about, but one was knocked from its feet as it tried to dash between the legs of a knight's horse and was trampled instead. It rolled sideways and struggled to its feet, but one leg appeared to be broken, slowing it down.

As it limped after its fellows, a squadron of knights burst through the rapidly thinning line of aalvarg berserkers, and one of them casually drove his lance through the beast's body, behind the shoulder. The lance broke off, and the wolf slumped to the ground, its body convulsing violently. Gradually, the erratic movements slowed until they finally stopped, and as Fjotra and the two mages looked on in amazement, the dying wolf transformed back into its monstrous half-man, half-wolf form at the moment of death.

"Can they all do that?" Patrice wondered.

"The shape-shifting or the magic?" Blais asked him.

"Both, I wonder," Patrice replied. "Hopefully not the latter, or we're in for a world of hurt. I'm not sure they're related. We both felt the spell when it was being prepared, but I didn't notice anything when the first one changed, or when the others did."

"I felt nothing either, not even when that last one died, and I'm sure I would have noticed. It might be a good sign if the magic isn't related to the transforming ability. Perhaps the shapechanging is some sort of intrinsic magic for some of them, or perhaps even all of them. If so, then the likelihood that every single one of them is a mage of some sort is low."

"We need a prisoner," Patrice concluded, and the other mage nodded as he banished all three of the magical lenses he had created.

"One of the shapechangers would have been best, but even a common beast could prove useful. We had better get down there quickly before they finish killing all of them. It's going to be difficult capturing one when they've all been driven berserk by that spell."

Fjotra gingerly touched with her finger the water that had fallen on the grass. It looked for all the world as if it were simply dew, albeit late in the day as well as the season.

Patrice rose stiffly and extended a hand to help Fjotra to her feet. She took it gratefully, for after lying so long in the cold grass, her legs were stiff and unsteady too.

"It shouldn't be difficult to break the spell," Patrice said. "And we can always put one to sleep with a soporific."

"Absolutely not! We don't show them anything." The older mage's tone was uncompromising. "I can only imagine how many eyes are upon us. We know they have at least two mages, perhaps as many as seven, and most likely dozens more. Even if we're stronger than them, and I think we can safely assume that we're better trained, we don't dare put ourselves in a position where they will target us. Besides, it's always wise to hold your cards until you have no choice but to reveal them."

They made their way down the hill, which was steeper on the northern side that abutted the battlefield. Fjotra slipped several times, but she waved off Patrice's attempt to take her hand. His constant attentions were well within the bounds of propriety, but they were beginning to annoy her. She didn't know how it was in Savonne, but it was not the place of a shaman to pay court to a king's daughter no matter what eldritch powers he commanded.

The battle was still winding down, but the violence was too far away to be dangerous. About fifty or sixty aalvarg were still alive, having been surrounded and forced into a defensive circle that was steadily growing smaller as the knights and mounted men-at-arms repeatedly smashed into them and struck down four or five of the beasts, then rode away just far enough to regroup and do it again.

Twice, the Red Prince halted his knights and tried to convince the undaunted beasts that continued resistance was hopeless, but either the surviving aalvarg didn't understand his language and gestures, or else they were too maddened by the magic of the wolf-mages to consider surrendering.

Finally, Fjotra saw the prince's shoulders slump, after which he had a brief conversation with one of his nobles that was followed by half of the riders assembling themselves into what she could see was a large wedge formation. The final outcome of the battle was never in doubt as the heavily armored knights rode over the remaining aalvarg to the rousing sound of Dalarn cheers, as if the powerful beasts were little more than helpless kittens.

The battlefield, once Fjotra and the mages reached it, was even more ghastly than she had ever imagined one could be. Everywhere she looked, there was blood, mud, and furry bodies missing limbs or torn open. In some particularly awful cases, the dead were barely identifiable as corpses. Here and there, scattered in amongst the bestial creatures was a motionless human figure encased in bright steel—or worse, a slain Dalarn warrior. To her relief, there were not many of them.

But if what she saw was terrible, what she smelled was even worse. The stench was unbelievable, and she desperately fought the urge to retch. Many, if not most, of the ulfin-wolves had fouled themselves as they'd died. The blood, the horses, and the acrid sweat of the hundreds of men around her were blended into a hellish miasma that threatened to overpower her senses.

This was victory? It was more like a vision of a unthinkably gruesome Hell. There was no glory in this. There was nothing noble. Even the bestial demonspawn aalvarg were pathetic in death. They looked much smaller and scrawnier than she remembered them being during the terrifying flight from Garn.

The noxious smells and sights of death were finally more than her stomach could bear. She doubled over and vomited. Patrice grabbed her arm, holding her upright, and she was too grateful for the support to take any offense at his touch. The very last thing she wanted was to fall onto her hands and knees in the dreadful blood-soaked swamp.

When she finished, she pushed back the hair that had fallen over her face and spit several times to clear the taste from her mouth. The air didn't smell any better, but at least the insidious pressure in the pit of her belly had been relieved.

"What are you cretins doing bringing the reaver princess down here?" she heard someone demand in a loud and angry voice.

She turned around and was startled to see the Red Prince, his armor already clean and wet from a recent sluicing, standing before her on foot. He was unhelmed, and his hair was wet, but there was still an amount of dark blood on the armor that protected his right hand and arm. He wasn't as tall as the warriors of her people, being not much taller than she was, but he radiated such magnificent confidence that she found herself almost in awe of him.

She instinctively curtsied, as the comtesse had trained her.

The act drew a wry smile from the royal Savoner.

"I daresay that is the first time anyone has curtsied to me on a battle-field. I think I rather like it. I may very well demand it of my captains in the future. But Your Highness, you should not be here. It is no place for a lady."

"I am well, thank you. I was ill at first, but I am much better now. We came down because your lord mages want a prisoner, and they did not think it wise to leave me alone on the top of the hill."

"Bloody damned fools, mages," the prince growled, and despite all the horror surrounding her, Fjotra found herself smiling at Patrice's discomfiture. "Well then, did you at least manage to keep your magic to yourselves as I told you?"

Fjotra saw Patrice nod, although she wondered if the magical far-seeing lenses counted.

The prince looked satisfied, though, and waved over a knight who was still mounted. "Michel! See if you can find two wolves that aren't dead. Bind their front legs, tie their jaws shut, and get them cleaned up. You'll probably have to march them back on foot, since the horses don't seem to like the way they smell. Can't say I blame them either. The cursed monsters reek to high heaven, and that's before they shit themselves! Bring them to our noble battlemages here once you've found a likely pair. See if they meet with their liking."

"At once, your Highness."

"Are you satisfied, my lord mage?" The prince's tone seemed to indicate that Patrice had damn well better be.

"Entirely, your Highness. And at the risk of belaboring the obvious, I should like to point out that the wolf people appear to have considerably more magic at their disposal than we had previously believed."

"Yes, you know, I actually noticed as much when their warleader unexpectedly turned into a right proper wolf right in front of me." The Red Prince removed one of his gauntlets and rubbed his eyes. "I nearly pissed myself. What the Hell was that? I suppose you're going to tell me now that those two other wolves that ran off with the big bastard weren't actually wolves either."

"That's correct, your Highness. We believe they were the actual mages. We observed them preparing the spell that appeared to infuse the rank-and-file troops with so much courage and aggression. It was remarkable, actually. Their magic appears to be urine-based, at least with regards to the preparatory rituals. I was even thinking that—"

The prince raised a hand. "I have no doubt it is entirely fascinating, Lord Patrice, but let us save this discussion of ulfin urinary habits for after you have interrogated your prisoners. I can't imagine the men have finished butchering all of them as yet. Sieur de Platins is finding a pair for you, so why don't you chase after him and see what sort of shape they're in? I will see that Her Reaver Highness is returned to the castle immediately and with proper escort."

Patrice looked as if he wanted to protest, but he bowed obediently, then bowed again to Fjotra before striding off through the muck in the direction that the knight had ridden.

No sooner had the battlemage departed when another man took his place. It was a face she knew well. Steinthor Strongbow was one of her father's best and bravest fighters, and he was the man who had been commanding the Dalarn rearguard. Between his height and his long, waist-length blond braid, he had been easy to see from afar.

"Well met. Captain Strongbow, isn't it?" The prince looked genuinely pleased to see the bold warrior and clapped the taller man on his shoulder. "You and your men cut it a little closer than I'd anticipated, but then, you've been fighting these creatures for a long time, haven't you?"

Fjotra quickly translated the gist of his words to her father's man.

"Tell him to call me just 'Steinthor,'" the big Dalarn told her, but he was grinning, and to Fjotra's surprise, he even ducked his head respectfully. "And say the men asked me to thank him and his officers. We were holding strong, but they were pressing us hard, and we would have lost twice as many men if they hadn't come so quickly."

Fjotra conveyed the message as precisely as she could manage and was gratified to see the prince smile even more broadly.

"You and your men are damned fine fighters, and you can fight with me any time!" he declared.

The victorious bonhomie was broken, however, by the sound of hoof-beats pounding toward them from the direction of Raknarborg. Fjotra could tell it was one of her father's riders, as it didn't sound like one of the heavy-boned southern horses capable of carrying a steel-armored man on its back.

Sure enough, the rider rounded the curve of the hill to her right, and she could see long hair that was very nearly white trailing behind him. His clothing was the drab browns and greens of her people, not the bright hues favored by the Savonders. The rider initially made for the crowd of warriors clustered around Asmund Hairy-Arse, but upon seeing Steinthor and the Red Prince, he changed his course and very nearly rode all three of them down before reining his horse in, such was his haste.

But the young man ignored the prince and the veteran warrior alike in favor of Fjotra.

"There you are, Fjotra!" he cried, breathless.

"Yes," she nodded slowly. "Do you bring word from the Skull-breaker?"

"Your father told me to tell you that everyone must return to the fortress at once! All of you! Do not delay or the wolves may prevent your retreat!"

Steinthor, hearing the urgency in the voice of the king's messenger, stepped forward. "Retreat? Look around you, boy! We smashed them. The few that survived are still running through the woods with their tails between their legs!"

The rider shook his head. Fjotra recognized him now, he was the cousin of her uncle's second wife. His name, if she recalled correctly, was Neri.

"The scouts have returned. Three more of their kings are marching toward Raknarborg." He looked at the wolf bodies on the ground. "This was the smallest of the four armies. You must ride back now at once! The Skullbreaker demands it!" His eyes pleaded with Fjotra's. "He told me that you must convince the Savonders to return or they will be trapped outside the walls."

She glanced at the Red Prince and saw he was watching the exchange with narrowed eyes and a suspicious expression on his face. Seeing that she was looking at him, he pointed to Neri and spread his hands.

"There are more of them," the prince said. "More wolves."

"Yes, how do you know?" She was amazed. Was he already learning her tongue?

He seemed to read her mind, for he laughed and shook his head. "I didn't understand a word that either of you said, but the only thing your father and I feared was that this camp might be a trap and we could be cut off if we rode out this far. What else could be so urgent? Do the wolves stand between us and the castle?"

"No," she said. "He come from my father. The Skullbreaker only say all must return, very fast. There are more, many more, who come."

The prince nodded, seemingly unconcerned. "The sooner we get the men out of this gruesome mire, the better. I think they have had enough for the day. What about your men, though? They have no horse, and their wounded are going to slow them down."

Fjotra turned to Steinthor and put the prince's question to him.

The big warrior shrugged. "We leave behind those who can't march fast. Perhaps they make it. Some men will stay with them."

But there was a flash of anger on the prince's face when she gave him Steinthor's answer. "No," he barked immediately. "How many wounded does he have? How many who cannot keep the pace?"

Somewhere between fifteen and twenty was the response.

The prince gestured at his big flag bearer and removed his other gauntlet. He was speaking too quickly for Fjotra to follow what he was saying, but she could see neither the flag bearer nor the two captains who were similarly summoned a few moments later were at all happy with his orders. But after a brief and furious exchange of words, which culminated in the prince hurling his gauntlet in the mud at Sieur de Platins's feet, the two men rushed off and began gathering their men. The flag bearer, meanwhile, lifted the horn that was at his belt and blew four long notes.

"I do not understand," Fjotra told the prince. "Will you not come as my father say?"

"Yes, yes, of course we will. But we're not going to leave your wounded behind. Tell your captain here that we will put on our horses as many of them as cannot march, along with our armor, and lead them back to the castle. Now, where are those damned mages? I want you to leave now and ride ahead with them, your Highness." He turned and looked about the battlefield, which was suddenly full of activity again, searching for the distinctive royal blue cloaks of the battlemages. "Blancas! De Foix! Get your sorcerous derrières over here at once!"

"Bring your wounded here, to the prince," Fjotra ordered Steinthor, who had been quizzing Neri concerning the approaching aalvarg armies, apparently to little avail. "The Savonders will put them on their horses and march with you."

"They will?" the blond warrior's bearded jaw dropped with astonishment. He turned toward Prince Karl, who was simultaneously arguing with the two mages while having his flag bearer help him out of his blood-red armor. "He would do that for us?"

"He will if you bring your men here quickly, son of Halfgarm." Fjotra snarled at him as ferociously as her father would. "Hurry! I'll not have the Skullbreaker lose his best men and his only ally because you tarried!"

Steinthor nodded and ran toward where the wounded Dalarn warriors were gathered, receiving whatever rudimentary care their fellows could provide.

Fjotra whirled around and found Neri, wide-eyed by the chaotic response to the message he'd delivered. "Ride back to Raknarborg now," she told him. "Tell my father the Savonders are riding to protect our men and they'll be slowed by the wounded. Tell him he must come out in force and protect their line of retreat. And if need be, remind him that no Dalarn king is less brave than a southern prince."

"Fjotra, I can't tell Skuli that!"

"You'll tell him exactly that!" she shouted at him. "Now go, damn you!"

He turned his horse and kicked it into a full gallop.

The prince was already free of the armor that covered his upper body. He grinned shamelessly at her as he slipped off the leather padding that had protected his pale skin from the steel. He was hairier than most of the men of her people. A moderate sprinkling of black hair, slick with sweat, covered his chest and made a line down over his belly. It both repelled and fascinated her, especially since underneath the dark hair he had the hard, rounded muscles of a true warrior.

"Do forgive my informal attire, my lady reaver, but it is blasted hot under all that steel. I fear my lord mages are unhappy about leaving their prisoners behind, but it's more important to get you back to your father. And them as well, seeing as the enemy appears to have their own magical resources."

Fjotra found it hard not to stare at him, especially since he was now unbuckling the metal skirt that guarded him from his waist down to his thighs. She wasn't entirely sure if she was relieved or disappointed to see that he was wearing soft leather leggings underneath his armor.

"I thank you for what you do," she finally said. "Is very noble, when save my father's men. I pray the gods you will be safe to Raknarborg."

"Noble?" He raised one black eyebrow quizzically. "Downright bloody regal, I should say. But your men earned it. And if what your rider said is true, we'll need every one of them. Now, it's sweet that you should pray for us, but never fear, I'll dine with you and your father in the castle this evening. I'd just as soon not subject the men to a second battle today, nor lose any men I need not. Besides, I wouldn't be worried even if there were five more of their armies on our heels."

He gestured toward the hundreds of wolfish bodies lying hacked apart and scattered throughout the field around them. The gesture spoke eloquently of his genuine lack of concern.

"Now get you gone, my lady, and you have my thanks for your courage. I really must have a few of my men learn your damned northern tongue, but in the meantime, I could not ask for a lovelier translator." To her surprise, he stepped forward, took her hand, and kissed it, just as he often did with the comtesse.

The sensation, combined with the nearness of his half-naked presence and his pleasant, musky scent that somehow drowned out the hellish stink of the incontinent dead, nearly caused her to swoon. She felt a strange warmth deep inside her that unsettled her even more than she could have imagined, and his grasp on her hand tightened as the world seemed to wheel about her.

"De Foix!" she heard someone shouting, but very far away. "Take her and get her out of here now. Are your horses nearby?"

"Close enough. We'll keep an eye on her, your Highness."

"Do, or I'll have your head."

"I'm fine," she tried to protest, but no one was listening to her. Patrice had a strong grip on her arm, and he was already dragging her back in the direction of the hill from which they'd descended.

When she looked back, she saw the Red Prince had turned his back on her and was issuing orders to his men as they began to help the first of the wounded Dalarn onto the backs of their war steeds turned pack horses. She could see that he truly wasn't afraid. He was like a lion. No, he was actually more like a very powerful black bear before whom the wolves of the forest would tremble.

And suddenly, to her surprise, she found herself again feeling more than a little envious of the comtesse.

MARCUS

MARCUS grew sweatier and tenser the closer he came to the rostrum, but somehow, the murderous attack he feared never arrived. When he reached the wooden steps and the sun's glare was no longer in his eyes, he saw that Honoratus was the only officer wearing his helmet. The four centurions were the primi ordines, the senior surviving officers of the legion behind himself, Trebonius, and the primus pilus.

Marcus studied their faces as he approached. He saw anger, he saw fear, and he saw doubt that was almost certainly directed at his ability to lead the legion. But what he did not see was guilt or secrecy or shame. There was relief and something akin to joy in the face of Trebonius. If he knew his friend at all, Gaius Trebonius would have been all but wetting himself over the thought of having to take command of the headless legion. He wasn't a Valerian, he wasn't born to rule over Amorr, and he didn't regard leadership as his natural birthright.

But when he met the dark brown eyes of the primus pilus, he saw something he had not expected. The senior centurion was angry, just as Cassabus had told him, but it wasn't the clean, honest wrath of a man whose beloved general had been treacherously murdered. Unless he missed his guess, it was the furious rage of a man whose plans had been thwarted.

For just a moment, at the very moment he reached the direct line of sight from the men on the platform, Marcus had seen the senior centurion's eyes widen with surprise. It must have been the decurion's helm that had fooled the centurion about Marcus's identity as he approached through the crushing mass of legionaries. You were not expecting to see me, Gnaeus Junius, he thought to himself. And you are not at all happy to see that I survived.

Marcus leaned toward Barbatus and whispered into the decurion's ear. "Slip off while we're addressing the men and search the tent of the primus pilus. If you can't find that wounded man or his body, search every tent of the first and second centuries."

The decurion didn't blink or say anything. He merely continued to look straight ahead at the men on the rostrum. But he nodded once, firmly, and Marcus knew he would obey.

When Marcus stepped upon the platform, Honoratus was the first to salute him, unhesitatingly thumping his fist against his chest. The rest of the primi ordines followed suit, as did Julianus and Trebonius. And if any of them wondered why he was surrounded by armored knights with their hands on their hilts, they did not ask.

Marcus merely nodded in response, knowing that a refusal to return their salutes would irritate one or two of them, but it was more important to establish his authority over them right here, right now.

"It's good to see you alive and well, Gaius Trebonius. You too, Gnaeus Junius. Is there any word of Castorius yet?"

"I sent seven of my men to search the pubs and brothels, Tribune." The primus pilus was a big man. He wasn't any taller than Marcus, but he was nearly twice his girth, and very little of it was fat. His arms were especially large, and although his torso was covered with much-bemedaled armor, the easy—uninjured—way he moved made it clear that he could not have been the night assassin even if Marcus had not seen him the night before. "They have not returned as yet."

Marcus nodded, but he was silently cursing his morning slumber. Sending men to look for Castorius was the first thing he should have done. But before he could reply, Julianus interrupted.

"I sent two riders over not long after sunrise. They came back before the horn and reported that no one saw the praefectus last night."

"Very well." Marcus cleared his throat. "In the absence of Sextus Castorius, it appears I am the senior officer surviving last night's attack. Therefore, I will assume command of the legion until such time as he returns to us. I assume I can rely on the support of the senior centurions and decurions, as well as you, Tribune Trebonius?"

"Of course, sir," Trebonius replied. Julianus too was quick to assent. The five centurions also indicated their compliance, one by one, although both Honoratus and the pilus prior of the third cohort had visible reservations.

"Then, gentlemen, I had better inform the men of the tragic events of last night. I would appreciate it if you would stand on my left, Gaius Trebonius. Gnaeus Junius, if you would do me the favor of standing on my right, I should appreciate your support." As well as not stabbing me in the back, he added to himself. He could only hope that the centurion would not be so bold as to strike in front of everyone.

The primus pilus grunted his agreement, but a faint flicker of a smile touched his lips. Gaius Trebonius, on the other hand, looked as if he was about to vomit, but he was still sufficiently aware to point to Marcus and tap at his own helmet.

Ah, yes. Marcus removed the helm and tossed it to Julianus, who caught it easily. It would not do to appear as a decurion, and anyway, it might better serve his purposes to show his face and remind the men that, however young he might be, he was still a patrician and the son of a House Martial.

He took a deep breath and prayed a short silent prayer for courage. Then he stepped forward to face the legion.

Nearly five thousand men stood in front of him. He looked out over the sea of hardened, unshaved, sunburned faces, all staring up at him and waiting for him to speak. But he did not talk right away, instead he slowly scanned the crowd, wondering if this was how Corvus had felt the first time he'd addressed an entire legion.

And in that moment, his nervousness disappeared. It was as if everything he had ever done, everything he ever was, had led him here. The thought that his father and his father's father had stood in exactly this position in a camp almost identical to this one filled him with a sense of tranquility and his fear seemed to slip away. He felt almost reluctant to break the spell that held so many brave and worthy men enrapt in such solemn silence, waiting upon his words.

"Men of Legio XVII, I am Marcus Valerius, the son of Sextus Valerius Corvus, tribunus militum by the voice of the People, your sworn brother. And, as of this morning, the senior surviving officer of this legion."

When he gave them the bad news, there came a sound like a rushing wind, as five thousand gasped as one. Except for a few involuntary cries of dismay that followed it, however, the men remained largely quiet even though he could see dismay and confusion on most of the faces of the men near the rostrum.

"Like the crow for which my father is named, I bring you dreadful news. Many of you will have heard the rumors, and I am sorry to confirm that they are true. The legate Marcus Saturnius is dead, murdered in his tent, along with two of his guards. The tribunus laticlavius, Aulus Crescentius, is dead as well. The praefectus Sextus Castorius is missing. Lucius Volusenus and two more of my tribunal colleagues are also dead. Gaius Trebonius and I are the only senior officers to survive what appears to have been a deliberate attempt to assassinate your entire command staff."

Anger, disbelief, and fear rose and crested on a chorus of what had to be at least three thousand voices all speaking simultaneously. He waited until the noise had died down enough to permit him to be heard, then jabbed his finger accusingly toward them.

"These foul deeds were committed by someone in this camp! Some-one in this camp has your legate's blood on his hands!"

A fury arose in response to his words. It was deafening, and it rocked the wooden platform on which he was standing. It was at once invig-orating and terrifying. As the angry legionaries shouted their futile but feverish denials at him, he began to understand why the ancient dema-gogues tended to describe a crowd as if it was a being in its own right, with a discernible spirit that could be mastered and manipulated by the sufficiently skilled.

"I myself was attacked by the assassin who murdered my fellow tribune, Gaius Marcius, last night. Fortunately, I had been on night patrol at the command of Marcus Saturnius and was still wearing my armor. It saved me, or you would be burning me in company with my colleagues, and Gaius Trebonius would be addressing you today. But the assassin did not succeed, and so I promise you this, men of Legio XVII: Together we will find those responsible for these evil deeds, and we shall have our vengeance for our murdered brothers and for the noble Marcus Saturnius!"

There were cheers and cries for revenge, but they were fewer and rather less fervent than he would have liked to hear. Perhaps it was too soon to speak of vengeance. Or more likely, the men believed it would be difficult, if not impossible, to determine who had committed the crimes, and they feared that the legion would be riven by suspicions and misgivings of the sort that are impossible to disprove or otherwise allay.

Marcus resisted the urge to glance at the primus pilus. He had no need to waste any time on a search for the killers. The man responsible was standing right beside him, and there were more urgent matters at hand. "Now I will demand that you prove yourselves worthy of your fallen general. I remind you of the oaths you swore when you joined the legion, that you are sworn to House Valerius, and that I am a true Valerian. I am telling you this because, in less than one week, we will be under attack."

He was pleased to see that the soldiers accepted his statement calmly, with little more reaction than to exchange a few significant glances with those around them. They were accustomed to being kept in the dark, after all. The reaction of the officers beside and behind him, on the other hand, was one of pure astonishment.

Trebonius blurted out his surprise, and Junius's head whipped around to glare at him as if he had sprouted scales and a forked tail. He could hear the shifting and muttering of the senior centurions behind his back. He imagined they were wondering if he had gone mad with fear and power.

He glanced back at the pilus priors and smiled at them. Strangely, he found the somber attitude of the legion filled him with more confidence rather than less. He was House Valerius, and this was a legion sworn not to Magnus, not to Corvus, but to the House. They were not only his men, they were his right—and they were his responsibility. He could win them over. He would win them over. It hadn't happened yet, but it would come soon. He could feel it.

"The assassinations last night were not happenstance or some cruel trick of fate. They were a desperate and cowardly attempt to destroy the leadership of this legion. And do you know why your enemy attacked Marcus Saturnius, Aulus Crescentius, Castorius Spina, Lucius Volusenus, Gaius Marcius, Gaius Trebonius, and Valerius Clericus? Because they feared to face you in honest battle under the command of such men!

"They know you defeated the Vakhuyu. They know you defeated the Chalonu. Like the Insobru—they fear to face you! They know what Marcus Saturnius told you, that the men of Legio XVII are no longer green, the men of Legio XVII are no longer mere men—the men of Legio XVII are the blooded and unbeaten soldiers of House Valerius!"

He waited for the soldiers. He had invoked the word that the late legate had imbued with such power in this newly blooded legion. The chanting began slowly, but gradually grew stronger, from century to century, cohort to cohort, until the entire mass of men was chanting. "Saturnius! Saturnius! Marcus Saturnius!"

Marcus nodded, well-satisfied now. In time, if all went well, perhaps the Saturnius they were chanting would one day be Valerius. But not today. A general had to earn the respect of his men before he could hope to win their love. But their chanting of the legate's name was a significant step. It was more than a just a reverential dirge for their fallen leader— it was the soldiers' way of announcing that they would accept Marcus Valerius in his stead. And only now, emboldened by that acceptance, did he dare to tell them of his plans.

"This morning, the first and second centuries of the tenth cohort will inform all the residents of Camp Meretrix that they must relocate

to Gallidromum immediately for their own safety. All those who have
not departed by tomorrow morning will be lashed, and all goods not
removed from the camp will be confiscated or burned. Legionaries with
camp wives or children may request three hours' leave this afternoon from
their century's tesserarius to go and aid them with their preparations.

"Centurions, your centuries are to be made ready for combat by this
evening. I will be requiring status reports after nightfall. Decurions,
prepare your squadrons for extended patrol duty, including night patrols.
I am promoting the decurion Julianus to praefect equitatus, since we are
presently short several tribunes in the cavalry. See him for the patrol
schedule. For the same reason, Tribune Trebonius is hereby promoted
to tribunus laticlavius. The primus pilus, Gnaeus Junius Honoratus, will
act as our praefectus in the absence of Sextus Castorius. And the optio,
Titus Cassabus, is promoted to praefect ballistarius."

After an initial wave of groans in response to hearing of the eviction
of the camp followers, the men cheered the news of the four promotions.
Marcus very much hoped his elevation would lull the primus pilus to
sleep, or at least prevent him from striking again today. He had to admit,
as Honoratus stoically accepted the loud homage of the legion as if it were
nothing but his well-merited due, wearing enough gold and silver medals
to comprise a second layer of armor, he had never seen a man who looked
less likely to betray his eagle.

"Men of the legion, more than one battle lies ahead of you. More
than one test of your courage and your honor awaits you. And you will
pass those tests, just as you passed the test of battle when you defeated
the Insobru, the Vakhuyu, and the Chalonu. Remember this. In seven
centuries, House Valerius has never surrendered to an enemy. And it has
never once abandoned its loyal soldiers. I am Marcus Valerius Clericus
of House Valerius. Will you follow me as you followed my father, and as
your fathers followed my grandfather?"

"Ave, Valerius!" the legion roared back. Marcus slammed his fist
against his chest and hurled out his right hand in a salute so crisp he hoped
it looked like a slashing sword. The sound of five thousand men returning

his salute thundered like a force of nature, a deep metallic crashing so loud it seemed to shake the sky.

Expressionless, but triumphant inside, Marcus turned on his heel and marched down the steps at the back of the rostrum. The four pilus priors followed him instinctively.

Junius Honoratus bellowed the end of the assembly with a voice like an angry bull. "Legion dismissed!"

One of Barbatus's men was waiting near the base of the steps. When Marcus looked quizzically at him, he nodded and stepped forward. "Sir, the decurion sent me to tell you that he will meet you at the legate… uh, at the legionary commander's residence."

"Tell him I will meet him there in the company of the senior centurions." Marcus assumed Barbatus would understand that he intended to arrive with the man guilty of ordering the murder of Marcus Saturnius and the tribunes. But with that man right at his shoulder, he did not dare to be any more clear.

"Well done, Tribune," Tertius told him.

Marcus was particularly pleased to hear praise from the centurion, since the chief of the third cohort had been the other skeptic to greet his unexpected ascension to what could still be a temporary command. But Castorius must be dead or else he would have already been found by now.

A thought struck Marcus: What if Honoratus wasn't the brains of the murders, but merely the brawn? What if it was the missing praefectus who was behind the attacks? Castorius was a quiet, hard-working man who oversaw most of the practical details required to keep the daily operations of the legion moving smoothly, and he was certainly clever enough to stash a wounded man in a place that would mislead the hunt for the murderer or murderers. There was only one means of finding out. But before he could thank the centurion for the compliment, he discovered to his dismay that he had failed to grasp Tertius's sarcastic tone.

"Yes, well done indeed. It appears you have not only panicked, but you may have managed to put a scare into the entire legion. Are you mad, Marcus Valerius? What were you thinking?"

What was I thinking? I was thinking that we're going to have either the Cynothii or that bloody Severan legion arriving at our gates in a matter of days. Or, if we're less than fortunate, both of them at the same time. He cleared his throat and stared levelly at the angry centurion.

"I shall be pleased to explain my intentions to you in the quarters that previously belonged to Marcus Saturnius, if you will all be so kind as to accompany me there. Gnaeus Junius Honoratus, will you please come with us as well?"

The big centurion was just coming down the steps from the platform, having overseen the departure of the men from the forum, and he stared narrow-eyed at Marcus for what seemed like a discomfitingly long time before he nodded once, sharply.

The tent that had previously housed the deceased legate was not far away. It was to the left and behind the giant canvas of the headquarters tent. It was large, of course, and could easily accommodate twenty men standing as well as an amount of furniture in the meeting room. Four of Barbatus's men were standing guard outside, and by their grim expressions and the dark looks they gave the primus pilus when they thought he would not notice, Marcus assumed that they had come across something damning in their search of the first two centuries of the first cohort.

Marcus pushed the tent flaps aside and saw that Barbatus and six of his men were standing inside waiting for him. Before them, lying on the ground, was the body of a dead legionary naked to the waist. His face looked vaguely familiar to Marcus, but what was much more recognizable was the deep wound in the man's left side. This was the man Marcus had struggled with in the tent. But Marcus had not struck the mortal blow, as the man's throat had been slashed with a powerful blow that had nearly severed his head.

The seven knights leaped to attention as Marcus looked over the corpse.

He wasn't really looking closely at it, though. He was mostly listening to learn if the primus pilus was going to react in any way. When no immediate reaction appeared to be forthcoming, he drew himself up and nodded to Barbatus.

"Where did you find this man, decurion?"

"In the tents of the first cohort, second century, sir. The body was covered in a blanket on the floor of the tent next to that of the century's commanding officer, Gnaeus Junius Honoratus."

Still no reaction from Honoratus.

"And he is a legionary?" Marcus asked. "That is a legion tunic he is wearing, isn't it?"

"Yes, Tribune. I believe his name was Narbonio, sir."

"Is that correct, Gnaeus Junius?" Marcus turned around and did his best to appear as if he had been surprised. The senior centurion was never a cheerful man, but now he was almost glowering, like a bear surrounded by the hounds waiting for the hunter's approach and knowing it has no chance to escape.

"Yes, sir, that's Narbonio. Not a good man, but not a bad one neither. Had a gambling problem, as I recall. Except he couldn't have been in the tent near mine. That weren't his. His contubernium were a few rows back from mine."

Marcus turned to Barbatus.

Barbatus shrugged. "That's as may be, Honoratus. But that weren't where we found him. Somebody killed him, but they didn't kill him there because there weren't enough blood around the body."

"Did you find where he was killed, then?"

"Not yet, Tribune. But we will. The rest of my squadron are searching the tents in the area. That much blood can't be hidden easily."

"No," Marcus said as he met the head centurion's eyes and held them, daring the other man to look away first. After a long moment, the centurion looked down. "It can't. Now, everyone except Trebonius, Julianus, and Honoratus: Out of the tent. Barbatus, go and find Claudius Hortensis from the fifth of the second knights. He has two prisoners in the stockade I wish to interrogate with the help of the new praefectus."

Barbatus shot him a significant look, and Marcus nodded in silent confirmation. As his knights filed out of the tent, Barbatus stopped in front of Honoratus and held out his hand. After a momentary hesitation, the big man drew his gladius and handed it to the decurion. Barbatus nodded in response, not entirely without respect, and closed the tent flaps behind him as he withdrew. Marcus waited until the heavy canvas flaps had been tied shut, then walked over to the table and sat on its edge.

He stared at the centurion and allowed himself to smile a little contemptuously. He wouldn't have wanted to face the man with swords or fists, but here Honoratus was as overmatched as Marcus would be in a physical contest. The key was to keep the big man off-balance.

"Do you love learning, Gnaeus Junius?"

Judging by the expression on the centurion's face, this was possibly the very last thing he was expecting Marcus to say. Honoratus stared at Marcus in mute astonishment. "Do I love what?"

"Learning. The acquisition of knowledge, the voyage of intellectual discovery. Do you find that it appeals to you?"

"I suppose," Honoratus said warily.

"Why then, I think we shall understand each other," Marcus declared brightly. Both Trebonius and Julianus were staring at him now, nearly as dumbfounded as Honoratus. "They call me Clericus, you know. It's an amusing witticism, because, you see, I spent my youth preparing for a career in the church. Very clever. But the interesting thing about a career in the church is that one spends most of one's time learning, pursuing knowledge, and travelling on the aforementioned voyage of discovery. Like you, I found that I rather enjoyed it." Marcus smiled at the centurion and sat on the table. This time, he let his full disdain for the man show.

Gnaeus Junius was not smiling at all. The merest spark of what might just possibly be fear appeared to have entered his eyes. The veteran of three dozen battlefields, he did not know what to do in a battle where his enemy wielded words, not swords, to cut.

"Now, I am tribune in my year, Gnaeus Junius. Which is to say that I have taken the first step on that illustrious path known in patrician circles as the cursus honorum at the youngest possible age. Indeed, thanks to some mysterious benefactor, I find myself promoted much sooner than I would ever have imagined. Who would have thought at the age of only twenty, I would find myself in command of an entire legion? Being an ambitious man, I am naturally grateful for this, as you can surely understand. And now I have a desire to express my gratitude toward this benefactor."

Marcus waited expectantly, but no answer was forthcoming. So, he spread his hands and continued.

"To return to our earlier theme: During my clerical studies, I was introduced to some of the great minds of history. Oxonus, Patroclus, Occludus, Quadras Empiricus, and greatest of all, Aristoteles. Aristoteles was an enthusiastic categorizer, and in one of his more important works, with which I have no doubt as a learned man you are intimately familiar, he divided men into two categories.

"You may recall that he concluded there are men who are capable of being persuaded of a truth through dialectic, which is to say sweet reason, or if you prefer, the inexorable progression of logic. And then, he asserted there are also those who cannot be instructed and therefore cannot be convinced of anything through argument based on knowledge, but rather require manipulation and persuasion through having their emotions played upon, which device he calls rhetoric. Would you say that you agree with this, Gnaeus Junius?"

The big centurion was bewildered and all but cringing before Marcus now. He shook his head slowly back and forth. "I would say... I would say I don't know. That is, maybe, I suppose. Yeah, why not?"

"Ah, but then here is where we must part company, you and I," Marcus leaped from the table and began pacing back and forth. "Although you are in the most noble of company and I stand alone, I will nevertheless insist that you are incorrect. In my view, there is a third category which Aristoteles uncharacteristically failed to investigate. And since there is at present no word to accurately describe this third category of men, it falls to me to coin it. So I ask you, if a man who is persuaded by knowledge is susceptible to the dialectic, while a man who is persuaded by the verbal arts is susceptible to the rhetoric, how then shall we describe a man who may be persuaded only by pain?"

"A masochist," Trebonius burst out enthusiastically. Marcus stopped pacing and shot him an irritated look. Abashed, Trebonius shrugged and muttered an unintelligible apology.

"This is not a discussion open to the public, Gaius Trebonius, it is a dialogue. From duo, or two, you understand, and while I can only applaud your enthusiasm concerning this discourse, I am much more interested in hearing the considered opinion of Gnaeus Junius on the subject."

The big centurion's face was increasingly coming to resemble that of a sacrificial ox as it was led to the altar. He shook his head again, clearly confused by Marcus's flights of scholarly references.

"The word I had in mind is dolorectic, Gnaeus Junius. Dolorectic. Would you say that you are a dolorectic man? I myself am not. I happen to prefer the dialectic. But, as you can no doubt see, if you cannot be convinced by either logic or emotions, this leaves only pain. And I am sure you realize, Gnaeus Junius Honoratus, that it will not be long before Barbatus returns with Hortensis and his prisoners. So, I am hoping that you will aid me on my voyage of discovery, that you will consent to serve as my Vergilius and help me understand if you are a man of the dialectic, the rhetoric, or the dolorectic. Because I wish for you to tell me to whom you are sworn, and I simply do not know which method you require."

"I took the legion's oath," Honoratus growled.

"I am aware you did as much. But what I really want to know is to whom you were sworn before you took that oath. So I will give you a choice: Either tell me why you assassinated Marcus Saturnius, tell me who was involved in the plot and to whom you are sworn, or I will put both men to the question as soon as Hortensis arrives. And if they happen to implicate you, I will have you beheaded immediately, right here in this very tent, where with my own eyes I saw you kill the legate!"

The centurion didn't say anything, but his eyes narrowed, and he glanced first at Julianus, then at Trebonius as if he were trying to decide if he could take all three armed men without a weapon. For a moment, Marcus wondered if he had blundered badly by not keeping two or three more men inside, or at least ordering the centurion bound. But the fewer men who knew about the treachery of a senior officer, the better it would be. Julianus obviously read Honoratus's thoughts, as he shook his head and caressed the hilt of his sword, smiling as he did so.

"Let me be clear, Gnaeus Junius," Marcus told him. "I don't give a rat's arse for your life one way or the other. I want the truth. If you give me that, you live. You and the others involved in the plot will be sent out of the camp tonight with sufficient supplies to see you to Cynothicum. I value the information far more than I value your wretched life. And if you remain silent and force me to make the others speak in your stead, you will die. Today. Here. Before the next bell. Now, I suppose you imagine I am bluffing, but recall, you beheaded my cousin at the orders of my father. I may be green, but I am the son of Valerius Corvus. Do you truly believe I will hesitate to do the same with you?"

"No, Valerian," the centurion growled. "I don't doubt you. I know your like. All fine words and pretty manners, but you'll order the deaths of a thousand brave men without even learning their damn names. They ain't even real to you blasted patrician bastards. You'll spill a sea of red before you'll risk a drop of that precious blue blood!"

Marcus saw no reason to point out that Fortex's blood had been as blue as his own, and yet Corvus hadn't hesitated to spill every last drop of it. But the bitterness and hate in the centurion's voice told him he had the man now. The centurion was above all a survivor, his encrustation of battle medals testified to that, and he clearly understood there was only one way he was going to walk out of this tent alive.

"I will do whatever it takes, Honoratus, you can be sure of that. Now speak. Is Castorius dead?"

"What assurances do I have that you won't kill me as soon as I tell you everything?"

Marcus smiled. The man might be brave and an efficient killer, but he simply wasn't bright enough to realize that he had already condemned himself with his question. "You have the word of a Valerian. That will suffice. Furthermore, I have no interest in your hairy hide. I have a legion to command, and if I am correct, I will soon have far more urgent concerns than seeking revenge for a few murdered officers."

"Aye, you will at that," the big centurion said. Then he shrugged fatalistically. "My men were on the Praetorian gate last night. They saw Castorius returning from one of the brothels, took him aside and killed him. You'll find him buried under a rock near the southern edge of the forest you can see from the gate there."

"Did you kill Narbonio?"

"He was wounded and the gate was due for a change so we couldn't get him out. I don't know if he would have lived anyhow, since we couldn't take him to the medicus. Anyhow, yeah, I killed him."

"Was he the only assassin? Who killed Saturnius?"

"Narbonio and me. I killed the legate myself. Didn't want to. I respected the man. He was a damn good general. But that's why they wanted him out of the way, he was too dangerous. Narbonio killed the tribunes. He should have killed you. How did you get him first?"

"Never mind that. Who wanted Saturnius out of the way? Who is they? Who thought he was dangerous?"

"The Severans."

Marcus inhaled sharply and glanced at Trebonius. The younger tribune looked troubled, while Julianus was shaking his head grimly. This meant war. And not just war, but civil war.

"I don't know what they're planning," Honoratus said, "but they're up to something. And I can tell you this, they been up to it for a while. They paid me real good to sign on with the new legion when Corvus was forming it, and I also knowed I'd have to kill someone. But I swear, Valerius, I didn't know it was going to be the damned legate!"

"What's the matter, Trebonius? You heard the man. He confessed."

Trebonius nodded. "Yes, I know."

"You don't think we should let him go?"

The tribune shrugged. "Like you said, the information is more important. No, I was just thinking that the root of dialogue isn't *duo*, for 'two'—it's *dia*, for 'across.' As in, to speak across."

"Oh, is it? I suppose you must be right."

The big centurion stared at them incredulously. Then he threw back his head and laughed. "Listen to the two of you. Blood and bones, Buteo is going to eat you little clowns alive!"

The dawn sun rose over a cold and quiet castra. Marcus started as one of the four decurions he had left in command overnight softly called to him. Before he turned in, he had given them orders that he be woken at first light. That had seemed like a much better idea at the time than it did now. After having slept the night before in his armor, the thought of getting out of his warm wool blankets was almost painful. But, he reminded himself, he had an example to set. Like it or not, at twenty, he was officially the Old Man of the legion.

So, he rolled out of his blankets, off his cot, and stretched. A large bucket had been brought in from the water troughs in the stables, and he splashed the ice cold water on his face to wake himself up. He would be shaved later, he decided. First, he had to decide if the legion would stay in its camp and await the foe or not.

Two days. He could only be sure that he had two days before Legio XVII would be under attack. It might be more, he hoped it would be more, but it could not be less.

He didn't know how aggressive a general this Secundus Falconius Buteo was, except that whereas the Rullianus branch of the Falconians favored the governing side of politics, the Butean branch had been able to boast no less than two consuls of the legions during his relatively short lifetime. He seemed to recall there was another Falconius who had also been consul aquilae as well, but that had been a Falconius Licinus, not a Buteo or a Rullianus. House Falconius might not be as famous for its martial virtue as House Valerius, but they did have a long tradition of military service, and it was quite likely that the Severans' Falconian general would be competent. He had to assume the man would be that at the very least.

The best defense is an ignorant enemy, he thought to himself. Failing that, an incompetent one. If it wasn't already a military maxim, it should be. He would give much to know that the Severan forces, quite possibly allied to the rebel Cynothii, were generaled by one of the great incompetents of the past, such as Lapenius or the infamous Varrus. But that would be expecting far too much of Fortune, who had already dealt him some very troublesome cards. He'd weeded out most of the traitors the Severans had planted in the legion at the time of its formation, or he believed he had, but there were surely others of questionable loyalty still in their midst.

But they were of no concern now. Fulgetra was the more pressing issue, assuming that he was correct. If he was wrong and he'd put the legion on alert for nothing, that would be humiliating and would call his judgment into question, possibly his authority as well. But nothing would be worse than sitting idly in camp while the Severans marched south to catch them unprepared. He doubted either Honoratus or Buteo would put much store in the lies he'd told Honoratus about the legion returning immediately to Vallyrium, but at least it might sow some seeds of doubt concerning his real intentions.

The problem was that he had no idea as yet what those real intentions should be. That was why he'd risen early today, to scout the area and figure out his options. Fully dressed now, and wearing his gladius at his side, he nodded to the guards and indicated that he wanted the tent flaps to be untied. They had to give battle, they might be outnumbered, and the first question that required answering was if the legion should spend the next two days fortifying the castra and preparing for a siege. He decided to ride out and take a closer look at the surrounding terrain before breaking his fast and so he headed for the stables.

Two of the guards followed him. They were knights from the Second, so he knew they wouldn't have any problem accompanying him. There was a brief delay as it turned out that Bucephalus had somehow managed to lose a shoe, so he ordered the groom to bring him Incitatus, whom one of the more enterprising decurions—he suspected Julianus—had arranged to keep in the Second's stables after Fortex's execution.

After acknowledging the salutes of the gate commander and his men, he rode through the brick arch and mentally measured the thickness of the walls. They were ten feet thick and fifteen feet high, with additional three-foot battlements every six feet. He was fortunate in that this castrum was of the sort known as a castra stativa, built to serve as a permanent home for two legions. With forty operational artillery pieces, Marcus could hold it for an eternity, or at least until the food ran out, against any enemy unfortunate enough to lack powerful mages capable of tearing down the walls.

The six wells inside the walls provided an adequate supply of water, and since he intended to send an entire cohort to Gallidromum to commandeer enough grain and meat to see them through the winter, they would be very nearly impregnable no matter how many rebellious Cynothii appeared. They could bring ten men to his one, and it would accomplish little more than the waves of the ocean breaking one after the other on a solid rock face.

The problem was that he could not be certain that the rebel provincials would come alone. Those walls that were so impregnable to barbarians, even half-civilized barbarians who had been dignified with the title of imperial subjects, would provide little defense against skilled architecti who had probably overseen the building of one or more castra very much like this one, if not exactly like it.

But if the Severan legion came, how would they attack? They would be arriving from the northeast, which meant that they would not have to cross the river, which was far enough to the west that he needn't fear it being diverted to undermine the walls. There was a hill to the south, but it was too far away to serve as an elevated platform for enemy artillery. However, the woods to the northeast and south would provide plenty of material for building rams, ladders, and siege towers.

Marcus stopped and sighed, trying not to give into either despair or the foolishness of wishful thinking. Right now, it seemed very hard to imagine the peaceful quiet of the morning being shattered by the chaotic roar of battle, the frost-covered ground crunching crisply beneath Incitatus's hooves transformed into blood and mud by the boots of men come here to kill and die. It was tempting to assume that all the preparations he was contemplating would be unnecessary, but he could feel it in his bones that they would not only be necessary, they would be insufficient.

What he needed, he decided, was more information. How many Cynothii were there? Assuming they had defeated Legio XIV and Caudinus without any assistance from the Severan legion, there were probably a lot of them. At least fifteen thousand, more likely twenty. Even if Caudinus had bloodied them well in defeat, and the odds were that he had, the enthusiasm that a victory over a genuine Amorran legion would have caused to sweep across the rebellious province meant that any Cynothi losses had probably already been more than replaced. On the other hand, he doubted they had more than a few thousand horses, which meant they would not be able to simultaneously make use of both their mobility and their numbers.

A thought struck him. He looked back at the two knights who were accompanying him. Out here, in the meadows that stretched to the river, they were lagging back, trailing him by more than one hundred feet. If any enemy were to somehow burst from the ground or fall from the sky, they were too far away to be able to defend him. The point was that to accompany someone, even to guard him, does not necessarily mean staying close enough to him to do so effectively.

Therein lay his one opportunity.

There were four possibilities. First, neither the Cynothii nor the Severans attacked. He dismissed that option immediately. If the legion was not attacked, there simply wasn't a problem. Any preparations made would serve well enough as a drill and he might even be able to pass them off as one, at least in the minds of the men.

Second, the Cynothii alone attacked. In that case, the correct strategy would be to stock the castra, prepare for a long winter siege, and hope that Durus would not be too tardy in his arrival come spring.

Third, they were attacked by the Severan legion alone. Due to their siegecraft and Marcus's larger cavalry force, two to their one, the right strategy would be to find advantageous ground and meet them in the open field, or perhaps to ambush them on the march.

Fourth, both the Cynothii and the Severans marched against him together. In that case, the castra would be a death trap.

Ironically, the most daunting challenge had the most obvious solution. Regardless of what was in the works, his course was clear, and he now knew what needed to be done. The problem would be convincing his officers that it was not only their wisest course of action, it was their only real chance of survival.

LODI

EVEN to Lodi, it was remarkably stupid to be travelling east into the unknown instead of west, especially when the heavy weight on his back was a constant reminder that he'd already accomplished what he'd set out to do. But the bloody encounter with the four plains orcs had triggered a memory that he simply couldn't set aside or ignore.

They had been walking parallel with the path for most of the afternoon, not wishing another accidental meeting, and while they hadn't actually seen any more orcs, Lodi had noticed signs that they were getting closer to wherever the orcs were headed. Small bones, bits of refuse, the acrid scent of orc urine, and unmistakable piles of orc shit increasingly littered the path—most of it several days old by the look of it, but a few were quite obviously fresh.

"What are you looking for," Thorald said, wrinkling his nose as Lodi examined a large pile so fresh it was still warm.

"I'll know it when I see it." Lodi stood and stepped upwind before he stopped holding his breath. "If we're lucky, it will just be an avalanche of orcs getting together for some sort of inter-tribal competition or perhaps one of those festivals where they choose the new chief shaman or whatever."

"And if we're not?"

"Then we have to figure they're gearing up to attack somebody somewhere. And if it happens they've got their eye on finishing what the

Goblinsbane started, don't you think the king might prefer to know about it before a bloody orc army shows up at his gate?"

"I suppose so," Thorald admitted. Then he frowned and looked around. "Do you hear that?"

"Hear what?" Lodi asked, even as he quickly retreated back into the forest and started to unsling his axe.

Thorald followed him, but without any sense of urgency.

"No, no one's coming. Really, you can't hear that? There's sort of a deep rumbling or thudding, but it's repetitive. Sort of a boom-boom-boom. Like thunder that's far away. Only it's too regular to be thunder."

"Like the sound of a drum?" Lodi suggested dryly. He wasn't surprised that the young dwarf's ears were better than his own. Like most survivors of the siege, he'd lost an amount of hearing as a result of all the mines, firepots, and spells that had left his ears ringing on more occasions than he could remember.

"Yes!" Thorald exclaimed, completely failing to realize Lodi was laughing at him. "It's a drum. Or maybe drums."

"Drums. I imagine we'll find quite a lot of them." Lodi gestured for Thorald to take the lead. "Just follow the sound, lad. Very considerate of them, you know. Now we don't need to worry about running into anyone on the trail... or stepping into orc shit again."

"You're not going to let me forget that, are you?" Thorald raised a skeptical eyebrow.

"Merely a helpful reminder that you ought to look where you're going, lad."

His young companion led them through the woods until Lodi too was able to hear the drums pounding. It was tough going, as the terrain was steep, and they found themselves alternately pulling themselves up the wooded hills by the occasional exposed tree root and using tree trunks as a brake when sliding down the other side.

Before long, both of them were scratched and bleeding from branches that had caught them in the face as they were going downhill. But Lodi didn't mind, and Thorald didn't complain. It was hot, exhausting, and mildly painful work, but even so, it was a damned sight better than risking another heart-stopping and potentially fatal encounter with another group of orcs on the trail. All the while, the drums continued to grow louder.

At last they reached a point which Lodi surmised was approaching the edge of the forest. The light ahead was much brighter, and so they proceeded cautiously, determined to stay well inside the shadowy safety of the trees. But as they came closer to the edge, Lodi realized that the open space ahead wasn't a meadow: It was a cliff! And at its base was a wide open space that appeared to be serving as a gathering place for more orcs than Lodi had ever seen, not even in Guldur Goblinsbane's mighty army.

They stretched out in a vast array, in large, irregular groups that must have consisted of tens of thousands of orcs in each one. The banners of their chieftains and kings waved over the great circular tents that they used when on the march, although there were three giant flags mounted on huge poles that stood atop a large hill that appeared to be the center of the gathering. Upon it were set up three of the queer stools that the orcs customarily used in the place of chairs. The leather and the bones used to make them were goblin, although Lodi had seen stools made from the hide and bones of men and dwarves as well.

"Ugh, what is that?" Thorald pointed to an uneven pyramid behind the hill.

Lodi recognized it immediately even though he had seen something like it only once before. But it was the sort of horror a dwarf didn't forget easily.

"It's an offering. I don't know what it's called, but this is a convocation of sorts, almost a religious thing. It's called a golshoggru, and it's a big ritual they do when they're trying to summon one of their demon gods, usually Gor Gor."

"Gor Gor?" Thorald looked skeptical. "That's supposed to be their god's name?"

"I wouldn't laugh, lad. Their shamans call upon a number of hell bastards, but he's the worst of a bad lot. He ain't the most powerful they call up—the alchemists say Khemash is—but Gor Gor is the one the warriors worship. He's the one they call upon when they's gearing up for war."

"How do you know about orc magic?"

Lodi looked at the young dwarf and shook his head. "You think you're gonna forget what it felt like when you split that orc's head open like it was nothing but rotten fruit?"

Thorald shivered and made a face. "No, never."

"Then you should understand why I know all about filthy orc magic. Next to elven witchery, it's the worst there is." He pointed to the golshog-gru. "The last time I saw a mound of heads that size, they was piled up in front of Iron Mountain. After about six months, when they saw we wasn't going down easy, they started chopping heads and stacking them, trying to get their bloody demon-god to do the dirty work they couldn't."

Even as he spoke, two large mountain orcs dragged a furiously struggling smaller orc behind the hill. The nearer bands began stomping their feet in time with the drums and chanting the same short phrase over and over again, although Lodi couldn't quite make it out.

As the mountain orcs forced the smaller one to its knees, one of the biggest orcs Lodi had ever seen came strutting out of one of the round tents, followed by two more mountain orcs, both bearing massive axes that made Lodi's battleaxe look like a toy. The big orc was wearing a black ornamental device on its head that looked as if it might be a mad artisan's notion of a crown. But of rather more concern to Lodi was the fact that it was also wearing the robes of a shaman.

One of the few advantages they'd had during the siege was that the warleaders among the tribes didn't trust the shamen, and the shamen had refused to obey the warleaders. So, for all the dark spellpower available to the invaders, it was seldom utilized effectively and had been easily countered by the alchemists and Deep Ones of Iron Mountain. But if the warleader was a shaman himself....

The drums crescendoed, then stopped suddenly before starting up again with a slow, ominous rhythm. Lodi didn't have to look down to see what was happening, he knew another head had been harvested for the grotesque pyramid. He remembered watching similar scenes long ago. Sometimes the orcs being sacrificed went to their deaths gladly. At other times they kicked and screamed right up until the moment the blade descended. It seemed Gor Gor didn't care about the attitude of the sacrifice as long as he got his head.

"How can they worship monsters like that?" Thorald was visibly distressed.

"Talk about monsters! Did you see that one! Looks like his dada was a troll and his mama weren't willing." But the nightmarish vision was nothing Lodi hadn't seen before. And disgusting as it was, as appalling as it was, it made its own sort of twisted sense. After all, what was easier: to raise up, train, and pay for a well-disciplined army, or to breed like rabbits, cut off a few heads every now and then for the benefit of your war god, then roast the remains for dinner over a roaring fire?

The most recent sacrifice had already been forcefully spitted by its executioners and was now being carried off in triumph by four orcs who looked as if they might have belonged to its tribe. Well, it might make sense, but even so, Lodi's stomach roiled in protest at the sight. As much as he despised the Amorrans who had enslaved him and forced him to fight for their entertainment, they probably had the right of it. Good magicians, bad magicians, it was only a matter of time before they turned to the dark side in search of more power. Better to be safe and kill them all.

"We seen enough," he declared. "Once they got Gor Gor raised, they'll be on the march. We'll head for the easternmost watch tunnels. They'll be able to get word to the king and maybe send some proper scouts out to see where these orcs are headed."

"Wait!" Thorald said. "Something's up!"

The big shaman was standing in front of the vast pile of heads with its arms stretched out high above its own head, still safely attached to its neck. In one hand it held some sort of rod, in the other a large black goblet. It looked as if it was chanting, although it was impossible to hear anything at such a distance, especially over the constant booming of the drums. When it stopped, it took a large drink from the goblet, then flung the rest of the contents over the golshoggru. The mass of orcs, at least those who were watching, cheered in response.

"Blood, most likely," Lodi mused. "The damned buggers never can get enough blood."

"Orcs? Or demons?"

"All the same in the end." Lodi frowned.

The big shaman turned a little and now appeared to be almost facing the cliff upon which they were standing. The drums stopped. Then it raised an arm and pointed upwards. It was impossible, and yet it seemed as if the giant orc was pointing directly at them.

"Can you hear what that big one's shouting?" he asked Thorald.

"Yeah, a little, but I don't speak no orc, Lodi."

"I know, just tell me what it's saying! The words!"

The young dwarf leaned forward and put his hand over his ear. "I'm not sure. He's said the same thing a few times, though. Something about 'ghorag' or maybe 'ghorakh.' And then he said 'nanakh' a couple times."

"Dammit, dammit, dammit," Lodi swore, grabbing Thorald's arm and backing away from the edge of the cliff. "We got to run and run now, lad!"

"Why?" Thorald was confused, but he willingly followed Lodi's lead. "They can't possibly have known we were up here!"

"I don't speak orc neither, but I know what nanakh means. It means 'dwarf.' And I don't think the big one saw us. I think that damned demon they're calling up probably told him!"

"So where do we go? North, into the mountains?"

"No, those mountain orcs will move a lot faster though the mountains than we can. First we go back to the stream. They can't track us through the water. Then we find a place we can hole up for the night. We got a long way to go, lad, and we aren't going to outrun them. They won't all come after us, but the ones that do will know these parts a sight better than we do. But we can bloody well outsmart them, right?"

Thorald nodded, but his eyes showed his fear when the drums abruptly stopped and deep, evil-sounding horns began to sound.

Lodi smiled at the young dwarf and clapped him on the shoulder as they jogged, side-by-side, through the dark, sun-dappled depths of the forest. "Don't be afraid, lad. Remember, I spent seven years crawling through tunnels and killing the bastards. Hundreds. Maybe thousands. They didn't get old Lodi then, and they ain't going to get him now. So just stick close, do what you're told, and you'll be all right."

They didn't see any evidence to confirm they were being hunted until late in the afternoon two days later. After wading along the stream for about an hour the previous day, they came across a half-uprooted tree with heavy branches extending out over the water. First Thorald pulled himself up and out of the stream, then Lodi did the same, a little more awkwardly. Wading through the stream had been slow going, but Lodi calculated that breaking their scent trail was more than worth the ground they'd given up to their pursuers. They'd spent the remainder of the night sleeping in some shallow scrapes quickly dug out from under a large and rotting fallen oak tree, then rose with the first red rays of the pre-dawn and began moving again.

It seemed, however, that at least one party of orcs must have passed them during the night, as the sun was well past its peak when they came across the unmistakable indications of an orc encampment.

Thorald grabbed Lodi's arm to stop him.

"I smell something. I think it's orc stink, but it's not real strong."

Lodi nodded, unslung his axe and then slipped both his pack and the shield off his back. "Stay here. I'm going to circle around and see if anyone's there. You hear me whistle three times, it's safe. If anything

happens, if you hear a scuffle, don't come helping me. Take the shield and
my pack, then hide and wait until they go on. Remember, we got to get
word back to Iron Mountain!"

Thorald nodded, looking scared.

Lodi took a deep breath, gripped his axe tightly, then started in a
direction that would keep him north of the suspected orc party. When
he thought he'd gone far enough, he angled to his left. The scent that
Thorald had mentioned was there, but it wasn't as strong as it should be,
not when he could see there was a small clearing barely twenty paces in
front of him. He crouched and edged closer, moving from tree to tree,
until he was nearly to the edge of the clearing. Then he grinned, stood
up, and whistled three times.

Thorald came crashing through the brush with all the stealth of a
wounded troll. He couldn't fault the younger dwarf too severely, however,
as Thorald was weighed down with the shield as well as Lodi's pack in
addition to the warhammer and his own pack.

"They're gone?" the young dwarf asked, looking around the abandoned campsite.

"They're gone, but not too long ago," Lodi confirmed. Judging by the
size of the fire, the number of indentations on the ground and piles of fly-
festooned leavings scattered toward the perimeter of the clearing, about
twenty orcs had passed the previous night here. The embers of their fire
were still faintly warm below the well-charred bones of their evening meal.
"I'd say they left here a little before midday."

"Ugh, what's that?" Thorald pointed to a half-burned skull that was
lying on the ground not far from the fire. It still had hair and flesh attached
to it.

"Looks like they had kobold for dinner." Lodi prodded at the head
with the spiked tip of his axe, rolling it over to expose the small, sharp teeth
that distinguished that vicious breed from the goblins who also sometimes
served as meals for their larger, carnivorous cousins. "I didn't see none at
that gathering with the golshoggurath, so they must have caught one along

the way. Too bad. We'll know they're running out of steam when they start eating the smaller ones in their party."

"They eat their own?" Thorald suddenly turned nearly as green as a goblin.

"They eat anything. You get hungry enough, you'll eat anything too, lad. Suppose it come down to eating rocks, metal, or another dwarf? Then a roasted leg of orc suddenly don't look so bad, does it?"

"You never ate an orc!"

"Well, of course I did! When your belly's been empty for days and all the rats and the bugs've been ate, then you just do whatever you have to do. Hell's embers, lad, but if your mother didn't, and if your father didn't, you wouldn't be here!"

Thorald was silent for a moment. Lodi took the opportunity to retrieve the shield and his pack. "Why do you think they do it?" Thorald finally asked. "When they don't have to."

"That'll be the line between savage and uncivil," Lodi grunted as the weight of his pack pulled at his shoulders. He began walking west, following the trail of broken branches left by the orcs. "Orcs, kobolds, goblins—they're all savages, meaning they always take the easy way and don't never think about tomorrow. Orcs especially. The way they breed, they'd all be starving if they weren't cannibals. What's easier: growing plants, baking bread, and keeping your pizzle in your pants, or futtering every damn thing that moves and eating anything that's smaller and comes close enough for you to grab? It's a cycle, lad, and they can't stop eating each other any more than the Deep Ones can go live atop the mountains."

"It's just as well we're civil, then. Even if we run out of stonebiscuit, you're probably about as edible as quartz. If we end up in their pots, at least we know you'll break their teeth."

"Now you're learning, lad!" Lodi nodded approvingly at the young dwarf. "The gods are hard, but the dwarves are harder. When it all turns to shit and sorrow, you just remind yourself of that."

FJOTRA

TRUE to his word, the Red Prince reached the safety of Raknarborg's walls with both his and the Skullbreaker's forces intact well before nightfall. Her father was much impressed that the Savoner prince had troubled to bring back the bodies of the Dalarn fallen as well as his own, and he admitted to Fjotra that if it was necessary for their people to accept a king, they might do considerably worse than Prince Karl.

It had been an anxious few hours for Fjotra, as she and the mages had reached the fortress long before either the exhausted Dalarn or the exuberant Savonders did.

Rather than take her father's advice and order a tub warmed for herself, Fjotra had climbed to the summit of the North Tower in order to keep watch for the returning warriors.

She could see the cause for his concern: There was a large mass of what looked to be four or five thousand aalvarg that were potentially in position to interfere with the prince's line of retreat. But they didn't appear to be moving toward the fortress, and she relaxed considerably when she saw several hundred Savonder footmen, accompanied by a few dozen riders and led by a blue-cloaked man at the fore, being slowly disgorged from the great black gate below her to her left.

Her stomach was beginning to remind her that she had eaten little today when she first caught sight of the bright scarlet pennon borne by the prince's stoic flag-bearer, followed by a squadron of knights escorting the uneven column of Dalarn warriors. She gave a short prayer of thanks to the All-Father and to the Giantslayer for their safe return, but she waited until she was able to lay eyes upon a red-armored man on a big black horse bringing up the rear of the march before descending from the tower.

After taking a lukewarm bath and spending a frantic few minutes searching through the dresses that she'd already packed for her return, she brushed her hair and presented herself to her father in the hopes that Prince Karl might soon be doing the same.

As darkness fell and the oiled rushlights were lit, the mood in the Skullbreaker's hall was cheerful, if not entirely celebratory. Their victory had been complete, but there wasn't a man or woman in the hall who didn't realize that they would have to fend off their besiegers at least once before the last man, most likely the Skullbreaker, would board ship and abandon the isles to the bestial mercies of the aalvarg.

Fjotra worried too about the discovery that the aalvarg possessed magic of their own. The last known troldmand had been killed before she was born, and the few wizened *troldkvinde* who survived had been sent on the first ships along with the other women in order to watch over the pregnant ones as well as the sick children.

But surely wolf urine could not bring down the mighty walls of Raknarborg, no matter how magical it was! She decided she would ask Blais about it when she saw him. If anyone on this side of the sea might know, it would be him. She wished Lord Theuderic and his Lady Everbright were there, both of them seemed to possess significantly more knowledge of the runic arts than either of the two young battlemages.

The Skullbreaker had ordered a victory feast in the great hall. She was disappointed to find herself seated on the other side of her father from the prince, who had taken his place at the Skullbreaker's right hand with the royal admiral on the other side. She was further disappointed to find herself between Steinthor Strongbow on her right and Patrice on her left. Steinthor made for poor company, as he was heavily involved in the conversation about the day's battle with her father and the prince, but the young sorcerer was more than happy to take advantage of the Dalarn warrior's disinterest in talking to her.

As if by way of compensation, the meal itself was surprisingly lavish. Prince Karl had brought over a considerable quantity of wine, which was almost unknown to a generation of Dalarn warriors who had grown up defending their people against the aalvarg instead of raiding the northern coasts of Selenoth. It was well received by Savoners and Dalarn alike, as was the spit-roasted beef, which was served in such quantities that even the lowliest kitchen drudges would be able to eat their fill tonight.

The Skullbreaker had laid in supplies intended to last his men for two years, but now that the decision to abandon the fortress was settled, there was no longer any need to ration them out. And because not all of the pigs, cows, and chickens could be transported on the ships, they would dine as if they were kings across the sea throughout the final days of Raknarborg.

"Will you stop that?" she snapped, rather too harshly, as Patrice offered for the third time to refill her cup.

"I beg your pardon, my lady," he said, flustered.

"There be twenty other women here in the hall, why must you always talk to me? Why you not bother them, not me?"

"I had no idea I was bothering you," he said, pulling back from her and holding himself in a stiff and unnatural position. "I do apologize, of course. In my defense, I hope you will allow me to point out that I can't speak to any of those other women, as I don't speak your tongue, and they don't speak mine."

Fjotra stared at him for a moment, then burst out laughing. Of course the poor man hadn't tried to speak to anyone else. He couldn't! She shook her head then lifted her cup and held it out toward him by way of apology.

He grasped the gesture, and grinned ruefully as he poured the wine.

"I fear you must have thought that I was being rather forward in my pursuit of you."

"Like a dog after a bitch."

He winced. "Never fear, my lady. Prince Karl would have my head if I even thought to attempt seducing you, much less managed to succeed. I don't know what his plans are for you, but he made it clear to all of us that if we were to offend you in any way, he'd give us to your father, which fate I am given to understand can be arguably worse than death."

"The blood eagle," Fjotra said, nodding. She'd seen him offer sacrifices of his enemies to the All-Father before, usually rival chieftains who had refused to submit to him peacefully. "You don't want that."

"No, I most certainly don't, whatever it is."

"You say the prince have plans for me? Why he do that? Why he always call me princess when everyone else call me lady?"

The mage glanced over at the prince, who was out of earshot in the noisy hall and engaged in an animated conversation with his admiral. "You have to understand that I don't know what his intentions are. His Serene Highness is not in the habit of taking lowly battlemages into his confidence. But if his father seeks to add the Wolf Isles to the realm, which I can only assume is why we're here, then it would make a good deal of sense to establish a more lasting claim to them than merely receiving homage from your father. Especially since he's going to have to grant your father a fiefdom from the existing crown lands where your people can settle."

"Homage? Fiefdom? I do not understand these words."

"No, of course you don't." The young mage pursed his lips then reached into the bread basket and withdrew a piece of bread, which he began breaking into pieces. "Here, these four pieces are the isles, and all these other pieces belong to Savondir. Each piece is a fiefdom that belongs to one noble or another. The big pieces belong to the great lords, whereas the little ones belong to the minor nobility. So, even though everything belongs to the king, since your people can't live on any of the four pieces anymore, they have to live on one of these other pieces. *Homage* is what your father must do in order to receive the land from the king. It's a simple ritual."

"Like he promise the king will be his chief."

"Exactly. Now, your people don't really have a structured system of nobility, so your father will need to be incorporated into the Savondese aristocracy. I mean, he has a certain status by virtue of his several thousand warriors, which will make him one of the most powerful men in the realm right away. Since the king won't want your father using his warriors to take the lands he needs to settle your people on, he'll simply give them to him. And since he'll want to formalize your father's status, he'll make him a comte, or more likely a marquis, considering his following. He could even make him a duc, but I can't imagine that happening since it would offend far too many of his lords, and perhaps more importantly, their ladies."

"So I not to be a princess? What about Brynjolf, will he not be a prince?"

"Brynjolf won't be, no. He'll receive a title one level below your father. If the Skullbreaker is made a marquis, then your brother will be made a comte. Can you imagine that? What would he be called, the Marquis de Tête de Mort? Still, I doubt anyone would dare titter at him at court, for fear of getting brained by an axe. On the other hand, if your father is made a comte, your brother would likely be named a viscomte."

Fjotra considered it. She didn't think either her father or her brother would mind what they were called, so long as they were provided sufficient land on which to settle safely. Until nine months before the fall of Garn, when her father had begun preparing Raknarborg for the last stand of the Dalarn, he'd never held the allegiance of more than two hundred men and their families. To her kind, men, money, and power were much more important than titles. All the same, she couldn't help asking about herself.

"I will be a comtesse?"

Patrice shrugged. "At the least. I suspect you'll be more valuable to the king as 'the Princess des Îles du Loup.' Whereas your father and brother are worthless as claimants to the islands, he can declare them to be your dowry and either give you to the man who can take them back for him, or, if he prefers to keep them for the crown, marry you to Prince Karl."

"Marry me?" It wasn't a horrific thought, but Fjotra was alarmed at how the comtesse might react. "What if he loves someone else?"

"Kings and princes are much more interested in what a woman brings with her to the wedding than anything else, my lady. You're a pretty girl, to be sure, but it's not your face that will have every adventuresome noble seeking your hand in marriage. I daresay even a few peers of the realm would be interested, were it not for their wives getting in the way. And besides, from what I've seen, you and the prince appear to like each other well enough."

He did? "You think he likes me?"

"I think you know perfectly well that he does." The mage's voice was measured, but his eyes betrayed his amusement. "I merely hope that my lady will look upon me with favor should she one day find herself Queen of all Savondir."

She snorted. "Queen of Savondir? No, I don't believe you. But I need friends in Savonne, I think, no matter who marries me. Should we be friends?"

"Done, my lady," Patrice declared, and they raised their cups together by way of sealing the pledge.

Fjotra was certain the young battlemage was not quite as disinterested in her as he feigned, but she was pleased to know that she would have at least one genuine friend in Savonne if a marriage to the Red Prince caused even the comtesse to turn on her. So it was with a light heart that she subsequently retired from the hall and made her way toward the bedchamber she shared with four of her friends.

Fjotra had already repacked her dress and slipped on her thick woolen nightshift when there was a knock on the door.

It was Grenjar, the young thrall who had been freed upon reaching Raknarborg and who was now serving her father as what the Savoners would call his squire. He had unusually dark hair for a Dalarn and was sometimes called Stormcrow, as the Skullbreaker seldom summoned someone because he was pleased with them. But his presence held no terrors for Fjotra. Quite the opposite, actually, as she had seen both her father and Prince Karl looking over at her after engaging in a long and apparently intense discussion. Dared she hope that they had been speaking of her betrothal? She would find out soon, it seemed.

"Your father wants you," the dark-haired young man told her. He wouldn't meet her eyes, and she knew that, like most former thralls, he would not see himself as a true man until he had stood with the shield wall and proven himself worthy of a warrior's regard. "He's in his chambers."

She followed Grenjar up the stairs that led to the room at the top of the tower that her father had claimed once the Red Prince and his retinue had arrived. Since the self-styled King of the Wolf Isles had neither servants nor court, he simply didn't require the space that the southerners considered an absolute necessity. Pride might have demanded otherwise, but then, it was the Skullbreaker's fondest hope that they would soon abandon what presently passed for his entire royal demesne. She also knew that he liked being able to look out over the sea to the south, toward the lands that they would soon be forced to call their home.

Grenjar had nearly reached the final landing when the sounds of a struggle could be heard coming from one of the rooms above them.

The young man glanced back at her for a moment, confusion on his face. Then he turned and leaped up the remaining stairs two at a time.

Fjotra wrinkled her nose, smelling something unpleasant but vaguely familiar. Then horror struck her heart as she realized where she had smelled it before.

"I'm coming, my lord!" Grenjar shouted.

"Father!" Fjotra gathered up her shift on one hand and ran up the stairs after Grenjar, and she screamed again when she saw the creature that had her father pinned beneath its grey-furred bulk.

It was an aalvarg, though she couldn't see how it could possibly have entered through either of the chamber's two small windows, much less climbed more than one hundred feet up the walls that rose from the stony shores of the White Sea.

With a battle cry that might have done credit to a veteran berserker, Grenjar drew his dagger from his belt and leaped at the monster, stabbing it once in the back of the neck and again in its right shoulder.

The half-wolf, half-man roared, releasing the Skullbreaker's shield arm from its bloody jaws, and twisted its torso, causing Grenjar to tumble from its muscled back.

Her father took the opportunity to roll out from beneath his attacker, but Fjotra could see that he couldn't use his arm, and there was blood covering most of his naked upper body.

"The axe!" he shouted, pointing with his sword arm as the aalvarg swiped its long claws at Grenjar, raking him across the chest.

Fjotra whirled around and saw the weapon that had given her father his name suspended on four iron rods driven into the wall. She lifted the battleaxe off its supports—it was heavy, and she could barely hold it aloft over her head. When she turned, groaning under its weight, she saw that the aalvarg was back on top of her father, snapping madly at him and lunging for his throat.

She cried out as she staggered toward the embattled pair. Then gravity came to her aid, and she brought the axe blade crashing down squarely in the middle of the aalvarg's back. A fountain of dark blood splattered in her face.

The beast threw its head back and shrieked, scrabbling madly at the giant blade that was now embedded deeply in its flesh.

Skuli managed to push it off him, and no sooner had he done so than Grenjar dove at the aalvarg, driving his knife into its throat, ripping it back and forth with murderously unrestrained violence, and sending the unnatural monster back to the Hell from whence it must originally have come.

Fjotra rushed to her father's side and kneeled down beside him, heedless of the blood that was staining her white shift.

"Let me see, Father. Let me see you!" She gasped at the sight of his shield arm, which was badly mangled all around its circumference, torn from his wrist to his elbow by the long, wolfish fangs. A pair of claw marks ran from his left cheek down to his breast, and three more, much deeper wounds marked his side where the beast had very nearly slashed open his belly. "Grenjar, run and find one of the troldkvinde! Wait, first take the blankets from his bed there and throw them to me!"

The young man was bleeding from his face and favoring his left leg, which was slashed below the knee. But he quickly stripped the woolen bedding from the Skullbreaker's bed and tossed it to her. Then he bent over, pulled his knife from the dead aalvarg's throat where he had left it, and handed it to her.

"You'll need this in case there are more of them about," he said. "I'll send some men up while I look for a witch woman."

Fjotra nodded. It was a good thought. She wiped off the blade as he departed, then used it to cut long strips from the thinnest blanket. Her father had lost a good deal of blood, but judging by the astonishing number of scars on his body, from the long-healed and barely visible white lines to the newer ones that looked like fat pink worms, he had seen worse in the past.

"Tighter," he hissed as she wrapped a makeshift bandage around his torso. "I think he may have broken a rib or two. It hurts when I breathe too deeply. Reminds me of the time Gunnlaug Sigurdsson caught me with the edge of his shield. Took me a month before I could breathe properly again and cost me a ship to ransom myself. He was a clever one. We could surely use that old bastard now."

She dabbed lightly at the wounds on his cheek, which turned out to be little more than scratches, then carefully reached out and began to examine his arm. It was a horrific sight, and she didn't really know where to begin bandaging it, so she decided to concentrate on getting the bleeding to stop, especially near his wrist.

"At least it wasn't your sword arm," she commented.

He nodded, his eyes tightly closed. His breathing was irregular and forceful in her ear. She had just finished bandaging his arm when she felt him push her away from him. "The Savoner prince," he said. "Go and make sure he has guards in his chamber. If they found me here, they might have attacked him too."

"I can't leave you here alone! We don't know how many of them there are inside the walls! And surely someone will alert the Savoners once Grenjar sounds the alarm."

"None of them speak the bloody southern tongue, girl! I'll be fine. You take the blade. I've got the axe in case I need it. Now go, he's our guest and our liege lord—we have a duty to him."

She looked dubiously from him lying in a pool of his enemy's blood to the heavy axe that she had barely been able to lift with two good arms. How could he ever lift that with one arm, wounded as he was? But then, he was not only right, he was her father. And they did have a duty to the Red Prince.

"I'll warn him and come right back," she said, kissing him on the forehead and pushing herself to her feet. "Don't die before then."

"It will take more than one damned wolf to kill the Skullbreaker, my girl. Go, then, go!"

She ran from the room, reversing the knife in her hand as she did so. She knew she was on edge, and the last thing she wanted was to stab people instinctively if they startled her.

She was barely out of the room when she saw a group of half-dressed but fully armed Dalarn warriors with Steinthor Strongbow at their head charging up the stairs toward her. Relieved that her father would at least be safe from another attack, she quickly told Steinthor where she was headed. After ordering most of the men to go and assist the Skullbreaker, the captain insisted on accompanying her to the prince's chambers, along with three of his men.

The Red Prince had been given the great chamber, which was in the central tower, so it took some time to descend the stairs of the South Tower, run through the courtyard, then ascend another set of stairs.

There were no signs of any alarm, however, which was a relief to Fjotra, since she was getting out of breath before they reached the landing upon which the prince's room was located. But her relief quickly faded as they turned a corner in the corridor and saw an unfamiliar man staggering toward them holding a bloody shoulder.

"Dammit!" swore Steinthor, and he drew his sword, racing past the man into the room.

His men followed, but even as Fjotra tightened her grip on her knife and steeled herself for what they would find there, a familiar scent caught her attention. She frowned and sniffed the air to see where it was coming from, then turned around and realized that it was the wounded man, who was neither Dalarn nor Savoner, but what looked like a strange blend of the two peoples. It was the eyes that were the wrong color, they were black like some of the dark-eyed Savoners', but the skin and hair were fair.

"*Sigskifting!*" she screamed.

The false man growled and bared teeth that were much too long, thin, and curved to be human.

Terror filled her, but she didn't hesitate to throw the knife in her hand. The aalvarg was only steps away, and at that range, she did not miss.

The man howled like the wolf he truly was as the blade sank hilt-deep into his left shoulder.

Fjotra ran toward the room into which Steinthor and his men had disappeared. She was almost to the door when a heavy weight struck her in the back and smashed her to the floor.

The force of it stunned her, leaving her more conscious of the beast growling and snarling on top of her than of any pain from its attack. And then, almost as soon as it had come, the heavy weight was gone.

A high-pitched shriek resounded throughout the stone corridor, and when she rolled over onto her side and looked behind her, she saw Steinthor Strongbow standing over the dying figure of the aalvarg, now shifted back into its terrible half-form, holding it up by the sword that ran all the way through its throat and out the back of its neck. Two of his men stood behind him, already sheathing their swords.

Twitching and thrashing, but unable to escape from the iron blade that held it as firmly as a kitchen spit, the dreadful beast finally slumped to the ground, apparently dead.

Steinthor lifted his hilt toward the ceiling, then placed his boot on the lupine face and withdrew his sword.

"These things are magic. We'd better burn it, just to make sure it's true dead."

He extended his shield hand to Fjotra and effortlessly pulled her to her feet.

"Thank you," she said.

The Dalarn warrior only shook his head. "How did you know? I thought it was one of the Prince's men."

"Oh, by the gods, Prince Karl!" she cried, and she ran into his chamber.

It looked as if a cow had been slaughtered inside, perhaps two cows. Steinthor's third man was standing over the body of a man that Fjotra recognized as one of the Red Prince's servants. His throat was torn out, although it was impossible to tell if it had been the aalvarg's teeth or claws that were responsible. Another servant was unconscious. He appeared unmarked, but he was clearly breathing, and the broken wooden chair lying in several large pieces around him made it obvious how he'd been attacked.

"He's not here!" she cried, more relieved than she ever would have imagined. But then she heard a groan from someone lying out of sight on the other side of the chamber's large bed. She leaped upon it and felt something wet and a little sticky under her hands, but she paid it no mind. For there, lying on the floor with his eyes closed and his face half-covered by a blanket, was the prince. His gold-hilted dagger lay by his side, and its blade was covered to the hilt with blood, but Fjotra couldn't tell if it was his or if it explained the monster's wounded shoulder.

"No, no, he's here, behind the bed," she shouted, throwing aside the blanket and pressing her hands frantically to his face and his chest.

His face was scratched, but not badly, and his throat was unmarred. Then she saw his stomach, or rather, what was left of it, and her heart sank. A deep wound to the gut usually sufficed to kill a man, and she knew that no man could survive the terrible mauling that had left the prince's insides torn into an obscene ruin. Fighting back tears and biting her lip to keep her horror from showing on her face, she gently pulled the blanket back over his torso.

"My reaver princess," the Savoner prince said, but his smile turned into a grimace. "I fear I shall never be king over your isles."

"I am sorry, your royal highness. They would think you well for their lord."

"They would have, would they? Did you see it? The creature, the ulfin—it turned into a man!"

"Yes, my prince. It is dead now. The Strongbow killed it."

Steinthor was standing at her side now. He nodded to the prince, his face grave, then glanced at Fjotra. His question was obvious. She shook her head by way of reply, and his eyes grew dark with impotent anger. He kneeled down and took the prince's hand in his own.

"Tell him that the Dalarn will not forget him. Tell him that his name will be honored among us. Tell him that one day, he will be avenged, that we will cross the sea and grow strong again, and then we will come back and wipe out their accursed race. And tell him that if his gods do not want him, ours will be proud to host him in the Hirdhal."

She told the prince as best she could manage in the southern tongue.

It made him cough with laughter, and smile at the grim-faced warrior. "Tell the man I am well-pleased. If the Immaculate will not have me, then perhaps we shall meet each other on the battlefields of your gods." But when he coughed again, there was blood on his lips.

"My lady, tell your father to be loyal to mine, and all will be well. And tell my father that one day, your people must come back here and claim these lands for the realm. The comtesse..." His eyes closed, and his face suddenly turned even whiter than it already was. "God, it hurts. A priest, I need a priest!"

"He wants one of their spirit men," she told the Strongbow.

"There is no time. He'll be dead soon."

"You tell me the words," she suggested. "You say again to priest when he come."

"Are you purified?" he asked, his voice growing weaker.

She didn't understand his question at first, then she realized he was asking her if she worshiped his god.

"Oh, yes," she lied without hesitation.

A faint expression of relief flickered across his face, then he began talking in a low voice, telling her of things he had done, of things that he had not done, and of things that had shamed him. Most of it went completely over her head, but one thing was very clear: The comtesse had, without question, been his mistress.

It seemed mad that jealousy should strike her, even now as he lay dying, but she could not help it. Behind her, she could hear that others had entered the room. But Steinthor, understanding the essence of the ritual if not its substance, permitted none of them to interfere, until she felt a hand upon her shoulder and saw that it belonged to an older Savoner wearing a long black robe.

"He has confessed his sins to you?" the priest asked her.

"Yes, my lord." She tried to move out of his way, but the prince, still mumbling unintelligibly with his eyes closed, was holding onto her hand.

The priest indicated by gesture that she could stay where she was, and he knelt down to place his hand on the prince's brow.

"Prince Charles-Phillippe de Mirid of Borgoune, the Almighty God, the giver of all mercies, through the fall and rise of His Immaculate Son has reconciled the world to Himself and sent His purified Spirit among us for the forgiveness of sins. Through the ministry of the Holy Mother Church, may the most merciful God give you pardon and peace. And I absolve you from your sins in the name of the Holy, the Immaculate, and the Sanctifier."

With his index finger, he drew a shape on the dying man's forehead, and both Fjotra and the Strongbow gasped as the prince's flesh began to glow in the shape of a vertical line crossed with two smaller, diagonal lines, precisely where the priest's finger had drawn them.

"Be at peace, my son. May the Immaculate Lord be your advocate and usher you into the life eternal."

The prince's eyes were closed, but his face relaxed. Whatever pain he had been in appeared to have vanished. The movement of his chest slowed, then stopped entirely. A few moments later, the glowing light on his forehead began to dim.

When the last vestiges of the light disappeared, the priest rose unsteadily to his feet. His face, Fjotra noticed, was streaked with tears that she had not heard in his voice.

"He is gone to glory now, to the very great loss of the realm."

"What does the priest-man say?" Steinthor asked her.

"I think he says the prince is dead. I'm not sure. It is hard to tell. They always say so many things that don't mean what they say."

"Well, he is dead, anyway," Steinthor assured her with the nonchalant certainty of a man who had sent dozens of men and scores of aalvarg to their graves.

Fjotra, her shift torn and covered with blood, nodded and swallowed hard, looking down at the peaceful face of the man who might have been her husband. He had been so strong, so commanding, so warm and full of life. And now, there was nothing, nothing except an empty shell of what had once been a vigorous, handsome leader of men. The hand she held was dead weight. It was an object, not a person.

For the moment, the waste and the tragedy of it struck her more than her own sorrow. Everything depended on the king's response to his heir's death, and only the gods knew what that would be. She leaned forward and kissed Prince Karl, for the first and last time, on his bloodied lips.

AULAN

THE road from Cynothicum to Gallidromum was longer and colder than it had been when Aulan traveled it the previous summer. Winter had not yet arrived, but it would come in a matter of weeks, and already it was much colder than he and his knights found comfortable. The hardiness of the provincials with whom they were riding impressed him, as neither they nor their shaggy, stump-legged horses that looked more like oversized ponies seemed to mind the weather in the least.

They made good time too. At first, Aulan had been inclined to join with the rest of his knights in sniggering at the ugly, ill-bred beasts as well as their mounts. But after seeing how they managed to not only travel farther in a single day than even a veteran legion could march, but also nearly keep pace with the sixty riders of his command, he had to admit that the Cynothii appeared to be on to something with this idea of rapidly moving infantry around.

It would be impossible to fight from the backs of the rugged little horses with one's feet all but dragging on the ground, but they served perfectly well for rapidly moving the provincials' infantry from one place to another. If being there first with the most was the key to winning battles, such a tactic would go a long way in ensuring the former.

Not that being there first applied in this particular situation. The Valerian legion wasn't going anywhere, being comfortably settled into the castra stativa near Gallidromum for the winter. Neither Aulan's half-wing nor the Cynothii they were accompanying were to attack Legio XVII.

Their orders were to bypass the fortification and secure the roads leading to the south against any messages being sent to Amorr alerting the Senate and the Consuls about the presence of a second legion inside Cynothicus.

Strictly speaking, there wasn't much that either the Senate or the Consuls could do about where House Severus, or any of the other Houses Martial, chose to march their legions. But his father had made it very clear that he did not wish to be called upon to explain himself before the Senate until spring. No doubt this would upset one or more of the countless strands of the web that the old spider was always spinning. Aulan didn't even bother trying to keep them all straight anymore. He had given that up as a lost cause several years ago.

He heard unshod hooves cantering on the hard surface of the frozen dirt road and sighed. It was sure to be Vestremer, who was the Cynothi equivalent of a tribune. Neither of them was entirely sure who was supposed to outrank the other, but since the Cynothi was, despite himself, a little in awe of an actual Amorran tribune, whereas Aulan found it difficult to take a precariously balanced provincial on the back of a shaggy pony very seriously, they had reached a functional accommodation. Vestremer commanded his pony riders, Aulan commanded the cavalry, and whenever their different perspectives diverged too far from parallel, Vestremer would track down Aulan and complain. Aulan sighed. Sweet sanctification, but how the man could complain!

"What is it now?" he asked wearily, trying to keep a sharp tone out of his voice. He'd been counting: This was the eighth time today that the Cynothi captain had sought him out. No doubt it would concern something about as vital and as relevant to the task at hand as the previous seven times.

The Cynothii were a touchy, prideful bunch, and, thanks to their victory this summer over the Andronican legion, they weren't inclined to behave in what a patrician might consider to be an appropriately submissive manner on the part of a mere provincial. After the most recent fight, in which blades were actually drawn, though thankfully unused, Aulan had finally been forced to tell his decurions to whip the next knight who came to blows with one of their loyal provincial allies.

"I'm worried about the outriders," Vestremer said. "They should have been back already. I sent a pair out to ride ahead at midday."

Aulan looked around. The road was making its way through a wooded valley of sorts. The trees were thick on both sides, and when he looked back he could see that the men and horses were descending somewhat, though the slope wasn't steep enough to really notice as you were riding. They couldn't possibly have gotten lost. However far out they had been ranging, they wouldn't have difficulty finding the road. And once the road was found, it was a simple matter of checking the markers laid at one-mile segments of the roadside and determining if you were closer to Cynothicum or Gallidromum.

"Bandits?" Aulan didn't think even a good-sized pack of bandits would dare to attack a pair of armored Amorran knights. But except for their short, curved swords, the Cynothi scouts didn't look much different than any of the bearded farmers past whom they'd ridden over the last two days. "Or some peasants might have killed them for their horses."

Vestremer stared at him for a moment, his jaw slack with surprise, and then he smiled. "Lord Severus, there are few farms near here. Few peasants. Few people. Not until we get closer to the river will we see much in the way of civilization. It must be the Amorrans from the Gallidromum fort."

Civilization? Aulan nearly choked as he repressed the instinctive snort that the other's words had provoked. There were many words that he would consider applying to Cynothicum, but that would have been among the very last.

"Very well, then. It seems likely that they were taken by a Valerian patrol. But what of that? Whoever took over for Marcus Saturnius would never be mad enough to leave the safety of the castra. They couldn't know how many we are. Besides, legions fight on foot. Even if their commander was foolish enough to march out against us, we're mounted, and we could easily ride around him. We might even be able to capture the castra. With my sixty and your five hundred, we could surely hold it until Buteo could relieve us with the rest of the legion!"

"The rest of your legion are two days behind us. And the Valerians would leave a large garrison behind."

"Not if they think they are coming out to meet an entire legion."

"I don't believe we could hold for two days against an entire legion, even with stone walls. My men aren't trained in siegecraft. And neither, I should think, are your riders. It's your footmen who do most of the manual labor, is it not?"

Aulan shrugged, but he couldn't argue with the hairy little man. "I suppose you're right. Even if we could take the fort, Buteo's appearance would force them to retreat toward Amorr, which is the last thing he wants now."

"And is the very thing we are riding ahead of the legion to prevent, if I understood him rightly."

It was annoying, but the Cynothi was correct. Secundus Falconius had made his feelings very, very clear. He was not a legate who wished to see a great deal of initiative out of his tribunes and auxiliaries. "You win, Vestremer. Send out four pairs of yours, and I'll send out a squadron. Let's see if we can scare up this patrol of yours and find out if there is anything waiting for us in these woods."

The Cynothi nodded and turned his horse around to return to his men, who were plodding along on their little horses behind the Amorran cavalry. Aulan called a decurion over and ordered him to take his men and ride ahead in search of either the missing Cynothii or the hypothetical Amorran patrol.

Actually, if the squadron could capture a knight or two, that would be useful indeed, as Aulan could learn who the Valerian commander was and perhaps gain some insight into his thinking. Buteo was a hard man, and he wasn't easily pleased, but Aulan imagined even the Falconian would appreciate that sort of information.

The ride through the forest continued uneventfully. They stopped once, upon crossing a stream, to water the horses and relieve their cramped legs for a while, then rode on. What appeared to be the edge of the forest was just coming into sight, judging by the brighter light ahead, when he heard the distant sound of metal clashing on metal, followed by angry shouting, and then the sound of hoofbeats rapidly approaching them from the direction they were headed. It was the squadron he'd sent ahead, he could tell from the sound of the iron horseshoes on the hard-packed earth of the road.

Aulan stopped and raised his fist. The column of riders behind him stopped amidst the creaking of men in their leather saddles and the explosive equine complaints of their mounts at being so abruptly halted.

Aulan saw the decurion come into view as he rounded the corner of the curving road, followed by five of his fellows. There was an arrow jutting from the decurion's armored shoulder, and as Aulan looked on, alarmed, there was a gasp of dismay as the knight bringing up the tail of the squadron slumped to one side and collapsed, falling off his horse without making any attempt to break his fall.

"Report," Aulan barked at the decurion and urged his horse forward to intercept the officer, who was yanking hard on the reins of his horse to slow the gelding before it crashed into the Amorran column. "What happened up there?"

"We didn't find the patrol, we found the whole bloody legion!" The decurion was no blushing battle virgin, but he was wide-eyed with shock and trembling with a surfeit of excitement. "We saw their lines when we came out from the trees. They were far enough away that I thought we could ride closer and see how they were arrayed, but they had a whole squadron in the woods behind us. We had to fight our way through them."

"I see that." He reached out and tried to pull the shaft out of the decurion's shoulder, but it was buried too deeply in the thick leather underneath the steel, so he had to content himself with breaking it off. "How did you get this? Did they have archers behind you in the woods too?"

"No, two of their riders had bows. I don't think they were horse archers, though. They just looked like regular knights, and their bows were longer than those the pagans use."

"Are you sure it was the whole legion?"

"I'm not sure. We didn't have time to count. But there had to be at least four or five cohorts. Except for the squadron behind us, their cavalry was on the left. Looked like five squadrons, maybe half a wing in all. They had a ballista with them too, but I think they must have broken a rope. They loosed a firepot, but it flew a mile over our heads. Didn't come anywhere near us."

"Strange," Aulan mused. "Why would they decide to come out when they were already in a perfectly defensible castra with stone walls? Vestremer, it would appear that we are indeed dealing with a madman."

"He's an Amorran. Of course he's mad," said the Cynothi captain, who had ridden up to discover why the column had stopped. "I see you found the patrol," he told the decurion.

"Found a damn sight more than that." The decurion spat. "There's half a legion waiting for us once we come out of the trees."

Dismayed, Vestremer turned to Aulan. "You said they'd have to be mad to leave the fort!" he said accusingly. "Half a legion is three thousand men. We can't fight them. We have to turn back!"

Aulan knew he had little choice but to agree. The Valerian commander might be mad, but there was an element of shrewdness to him as well. By sending out only half his men, the Valerian had prevented them from simply riding around him and taking the castra. That probably meant the Valerian had been expecting to face a mobile enemy, which meant that he was anticipating the need to fight the Cynothi infantry as well as the legion. But how could he have known that the full legion was two full days behind them, rather than at their heels? No, he hadn't known, he had merely guessed correctly, because today was the first day that mounted troops could have travelled the distance from here to Cynothicum.

"I'll bet you the other half of that legion arrives the day after tomorrow, before midday," he mused aloud.

"What's that?" the Cynothi asked.

"By your leave, tribune?" The decurion indicated the blood flowing down his arm. It appeared the arrow must have penetrated the leather on his shoulder after all.

"Yes, yes, of course. Get that removed and cleaned up, by all means." He returned the man's salute and frowned as he turned to his colleague. "You were saying?"

"You said the legion would arrive tomorrow. They can't possibly march that quickly!"

"Tomorrow? The legion?" Aulan was confused. Then he laughed. "No, not Buteo's legion, I was talking about the other one: the Valerians. Their commander may be mad, but he isn't stupid. He knew we could either arrive quickly or in numbers. One or the other, but not both. So he sent out only half his troops to stop us from stealing the castra out from under his nose. If he decides to make his stand in the field, and that must be his intention, he'll stop us and arrange to bring the rest of his troops here before our combined forces show up. He's clever enough, but he's probably young. No experience. It's one of Saturnius's surviving tribunes. I'd bet my life on it."

"So long as you're not betting mine," the Cynothi said sourly. "Or my men's."

"You should have thought of that before you decided to start killing Amorrans, my provincial friend." Aulan slapped the smaller man on the shoulder. "You didn't beat a real legion. You defeated a green, half-trained army of battle virgins that hardly merited the title. And even though you outnumbered them four-to-one, they still slaughtered half your men."

"We still won. We'll hold our own, Amorran, be certain of it."

Hold your own? You'll do more than that, Aulan thought. Falconius will dash you against the Valerians like water against a rock. But water costs nothing and enough of it will erode the hardest stone.

"I have no doubt. But today, I think discretion shall serve as the better part of valor, loath though I am to admit it. We can't attack them, we can't take the fort, and I think it is safe to assume that the foolhardy young tribune there isn't about to go running back to Amorr. Tell your men to turn around. We'll ride back and rejoin Buteo. He won't thank us for throwing half his cavalry away."

"You don't know who is commanding. Why do you say he is young?"

Aulan smiled, thinking of how a young Amorran tribune had eagerly led two legionary squadrons across a river in pursuit of a fleeing pack of orc raiders, only to find himself nearly surrounded by what appeared at the time to be every wolfrider on Selenoth.

That was nearly four years ago, but he'd never forgotten that dreadful moment when he'd learned the difference between being bold and being foolhardy. To this day, he still didn't understand why the goblin commander hadn't attacked and killed them all. Perhaps the little greenskin had simply enjoyed witnessing the discomfiture of their bigger, nastier kin. Regardless, it had left him with a healthy appreciation for goblins and an even healthier instinct for retreating when it seemed in order.

"Because I have a good deal of personal experience in how foolhardy young tribunes think. They all dream of making a name for themselves as the next Magnus or Victorinus. Anyone with more than a lick of common sense would already be marching double-time in the direction of Amorr. But he's going to fight."

"What's that?" Vestremer held very still. "Hush! Do you hear that?"

"Hear what?" Aulan said, confused. But there was something happening off in the distance. It was muffled by the trees, whose leaves were red, yellow, and brown but still mostly attached to the trees. It was the sound of combat, he realized, but it was coming from the opposite direction than it had before.

"The rear is under attack," the Cynothi said just as Aulan reached the same conclusion.

"By whom?" Aulan asked. "The other half of that legion! They weren't behind us, so how could they come through the forest so quickly?"

But Vestremer didn't answer. He was already galloping alongside the column toward the rear.

Aulan booted his horse in the sides. Its longer legs helped him rapidly gain on the Cynothii as first knights, then provincials, milled around in confusion. Then the captain abruptly slowed, and Aulan was forced to rein in his mount and slew it sideways in order to avoid colliding with the smaller horse. What he saw astonished him.

Cavalry, Amorran knights, were slashing their way through the Cynothii that made up the rearguard, who were almost helpless to defend themselves on horseback. And there were a lot of them—it wasn't just a few squadrons. His view was partially obscured by the trees and the mass of confused provincials, but it looked as if they were being attacked by an entire cavalry wing!

"I thought you said the cavalry was out in front of us!"

"I did! They are! The decurion said there was half a wing on their left. That's seven squadrons. How they can have so many horse?"

The two commanders stared at each other, more astonished than angry or even afraid. Vestremer was the first to collect himself. "I have to get my men off their mounts and into line. They can't fight like this. Now do something, Amorran, before the other half of that legion traps us in here and they butcher us like hogs." He urged his horse toward the clashing, shouting, shrieking chaos of the fray, bellowing orders in the bastardized tongue spoken by the hairy little men.

Aulan turned his horse around and galloped along the side of the road, desperately casting about for a way out of what was beginning to look more like a wood-lined deathtrap than a road through the forest. How had the Valerian horse hit them from behind? Different notions suggested themselves, but with a determined effort he put the problem aside for the time being. How they got there didn't matter now. What mattered was how to extricate his men, and if possible at least some of the Cynothii, from the jaws of the enemy legion.

When in doubt, move forward. It was a concept that ran counter to every man's instinct to freeze and hide, but he'd learned the lesson the hard way when ambushed by orcs on the frontier. The Valerians to the fore might already be moving forward, so he had to escape the confines of the forest before they sealed him in. His riders couldn't hope to fight them, but they could most certainly outrun the legionaries. The Valerian's

cavalry squadrons might try to engage them and slow them down, but
Buteo was not the only one who could afford to spend Cynothi lives like
water.

"Publius Terentius!" he shouted for the draconarius when he reached
the front of the column. "Get ready to sound the advance. Decurions,
you've got to keep your men moving at full speed. We're going to ride past
them and make for Curcomelis. If you get separated, we'll meet there. Pass
the word on to the others further back."

He reached out and grabbed a red-haired knight, who was, predictably
enough, named Rufus. "Ride back and tell the first Cynothi officer you
can find at the front of their column that we're riding past the Valerians
to Curcomelis. Tell him his captain is engaged with the cavalry attacking
us from behind, so he's going to have to leave a second rearguard behind
once we clear the forest to slow their cavalry down to let the rest escape.
He's got to leave enough men back to handle sixty of them, but tell him to
move fast or they'll be trapped in here. Have them sound a horn as soon
as you've delivered the message."

"Rearguard against sixty cavalry, then a horn. Yes, sir!" The knight
saluted and rode back toward the end of the Amorran column, in search
of an officer.

Aulan knew he had just doomed one hundred and fifty, or perhaps
two hundred men, assuming that his orders were followed. And that was
if they weren't all trapped and slaughtered together. Whereas Vestremer
and the first rearguard could reasonably hope that the Valerian knights
with whom they were engaged would withdraw once the Cynothi defense
organized and stiffened, thus leaving open the path to retreat, the second
rearguard would also have to dismount if they were to hold back the rest
of the Valerian cavalry. But on foot, they would not be able to escape
the thousands of legionaries who would be following in the wake of their
mounted wing. Those fortunate enough to remount in time to escape
the slaughter on foot would rapidly be ridden down by the bigger, faster
horses of the Amorrans.

He shrugged. It was a pity, and he regretted the need to issue such bloody orders, but sacrificing a few hundred Cynothii was simply the price he would have to pay to save his men. If giving the order meant his soul was damned, then so be it. Anyhow, every Cynothi slain today would probably save him, or some other Amorran commander, the trouble of having to kill them later if the flames of their futile rebellion did not eventually die down, in keeping with his father's plans.

Behind him, a horn blew. He snapped his fingers to draw Publius Terentius's attention, then pointed forward. The draconarius nodded, took a deep breath, and responded to the horn in kind, sending the deep, penetrating sound through the forest.

Aulan normally loved the sound of the advance, but tonight, in these circumstances, it sounded disturbingly like a dirge to him. He drew his sword in case the squadron reported by the decurion was still to be found on the edge of the woods, and he urged his horse forward, first permitting it to trot until it was well clear of his men, then kicking it up to a comfortable canter, then a gallop.

The ride to the forest's edge did not take long at the speed they were riding. Once the open field came within sight, he saw what he'd suspected. The enemy infantry cohorts were advancing, and they were less than one hundred paces away as Aulan and the leading riders burst out of the woods within clear view of them. Fortunately, the Valerian commander had withdrawn his own cavalry, and the infantry stood between the two mounted forces. Aulan looked quickly to the left and saw they would have just enough space to ride past the enemy infantry and back onto the road before the Valerian horse would be able to cut them off.

He pulled his horse off to the side and furiously waved his arms at his riders. "Ride, damn you, ride!" He knew their instinct would be to rein in their mounts when they saw the nearby mass of the approaching enemy. Horse after horse pounded past him, mostly blacks and browns, with the occasional grey flashing past his peripheral vision. But he was focused on the activity taking place behind the Valerian lines.

He rapidly discerned three concerns. First, the decurion leading the enemy knights had been a little slow to respond to their appearance, but once the man had realized that Aulan's knights would be able to escape being cut off by the lumbering legionaries, he turned his riders around, then led them on a path behind the infantry in pursuit of the Severan horse.

The second concern, and the most pressing one, was the infantry, who were still marching inexorably toward his position. Soon, very soon, the enemy would be upon them, and, considering that there were hundreds of men at the fore of the enemy line, they wouldn't even need their swords—they could simply trample him under the iron-nails of their sandals.

But he had no choice except to wait until the first Cynothi began to emerge if he hoped to augment his seven squadrons with them. He decided to count to thirty before following his men. If the Cynothii had ignored his order to move out quickly, there was nothing he could do about it now.

It was with an amount of genuine awe that he looked over the front lines of the Valerian cohorts. He had reviewed troops before, but he had never seen an Amorran legion deployed for battle and advancing into combat from the other side.

Their black armor and the helms with their face-obscuring cheekpads made the legionaries look like some sort of inhuman, insectoid demons, an effect that was powerfully enhanced by the beaked silver faces of the centurions. The long rectangular shields they bore were painted with the Valerian insignia in the center, with the number XVII above and the number of the cohort and century below. He was a little surprised to see their commander had established cohort VI in the center, which would be the best and most promising of the young men. But this was the sort of situation that was perfectly suited to a green cohort in need of seasoning, he noted with reluctant approval.

His third concern obliterated several trees with a series of loud, splintering crashes as a large rock hurled by the Valerian onager smashed into the forest off to his right. He could see the crew had already adjusted their aim and loaded another massive stone into the sling. The Valerians were just beginning to winch back the arm when the steady stream of horses galloping past him slowed to a sporadic trickle, then stopped entirely. He glanced back into the gap between the trees and saw the first Cynothii approaching. Not quite as rapidly, given the shorter legs of their horses, but quickly enough.

"Dismount! Dismount!" he shouted at the first Cynothi he saw bearing a horn.

Fortunately, the provincials were as astounded as his knights had been at the proximity of the approaching legionaries. But the gap to the left between the woods and the right edge of the Valerian line had narrowed considerably, and the threat from the infantry was that much more imminent. The Cynothii reacted precisely as he hoped they would, springing from their horses and rapidly forming themselves into a line. They would be crushed by the heavier armor and greater number of the legionaries, of course, but even if he could save only a few hundred of the little bastards, they would likely prove useful in harrying the Valerians and keeping them penned in their castra until Buteo and the rest of the provincials arrived.

The rider with the horn was still blowing something that the rest of the provincials seemed to find meaningful, as their line had grown to nearly fifty strong. He heard a shout from the Valerian lines, and they suddenly stopped their approach, ready to hurl their pila.

Dammit, he had left it too long, he realized even as the onager loosed a second time and the rock it threw evoked screams from the Cynothii as two riders that had just ridden up behind the newly forming line were smashed backward, along with their horses, as if swept from the ground by an invisible giant's fist. They vanished, but their blood spattered the men on either side of them.

It was too late. He saw that now, he couldn't possibly hope to ride past the long black line of Valerian legionaries, their faces mostly obscured by the cheekguards that dangled from the familiar helms. He'd been thinking like a cavalryman too long and he'd stupidly forgotten that he couldn't simply ride past hundreds of men carrying pila and trained to throw them accurately. He'd be lucky if he was transfixed with less than ten of the short throwing spears if he tried to follow his squadrons around the Valerians' right flank.

But where squadrons and armies couldn't quickly go, one man alone could make his way. As a centurion shouted a command, several hundred Valerians hurled a black cloud of pila directly into the face of the assembling provincials. More than a few of the lightly armored men fell, pierced through.

Aulan himself was unscathed, though, as he had already urged his horse back into the forest and was working his way as fast as he dared just inside the forest, safely obscured from the view of the nearest Valerians, ducking his head as small branches whipped impotently across his helm and armored forearms.

Behind him, he could still hear the shouts of centurions and the crash of the onager as Vestremer and his infantry began to learn that it was one thing to fight Amorrans with the numbers on your side, and something else entirely when the advantage ran the other way. Despite his chagrin at losing five centuries' worth of potentially useful provincials, he couldn't help but feel a small burst of patriotic pride as behind him, he heard the sounds of his enemies killing his allies.

MARCUS

THE legion's new primus pilus glared at him impatiently. So too did the draconarius he'd commandeered from Julianus. Julianus himself would no doubt be growling at him now if he were not already occupied with chasing the Severan cavalry that had boldly ridden right across the face of their front lines. Even Trebonius was occasionally glancing over at him with a quizzical expression whenever he took a momentary break from counting the force of Cynothi infantry that was increasing before their eyes.

The enemy had nearly two centuries' worth dismounted and assembled in two lines about thirty paces in front of Hosidos's cohort. That cohort hadn't seen any combat against the goblins, having been held in reserve that day, so Marcus thought the experience of being exposed to the threat of it might serve them well. So far, they were maintaining flawless discipline. Not a single legionary had so much as thrown a pilus beyond the initial two volleys, although the temptation to charge and break the enemy had to be almost overwhelming.

Marcus grinned at Didius, who was practically shaking with his eagerness to come to grips with their outnumbered enemy. He had promoted the primus pilus from Cohort VIII instead of simply permitting the second centurion from Cohort I to replace Honoratus, as was the practice in ordinary circumstances. But these were no ordinary circumstances, and, even with Honoratus and his known associates gone, Marcus could not be sure how far the rot of treason had penetrated the first two centuries. Didius might have significantly less experience then a number of the centurions in the first cohort, but unlike his more senior colleagues, Didius had only ever served in another Valerian legion.

There had been some grumbling amongst the centurion corps concerning his promotion. Being well aware of it, Didius was anticipating the chance to prove himself to his new subordinates.

"Gentlemen, relax," Marcus said, shaking his head. He could feel the strange weight of the yellow general's plume bobbing as he did so. "That's an order. I have no intention of engaging with the Cynothii today if they don't force me to it."

The three officers near him looked at each other as they attempted to digest his statement.

Trebonius cleared his throat, then pointed toward the onager, which had found its range and was killing one or two helpless provincials with almost every missile it threw. "Sir, with all due respect, you have not forgotten the squadrons you sent to ambush their column in the forest, have you?"

"I wasn't referring to the cavalry, Tribune. The ambush was merely to ensure they were not able to withdraw easily once they discovered we were here in force." He pointed to the Cynothi lines, which were now stretching nearly far enough to reach cohort II on the right side and cohort X on the left. "The context was in reference to the Cynothii who happen to be right in front of us at the moment."

"What are you waiting for?" Didius asked, almost wailing in his distress. "We can smash them right now!"

"Of course we can. And we can smash them almost as easily once all of them have arrived, dismounted, and taken their positions. But unless I am very much mistaken, their commander will have sufficient wit to surrender to us once he sees his position is untenable. We've already bloodied their noses, and that should be enough to demand his attention."

"I wish we could have at least caught those damned Severans that got past us," Trebonius said, looking in the direction the enemy cavalry had escaped. "We were so close too. Just a little sooner, and we would have had them."

"And done what?" Marcus shook his head. "Killed our fellow citizens? I have no interest in the Severan horse today. They can do us no harm."

"Then why did you order Julianus to pursue them?" Trebonius asked.

"Because I know him. He was going to chase after them whether I ordered him to do so or not. Magnus always told me to never give an order you know will be broken, or fail to give an order you know will be followed. So, I told him to do what he was going to do anyhow."

"You're not always going to be able to anticipate insubordination," Trebonius said.

Marcus smiled coldly. "I'm not always going to be as tolerant of it either. Julianus has earned my trust to an extent that very, very few of my officers ever will. If Hosidos is foolish enough to attack, I'll have him flogged."

By Valerian standards, that just about qualified as being soft, Marcus thought wryly. He was a little disappointed in Trebonius, but he wasn't surprised that the others didn't understand why they needed Cynothi captives more than they needed Cynothi corpses.

"Is that their commander over there?" the primus pilus asked, pointing to a new arrival, who was riding a grey horse. He appeared to be a man of some importance, as various dismounted men, presumably the equivalent of whatever the provincials called their centurions, approached him. Judging by their gestures and widely swinging arms, they were either informing him that the large mass of armored men poised to overcome them were not friendly or complaining about their abandonment by the Severan cavalry.

"Gaius Trebonius, will you send someone to tell the onager to stand down? I imagine the spotter already has his eyes on that one."

"At once, sir," the tribune said, and he turned his horse toward the six message riders who were waiting at the ready about twenty paces behind them.

"You don't want him dead?" Didius was aggrieved, but Marcus, understanding the centurion's frustration, decided to overlook it.

"Yes, it would be difficult for him to surrender in that case, would it not?"

Marcus nodded with satisfaction as, after some additional deliberation on the part of the Cynothii, even more exaggerated arm-waving, and some activity on the ground that couldn't be seen behind the two lines of enemy infantry, a young Cynothi on horseback was handed a spear shaft. When the lad held it up, it could be seen there was a large piece of white fabric attached to it.

"Mirabile dictu, it appears as if someone over there can count," Trebonius commented, having sent off a rider as instructed. "What are the terms? Unconditional?"

"I don't know if that's necessary," Marcus said. "I think it would be more useful to talk to the man. Take Dardanus with you under a herald's flag and offer him safe passage to a parley. Didius, since you were so eager to get at them before, why don't you accompany them and act as his surety while we're hosting him? Take Hosidos too. They have to know we're not going to sacrifice two of our senior centurions."

Didius raised a skeptical eyebrow in his direction, causing Trebonius to burst out laughing. "Never fear, primus pilus. If the tribune already finds you tiresome, he's hardly likely to murder the Cynothii. After all, he only has to wait until Fulgetra arrives to deprive himself of the pleasure of your company."

The centurion smiled sourly and thumped his chest. "God and Amorr, sir. Hosidos and I will see if those damned provincials have anything worth dicing for."

"There are worse ways to spend an afternoon, Centurion." Marcus saluted back then nodded to Trebonius and Dardanus. "He can bring his sword and four men, if he wishes."

But the Cynothi commander came alone, Marcus was pleased to see, riding alongside Gaius Trebonius and exchanging pleasantries with him as if they were out for a summer evening's ride, not riding past three thousand legionaries who were still poised to wipe out him and his entire force. If the man was concerned for his safety of the lives of his men, he certainly hid it well. Marcus had seen more defeat on the faces of men who had lost bets on the legion's fist-fighting champion.

"Trebonius, I'm going to want notes," he said without taking his eyes off the man.

The Cynothii dismounted with the easy grace of a man born to life in the saddle. He was short and fair, with long light brown hair and a shaggy beard that covered most of a rather nondescript face. Like most Cynothi men, his legs bowed outward at the knees. But even in what could reasonably be considered desperate circumstances, his demeanor appeared to be lighthearted. An enemy, to be sure, but a likable one perhaps. He bowed to Marcus, who nodded his head in polite response as Trebonius and Dardanus both dismounted and took up positions behind Marcus.

"I thank you for the invitation, General," the Cynothi said. "I imagine it has not escaped your attention that you appear to have us at a distinct disadvantage. I am called Vestremer, son of Nervutachs, Captain of the Royal Infantry, in service to King Ladismas the First."

"I noticed something of the sort," Marcus said. "I am Valerius Clericus, son of Valerius Corvus, Tribune of the People and the commander of Legio XVII. And while it may surprise you, the Senate and People of Amorr have long made a practice of requiring that its legionary officers are able to count without using their hands and feet."

Vestremer grinned. "And here I thought that's why you Amorrans wear those open-toed sandals. So you're the Crow's son, are you? I suppose that takes away a bit of the sting of being outfoxed by a mere stripling. No offense intended, Tribune of the People and commander of Legio XVII."

"None taken, Captain of the Royal Infantry." He glanced at the decurion, who had taken an aggressive stance with his hand on his sword hilt. "Stand down, Dardanus. I will be the judge of what I find offensive. Now, Captain, you would appear to have a large quantity of horses for an infantry unit."

"Walking gets tiresome."

"And I must confess to be a little curious concerning this king in whose service you claim to be. Is Cynothicus no longer a province of the Amorran Empire?"

"Not since Ladismas beat your consul and was acclaimed king by the nobles and commoners alike. The Cynothii were a free people for centuries before your Empire, and we're the first to free ourselves from it. But we won't be the last."

"A noble dream. You understand that the Senate and People tend to see it a little differently, of course. And they not only object to rebellions, they particularly object to rebels killing our consuls." Marcus smiled. "Of course, in this one instance, I may be able to find it in my heart to forgive your people the latter, seeing as the Senate saw fit to replace the late Lucius Andronicus Caudinus as consul of the legions with one Sextus Valerius Corvus."

Vestremer smiled back, but the smile didn't quite reach his eyes this time.

Marcus almost laughed at the consternation that the man almost managed to hide. *You were hoping for an incompetent or a lazy, vainglorious fool, weren't you, my provincial friend! I'll bet you don't like the idea of the Crow coming after your infant kingdom with eighteen thousand swords as soon as the snows melt.*

The Cynothi bowed. "I am pleased my people could serve your father in this manner. In fact, I believe my king would wish for you to convey his congratulations to the new consul aquilae and to express his wish that if he can ever be of future service to him, or any of his House, he would be pleased to do so."

Marcus affected surprise and pleasure. "How very kind of him! And do you know, it occurs to me that there may in fact be a way in which he could be of service to House Valerius in the future—in the very near future, as it happens."

"I'm sure that would be his fondest wish."

"You see, Captain, although we have lamentably found ourselves facing each other with swords drawn in anger, we both appear to have problems for which the other party might be able to offer a solution. For example, I am given to understand that my men and I may be soon facing a winter siege due to what appears to be an inexplicable alliance between your new king and a rogue legion belonging to House Severus. You happen to have a great quantity of horses in your possession, upon which I could feed my men for most of the winter."

"You want my horses?" Vestremer was clearly puzzled. "If that's all you want, why not simply kill us all and take them?"

"For one thing, battle can be very hard on horses. Who knows how many would be killed, only to lie there rotting, of no use to anyone? And for another, who said that was all I wanted? I am merely pointing out one area of potential cooperation. Perhaps not even the ideal one, since I imagine your king would be very loathe to lose so many horses. How many do you have, six hundred?"

"Five hundred."

"That's more than four Amorran legions' worth. Horses are expensive, and it wouldn't surprise me if those five hundred horses amount to half the king's horses."

"More like a quarter."

"Let's say a third, then. Even if he has another thousand, losing one-third of his cavalry, or whatever you call it, isn't going to advance his rebellion, is it?"

"More horses can always be acquired. But yes, he'd rather not lose them."

Marcus nodded and gestured to Trebonius. "Captain, this is Gaius Trebonius, tribunus laticlavius of the legion and my second in command. Gaius Trebonius, it occurs to me that we have been lamentably inhospitable. While we are speaking, would you be so kind as to secure the three of us a wineskin or two? I believe you have already met our primus pilus, who is being hosted by your men for the duration of this conversation."

"Enchanted, Tribune," Vestremer said with a smile. "Yes, Tribune Valerius, I did indeed have the opportunity to meet the centurion— Claudios Didios, or something to that effect, I believe—and I hope he is being as well-received as I am. I have to say, I am somewhat amazed by the youth of your legion's executive staff."

"Does a star shine any less bright for its youth?" Marcus asked. "We are young, Captain, but does not our very youth testify to our accomplishment?"

"Or potential," the Cynothi shot back. "And what a true loss to Amorr it would be should that potential be snuffed out unrealized."

"I could not agree more," Marcus replied calmly. "Have you any ideas how we might arrange to avoid such a tragedy? You see, Captain, I have no wish to harm you or your men. I will not hesitate to do so, of course, if it becomes necessary in the course of my duties. I am my father's son. But I fail to see how involving yourself and your self-declared kingdom in the internal affairs of the Senate and People could be of any benefit to the Cynothii."

"Defeating an invading legion sent to suppress us and keep us under the heel of the empire can hardly be described as interfering in the internal affairs of Amorr, Tribune."

"I concur. But we are not discussing the defeat of Lucius Andronicus and his legion. That is a tangential matter that will surely merit consideration one day. But today, I am simply attempting to understand why a band of provincial rebels should be moving to attack one Amorran legion in the company of another Amorran legion. I fail to see how I am supposed to interpret that as anything but aggressive interference in Amorran affairs."

The Cynothi was silent for a long moment as he gathered his thoughts. But before he could speak, Trebonius returned, followed by three legionaries carrying a standing table, several crude silver goblets, and two flagons of wine.

Marcus took the opportunity to sit on the ground, and he indicated that the other two officers should do likewise. Trebonius poured the wine and offered the first goblet to Vestremer. When all three goblets had been poured, Marcus raised his to the Cynothi.

"To your health, Captain."

"Likewise, Tribune," Vestremer responded. "And yours, Laticlavius."

Marcus took a moderate sip of the wine. This far north, the wines were barely drinkable, but it wasn't quite as bad as he expected. Though it was close. "I hope you will understand we are not actually attempting to poison you, Captain. We merely happen to find ourselves reduced to these desperate straits."

"I've had worse," the Cynothian admitted. "There is a reason we tend to prefer beer in these parts. Now, am I understanding you correctly if I infer that House Valerius might be willing to recognize King Ladismas if he breaks his alliance with Buteo?"

"Buteo... Falconius Buteo?" Trebonius asked.

"Secundus Falconius is commanding Fulgetra," Marcus told him, pretending that he had known this already. But there was only one Buteo among the generals of Amorr. "However, it is not Buteo who is our primary concern, Captain. He is merely the puppet in command. His strings are pulled by House Severus."

The Cynothian nodded. "Aulan did appear to have an unusual amount of leeway with his cavalry. That would explain it. You understand that my grasp of Amorran politics is quite limited."

"All the more reason to keep your king's nose well out of it," Marcus commented agreeably. "And by Aulan, you are referring to the younger Aulus Severus?"

"He's the only Aulus Severus I know. He was the tribune in command of the legionary cavalry. He is here. Or rather, he was with those knights that made it past your infantry before they cut us off. I was riding next to him just this morning."

Marcus and Trebonius looked at each other. Marcus had to restrain the urge to curse or otherwise betray his frustration. Any Severan prisoner would be useful to him, but Patronus's own son and namesake would have been a prize indeed. And here he had ordered his men to let the Amorran riders pass safely before his trap slammed shut!

"I think we may have seen him, sir," Trebonius said. "There was a tribune who was among the first to ride out of the forest, who then waited with the Cynothii for a while as his men rode out. I saw his helm. I didn't see what happened to him, but he must have fallen in with the mass of them, because he wasn't there when Dardanus and I arrived."

"That was Aulan," Vestremer confirmed. "Buteo only sent one tribune with the joint force. There was some question as to who was in command, but we reached an understanding. Aulan commanded the Amorrans, and he left my men in my hands."

"And subsequently in mine, it would appear," Marcus noted.

As he spoke, the Cynothi met his eyes, and for a moment, Marcus felt they understood each other very well. Neither of them could reasonably doubt that House Severus would not hesitate to treat the Cynothii and their new king in much the same manner that Aulan had treated Vestremer's infantry.

"Captain," Marcus said, "I neither want, nor need, your horses. Nor am I asking for your assistance, much less an alliance with your king, which I very much doubt you could deliver in any event. And as I have already said, I have no interest in your lives either."

"Then what do you want, Tribune?" Vestremer asked it casually, but his hand on the stem of his goblet was shaking, almost imperceptibly.

"I want straightforward answers to a few specific questions. And then I want you to go home. Not only you and your men, but your king and his army as well. Go back to Cynothicum. Go back to your farms and your families. Your king should enjoy his reign while it lasts. Let the evils of the day suffice, and leave Amorr to sort out her own affairs, however they might turn out. And most of all, I would very much like to know what House Severus is up to that involves a legion marching through the provinces in the company of a rebel army."

The Cynothi smiled ruefully. "Would that I could answer the last one for you, but I am a mere captain of infantry, and the king does not invite me to attend his councils. As for me and my men, I will gladly swear that we will return to our homes as soon as you give us leave to do so. And we will swear as well to never draw our swords against House Valerius— against Amorr, rather—again, so long as our borders remain inviolate."

Marcus raised his glass to his adversary. "A good start, but not enough, I fear. I will need assurances, of course. I assume you have some nobles or young men from influential families in your command?"

"Of course. You shall have your hostages. How many do you require, and when will they be returned?"

"I want ten. None over the age of twenty-five, preferably from families with whatever your equivalent of patrician rank might be. Five will be permitted to accompany the king upon his return to Cynothicum, should he have the good sense to do so; the remaining five will be released by the end of next summer. I will send them back sooner, unharmed and in good health, if the legion is required elsewhere for some reason."

"Very generous, Tribune. May I ask precisely for what they will stand as security? Their families will want to know."

"Your withdrawal. I will send five knights with you. If they do not return within ten days with news that you and your men have crossed the provincial border and subsequently remain within it, I will execute them. As I will do if you or your men attempt to engage any Amorran forces in battle outside of the borders of your new kingdom."

"Ten days? It's only a two-day ride from Cynothicum to here."

"I'm giving you time to convince your king to go home instead of joining Buteo in battle against me. Leave Amorr to fight Amorr. Even if the Severans win, joining them could prove to be a very big mistake for him. Defeating one legion can perhaps be overlooked, particularly if the rebellion fever does not spread to other provinces. Defeating two in succession, even if it involves an amount of Amorran complicity, will inspire fear in the Senate and wake all the furies of Hell against your king. Amorr is slow to wrath, but her anger is terrible indeed."

"Very poetic," Vestremer said lightly, but the gravity of his expression belied the tone. "Will there be any negative consequences for the hostages if I fail to persuade the king to withdraw as you wish? And what support are you willing to provide if Buteo turns on the king if he refuses to march with the Severans?"

"If Buteo attacks your king, or even threatens to attack him, I'll provide him with a full legionary cavalry wing and four cohorts. And I'll prevent Buteo's cavalry from rejoining his legion as well. So, even if Buteo refuses to respect Cynothi neutrality in this matter, your king should be able to escape him unmolested unless he can't outride an infantry march.

"As for the hostages, I understand you cannot guarantee your king's compliance. If he refuses, the only consequence to them is that they will remain the honored guests of House Valerius. There may be more dire consequences to the king himself, of course, as I will defeat him and Buteo together if I must. Which leads to my next question: how many men does your king have under arms with him now?"

"Ten thousand, twelve hundred of them mounted," the Cynothian answered without hesitating. That was two thousand more than Marcus had been privately estimating, certainly more than enough to cause him some difficulty if he could not separate them from the Severan legion.

"All mounted infantry?"

"The kingsguard is one hundred strong. They are the only real cavalry we possess in the sense that you Amorrans think of it."

Marcus nodded. The Cynothi commander didn't know quite as much as he'd hoped, but the information he'd divulged wasn't entirely useless. Of course, Marcus would forgive him for sharing nothing at all if he could only convince his king to withdraw with him. One day, an Amorran legion or three would likely have to invade Cynothicus in order to bring its proud people to heel again, but if Marcus's fears were well-founded, it might be a long time before the Senate or the People—or more importantly, the Houses Martial—were free to concern themselves with the provinces again. They might be too occupied with fighting one another.

"What is Aulus Severus like?" he asked Vestremer.

"I was expecting you to ask about Buteo." He shrugged in response to Marcus's noncommittal gesture. "He's sharp, he's brave, and he's unbelievably arrogant. Not in such a way as to make you angry, though, as you find yourself more inclined to marvel at him in astonishment. He speaks to my king as if he's giving orders to one of his riders. It's almost beyond giving offense because it's so outlandish."

"So he's a typical patrician," Marcus couldn't help smiling. "I'm more interested in what he's like as an individual. Is he impulsive? Does he prefer to bide his time? Is he decisive, or does he dither?"

"He's only got sixty men. I don't think he is of any concern to you."

"He isn't, today. Or tomorrow. But he is Aulus Severus, the second son of Aulus Severus Patronus. He may not always have a mere sixty knights at his disposal. Who is to say he will not one day become a matter of serious concern to me? You haven't answered my question."

"Ah, my apologies, Tribune. I understand now. It is a long game you play! I should say he is by nature impetuous, but experience has taught him to rein it in a little. I think with a bit more seasoning he will provide you with a formidable opponent one day. In fact, I think I should rather like to see it. I don't think he is as well-spoken as you, perhaps, but he might be a bit more ruthless. And almost certainly more reckless."

Marcus laughed. "Don't mistake civility for weakness, my good captain. I would have had you all killed this morning if you weren't so much more use to Amorr alive than dead."

"I am delighted you should think so," Vestremer said with a faint smile playing across his lips. "In any event, my impression is that Aulus Severus does not think much of Buteo, either personally or professionally."

"No, I can't imagine he would. From what you've said, I imagine Secundus Falconius strikes him as too stolid and conservative. But slow and steady often wins the race, or so I've been told."

Marcus returned his empty goblet to the table and nodded to Trebonius, who was still scribbling on a piece of parchment. "Well, Captain, I think it is time to return you to your men. Your officers will be wondering if I am trying to convince you to volunteer for the legion, and I shudder to think of how many horses Didius and Hosidos will have won off your men at dice."

"None, I hope. Gambling his horse away is not a mistake any Cynothi can make twice. My thanks to you, Tribune, for your civility and for your generosity. I will not play you false, and I will do my damnedest to convince my king to leave you Amorrans to settle your disputes without our involvement. And if you will indulge an old soldier who wishes you no harm, let me offer you a piece of advice. You are a bright lad, it's plain to see. But do not forget that there is no substitute for experience. You have a keen mind, but only time and bloodshed can season you."

The infantry captain bowed, and this time Marcus returned the bow as deeply as it was offered. He rather liked the little man, who struck him as more sensible than many of his own officers. He made a mental note to remember that the Cynothii might make for suitable auxiliaries one day, once they were tamed again and their wings had been properly clipped.

"It was an honor to meet you, Captain, and I hope we shall not have the pleasure of meeting again on the battlefield."

"The honor was mine, Tribune. My only fear is that if you manage to defeat Buteo, I shall find myself one day boasting to my grandchildren that I was once defeated by great Valerius Clericus himself!"

Marcus chuckled. "I shall do my best to ensure that you will one day have that honor, Captain."

SEVERA

I T was good to be back in Amorr. Despite its distinctly unflowery perfume that assaulted the nose, the importunities of daring men both young and old, and the sense of lurking danger that her father had instilled in her, Severa had seldom felt more alive than she did now. Walking down the ancient cobble-stoned streets arm in arm with her friend Falconatera, daughter of the younger Gaius Falconius Aterus, studiously examining the various wares, edible and otherwise, that she had no serious interest in buying, filled her with a bubbling sense of delight.

They walked through a square, the Quadrata Aqueducta, with a large statue of a man bearing two water buckets over his shoulders that gave it its name. Severa was never quite sure if the statue was supposed to honor the man who had designed the great pipelines that supplied the city its water, the man who had started building them, or the man who had finished them. But whoever it was, she doubted he had been missing a nose as his marble representation did now. She didn't bother asking Tera, as her friend not only had no interest in such things, but was entirely unlettered.

That was something she had never considered before, but now that her ill-fated imaginary affair with Clusius had made her conscious of the distinction between those who could read and those who could not, she realized that her father had flown somewhat in the face of patrician tradition in seeing to her education. She wasn't entirely sure he had done right by her, seeing how happily Tera prattled away about the new jewelry she had seen on various women at the theatre the previous week. There was something to be said for the careless, cheerful life of the beautiful butterfly.

The danger of having your eyes opened was that you could not choose to unsee what your eyes had seen. Innocence was like virginity: Once punctured, it was gone forever. Two months ago, Severa would have walked to the baths alone without a second thought, secure in the certainty that no one, not even the street ruffians, would dare lift a hand to the daughter of Patronus. Every time anyone had raised their eyes to her or turned to watch her walk past, she had assumed they were simply admiring her beauty, or perhaps the tastefulness of her attire. Now, despite the sunny skies and the familiar bustle of the city, she found herself wondering if every smiling face concealed deadly thoughts, if every cheerful wave might mask a hand that would one day be raised against her father or her brothers.

Falconatera seemed to sense the darkening of her mood. "Is it true that your father took you away because he thought you were having an affair with a poet?" Like most women of their class, her friend was an inveterate gossip. Severa had already learned so much about the various deeds and misdeeds, both social and amatory, of their acquaintances since the morning that she was better informed than if she'd never been away.

She knew she had to be careful, because telling anything to Tera was tantamount to shouting it out from the sands of the arena.

"Is that what people are saying?"

"Well, some say it was an actor." Her friend wasn't so easily put off. "Were you?"

"Was I what, having an affair? Of course not! I will confess that I was a little enamoured of that handsome young gladiator. You know, the one from the Blues? But there is no more harm in admiring a gladiator than there is in admiring a fine horse!"

"A handsome gladiator from the Blues. Oh, do you mean Clusius, the one who died so wonderfully fighting against Montanus?"

Severa closed her eyes for a moment, then forced herself to smile. "Yes, Tertius tells me he was killed. What a shame. I did think he was the most beautiful specimen."

"I never saw him fight, but I was most affected by one of the poems that was written for him. I cried and cried to think of Montanus kneeling down to cradle his head in his arms. They say he wept, you know, Montanus."

Severa looked away and smiled wryly to herself. A month ago, she too might have wept copious tears at the tragic romance of it all. Damn all poets! They lied and made their lies sound sweet. It was much more likely that Montanus had simply knelt down to ensure that the wound he'd given his overmatched opponent was mortal, and was readying himself to snap poor Clusius's neck if need be. She wondered how her father arranged such things, and if she'd ever see Montanus at the domus now that he was free. She imagined the man would make for a perfectly fearsome bodyguard.

"I've heard women sometimes arrange to meet them at night, you know," Tera said in a voice that was very quiet, but rich with excitement. "Very wicked women! Can you imagine?"

"Arrange to meet gladiators?" Severa feigned shock. "At night! How awful!"

"I know! But Lucilla says that the child Julia is carrying—I mean Sempronius Blasus's wife, not Gaius Nautius's—that the child actually belongs to a charioteer of the Reds, not Blasus!"

"That's not what I heard. I heard it was a gladiator of the Greens," Severa said with a mischievous smile.

"Severa! You're terrible!" Tera looked absolutely delighted, and Severa laughed. By the time Julia finally had her baby, half of Amorr would be expecting it to have mottled green skin or a dwarf's bulbous nose.

The dark spell that had held her in its grip dissipated before her friend's laughter. She had nothing to worry about. When she glanced behind her, she could see the familiar faces of the House guards her father had ordered to henceforth accompany her outside the domus given the recent unrest that was said to have followed the Holy Father's death.

The two brutish young men were occupied with glaring at random people in the street as if they were potential kidnappers. Severa had thought they would be a bother, but as it happened, they were no trouble at all. They kept a good distance behind, so she and Tera could speak freely. And in truth, she had almost forgotten that they were there before they had even reached the grand Quadrata.

"Have you finished your dress for Hivernalia?" Falconatera asked about the upcoming festival. "I hear that blue will be the color this season, a sort of sky blue. I do wish it was green, though. That would suit my eyes better. But I suppose all the romance about your poor gladiator's death will only make the blue all that much more poignant."

"He's not my gladiator!"

"Well, you did say you quite admired him, did you not?"

"I haven't been working on it. To be honest, I've barely given the festival a moment's thought. Father is all in a dreadful stir about the winter elections this year for some reason, and Mother is naturally distracted as a result, so I wasn't about to start making a dress without her help. I suppose I probably should get started soon if I don't want to be stitching until my fingers bleed, and I'm sure Amarapora will have whatever material I need. It just didn't seem all that urgent down in Salventum."

"But don't you find all those stinking pigs and cows to be ever so inspiring?" Falconatera's laugh was filled with the lifelong city dweller's blithe certainty that the country was one large, foul-smelling place inhabited only by impoverished peasants and their animals. She would be astonished, Severa mused, if she were ever to learn that Amorr was far more unpleasantly odiferous than Salventum or any other agricultural province, even when the manure was spread on the fields in the spring and fall.

It was strange. When she had first been approaching the city, its smell struck her with an almost palpable force while she was still miles away from it. It grew stronger and stronger as the walls grew higher and higher, only to begin weakening within hours of entering the city gates. And yet, by the third day, she couldn't even imagine why she had thought it smelled bad.

But then, one only needed to observe the way in which both street beggars and rural mendicants managed to survive in their very different squalors to realize that men could very rapidly accustom themselves to almost anything. Severa had seen it in her very own house. There were several servants, people who had once been fine ladies in their own lands, reduced to slaves and whores by her father's legions, then rescued and raised up again by her mother or the majordomus's wife. And now, as proud and happy servitors of House Severus, the once-sullied women carried themselves as grandly and turned up their noses as splendidly as any provincial noblewoman ever had.

"So I think I'm going to be married this festival," Tera said, startling Severa, who suddenly realized that her friend had been prattling happily away the entire time.

"Wait, did you just say you're getting married?" Severa was astonished. She hadn't even heard her friend was engaged. Was that something she'd somehow missed in her absence?

"Well, not so much married as betrothed."

Ah, that sounded rather more likely. A betrothal at Hivernalia was generally considered to be either lucky or divinely blessed, depending upon whether you asked a midwife or a priest.

"To whom?" she asked. She hoped for her friend's sake that it wasn't to an elderly patrician. Tera had been somewhat optimistically named, as her mother was a Falconius, albeit hailing from one of the lesser branches of the House Martial, and her father, although a senator, was a plebian whose great-grandfather hadn't even been a citizen.

Falconatera blushed, and there was a hint of eagerness in her smile. "I don't know that it's been properly settled yet, but last week, Quintus Fabricius was paying attendance on Father, which has never happened before, and I was allowed into the triclinium after they ate. From the way he was staring at me, I rather thought he just wanted to see what I looked like. And Father was serving him pheasant stuffed with duck."

"Isn't he the eldest son of Luscinus?" Severa clapped her hands and embraced her friend. "Oh, Tera, how wonderful for you! Even if Gaius Fabricius doesn't accept whatever your father is offering, just the news that a consular family considers you worthy of their son will soon have a century of knights and senators perking up their ears!"

"He wasn't just an ex-consul: He was the consul civitas! It's a pity Quintus didn't win when he stood for tribune. But he's very handsome, and he's only five years older than me. I think I should be ever so happy if I married him, don't you agree?"

"Of course, my love!" Severa thought about whom her father might give her own hand. A daughter of House Severus would be considered a prize by nearly any House in Amorr, let alone the petty patricians. A plebian like Fabricius would do very well for Tera, especially one of consular rank, but wouldn't enter into Father's thinking even if his family offered a husband's dowry. She hadn't given the matter much thought over the summer, having been wholly caught up with thoughts of her gladiator lover.

Almost-lover, she corrected herself. Should-have-been lover. Or, if she was honest with herself, never-was lover. She had never had the chance to run her hands over that marvelous, beautiful body, to feel herself overpowered in the embrace of those muscular bronze arms. She still dreamed about him, though. Dreams were one thing neither Father nor death nor the ugly truth could steal away from her.

At least Father hadn't overreacted to her indiscretion and married her off to some aging greybeard, or worse, a stripling boy too young to even win election as tribune yet. It was a pity that neither House Falconius nor House Andronicus had any young men near to her age. It was even more of a pity that House Valerius seemed to have a surfeit of them.

But there was little chance that she would be forced to marry any of them, since there wasn't a man in Amorr who despised the stiff-necked Valerians more than Aulus Severus Patronus. Her father wasn't a man much given to refighting past battles. But even now, twenty-some years after the fact, he still occasionally complained of the vote in which the Senate had declared that Valerius Veheminus was worthy of the accolade "Magnus."

"Has the lord princeps spoken to you of your marriage yet?" Tera leaned into her shoulder in order to stir her from her thoughts. "I was wondering if you might be betrothed this winter, as well."

"Father hasn't said a word to me about it. But there are suitable men in House Crescentius, House Tarquinius, and House Volsius. I think I should prefer to marry into one of the Houses Martial, you know."

"I supposed you would almost have to."

"Not necessarily. But I think it's much better to be married to a man like my brother Regulus than one who is always in the courts or the Senate. Regulus spends nine months of the year wandering around the provinces killing provincials, or reminding them that they are liable to find themselves facing the sharp end of a sword if they refuse to pay their taxes. And then, when he's in the city, he spends nearly all his time in the Forum or at the baths. He hardly bothers Volsilla at all."

"I think the people of the provinces must be very stupid indeed."

"Why do you say that?" Severa didn't quite follow her friend's train of thought.

"Well, they always seem to find it so very difficult to remember that if they don't pay their taxes, sooner or later someone is going to come and be sure they do. And you know, Regulus is very handsome. I was so unhappy when you told me he was going to marry that Volsian girl. I thought she was so much prettier than I was. Although I don't think so anymore, now that she's gotten fat. Is she nice?"

Severa shrugged. "She's nice enough. She spends most of her time fussing over the children, so I don't see her very often. Father gave them a domus after the wedding, but it's over near the Trentanian Hill. I think he was glad to get Regulus out of his hair. He used to say that Regulus was more quarrelsome than any ten plebian senators."

"Do you think he'll have you marry a Volsian too? I should think you'd be more interested in Crescentius Rufinus's older son, Publius."

"Father says he'll be elected Aedile this winter."

"Really? That's in his year too. And Rufinus isn't just an ex-consul. They say he would have been elected censor if he'd put his name forward. Don't you think he's handsome?"

"Yes, he's rather good-looking. Though he's no Clusius."

"Clusius wasn't tall and rich and powerful. Publius Crescentius will surely make consul one day. And afterward… wouldn't it be wonderful to be governor's wife!"

Severa smiled. "I suppose it depends upon the province. Can you imagine being married to the poor man who is supposed to be governing the Cynothii right now?"

Her friend shivered. "I'd be terrified! I heard that after they defeated the city legion, they put the consul's head on a spear! I'll bet they would have done it to the governor and his wife too, if they hadn't fled first."

Severa wrinkled her lip. That was what came of the Senate sending out governors from the lesser Houses. She'd rather risk her own head on a spear than suffer marriage to such a coward. At least the Valerian House legions would set things right there in the spring. Even her father would admit that the one thing the bloody-minded Valerians did well was fight.

Then she heard something in the distance. Severa frowned. It was a sort of dull roar coming from somewhere, although she couldn't tell if it was from in front or behind. They were in a narrow street that connected the Quadrata to the river, but it turned a corner not far ahead, and so there was nothing to see except brick, stone, others who were passing through, and five shopkeepers standing outside their shops, engaged in desultory conversation.

"What do you think that is?" she asked Tera.

Her friend looked around with a worried look on her face. "I don't know?"

But when Severa looked at the shopkeepers, she saw their faces betray alarm, and almost as one, they turned and ran inside, slamming and locking their doors behind them.

"Oh, Goddess, this isn't good," she breathed.

"My ladies," one of the guards called out as they ran toward her and Tera. "We have to go back. Do you hear that noise? That's a riot ahead!"

The two girls looked at each other, perplexed. It sounded more like water rushing than a human-made noise.

"A riot?" Severa said. "Really?"

"What are they rioting about?" Tera asked.

"Who gives a damn!" the other guard said, grabbing her arm. "It's coming this way!"

And indeed, the roar was growing louder. It was clearly coming from the direction in which they had been headed, and now Severa could hear the sound of things crashing and being smashed.

"We'd better go," she told Tera.

But it was already too late.

Six or seven poorly dressed plebians came running around the corner, and fast on their heels were perhaps thirty or forty more plebs, not any better dressed but better armed with staffs, clubs, and other impromptu weapons. They seemed to be pursuing the smaller group. And indeed, when one of the men caught his foot in a cobblestone and fell, some of the pursuers stopped and began beating him. Severa stared, shocked by the violence and unable to believe what she was seeing.

She was yanked backward by one of the guards, who pushed her in the back as soon as he'd spun her around. He was holding his sword in the other hand.

"Run, you stupid girl. Run!"

The other guard had drawn his sword too and was standing in the middle of the street, ready to meet the onrushing mob. He didn't say anything, he merely spat and jerked his head to indicate that she should go back the way they'd come.

Still too stunned to say anything, Severa grabbed Tera's hand and began to run, even as she heard someone screaming behind her. In normal circumstances, even the most desperate criminal wouldn't dare to lift a hand to a patrician's daughter, but it was clear from the savage shouts of the rioters and the screams of those they'd either caught or dragged from the buildings that these were no normal circumstances. And the grim realization struck her that neither she nor Tera would need to worry about marrying future consuls if they were caught by these maddened animals. Even if they weren't killed, they would surely be raped.

"What are they rioting about?" Tera, terrified, asked her as they ran. She was beginning to lag behind.

Severa tugged her onward. "How would I know? We just got back to the city!"

The shouting behind them grew louder and angrier, and Severa assumed her guards were attempting to dissuade the mob from continuing on its path. She thought she heard a scream. Perhaps one of the men had struck down someone with his sword. But she knew that two men, even two well-trained men, couldn't hold off scores, perhaps even hundreds, for long. It would be like trying to dam a river with two wagons of dirt. And no sooner had they turned a corner when the roaring unexpectedly began to grow louder, and she realized the unruly mass of men was now gaining on them.

Or was it ahead of them now? She had no idea how big the riot was or how fast it was spreading throughout the quarter. She didn't want to be caught, but the next worst thing to do would be to run blindly right into it. She slowed down and frantically looked around the buildings to see if there was anywhere to hide.

"I can't... I can't run anymore!" Tera protested.

But even as Severa urged her friend on, something caught her eye and she stopped. It was a statue, an old and battered one worn down by years of wind and rain and stained by decades of avian disrespect, but she recognized it all the same. It was Saint Malachus, and it was standing outside of an old church.

"Tera, wait, we can go in there!" She fingered the solitary earring in her left ear. This church must be one of the places that the old witch had described to her. "The saint! The mob won't dare to come in here!"

"Okay," Tera gasped, half-doubled over with her exertion. "If you say so."

"Do you have a better idea?"

Tera didn't say anything, and she followed dutifully as Severa quickly mounted the four steps and tried the large iron handles on the dark double-doors. They opened surprisingly easily despite their massive size, and they entered a church that was rather brighter and more spacious inside than it had looked from the outside. Severa shut the doors behind them and turned to face the inside of the church.

The colored glass of the tall, thin windows was cunningly arranged in such a fashion as to catch the rays of the sun and permit bright jeweled colors to spill across the white marble floors and polished wooden pews of the nave. But instead of a single giant tree behind the altar, there were three trees carved in stone relief. The first was a sapling of some sort, the second was a tall birch with its leaves in bloom, and the third was a gnarled oak in winter, thick knots upon its bark and its naked branches all bent and twisted.

Severa smiled. Yes, unless she was completely mistaken, this was exactly the sort of place that had been described to her. Surely it was a sign! The goddess was looking out for her! And, as the old Salventian witch had said, it was hidden right in the very heart of Amorr itself! There were additional clues that further confirmed her hopes now that she knew what to look for. Each of the stained glass windows appeared to tell a familiar story: The Bull and the Centurion looked down from a predominantly orange-and-blue window on the north side while the Seven Seekers were memorialized in red, green, and yellow opposite. But unlike most bulls, this one had an udder. And three of the seven seekers were not only lacking beards, but appeared to be of three distinctly different ages.

It was amazing. This church had stood here for centuries, thousands of deeply devout Immaculines had walked past it, entered into it, and even worshipped within it without ever noticing that it was not a holy house dedicated to the Immaculate at all, but an ancient shrine to the Goddess.

"May I be of service, daughters?"

Severa was startled by a voice behind her. She turned around and saw a short, middle-aged woman wearing an uxora, the black garment intended to signify a woman's marriage to the immaculate.

"Or if you have merely come to pray, please allow me to show you to the saint's shrine."

"Thank you, sister," Severa said, though Tera raised an eyebrow at her. Severa grabbed her arm and urged her to go along with the nun, or priestess, whatever she might be. "Go with her, let her show you the saint. You can pray to him about your betrothal. He is the patron saint of maidens, and it can't hurt. I need to make confession."

Tera sighed but didn't protest. "Confession? And I'm still supposed to believe your father didn't have good cause to drag you off to Salventum? Or did you manage to find trouble out there in the country?"

Severa fled before her friend could conclude she was pregnant with the child of a field slave or something equally absurd. The confessional was on the near side of the nave, hidden well away from the statue of Saint Malachus, in rather better condition than the one outside, that presided over the shrine on the far side of the large hall. Glancing around and feeling as if many eyes were upon her, she slipped silently into the little box-like room and kneeled down upon its well-worn wooden surface.

But what was she supposed to say? She couldn't simply blurt out that she'd been told to come here by an old Samnian woman. Even if the church harbored a secret temple to the Goddess, there was no way of knowing there wasn't a proper Immaculine priest on the other side of the narrow wooden screen.

Then a thought occurred to her. The Goddess was triune. Everywhere around her, above and below her, the signs and symbols of the Goddess were given in threes.

"Forgive me, Father, for I have sinned. Forgive me, Father, for I have sinned. Forgive me, Father, for I have sinned."

"I cannot forgive you, daughter, for I am neither a priest nor am I ordained." The voice through the screen was low but feminine. "Father Hermogenus is not here today. Though I cannot grant you absolution, I am willing to lend a sympathetic ear if you are troubled at heart."

Severa was troubled, but only because she was unsure. The moment she'd heard a woman's voice, her heart had leaped with excitement. But the woman's words didn't seem to indicate that she'd noticed any significance to Severa's three requests.

"I am not troubled, Sister, I am merely a maiden...."

After her voice trailed off, there was a long pause. When the woman behind the screen spoke again, her voice was harsher, and more demanding. "You are a maiden. And whom do you serve?"

"One who is also a maiden."

"And?"

"One who is also a mother."

"And?"

"One who is also a crone."

Another silence. Then, another question.

"Who sent you here?"

"We came to escape the crowd. There was a riot... but I think I was meant to come here. An old woman from the temple of Saint Malachus in a village told me to come. It was in a village in Salventum, I can't remember the name. It started with an S. But her name was Idemeta Venfica. She was a woman of wisdom."

"And how do you know this?"

"By what my eyes have seen. She said she had a message for the Sisters in Amorr."

"A message. Are you the messenger?"

"I am. Are you one of her Sisters in Amorr?"

"All women are Sisters. But you may tell me the message. I am one of those for whom the message is intended."

"She told me to tell you to look to the skies. The black swan is flying."

The woman uttered neither an oath nor a gasp. Instead, she simply sat on the other side of the screen and continued to breathe in a loud and annoyingly nasal manner.

Severa wasn't sure what she'd been expecting, perhaps a scream of dismay or a thumping sound as the woman fainted to the floor, but this contemplative silence was anticlimactic.

"What is the black swan?" she finally asked.

"Something you are never likely to see or hear about," the woman answered. "And it is better that way. You do not sound like a Salventian."

"I am not."

"Then how do you come to be delivering a message from the sister?"

"My father has an estate there. We arrived back to Amorr yesterday. I came as soon as I could."

"Ah, I see. And your father is?"

Severa felt strangely reluctant to answer, but she felt it would be unwise to avoid the woman's question.

"Severus Patronus."

Another silence, then a chuckle. "So the patrician's daughter comes bearing the peasant woman's message. I sense the hand of the Maiden in this. The Mother has no humor, and the Crone's is dry and cruel. How are you called, and how many earrings do you wear, little sister?"

"They call me Severa. I wear only the one."

"Only one? Then you know nothing. And there may not be time for you to learn anything. Are you willing to serve, daughter of House Severus?"

"If that is what I must do to attain wisdom, I am willing, Sister."

"A proud answer," she heard the woman say, as if musing to herself. "A poor one too. And yet, the message was delivered.... Very well, daughter of House Severus, as you obeyed the Salventian woman, obey me now. You will not come here again until permission is granted you. Within three days, a woman will present herself to you. You will accept her into your service, but you shall obey her as your teacher."

"But Sister, I cannot! My father, or rather, his majordomus, makes all such decisions!"

"Trust in the Goddess. You and your mother will be needing dresses for the upcoming festival, will you not? The Sister who will instruct you in the wisdom is a superlative seamstress, and you need not fear your father's majordomus will not take her on. She speaks with the voice of the Mother. Obey her in all things, and say nothing to anyone."

"Yes, Sister."

"Go now, and may the Maiden enlighten you, the Mother nourish you, and the Crone guard you. You have done well in coming here, Severa. The Goddess's blessing be upon you."

Severa heard a rustling as the unseen Sister left her side of the confessional. She did the same, unsettled and a little frightened. What had she done? What was the black swan? The wisdom was real, that much she knew, but it had never occurred to her that there might be a darker side to the Goddess and her worship. She had a sneaking suspicion that her father might be even less happy with her involvement with the secretive old women than he had been about her aborted affair with a gladiator. And yet, how could the old witch woman have known about Clusius if there wasn't a real power there, and the sort of power that even an influential man like her father could never hope to understand, much less access?

As a Moon-blooded woman, she owed a duty to the Goddess. That much was certain. But even a female member of House Severus owed her duty to the House. Perhaps she could serve both allegiances this way—not only serving the Goddess, but in doing so, giving House Severus the same sort of access into the women's temple it had into the Church and the Alabaster Palace. The Sister had said she'd done well, and she had blessed her, after all. Her conscience clear, or at least sufficiently confused, she went to meet Falconatera.

Her friend was waiting for her near the vestibule.

"You must have a lot to confess," Tera said with an inquisitive look.

"They say sin abounds in us all, my dear. Even in the boring countryside." She slipped her arm into Tera's and walked with her from the darkness of the secret temple into the bright light of the brisk autumn day.

The rioters had passed, leaving a visible trail of destruction that had somehow left the church, even the statue outside, entirely unharmed. The Goddess, it seemed, could protect herself.

Tera looked around in dismay at the wreckage strewn about the street. Doors were kicked in, shutters were hanging by their hinges, and the body of a woman not very much older than them lay face down in a pool of blood. Her dress was hiked up well past her waist. They could still hear shouts, but they were off in the distance now and growing gradually more faint.

"What do we do now?" she asked Severa. "Do you even know where we are?"

Severa smiled, pointing to two men who were limping down the street toward them, one with an arm around the shoulders of the other. It was her father's men, battered, bleeding, and much the worse for wear. But she was delighted to see they were still alive, even if she didn't know their names.

"No, but I imagine they do." She waved to them.

After a moment's hesitation, one of the young men waved back.

"My lady, thank God you're alive!" the shorter man said when they finally reached her. It looked as if his ankle might be broken, but he still had his sword. "Your father would have flayed us and rolled us in salt if we'd returned without you!"

Severa was touched by his heartfelt relief. But don't thank God, she thought, even as she offered him and his companion her prettiest thanks. He didn't save us. Thank the Goddess.

FJOTRA

AN impromptu council gathered in the main hall amidst the remains of the earlier feast that was still being cleared away by
the kitchen thralls. But there was nothing festive about the
haunted eyes and stricken expressions that could be seen in all of the
Savoner faces, and more than a few of the Dalarn ones as well.

The Skullbreaker's wounds were clean and bandaged, and, much to
his disgust, he had been carefully carried down the stairs by two of his
strongest warriors. He now presided over the makeshift gathering with
his feet propped up on one of the table benches and goosedown-stuffed
pillows supporting him on either side. Fjotra sat between the two sides, as
she had to supply the translations required for them to talk to each other,
which slowed the conversation considerably.

"How did this happen?" her father demanded of no one in particular.

"I went down and looked at the cells in which the two captive ulfin
were placed," Patrice said. He had taken the news of the prince's death
very hard and his uncharacteristically low voice made it hard for Fjotra to
understand him. "There were two gaolers. Both were dead. I don't know
how the creatures managed to get out, but both gates were unlocked, and
I didn't find any keys on either body."

"They've got a demon's strength, and they have long arms too,"
Steinthor Strongbow commented. "If one of the guards got too close to
the cell, they could have reached through the bars to catch him, kill him,
and take the key from his body."

"That seems plausible," the battlemage allowed. "And one of them did have wounds to his arm that could have been caused by their claws. But what's harder to understand is how they knew to attack both you, my lord Skullbreaker, as well as the prince. The guards' bodies were cool, but not rigid, so the beasts didn't escape long before the feast. That would have given them enough time to explore the keep, and of course, if they slipped into the hall, they would have seen both the prince and my lord at the high table."

"It doesn't matter how the prince was killed!" Gerard de Coucy, the Comte de Montbrelloz and the prince's captain of cavalry, exploded. "This is the Red Prince of whom we speak, the heir to the realm! Why are we wasting words on how the cursed demonspawn murdered him? Our liege lord now lies dead, and instead of avenging ourselves upon his killers, we sit and babble about how they managed the trick! When a knight falls on the field, do we stop fighting, sit on our arses, and parley about whether it was the sword through the gut or the axe through the helm that slew him? Or do we drive the cursed enemy from the field?"

Before Fjotra could even begin translating the comte's words, Blais de Foix was shaking his head. He had been silent until now, but his eyes were dry, and he was visibly less perturbed than his younger companion.

"His killers are dead, my lord captain. The prince has already been avenged."

"To kill the dog that slew him is no avenging. Such infamy demands a reckoning of the sort these islands have never seen! To return to Savonne without ten thousand skulls to place upon his grave would be an insult to his memory!"

Her father and the other Dalarn looked at her as the Savonners argued, but she only shook her head and let them vent their rage and frustration for a few moments without attempting to translate their actual words, only half of which she could understand anyhow as they shouted over each other. She did her best to summarize the situation for them.

"The horse warrior wants to take the field and collect aalvarg skulls to take back to the king, and the witch men tell him he's mad."

Her father waved his hand, unconcerned. "They're angry, that is all. No one will take the field, not unless they don't wish to re-enter my gates. You're sure the one you saw looked like a proper man, both of you?"

Fjotra and the Strongbow both nodded. There was no doubt about it. Even in death, the aalvarg that the Strongbow had slain remained half-changed between its man shape and its bestial form.

"So we know they can change their shapes to look like men as well as beasts," her father said. "Or at least some of them can. That might explain how they were able to take Trandhus and Aarborg so easily in the summer. Ambush a villager when he's out, return wearing his face, and then open the gates to the others at night. I found it hard to imagine how two cunning old warriors like Olaf the Fat and Randver Longreaver could be wiped out to a man before even managing to get a messenger out. But if they were attacked at night in their beds by sigskifting that were able to get past their walls, that makes a little more sense."

"We know one thing more," added the Strongbow.

"We do?"

"They're stupid."

"Why do you say so?"

"If you infiltrated a fortress like this, Skuli, would letting the enemy know you're inside be the first thing you'd do? Sure, they killed the prince, and they damn near killed you, but if they'd only bided their time and begun with the guards at the gate, they could have taken the place and both of you before anyone realized anything was wrong."

It was a sobering thought. As the two veteran warriors stared at each other, realizing what a close escape it had been, Fjotra noticed that the argument between the Savonners had cooled somewhat.

However, the Comte de Montbrelloz hadn't given up on his desire to take the battle to the enemy. He was gesticulating energetically as he attempted to convince the two mages of their need to take the offensive.

"Even if we don't send out an army, we can enlarge the size of our mounted patrols and hit their smaller groups. You saw how easily we rode them down! I propose that each morning we send out two patrols, each containing four squadrons. Eighty knights should permit each patrol to easily defeat all but the primary ulfin forces. And we have the speed to disengage at will in order to avoid those. I will lead one, and the Baron d'Angennes the other. And, of course, we'll each take one of you with us in case we run into any more of the sorcerous beasts."

"I'm not going on any patrols. And if the lord captain is wise, neither will he," Blais firmly rejected Montbrelloz's idea. "We were already in a difficult position before the prince's death. Taking the risk of losing nearly two hundred of our men and betraying the secret of our magecraft just to let you whet your appetite for vengeance would be insane."

While the comte spluttered in impotent anger at the mage's calm refusal to participate in his mad scheme, Fjotra quickly explained his intentions to the Dalarn.

Her father laughed contemptuously. "Tell that southerner the aalvarg aren't like his turtle-shelled knights. They won't line up out in the open and stand there waiting to be killed. They will stalk you like prey, look for the chance to ambush you wherever they can, and use darkness as their armor. If he rides out in the daylight, he'll find nothing until the day he rides out and turns around to find himself cut off from our gates by a thousand wolves."

"So you haven't even sworn an oath to the king and already you would betray him?" the comte demanded once the Skullbreaker's opinion of his plans had been conveyed to him.

"No, it would be a betrayal to cut the throats of eight squadrons of his liegemen, including the lord captain's, while they slept under my care. And that wouldn't be much more fatal than were I to permit the lord captain to ride out from the safety of my walls. Maybe he won't be caught out the first day, maybe not the second or third day either. But sooner or later, they'll catch him out, cut him off, and his patrols will be wiped out to a man.

"Look at their numbers. We've counted more than five thousand already. Given how they skulk about, you can be sure there are at least twice that many. Tell the comte that if he has the sense the All-Father gave a fish, he'll heed my words. And if he doesn't, he'll damn well heed them anyway, because I am not opening Raknarborg's gates for him or anyone else!"

The comte glared at her father, but even wounded as he was, the Skullbreaker's gaze was an intimidating one. Before long, the Savonner looked away and nodded in reluctant acceptance of her father's verdict.

De Foix cleared his throat to draw Skuli's attention.

"Your Majesty, may I have leave to take the prince's body and prepare it for the return to Lutèce? Since the cavalry will not be riding out against the ulfin, I expect you will want *Le Christophe* to depart for the north coast on the morrow with as many men and mounts as it will carry."

"You may take the prince's body and prepare it as you see fit. And you should prepare one of the aalvarg bodies as well, or else the king might not believe your story. However, the cavalry stays here until the fleet returns. So does one of the mages—the older one, I think. I will permit an honor guard of twenty men to accompany the prince's body on board the ship, which will depart tomorrow morning. Another six hundred women and children will be ready to board at first light, as well."

Fjotra repeated his words to the Savonners to the best of her abilities.

The comte drew himself up stiffly before she'd even finished, clearly displeased by her father's decision. "*Le Christophe* belongs to his royal majesty, the King of Savondir, Your Majesty. It is for the Lord Admiral of the Sea Nordique to decide who will, and who will not, board the ship, not the Reaver King of Raknarborg!"

Her father was smiling dangerously even before she translated the captain's words. "The Lord Admiral is not here. The Reaver King is. And while the ship may belong to—how do they say it?—to his majesty the king, Raknarborg is mine, and no one, including the Lord Admiral, leaves or enters its walls unless he does so with my permission. Now, Daughter, tell those southerners to see to it that the prince's body is prepared for travel, select his honor guard, and leave the rest of the ship's cargo to me!"

Fjotra dutifully told the Savonner, who despite his fury was wise enough to avoid further argument with a wounded and increasingly

irritable king of reavers. The comte nodded briskly, bowed in a perfunc-
tory manner, then turned to his two mages and told them to accompany
him to the prince's chamber.

She wanted to go to Patrice, as the friendly young battlemage was
looking downright nauseated at the thought of returning to Lutèce and
telling the king of the loss of his heir. But her father leaned forward and
placed his hand upon her forearm.

"Fjotra, you will prepare your possessions and select four of your
friends to serve as your attendants in the south. Choose girls you can
trust, young ones with the wits to learn the language quickly, but no sluts
or silly ones with slanderous tongues. You will be on that ship tomorrow
too."

He unbuckled his belt, slipped it gingerly from around his waist, and
held it out to her, his sword and dagger dangling from it. "You must bring
this to Brynjolf. If Raknarborg cannot hold out until the ships can make
the crossing three more times, he will be ruler over the Dalarn. Tell him
I will hold him to these three vows, which he must swear to sea and sky:
He must marry, he must father at least three sons, and each of his sons
must be taught one thing with their mother's milk—we will return. The
Isles belong to us, not the wolves."

"No, Father," she protested. "You must not talk like that. I don't want
to go, I want to stay here with you. It is my duty too! And you need me
to translate when you need to talk to the Savoners, especially if there is
fighting."

"We will make do." He shook his head and pulled her closer to him,
then placed his large, scarred hands on her shoulders. "It's not only that I
want you to be safe on the other side of the sea. I need you there. Who can
tell how the prince's father will react? Perhaps he will blame our people.
But you were there. You saw what happened. So you must go there to
tell him the truth of it and assure him that we feel his loss as our own.
The Savonner prince, he was a good man. He was a brave warrior, and
he earned the respect of our men. You tell the king I said that. Tell him

that I said his son would have made a strong king. And tell him of the sigskifting. They must know of the sigskifting!"

"You will tell him yourself, Father." Fjotra's vision was blurry with tears she could no longer resist. "I can't bear it. You talk as if you will die here! How can you fight without your sword?"

"I have other swords. What I don't have is other daughters." He smiled at her. "My darling, do you not know I love you far more than life? Brynjolf is hurt, but he is safe, and I thank the gods that I can send you away from here again before it is too late.

"Now, I have much to do. The aalvarg will be coming soon, perhaps even tonight. So go. Tell your friends who are to accompany you to prepare themselves. I will also send five of my best young warriors to serve as your bodyguard. But you will marry none of them. You will not marry any Dalarn, because you must marry a southern noble—the higher his rank, the better. A prince, if you can. If we are to survive among them, we must become Savonners, at least on the outside. And listen to your comtesse, let her be your star, and follow her lead. She is a reaver at heart. I think she will steer you well."

"What about Mother?"

"Be sure to say goodbye to her tonight. She will stay with me." Her father smiled ruefully and shook his head. "I tried to tell her she would go with the last ships, but she drew her blade and threatened to cut off my manhood. You will forgive me if I found the argument persuasive. Sweetling, your mother and I have lived our lives together, and if the gods require that we must end them together too, I will not deny her that right.

"But do not be afraid! Raknarborg's walls are tall and strong, and they are held by many brave men. I think we can hold them off long enough for the ships to return, and then we will cross the sea ourselves to join you. If not, then we shall live on through you, through Brynjolf, and through your children. The demons may have driven us from our homes, but I have done my best, and I have saved my children. I am content. I have sent many a man to his grave who could not say the same."

Fjotra rose and buried her face in her father's chest, hugging him hard and inhaling his familiar scent. Remember him, she told herself fiercely. Remember how he feels, how he smells. Remember the strength of his arms around you. Somehow, she managed to keep herself from sobbing hysterically.

"I love you, *far*," she whispered.

"I know, *kælebarn*, I know."

No one slept that night as thousands of howling aalvarg tried to storm the high walls of Raknarborg using crude ladders constructed in the nearby forests. Fjotra stayed in her chamber, two guards standing outside her door, in the company of a group of young women and children who huddled together for comfort and shivered with fear throughout the dark and terrible hours.

The dawn was near by the time an exhausted young warrior, who had come to reassure his betrothed after the battle, told her that the wolf-demons had been driven back, but at the cost of fifty-seven northern dead and one hundred twelve southern lives. Nearly three hundred men were wounded, though less than a score seriously.

Not long after first light, *Le Christophe* set sail, accompanied by ten of the Skullbreaker's eleven remaining longships.

As the sun rose from the green-blue waves into the lighter blue of the heavens, Fjotra stood on the aftcastle, holding hands with Geirrid and Svanhvit, two of her closest friends from childhood, who would henceforth serve as her ladies-in-waiting. They watched together in silence as the great black towers of embattled Raknarborg drew slowly away from them, fading into sea and sky.

CORVUS

As Corvus followed Vecellius through the streets of Amorr under the last rays of the setting sun, he reflected that his decision to accept a third goblet of wine may not have been the height of wisdom.

It was not yet dark, but the two leading fascitors already bore torches, which had the result of turning his escort into something of a procession. Several of the clients he had not had time to see today were following in his wake, and as the journey to the elven embassy progressed, they gradually collected curiosity-seekers, until Corvus found himself accompanied by the greater part of a century.

The embassy was new, having been established only a few months ago after the release of Immaculatus Dei and the return of the legionary eagles lost by Lucius Varrus two centuries ago. It had once been a private residence, but Publius Licinius Dives had not become vastly wealthy by overlooking opportunities.

When the Senate had met to discuss the High King's request to establish a permanent embassy following the return of its Amorran counterpart, and when concerns had been raised about the potential unwillingness of property owners to rent a suitable building when its inhabitants would almost surely be engaging in occult and illicit arts, Publius Licinius absented himself from the debate, tracked down the elven ambassador, and placed one of his larger domuses near the city wall at the High King's disposal.

It was said the elves were paying five times the rent of the previous tenant, who was summarily evicted by Dives the following day.

Maximus, who was married to Dives's younger sister, Licinia, had assured Corvus the story was untrue. He was entirely confident that Publius Licinius was receiving at least ten times the rent he'd been getting before.

The elves might be much reduced in numbers and in power from the days when their legendary Seven Kingdoms ruled over most of Selenoth, but the Church embassy had confirmed that their legendary wealth yet remained.

However, very little of it was on display outside of Elebrion House, he saw as they approached its gate, affixed with an ornate brass symbol that was the only indication of those who resided within. The grounds of the domus were walled, which no doubt had recommended it to Lord Silvertree, and as the property backed up on the city wall, it was as defensible as any residence in the city.

The gate doors unexpectedly swung open at their approach, alarming Corvus, his fascitors, and the crowd following them alike. Vecellius swore under his breath, others behind them cried out loud in dismay, and Corvus couldn't help but agree with them as he, like nearly everyone else, instinctively sketched a tree over his heart to protect himself from the invisible evils of the elven magic.

There were no guards, man or elf, in view, but Corvus had the distinct impression they were being watched. No sooner had the last fascitor entered the grounds than the gates swung shut again, as silently as they had opened. The crowd gasped, sounding for all the world like spectators at the stadium witnessing a gladiator receive his death wound.

"A neat trick, wouldn't you say, Captain?" His guards might be disciplined enough to conceal their nervousness, but Corvus had been with the legions too long to miss the signs of a body of men nearing a state of panic. The wide eyes, the rapid blinking, the convulsive swallowing. The only thing unusual was seeing it here in the city.

"I heard they have ghosts to serve them, my lord consul, but I never thought I'd see the like!" Caius Vecellius's hands on his axe were white-knuckled.

"I hear they trap souls and make things from them," one of the men muttered.

Cursed bloody elves, Corvus thought. Lord Silvertree seemed a reasonable sort, but he wouldn't put it past the elf to be putting them to the test. Or simply amusing himself at their expense. Damn his golden eyes.

As they crossed the well-maintained grounds toward the entrance to the domus, Corvus forced himself to laugh.

"My good men, I fear in your alarm you are overlooking the good news here!"

"Good news?" someone asked.

Corvus couldn't help but smile at the sight of eight pairs of extraordinarily skeptical eyes aimed in his direction. "Do you not understand what this means? It will be months before any of you need pay for your own drinks! Every man in the city will want to hear your tale."

No one laughed, but Vecellius nodded slowly, and several of the men exchanged speculative looks before shrugging and visibly relaxing. Nevertheless, they were startled again when the front door to the domus opened.

This time their surprise was not due to the magic, but rather to the sight of Lord Silvertree.

The elvish ambassador was resplendent in a white tunic, white leggings, and silver cape that looked as if it was spun from the metal itself. Being nearly a head taller than Corvus, who was himself considerably taller than his fascitors, the elf made an imposing sight despite his slender build, especially when both torches happened to go out at the very moment that the ambassador raised his left hand in greeting.

"My lord consul, I bid you welcome to the residence of the High King of Elebrion. And I do apologize if the spell on the gates should have taken anyone by surprise. I fear it was necessary, as I have but the one companion, and he has been preparing refreshment for your guards."

The men brightened considerably at the mention of refreshment. If they were anything like the legionaries, Corvus knew, they would brave a lot more than a bit of soul-threatening magic if there was a reasonable prospect for free alcohol in sight.

"Has my colleague arrived?" Corvus asked.

"He has not, but I expect him soon. He sent a messenger informing me that he was momentarily delayed but would be with us before long."

Corvus glanced at Vecellius, whose face was unreadable.

"I wouldn't wish to offend the High King, of course," Corvus said wryly. "Nor should I wish to unnecessarily imperil anyone's soul with what I fear will touch upon some unseemly matters, so, if you would be so kind, Lord Silvertree, I should be pleased if you would inform my men where they might find these refreshments."

The elven ambassador nodded gravely and held up his hand. When he opened it, a disc of soft blue light appeared and hung suspended in the air without support when he lowered his hand again.

The fascitors looked at each other, astonished, but this time there was none of the trepidation that had filled them at the sight of the ensorcelled gate.

"Follow this," Silvertree said, "and it will take you to the dining hall. Pray relax and enjoy yourselves. I believe you will find the wines well worth drinking."

The blue disc began to move, and after a mere moment's hesitation, Vecellius and his seven men followed.

When they had gone, Corvus shook his finger at his host.

"You can't possibly convince me that was necessary. My understanding was that you were to keep your sorceries to a minimum."

The elf laughed. "I'm not attempting to corrupt your people, my lord consul. But I don't find it conducive to intelligent conversation to have twenty frightened men armed with axes standing over me. If one of your men happens to be murderously inclined toward those skilled in the arts, my preference is to learn that before I'm absorbed in discussing more important matters—such as the reason for your visit here this evening."

"Are you sure pouring wine down their throats is the wiser alternative?"

"A salient point, to be sure. I don't suppose you would like a tour of the residence?"

"My wife will be disappointed, but if you don't object, I'd much prefer to get your thoughts on the murders in the chapel. Brother Ignatius appeared to be rather out of sorts, which was disturbing."

"Very well, then. I trust you won't mind if we take some wine ourselves while we speak?"

The elf led Corvus through a high-ceilinged entryway, past a wide set of steps that revealed an unexpected lower level to the domus, then down a corridor with exposed wooden beams overhead. The corridor terminated in a large, rectangular room that spanned two floors.

The walls of the room were lined with a vast collection of leather-bound books that filled shelves all the way up to the ceiling high overhead, broken only by a fireplace on the far side of the room and wooden stairs that led to a narrow walkway lining the walls where the first floor had once been. The stairs continued in a highly unusual fashion to what appeared to be a large trapdoor on the ceiling. The room was warm, as the walls were lined with thick, colorful tapestries depicting events and places Corvus had never seen, and flames were leaping high from the wood that had been generously stacked to form a sort of ziggurat within the fireplace.

Lord Silvertree walked toward a table upon which rested a clear crystal decanter full of a lightly bubbling golden liquid and three impossibly delicate transparent goblets. "I think you might find this wine from Kir Donas to be interesting. The spirits within the wine are stirred to animation, which produces the movement you see within the liquid. It's more of a sensation than a flavor, but you'll find it does enhance the taste."

He poured two goblets without losing a drop.

Corvus took one from him, sketching an abbreviated tree from his forehead to his heart in the hopes that accepting his host's offer would not be viewed by the Almighty as dabbling in the forbidden. He raised the glass as if to offer a toast, but then his conscience overcame him and he lowered it again.

"They're not spirits of the dead, by any chance?"

The elf looked startled for a moment, then burst out laughing. "Oh, do forgive me, my lord consul. What you must think of us! No, the spirits to which I refer are merely spirits of the grape, very small ones and utterly devoid of anything you or I would consider sentience, much less animus. I will confess to being no theological expert, as my esoteric studies were rather more concentrated on alchemy than animalogy or what the Savondi sorcerers call diablerie, but I am certain you can safely drink it without offending either your god or your Church."

"How would an elf know what would or would not offend the Almighty or His Church?"

"You'd be very surprised to know how often such matters are discussed in Elebrion these days. Thanks, in part, to the good services of your son. I trust he enjoyed our city?"

"He still talks about writing a monograph about it. And one of your ladies appears to have made a particular impression on him. I believe they write to each other still."

"Ah, yes, the Lady Shadowsong." Silvertree drank from his glass. "Such an encouraging sign of friendship between our two peoples. It can never go anywhere, you understand."

"I should be very unhappy if it did."

"Then you will be pleased to know the High King shares your opinion, my lord consul."

Corvus raised his glass and tasted the wine. It was a most unusual sensation. It didn't burn like the similarly colored wine from Savonderum, but it seemed to almost move and swell inside his mouth. It was like drinking a living thing. It was startling, not unpleasant. And as the liquid tide flowed around his teeth and his tongue, the flavor changed, almost imperceptibly, with the motion.

"It's like... like drinking the ocean!" he cried despite himself. "I've never tasted, or felt, anything like it!"

"Do you like it?" his host asked with an amused expression on his face.

"God help me, I do!" he confessed. "It's truly remarkable. I imagine you won't have any trouble finding a market for it here."

"No, the landlord appeared to be most enthusiastic about its prospects." Silvertree looked so self-satisfied that a thought occurred to Corvus.

"You know you overpaid for this residence, don't you."

"Let us simply say that I am aware that one is unlikely to take advantage of the richest man in Amorr. Or expect much in the way of a bargain from him."

Corvus reflected that, by the simple mechanic of one seemingly bad deal, the ambassador had managed to purchase close contact with House Dives, the wealthiest in the Republic, if not the Empire, as well as disarm a public that otherwise might have been inclined to fear his centuries-old wiles. No doubt Silvertree would think his rent cheap at three times its current, exaggerated price. Corvus reminded himself that the elf sitting so affably across from him had been alive for more than a man's lifespan when the Houses Martial had first risen against King Andronis. He had not only seen every trick in the book, he was old enough to have invented some of them.

"Do you know, my lord consul, it is not only the faith of your people that is of much interest to Elebrion, but your House as well?"

"House Valerius?"

"Indeed. You are well aware of the part your son played in averting what could have been a very costly war between Amorr and Elebrion. And the correspondence between the Lady Shadowsong and your son is of potential use to our two nations, so long as things are not permitted to get out of hand."

Corvus nodded. "For my part, I am deeply indebted to the lady. I'm convinced it was encountering her that persuaded him to refrain from taking vows. I could have kissed her myself when my wife wrote to tell me that Marcus wasn't entering the priesthood."

"You speak as if his entering the Church would have brought shame upon your House. But is it not a great honor if a family member devotes himself to the service of your god?"

"Of course it is, of course it is." Corvus took another drink of the strange but compelling wine. "But each House has its tradition, and the tradition of House Valerius happens to be the legions. Naturally, a father wishes for his sons to continue the customs established by his forebears. But his calling wasn't genuine. It wasn't God that was calling to him—it was the Church library."

"We have one of some note in Elebrion."

"I know. My son was almost as taken with it as with the girl."

Silvertree leaned forward in a conspiratorial manner. "You do realize that the girl, as you call her, is eighty-two years old, do you not? She is still quite young by elven standards, of course, but nevertheless, she is old enough to be your son's grandmother. And in addition to being a sorceress of some skill, she also happens to be cousin to the High King."

"You needn't convince me that she's unsuitable for the boy, my lord ambassador. My wife and I were discussing various marital possibilities for him just last night. You can assure the king that there were no elven maids, royal or otherwise, on my wife's list of suitable matches."

"No doubt you will receive some interesting offers now that you have reached your present standing." The elf leaned back and regarded Corvus with amusement. "I realize that the idea we might be possessed of souls and are therefore worthy of some modicum of regard is a relatively new one for your people. But you should understand that we elves have had similar debates amongst ourselves in the past. And whereas your debates tended to concern whether my people were angels or mortals, ours were more likely to revolve around the possibility that your people were genuinely sentient or only talking beasts with little more capacity for true reason than those birds that mimic the sounds they hear."

Corvus laughed. "Don't spend too much time at the arena, or you'll be forced to conclude the latter."

"Indeed?" The elf chuckled. "You are a young race, a young society. Such forthright customs become increasingly embarrassing to the more sophisticated, but sophistication leads to problems of its own. Which is why I broached what I understand must be an uncomfortable subject. I wish to ensure that if there is any such future rapprochement between our peoples, whether it involves your son and our royal family or not, there will be no unfortunate incidents such as the one that sparked the last war between Elebrion and Amorr."

Corvus frowned. He was much better versed on what had happened during Amorr's past wars than the various events that had led up to them. But if he recalled correctly, the elves hadn't initially objected to the destruction of the little colony of half-elves in Pannonia. "Unfortunate incidents? I was under the impression that the Sanctiff of the time had written to the High King informing him of his intentions to declare Crusade, and when he received no response, assumed there were no objections."

"There were no objections to eradicating the half-breeds," Silvertree said with a pleasant smile. His eyes, however, had gone strangely dark. "The misfortune to which I referred was that the general responsible—a Lucretian, I believe—did not content himself with killing the half-elven, but massacred their true-blooded kin, as well. I lost a sister there."

"I'm sorry," Corvus said reflexively.

"There was much anger, particularly among the families who had lost sons and daughters. You see, for many of the elves there, it was little more than a game. What is thirty, forty, at most fifty years to an elf? That is why the colony grew so rapidly: It was a fad among elves and a few elfesses like my sister, which turned out to be a fatal one."

Corvus nodded gravely. He really didn't know what to say. It seemed a little much to apologize for something that had happened so long ago.

The elf seemed to read his mind.

"You needn't apologize. I am aware it happened long before your great-grandfather was born. An elf would have to be a fool to hold the Amorrans of today responsible for the excessive zeal of a single man who has been dead and all but forgotten for centuries."

"Though not by the elves."

"Though not, as you say, by the elves."

"Why is the High King interested in a rapprochement now?"

"We are a dying race, Consul. Our warriors don't wish to marry and are more interested in making war than children. Our elfesses are too enchanted with their freedom and their sorcery to devote the thirty years or more required to properly raise a child. Our poets are but a limpid shadow of their predecessors. Our aristocracy is decadent to the point that half our nobles only manage to get out of bed to crawl into another one. And our mages are too caught up in their esoteric interests to care what happens to the race. What were once seven great kingdoms have now been reduced to three moderate powers, and Elebrion is more a collection of tombs and tomes of past deeds than a proper city, let alone a kingdom.

"We need something to spur us to life again. There were those who favored encouraging another crusade against us, as perhaps the sensation of a sword at the throat might be enough to awaken the insensate. The problem, of course, is that this time we might not be strong enough to defeat the legions so easily, especially now that we would also have to contend with the Order of Saint Michael. Our most powerful mage, Bessarias, was so impressed with them that he actually adopted the worship of your Tree God."

"The Immaculate is not a tree!" Corvus hastened to correct the ambassador.

"No, of course not. I misspoke. Naturally your Lord Immaculatus is not a plant of any kind. In any event, the party that favored peaceful engagement with your young and active race had the favor of King Mael and won out. Because even if our increased contact with Amorr goes terribly awry, we can still hope to gain the prospective benefit from your hostility and inevitable invasion at a later date."

"That is an unusual perspective," Corvus said, thinking that the elven mind was a strange one indeed.

"The alternative is to embrace the half-elven idea." Lord Silvertree shrugged and emptied his wine glass. "Which would be the ultimate irony, considering that the royal policy has always been to eliminate any half-breed discovered. And the non-elven mother, of course."

"Mother? What about fathers?"

"There are very few elfesses who find mortal men to be the least bit attractive. I suppose if you imagined how attracted you are to an female orc, or perhaps a goblin, you might have some idea how little appeal humans present to most of us. No, it's not quite that bad. Perhaps dwarves would be a more apt comparison."

Corvus nearly choked on his wine. He found it very, very difficult to believe that he was the consul aquilae suffectus, he was meeting the Lord Ambassador from the High King's Court of Elebrion, and he was being lectured on comparative breed shagging from the elvish perspective.

"I take it my son need not worry about the Lady Shadowsong becoming overly enamored of him, in that case?"

"I don't believe I, or any other elf in any of the three kingdoms, would dare to attempt to say what the Lady Shadowsong will or will not do in the future. I would sooner attempt to predict the wind. I don't pretend to fathom her interest in your son, nor could I possibly tell you what it entails. But you need not fear their friendship becoming overly close. She will not sacrifice her magic for a few short years with your son."

That was good to hear, although Corvus didn't understand what the contradiction was. "What of Savonderum? Would not an alliance of kings be more palatable to your sovereign?"

"No." Silvertree's answer was succinct and decisive. "The king of Savonderum covets our magic. The crown there has long claimed ownership of all those with sufficient magical talent, and this is accepted by the royal mages there. They live their short lives like birds in gilded cages, and their very existence is seen as an offense by our magisters. For every war we have waged with your people, we have fought three against them. And, moreover, we are more valuable allies to Amorr, since the use of magic is anathema to you. The time is coming, I fear, when you will find that you cannot be so delicate in forswearing it."

"We provide the armies, and you provide the sorcerers? It makes sense." Corvus toyed with his glass, then met Silvertree's inhuman eyes. "Against whom?"

"That is the pertinent question, is it not?"

But the question wasn't answered, for at that moment the elven ambassador's eyebrows rose as if he had heard something. A sparkle of light
floated through the air, unattached to anything and devoid of any support.
At the sight of it, Silvertree pushed himself gracefully up from his chair.
"It appears the consul civitas has arrived. Please excuse me while I ask him
if he will consent to join us."

"Of course," Corvus nodded.

Truth be told, he was glad to have a few moments to consider his
thoughts. While Marcus's familiarity with the elves was no news to him,
he was surprised and a little concerned about the extent of it. He'd been
proud of his son's part in the successful embassy, but in its aftermath he
had probably devoted more time thinking about the consequences of what
that success might mean for his son's future career in the Church, and
about the unsettling problem of the false Michaelines, than he had about
the implications of any future relations between Marcus and those elves
he had met in Elebrion.

And once Marcus had decided against taking vows, Corvus had almost completely forgotten about the entire affair in the course of helping
the boy take his first steps on the cursus honorum while simultaneously
overseeing the creation of the third House legion.

As he was privately debating the wisdom of marrying off Marcus to
one of the available Andronicans, Torquatus entered into the large library
room, followed closely by Lord Silvertree, and nodded to Corvus. It
was an inward-focused, distracted gesture, and despite an initial surge of
annoyance, Corvus wondered what business could have been so urgent as
to delay the man in the present situation.

"My apologies to you both, especially you, my lord ambassador. You
will forgive me, I know. I had several insistent visitors whose business
required immediate attention. A delegation from the Church arrived at
my home just as I was setting out to come here and begged me, as consul
civitas, to name the next Sanctiff for them."

"Who was in the delegation?"

"Oh, Eusebius, Vizantus, and four or five other celestines. They're all terrified, of course. Vizantus kept going on about Satanas invading the sanctity of the temple, and apparently everyone suspects everyone else of being possessed or in league with the dark powers." He grimaced and shook his head at Silvertree. "It may have been a mistake asking you to come to the chapel, you know."

"Why is that?" The elf's pale eyebrow rose ever so slightly.

"You know how word gets around, especially when there's bad news and people are frightened. Merely hearing the word elf associated with the murders has half the priests there convinced that you killed the celestines with your evil elven sorcery."

"It is to be expected." Silvertree did not appear to be concerned. "I trust you informed them otherwise."

"I did a lot more than that. I told the sackless chicken-livered eunuchs that if they didn't decide amongst themselves who would be the next Sanctiff that I'd bloody well name you the head of the Church and see them all damned! This has gone on far too long, and with the recent events, we need to have a Sanctiff named and sitting on that throne of old bones before the people start getting restless."

Corvus was startled, but the astonished expression on the elf's face almost made him choke on his wine.

"Please tell me you didn't actually tell them that, my lord consul."

"You can bet your sorcerous elven arse I did, Ambassador!" Torquatus's face was red. The walk from his domus clearly hadn't been far enough to calm him entirely. "And if they don't give me a name to announce to the Senate tomorrow, I'll damn well put the crown on your head and slip the Fisher's Ring on your hand myself!"

"Don't worry," Corvus assured the speechless elf, who was at a complete loss for words. "The princes of the Church are not about to permit Titus Manlius to name the new Sanctiff. They will provide him the required name. Indeed, I expect they'll present him with several in order to prevent him from making the decision for them."

Silvertree regained his customary composure. "If you require an elf,
I have heard the archmage Bessarias now shares your faith. No doubt he
would make for an admirable Sanctified Father. Indeed, an unforgettable
one. But I shall heed your advice, lord consul Corvus, and put my mind at
ease concerning the matter. It is only that I was thinking of the potential
difficulties in explaining such a turn of events to my liege."

"Hell, he'd probably be delighted," Torquatus said sourly. "In any
event, Corvus, I've sent a message to Patronus asking him to convene the
Senate tomorrow afternoon. If those blue-skirted ninnies can manage to
stop their teeth chattering long enough to pronounce a name, we should
be able to have him safely enthroned and installed in the palace before
the winter festivities begin. Now, my lord ambassador, what can you tell
about these murders?"

Torquatus picked up the glass that their host had set on the table
for them without looking at it. Lord Silvertree smiled as Torquatus,
unsurprisingly, was even more startled by the spirited elven wine than
Corvus had been and nearly dropped his glass as a result.

The elven ambassador took advantage of the consul's momentary discomfiture to answer his question.

"If I may safely assume now that I will not be expected to take on any
religious duties during my sojourn here, I must ask if you are familiar with
the race of sorcerers once known as Witchkings."

"Not in the least," Corvus confessed.

Torquatus shrugged and glared suspiciously at his glass. "They ruled
in the north long ago. They were men but corrupted by their sorceries.
Their name has been a byword for human evil for centuries, but I don't
see that they were very different than the men of Savonderum are today.
What does that have to do with what happened in the palace last night?"

"Possibly nothing. Possibly everything," Silvertree said. "But you are
correct: They were men, and their sorceries did corrupt them. Now, I am
old enough to remember the end of the last war against them, although I
had not yet begun my studies in the arts. I served as an archer under Prince
Newellyn, who was cousin to King Mael. At the time, Mael was merely

the crown prince. Rather foolishly, we underestimated the Witchkings, and two of our four lost kingdoms fell to them. Although we considered ourselves to be masters of every form of magic, we learned to our great cost that we were wrong. Their great sorcerers had developed a new and more deadly magic that was very difficult for us to effectively counter."

"That must have been a shock," Torquatus commented.

"It was more than a shock—it was a terrible blow to our pride. For four thousand years, we had reigned our corner of the world unchallenged, the boundaries of our lands set only by the will of our kings rather than the strength of our enemies. War has always been the noblest game in the eyes of the elven race. But suddenly it became apparent that it was a game no longer, that we were engaged in a brutal struggle for our very survival with a vicious and depraved foe who would stop at nothing, absolutely nothing, in their quest for mastery."

"They sound like ogres." Corvus found it hard to imagine any foe more ruthless than an ogre lord. Not that orcs ever shirked from devouring their smaller cousins on occasion, such as when their logistics failed and their supplies ran low, but only the ogre lords were callous enough to knowingly begin a campaign with a plan to feed half of his troops to the other half.

"They were worse. Ogres may feed upon the flesh of elf, man, and beast alike, but the Witchkings didn't hesitate to devour their spirits. And their ambitions were outrageous. They didn't dream of ruling over merely the material world but over the spiritual realms as well."

"You can do that?" Torquatus looked skeptical. "Forgive me, my lord ambassador, but this sounds like a lot of arcane nonsense, and I don't see what it has to do with the princes of the church murdered last night. Which, if you don't mind me reminding you, is what we've come here to discuss!"

"So you have. My apologies, my lords consul, but at times I forget that men often find elvish forms of expression to be tortuous and more than a little tiresome. I shall attempt to proceed a little more expeditiously to the salient point. And while the cruel character of the Witchkings is,

I admit, not terribly relevant here, I am afraid the specific form of their peculiar and pernicious sorcery may be extremely pertinent to the events with which you are concerned."

"The ritual patterns in the blood," Corvus guessed. "And you think it was Witchking magic, only that's not possible, since they were wiped out long ago."

"Not quite, but you are thinking along the appropriate lines, Consul. The unique aspect of Witchking magic was their approach to the plane that men conventionally describe as demonic. They were far from the only ones to make use of a connection to the entities of that dimension, as the Collegium Occludum has long had a school devoted to it, the occasional Savondese mage has been known to dabble in it despite the formal royal proscription, and of course, it is the basis of the greater part of orcish shamanism."

Torquatus glanced at Corvus. His expression of dismay mirrored the emotion Corvus himself was feeling. "You're talking about demon worship."

"Not at all." The elf shook his head. "Quite the opposite, for the most part. Obviously many of the lesser races such as goblins and kobolds worship gods that are clearly nothing more than petty demons that managed to make an impression on various tribes at one point or another. The relationship between, for example, the diableriste and the various demons he summons is more akin to master and servant than worshipper and god. Demon worship is supplication and propitiation—but to summon a demon and force it to serve your will instead of its own, that requires mastery."

Suddenly, the affable elven lord struck Corvus as being rather more dangerous, rather more corrupt, than he had just a few moments before. "Have you ever done that?" he asked tentatively.

"Yes, of course. One must master summoning from the less nefarious nether regions as part of one's training at the Collegium. It wasn't an area of interest to me, so I doubt I ever summoned more than ten or twelve of the wretched things. Mostly very minor, very harmless ones, as you can imagine. I was simply attempting to get the requirements out of the way as quickly as possible since I was, as I previously mentioned to the consul aquilae here, much more interested in the alchemical arts. Demons are inveterate liars, after all, and the lesser ones aren't very intelligent. So, as far as I am concerned, unless one is going to truly master the art, there is little utility to it."

"It would be hard to argue with your logic, Ambassador," Torquatus agreed easily. "Since I have no idea what you're talking about."

"But do you understand that Amorran law requires that those who consort with demons be put to death, Lord Silvertree?" Corvus asked. "It is one thing to look the other way if you happen to indulge in some minor magics from time to time. As you are the representative of the High King, Elebrion law holds sway in this residence. But there are some things that simply will not and cannot be permitted here in Amorr, and one of them is voluntarily trafficking with the enemies of God and the darkest forces of evil!"

"I understand, my lord consul," the elf said gravely. "However, would it ease your conscience if I informed you that the last time I engaged in any such occult concourse was more than three hundred years ago? I am, of course, willing to give any amount of assurances required that I will not do so again while I am a guest here in your lands."

Corvus and Torquatus looked at each other. The Amorran Empire had been founded only four hundred years ago. "Yes, I think that should do," Torquatus said.

The elf smiled. "Elven ways are not the ways of men. Nor, I hasten to add, are they the ways of the Witchkings. My lords consul, your church and your god speak firmly against consorting with demons, and I will not say they are wrong to do so. But if you believe that even mere discourse with them is evil that merits punishment by death, then I think you will readily admit that the sins of the Witchkings were far graver, far more despicable, and far more dangerous than anything we elves have ever done. Well, except for Bessarias, but that is another matter. For you see, they did more than summon demons: They discovered a means of bringing them into the material plane and keeping them here by binding them to the flesh."

The elf raised his narrow, pointed eyebrows, but neither Corvus nor Torquatus understood the distinction he was making.

"Do you mean something like demonic possession?" Corvus asked.

"No, possession is a temporary and artificial state. In such cases, the extraplanar being is only acting through the physical being like a puppeteer pulling the strings on a puppet and making it appear to dance. I am speaking of a chthonical wedding between a demonic spirit of the nether planes and the physical bodies of one or more living beings, which has the result of permitting the spirit to live and interact in our world while simultaneously permitting the bodies with which it had been merged to draw upon the dark powers provided by this unholy bond."

"That sounds like something straight out of Hell," remarked Torquatus.

Corvus couldn't have agreed more. He knew the depravity of Man knew no bounds, but this was something altogether more distressing than he'd ever imagined. It was even worse than the nightmarish images of the bloody massacre in the chapel that still occasionally flashed into his mind's eye without warning.

"I suppose that would depend upon which of the nether planes you would regard as your Hell, but yes, that's essentially true. And through this occult marriage of spirit and flesh, the Witchkings were transformed into creatures that were less than demons but more than men. They became formidable fighters and, much to our horror, we learned their mages had become very nearly as strong as our own, at least, as strong as the younger elven mages who customarily went to war. Their sorcerers were no match for the magisters of the Collegium Occludum, of course, but the magisters seldom bestir themselves in the service of anyone or anything except their own interests. If I recall correctly, Lord Consul Civitas, you had some experience warring against my people in your youth."

"A little," Torquatus answered. "Nothing more than a few skirmishes, really."

"And yet perhaps you will understand that even though our armies were larger and our warriors more skilled than they are today, we found we needed to maintain a ratio of one-to-two if we were to expect reliable success against them in battle."

"Legionary doctrine still considers that one must have a five-to-one advantage before engaging elves, and that a ratio of seven-to-one is necessary to guarantee success."

"Accompanied, one imagines, by your doughty thaumaturges." The elf smiled. "I can still recall those terrible battles against the Witchkings. Nothing had been seen like it before, and nothing has been seen like it since. Villages, cities, even mountains were destroyed by their demonic sorceries or the mighty retribution of our greatest magisters.

"That was how we finally defeated them in the end. We could not beat them by force of arms. The kingdom of Glaislael had fallen, and those who were privy to the truth of the situation were lost to despair. Finally, the High King humbled himself and went to the Collegium in supplication. He went down on his knees before the council of magisters and begged them to intervene, which was without precedent in the three thousand years since Vilthoniel the Wise first established it as a library and a center for arcane scholarship. Even so, the vote was close, as the magisters only deigned to join the war effort if the High King was willing to heed its counsel and obey its commands for the remainder of the war."

"Why did they do that?" Corvus asked, curious despite himself. "That seems to make little more sense than a group of Church ecclesiasticals suddenly deciding to assume command of the legions! What would a group of mages and scholars know of war?"

"How to win them," Silvertree answered simply. "The High King and his generals made the mistake of attempting to use natural means and natural tactics to defeat an enemy that was, at least in part, supernatural. The magisters had no interest in troop movements and battlefields. Instead, they struck directly at the heart of the Witchkings' power, which is to say, at the demons that had been bound to them."

"Sounds almost like a Michaeline approach," Corvus mused aloud.

"It was very similar. To deny the enemy the core of his strength is the shortest path to victory. After forty years of vicious war and three defeats for every victory, in less than three years, the magisters completely defeated the armies of the Witchkings. And by completely, I mean just that. Using the power of their sorcery to augment the High King's armies, they eliminated every man, woman, and child throughout the land of that abhorrent people. The few who escaped the initial slaughter were tracked down and killed over the next two decades. Selenoth has been rid of their cursed race for centuries."

"Then why are you telling us all of this? You're not saying that the murders of our churchmen were committed by the Witchkings, are you?" Corvus was surprised to see Torquatus looked genuinely alarmed. "If their defeat was as complete as you're saying, that's clearly impossible!"

"It is," the elf admitted. "And I am not suggesting the Witchkings were responsible. What I am saying is that the murders appear to have been committed through the use of a magic very similar to theirs. Since the Witchkings are no more, I imagine you can understand that this poses somewhat of a puzzle."

"Somewhat? I'd say either your precious Magisters missed a few of them, or you made a mistake about the magic involved." Torquatus placed his empty glass on the table. He blinked with unvarnished astonishment as Silvertree refilled it with a flick of his finger. "That's a useful trick."

"They didn't miss any of them. And I don't make mistakes, my lord consul, not of that sort. Their magic was... very distinctive. In fact, I can tell you exactly what happened to your priests, and I can also tell you that you need not concern yourselves with any search for the goblin involved in the murders. By this time, the creature will be dead. I expect those who collect the refuse in the morning, or perhaps those who drag the river by night, will come across its body on the morrow."

"You said 'goblin,'" Corvus said. "As in only one. We were under the impression that there were several of them. I've fought goblins before. One couldn't possibly have been so lethal as to have slaughtered the celestines like that, especially bare-handed. The men were old, admittedly, but there were six of them! At least one or two should have survived an attack during daylight hours by just a single goblin. They had only to run outside the chapel—there were guards all over the palace."

"A simple goblin, yes, but they could not have escaped one infused with demonic power. Especially one whose mind had been given over to the demon." Silvertree folded his hands. "Forgive me, my lords consul, I realize you are both experienced men of war, but this is something far beyond simple battle magic or anything you have ever known. I confess it is even somewhat beyond my experience. I have never studied this form of magic, never practiced it, and what I witnessed of it as a young archer was mostly from a reasonable distance some five hundred years ago. But the reason I am certain it was Witchking magic is that the blood that was smeared in the ritual pattern was neither a summoning nor a banishment—it was an attempt to reverse the spell that had bound the demon with the goblin."

"I don't understand," Torquatus said. "Who was attempting to reverse it?"

"The demon inside," answered the elf. "I have seen elegant and stable forms of this spell. The Witchkings perfected it to the point that the spiritual bonding was transferred across generations, fragmenting the demon and infusing their descendants with substantial power that was entirely under their control. But this appears to have been a slapdash effort, though whether it was amateurish or simply careless, I could not say. The ritual was the demon's attempt to break the bond and free itself before the goblin died as a result of the spell."

"Why would it care about the goblin's life?"

"Presumably, Consul, it was either bound to return to its summoner or to the plane from whence it was originally summoned upon the dissolution of its anchor, which in this case would have been the goblin. But it failed, and the careless nature of the original spell indicates what I said earlier: The goblin is most likely dead and the demon back where it belongs. Of course, this leads us to certain intriguing questions. Such as, who the demon's binder was, why he used it to murder the princes of your Church, and, most of all, where he could have learned Witchking magic?"

Corvus shook his head. "How could anyone learn something that doesn't exist anymore? Books, one presumes, but I assume you burned them back in the day, or you wouldn't consider it a question."

Silvertree nodded at Corvus. "Precisely. I asked myself that very question this afternoon. And I reached a conclusion, but it is one I suspect you are not going to like. I don't like the implications myself. Now, you must understand that some of our ideas about the Witchkings have proven to be false."

Torquatus sighed impatiently.

Corvus nodded to the ambassador. "Go on."

"The magisters at the Collegium have long asserted that the Witchkings had been nothing more than normal men who, by virtue of sheer chance combined with steadfast devotion to their dark arts, had reached an unusual level of skill that has never been matched, before or since. But we now know this is not true, and that someone has been able to replicate their efforts. We know this because the Amorran embassy of last year was kind enough to gift the High King with one of the wolf creatures. It was the one that attacked your son, Lord Consul Valerius."

"Ah, yes?" Torquatus glanced at Corvus. "You'll have to tell me more about that one day, Sextus Valerius."

"Why is that?" Corvus asked Silvertree. "How were you able to determine that?"

"Because the beasts are the product of the same demonic magic that once created the Witchkings. It is a sorcery akin to the one that made use of the goblin here in Amorr last night, albeit a more sophisticated one. This suggests to me that the Witchking magic wasn't developed by the Witchkings any more than it was developed by wolves in the wild. While the Witchkings made use of the magic to great effect, I strongly suspect they were its product, rather than its author. Someone else, something else, used it to create them. Quite possibly the same being or beings responsible for creating the wolf creatures."

"And the same that did whatever you said happened to the goblin?" Corvus asked.

"No, almost certainly not. The spell utilized there was too crude, too haphazard. So we are speaking of at least two, and quite possibly three, different sorcerers over the centuries. There is the creator of the Witchkings. There is the creator of the wolf-creatures. And then there is the murderer of your priests."

Corvus rubbed his lip with his index finger. It was a lot to take in. "Could they all be the work of the same hand? I know it's an awfully long time, but then, you elves are damn near immortal."

"It is unlikely. The difference between the wolves and the goblin, to say nothing of the sophistication and subsequent mastery exhibited by the Witchkings, is profound. But as it happens, I have an idea about a certain group from whom the sorcerers responsible may very well have hailed."

"What group is that?" Torquatus asked.

The elf smiled mysteriously. "We call them the Abandoned. But men, as well as orcs, goblins, and other breeds have usually called them by another name over the centuries. Your race, in particular, has been known to worship them as gods."

MARCUS

THERE were few things more intimidating than an Amorran legion arrayed for battle, Marcus thought to himself. Perhaps only the steep mountainous approach to the elven city of Elebrion, with its silver-helmed hawk riders patrolling the blue skies overhead, was more impressive.

The heavily armored cohorts stood evenly in their black-armored lines, identified by their banners as well as the numbers painted on their shields. The crimson crests of the centurions made it easy to distinguish them from their men. There was one for every hundred infantry, and the veteran officers on the front lines looked as if they were encrusted in gold and silver, with their armor well nigh covered by the medals they had won in battle over the years. There were few battlefield prizes so rich as a fallen centurion. The scorpios and onagers were grouped in six locations, each manned by three ballistarii, although none of them were loaded yet with the giant bolts and rocks they hurled to such devastating effect.

All that was missing was the cavalry wing. But the huge quantities of Cynothi auxiliaries positioned on either flank were more than an adequate substitute, since both flanks actually outnumbered the legionaries stationed in between them. Altogether, the legion made for an awe-inspiring sight, particularly when one found oneself standing in front of it, as Marcus now found himself doing.

"It would appear we made a mistake in failing to abandon the castrum when we had the opportunity," Trebonius remarked, as they looked out over the Severan legion and its auxiliaries from the safety of the thick walls of the legion's fortified camp.

"I don't recall you advising a withdrawal," Marcus replied mildly. "What you may recall is my desire to meet them in the field, while you and Julianus advised remaining here inside the walls. Now, I admit, I may have been too optimistic about the Cynothii returning home."

"Better to meet them behind these walls than out there, Clericus. Three hundred horse can't be expected to counter ten thousand foot. I recall Vellius Maccius to you: Foot-soldiers, if rightly handled, can hardly be beaten except by other soldiers fighting on foot."

"I am perfectly aware that the geometry is not in our favor!" Marcus snapped.

"Geometry? I should say simple subtraction is sufficient to illustrate the challenge."

Marcus closed his eyes and allowed himself to indulge in a momentary fantasy of strangling his fellow tribune and second-in-command. Was it ever like this for his father and Saturnius? No, probably not, he concluded. The two of them had won almost all their battles, whereas he and Trebonius bid fair to be defeated, if not wiped out to a man, in their very first command.

What would Corvus do in this situation? That was a useless question. His father would have avoided it in the first place by retreating when he still had the time. But Saturnius was the tactician, so what would he have done if he were facing a siege by an enemy that outnumbered him nearly three to one?

Marcus had absolutely no idea. He found himself wishing he'd paid more attention to Father Aurelius when his tutor had been lecturing on the Iamblichus and the Ychaian astrologers. He did his best to imagine what Saturnius would have done. Simplify the situation. Ignore the details and see the geometry. But try as he might, all he saw before him were three very large rectangles facing one rather thinner rectangle.

"I suppose we had better see if they're amenable to a parley," he told Trebonius. "We are all Amorrans, after all. I'll go talk to Buteo and the cursed Cynothi who calls himself a king. Perhaps this is all one tremendous misunderstanding, and Secundus Falconius will join us in suppressing the provincials. He can't be so mad as to want to start a civil war. I haven't received a single message even hinting at any conflict in the city or the Senate!"

"Maybe one of the king's grandsons is among the hostages we're holding." His fellow tribune shrugged. "Well, we can hope, anyhow. Good luck, Clericus. We'll be praying for you."

Marcus elected to ride over to the enemy lines with only a draconarius by his side to bear the white flag of truce under which he was riding. No spear was hurled at him and no iron bolt punched through his breastplate, but the contemptuous stare of hundreds of veteran legionaries, their faces bearded and weather-beaten, drove home to him how badly he had already been beaten without a battle.

He had better learn to be a superlative tactician, he told himself, because it appeared he was already a failure as a strategist. The maneuvers before the battle were as important—no, even more important, he understood now—than the fighting that eventually followed. And as he rode through the lines that had been parted for him, he could also see that the men of Fulgetra were battle-hardened in a way that Legio XVII was not yet. He began to think that, even if by some miracle he could convince the king of the Cynothii to withdraw from the field, he and his men would likely find themselves outmatched by the experience of the Severan legion anyhow.

Fulgetra's legate received him in a canvas tent that was set up behind the legion's right flank, accompanied by the provincial king and four of his tribunes, each of whom appeared to be a decade older than either him or Trebonius. Buteo was a big man, who, given the way his bulk strained against his well-worn armor, looked rather like a sausage. But Marcus didn't smile. There was nothing amusing about the man. His pyramid-shaped head and small, predatory eyes gave him an intimidatingly brutal appearance. The Severan legate didn't bother introducing his companions. He only grunted in what appeared to be a satisfied manner.

"Secundus Falconius," Marcus nodded to him as if they'd encountered each other in the Forum. "How good it is to see a fellow countryman so far from home."

Buteo wrinkled his lip in what could have been a sneer or a failed smile. "You should have run home to your daddy after Saturnius got himself killed, Valerian whelp."

"That does sound like good advice at the moment. Are you going to let me?"

"Not now. You should have run when you had the chance. You're too late."

"Pity," Marcus sighed. "I suppose I'll just have to kill you all, then."

"Spare us the brave words, puppy. There's naught to discuss. Surrender, and your men will live. Fight, and many of them will die. Either way, the XVIIth comes under my control. But if you surrender, I won't kill you and I'll even keep you out of Severan hands too."

Marcus ignored Buteo's offer and turned toward the newly crowned king of Cynothicum, a spare, balding man who looked more like a priest than a rebel king. "What is your interest in this internecine squabble, Your Royal Kingliness? Or am I to address you as 'Your Majesty'?"

"Don't answer the boy," Buteo interrupted, and the Cynothi obediently closed his mouth. "You should thank me, Valerian. I've got no wish to kill you or your men. All you have to do is keep your nose out of affairs that are none of your concern and turn your legion over to me. If you don't trust me to keep you safe, why then, you can just run along to Amorr. Or Vallyrium, if you prefer, it makes no difference to me. I'll even give you a scroll with my stamp on it to make sure that arrogant Severan pup doesn't kill you on the road if he finds you."

"You are most generous, Secundus Falconius." Marcus didn't mean for that to come out quite as sarcastically as it sounded. Buteo's offer was a fine one, and no doubt he had no more desire to risk his soldier's lives against a trained Amorran legion than Marcus did. Buteo would win, to be sure, though he would pay a heavy price in blood. "But if you don't mind, before I answer, please allow me to pose one question to your provincial friend here. You won't find it objectionable."

Buteo shrugged.

"Your Majesty," Marcus said to the little king, "are you aware that I hold inside those walls ten young men of noble rank who are your loyal subjects? I mean them no harm, of course, but you will understand that I cannot guarantee their safety if an attack is made against the camp."

"The captain you captured a few days ago told me as much." The king's accent was thick, but he spoke clearly and was perfectly intelligible. "He also said you pledged not to harm them if I did not withdraw with him."

Marcus mentally kicked himself for promising the Cynothi captain that he would not use his hostages in an attempt to compel the king's acquiescence. But before he could point out that accidents were known to happen even with the best-intentioned gaolers, especially in the midst of a siege, the king continued.

"However, you may kill them if you like, General. As it happens, if you would cut their throats as soon as you return to your army, you would be doing me a service."

Marcus blinked. He had not really expected the king to slink away in fear for the hostages, but the Cynothi's cold-blooded willingness to see the young men dead took him by surprise.

Buteo laughed, seeing Marcus's unsettlement. "What else would you expect, puppy? His throne is newly established. He's the first of his line, and he was only crowned king six months ago. Killing a few young nobles, half of whom are potential claimants to his crown, is less a threat than a favor. I recommend you make him an offer before you surrender. I daresay you'll profit nicely from it."

Marcus looked from the Amorran legate to the Cynothi king. They were powerful men. Dangerous, even. But both were men without honor.

Was this what he would have to become if he wished to survive and prosper in a fallen world?

"Just to be sure I understand you correctly, Secundus Falconius: You are advising that I first enrich myself by murdering the young men under my protection, then betray my House, my country, and my men by turning over Legio XVII to you."

"They said you was a quick-witted puppy, Valerian." Buteo rubbed his stubbled chin. "I don't know about that, but you ain't as stupid as I thought, getting yourself caught so easy. I see you understand the situation. The question is, do you have the sense to take the only deal you're going to get?"

"My life, a little gold, and the chance for my men to die in battle fighting whom, goblins? Orcs? Or the other Valerian legions? With all due respect, I must decline your generous offer. If it profiteth not a man to gain the whole world at the cost of his soul, I can't see that a single legion is worth the price."

The Cynothi's eyes narrowed.

But Buteo only laughed. It was a harsh, triumphant sound, and the man wasn't feigning his amusement either. He was genuinely amused.

"You don't know a damn thing, Valerian. You're still a cleric, not a soldier. The men don't give a damn about their own souls, much less yourn. I'll have your head within the week, and it'll be your men who will give it to me. They didn't kiss the eagle this spring thinking they'd face a bloody Amorran legion and an army that whipped the consul of the legions. They thought they'd be slaughtering farm boys and raping their way through a provincial city or two. I'll give them the same offer I gave you: Surrender or die. And if you stand in the way of their surrender, why, I'll just have to remind them that all they have to do is get you out of the way."

"I fear you sell the men short," Marcus said bravely, but he was think-ing absolutely nothing of the kind. He had no doubt whatsoever that the centurions who had seen one legionary commander dead and burned wouldn't hesitate to kill a second one themselves, not if their lives hung in the balance. They probably wouldn't even see it as surrender per se, more of a change in command, and arguably, a sensible one. The youngest of Buteo's four tribunes had at least a decade on him, and any one of them would have more experience and a stronger claim on commanding a legion as well. "Perhaps you will find that the men of Legio XVII are more loyal and honorable than your own, Secundus Falconius."

"More likely I'll find your head lying on the ground after they throw it over the walls." Buteo made a dismissive gesture with his hand. "You're a brave little boy, Valerian, I'll give you that. I'll be disappointed if I hear you died crying and begging and pissing yourself. Now, go back to your men and try to explain to them that you're expecting them to fight an army three times their number and ten times their experience."

"Yours is a tender heart, Falconian. Never fear: I shall endeavor to face my fate in such a manner as to spare you any distress. Legate, tribunes, Your Majesty."

Marcus was careful to show a fearless face to Buteo and the others as he turned around smartly, walked toward his horse, whose reins were being held by his draconius, and mounted it as casually as if he was on his family's estates. He neither looked back nor so much as glanced at any of the legionaries through whose lines he was riding as he returned to the castrum.

A single thought weighed heavily upon his mind as he rode half a horse's length in front of the subdued companion. How did Secundus Falconius, or the man who appeared to be pulling his strings, Severus Patronus, merit such deference and obedience from a half-barbarian rebel like the king of the Cynothii?

"How did it go?" Trebonius asked him as he helped Marcus shed his heavy leather-and-steel armor. "Does he intend to besiege us?"

"Buteo appears to be about as imaginative as my father once told me Marcus Saturnius was." He held up a hand to forestall what appeared to be an immediate protest from his friend, who had greatly admired Saturnius. "Corvus meant it as a compliment. He thought that the best tacticians saw the battlefield more clearly because they lacked imagination."

"Oh, I see. Yes, I suppose that makes sense."

"Anyhow, if that's the case, I fear Buteo must be tactical genius. He obviously expected me to surrender. I believe his intention is to publicly demand our surrender tomorrow, in a manner that all the men can hear. When I refuse, he'll call for them to mutiny, kill me and any officers who support me, and then accept him as stragister militum and one of his tribunes as legatus. It's a perfectly reasonable approach. It won't cost him a single man, and he can always try storming the walls if the men don't prove amenable."

Trebonius frowned at Marcus's relaxed tone. "That doesn't bother you at all? It's not like you to be this fatalistic, Marcus. I don't know if you're going to be able to keep the men in line. Half the centurions have told me their men started grumbling as soon as the Severans showed up with the Cynothii in tow. I have to tell you, Marcus, they may turn on you, Valerius or no. They're willing to follow you to a point, but I don't think that extends to taking on another Amorran legion. Especially not one that outnumbers us so badly."

Marcus laughed. "I'm not at all concerned about the men turning on me. Julianus tells me Aulan and his horse is nowhere near here. He may be halfway to Amorr already. Buteo has no horse, and he hasn't shown any sign of investing us. See how he's got his men building their own castrum already? He doesn't expect me to wait around to be murdered—he expects me to take the knights and ride clear of here tonight. He's even leaving the Porta Decumana free to make it easier for me."

"Is that what we're going to do?" Trebonius looked as if he couldn't decide if fleeing with the horse was a wise decision or a cowardly and dishonorable one.

"Only if we have no other choice. But we have to try to find a way to keep the legion out of Buteo's hands. If there is some sort of civil war brewing, just running away and handing the men over to House Severus would be worse than losing half of them in battle and giving Fulgetra a bloody nose in the process."

"But I just told you, the men aren't going to fight for you against Fulgetra!" Trebonius's voice rose a little in protest. "You can make all the speeches you like, Marcus, but it's not an option!"

"I know." Marcus grinned. "Have you ever heard of the Siege of Iron Mountain?"

"Of course. Who hasn't?"

"Well, you haven't heard the half of the actual siege. And the half you've heard is mostly tall tales invented years later by Sir Alwys d'Escard, a troubadour-knight who wasn't ever near the place."

"What does a seven-year siege have to do with anything? We can't realistically expect to hold off the Severans for even seven days! The dwarves at Iron Mountain didn't have a choice: They were fighting for their lives, and they couldn't expect any mercy from the Troll King. Buteo is going to give the men an easy way out, and they'd have to be mad not to take it!"

"Not if we give them an easier way out." Marcus smiled again and pointed toward the south, to the fields beyond the Porta Decumana. "How far out do you think their lines are going to extend on that side when Buteo decides to begin circumvallating us?"

"Two acti, perhaps. Just out of spear range, but close enough for archers."

"I agree. Now, do you recall how I told you that on the embassy to the elf king, my uncle bought me a dwarven slave?"

"Yes, I remember. Laudus or something like that?"

"Lodi, yes. Well, he was at Iron Mountain. And believe it or not, he was one of the dwarves who killed the Troll King."

"I thought the elven prince killed him," Trebonius protested. "When the elven cavalry broke through the orcs and charged the royal body-guard."

Marcus shook his head. "I told you, everything you know about it is wrong. The elves never fought at Iron Mountain. They showed up, took one look at the size of the Troll King's army, and rode back to the

Three Kingdoms. That's why the dwarves, at least the Iron Mountain ones, despise them now."

"Really? That's astonishing! So the elves ran away? I'd never heard that!"

"It's not very romantic. And d'Escard was, above all, a romantic. But here is the significant part: Lodi was part of a team that tunneled out from the mountain and set up a sort of giant scorpio in the troll army's boneyard. That's how they killed the king—they put a giant bolt right through his chest. And that's what broke the siege."

Trebonius looked dubious. "I don't think much of that as a plan, Marcus. Maybe killing the Troll King was enough to break apart his army, but Fulgetra isn't going to fall apart just because we kill Secundus Falconius. And I doubt it's his honeyed tongue that convinced the Cynothii to serve as his allies."

"We're not going to kill Buteo, you idiot," Marcus punched his second-in-command's shoulder. "What we're going to do is dig our way out of here and steal a march on him! Tomorrow night, we'll march out underground. All we need is a solid head start. If we leave around midnight, that should give us until sunrise at the very least. Once we have a lead on them, our horse will be able to harass them and slow them down enough so they won't be able to catch us."

Trebonius frowned and looked up at the sky. "That's either mad or brilliant, Marcus. Quite possibly both. It sounds like something out of Frontinus!" He punched his palm with his fist. "I think it will work! All right, I'm with you, but you're going to have to convince the centurions. And if they think it's too risky or if they won't go along with it, I think we should take the cavalry out the Porta Decumana before Buteo starts digging his ditch and slams the door shut on us."

"We can dig faster than he can, Trebonius. My father was right: It's all in the geometry." Marcus hesitated for a moment, then shrugged. "All right, that's not exactly what he meant, but it's true nevertheless. The straight line we need is shorter than the circle they require. And we'll start tonight, whereas they wouldn't start digging their ditch until tomorrow at the very soonest. What's more, you're going to delay them even longer."

"I am?"

"Yes. Tomorrow morning, you'll ride out to him and tell him that you and the senior centurions have arrested me and want to discuss the terms of surrender. That will buy us the second night we need. Buteo will be so certain of taking the castra that he won't bother with starting his circumvallation right away. Why should he? He knows he has us trapped, so he can afford to be patient."

"Yes, I suppose if I were him I wouldn't set the men digging right away, either, not if I was hoping to avoid a battle," Trebonius said. "I agree, we can probably get out underground. The earth isn't rocky hereabouts. But he's still got twelve hundred Cynothi horse that could catch up to us and slow us down until Buteo catches up."

Marcus winked at him. "I have an idea about that, as well."

"More geometry?"

Marcus shook his head and waved Trebonius out of the command tent. "No, more Frontinus. Tell the primi ordines I'll want to see them here at the fourth hour. I want you and Julianus too. And bring a pair of messengers. I've got to write some letters now."

Trebonius saluted and slipped out through the tent flaps.

Marcus sighed and flexed his hands. He could almost imagine them aching from the letter-writing already. There were men to be convinced, there was tonnes of earth to be moved, and there were enemies to be bamboozled and escaped. But first, and foremost, he had to get word of his suspicions to his father and uncle in Amorr.

And, he thought grimly, if he couldn't accomplish all of those things, this might be his last opportunity to say farewell to Sextus, Marcipor, his mother, and a certain royal elfess in Elebrion.

AULAN

To A. Severus Patronus, Senator, Primus Consul, and Princeps Senatus

at Amorr (Novembris)

I regret to inform you, my dear father, that your confidence in II. Falconius appears to have been misplaced. Not only did Buteo fail to bring Legio XVII to heel, he somehow managed to lose them entirely despite the demise of the legatus, M. Saturnius. I cannot attest to precisely what happened, as I was not an eyewitness to his actions, my knights and I having been separated from the main body of the legion by one of his earlier brainstorms, which story I related to you in my previous letter. But I shall endeavor to provide you with an accurate picture of what happened according to my subsequent conversations with Buteo and the other tribunes.

Fulgetra arrived at the castra stativa near Gallidromum on the afternoon of the Nones, accompanied by King Ladismas and the Cynothi infantry. The tribune who happens to be the son of Sex. Valerius Corvus, one M. Valerius Clericus, rode out to meet him under a flag of truce. Buteo demanded the Valerian surrender the legion to him, but he met with some defiance. The next morning, Buteo sent a herald to the Porta Praetoria and demanded the surrender of the legion by the senior centurions, presuming they would either kill the Valerian or send him out with their cavalry prior to submitting. You will understand that Buteo had no reliable means of preventing the cavalry's escape, if you recall that neither I nor my cavalry were in the vicinity.

No answer was forthcoming until the evening, nor did the Valerian horse issue forth from the gates, until another tribune, one G. Trebonius, rode forth under a second flag of truce and indicated that he was now the legionary commander, that Valerius Clericus had been taken into custody, and that therefore he wished to negotiate the terms of the surrender. Buteo was much pleased by the prospect of obtaining the legionary cavalry as well as the infantry without loss, and so he freely granted the tribune's request to open the gates of the castra at noon the following day. At no point did he order the men to begin circumvallating the castra or otherwise prepare to besiege it. I suspect it was his intention to storm the walls if negotiations failed. This failure to invest the fortress may have been understandable, but it was negligent nonetheless.

As night fell, the troops inside the castra were heard to be engaged in some degree of license, as it appeared the customary legionary discipline had been relaxed. A number of large bonfires were noted, and a small body of horse was observed to depart from the Porta Decumana after dark. No attempt was made to stop them, it being presumed that this group consisted of the Valerian tribune and whatever officers were reluctant to serve under Secundus Falconius. No further activity was detected, and the customary guards were observed in their positions on the walls throughout the night. However, just before first light, a large body of horse, estimated at some 15 squadrons, attacked our auxiliary camp. The assault was focused on their horses. More than two hundred horse were slain or injured so severely they had to be put down, while another seven hundred had their tethers severed and were driven off.

As you can probably imagine, this caused an amount of confusion. I believe Buteo was initially under the impression that a second legion had arrived in relief of Legio XVII, presumably one of the two Vale-

rian legions thought to be wintering in Gorignia under the command of T. Didius. The legion immediately fell to arms and marched out of camp to go to the assistance of the Cynothii.

Therefore it was well after mid-day when two of the tribunes, accompanied by a century from the first cohort, finally went to the Porta Praetoria to demand the surrender. They found the gates still closed. A pair of guards eventually appeared in response to their demands for entry, but when the gates were opened, it was discovered that the castra had been entirely abandoned and the guards were actually ten Cynothi hostages who had been taken during the same battle that resulted in my separation from the legion.

About which, more anon.

The more important discovery was a large tunnel that had been constructed to run under the walls of the castra, a tunnel which proceeded nearly half a stadia to the south. It was wide enough for four men, tall enough for a horse being led, and its exit was on the far side of a hill that could not have been seen by anyone in a position to watch the castra itself, particularly at night. The false guards said the infantry had departed first, followed by the cavalry, about the same time that the first body of horse had ridden out of the gate. Buteo estimated therefore that Legio XVII had the advantage of at least one day's march. And, considering that his auxiliaries were in some disarray and my own whereabouts were unknown, he declined to pursue. In my opinion, this was probably the correct decision, but it in no way excuses his previous errors in judgment.

I myself witnessed Legio XVII marching along the Via Axicia, which is what inspired me to ride to Gallidromum in search of Buteo. From their course, I conclude that the Valerian tribune does not intend to march toward Amorr or to winter his troops in Vallyrium, but rather join with T. Didius and his two legions in Gorignia. That being said, you must assume that he will have written to his father, and that Valerius Magnus will not hesitate to make use of the news that the *very Cynothii who defeated Caudinus are now serving House Severus as auxiliaries. I do not know how this affects your plans, dear father, but enough blood has been shed that I do not believe denial is an option. Even so, I trust you will find some way to turn this setback to your advantage, as you have done so many times in the past.*

As II. Falconius has no need of my services at present, I shall ride directly to Amorr in the morning. I shall bring two squadrons with me. If you are not already in the city, I expect you will arrive there soon. Greet Mother and my sisters for me, and tell them I am well.

A. Severus Aulan
tribunus militum, Legio III Fulgetra

CORVUS

THE face of the tall elf loomed over Corvus. The elongated alien eyes held him transfixed in place. He tried to move, but he was held fast by invisible bands of iron. Frantic, he struggled against them, desperately trying to reach the gladius he knew was at his side, but he could not free his arms. The spell, if indeed a spell it was, was stronger than a man's grasp.

"The gods are coming!" the elf said in a voice like thunder. "They are coming, they are coming!"

Closer, closer came the face to his own. He could smell its fetid breath, the rotten scent of carrion emanating from its broken, jagged teeth. The elven features began to ripple and blur. The skin began to rip and tear like a bloodless mask as if the beast were a snake shedding its skin from the head. Was it a kobold or a demon? He couldn't tell. Fear exploded within him, and the force of the terror somehow freed his arm. He cried out to Saint Michael as he drew his sword and thrust it toward the yawning jaws that were lunging for his throat.

But no sooner had the blade struck home than it vanished in a cloud of stinking red smoke. The demonic kobold smiled, and the horrific smile widened as the monster began to laugh. It reached out and seized his shoulders in its outsized claws and began shaking him, methodically, rhythmically, back and forth, back and forth, up and down, up and down.

"Corvus!" the terrible beast hissed at him. "Corvus, wake up!"

He blinked, and with a shrug of his shoulders, managed to break free of the hands that were pressing him down upon the bed, batting them away with the feeble remnants of his strength.

"Corvus, you were dreaming. Wake up now. He's here to see you before he goes."

"Romilia?" he asked, his heart still racing.

The curly tendrils of his wife's dark hair were tickling his face as she leaned over him. She sat down on the bed beside him and stroked his cheek.

"Corvus, you need to get up now. He's waiting for you."

He groaned. Whatever spirits had been in that elven wine were now located somewhere behind his left temple, and they were not happy to be there. "Oh, good Lord, Romilia. Tell Nicenus I'm not seeing any clients today. He can tell them whatever he likes. Just make them go away!"

She leaned over and kissed him, her lips feeling soft and plump against his own. He reached for her.

But she only laughed and batted his arms away before leaping up from their bed.

"I thought that might wake you up. Now get out of bed and put some clothes on. Caius Vecellius is here to escort you to the Sanctal Palace. And Lucretius Siculus is here to see you. He said he's leaving for Marcus's legion today."

"Siculus?" All thoughts of a morning dalliance vanished. "Did he say if anything is wrong? Did the Cynothii move against the XVIIth?"

"I have no idea," she said as he slipped a tunic over his head. "I don't think it's an emergency, though. He seemed relaxed to me."

And indeed, while Siculus was dressed for travel, the tribune's only armor was his stained leather lorica. He wasn't even wearing his sword. He was a legionary veteran and patrician whose path along the cursus honorum had been more of a leisurely stroll than a march. He stood eating a handful of figs liberated from the table in the triclinium and smiling at the pained expression on Corvus's face as he stumbled awkwardly into the room with Romilia trailing rather more gracefully behind him.

"It would appear you sit uneasily upon the Eagle Chair, my lord consul aquilae."

"Do shut up, Siculus," Corvus groaned. "What possesses you to ride off in such haste? Is there word from any of the legates?"

"Nothing out of the usual. Scato is complaining again about a shortage of olive oil, and he says the quality of the last wine shipment from the Thursian merchant holding the contract has reached a new nadir. Apparently there is some dispute over which is the inferior vintage, the Thursian's wine or this year's horse piss. He also said the signifers from four or five of the centuries anticipated running short of coin soon, so I'm bringing three chests of silver and another of gold with me to Aviglianus. Then I'll ride east and join up with Marcus Saturnius. We'll need to pay off our winter suppliers."

"I assume you aren't traveling alone?" Corvus asked. The ex-quaestor was trustworthy enough, but they were hardly capable of defending such a treasure alone.

Siculus grinned. "Surely you don't think I'm going to lug those heavy monsters around myself! No, a group of Petrines are bringing the winter supplies to one of their monasteries in Gorignia so I've arranged for us to travel with them, and we'll meet a squadron from the VIIth there."

Corvus nodded with approval. Although smaller and less renowned than their fraternal colleagues, the Order of Saint Peter was the oldest military order and was primarily comprised of ex-legionaries who had taken vows after retiring into the service of the Church. They were tough as the leather armor they wore, eschewing both steel and iron for reasons that Corvus had never understood. They were nigh on incorruptible, having little in the way of ambitions or material wants. The legion's money would be safer in their company than in the banks of Amorr.

"So you know where Saturnius decided where to stow XVII for the winter?"

"Yes, at the castra stativa near Gallidromum. It's a good choice, in my opinion. It should serve well as our primary base of operations in the spring."

Corvus closed his eyes, attempting to envision the territory surrounding the northeastern province. He'd been over the map of it so often, he
could see it almost as clearly as if it were spread out before him. "The castra
at Gallidromum will hold two legions. Why doesn't he bring another
one up? That would be safer than leaving the other two in Vallyrium.
Remember, that mounted infantry the Cynothii have can move faster than
our infantry can march."

"I know," the strategist admitted. "But half of Caudinus's men are
out there somewhere, and we'll need to find a place for them once they're
located. I imagine an amount of retraining will be in order too. Arvinus
is the best praefectus in the three legions, and all the centurions of the
XVIIth are fresh from training up their recruits last summer. In light of
how they performed against the goblins, we can be sure they'll do a good
job with the XIVth, once we find them."

"What will Saturnius do if he finds out they ran?"

The two men locked eyes for a moment, each daring the other to
admit what neither wanted to say aloud.

Siculus shrugged.

"I don't know if he can justify not decimating them," he said quietly.
"But if Caudinus lost three thousand, what do we gain from eliminating
another three centuries worth? That's half a cohort!"

Corvus shrugged. "I don't know. Saturnius will think of something.
If not, remind him that he knows what to do. The honor of the eagles
must be preserved."

Siculus nodded and was silent for a moment. Then he grinned.
"Would the lord consul happen to have letters for any of his junior officers?"

"I do," Romilia called from behind him. She slipped one arm around
Corvus and extended a tightly rolled scroll with the other. "Tell my son
to keep himself well-wrapped and warm, Gnaeus Lucretius. And tell him
to stay away from those filthy women at the baths!"

The tribune laughed. "The men call him 'Clericus,' my lady, so I
think you need not concern yourself overmuch with fears for his virtue.

I happen to know he spends his free evenings reading in his tent, as he robbed me of the only book in my library!"

Corvus gripped the younger man's forearm and clapped him loudly on the thick leather covering his shoulder. "Tell him the consul suffectus is following his career with interest and that I will see him in the spring. And keep your eyes open, Gnaeus Lucretius. Write me once someone finds Caudinus's men, and tell me exactly what happened to Caudinus too. I won't have anyone following his example."

"Ave, my lord consul," Siculus said mockingly as he gripped Corvus's arm firmly in return. "You keep your eyes open too, General. You've made enemies of the first two men in Amorr. Be sure to make some friends as well."

"If you'd been here with the clients yesterday, you'd know I have far more friends now than I ever wanted," Corvus said with a rueful smile. "Now go, lad, and may God go with you."

Siculus nodded, kissed Romilia twice, once on both cheeks, then turned and marched from the triclinium. They could hear the horses outside stirring as he rejoined his waiting men, mounted his horse, and rode off through the gate and over the cobblestones of the street.

"He's a good man," Romilia said. "But Lucius Andronicus was a good man too. Do you think Marcus Saturnius can defeat those northern barbarians?"

"He damned well better. He's ten times the tactician that Caudinus was. And he'll have three legions—three and one-half if you count the XIVth—to Caudinus's one. I don't doubt his ability to beat the Cynothii, but I am concerned that no one can seem to figure out where the rest of the bloody XIVth is. They can't simply have vanished, and if there had been another battle anywhere near that province, I can't imagine we wouldn't have received word of it yet. But we will. The snows will start soon enough, and nothing is going to happen up there until the spring thaws anyway."

She slid past him, slipped her arms around him, and pressed herself against him. "Well, I, for one, am delighted to hear that I'm actually going to have my husband keeping my bed warm in the winter for once. It's one thing to be lonely during the summer, but in the winter, a woman gets cold!"

He ran his hands up her sides. She wriggled to escape his grasp, but he flexed his arms and held her fast. He leaned down to kiss her, and she kissed him back for a moment, hard, then used the moment of distraction to break free.

"Come back to bed," he urged her, still holding one arm captive. "I'll warm you up."

"I'm not cold now!" she protested. "It's a lovely day, and I have to go to the market. Valerilla is coming over this afternoon, and she's bringing both the little ones. You haven't even met her Decia yet. You were too busy gallivanting around the allied cities trying to find centurions for your new legion last spring when she was born."

"Valerilla is here?" Corvus released his wife's hand, delighted at the news.

He loved all his children, but he had a particular affection for his younger daughter, whose shy and sensitive personality had always stirred the protective side of his nature. He had given her to Gaius Decius Mus, the elder son of Publius Decius Mus, twice consul provincae, in exchange for a larger dowry than he could really afford as well as a collection of dire threats and apocalyptic vows if the man should ever so much as inspire her to tears. He need not have worried, though, as Gaius Decius, who served as curule aedile last year and was widely expected to win election as praetor two years hence, was slavishly devoted to his young wife and the two children she had already given him.

"Yes, she wasn't planning to attend the Hivernalia. You know how she detests a crowd. But when she heard her darling papa was deigning to show his face in the city for once, she talked Mus into bringing the family back from his Clusian estate. I don't know if Valerilla is a bad influence on him or if he simply can't face the thought of enduring one more social event after having to put on all those games last year, but he's been hiding out there ever since his year as aedile ended."

"I can't say I blame him." Corvus snorted. He remembered his year as curule aedile and the job had made the legionary logistics look like a mere tutor's exercise by comparison. His aedileship hadn't been a disaster, but neither had it been a triumph, and it had put him deeply into a debt that only a very profitable campaign against the wealthy kingdom of Pharesiya, during which he captured and ransomed two of the heirs to the throne, permitted him to pay off six years ago. "Do you remember that time that Ilkubran merchant brought twelve lions to the house and left them with Nicenus? I was terrified he was going to quit my service."

"I wouldn't have blamed him. I was about ready to quit your service too. I was terrified one of them would get loose and eat the children before the beastmaster arrived to take them away. Now, speaking of children, you need to collect your little army of axemen and run off to the baths before you do anything. Your face needs shaving, and your daughter will be dreadfully disappointed if you don't look like a proper consul when she arrives."

"It's good to know someone properly appreciates me," Corvus said, laughing. Romilia wasn't jealous of how close he was with their younger girl, but he knew Valerilla was a closed book to her and sometimes she felt a bit excluded. "Oh, and that reminds me! I brought something back for the children from Gorignia. They were in my saddlebags. Tell Nicenus that I'll want them when I return."

"You brought something back?" Romilia said suspiciously. "From Gorignia?"

"Yes, a real goblin war club for Gaius and a black wolfskin for Decia!"

"Oh, Corvus." Romilia shook her head then pressed her forehead against his chest. He could feel, rather than hear, her laughing. "Only you would think those are suitable toys for babies. Please tell me you at least cleaned all the blood and all the other nasty bits off it."

"The wolfskin or the club?"

"Both!" She kissed him, then pushed him away. "I'll tell Nicenus to have one of the girls clean them again while you're gone. Now get yourself dressed properly and be on your way, my lord consul. And tell Captain

Vecellius to arrest anyone who tries to detain you on your way back. Your daughter is desperate to see you."

The great bell was just ringing for the second time when Corvus strode into the White Palace, followed by Vecellius and his axe-bearers. The Sanctal guards stood aside at his approach, their demeanor entirely different than the last time he'd been here. They lined the corridors, one positioned every twenty paces or so, and their white cloaks over their bleached leather armor made them look like statues as he marched past them. It wasn't customary for the Senate to meet in the Sanctal throne room, but then, this was no common meeting of the Senate.

The doors to the great chamber stood open, and he could see that most of his fellow Senators were already seated in a grand semicircle facing the central dais. The three consular seats had been arrayed upon it, below an elevated platform upon which rested the great gold-and-ivory Sanctal throne, nearly twice the size of the three below it. Like his own Eagle Chair, it was unoccupied—although not for long, God be praised. A new Sanctiff would go a long way toward keeping the unruly city from devolving into too much chaos during the winter festival. His two colleagues were already seated, although the blue-robed celestines for whom the first rows were reserved were not.

He nodded at several of his clients and other acquaintances as he walked down the length of the central aisle. But he nearly stumbled and broke his stride when he saw who was seated in the front row next to the princeps senatus on the right side of the aisle, across from the princes of the Church.

It was his brother, Magnus. He was deep in conversation with Severus Patronus, of all people. Their heads were so close they were almost touching, he saw to his astonishment. Unlike the last time Corvus had seen him, his brother was clean-shaven, but his face was still drawn, as if he had not eaten in several days. But what was he doing seated next to the man who had been his chief political rival, if not outright enemy, for more than ten years?

Well, he wasn't going to find out now. Corvus looked quickly away, not wishing either to meet his brother's eyes or to draw undue attention to the unholy union of House Severus and House Valerius that appeared to be taking place. As his escort smoothly split in two and moved to join their counterparts ringing the dais, he mounted the stairs then nodded to Titus Manlius and Marcus Fulvius before turning around and seating himself in the Eagle Chair. No sooner had he sat down than the doors to the chamber closed and the celestines, most of them white-bearded and stooped with age, were helped to their seats by the four young senators charged with assisting them.

Patronus rose and declared the Senate in session. He then sat down again, and an elderly celestine took his place between the platform and the assembly—the cerulengus, if Corvus interpreted the gold stripe on his sky-blue robe correctly. He raised his hands and the senators fell silent. This had not been the first intersanctum in the history of the Republic, but neither the Senate nor the People were comfortable without a Holy and Sanctified Father to guide them, and perhaps more importantly, to intercede with the Immaculate on their behalf.

"Immaculate, Son of Man, Son of God, most holy and perfect Savior of Mankind, we pray You hear our call!" The cerulengus's voice echoed throughout the chamber despite his age. "We follow You, You who are both God and Man, who left Your first estate and became flesh so that Man might know and see and hear and touch the Eternal and Almighty God. You lived, You healed, You loved, You taught, and yet You were betrayed and hung upon a Tree for the wickedness of Man. But just as Death could not hold You, and You rose again to life eternal, so we now raise up a Man to stand in Your stead and guide Your Most Holy and Sanctified Church in, but not of, this Fallen World."

When the cerulengus returned to his seat, Patronus rose again and stood before the dais, facing out toward the rows of senators. "City

Fathers, I bring you the best of news: By the grace of God and the mercy of Our Immaculate Savior, the Sacred College has spoken with one voice. We have a Sanctiff!"

A great cheer went up from the assembled Senate.

"Who is it?" Corvus whispered to Torquatus.

"A Falconian, Valens," the consul civitas leaned toward him and replied. "It's unexpected. He's young, not even fifty. After an impasse of this length, they usually compromise on the oldest goat in the flock in the hopes that he'll need a successor before long."

"A Falconian… well, at least it's not a Crescentius or a Colonna."

"Or Severan," Torquatus shook his head.

There came a thunderous blaring of horns. The double doors swung open, and the new Sanctal nominee, Falconius Valens, entered the throne room. He was preceded by the Grand Masters of the four knightly orders, the Priest-Captain of the Redeemed, and two other tall, stiff-backed men of martial appearance whom Corvus assumed to be the commanders of the Sanctal Guard. He was followed by a phalanx of twenty-one archbishops, all wearing towering white mitres and sky-blue mantels over their white vestments. As one, the Senate rose to its feet and began to applaud, including Corvus and his two colleagues.

In contrast to the splendor that surrounded him, Falconius Valens was clad in nothing more than an unadorned white robe, and he walked barefoot over the crimson carpet that led to the dais. But he stood out like a bird among butterflies and looked all the more noble for his humble attire. He was so tall that his head was nearly on a level with the top of the mitres worn by some of the shorter archbishops, and his short, neatly-trimmed beard accentuated, rather than concealed, his fine, aristocratic features. If there was no palpable sense of holiness surrounding him, neither was there the vague impression of frivolity his predecessor had occasionally conveyed.

"I see Patronus is displeased," Torquatus muttered. "Whatever his shortcomings, at least we know he won't be a Severan pet."

"How can you tell?" Corvus had also glanced at the princeps senatus, and although he could see only the man's profile, he couldn't detect any sign of satisfaction or disgruntlement.

"Because he doesn't look like a cat that caught a mouse."

Corvus was willing to trust his colleague's judgment. After more than two decades battling each other in the Senate, no doubt Torquatus knew how to read Patronus well. But Titus Manlius would never go over to the auctores, so how was it possible that Magnus, who had been a more bitter opponent of Patronus and his party than Torquatus, could have done so?

But whether he was pleased or displeased by the college's choice, Severus Patronus did not shirk his duty. When the procession reached the dais, the military commanders took their positions around it on the left, whereas the archbishops stretched out in a semicircle nearly half around it to the right.

Valens himself mounted the first step, then turned around to face the senators. He extended his ringless hand to Patronus.

The princeps senatus took it, but he did not kiss it. Instead, he raised it above his bald head and called out to the Senate in a loud and well-practiced voice.

"City Fathers, I present to you the Most Eminent and Most Reverend Lord Giovannus Falconius Valens, celestine of Our Lord and Savior's Sanctified and Immaculate Church, the chosen of the Almighty God and the Sacred College. Will you have him as your king?"

"We have no king but God," the group response echoed through the chamber like thunder. It sparked a sensation of fierce pride in Corvus. This was the faith of their fathers that had made Amorr great. This was the unshakable faith in God, not Man, that had raised this city above all the other nations and cities of the world.

Patronus continued with the ritual. "City Fathers, if you will not have this man as your king, will you have him as your prince?"

"We have no prince but the Immaculate, the Son of Man, the Son of God, the most holy and perfect Savior of Mankind!"

"City Fathers, if you will not have this man as your king or your prince, will you have him as your guide, as your guard, and as your advocate before the Most High God?"

Corvus counted to three. Then he, Titus Manlius, and Marcus Fulvius called out together as they had been instructed. "We will have him!"

A moment later, the five hundred voices of the Senate echoed them. "We will have him!"

The horns sounded three times. Then triumphant stringed music began to play from the musicians hidden behind the dais, somewhere toward the front of the chamber.

The new Sanctiff, who would be crowned publicly before the people in an open mass next Domenicus, raised his free hand in blessing the applauding senators, waited for a moment as his military commanders moved into position in front of him, then began to proceed down the aisle, followed this time by the twenty-six celestines, behind whom the archbishops fell in line. Giovannus Falconius would not receive the Sanctal ring nor take his seat upon the Sedes Ossus until he announced the name by which he would henceforth be known and the Senate's three consular thrones had been removed from the house of God.

Two hours later, Corvus was clean, shaved, scraped, confessed, absolved, and sitting happily on the floor of the triclinium, holding his six-month-old granddaughter for the first time.

It hadn't been easy to escape the crowds of senators outside the palace. His fascitors had been forced to call upon the help of ten or twelve of his more loyal clients to extricate him from the rest of them without incident or too much delay. Or any violence, for which he was grateful, as it would have broken the uplifting air that still filled his soul after the stirring sight of seeing the most powerful and prideful men in Amorr bowing their heads and bending their knees in humility before God's newly chosen viceroy.

"And if I'd stayed there, I might have missed you," he said to the little girl in his arms. "And we couldn't have that now, could we, beautiful?"

She truly was a lovely baby, with huge brown eyes that stared up fearlessly at him. He felt unexpected tears rising behind his eyes. Looking down at her was like going back in time. It was as if all the intervening years had never passed, and he was a man in his mid-twenties again, holding his younger daughter in his arms. There were times in the past when he'd thought he might have sold his soul to again experience one of those precious moments seared into his mind for all time. And now, holding little Decia, it was almost as if he was.

"Father, what's wrong?" Valerilla asked.

He had to clear his throat before he was able to respond to her. She had grown from a tiny and helpless little creature very much like the one in his arms into a paragon of Amorran womanhood, but her brown eyes were still enormous, and they still danced with the happy humor that had marked her personality from the start. She didn't have her mother's striking beauty, but she was pretty, and her natural charm and easy smile more than made up the gap. Everyone loved her. Everyone always had. And although she was a mother herself now twice over, Corvus still found it absolutely impossible to think of her as anything but his little girl.

"Not a thing," he answered truthfully, if a little huskily. "Not one single thing. I'm only astonished by how much she resembles you when you were her age."

He felt a soft hand squeezing the back of his neck. His wife always knew when he was concealing the depth of his true emotions. But she respected his preference not to display them openly, for which he was grateful.

"Well, she knows her grandpapa," Valerilla declared. "Look at how she smiles at you!"

The combination of his granddaughter's cheerful, toothless smile with her happy, enthusiastic eyes was almost too much for Corvus. He cuddled her to his chest, knowing that if he held that infant stare one moment longer, he would break into decidedly unconsular tears. Bless her with beauty and love, God, he prayed silently, breathing in the pure, innocent scent of the recently bathed baby. Bless her with long life and happiness and joy. And do not hold my sins against her or her mother, Almighty Father. If there is a price that must be paid for them, let it be paid by me and me alone. Not her. Never her.

Lost in his thoughts and prayers, he had lost track of the women's conversation. Now, a sharp tone in Romilia's voice caught his attention, and he tried to figure out what they were talking about. Then he heard a familiar name, and he realized at once what the subject of their discussion concerned.

"It's not right to speak ill of the dead, Rilla," his wife said to his daughter.

"It's not about the dead. It's about whether Papa was right to do what he did or not! Mama, everyone has been talking about it, but none of them knew Fortex like Rina and Corvinus and me. We grew up with him, after all! I heard him talk about the honor of the legions and how frightfully disciplined they were and all that sort of nonsense a million times! Did you know he used to hit me all the time with a stick that he pretended was a vinestaff when we were playing legion and he was the centurion? He was always the centurion! So, it's just silly to pretend that Fortex was this poor naïve young officer who simply didn't know any better. He knew better. He just assumed all those rules he used to think so grand didn't apply to him."

"I just think you could be a bit more sympathetic, at least to your aunt and uncle, if not Gaius Valerius."

"Sympathetic to Magnus and Aunt Julia? Mama, it's their fault he was such a spoiled brat, not Papa's! They filled his head with all sorts of stupid ideas about his birthright and his destiny, as if his birthright were different than Sextus's or any of his other brothers!"

Corvus carefully rose to his feet without using his hands, still cradling Decia in his arms. "Well, there's naught to be done about it now. Did anyone see where my little warrior ran off to?" He kissed his granddaughter on the forehead then placed her gently in the arms of his wife. He started to leave the triclinium in pursuit of his grandson, but Valerilla placed a small hand on his chest.

"Father, Mama has told me how busy you are, but would you be free to take me to the Ephoran amphitheatre this evening? Laevius is reading twelve of the latest stanzas he composed for his *Amorriad*, and I thought you might like to hear it. Decius says they include a section about Valerius Victus and his conquest of the Marmori."

Corvus started to shake his head, but the hopeful expression in Valerilla's big brown eyes was more than he could resist. He hesitated.

Romilia took the opportunity to argue their daughter's case.

"You must go, Corvus. You haven't shown yourself to the people once since you've been back from the field. You really must give them the chance to see their new consul and show their appreciation for your victory over the goblins. The city is restless. They've lost a consul and a sanctiff in the last three months, and now everyone is talking about the murdered celestines and how the new sanctiff is much too young to be anything but a disaster. Give them something else to talk about, something else to think about."

He glanced from his wife to his daughter. Valerilla nodded expectantly, enthusiastically, and he burst out laughing. How many times had she effectively lobbied him in that manner?

"Very well," he declared. "I should be delighted to hear Laevius give our ancestor his due. Romilia, are you coming too, or are you going to watch the children?"

"And miss my first opportunity to see the Consul Aquilae finally receive his due? I'm not the one who is a stranger to our grandchildren, Corvus. Maronna will watch the children tonight. Now, do you have time to eat something before you have to run off to the Senate, or will you find something along the way?"

"I think I have time," he said, winking at Valerilla.

"Oh, Father, I am glad!" she beamed, throwing her arms around him and nearly knocking him off balance. "And I'm so very proud of you! I always wanted to be a consul's daughter."

"I always said you were a princess," he reminded her. "And given how quickly your husband seems determined to walk the cursus, I doubt it will be long before you're a consul's wife as well, darling."

The sun was just beginning to set when the poet, Laevius, walked out into the center of the wooden theatre that had been erected for Hivernalia in the Forum.

Corvus had to admit that Romilia was right: The applause that greeted them as they took their seats in the middle of the second level was even more rapturous than that which the senators had given Amorr's new Sanctiff. And, judging by the comments and compliments that were directed to him, he began to realize that it was his defense of the clausores, and not his defeat of the goblin tribes, that was the source of his unexpected popularity with the public. Severus Patronus and the auctores might be the most powerful faction in the Senate, but the common folk of the city were clearly less than enthusiastic about seeing the people of the allied cities raised to their level as full citizens of the Republic.

There were only a few other senators present. Laevius was much more popular with the plebs than he was with the patricians. Despite having been seated on a consular throne only hours before, Corvus felt uncomfortably self-conscious when the poet, upon reaching the candle-laden stand that had been set up for his manuscript, first acknowledged the audience to the left and right of the theatre, then threw a legionary salute in Corvus's direction. Laevius was short and rotund, with a round face like a full moon, but he was blessed with a voice that might have done credit to a centurion. Even those seated in the heights of the theatre had no problem hearing him.

"Although, Amorrans, it is not ordinarily my custom at the beginning of a reading to explain my art, tonight I shall make an exception. I am pleased to present to you the sixth book in my poetic tribute to the history of our great city, which I have entitled *Amorriad* and which purports to chronicle the mighty deeds of our ancestors, to whom we owe an everlasting debt.

"We begin with the war against the treacherous king of the Marmori, Arsanius Tiranus, in which two legions, led by the consul civitas, Titus Valerius Victus, finally called him to account for the foul murder of Quintus Accius Plautus, an ambassador sent by the Senate to Marmorus in an attempt to negotiate an alliance between Amorr and that kingdom. But before I begin, I observe that we are honored by the presence of a descendant of that noble hero here in the audience tonight. So, I should like to dedicate this book to the new consul aquilae, Valerius Corvus, as well as to my patron, Licinius Lucretius."

The audience again applauded, but more hesitantly this time and with an anticipatory air. Laevius did not wait for it to die down, but began declaiming in his deep, resonant voice, causing the crowd to fall silent in an instant.

> *The Senate spoke, and in one voice acclaimed*
> *Quintus Accius of silvered tongue enfamed.*
> *"Go you, now, to the land of Marmorus,*
> *And eternal friendship with their folk discuss."*
> *Willing, Plautus obeyed; and, hither bound*
> *To Marmorus, its king at length he found...*

Something stabbed into his side, and Corvus nearly leaped to his feet, wondering where he was. Then he realized he wasn't being attacked, he was in his seat, safely ensconced between his wife and daughter, and the weapon with which he'd been assaulted was only his wife's sharp little elbow.

"Do wake up, my lord consul. He's just reached the climax, where your ancestor is confronting his sworn enemy. And mind your mouth!"

Corvus wiped at the left side of his mouth. It seemed he had been drooling a little, and he was exceedingly grateful that the reading was taking place under the cover of night, as not even his daughter, sitting on his left, appeared to realize that he'd fallen asleep under the mesmerizing flow of the poet's verse. He cleared his throat and straightened his back, thinking that he really must pay close attention to this particular part of the poem, as the slaying of the Marmorite king was generally deemed to be one of House Valerius's proudest achievements.

Laevius seemed to have hit his stride. He gestured grandly, and his voice showed no signs of weakness as he told of the bloody battlefield of Lausentius, where the Amorran legions shattered the army of Marmorus and the consul confronted the royal villain of the piece.

> *Titus Valerius brandished his long spear*
> *Against the foe, and so inflamed his fear:*
> *"What further course can you hope to find?*
> *What empty hopes are hidden in your mind?*
> *There is no swiftness to secure your flight;*
> *Not with their feet, but arms, the valiant fight!*
> *Vary your shape in many forms, and run*
> *All across the world under the scornful sun;*
> *Pray for wings or winds to mount the sky;*
> *It will avail you naught, for today you die!"*
> *Tiranus shook his head, and uttered reply:*
> *"No threats of yours could ever give me pause;*
> *For mine the right and the gods' own cause!"*
> *The king fled not, but firmly stood his ground*
> *Before the man that him had hunted down.*
> *The Marmori king was sworn never to yield*
> *And, as he cast about the bloody field,*
> *A javelin lay, broken, but free to wield;*

He drew it from the earth, and, poised on high,
　Charged toward his foe with a loud war cry,
But so shattered in spirit that he scarcely knew
　His way, or what unwieldy spear he threw.
He hurled it forth, but it fell well short
　And, want of vigor, mocked his vain effort.
He sought to stand, but destitute of force,
　His sinking limbs failed him amidst the course:
In vain he heaved, in vain he cursed;
　His last strength failed, by his wounds dispersed;
On royal tongue the futile curses died.

　Tiranus failed; whatever means he tried,
All force of arms and artful skill employed,
　They went for naught and the endeavor void.
Death's cold whispers through his soul resound;
　He shouts for aid, no help nor succor found;
Encircled, legions all his men surround;
　Once more he pauses, and looks up again,
Calling to his pagan gods all in vain.

　Trembling, he views the Valerian advance,
Brandishing aloft that most deadly lance:
　In despair he retreats before the conquering foe,
Forsaken by all, awaits the coming blow.

　Alone he stands, as ruthless Death draws near,
From behind his shield sees he the flying spear.

　The hero marked first, with an eagle's view,
His intended mark; and, rising as he threw,
　From his right hand the fatal weapon flew.
Not with less rage the rattling thunder falls,
　Or stones from war machines shatter walls:

Swift as a whirlwind, from an arm so strong,

    The lance flew past and bore grim Death along.

Naught could the king his silver shield avail,

    Nor aught, over his breast, his coat of mail:

It pierced through all, and with a grisly sound

    Transfixed his thigh, hurling him to the ground.

In pain, Tiranus rent the vaulted sky:

    With howls and curses did he his gods decry

Now upon earth the haughty king is laid,

    With face cast up, lost in the victor's shade,

Humbled, he thus to the conqueror prayed:

    "I know my death deserved, nor may I hope to live:

Save what the gods and your grace may give.

    Yet think, Amorran, if there may not be

That which you claim from your god, mercy.

    Pity my people, ten thousand in the grave;

And for your soul's sake your sworn foe save!

    Though if your vengeful vows require my death,

Give my folk a body void of breath!

    But all your legions see me beg my due;

Yours the victory, the crown belongs to you:

    Against one fallen, the strike is no virtue."

In suspense the Valerian held his hand

    Although eager to strike this foe of God and land.

He searched his heart, and at that moment felt

    His angry soul with more compassion melt;

When, casting down his eyes, he spied

    A medallion glittering at the king's side,

A fatal spoil which Tiranus himself tore

    From Quintus Accius, and in triumph wore.

Born again to wrath, angry flames did blaze
  From the fiery rage of the Valerian gaze.
"Traitor, I say, you are to grace pretend,
  Clad, as you are, in trophies of my friend!
So now, to him, a fitting offering go,
  It is for noble Plautus give I this deadly blow."
He raised his arm, and at the final word,
  Into Amorr's enemy drove his iron sword;
Valerius Victus killed the king abhorred.

Valerius Victus. Corvus liked the sound of it. He would give much to be able to claim such a name for himself. Then he glanced at his wife on his one side and his daughter on the other. He would give much. But he would not give everything.

SEVERA

S EVERA had spent three anxious weeks waiting for the seamstress
that the Moon Sisters, as she had privately come to think of
the followers of Saint Malachus, promised to send her. As it
happened, all her worries had been in vain, as the woman who showed
up at the manor, Quinta Jul, not only won her mother's affection with
effortless ease from the moment of her arrival but even earned a favorable
word from her father after patching his favorite tunic with such skill that
it didn't even look as if he'd torn it. She was a short, plump woman with
a ready smile and a grandmotherly demeanor. Within a week, it was as if
she'd been there for years.

Indeed, the only real problem appeared to be that the Sister had very
little time in which to instruct Severa in anything, much less the secrets of
the Goddess. With the Invernalia fast approaching, the newest member of
the household was immediately drafted into service preparing the ornate
outfits that the members of the family would be wearing.

Which was a pity, as far as Severa was concerned, because she was
alarmingly behind schedule on her own dress. She had chosen an asym-
metrical design with a high collar that would cover her throat entirely—
only because her mother had rejected as being too common the low-cut
one that would've shown off her cleavage. Now she regretted her short-
sighted reaction, but it was too late to go begging for the material to make
a new dress with only a week before the festival.

While the gown itself was mostly done, there was still an amount
of tedious embroidery that was necessary, and the silver thread she had

foolishly chosen for it was heavy and awkward. While the thread looked spectacular on the deep shade of blue, its thickness made the working difficult, and she found it all too easy to set the dress aside once her fingers started to cramp and leave it for the rest of the day.

"That dress really isn't going to suit you, my lady Severa," Quinta Jul said as she cast a skeptical eye on the disorder of Severa's room. She was a small, round woman about her mother's age with grey-streaked hair, bronze skin that was deeply lined and tanned by the sun, and dark, piercing eyes that one would have expected to see on a senator or bird of prey, not an elderly freewoman. "The blue goes nicely with the silver, I'll give you that much, but it doesn't suit your skin."

"It doesn't?" Severa was horrified. Why hadn't her mother said anything to her? Then she remembered the bright orange gown her mother had worn for the spring festival two years ago and was reluctantly forced to conclude that she had better look elsewhere for a sartorial guiding light if she wasn't going to make a fool of herself. "But what am I going to do? I barely hoped to finish this in time! What have you been doing for the last two weeks anyhow? Aren't you supposed to be teaching me?"

She was mortified to realize that she had tears in her eyes, but thankfully, her new lady didn't laugh at her or even smile. She simply smiled and ran her fingers through Severa's long curls. "Such lovely thick hair you have, my dear. Ah, I remember when mine was like that. Where did it go? You have the raw material to be beautiful, my lady, but even the finest gold ore requires an amount of work before it is worthy to be called jewelry or adorn a woman's throat."

"I don't understand."

"Always first things first, Lady Severa. Remember that. If I had spent my first few weeks in this house attending your needs, then I should always fear for my place here. But since I have been careful to first attend the lord and lady of the house and to win them over by anticipating their wishes, I need fear nothing. And moreover, I have learned a great deal more than I would have if I spent my days in your company, for which you shall soon be very grateful."

Severa caught her breath. What now? Her father hadn't mentioned the Clusius incident since the day before they'd returned to Amorr. Had he learned some dreadful new revelation to displease him? Or, since Quinta Jul didn't appear to be concerned about her ill-colored dress, was it possible that he would deny her the Invernalia? Father was capable of it, she knew, for he had once forbidden her brother Aulan to attend the festival when he had spoken back to him.

"You look pale, Lady Severa. Are you sure you are well?" Quinta Jul reached out and touched her forehead.

"He's not going to deny me the festival, is he? Is that why you don't care about helping me finish my dress that will look so terrible on me even if we do?"

The older woman laughed. It was a dry, throaty sound.

"Don't be a goose, my lady. No, your father has no intention of denying you the festival. In fact, I suspect your attendance will be demanded of you."

"Really?" Severa thought quickly, then gasped. "Has he decided upon my husband?"

Quinta Jul nodded. "That is the rumor among the household staff. And that is why I saw no reason to concern myself with your blue dress, since I had cause to suspect that you would not be wearing it at the festival."

"So you just left me to work on it without you anyhow?" Her indignation faded in the face of Quinta Jul's skeptical stare, a raised eyebrow her only response. "Very well, you knew I wasn't working on it either. But you haven't told me who it is! Oh, please tell me it's not some old plebian merchant with a purse as fat as his belly!"

"Lady Severa, you know perfectly well that your father is not going to bestow you upon anyone of insufficient rank. I don't know which of your suitors he has settled upon, but I am given to understand there appear to be three leading contenders, one from House Andronicus, one from House Valerius, and one from House Crescentius."

"What?" Severa shook her head. "Did you say House Valerius? You must mean House Volsius. Father would never marry me to a Valerian!"

Quinta Jul shrugged. "I surely couldn't say, my lady. I can only say that is what I heard. But my lady, if you are indeed to be betrothed, then we must begin discussing your betrothal dress for the Invernalia."

"There isn't going to be any betrothal if Father is talking to the Valerians! I can't believe it. I won't!" Severa turned to flee the room at once.

"My lady, where are you going, my lady?" she heard Quinta Jul call to her back.

"Where do you think!" she shouted back as she stomped down the stairs in search of a parent who could explain to her what was happening.

She found her mother in the kitchen, giving instructions to the cooks for the evening's dinner.

"I do think the Volsian sauce would better complement the fish, don't you? And besides, I imagine it will be taken as a compliment of sorts to young Numerius Volsius, who, if I understand my lord's intentions correctly, will have House support for the quaestorship this season." Her mother shot her a quizzical look. "Oh, Severa, whatever is the matter now?"

She was overweight and half a head shorter than Severa, but her hair was still thick and mostly black, and her wits had not been dulled by more than thirty years of overseeing the household of the most powerful man in Amorr.

"Mother, do tell me that Father isn't throwing me to the damned Valerian dogs this festival."

"Language, Severa. Society may forgive the occasional youthful indiscretion, but it will never accept a young woman—I will not say lady—who swears like a camp follower. And precisely whom do you think you are to object to any husband from a House Martial, when not six months ago you were willing enough to plight your troth to a slave from the fighting stables?"

Her mother's voice was conversational, but her words cut Severa as if they were iron-forged. She actually felt as if she had been physically struck. She would have preferred to have been physically struck.

"You knew about that?"

Her mother sniffed and gestured around the kitchen. The senior cook, a freeman, and the three kitchen slaves were all studiously pretending not to be hearing anything, but Severa had no doubts that they would be reciting the whole conversation, word for word, for the entire household by nightfall.

"Yes, I knew about it, Severa! I daresay the entire household knew about it. Do you honestly think a mother doesn't notice when her hot-blooded daughter is mooning after some hopelessly impossible young man? I was the one who told your father that you were up to something, but I never imagined you would sink so low. A gladiator, Severa, really? A gladiator? You might not have the sense that God gave a goose, but I would have thought you would have at least been a little more original."

"There's a first time for everything, Mother."

"You should have been married two years ago. Two years ago, I told your father he should marry you off to the first noble he found the least bit useful to him. Look at you! You're made for love, for marriage, for breeding and babies! I told him again last year, and then after your little escapade, I told him to do it now or lock you in a nunnery. The problem is he's too soft-hearted. He can't bear to see that his little girl has grown up—or believe that she's panting after unsuitable young men."

"Too soft-hearted? Father?" Severa was having trouble getting her mind around the concept.

"Yes, your father is much too soft-hearted where you are concerned. All five of you. Children are blind where their parents are concerned. The rest of Amorr looks at him and sees the head of a House Martial and the princeps senatus, so they are wise enough to fear his wrath and power. But because he's always been too easy on you, you see only a doting father. He spoiled you terribly. You, your sister, and all your brothers. And now, you and Regulus are forcing him to see that it was a mistake."

"I see that your heart, at least, is hard where we are concerned."

"Don't affect martyrdom, Severa, it doesn't suit you in the slightest. You know perfectly well that I love you from the very bottom of my heart. But your father's indulgence has not served you well, and at long last, he finally admits it. So he is going to betroth you this winter and you are going to make an excellent marriage that will be the talk of all Amorr. If you're lucky, you may even find yourself married to a man possessed with sufficient spine to make a proper wife of you, though the Immaculate knows that will take some doing."

Severa fought off the urge to pout. She was confident any such behavior would fail to impress her mother, especially when she was in the middle of such an uncharacteristic rampage. "And to whom might this excellent marriage be, Mother?"

Her mother waved her hand. "Go ask your father. He's in the garden. I don't believe he has made his mind up yet. And remember that the Valerians are only one of several possibilities, so you needn't work yourself up to a tantrum over it yet. Now go. Your father is entertaining tonight, and if I don't whip this kitchen into shape now, I have no doubt there will be some nicely striped backs around here on the morrow."

"Very well." Severa sniffed and walked out of the kitchen with whatever shards of dignity she could manage, ignoring the glares of the gathered kitchen staff. They looked as if they blamed her for her mother's sharp tongue, which was unfair since they were the ones who had put Mother in a mood. Mother was usually sweet and sympathetic, but it seemed the need to oversee the kitchen today had obviously put her in a poisonous mood.

She caught herself stomping through the hall that led to the rear door, and she took a deep breath, forcing herself to calm down. If she wanted to convince Father not to marry her to a Valerian, she knew that anger wasn't going to get her anywhere.

The door opened out onto a tiled platform overlooking the walled garden that brought a little of the tranquility of the Samnian countryside to Amorr. There were armed guards standing on either side of it. They both glanced over as she walked through the door, but, seeing that it was only her, immediately lost interest. Or, in the case of the older one standing on the right, pretended to lose interest. She could see him eyeing her body out of the corner of his eye. She smiled at him and laughed to herself as he glanced away and straightened his back uncomfortably.

Her father, Patronus, was standing toward the rear of the garden in front of his favorite lemon tree with his hands crossed behind his back. Severa never quite understood why it was his favorite, as he never ate lemons and seldom touched the sweet drink her mother made from their juice. But whenever he was in a contemplative mood, she could find him here. In the spring and summer, the lemons gave the arboreal garden its only color. It was more of a forest glade planted in the heart of the city than a garden with proper flowers. She wondered what he was thinking about, knowing that it almost surely had nothing to do with her prospective marriage.

Suddenly, she felt a burst of great affection for him, followed almost immediately by a moment of sadness. If she was to marry in the spring, this would be the last winter she would call the Severan domus her home.

She walked up behind him and put her arms around him, pressing her cheek against his protruding shoulderblades as she embraced him. He felt thinner than she remembered.

"I don't want to get married. I want to stay here forever with you and Mother and Severilla."

He turned, put his arms around her, and pressed her face to his chest. "Oh, my little one, my beautiful, perfect girl. If it were only possible, I would ask God for nothing else."

"Mother says you are too soft with me. But I wanted to tell you I will marry anyone you choose for me. I trust you."

He held her out and pretended to inspect her face. "What has brought about this sweet compliance? I had thought your new servant would instruct you in embroidery and other wifely skills, not philosophy."

She smiled. Her new approach was working. "I don't understand one thing, however. I've heard the servants talking. You can't seriously be thinking of giving me to House Valerius. Have I been so much trouble that you would punish me by turning me over to our enemies?"

"Severa!" he remonstrated. "The Valerians are not our enemies. Tell me, what is the difference between a dog and a scorpion?"

"Two legs?" As she intended, the answer made her father laugh. He shook his head.

"The difference is that a dog, no matter how inimical its nature, can be trained to love, or at least to obey. All it requires is time and the patience of its master. A scorpion, on the other hand, will sting even him who treats it with the utmost respect and affection. That is its nature, and its nature cannot be altered. That is the difference between a rival and an enemy."

"So you're saying that the Valerians are dogs, which I will not deny. But because they are dogs, they can be trained, and therefore there is hope for them."

"I should say, rather, there is potential utility to be found in them."

"Potential utility then. I understand, but I fail to see how my being thrown to the dogs—potentially—is something to be celebrated."

Her father smiled. "You have grasped the metaphor but failed to understand your place in it. They may see you as the bone, the reward, but I intend you to be the master. I intend that it is you who shall do the training."

"So you have chosen the Valerians, then." She wondered if this was the right time to throw a legendary tantrum that would leave all its predecessors in the shade, then she decided against it. Instead, she smiled even more sweetly than before. "May I ask which of the dogs you have in mind for me? I understand there are several. I should prefer one that is spotted, with a little tail that curls upward, if you care to take my wishes into account."

Her father smiled fondly at her. "I have decided nothing, except that you are to wed in the spring. Which means that you are to be betrothed at the festival, so naturally you will require someone to whom you may be betrothed. You are an intelligent young woman, and one day you will have to consider similar questions on behalf of your own children, so I see no reason why you should not be privy to my thoughts on the matter if you are inclined to hear them."

She nodded. "Please go on."

"There are eight Houses that have offered alliances; I am presently considering the two that are the most advantageous and possess men of an age I deem suitable for you. There are, of course, any number of requests for your hand, or Severilla's, from a variety of knights and even a few men of rank among the allied cities, but that would not be appropriate. And then, as you have apparently heard, I have had a conversation or two— nothing more—with House Valerius."

"What age do you deem suitable?"

"I want you to have a degree of influence over him, so he must be near to your age. Below twenty-five, to be precise. House Caerus has made what would otherwise be an attractive offer, and while I am interested in binding them closer to us, no matter how he might dote on you, your voice will count for nothing with a husband who is nearly fifty years of age and secure in his power." He smiled at her. "You see how our interests coincide?"

"Nearly fifty?" Severa winced, relieved that she had escaped that dire fate. "May I ask about the two candidates you are seriously considering?"

He nodded and released her, then began to pace back and forth as was his custom when lecturing her. "There are five, actually, from Andronicus and Arrianus. Three of the former House and two of the latter. The Andronicans are all sons of ex-consuls, and one of the Arrians is the son of Arrianus Lepidus, who was consul provincae sixteen years ago. But with Caudinus's death, I fear things may become a bit complicated."

"I didn't know Caudinus had a son older than me."

"No, two of the young men are the younger sons of Andronicus Geminus. The other is Albinus's lad. I've heard nothing ill of them, although one does occasionally worry about the madness that seems to taint their blood. Geminus was a great man in his day. He sat the Eagle Chair twice and defeated the dwarves in the Underground War, but about ten years before that his father had to put down his brother as if he were a mad dog. His twin brother, no less."

"Oh, that's dreadful!" Severa shivered, but she was fascinated too. "Why did he have to do that?"

"Some say it's a curse that goes back four hundred years to the old royal line. They never tire of reminding everyone that they were kings before the Houses rose against them, but they're not so proud of their legacy of madness. There were all sorts of horrific stories about Titus Andronicus, Publius Andronicus's twin, but I never put too much stock in any of them. If I recall correctly, he had a nasty habit of tormenting the slave girls. Torturing them, to be honest. The family looked the other way for a while and sent him off to the countryside, but he killed one of his aunts in a rather brutal fashion during her visit there, and his father had no choice but to act. Brilliance or madness, it's usually one or the other with the Andronicans."

"What killed the consul aquilae, then? Brilliance or madness?"

He flashed her a weary smile. "Something much more prosaic. Stubbornness. Let that be a lesson to you, little one. There are careless missteps anyone can make, however brilliant one might be. However beautiful."

"Even you?"

"Especially me. The more power one has, the easier it is to be careless. The higher one rises, the easier it is to be seduced by the idea that the path one has chosen is right by virtue of the chooser. It's nonsense, of course, but astonishingly seductive nonsense."

"That sounds like Regulus. He always thinks that whatever he does is the right thing, just because he's the one doing it."

"Yes, it is a common problem among the sons of the Great Houses. The legions have a way of beating it out of most of them, but then, martial success can sometimes make it worse. It probably wouldn't do your brother any harm to lose a battle or two."

"What a pity he wasn't with Caudinus, then."

"Cruel, daughter, very cruel." Her father smiled at her again. "As much as I cherish you as you are, it is rather a pity you weren't born male.

Perhaps it is a blessing. I cannot decide if you are more clever than Tertius or more reckless than Aulan."

"Or more enthralled by my own beauty than Regulus?" She tossed her hair. "So you have seen through me again…. Now tell me why you would consider the Valerians for even a moment! I still cannot believe that you might give me to a son of Magnus, or were you thinking of one of the lesser Valerians?"

"Until recently, I was considering Corvus's youngest, after I heard he'd abjured his vows. But now, I am not so sure. Even as consul suffectus, Corvus has considerably less weight in the Senate than his brother. After more than twenty years of battling Magnus, I've come to have more than a grudging respect for the man. He knows how to compromise, and he knows how to build alliances. He's much wealthier than Corvus too, but the main attraction of an alliance is that I need him. Not to join me, you understand, but to simply stand aside and refrain from opposing me. I think, with your help, that much can be arranged."

"But why, Father?" Severa complained. "House Valerius have been our enemies—all right, our rivals—for ages!"

"The world is changing, Severa. It's changing in ways you can't possibly understand, in ways I don't understand myself. There are strange forces at work, powerful forces that go well beyond Amorr, or its allies, or even the race of Man. And my fear is that we are going to see drastic changes of the sort that haven't been seen in Amorr since the City Fathers rose against King Andronis.

"I can't prevent them from occurring, but I have to believe it is my place to help Amorr prepare herself so that the Senate and People will survive, and perhaps even thrive, during the disorder to come. And to do that, I need to win over the conservatives and traditionalists, those who oppose change reflexively. If I can remove the Valerians from the ranks of the clausores, especially Magnus, then the rest will fall in line."

"You make it sound so frightening, Father. Strange forces, things that haven't happened in four centuries… do you actually believe awful things are going to happen?"

"I don't know precisely what is going to happen. But I know that whatever is going to happen will take place within the next two years. I thought to have more time, but as I look at the various events outside the empire, I don't think that will be the case."

Severa shook her head. There was so much he wasn't telling her. "But why, Father? You haven't said why you believe any of this!"

"Nor will I. I wouldn't have told you this much, except that it's important for you to understand that I need your acquiescence to whatever marriage I make for you. I want more than that, I want your cooperation, I want you to do everything you can to ensure that your husband's family doesn't oppose my actions, as many in the Senate will. Few will understand the actions I've taken until it is much too late. That's the way it usually is. Those who see the coming storm are called madmen and fabulists, and those who attempt to prepare for it will be denounced for being self-serving. But what else can I do? I can't simply retire to my estates and let the city collapse. What sort of legacy would that be for my children, for my grandchildren?"

She stepped forward and kissed him on the cheek. "You'll find a way, Father. You always do. Are you certain you don't want to tell me more about it?"

"The less you know, the better. There is some knowledge that can be dangerous, and I would not have you bring yourself to the attention of... to the attention of those whose attention can be perilous."

Severa nodded, knowing that this was the time to play the dutiful daughter. She decided to talk to Quinta Jul. Perhaps the Moon Sister would be able to make some sense of her father's arcane references. Or perhaps Tertius might know something. He was always poking around in the same old books their father did.

"If you think it will help you save Amorr, Father, I will willingly marry any Valerian you name, even if he is ugly and old. If my brothers are brave enough to risk the sharp swords of Amorr's enemies, then surely I can face the rusted blade of an elderly Valerian."

He shook his head and smiled at her. "I think we can spare you that unseemly sacrifice. Magnus has two unmarried sons left after losing the one. Corvus has the priestling, and Pardus has either two or three lads, I can't recall. The young men are all tall and more or less well-formed. I mislike the notion of the priestling, though, and in any event, Magnus's line is the more significant one. Corvus is consul now, but only as suffectus, and he'll be back in the field when the new consul is elected in a few weeks.

"But it all may be moot. I made an overture to Magnus concerning the possibility of a marriage about a month ago and have heard nothing from him. And he's been in mourning since the word arrived that his son, the tribune, died in the campaign against the goblins. Naturally, I am loathe to press him further for the nonce."

"Oh, that's awful," Severa exclaimed, genuinely upset by news of the fallen young Valerian. With both Aulan and Regulus serving with the House legions, Aulan being a tribune himself, she couldn't bear to think about the death of even a hated Valerian without feeling a sinking sensation in her stomach. It was strange, too, to think that the dead young man might have been chosen as her husband, had he survived.

"Yes, well, House Arrianus always had the most likely prospects, to my mind. They would be the safest choice, for both your interests and mine. I think you will not be displeased with Lepidus's son. He is well-formed and will be quaestor in his year next year."

So he was twenty-seven, only nine years older than her. That wasn't too much. And the son of a consul too. House Arrianus might not be the most influential House Martial, but she'd prefer it to the too-numerous Falconians or the ancient, but unstable Andronicans.

The sound of a door being opened caused them to turn around and look up toward the platform. The two guards were saluting a man whose position in the household had never quite made sense to Severa. Domitius was a fighting slave and wore leather armor like the rest of the guards but never seemed to actually be around the domus very often or guard anyone.

He was older than most of the guards too, and seemed considerably more intelligent than them as well.

He spotted Patronus at once and hastened down the stairs. His lean face was red with effort as he half-ran across the length of the garden toward them, holding a little scroll in his hand. He was out of breath too. Something is wrong, Severa thought instantly.

"My lord princeps, I pray you, forgive my intrusion."

"Of course," her father said. "What is it, Domitius?"

"A letter. From Lord Aulan."

Her father nodded calmly, took the letter from the slave, and dismissed him. He broke the seal and unrolled the scroll. Severa watched his face closely as he quickly scanned its comments. There was only a flicker of irritation before the familiar, imperturbable mask returned.

"Is Aulan hurt? Was there a battle?"

"No," he said curtly. "And that is precisely the problem. But what is done is done. Let this be a lesson to you, Severa: Both the truth and mediocrity will always come out in the end, and we are fools to imagine they will not." He shook his head and stared out over the garden, not bothering to conceal his vexation from her. It was clear he had deeper concerns than her prospective betrothal.

Severa reached out and took his free hand in her own. "I'm glad Aulan is well. But I don't know what you mean by that."

"It means that I made a mistake," her father told her grimly. "And it means I may have to reconsider your betrothal."

LODI

THREE days and two abandoned campsites later, Lodi and Thorald discovered why the orcs had been moving so quickly.

Lodi hadn't thought twice about the Ludareka, a wide, aggressive river that ran down from the mountains and eventually made its way into the Elvenlands, where it was known as Elf River. Swollen with snowmelt and the rains that had made their journey eastward a slow and miserable one, the river raged and boiled its way south. They'd previously crossed it much further to the south, over a decaying stone bridge that had been built by the elves of Glaislael many centuries ago and still stood, spanning the river, a mute testament to a defeated and departed civilization. The orcs showed no more inclination to guard that bridge than repair it, so Lodi had assumed it would be a simple matter to travel south along the river until they found a similar bridge and crossed back with the same ease.

However, it seemed that whoever had set the orcs to hunting them had anticipated their need to get across the river and had therefore sent them directly to the nearest bridge. It wasn't that his little trick of climbing out of the water without leaving tracks had prevented the orcs from picking up their trail. It was that they had never wasted any time searching for it. They knew that this rickety wooden structure that hung above the tempestuous, fast, moving water would draw any dwarf hoping to make his way out of the orclands and back to the Underdeep.

With a deepfelt sigh of frustration, Lodi began counting orcs. There were eighteen of them, which gave him a momentary sense of satisfaction that he'd estimated their numbers correctly, more or less.

The sight of the orcs lounging about the wooden supports of the bridge, their boisterous bickering interrupted periodically by the occasional brawl, sent a shiver down his spine.

There was no typical orc intelligence directing them, of this he was certain, although he didn't know if it was the huge shaman, the summoned demon, or something else that was behind this unexpectedly anticipatory action. Regardless, he was worried now in a way that he had not been when they were hiding out before. Because he expected that, in addition to this group that had been ordered to rush to the bridge to cut off their retreat, there were probably one or more similar groups carefully combing the forests behind them, looking for signs of their passing. This required thought, but first they needed to put some distance between them and the orcs.

He indicated that Thorald should follow, and they walked north along the river until Lodi felt they were sufficiently far from the guarded bridge.

He went to the river's edge and sat down.

There were too many of them to openly attack. If they got lazy and the guards fell asleep, they might be able to sneak across, but even then, he had to assume they'd been ordered to sleep on the bridge itself. They couldn't fly across, and the river was too wide to loop a rope across a branch on the other side. He could attach a rope to a crossbow bolt and fire it into a tree, and they could use it to pull themselves through the rapids and across the river. But he doubted it would hold the weight of a dwarf, given the force of the rushing water.

Building a raft seemed their best bet, but it would be risky. Very risky, since they'd have to enter the water at night. He couldn't swim, and he doubted Thorald could, so even if they weren't spotted by the orcs or smashed onto rocks, a simple upsetting would be enough to finish them. What were their chances? Perhaps one in ten? There wasn't even any guarantee they'd be able to make it to the other side. They might float miles down the river, only to end up on the same side of it on which they'd started. And poling across wasn't an option either, given the depth of the river.

Then a thought struck him. The river was deep, and if his memory served him correctly, it flowed all the way to the sea. So there was a chance—perhaps not one in ten, more like one in a hundred, but at least failure meant only that he'd have to figure out something else. He dug through his pack and withdrew one of the two gold coins he'd rescued from the dragon's hoard, then he took the waterstone he used for keeping his blades sharp out of his belt pouch.

"What are you doing?" Thorald asked.

"I'd think it was obvious. I'm grinding gold dust."

"Yes, I can see that! I mean, why are you doing that?"

"Got an idea for crossing the river."

Thorald looked from the bowl to the river, perplexed. "You can't think we'll get across that river without a bridge!"

"No, I don't. We won't."

"Do you think there might be a ford?"

"Nope. Too close to the mountains. That water is coming down hard and fast. And it's deep. I bet we could go south a hundred miles without finding a place shallow enough to walk across it."

Thorald watched him work. "How are you going to make a bridge out of a little gold dust?"

Lodi ignored the question and drew his knife from his belt. He ran the wickedly sharp blade across the tip of the little finger on his left hand, then squeezed it until there was a small quantity of blood in the bowl.

"Are you some sort of alchemist?" Thorald asked, seeming a little alarmed by the sight of the knife and the blood.

"Nope," Lodi said, still squeezing his fingertip. "See, they got keen noses, especially for blood. But they love gold almost as much as we dwarves do. So if there are any of them within a few miles of here, this here mixture should bring them in a hurry."

"Bring what, naiads? Who is 'they'? The river god?"

"The river god? I hope not, we don't want the bridge washed out—
we got to cross it!" Lodi scoffed as he poured out about half the bloody
contents of the bowl into the river. "And what use would river sylphs be
against a troop of orcs? Just keep your eyes open and be real civil if they
show up. Don't be waving your hammer at them or anything stupid, all
right?"

"If what shows up?" Thorald asked, exasperated.

"You'll know. I guarantee, you'll know. Now, I'm going to get me
some sleep. You're on watch. Keep your eye on the river. And make
yourself useful. Maybe see if you can catch some fish for dinner."

Lodi woke to the sound and scent of frying fish. For a moment, he lay
back and luxuriated in the almost euphoric sense it inspired in him, after
days of eating nothing but stonebiscuit and the occasional raw mountain
squirrel. Then he realized where he was, and he sat up in a panic.

"What are you doing?" he hissed. "Are you mad? Put that out!"

Thorald stared back at him unrepentantly and reached out with his
knife to delicately flip over one of the fish that was roasting on the glowing
coals. "Look at the direction of the wind, Lodi. Even if someone is there
to smell it, there ain't nothing they can do from the other side of the river."

Lodi licked a finger and held it up. Sure enough, the wind was coming
from the east, and it was carrying the smoke from their fire across the
river. Even in the unlikely event that the wind changed slightly and started
carrying the smoke downriver, they could be confident that the orcs at the
bridge to the south wouldn't notice the smell, not with the size of the fires
they made every evening. And considering the odds that were presently
stacked against them, this might be his last chance to get a decent meal in
this life.

"All right, lad. We could use a good meal before we deal with those
buggers at the bridge. How'd you catch them?"

"Dug up some worms and undid a link from my chain. Worked like a trick. This river must be so full of trout I'm surprised we can't just walk over on their backs. I caught two before you even started snoring."

"Smells good." Lodi crouched over the riverbank and poured the remainder of the blood and gold into the rushing waters. "No sign of anything bigger than trout?"

"Nothing except that pike there," Thorald said, pointing to a slender, evil-looking fish that was half again as long as the two trout still waiting to be put on the fire. "These look ready. I wish we had some oil though. Do you want that one?"

Lodi speared the fish with his knife, peeled back the blackened skin, and began eating the flaky white flesh inside. It was marvelous, and if it wasn't the finest meal he'd ever eaten, it was perhaps the one he'd appreciated the most.

He was looking up at the night sky, thinking that tomorrow might not be such a terrible day to die, when there was a large splash right in front of him.

Thorald made a noise that was as close to screaming as it was possible for a dwarf to make and still call himself a dwarf.

"Lodi, what in the blackest name of the Deep Dark is that?" The young dwarf was pointing at an expanding circle that was rapidly flowing downriver and out of sight. Admittedly, it was a very large circle.

"That's something splashing in the water," Lodi said, suddenly feeling that luck might be back on their side. "Apparently something just a bit larger than your pike."

The creature that made the splash suddenly popped up from the water not three armslengths away from him. Despite himself, Lodi very nearly let out a very undwarven sound. It had the head of a dwarf, only smaller, beardless, and more streamlined, the upper body of an elf, though more muscular, and its hips were covered in scales. Several feet behind it in the water, a tail lashed the water.

"What is that?" Thorald said in a hushed voice as the fish-creature pointed downriver and made weird clicking noises at them, punctuated by the occasional eerie screech.

Lodi ignored him and clicked back, albeit much more slowly and without any of the screeches.

The creature rocked back in the water, its dwarf-like features betraying shock, then dove down into the water and disappeared.

"You know how to talk to that thing?" Thorald said, incredulous.

But before he could answer, the wild mer reappeared. This time, it was calmer, and it cocked its head to one side as it stared at Lodi and clicked slowly at him. Lodi clicked back, and it beat its tail against the water in excitement. Lodi used his hand in a similar fashion. They were communicating! He offered it a piece of the cooked fish that had cooled off a little, and the mer wolfed it down in a single bite, revealing two rows of sharp, jagged teeth that looked as if they were capable of biting through a dragon's hide.

Lodi pointed downriver. They exchanged some more clicks. And when it smiled, seemingly pleased, Lodi took a gold coin out of his pouch and gave it to the river monster. It fairly leaped backward, turned a somersault in the water, then surfaced again, clicking madly at him. It slipped into the current, and with one last flick of its tail, disappeared beneath the surface of the water.

"Were you bargaining with it?"

"You can bargain with everything except trolls and devils. Trolls are too stupid, and devils are too damn smart."

"How can you bargain with a fish-man?"

"Well, he thought you were real pretty, so I offered you for its wife if he'd help us clear the bridge in the morning. I gave him the coin to make rings, so he's off to fetch the priest now. He wants to make it all good and proper-like."

"Lodi!"

Lodi chuckled. "Hey, I told you they loved gold. The mer got big kingdoms and all sorts of things going on under the sea. They say they got buildings even bigger than the ones men build in Amorr and Savonne. But they can't smelt metal under the sea, what with it being wet and all, so precious metals are a particular rarity. They mostly get them from trade with sea elves or from shipwrecks. They love shipwrecks! But the river mer, they're the wild ones, and there ain't no shipwrecks in the rivers, so they'll do just about anything to get their hands on some."

"And he smelled it from that dust you put in the water?"

"Well, it was probably the blood that got his attention first. I just put the gold in to make him curious. They don't get a lot of meat other than fish, and they've got noses like sharks."

"What's a shark?" Thorald said. "Anyway, I don't understand how you can talk to them."

"When I was a slave in Amorr, they had this huge stadium called the Colossus where they'd make us fight. Sometimes they'd fill the whole ground with water and bring in ships—to have naval battles, you know. Once, for one of the special ones, they brought in about a score of mer captured by fishermen. The mer fought real good and real clever, so I got to know two of them that survived the bout because we were owned by the same stable. I learned a few words."

"Do you think he understands what you want?"

"Yeah, they're probably smarter than gobbos and orcs. I think he got it, because most of the words I know have to do with fighting, us being fighting slaves and all. He'll bring some others, and they're going to attack the orcs at the bridge in the morning, so we need to be in position to run across."

Thorald frowned, looking dubious as he put the remaining three fish on the coals. "Do you really think they'll come? And how can they attack the orcs from the water?"

"You'll see." Lodi picked a little bone from his teeth and flicked it into the river. "They'll be there because I promised him another coin and some fresh meat. No way they'll want to miss out on that."

"Meat? It's already dark! How are we going to find any squirrels or deer now?"

"No need for that." Lodi smiled grimly. "When we cross that bridge tomorrow, just be sure to throw an orc or two in the water for our new friends."

AULAN

I T was with more trepidation than relief that Aulan slid off his horse at the foot of the steep slopes of the Quinctiline and handed the reins to one of his father's stable slaves. It was good to know that he wouldn't have to spend another day in the saddle, fear his horse breaking down under their merciless pace, or get caught up in whatever plebian lunacy had caused the fires and destruction he'd seen riding through the Vicus Anser.

Still, he dreaded facing Patronus's reaction to the news that the Valerian legion had escaped the traps set for it. Not being privy to his father's plans, he had no idea if this was nothing more than a minor setback or a disaster that could trigger a civil war between the Houses Martial, but regardless, there was no chance that he would be pleased.

Aulan wasn't much happier about the familiar climb uphill he now faced on legs that were bowed and aching from nearly two weeks on horseback. It had taken several generations of persistent effort, and ultimately an appointment as the pro-praetorial governor of Ptolus Triticus, for his great-great-grandfather to convince Quinctilius Quantuvis to sell him the great manor that now served as the heart of House Severus in Amorr. It held a commanding view of the western half of the city, one that was second only to that possessed by the Sanctiff in his palace atop the Inculpatine. And while its location served as a useful reminder of Severan power to visiting clients and rivals alike, Aulan had come to loathe the tiring ascent from the base to the peak even as a child. Even if it weren't for his reluctance to face his father, the long march uphill would have been very nearly the last thing he wanted to do.

"It's not my fault," he told himself as he removed his leather gloves and beat them against his thigh in a mostly fruitless attempt to shake some of the caked-on dust from them. "I wasn't in command. I wasn't even there, for the most part. And I didn't have enough horse to hunt that damned legion without risk of being caught by their cavalry. Coming back here to give a few days' warning was the only sensible thing to do!"

It had been the only sensible thing to do. He was sure of it. But if he was right, why had he spent most of the exhausting ride back to the city trying to convince himself? Why was he still trying to convince himself now? Perhaps, he thought, because in his place, Patronus would have simply stripped Falconius Buteo of his command and ordered the young Valerian tribune to surrender his legion by virtue of his own self-declared authority—and somehow it would have worked. Regulus, on the other hand, would have launched a bold, dashing, and suicidally insane attack with his badly outnumbered cavalry wing. In that case everyone, including their father, would praise his brilliant heroics despite the loss of all his men while accomplishing precisely nothing.

A pretty house slave's double-take as he entered the front door and walked past her made him smile and helped distract him from his worries for a moment. She had the sort of dark, sensual eyes he hadn't seen during several months in the north, and he made a mental note to discover her name in the unlikely event his father left him with his evening free.

He turned a corner, saw there was someone in the smaller of the mansion's two triclinia, and frowned at whom he saw dining there. It wasn't the sight of his older brother reclining on a coach that offended him, pompous ass though he was, but the six men with him whom he recognized as being men of the principalities, not the city. One of them might have even been a provincial, judging by the outlandish cloth cap he was wearing on his head as if he were some sort of jester.

"Have you turned merchant, then, Regulus?" Aulan asked, drawing himself to his full height and placing his hand on his sword hilt. "Or are you going considerably further afield these days in search of your debaucheries?"

"Aulan?" His brother's eyes widened, and he was sufficiently startled to sit upright with such suddenness that he upended a wooden cheese tray and sent its contents rolling across the marble floor. "Saint's bones, what are you doing here? Shouldn't you be with Falconius Buteo?"

Aulan scowled at his older brother, whose face was flushed with wine already though the sun was barely past its zenith. "I'm hardly going to discuss either House or legion business in front of your friends, Regulus. Who are they, and what are they doing here?"

"We are guests of your father, Lord Severus." One man rose from the couch he was sharing with the man in the oversized cap and bowed to him. "Your lord brother has been kindly keeping us company as we wait for our audiences with the most noble princeps. I am Opelius Macrinus, and I am here representing the interests of the High Prince of Oscium, if it please you, my lord. Am I correct in understanding you are Aulus Severus, the younger?"

Aulan had no idea what the man was babbling about, nor was he pleased, but the idea that their presence here wasn't Regulus's fault did manage to penetrate the red fog of his irritation. And if they were indeed his father's guests, then he had damned well better stop embarrassing himself. Even a son had no right to question the dominus of the household, still less if that dominus also happened to be the head of a patrician House.

"You are correct, sir. I apologize for my rudeness, Macrinus, and beg the pardon of you gentlemen, as well. I have been away from Amorr for some time with my legion and, as you can probably tell from the state of my attire, have only just now arrived in the city. I did not mean to be a bore."

The Osciite and the other five men were quick to assure him that they had taken no offense and that it was indeed a veritable pleasure to make his acquaintance, however unexpectedly. And they were all obviously intrigued, Macrinus in particular, by the fact that Aulan was wearing leather armor bearing the unmistakable signs of a long and hurried journey. Given the practiced eye with which the Osciite looked him over, Aulan had little doubt that the man had identified him as a tribune and a knight.

He was tempted to ask the man what his business was that had brought him to the heart of House Severus, but resisted the urge, knowing that the attempt to pry would only make him look weak. And besides, if he cared to, he could learn it easily enough from his father or the one of the slaves later.

"Well, gentleman, if you don't mind, I am eager to see my mother and sisters, so I shall take my leave of you now. Regulus, I imagine we shall see each other later."

His brother waved a languid hand in dismissal. One of his reclining visitors sat up and poured yet more wine for him. It was just what Regulus needed, Aulan thought sourly. If they were lucky, he'd pass out before saying anything he shouldn't.

"Lord Aulan," he heard a familiar voice call.

He turned and saw Delmatipor, the majordomus, walking quickly toward him. The bald slave smiled broadly and held out his meaty arms to embrace him despite the immaculate white robes in which he was clad.

"Delma, your robes," Aulan protested.

But the majordomus was having none of it.

"The laundry girls are too lazy anyhow," he said, thumping Aulan's back as he hugged him. "It's good to see you back safely, boy. The household has been praying for you every night since we heard about the legion's defeat in the north."

Aulan grinned. Regulus was his father's favorite and Tertius his mother's, but he'd always been the closest to Delmatipor, the true master of the manor.

"Is it safe to assume you will profit from my return, Master Delma?"

"There may be a few guardsmen who won't be as delighted to see you as perhaps they should be, my lord."

"I suppose it's just as well I came home unannounced, then, isn't it?"

Delmatipor only smiled and shook his head. "There's no harm in it. You've been in the legions long enough now to know the way of it."

He had a point, Aulan decided. "Yes, well, I suppose you must be right. It's good to see you too, Master. Is my father here? And speaking of Father, who are those men drinking Regulus off his couch in the triclinium minus? Are they truly his guests?"

"I am afraid so, my lord."

"What are they doing here?"

The majordomus spread his hands and shrugged. "I really couldn't say, Lord Aulan. Your father trusts me to oversee his household, but he seldom confides in me concerning Senatorial business, much less foreign affairs. Though I don't think I would overstep myself to observe there have been a remarkable number of provincials passing through of late. If you'll just follow me, I will take you to him, and you can ask him yourself."

As they strode through the marble floored halls together, Aulan occasionally being welcomed home by slaves who recognized him, Delmatipor filled him in on the latest family gossip. He would not, however, reveal the name of the man Patronus had chosen as his sister's betrothed, and Aulan's curiosity grew with each stubborn shake of the majordomus's head. The door of the scriptorium was closed, and to Aulan's surprise, Delmatipor knocked rather than simply entering.

"We've had some unusual guests of late," he replied in response to Aulan's querying glance.

Aulan heard his father's voice bark a less than courteous invitation to enter, and when the majordomus opened the door for him, he was astonished to see, seated across the desk from his father, a large man he had seen many times in the Forum, but one whom he would never have expected to make the arduous Quinctiline climb. He was too surprised to say anything, but fortunately, his father was nearly as surprised to see him.

"Aulan!" he exclaimed, rising from his chair. "You're filthy, did you just arrive? You must have ridden hard—I only received your letter the day before yesterday. Delma, see that you make sure the boiler for the caldarium is stoked. I imagine he'll be wanting to bathe soon."

The other man had risen too. "You must be Severus Aulan," he said, assessing him with the practiced eye of a former legionary commander.

"At your service, Senator."

The big senator exchanged an amused glance with his father. "I take it he has not heard the happy news? You must address me as Magnus, my boy, as we are all but family now. Your sister will be marrying my youngest son, Sextus, in the spring."

"That is… wonderful news indeed, Magnus. Please convey my sincere congratulations to your son." Aulan managed to simultaneously smile and get the words out without either choking on them or glancing quizzically at his father. What the hell was he thinking, marrying Severa to a Valerian?

"Cool young customer, isn't he?" remarked Magnus approvingly. "Patronus, if his commander can spare him an additional day or two, he might be the very one to seal the deal we were discussing."

"Indeed," his father commented noncommittally. "Aulan, did you bring any of your men?"

"A few," he answered truthfully. He didn't wish to mention in front of the head of House Valerius that in this case, a few happened to mean two squadrons. That would tend to raise serious questions as to why those twenty knights were missing from their legion, and it wouldn't take long for a well-connected retired general such as Valerius Magnus to find the answers.

"Consider it done," Patronus promised Magnus.

Magnus had the good grace to bow slightly.

"Excellent. If your son has any interesting news of developments in the north, I should appreciate being informed of them at your earliest convenience. In the meantime, I will ensure that Sextus is on the tribunal ballot, as we agreed."

"I rejoice to hear it," Patronus averred drily. "You will be at the next assembly?"

"I look forward to it, my lord princeps. Until then."

"Until then." Patronus gestured toward the majordomus. "Master Delmatipor will escort you to the gate, and if you should require anything further of House Severus, you have only to ask, Magnus."

The Valerian nodded to the bald slave and preceded him from the room.

Aulan stared at his father in silent disbelief as Patronus went to the door and closed it, then turned around.

"You look rather like a fish, with that expression," his father commented. "Albeit fish are seldom so covered in dirt, seeing as they tend to dwell in the water. You look as if you've ridden hard. What does 'a few men' mean?"

"Two squadrons." It was easier to focus on the small things. "I'm sorry, Father, but as I wrote you in my letter, the Valerian legion escaped. The assassins missed two of the junior tribunes, who then contrived to get past Buteo and the Cynothii."

"By digging a tunnel under the walls? How on Earth did Buteo miss that? Is the man a cretin?"

"No, but he was too confident in his position. Corvus's son is the tribune commanding, I think, and the lad managed to cut me off from the legion when he captured Vestremer and his men. Vestremer was the captain of the Cynothi mounted infantry, which I really have to say were actually a rather good idea for all that it didn't turn out well in this situation...."

"Aulan," his father broke in.

"Right, I'm sorry. Anyhow, I was trying to work my way back to Buteo when, fortunately, one of my scouts spotted their outriders. I sent a pair of riders to see what was going on and saw that the whole bloody legion was on the move, marching west. As soon as I reported to Buteo to let him know which way they were headed, I rode hell for leather here to warn you. I didn't dare try to shadow them, since Corvus established two wings of cavalry when he raised the legion, and I had only half a wing."

"West. I would have thought they'd make directly for Vallyria to winter there."

"My thought was that he's hoping to join forces with the two Valerian legions that remained in Gorignia. Do you know who is commanding them?"

"Yes, of course. Titus Didius succeeded Corvus. He's officially the general responsible for the goblin campaign. But Didius didn't remain in Gorignia—he marched them south to Vallyria. Your young tribune will find their castras abandoned and empty. It's a pity Buteo is so incompetent. I'd hoped we could take control of XVII now. That would have given us nearly three full legions in the north bolstering the provincials. But now, with Corvus holding the City legion plus his three House legions, we might be looking at our one and one-half legions against their four, come spring."

"But that's a disaster!" Aulan cried, suddenly realizing how precarious their situation had unexpectedly become. "Even if we could get the other provinces to join with the Cynothii, we still wouldn't have enough men to make up a difference of three legions!"

"Two and one-half," his father corrected. "It would certainly be a military disaster, my dear tribune. But fortunately, this is not a matter to be settled on the battlefield. Don't worry too much about the tactical aspects while the strategic battle is still playing out."

"I don't understand what you're doing," Aulan said. "How can you be so unconcerned about that failure to take the Valerian legion? That leaves the balance of power in their favor! And where does Magnus come into all of this?"

"I wasn't unconcerned, not initially. I was very worried, especially if our part in the untimely deaths of Marcus Saturnius and the others became public knowledge. But the loose ends have been dealt with, and some new developments have potentially rendered even Buteo's incompetence a matter of little concern."

"Valerius Magnus, I assume." Aulan folded his arms and eyed his father skeptically. "What sort of deal could you possibly strike with him? He's been a thorn in your side for decades. It's not as if he's going to come over to your side."

"Our side." His father smiled enigmatically, looking rather like an eagle about to strike. "And yet that's precisely what he's done."

Aulan was astonished. House Valerius was putting its not inconsiderable weight behind the auctores? That would leave the Falconians as the only House Martial of any significance supporting the clausores, a shift so significant it might even justify calling off the civil war they'd labored so tirelessly to prepare.

"The Valerians are with us?"

His father shook his bald head. "Sadly, no. Only Magnus himself. He may be the Head of the House, but that is a step he can't force them to take with him. The feelings run too deep. The bitterness is too severe."

"Even so…" Aulan's voice trailed off as he marveled at his father's ability to persuade even his worst enemy. "How did you do it? What do you have to do to seal the deal you were discussing?"

"Ask, rather, what you will do," Patronus said. Unexpectedly, his face tightened with distaste. "It's an ugly business, son, make no mistake. But when Domina Fortuna offers you her hand, take it you must, for she will seldom make the same offer twice. The opportunity is simply too great to be declined out of delicacy."

"What does Magnus ask of you?" Aulan had no idea what the answer would be. He was, however, fairly certain he wouldn't like it.

"Magnus has a nephew by the name of Corvinus. He left Amorr about six years ago and manages some family estates in Vallyria. He's a good man, from what I'm told, for all his lack of ambition. Married, two children. And it seems Magnus would be very grateful to House Severus, very grateful indeed, if you would kill him."

Aulan stared at his father in silence for a long moment, until it became clear that he wasn't joking. "You're not seriously intending on doing the man's dirty work for him, are you? I'm a soldier, Father, I'm not a damned assassin. I'm not a murderer! Why the hell would Magnus want his nephew dead anyhow? Did auntie visit the farm and get herself raped or something?"

"He has his reasons." Patronus shrugged. "You're not merely a soldier, son: You're an officer, a tribune. You've killed men with your own hand, and you've killed men by ordering them to their deaths. Dead is dead, Aulan, whether it comes to a man on the battlefield, in his bed, or on the street. We kill this one man for Magnus, and we may prevent a war that will see legion pitted against legion, House Martial against House Martial, and Amorran against Amorran. I've been speaking for peace in the Senate for twelve years, Aulan—twelve years, and the wretched old fools are no more inclined to listen today than they listened to me then. Maybe one life sacrificed for peace won't be enough to please the fates. God knows they are cruel, cruel bitches. But we have to try. We really have to try."

Aulan sighed. He saw his father's point. They'd shed enough Amorran blood, sacrificed enough Amorran lives, in trying to save the Senate and People from themselves. Why shirk at one more? Still, the notion of simply murdering an innocent man, even if he was a Valerian, stuck in his craw.

"Isn't there someone else you could use? I just got here—I really don't want to ride all the way to Vallyria now." Aulan knew he was whining, but he couldn't help it. For God's sake, he hadn't even managed to wash his hands yet and here his father was asking him to bloody them!

"Of course there are others I could use. But there is no one else I could trust so well. And you needn't complain. There is no need to ride to Vallyria. Magnus's nephew is right here, in the city, visiting his father."

Aulan gave up. It seemed both the fates and his father were conspiring against him. "Very well," he nodded with reluctant obedience. "I'll see to it. I suppose I should be happy that if someone needs to die, at least it's a damned Valerian."

CORVINUS

S ERVIUS Valerius smiled as a mocking toast was made to him by
his old friend Opimius. Opimius was only a knight, but he had
always been the smartest of his friends, and now that he had
cobbled together a group of investors to purchase the tax-farming rights to
Falera, Fescennium, and Solacte, the three largest cities in Larinum, he was
considered to be one of the leading up-and-comers of their generation. He
would never serve in the Senate, but it wouldn't surprise Corvinus in the
least if in ten years Opimius were more influential than half the patricians
in the Senate.

Opimius was a short, ruddy-faced, passionate man, with bright eyes
and the voice of a much taller, deeper-chested man. He commanded the
attention of the seven other men in the triclinium with ease, even though
he was the only plebian present. He gestured grandly with his goblet,
causing the wine within it to slosh audibly around, somehow without
spilling a drop. He was well into his cups, and yet his voice wasn't the least
bit slurred as he returned to abusing his friends for their lack of ambition,
a theme with which Corvinus was more familiar than most.

"What use are your noble bloodlines, my friends? What use is it,
Ponticus, to be treasured for that which runs so sluggishly within your
veins? What satisfaction do you find in displaying the painted statues of
your ancestors, an armless Arvina, a crumbling Caecus, a Calatanus who
has lost his forearm, or a Galus with neither ears nor nose? What does
it prosper you to boast a Maximus or a Magnus"—and here he nodded
at Corvinus—"in your family line and number consuls and censors and

Masters of the Horse among your rotted forefathers, if you carouse the night away and are woken by your slaves at noon?

"What valor do all the effigies of warriors past convey upon you, if the only bones you see are not on the battlefield but rolling upon the floors of whorehouses? You drink yourselves to oblivion and go to bed with the rise of the Light-bringer, at a bell when the generals of yore would be raising their standards as the legions began their march!"

He stopped to drink from his goblet.

Ponticus pointed to it, laughing.

"You would deny your betters the fruit of the vine, Opimius, when you yourself have drunk more than any man here?"

Opimius shook his finger and tilted his head as he fixed Ponticus with a somber stare. "Do not bind the mouths of the kine who thresh the grain, my friend. It is solely in your interest that I lecture you. Look at Servius Valerius here. He is the nephew of a consul, and now, the son of a consul!"

"Hail Valerius!" Rubellius Drusus cried, raising his goblet.

"Hail Corvus," Opimius agreed, joining the others in a toast to Corvinus's father.

Corvinus chuckled and sipped at his wine. He was pretty sure he knew where Opimius was going with all this. In fact, he rather suspected it was the purpose for the dinner Lucretius Ponticus had hosted tonight. He had no intention whatsoever of being yoked to serve his old friend's ambition, but he was determined to enjoy himself and see what madness Opimius had concocted now.

"My friends and countrymen," Opimius said, "though you bear the names of generals and heroes, you must know that virtue is the only true nobility. An aristocracy of aspiration, a society of public service—these are the eternal elites to which we must aspire! Model yourselves on a Paullus, a Causus, or a Demian. Do not spend your days languishing in the halls populated only by the lifeless statues of your ancestors. Let their noble spirits serve as your fascitors when you walk among the City as its consul!

"You owe me, my friends. You owe me the effort that my blood denies me. You owe me that walk that my humble ancestry forbids me! Leave your brothels and your baths, leave your stinking swine shit and whatever else it is you do in those savage and uncivilized lands, Corvinus, and I will name you a new Lucius Quinctius and acknowledge you as a lord among lords!"

"Lucius Quinctius went back to his farm, you know, Opimius," Corvinus drawled, amused by the fervor of his friend's appeal.

"After he saved his country!" Opimius wagged his finger again. "Only after he saved his country! Serve the Senate and People, Corvinus! Set your feet upon the path of honor once more, and you can return to your damnable pigs and chickens in their own time!"

"I'm not running for aedile, Opimius. I have no interest in it. Besides, there isn't time to raise the funds."

Opimius grinned and Drusus cleared his throat.

Corvinus swore under his breath. Dammit, he'd walked right into that one.

"Actually, Servius Valerius, you needn't worry about that." Ponticus gestured around the triclinium at the four other patricians. "We've arranged for the loans you'll need to secure the election. Gnaeus Palfurius is willing to wait a year in return for four hundred thousand sesterces and a promise of House Valerius's support, and Drusus has confirmed that House Falconius and House Horatius will throw their support to you over the Gaeran they were originally backing."

"How?" Corvinus demanded, wondering what that support would cost.

"Let's just say Falconius Metius and Horatius Pulvillus readily grasped the logic of putting their weight behind the new consul's son." Rubellius Drusus was thin and red-haired. His family called him Rufus. He was a moderately talented poet, and he waved his long-fingered hand theatrically as he reclined on his couch. "They know perfectly well that your father will win the next election without needing to buy so much as a single vote, and they don't see any point in wasting any more of their investment in Gaerus Balbus when the tribes that vote for Corvus will vote for Corvinus as well."

His six friends looked at him expectantly, waiting for him to say something. Corvinus merely stared at them in silence, wondering how on Earth he was going to convince them that he wanted nothing more than to return to his farm in Vallyria as soon as the winter festival was over.

"Come on, Corvinus," Drusus finally said. "How can you possibly think to keep yourself occupied on your estates?"

Corvinus stared in disbelief at his younger friend, who was expected to run for aedile the year after next. Were they really all so effete and hopelessly urbanized as to be ignorant of the back-breaking labor that was the agricultural life? He glanced from the gold necklace around Opimius's neck to the rich purple hues of Ponticus's tunic and realized they very probably were. He laughed and pointed to the remains of the fat turbot they had so appreciatively devoured over the course of the evening, lying in disarray on the large silver platter.

"Gentlemen, you do realize that, unlike that noble fish there, the countless pigs, cows, and chickens which contribute to your table do not wander to the city of their own accord. Opimius excoriated you for crawling back to your beds at sunrise, an hour when I am already feeding the swine and milking the cows. It takes six months of that to raise a hog to a size worth slaughtering. And let me tell you, butchering a beast twice the weight of a man is no easy task. This is to say nothing of sowing the fields, threshing the grain, mashing the grapes…. My friends, you should only marvel that I could find a few days to come here now that the harvest is done!"

Ponticus and the others stared at Corvinus in bewilderment.

But Opimius laughed. "See how his industry shames us! Is this not a man well worthy of one day sitting in his father's chair!"

"I don't see why he doesn't simply set a few slaves to the chores and have done with it," Ponticus said with a disdainful air. "Corvinus, you wretched man, only agree to run, and I'll send a score of slaves to your estate, each with more muscles than a gladiator, to milk your pigs and slaughter your grapes."

"Very well, in that case, I'll consider it," Corvinus promised, only half-insincerely, being genuinely touched by their faith in him.

His friends broke into a rousing cheer.

But he stopped them by raising a hand in warning. "I'm not promising anything, you understand. I'll need to talk to my wife, and I imagine it would be wise to take the opinion of the Consul Suffectus into account, as well."

"Of course, of course," assured Opimius, but he was grinning as if he'd backed the winning gladiator in an all-comers bout. "Just let us know by the end of the week."

"To Servius Valerius, the next Curule Aedile!" called Ponticus.

"Corvinus, Curule Aedile!" the others cried.

Corvinus rolled his eyes, but he had to grin at his friends' enthusiasm. They were truly the best of men, and it would be a pity to disappoint them. Had he not once shared their dreams of making the world a better place? And, he thought, it was even possible that a change wouldn't be the worst thing for him now. Julia would certainly enjoy moving back to the city for a while, and his mother would love to have the two grandchildren living where it wouldn't take her several weeks to visit them.

"No, to you, my friends," he raised his goblet to them. "I declare that no man has ever been more fortunate in his companions than me."

Two bells and several goblets of wine later, Corvinus was wrapped in his cloak and making his unsteady way through the winding bricked streets in the general direction of his father's domus. He was not alone. Ponticus had invited him to stay the night, as a severely intoxicated Opimius was already snoring on one of the couches, but when Corvinus had refused, Ponticus had insisted that he accept an escort of two armed slaves bearing torches. The cold winter air had somewhat shocked him back to his senses, and by the time he'd crossed the second street away from

Ponticus's residence he had firmly decided to refuse the aedileship and return to Vallyria.

Caught up in his thoughts, he didn't initially hear the men standing on the corner he was passing call out to him. Only when the slaves preceding him suddenly stopped and he nearly walked into them did he realize anything might be amiss.

"Keep your hands off them hilts, boys," a thickset bearded man holding a thick wooden staff warned the two slaves.

Corvinus felt a jolt of fear run through his body as he counted six, no seven, men stepping out of the shadows to confront them. He'd heard that the city had become increasingly chaotic of late. Even during daylight in some of the poorer quarters. But the thought that the crime and unrest might have reached this close to his family's neighborhood had never occurred to him.

"Pardon me, gentlemen, but I would ask you to step aside. I'm but a simple farmer. I have no purse or anything of value to give you."

"Don't sell yourself so short, Valerius Corvinus," he heard an educated voice behind him say. For a moment, he felt relief, thinking it might be one of his friends. But when he turned around, he saw a tall young man with deepset eyes and a bony face that, in the dancing torchlight, made him look rather like a dark angel. A Severan, unless he missed his guess. And he too was holding a staff, although his was more of a walking stick, painted black with iron bands on either end. "Value is entirely subjective."

"Who are you, sir?" Corvinus asked him, a little nervously. "And why do you know my name?"

"I know a Valerian when I see one." The young man grinned humorlessly. "I'm afraid you had the misfortune to be born into the wrong House. But for what it's worth, I do apologize."

"For what?"

The Severan, if he indeed was a Severan, grimaced. "For this."

Pain exploded under Corvinus's chin as the lower end of the black stick flicked up and snapped his head back. He could taste blood in his mouth and felt the rough brick surface of the nearby building smash against his back.

Corvinus tried to spin away from his attacker, but a second blow from the stick in his stomach doubled him over. He could hear the sounds of the two slaves struggling nearby, but it seemed they were as helpless to defend themselves as he was.

"No, please!" he cried out, barely managing to hold up one of his hands in desperate supplication. It was a futile gesture, as a third strike, this one to the left side of his head, dropped him to his knees. A moment later, the fourth one sent him into the merciful darkness.

SEVERA

HE was handsome, Severa had to admit as she watched her prospective husband walk down the stone steps and into the garden. Sextus Valerius carried himself with confidence as he approached her, and he didn't so much as glance at the armed guards who stood on either side of the staircase. His tunic was the maroon and light grey of his House, over which he wore a light blue cloak with a gold clasp in the shape of the crossed swords that indicated his was one of the Houses Martial. The cloak was perhaps a little much, especially given the easily recognizable colors, but the light blue went beautifully well with them, and the overall effect was both striking and effortlessly aristocratic. The only question was whether the deft touch was his own or someone else's?

She wished she had thought to wear Severan colors instead of the dark red gown her mother had selected for her the night before. It suited her well, but not half so well as his sartorial statement suited him. She felt at an unexpected disadvantage.

"My lady." He bowed gracefully once he had come within a few steps of her. His eyes were a very light brown, she saw as they met her own.

"Valerian," she replied, a little coldly.

"Ah," he said, raising his head, and a faint smile pulled at the corner of his mouth. It was, she noted with some annoyance, a rather charming smile. "Am I correct in understanding that I need not recite the various homages to your charms I had prepared?"

"As it suits you. You need not state the obvious. I am young, beautiful, and the daughter of the first man in the City. Otherwise you would not be here."

"Are you so certain, my lady?" he asked with a rueful snort. "Given the last, I suspect my father would have sought you for my bride even if you were old, ugly, and repellent. How fortunate for me that is not the case. We need not be at daggers simply because our Houses have long been enemies."

"Rivals, not enemies," she corrected him, just as her father had corrected her. "I concur, but there is a great distance between sheathed daggers and a marital alliance."

"A marital alliance? Say rather, a marriage, my lady. Houses and nations ally. Men and women marry."

She examined his face closely. His features were good and his bones were strong, but she could see the weakness of character beneath them. He was more horse than lion, wolf, or bear, with a slight skittishness that belied his apparent self-possession. He had the broad shoulders and slender waist of an athlete, but he had neither the rounded muscles of the gladiators nor the lean, wiry power of Aulan and other men of the legions she knew. His was the athleticism of the baths, not the battlefield. It gave him the soft appearance of a boyish innocence she had not expected from a son of the most warlike of the Houses Martial.

"You are not what I expected," she told him, a little more honestly than she'd intended.

"Are you sure you don't want to hear my homages?" Sextus smiled more openly now. "My father has some excellent poets who wrote some truly compelling verse. I swear, I very nearly fell in love with old Lucipor when he was reciting me my lines." He punctuated the self-deprecating remark by raising his eyebrows.

And suddenly she felt he had given her the key she required to understand him. He was the youngest son of a great man whose approval he could never hope to gain. That was why he had not embarked upon the cursus honorum and why he was so willing to portray himself as a clown. For all his seeming confidence and relaxed demeanor, he was an empty vessel of self-doubt. Most likely, he had figured out early in his youth that the only way he could avoid losing was to refuse to play the game. He was quick to diminish himself—so that his father, or perhaps his older brothers, could not do it for him. It was a habit she had long observed in Tertius, who, despite his keen intelligence, was never able to live up to the example set by their father or even the lesser examples of their dashing brothers.

And, it was something to which she could relate. No daughter, however ambitious, could hope to sit in her father's chair.

She nodded slowly, taking in his good looks and the tall, powerful frame he would impart to their children. His mind was not a dull one either, not with his easy wit and the vaguely mischievous sparkle in his eyes. He was something with which she could work, someone with whom she could work, that much was clear. His potential was unlimited, raw and ignored though it might be.

But would the clay be amenable to the potter's shaping? Did he harbor any ambitions of his own, or had they been crushed out of him under the considerable weight of his House and family?

"You are a gambler," she stated. It was not a question.

"Aren't we all? If I have heard correctly, even my lady has been occasionally known to place a wager or two at the games."

She caught her breath, taken aback by his unexpectedly cutting retort. How much did he know? Was his reference to her wagers the innocent and obvious response of one who had seen her at the games, or was it an oblique reference to her near-affair with Clusius? Could it even be that he was somehow connected to those behind the machinations against House Severus?

No, she realized as she looked closely at him. He was here to win her, not to prosecute her, and there was no expression of satisfaction on his face, instead, he looked almost comically wounded, as if a trusted hound had nipped him in the backside without warning. He was not counter-attacking—he was only lashing out in self-defense.

"I fear you mistake me, Valerian. I have no objection to a sporting wager. I find it adds somewhat to the spice of the event, don't you? What interests me is the extent of your gambling habits. Does it only extend so far as the plebian games of bones and stones, or do you wish to play for nobler stakes? I am the daughter of the princeps senatus, the grand-daughter of consuls, and the great-granddaughter of consuls. I have no regard for men, however noble their birth, however grand their House, who content themselves with children's games and end up as bankrupt clients dependent upon the largesse of their kin."

The Valerian folded his arms and frowned at her. But for the first time since he'd entered the garden, he was truly paying attention to her now, not to her face or her body, but to the woman inside.

"I may play what you call children's games, my lady. But I would not say I am content with them. Still, what would you have me say? Shall I tread the path of my fathers on the cursus honorum? Shall I join the legions, only to butcher men who have done nothing to me and want only to live their lives without Amorr's heel on their necks? One of my brothers died a tribune this summer, and for what? To teach a few wretched goblins not to harass a few miserable farmers? You have two brothers in the legions, my lady. Would you sacrifice them for such a gallant cause? Would you sacrifice your husband for it?"

"No," she shook her head. "I would not. But, my lord, I think you mistake the path for the destination."

"Do I?" Sextus asked. She could hear barely concealed pain in his voice. "Let us say I declared this fall and won election as tribunus militum, though I am well past my year. No doubt my father can arrange it. And then, I take my oath, and I join one of the House legions. My brother lived for the glory of battle and the honor of the legions, and my duty-mad uncle had his head for it. How long would someone like me survive? A week? A month? I'm no coward, Lady Severus, but neither am I a fool. I would risk the swords of the provincials, the clubs of the orcs, and the axes of the dwarves without flinching, but I have no desire to find myself under the executioner's axe of my own officers, of my own relations!"

She smiled to herself, more than satisfied with his answer. He wasn't merely intelligent, he was sensible, which her father had always told her was the rarer trait of the two. And who could fault him for lacking ambition when it seemed likely to lead him to an early grave? Better yet, he had an instinctive understanding for the inherent weakness of his House, their rigid pride in their outdated traditions.

"House Valerius is not the only House Martial, my lord. Have you forgotten that House Severus fields two legions of its own?"

"I had, actually. Or rather, I had never considered that I might serve with another legion besides our three."

"It is hardly unheard of, at least for those who aren't weighed down by Valerian pride. It may be your House tradition, but it does not hold the force of law."

"Tell my uncle that," he laughed, a little bitterly, but his demeanor brightened with unexpected hope. "Fulgetra, and what is the other, the third legion? Do you think your father would find a place for me in one of them?"

"For his son-in-law? I have no doubt of it. My brother Regulus was with Legio III when he was a tribune, and Aulan now commands Fulgetra's knights."

"My brother did the same in XVII," he said. "That's what got him killed. He defeated the enemy's captain of cavalry in a duel and led his horse in a charge that scattered the goblin army, and my uncle had him executed. For that, they made him consul suffectus!"

"I am sorry for your loss," she told him, and she found that she was almost sincere even though she had laughed when she'd first heard the news. "But I think you need not fear a general of House Severus doing the same. We revere courage. We do not sacrifice it to our pride or to cruel and stupid customs."

"Virtus et civitas," he cited her House's motto. Courage and citizenship.

"You see, you already know what it means to be a Severan, my lord Valerius."

Sextus tilted his head. "I had thought that, were we to marry, you should become Valerius, not I Severus."

She placed a hand on his chest and smiled up at him. "My name is Severa, is it not? And it will be Severa still, should I marry you. As yours will be Valerius, in any case. The question at hand, my lord, is whether you intend your name to one day be Sextus Valerius Illustris or something more akin to Sextus Valerius Pusillus. Do you wish to always be known as the wastrel son of Valerius Magnus, or do you want to become your own man?"

He grinned again, in that skeptical manner she was beginning to find increasingly appealing. "My own man, or your own?"

"If we two are to become one, is there a difference?" She stepped back from him and folded her arms. "I will be perfectly frank with you, Sextus Valerius: The man I marry will walk the cursus honorum, and one day, he will take his rightful place on a chair at the front of the Senate. His sons and grandsons will be soldiers, senators, and consuls in their year. If that is not the manner of man you intend yourself to be, if that is not a future to which you are willing to commit yourself, then you may walk freely from this place with your conscience clear and tell your father that you found me to be wholly unsuitable as a prospective bride."

He blinked at her, mutely. "Um, you come with an unusual dowry, Lady Severa."

"It's not a dowry, Sextus Valerius. It's a price. You are handsome, you are said to be charming, you have considerable promise, and my father has his own reasons for seeking this alliance between our Houses. So I have no objection to your suit so long as you promise me one thing. Just one thing."

"The handsome and charming young suitor quails before asking the obvious, until a phrase springs unbidden to his mind. Virtus et fortuna...."

"Don't play the clown, Valerian," she snapped.

"Very well, my lady of the notoriously sweet Severan temper, do tell me the price I must pay for your fair hand and a place in your father's legions."

She glared at him but found that it was hard to maintain her annoyance in the face of his insouciance.

"Promise me that you'll declare for tribune this year. Next year, if it's already too late. That you'll run for quaestor when you're of age, and that you'll aim for consul when the time comes."

"I can promise that I'll run," Sextus said slowly. "But you know I can't promise that I'll win. Tribune and quaestor, that's no problem. But a lot will happen before I turn forty. The giants of today's Senate will not rule tomorrow's. Magnus will not be there. Patronus may not be there. I won't have the benefit of having the support of the first and second men in Amorr and all their hundreds of clients."

"Don't you understand, Sextus Valerius? You won't need them, because I intend for you to be the first man in Amorr. When the time comes for you to run for consul, you won't have Magnus and Patronus behind you, but you will have me…. That is, if you still want me as your wife."

He regarded her coolly for a moment, his eyes unreadable. Then he smiled again. "Now that I've met you," he said in an unexpectedly husky voice, "I can't imagine wanting anyone else, my lady Severa."

To her surprise and more than a little alarm, he stepped forward without warning and pulled her to his chest, crushing her lips against his. The enthusiasm and practiced ease with which he kissed her sent the blood rushing to her ears. She felt as if the world had suddenly been reduced to nothing but heat and pure physical sensation. She wasn't sure what she was doing, or even what she was supposed to do, but she was entirely sure that she did not mind it.

When he broke off the kiss and stepped back, she found herself tottering, off-balance and confused. She was further surprised when, instead of kissing her again, he abruptly cleared his throat and bowed formally to her.

"My lady, I do thank you for your courtesy in granting me this audience. By your leave, I shall inform my father that I have no objections to the proposed marital alliance between our Houses."

She straightened out her gown and somehow managed to respond in an equally dignified manner. "Please do so, my lord Valerius. For my part, I shall inform my father of the need for House Severus to be prepared to provide its full support for a candidate in the tribunal elections this winter. However, I should be ever so grateful if you would first do one more thing for me."

"Anything, my lady."

She smiled demurely up at him. "Do that again, my lord."

CORVUS

THE walk from the forum to the splendid manor of Gaius Cassianus Longinus, the head of House Cassianus, was not a long one, but it was made longer by the respectful silence maintained by Caius Vecellius and his men as they marched alongside him and to his fore and aft. Their grim faces warned off senators and commoners alike, and they brusquely dismissed the few brave souls who dared to try to approach Corvus despite the silent warning.

Corvus barely even saw them.

His son was dead. Everything paled into nothing before that harsh, cold, unthinkable reality. His mind leaped from one image to the next. A red-faced squalling infant triumphantly presented to him by his wife's slave. A boy, confessing shamefacedly to stealing a pair of honey cakes and accepting his punishment without a murmur of protest. A military tribune, standing tall in his legionary armor. A man, standing proudly next to a pretty young woman, his left hand lashed to her right. What distressed him most was that in all the images his memory recalled to him, he could not clearly picture his son's face.

He wanted to fall to the ground, to tear his clothes from his body, to beat at the ground, to roll in filth and shriek curses at the heavens. Instead, he marched on, his head unbowed, his emotions controlled, and the howling rage in his heart tightly suppressed.

When they reached the gate, he parted company with Vecellius and the others and was escorted inside by Longinus himself.

The manor was splendid, both within and without, but its expensive statuary and intricately painted tiles barely registered with him. When they reached the triclinium, he saw that he was the last to arrive, and that the other four potential conspirators, including his fellow consul, Titus Manlius, were already there.

Aside from himself and Longinus, three other Houses Martial were represented. Andronicus Aquila and Lucretius Caecilius were the recognized heads of their houses, whereas Gaerus Tillius, like Corvus himself, was the military commander of House Gaerus. His father, Gaerus Albinus, was well into his dotage and would soon relinquish what little authority he still held. Titus Manlius was there as a representative of the Lesser Houses, but despite their greater numbers they were of little significance because they represented only Senate votes, not legions. Three of them, Longinus, Caecilius, and Aquila, were ex-consuls, while Gaerus was only thirty-eight and still two years shy of being eligible. At fifty-five, Longinus was the eldest of the group, but he was still hale and hearty, and a force to be reckoned with in the Senate.

Between the six of them, they were the effective council of the clausores now that Magnus had withdrawn from public life. Even a year ago, Corvus would have found it impossible to believe he would find himself a valued member of such an elite gathering, but any sense of accomplishment it might have given him was overshadowed by the emptiness that filled him now.

How he would face Romilia and tell her of the news seemed to be a much more urgent issue than the one they were there to discuss. That wasn't actually true, of course, they were hardly the first parents in Amorr to have ever lost a son, and yet the feeling of dread inspired by the thought of telling his wife rendered him nearly mute. Was this how Magnus had felt?

"You look grave, Sextus Valerius," Longinus said.

"These are grave matters," Corvus said. He had no intention of sharing his pain with them.

"Grave matters indeed," Aquila said. "I suggest the question is whether we are speaking of one grave or many. Between us, we represent no less than nine of the fifteen House legions. Eleven of the seventeen, if we count the two City legions. Even if Patronus has the full support of the other Houses, which he does not, he can mass no more than six."

Longinus frowned. "I fear you are getting well ahead of events, Marcus Andronicus. There is no call to speak of legion against legion now. We know little more than rumor and innuendo, some of which is deeply troubling, to be sure. But as yet we can't separate the truth from the fantasies. In every generation there have been whispers that this praetor or that proconsul is setting himself up for a king, and never once have the whispers been more than the fever dreams of an overly fearful Senate! Surely you cannot seriously contemplate the risk of a civil war over mere gossip."

"Mere gossip?" Tillius half-rose from his couch. He was the youngest participant, and he looked younger than his years, but he possessed a fearsome reputation that prevented his elders from discounting his opinion. His savage repression of a brief rebellion in Orontis four years ago had kept not only the Orontines in line ever since, but the inhabitants of the two neighboring provinces as well. "We all know what Patronus is after. Everyone knows. That ludicrous vision of Greater Amorr he was trying to sell with the Lex Ferrata Aucta was simply his way of trying to buy support from the allies and provincials. He's determined to put the crown on his own head before his pompous idiot of a son takes over House Severus!"

"Don't underestimate Regulus," Longinus advised. "He is young, pompous, and foolhardy, but I can remember when the same might have been said of your brother, Corvus. Speaking of whom, I do hope you can persuade Magnus to return to the Senate soon. You have been an admirable replacement—please don't think me ungrateful. But I am sure that, with both Valerian brothers leading the defense of the citizenship, we would not need fear Patronus's machinations."

"I'm afraid not even a fraternal alliance would help at this point." Aquila shook his head and reached for the wine to refill his goblet. "The

Lex Ferrata wasn't more than Patronus's attempt to sound out the Senate and demonstrate to the waverers among the auctores that his way is the only one that will work. I have it on impeccable authority that his real campaign will begin in the new year, as soon as the festivals are over."

"Impeccable authority?" Tillius asked.

"Indeed," Aquila answered, refusing to rise to the bait. "Make no mistake, my friends: The auctores will have their men among our party even as we have ours among them. That is why what we decide here tonight must never be shared with anyone else—not your clients, not your sons, and not your wives."

"In that case, I do hope we decide against civil war, Marcus Andronicus," Caecilius said drily. "While I have the utmost faith in our martial prowess, I fear we six shouldn't amount to much against the Severan legions."

Torquatus and Longinus laughed and saluted Caecilius with their goblets.

"Amorr has never known civil war, and it never shall, so long as we decide wisely," Aquila declared rather primly. "Or rather, if we have the courage to do what must be done."

Torquatus and Longinus fell silent, and the others looked around the triclinium at each other. Every man in the room had been a tribune and a general in his day. Each of them had fought with the legions, killed, and watched impassively as men under their orders marched forth to die. War was something they all knew well. But when it came to murder, that was a very different matter.

"And what is it that must be done, in your opinion, Marcus Andronicus?"

Corvus noted that his colleague's eyes were speculative and calculating as he awaited Aquila's response. Torquatus was curious, as were they all, whether the head of House Andronicus, the First House Martial, the only House that traced its bloodline to the ancient kings of Amorr, would dare to express himself openly and say the thing that could not be said.

But instead, he withdrew a small, tightly-rolled scroll from his under-tunic and silently passed it to Corvus.

"You have been silent, my lord consul aquilae," Aquila said to Corvus. "Read that aloud, if you will, and I think it will answer the question raised by my lord consul civitas. Be careful with it: I will have to arrange to have it returned on the morrow."

Corvus untied the red ribbon holding the scroll together and stretched it out as it unfurled. It looked like a hastily scribbled note, written in what appeared to be a half-literate hand. A missive from a slave, he thought, or perhaps a very plebian client, until he saw the signature and inked imprint of a ring at the bottom.

15 Sextilis, in the 416th Year of Our Immaculate Lord

I, Syrmis, son of Halos, by the grace and mercy of God, King of the Thursian people, do most solemnly vow, on their behalf, that we shall loyally serve as clients of Aulus Severus Patronus, from the moment we receive the Amorran citizenship. Upon his passing into the life that is to come, we shall faithfully serve whosoever shall be named the ruler of House Severus in his stead for the next 100 years.

This pledge we secure with the surety of our lives and lands, of our own free and certain will.

His Majesty King Syrmis I of Thursia

"I am told that there are at least six other scrolls just like that, four from the provinces and two from Utruccan cities," Aquila told the stunned patricians. "Allied cities. Salventum and Galabrus, to be precise."

"This is still not... this is certainly exceptional, I admit, but I cannot see how it is actually unlawful," Longinus said. "Towns and cities have taken patrons before. Is not the city of Nobonia sworn to House Falconius? And in the Salventum case—what is the difference between this client's pledge to Patronus and his existing rule over them as the Dux of Salventum?"

"The difference is that, as of right now, it makes no difference to anyone in Amorr what the Salventii think!" Torquatus snapped at the ex-consul. "But once they're granted the citizenship, they'll have to be assigned a House, which I suppose would be Severus. Whether it's House Severus or not, wherever they're assigned, they will comprise a very large voting bloc and one that is wholly owned by Patronus. That means that either the Senate must grow to accommodate all the new leading citizens who will demand a voice in it, in which case the voice of the City Fathers will be muted, or we'll see our sons denied entry into the Senate when they are outvoted for the magisterial offices by Patronus's hand-picked clients."

"Either option is unacceptable," Caecilius announced firmly. "And I agree with Aquila. This must be stopped, and there can be no question that Patronus is the man behind it all. But shall we seriously contemplate the murder of the head of a House Martial? Even if it can be done, do we not run the risk of unleashing the very civil war we hope to prevent?"

Tillius, Longinus, and Torquatus erupted into a simultaneous three-way argument that was as heated as it was incomprehensible. Corvus thought Caecilius looked deeply troubled, whereas Aquila simply reclined on his couch, his goblet resting on his ample paunch, watching the others through heavy-lidded eyes that were almost reptilian in their seeming indifference. Having thrown the torch, the old ex-consul was quite willing to sit back and watch it burn.

They were getting nowhere and accomplishing nothing. Corvus cleared his throat, and to his surprise, the three men fell silent almost instantly. "The civil war can no longer be prevented. In fact, there is good reason to believe it is already upon us." Corvus looked from one man to the next. He saw varying degrees of surprise on all of their faces, except Aquila's. Marcus Andronicus was merely moved to smile, a little bitterly, removing any doubt from Corvus's mind that the man already knew most of what he was going to tell the others.

"Marcus Saturnius is dead. He was murdered by Severan agents."

The news of the Severan connection appeared to surprise even Aquila. The others were visibly horrified, for to a man they thought well of the late legatus. Tillius in particular seemed outraged. He had once served as a tribune under Saturnius.

"He was murdered," Corvus said, "along with most of his command staff in the camp by a small group of soldiers led by the primus pilus. My son and one of the other tribunes were the only two officers to escape the assassinations. And after taking command of the legion, the lads found themselves under siege by Fulgetra—reinforced by more than ten thousand Cynothi auxiliaries."

"How long have you known this?" Tillius asked him, almost accusingly.

"My son's rider arrived at my house this afternoon." Corvus withdrew the scroll and handed it to the heir to House Gaerus. "There are more details you can read for yourselves, but the main import is that the auctores have been planning this for some time. This goes well beyond Severus Patronus. Fulgetra may belong to House Severus, but Falconius Buteo is commanding it. We have to assume that means House Falconius is involved somehow."

"They're not standing in his way, at any rate." Aquila sighed deeply. "I should have known. Patronus has never been one to risk everything on one line of attack, and he has a gift for making himself look the victim even when he's the one on the prowl. He's ten steps ahead of us, and I shouldn't wonder if he's been spending the last six months wondering why no one has tried to assassinate him."

"The Cynothii…" Torquatus began. "If they're serving as Severan auxiliaries now, what are the chances there was nothing more to Caudinus's death than a simple defeat on the field of battle?" Corvus was unsurprised to see him reach precisely the same conclusion Marcus had. "Has your son heard anything from any of Legio XIV's officers?"

"Nothing. He said Saturnius had scouts out looking for them before he was killed, but they found nothing. His assumption is that the same thing likely happened to them and that there never was a battle. I see no reason to doubt his conclusions. Patronus could do the legionary math as easily as Marcus Andronicus did earlier, so we have to conclude he has been actively seeking to improve his odds even as he builds a network of allies throughout Utrucca and the provinces."

Torquatus nodded. "With House Falconius behind him and as few as three or four of the provinces, he could reasonably expect to fight us to a standstill, especially if he's able to neutralize XIV and XVII—or worse, turn them. If the allies come in on his side as well, he may even conclude that we won't dare to fight him, and who is to say he is wrong?"

"We can't permit this," Tillius said, shaking his head in what was either disbelief or anger. "He has to die. He is the heart of the auctores and he's the one stoking all the provincial dissatisfaction of late. If we cut it out, we solve the problem. This requires surgery, not burning down our own homes, sacrificing our own sons, and salting our own earth."

"Is there a counter-argument?" Aquila asked, glancing around the room.

There was a long moment of silence.

Finally, Longinus slowly sat up, then grunted and pushed himself to his feet as if they were in the Senate. "There are two, I should say. First, can we truly take such an action? Assassinating Patronus, I mean. Second, assuming we can, do we have the right?"

"If not us, then who?" Torquatus asked. "We are all patricians. The rest of you represent five Houses Martial and the majority of the city's military might. Corvus and I rule the city as consuls. Three of you have sat in the very chairs we sit now. We don't seek power—we already hold it. But responsibility comes with that power. If we sit on our hands now out of fear for the laws or of making a mistake, our sons and our sons' sons will be right to curse our memories. We not only have the right to act, we have a duty to act!"

"You're proposing that we abandon the rule of law, Titus Manlius," Longinus said, "and jettison the traditions that have sustained this city for four hundred years. I can't believe I am hearing it from you, a reigning consul! Why not take that Thursian letter to the Senate? Why not send fascitors to House Severus to obtain the other letters, and proceed in a lawful fashion?"

Longinus looked as if the thought of taking the law into their own hands was causing him physical pain. "How can we throw stones at Patronus and claim he is seeking a crown when we are paying no more heed to the hallowed and ancient laws of our city than he is? How can we claim the right to lead the nation when we are every bit as immoral as our enemies? Creatures of evil must do their work in darkness. Is it not enough that we shine the light of truth on his insidious plans in the certain confidence that the Senate and People will rise and stand with us against such faithless ambition?"

Corvus saw Torquatus look at him and shake his head. Corvus nodded. It wasn't that Longinus was wrong in the great scheme of things, but it was already too late for ideals and legal processes. They could no longer afford them. Events had already moved beyond them. The time to expose Patronus's underhanded dealings was before Caudinus had ever marched north to meet his fate, before Marcus Saturnius had fallen, before the allies and provinces had been aimed at the city's throat like a giant dagger in the deadly Severan hand.

A thought occurred to him.

"What about the celestine deaths, Marcus Andronicus? Is there any chance that Patronus is behind them?"

The head of House Andronicus spread his hands. "I've heard nothing from anyone, either from my cousin Tarransus, who is in the Sacred College, or my brother the archbishop. There are two Severans in the Sacred College, Tigridus and Furius, but I can't see Patronus resorting to sorcery in order to create a Falconian Sanctiff even if they are knowingly backing his play for a crown, which I doubt. Whatever the nature of their alliance, I doubt it runs so deep. This new Sanctiff, I believe Valens was his name, doesn't appear to have much interest in the political currents."

"It could be useful if he had reason to be interested," Torquatus mused. "In his role as Censor, the Sanctiff can remove a senator from the Senate. That might be one means of cutting Patronus's legs out from under him once he reveals himself."

"Yes, yes!" Longinus said. "Surely the new Sanctiff will not tolerate such a grievous affront to God and the People alike! Once we array both the Senate and the Church against the auctores, surely Patronus will see reason and be forced to submit! And if he does not, he will learn that not even the princeps senatus may hope to stand against the law!"

"Are you not listening, Gaius Cassianus?" Tillius rose from his couch in a fury and jabbed his finger at the older man's face. "We cannot wait to array the Senate and Church against Patronus! He has already struck the first blow! We may have lost one legion already, and he's made a play for a second one, which might easily have succeeded. We are not discussing if we should take this to the Senate or not—we are deciding between assassination and civil war!"

"Calm yourself, Gaerus Tillius," Aquila snapped, and the authority in his deep voice was enough to cause the red-faced Gaeran to abruptly close his mouth and sit back down on his couch. "Gaius Cassianus, you have but a year on me. We are old, and I suppose we are as wise as we are ever likely to be. But in this case, I fear that our hot-tempered young friend has the right of it. This is no different than another uprising in the provinces. Once the tinder has caught fire, no amount of wishing or legislation will put it out."

"No different?" Longinus shook his head. There were tears in his eyes, and his voice was thick with emotion. "For four hundred years the Houses Martial have stood together. We have defeated men and elves, orcs and goblins, trolls and dwarves—and we have done so because we stand together as one city, one senate, one people. If we do this thing, if we take it upon ourselves alone to judge this traitor and give him his due, we may very well break Amorr in two!"

"It is already broken in two, my friend," Aquila said gently. "And if we do not act, and act decisively, it may well be shattered beyond all repair. We knew the provinces were stirring, and now we know why. If we do not assassinate this man, if we choose open war with House Severus instead, who knows how many rebellions we will face? Already Cynothicum is in revolt. If civil war breaks out, will we see five, ten, or perhaps even all fifteen provinces up in arms at once?"

Corvus whistled softly. Having spent the last few months arranging the logistics for two campaigns in the north, during the course of which he'd worried greatly about the Cynothi revolt spreading west or south, it was daunting to imagine having to draw up a plan to address an uprising the size of the one suggested by Aquila, even if he had all of the Severan and Falconian legions at his disposal. Depending upon how many provinces rose against them, it would be years, perhaps decades, before peace would be restored.

Torquatus saw his face and snorted. "You don't fancy fighting a civil war and putting down the provinces at the same time, do you?"

"It can't be done," Corvus said. "It can't be done!"

"What can't be done?" the others asked him.

"We can't afford a civil war now. The legions are scattered in their winter camps, and with the exception of Fulgetra, most of the legions belonging to our Houses are the ones that are wintering the farthest away. Two of the three Valerian legions are in Gorignia, and the other is in Thursia near the Cynothi border. Some of your legions are closer, but no closer than the Falconian legions… and I find myself suddenly wondering if Legio I was truly put out to pasture or not."

"Even if their retirement was genuine, all of those men are twenty-year veterans. It was only five years ago they were retired. They could probably beat two newly raised legions if Quintus Falconius were to call them to the eagle again." Aquila looked around the room. "My lords, it is time we decided. The law demands we take this matter to the Senate. The honor of our Houses requires that we raise our legions against our fellow

Amorrans. And Reason declares that we agree to murder one of our fellow senators, one of the leading magistrates of our city. How say you all?"

Tillius was the first to answer. "Patronus is the cause. Patronus is the poison and the power in the Senate." His eyes flashed. "Patronus dies."

Lucretius concurred. "Killing is killing. Patronus brought this on himself. Better him dead and rotting in the ground than ten thousand of the city's sons in his place. Once he is dead, we will have little trouble winning them over, especially after his secret agreements with the provincials are exposed."

Aquila looked at Longinus, but the old man held his tongue and looked away. Aquila nodded regretfully. "Though I wish it could be otherwise," he said, "I see no other option. Death for Patronus. My lords consul?"

"Death," Torquatus answered. "The consul aquilae knows whereof he speaks when it comes to military affairs. And better the risk of civil war than the certainty of it."

It was Corvus's turn. Immaculate, forgive me for what I am about to say. "The consul civitas is correct, but we should consider more than the avoidance of war. Marcus Saturnius is dead at the instigation of Patronus, if not his direct order. For that alone, he merits death. Patronus gave Saturnius no trial, so it is right and just that he himself should die without warning at the hands of an assassin."

"Well said, Sextus Valerius," Tillius interjected. Both Aquila and Torquatus grunted with approval. "Saturnius's death wasn't merely a murder," Tillius said. "It was an outrage that a legate who had so loyally served Amorr should die upon a legionary sword."

All eyes turned to Longinus. He was still silent, breathing loudly, staring pensively in the direction of the wall. Corvus wondered what the man was seeing in his mind's eye. Bloodshed? War? Burning cities ransacked by men in legionary armor? Finally, Longinus spoke.

"I agree. If there is any chance to bring this war to an end before it begins, we must pursue it. Aulus Severus must die. So how, my lords, do you propose to make this happen?"

"I will do it!" Tillius exclaimed.

"One of us can simply send a squad of fascitors to the Quinctiline," Torquatus suggested. "Once he's been arrested and is safely in our hands, he can be summarily executed. He is guilty of high treason against the Senate and People, after all."

Aquila shook his head. "No, Tillius, your attempt to kidnap his daughter through that gladiator has already failed. You are too fond of complicated machinations. And, besides the additional risk, there is no time for such antics. My lord consul, it will serve no purpose to attempt arresting Patronus. He is on his guard, he keeps more than fifty armed men at his residence, and whenever he is in public he is surrounded by dozens of his loyal clients who would never permit him to be taken easily. Moreover, any attempt to arrest him openly would be tantamount to declaring the very civil war we are hoping to avoid."

"You knew about the gladiator?" Tillius was astounded.

"Of course," Aquila answered. "I make it my business to know such things. But no worries, Lucius Gaerus: Patronus still does not know you were responsible."

"Corvus?" Caecilius turned toward him.

He shook his head.

"I would strangle him with my own hands without regret, but neither the Consul Civitas nor the Consul Aquilae can be seen to act in such a way. It is beneath the dignity of the office and would be seen as tyranny, not justice."

"It would set an evil precedent," Aquila said. "Very well. Leave it in my hands. You may be sure he will not survive the week."

"No," Longinus objected. "I will do it."

The others regarded him with varying degrees of skepticism.

"I will do it," he insisted. "Don't look at me like that, Tillius. Surely you have commanded enough men to understand that it is seldom the most reckless or the most eager who are the most effective. Patronus knows me well. He even, I daresay, trusts me, for all that we often find ourselves opposed in the assembly. I can get much closer to him than any of you without arousing suspicion."

Tillius looked doubtful, but held his tongue.

"Are you sure you can do it?" Aquila asked.

"I may be fat, Marcus Andronicus, but I have lost little of my strength."

"I have no doubt you can still wield a blade, old friend. The question is whether you can kill a man you have known for decades."

"How well do you know him?" Torquatus asked. "I did not know you were friends."

"I wouldn't call him a friend as such. He's ten years my junior, but we both served under Crescentius Metellus in his campaign against the hill dwarves. I saved his life once, when the century he was with got themselves cut off from the main body by a troop of axemen. I led our horse on three charges until the dwarves finally fell back and he was able to bring what was left of his century through to the rest of the legion." Longinus shrugged philosophically. "He was fighting for the city then. He's fighting against her now. I won't rescue him this time."

"I believe you," Aquila said, sounding sincere. "It needs to be soon, though."

Longinus nodded. He met Gaerus Tillius's skeptical eyes, and this time, Corvus noted, he did not look away. "I'll see it done before the end of the festival. Torquatus, Corvus, you should be prepared to call the Senate into session when you hear the news. If Patronus survives Hivernalia, Tillius, then you may consider the responsibility yours and act as you see fit."

The younger man stroked his chin and stared at the ex-consul before finally nodding in acquiescence. Corvus looked around the triclinium and saw emotion ranging from regret and sadness to anger and determination in the faces of the other men, but no lack of resolve. Nothing more needed to be said. They were committed.

It was strange, Corvus thought to himself as the talk in the room turned, with visible relief on the part of most of them, to the winter elections and who their Houses were considering throwing their support behind for the various magistracies. It seemed that planning a murder wasn't all that different than planning anything else. It bothered him a little that he didn't feel worse about it. And then the thought of his murdered son returned, and with it came the darkness.

FJOTRA

WHILE it was somewhat of a relief to exchange the terror and cramped quarters of Raknarborg and the ceaseless motion and cramped quarters of *Le Christophe* for the fish-stinking streets of Portblanc, Fjotra felt far from at her ease as she strolled aimlessly down the rudely cobbled streets, arm in arm with Geirrid and Svanhvit.

Upon reaching port, their captain had prevented anyone from leaving the ship or even going on deck while Patrice and the honor guard escorting the prince's body had debarked. After land had been sighted, Patrice had told her that he intended to commandeer a cart and a pair of horses from the portmaster and travel directly for the royal palace in the hopes of reaching it before any rumors of the prince's death could make their way to the king's ears. He would have to ride quickly then, she thought after she and her two handmaidens were finally permitted to make their way down the rickety wooden ramp to the shore.

No wonder the Savondese suffered so long from the depredations of her people, she thought. Ships like these might sail well and carry massive quantities of men and cargo, but they needed harbors and all sorts of special constructions simply to allow people to get on and off them, and the process seemed to take forever. It was so much easier and faster for men to simply hop out of a snekkja in waist-deep water and muscle it onto the shore. More importantly, they could do it almost anywhere the land met the sea. There must be some advantage to using the big boats and the deep-water harbors, but whatever it was, she couldn't see it.

Geirrid and Svanhvit were wide-eyed and slack-jawed with amazement at the size of the port city. It wasn't a particularly large city by southern standards, and it was considerably smaller than Lutèce, but Raknarborg had been bigger than the largest village in the Isles, and the thick, stumpy walls of Portblanc encompassed considerably more land than those contained by the walls of her father's grim fortress.

Unlike the little villages in which the three of them had lived prior to the coming of the wolves, the buildings here were almost universally made of stone, and the glass windows, in particular, struck her friends dumb with amazement. When the cathedral struck the midday bell, both of them screamed and nearly jumped out of their skin with alarm, only settling down when they noticed that neither Fjotra nor anyone else in sight appeared to be the least bit afraid of the jarring noise.

"It is loud," Fjotra admitted. "But it has to be, so that people all around the city can hear it. Do you see that building there, with the tall square thing pointing at the sky? The bell is inside there, at the top, and their priests hit it every so often to tell everyone the time."

"Why don't they just look at the sun?" Svanhvit asked. She was a pretty girl with long hair and skin that was even more fair than Fjotra's was now, after all the weeks Fjotra had spent in the southern sun.

"I don't know," Fjotra said. "They do many strange things. The bells are only one of them. But they create so many beautiful objects and they are so rich, I think they must have good reasons to do things the way they do."

And we will have to learn them, she reminded herself. They will not tolerate us for long if we insist on remaining reavers.

"Their clothes are so beautiful!" Geirrid sighed as a pair of women wearing homespun wool that was brightly dyed and neatly embroidered walked past them. She fingered the rough cloth of her own greyish-brown dress a little self-consciously.

"Just wait until you see the comtesse's silks," Fjotra said. "The material is so soft and fine, you would think a spider god wove it for her out of moonbeams."

The three of them were so caught up in all the wonderful and fascinating sights to be seen in this strange city by the sea that they forgot to pay attention to their surroundings. Their wandering had taken them away from the docks and the market area, and deep into a residential area that in a larger city would probably have been considered a slum. Here, it merely seemed to be a quarter in the early stages of decay. Fjotra had just noticed that the buildings were lower, less colorful, and increasingly devoid of glass, with their windows being covered with wooden shutters or iron bars, when two men wearing dirty clothes and predatory smiles approached them from the other side of the street.

"I'd heard a big fisherboat come in with a nice lot of reaver women, but I didn't know they was free for the taking!" The man's stubbled head barely came to Fjotra's chin, but his shoulders were thick, and he appeared to have no neck.

"You come looking for us, pretty gels?" asked his taller companion, whose long, stringy hair was dirty and streaked with grey. When he smiled, she could see that several of his teeth were missing, all on the left side.

"What do they want?" Svanhvit asked her, puzzled but not alarmed.

"Us, I would imagine." Fjotra reached into her bosom and drew the dagger her father had given her from the sheath she wore around her neck under her dress and spat at them in the southern tongue. "Go away, trash men. I kill you!"

She was taken aback when the two men simply laughed at her. But she understood their lack of concern when they pulled long wooden clubs out from their pants, where they'd been concealing them.

"Put the knife away afors you cut yourself with it, darling," the shorter man said, waggling his club. "Or I'll break your arm and make you drop it."

"Come now, is this any way to greet such lovely visitors to our fair land?" Fjotra heard a self-assured voice behind her ask. "Run along, my dear harbor rats. Such beauty should never be wasted upon those who cannot truly appreciate it. Go and find yourselves some poxied whores who won't openly object to your tender ministrations, and enjoy your-selves. No, really, you must, I absolutely insist upon it."

A pair of silver coins came sailing past her and landed on the cobble-stones in between her and the two men. She didn't dare take her eyes off the men in front of her, but out of the corner of her eye she saw a slender man with dark hair, about her height and wearing a black hat and a red velvet cloak, walk past her to confront the men.

"There's two o' us and only one o' you. Mebbe we'll take your purse and the reaver girls alike." The stubble-headed man whacked his club against his open palm. "Specially 'cuz it don't look like you ain't got no weapons, peacock."

"Don't I?" said the newcomer. "An unfortunate oversight, I admit." Then, without warning, both of the men facing them shouted in surprise as their clubs began to glow red. No sooner did the wood strike the stones on the street than they burst into flames, eliciting a little shriek from Svanhvit.

"How'd ye do that?" shouted the stubble-headed man, clutching at his hand. His taller companion was even more verbose, swearing energetically as he backed slowly away from their rescuer.

"I should be happy to lecture you upon the subject if your interest is genuine, my friend. But alas, your readily apparent lack of sanitary habits suggests to me that you would lack the necessary discipline to utilize the knowledge. No doubt this is why the mages of yore tended to set their apprentices to menial tasks for years."

"What?" Fjotra said almost at the same time as her erstwhile attacker did.

"I suppose I'm asserting my mistrust in the genuine nature of his intellectual interest in the subject," the strange man said, leaning toward her as if confiding in her. "It's just idle curiosity with no real thought behind it. Even a dog that burns its nose will sniff at the fire, after all."

"Ye're laughing at me, peacock? I'll cut yer damn todger off and futter the gels with it!" The stubble-headed man shook off his companion's

attempt to restrain him and produced a wicked-looking blade from somewhere underneath his filthy clothes. Fjotra gasped and felt her friends'
hands pulling her back, but their rescuer seemed to be more disappointed
than alarmed.

"Are you serious, my good man? Even the dog knows better than to
promptly stick its nose back in the flames!"

He made a circular gesture with his hand.

The knifeman's eyes widened as his right hand, seemingly of its own
accord, slammed itself into his own stomach.

The thug bellowed, with more shock than pain, but his roars rapidly
declined into wordless grunts as his arm mechanically punched the knife
one, two, three more times into his own chest before snapping the last
time on his breastbone. He fell to his knees, then collapsed limply onto
his face, as a pool of blood began spreading out from beneath his body.

"Josson!" shrieked his long-haired companion in horror, staring incredulously at his fallen friend.

"Josson, was that his name?" The magician spread his hands. "Weep
not, my good man. Find solace in the knowledge that our Josson's restless
and insufficiently inquisitive mind is now at peace. A man who fails to
realize that one is well-advised to use one's own todger to, how did he
so eloquently put it? Ah, yes, 'futter the gels' can hardly be considered a
tremendous loss to humanity."

"Ye've killed him!"

"Au contraire. You wound me, sir. As these lovely ladies will bear
witness, the man quite obviously attacked himself. The sad consequence
of a diseased mind, one fears. Wages of sin and all that. Given his observed
obsession with other men's todgers, I fear our Josson was not one for
leading the most pure of lives. Now, my good man, will you run along
and bear the sad tidings to the new-made widow and orphans, or must
I rack my imagination for some means of convincing you to leave these
charming young reavers to my tender mercies?"

But he was talking to the rapidly receding back of the man. Fjotra's surviving assailant was running away as fast as his feet would carry him, and the flapping sole of his right boot made the sight almost comical.

Their rescuer spread his hands as if mystified by the reluctance of the other man to continue the one-sided conversation, then he held out his hand, and the two coins leaped up into it from the ground as if his hand were a powerful lodestone.

"How you know he be married?" Fjotra asked their savior, a little afraid to address him, but too curious to remain silent.

"What a remarkable response," the man mused as he watched the tall man flee with a pensive expression on his face. "Of all the vast panoply of mysteries that life's rich pageant has provided for your entertainment today, that is what you consider to be the most curious matter? I weep for Man. In any event, I direct your attention to his hand, the visible one."

Fjotra didn't understand most of his answer, but she did see there was a simple silver ring on the man's left hand. That made sense, she thought, although it was strangely observant of the man to notice it in the middle of an altercation. And the ring still didn't tell her how he knew their assailant had children.

"Is he a troldmand like Patrice?" Svanhvit asked her.

"No, I am no king's sorcerer. I merely happen to know a few useful tricks," the man interrupted in perfect, unaccented Dalarn, causing all three girls to stare at him in even more disbelief, if that were possible. "Am I, on the basis of your courageous, if ultimately disastrous attempt to speak our most noble tongue with our late friend Josson, correct in ascertaining that you are Fjotra, the daughter of Skuli Skullbasher, the king soon-to-be-in-exile from the Wolf Isles?"

"Skullbreaker," she said reflexively.

"I stand corrected. As does my question. Stand, that is, it can hardly be corrected. Are you the aforementioned Fjotra?"

"Why you want to know?" she asked him in Savonnais. "How are you called?" It wasn't so much that she had any reason to distrust him. After all, if he wished her and the other girls any harm, he could have simply pretended not to see them being assaulted and walked on. But there was something deeply disconcerting about him. The friendly smile that so readily played about his lips never seemed to touch his dark eyes, and the way he carried himself reminded her a little of an actor she had seen at one of the plays to which the comtesse had taken her.

"Why does anyone wish to know anything? In my case, I should like to know because I am charged with the responsibility of bringing the maiden of the aforementioned name to her future husband. He awaits her even now, so that she may be betrothed within the bell, and I daresay he would be bitterly disappointed were he to find himself engaged to marry a reaver maiden given to frothing at the mouth, stripping naked, and biting at shields every time she loses her temper instead of the legitimate heir to the Iles de Loup."

"You make the mistake," she told him, both confused and amused by his words. "I am Fjotra, daughter to the Skullbreaker, but I have no husband and no betrothed."

"You will shortly," he assured her. "Now, if you'll be so kind as to come this way, your royal highness, I will escort you to your destination. My name, not that it will mean anything to you, is Donzeau, and I am in service to the Duc de Chênevin."

Fjotra nodded absently, her mind racing. Donzeau was correct that his name meant nothing to her, but she knew she had heard of the duc before. But where? There weren't so many duchés in Savondir that she should not be able to place the man's liege. The comtesse had taught them all to her, but it wasn't the sort of knowledge one needed in Raknarborg, so she'd forgotten. She mentally ticked them off. Savonne, Méridiony, Écarlate, Lutèce, Aubonne, Carouge, Vevenny…. Chênevin!

Her eyes narrowed.

"The Duc de Chênevin… he is the king's son, yes?"

"Indeed, he is of the blood royal, as are you, if one takes an extraordinarily broad perspective on the matter. But never mind that. Of such fictions are the grandest civilizations built. In my experience, be the blood red or blue, it all bleeds the same."

"Yes," Fjotra said. She did not trust this troldmand who smiled as he killed and called his victims friends. But she knew he could easily prevent her from fleeing, and besides, she was sure there was some mistake. Perhaps the Duc de Chênevin had misunderstood how matters stood and thought she was already engaged to marry Prince Karl. Since Le Christophe had only just arrived today, he did not yet know that his brother was dead and that he was now their father's heir. If nothing else, she owed it to Prince Karl to break the news to his brother as gently as she could. "You may take me to the duc."

Donzeau bowed, though whether he was mocking her or not, she could not tell. "The honor is mine, Your Highness." He led them back the way they'd come, until they were back in the more prosperous commercial quarter again, where she could smell the sea and some of the buildings began to look familiar to her.

And not just to her. As they turned a corner near a blue building that housed a butcher, judging by the ham hocks hanging suspended outside, Geirrid caught up to her and whispered in her ear.

"I know how to get to the ship from here. I'll go get help."

"No!" Fjotra whispered urgently back, and she tried to grab Geirrid's wrist, but her brave friend was too quick for her and adroitly eluded her. She didn't dare to look back, not wanting to alert Donzeau, but the rapid patter of the brown-haired girl's feet on the cobblestones as she dashed across the street seemed loud enough to drown out the pounding of her heartbeat.

Her heart froze as the troldmand, without breaking stride, raised his left hand and made a simple gesture. There was a crashing sound to her left, but Fjotra managed to keep herself from looking until she heard Svanhvit scream. She whipped her head around and saw Geirrid sprawled out motionless on the far side of the street. Next to her lay a cobblestone that had ripped itself from the street.

"What have you done?" Fjotra screamed in Dalarn.

Donzeau turned around, a half-smile on his face.

Seeing it enraged her. She leaped forward and grabbed his throat with one hand. "If she is dead, I rip out your eyes and feed them to you before I give you to the sky god!"

"And they say northern girls are ice princesses." The troldmand, unconcerned, calmly met her eyes. She felt a gradual but irresistible pressure forcing her fingers back. He answered her in her own language. "What I have done is show you the foolishness of defying the duc's will. Look. The girl is barely harmed—already she stirs. But the next time, I shall do worse than simply bounce a rock off her thick barbarian head, do you understand me, Princess Skullbreaker?"

Fjotra glared at him, but her fury was mitigated by her relief at the sight of Geirrid sitting up and staring at the blood on her hand. She switched back to Savonnais. "Yes, I understand. May Svanhvit go help her?"

"So long as they both come with us and don't try to run again." Donzeau waited, his arms folded, until the two girls had made their way back across the street to them. Then he addressed them in the northern tongue. "Ladies, her royal highness here is sufficiently brave, stubborn, and proud to place her life at risk. This means that other disciplinary means are required. So you two shall stand for her good behavior, and I trust you will remind her of that if need be, since it is your lives that are at stake. Do you understand what that means?"

Geirrid nodded. Svanhvit only looked confused.

"*Sacre Dieu!*" Donzeau shook his head in disgust. "It means I will kill you if she doesn't behave." He turned and walked away without waiting for a response.

The three girls stared at each other in shock for a moment, then quickly made haste to follow him.

AULAN

ACROSS the city, young men and women alike had been frantic with activity for the last few weeks. For the young patricians, it was the time when they declared themselves as candidates for the lower offices that would one day qualify them for the magistracies. There were only twenty-four tribuneships and twenty quaestorships available each year. However, the term of office was almost irrelevant, as once elected, a competent young man would find himself in demand for everything from legionary general staffs to provincial governorships. And while election to the first two offices in the cursus honorum were not absolutely required in order to find employment with the senatorial elite, it was rare for anyone not to do so.

Unless, of course, you were the son of the second man in Amorr and you were marrying the daughter of the first man.

Aulan examined his future brother-in-law with a slightly envious eye as they stood outside. It was dark, but the short walk to the Comitium, the large square that faced the senate house, was lined with torches. The December air was cold, but their thick wool cloaks provided them with sufficient protection against it, especially since there was little wind.

Sextus Valerius had never stood for tribune, had never spent a winter in the freezing filth of a legionary castra, and he would never need to ruin himself to entertain the public with a series of increasingly decadent spectacles or spend a year of his life poring through the highly fictional accounts of provincial officials, pretending as if his efforts would even slightly dam the river of moneyed corruption that began in the provinces and reached flood-like proportions in the city. A few ritual words, a simple consummation, and all the Senate would be at his feet as soon as he was of age, courtesy of his father and father-in-law.

For whatever that was worth, Aulan reminded himself. Amorr was on the cusp of the greatest change it had known since the Houses Martial had risen against the last Andronican king, and it was impossible to know exactly what form that change would take. He was no philosopher or historian, but in three years of legionary duty, he'd learned that nothing ever played out when or how it was expected. Killing that poor Valerian farmer had been the first mission to go as planned in months. He'd been half-shocked when he and his men didn't find themselves in the midst of a plebian riot or discover that the Valerian was surrounded by a bodyguard of retired ex-gladiatorial champions.

His father blithely assumed, no doubt correctly, that he would ride the inevitable chaos like a master charioteer, guiding it to take him precisely where he wanted to go. The problem was what would come after him. For all his ambition and arrogance, his father was almost wholly uninterested in the temptations that plagued lesser men. He'd been the only governor to end his term ruling Ptolus Triticus a poorer man than when he began. Governance of the wealthy, grain-rich province was much sought after by proconsuls, as one year there produced more tax revenue than four in almost any other province.

Aulan had no doubts that his father was right to bring the allies and provinces into the empire as the full citizens they should have been, in some cases, for centuries. Amorr couldn't hope to continue suppressing the sort of rebellions that had swept across its periphery for the last two decades. But he had spent enough time around the Cynothii to be uncertain that men accustomed to kings, princes, and other monarchs would make the transition to senatorial rule as easily as his father and the other leading men of his party assumed.

He groaned and looked at the Valerian in a new light. Aside from his younger brother, who was yet to prove himself, his future brother-in-law might well be his most reliable ally in the years to come, which was an alarming thought for someone who had grown up thinking of House Valerius as a collection of mindless warmongers. At least Sextus Valerius looked the part of a Senator-to-be, and Aulan took some comfort in knowing his sister thought well of the man too.

For all of Severa's near-embarrassment with the brave young gladiator, so fortuitously dead on the sands not long after that aborted rendezvous, she was normally a very sensible young woman. Even if the Valerian turned out to be an empty-headed ass, he would have a keen mind whispering in his ear, and, he hoped, guiding his public career in a manner advantageous to the various members of House Severus.

"Are you ready?" he asked Sextus Valerius. "You look good. But a little nervous. There's no need to be nervous. You're only one of thirteen or fourteen couples being announced. Once everyone realizes what two houses are connected to the betrothal, there will be so much commotion among the crowd that you could probably consummate the marriage right there on the table without anyone noticing."

"You have a delicate way with words, Aulus Severus the Younger."

"Oh, do call me that, brother. It makes me sound so philosophical."

Sextus grinned absently, but his eyes were far away.

"What are you thinking about?" Aulan asked.

"My brother: Gaius. He should have been the one to marry Severa, not me. He'd be running for quaestor in a few years. I'm only standing for tribune this winter because, well, because I'm supposed to."

"I'm sorry about Fortex," Aulan said, not entirely insincerely. "I once met a centurion who served with him. He said he was the bravest officer he'd ever seen."

"Yes, well, we all know how bravery is rewarded in the legions. Fortunately, I'm in no danger of that. With any luck, at the conclusion of my brief military career, the very few people who recognize my name will say that I never actually shit myself despite the popular assumption."

"I wouldn't worry about it. Most of the foot shit themselves sooner or later. It's not like anyone is excused from the ranks in the middle of a battle in order to visit the trenches. Of course, in the cavalry one can usually slide off one's horse, do the dirty, and catch up again."

"I wouldn't have thought it possible, but you make my future career sound even less appealing than I'd imagined. You'd make one hell of a recruiter, Aulus Severus. So tell me, does your sister actually like me?"

The Valerian glanced at him, and Aulan could see the vulnerability in the other's dark brown eyes. It almost made him wince; Severa would have the man eating out of her hand and performing tricks in public within a month.

"Strangely enough, Valerian, I do believe she does. You're tall, you're handsome, and you're not a fat, fifty-year-old heir to a minor house, which I happen to know is the fate she always feared would come to pass one day. She must have gotten offers for her hand from three-quarters of our father's clients, and he's got more than a thousand, you know. So, she's got every reason to be glad you're the one he chose for her. She's a headstrong girl, she knows what she wants, and she's probably the only one in Amorr besides my mother who can talk my father round. Believe me: If she didn't like you, if she didn't want to marry you, then she wouldn't go through with the betrothal, no matter how it served the political interests of our fathers."

That wasn't strictly true, he realized even as the words came out of his mouth. Severa would go ahead with the betrothal in their father's interests, if he told her to. She simply wouldn't follow through with the marriage. But there was no sense in telling the Valerian that. The poor man was nervous enough already.

"As for the tribuneship, if you like, I'll put in a word with Falconius Buteo for you. That's assuming you're willing to serve in a Severan legion, of course."

"I don't see why not." Sextus shrugged. "My cousin is with the new Valerian legion, but I don't think my father will be too keen on me serving under my uncle. Anyway, they're still on campaign in goblin country, which sounds absolutely dreadful. Not much in the way of local flavor, if you know what I mean."

"Depends on your tastes, I suppose." Aulan laughed at the look of horror on Sextus's face. "Not that mine run to breeds. But you do recall that you're about to get yourself betrothed to my sister, right?"

"From what you tell me, I'll be standing around shitting myself in some barbarian hellhole before I have the chance to make her any vows, let alone break them."

"Look, I'm only saying that if you want a place in one of our legions, you'll have one." Aulan didn't feel inclined to throw any stones, considering that he was half-contemplating returning to the legion by a circuitous route that would permit him to visit Lucarus's fat-breasted young friend with the red hair again. "Fulgetra would be best. In addition to the fact that the only women in the vicinity won't be goblins, I think I can assure you that no one will chop your head off for excessive courage, or anything else."

"No fear of that," Sextus said as they heard the crowd cheer the previous couple. It was time. "Aulan, thanks. I appreciate it."

"Thank Buteo. It will be his call in the end."

"No, not for that. For this. For standing by me here today. My brother should have been here, but you did a damned good job of standing in for him. For a Severan."

Aulan smiled and clapped the younger man on his maroon-cloaked shoulder. "It's my honor. We'll make a Severan of you yet, Sextus Valerius."

"*Virtus et civitas*," the Valerian replied theatrically. "See, your sister already has me trained."

"Good to see you lads are getting along," announced Valerius Magnus as he joined them.

The prodigious belly of the ex-consul strained against the tightly-tailored wool of Magnus's grey tunic. Like Sextus, he wore the Valerian colors, although his maroon cloak was embroidered with an elaborate pattern around the border that presumably had some significance that was lost on Aulan. He looked a little somber for what was nominally supposed to be a joyful occasion, but seemed to have otherwise recovered from the mourning period that had caused his withdrawal from public affairs.

"Now let's move along," Magnus said. "The archbishop has finally finished with the last of the equestrians, and there are only three other patrician couples being presented, so it's time for you to take your places."

They were close enough to hear the cheering that greeted the most recent betrothal, and Aulan wondered what sort of response would meet the news of the first Valerian-Severan alliance in two hundred and fifty years. No doubt word had leaked out to his father's more important allies and clients, most of whom would be there out of courtesy, but he was sure it would be a real surprise to most of the people gathered in the large square to see the newly betrothed couples presented to the public on the rostra.

Their flame-lit path circled behind the crowd. It was an unearthly experience, thought Aulan. It felt almost religious, and he wasn't even the one about to stand before the people at the side of his wife-to-be. How long would it be before he was the one making this silent, ritual march with his father and one of his brothers at his side? Next year? He hoped not, even though knew he would have little more say than Severa had had in the matter.

They reached the stone stairs and mounted them, with Magnus taking the lead. The archbishop was just raising his hand in blessing the last couple, a Falconian marrying a girl from one of the House's lesser branches—a Falconius Licinus it appeared—as the three of them reached the platform and looked out upon the gathered crowd.

Aulan nearly whistled, for the Comitium was as crowded as he'd ever seen it. There must have been five or six thousand people pressed together in the square. It looked almost like a legionary assembly. Presumably rumors that something unusual was in the works had attracted many who would be normally be celebrating the first night of the Hivernalia in a more conventional manner at one of the many parties and balls being thrown tonight. The Severan ball was traditionally held on the Tenth Night, though Aulan had always thought the Fifth Night would be more fitting, given its location.

Sextus was looking at something to their left, and Aulan grinned as he saw his father assist Severa in taking her place upon the rostra, followed by a slender young woman in a simple white gown who was serving as her honor maiden. He couldn't see the expression on Severa's face, as first she was looking out at the crowd, and then she turned to say something to his father.

Underneath her fox fur cape, her traditional betrothal gown was red, testifying that she was a woman capable of providing heirs, but even in the uncertain light of the torches he could see hers was the dark scarlet of House Severus rather than the lighter shade that was customarily used. Sextus didn't seem to notice, but Magnus did, and he raised a hairy eyebrow in Aulan's direction.

Then Severa glanced toward them and, despite the loud cheering that greeted the presentation of the newly betrothed Falconian pair, he could hear Sextus catch his breath.

Even Aulan had to admit his sister looked spectacular. Her face was painted boldly, almost like an actor's, to enable her to stand out before the crowd, and it gave her natural beauty an inhuman quality, as if she were not a woman, but a demigoddess. And when she smiled at her husband-to-be, her white teeth almost seemed to gleam in the dancing firelight. It boded well, he thought, for the future of their two Houses.

The cheers died down, and an anticipatory hush filled the air.

The archbishop turned toward the six of them. His deep voice echoed off the stones of the surrounding buildings as he asked the ritual question. "Who comes this First Night to offer this maiden to the men of the People? By what right do you offer her?"

"I, Aulus Severus Patronus, of House Severus, offer her, by right of fatherhood."

"And what price do you demand?"

"An alliance with my House."

The archbishop turned back toward the crowd and spread his hands dramatically. "Is there a man who will claim this daughter of House Severus and take her in pure and holy matrimony?"

"I will claim her!" Sextus said loudly, his voice cracking a little. A few people in the otherwise quiet crowd tittered a little at his nervousness. "I will meet the price."

"And you are...?"

"Sextus Valerius, of House Valerius."

An audible gasp swept through the Comitium like a wave. There were some cheers, hastily silenced, as well as a few cries of disbelief, although Aulan could not tell if they were from Severan or Valerian clients. It was clear there were many who had not heard the rumors of the unlikely alliance in the works.

"This man will meet your price, Severus Patronus. Will you accept his offer?"

He nodded imperiously. "I will accept it."

"Then come to me, Sextus Valerius. Come to me, daughter of House Severus."

Sextus and Severa stepped forward together and stood side by side. Sextus extended his left hand and Severa her right.

The archbishop bound them together with a long piece of red yarn that he quickly wrapped around their wrists, then tied off with an expert flourish. That accomplished, he took their joined hands in both of his long-fingered hands and pronounced his blessing upon the betrothal. "The contract is complete. May the Almighty God bless you and your Houses."

Both Sextus and Severa looked startled, even a little alarmed, at the roar of approval that greeted them from the crowd. Patronus and Magnus, astute politicians both, were quick to take advantage of the moment, stepping forward to stand on either side of their children and acknowledging the cheers with triumphant smiles and lordly waves.

The warmth of the people's reception to the news of this unexpected union brought home to Aulan how unsettled they had been of late. The defeat in Cynothicum and death of a consul followed by the loss of a popular and long-reigning Sanctiff, to say nothing of the celestine murders and the Sacred College's months-long indecision, was troubling enough to the average patrician who had some understanding of these affairs. But to the plebians, who could do no more than observe the travails of their betters and suffer through them in ignorance as best they could, it must have looked as if the world were going mad.

To see the two most formidable Houses Martial unite rather than fight must have come as a massive relief to them, a harbinger that the horrible events of the past year would come to an end with the year itself. What a pity that that was so unlikely to be the case, although the addition of Magnus would severely weaken the clausores even as it strengthened the position of his father and the auctores. But it was good to afford them at least one moment of hope. Indeed, an increased popularity with the masses could even be useful in forcing the necessary changes through the always-recalcitrant Senate. If Valerius Magnus could be won over, then who was to say that even the most conservative clausor might not see reason in time?

Aulan offered his arm to his sister's lady-in-waiting, and they descended the rostra in the wake of Sextus, Severa, and their fathers. He didn't recognize her, although she looked vaguely familiar and had a Crescentian look to her.

"What's your name?" he asked her as well-wishers engulfed the betrothed couple. She was rather pretty, he could see now that her face wasn't lost in the shadows.

"Pomponia," she said shyly, looking down.

"Pomponia? Your father is Pomponius Mathus? Why, I remember you! You stayed with us in Salventum one summer. Good lord, you've grown!"

She did not look up at him, but she smiled. "Lady Severa looks lovely tonight, don't you think? And Lord Valerius, he is so very handsome."

"Do you think so?" he asked, feeling somewhat deflated. Not that she wasn't right, damn it all, but he didn't see that she needed to sound so enthusiastic about it. "Yes, I suppose he is."

They reached the bottom of the steps, and now they too were surrounded by the press of clients and allies. All were eager to congratulate Patronus, not so much on the betrothal of his daughter as on the strategic political masterstroke it represented. The patricians in the crowd understood, as the equestrians and common plebians did not, that the balance of power in the Senate had just shifted as dramatically as if an earthquake had shaken the Comitium. But this was not a night to contemplate the consequences—it was a night for celebration.

House Severus was there in force, of course. Aulan saw his uncle Titus, as well as three of his older cousins, Septimus, Serenus, and Gallus. Pompilius Ferratus, who was some sort of distant relation to the girl on his arm, was there, as was the consul provincae, Fulvius Paetinus. To his surprise, he also saw that on this First Night the Senate appeared to have put its politics and party rivalries to the side. His father's most powerful ally, Falconius Metius, was among the first to greet Valerius Magnus, while two of the leading clausores, Cassianus Longinus and Laelius Flamininus, were warmly congratulating Sextus and Severa. Longinus, in particular, was complimenting his sister's beauty in such a flowery manner that she appeared to be uncharacteristically blushing.

Aulan found himself attempting to disengage himself from an effusive and somewhat wine-soaked Crescentian who appeared to have mistaken him for Sextus Valerius or one of the other betrothed young men, as the senator kept praising his nonexistent bride-to-be.

His father turned to say something to him, then suddenly cried out and clutched at his lower back. He stumbled forward into him and nearly knocked him over.

Aulan caught Patronus and prevented him from falling, though not without difficulty, as Pomponia was still holding onto his left arm. As he momentarily lost his balance, she instinctively tightened her grip on it.

"Father, what is it? Are you unwell?" For a moment, Aulan feared his father was having a stroke or perhaps some sort of fit.

But Patronus hissed from between gritted teeth and cursed under his breath.

"My back." He groaned. "In my back. I think I've been stabbed!"

A few of those in the immediate vicinity were just beginning to realize something was wrong and turn toward them. Ferratus was the first to react, and he pushed two senators as well as the consul out of the way as he leaped toward Patronus and caught him about the shoulders. Severus Serenus was also quick to respond, grabbing one of Patronus's arms and helping Aulan keep him upright.

"Who was it, Father? Did you see?" Aulan was frantically scanning the crowd, but more and more people were turning toward them, and he didn't see anyone running away. "Did you see who attacked you?"

"I didn't see anything," his father gasped, wincing as if in pain. "Ferratus, see if there is anything there, will you? In my back! Ah, it burns like fire! I was talking with Flamininus, and then Metius, and then I felt this terrible pain…."

His legs suddenly gave out.

Aulan was able to hold up his dead weight only with the help of Serenus, who wrapped both his arms around his uncle's chest and held him upright, supported by his armpits.

Regulus suddenly appeared in front of Aulan with a look of mixed irritation and concern on his face.

"Father, what's this I hear about you fainting? Dammit, Aulan, what happened? What's wrong?"

"I didn't see who it was," his father kept repeating. "I didn't see anyone. Put me down, damn you all. Put me down, and someone get that bloody dagger out of my back!"

Between them, Aulan, Serenus, and Ferratus managed to lay Patronus down carefully upon the hard stone of the Comitium. Pomponia, Titus Severus, Valerius Magnus, and Falconius Metius forcibly cleared out some space for him. Any instinctive objections to the actions of the latter two were swiftly rendered mute by the victim's realization that the large older man shoving him without warning or apology was a head of a House Martial.

"Daddy!" he heard Severa screaming. She wasn't the only one, but it was the only voice he recognized.

"Get her out of here, Valerius!" Aulan snapped without looking up. "Regulus, find some guards, or at least some clients, and keep Severa safe. And someone find a medicus, right now!"

"I found the knife, shall I withdraw it?" Ferratus asked him.

There didn't seem to be much blood, Aulan was thinking as he flipped the thick wool cloak his father was wearing out of the way. That was good, anyhow. He could see the dagger now, buried almost to the hilt at an upward angle. It looked as if it might have punctured his father's right kidney. But when he caught a glimpse of the hand that had moved the cloak in the firelight, he saw it was covered with a dark substance that it took him a moment to recognize was blood. Because the Severan cloaks were scarlet, he hadn't seen how much the wound was bleeding, and to his horror he realized the cloak was already soaked through with his father's blood.

He and Ferratus looked at each other.

"Better leave it in there," Aulan said finally as he shrugged off his own cloak and pressed it into place around the jutting knife handle. "There's a tavern near the other end of the plaza. Let's carry him there."

"You're going to be all right, Papa," Regulus assured their father as he bent down to grasp his right leg. Aulan couldn't see Severa, however, so at least Sextus had listened to him.

"Of course I'm going to be all right!" Patronus spat, sounding more annoyed than injured. "He only got me once, dammit. I've seen men stabbed twenty times and survive. But my God, it bloody burns!"

Eager hands reached down to help, so many that Patronus seemed almost weightless when Aulan counted to three and they raised him. But they hadn't gone more than three or four steps when he suddenly began convulsing, and, with a dreadful, subhuman sound, vomited blood all over the legs and feet of Aulan, Ferratus, and the others in the lead.

Startled, one or two of those carrying him released him and jumped back, forcing the others to stop as they fought to avoid dropping the stricken man.

"Put him down!" Aulan shouted. "Put him down gently." He reached out and turned his father's face toward him and was aghast at what he saw. His face was drawn in a rictus of pain. Blood covered his chin, and the eyes that had been so keen and conscious only moments ago were vacant and unseeing. Aulan sat back on his heels in despair.

"What is it? What's wrong? What's happening to him?" his brother shouted, sounding terrified.

"Poison," Ferratus said, standing over them with his arms folded as a violent spasm caused Patronus to curl into a fetal ball and vomit more blood onto the cold stone. "The bastards put poison on the blade."

"But what are you doing?" Regulus protested. "Pick him up again. We can't let him die!"

Aulan started to put his hand on his brother's shoulder, then he stopped himself. There was no need to ruin a third cloak tonight. "We don't have any choice, Regul. There's nothing anyone can do. I doubt even God could save him now."

A third spasm brought up another spray of blood, but it was smaller and less violent this time.

"Dammit, Patronus." Aulan looked up and saw Falconius Metius standing over him, in between Valerius Magnus and Laelius Flamininus. All three men were staring at his dying father. "I swear to you on the honor of my House and yours," Falconius said, "whoever did this will pay with their lives and the lives of their children!"

Aulan wished he could summon up a similar sense of rage, but instead he felt nothing except exhaustion. He wanted only to stand up, walk home, go to sleep, and wake up tomorrow to learn that this was nothing but a bad dream. But he couldn't find the energy to even rise to his feet. So he simply sat there, holding his father's left hand, feeling it alternately tighten and release as the poison wreaked its deadly havoc on his insides.

He might have sat there for hours, except a sudden commotion all around him drew him from his impromptu deathwatch. Even Regulus and Ferratus stood up and turned to look at something in the direction of the rostra. He ignored it until he heard a vaguely familiar voice calling his father's name.

"Let the histories proclaim, thus passed Aulus Severus Patronus, the Princeps who thought to make himself king!"

Releasing his father's hand, Aulan rose to his feet and saw Cassianus Longinus standing astride the platform, flanked by no fewer than thirty of his household guard, each aiming a loaded crossbow at the crowd below them.

"What have you done, Gaius Cassianus?" Flamininus shouted in anguish. "You have killed Aulus Severus!"

"Murderer!" he heard a woman shriek.

"Indeed I have!" Longinus thundered back, holding his right hand aloft for all to see. His palm was stained with Patronus's blood. "I do not deny it! But I deny the crime. This was no murder—it was an execution for the highest of high treasons!"

"And these," Falconius Metius said calmly, gesturing toward the crossbow-bearing slaves. "What is their purpose? Are they executioners too? Who else do you deem guilty here?"

"Merely a precaution, friend Metius. Have no fear, they are here only to ensure that I live long enough to be tried by the Senate."

"Do you really think we'll believe you're not going to run to Arretium, to hide behind your legion wintering there?" Magnus shouted, shaking his fist at the killer.

Longinus smiled and shook his head as if in pity at his former ally. "Are you so blind, Marcus Valerius, that you think I would hide from justice? I welcome it, and when the trumpeter comes to my home to summon me to the Senate and the trial that awaits me, you may be certain I shall be there! Your new ally betrayed you, Magnus. He betrayed all of you, as he betrayed Amorr herself. And I will prove this to the full satisfaction of the Senate and People!"

The crowd was mostly stunned into silence, less subdued by the thirty deadly bolts aimed at their faces than by the accusations and the unshaken confidence of the assassin. Longinus turned away and headed for the stairs at the rear of the rostra, still shielded by his armed slaves.

As he did so, Metius stepped forward and pointed his finger at the killer.

"It is you who are the betrayer, Cassianus Longinus! It is you who have shattered the City and the Empire alike and hurled us all into great danger! Do you not understand that Aulus Severus was the one man standing between us and the rebellion of the allies?"

Longinus seemed to hesitate a moment, then he disappeared into the night with his guards following him two-by-two.

"Avenge my father!" shouted Regulus as soon as the last armed slave had exited the platform. "Let them pay for his blood with their own! After them!"

"Stand where you are!" roared Magnus, who had swiftly moved toward the nearer of the two steps and mounted it halfway to block the easiest way to the platform.

The surging crowd stopped, instinctively obeying the authority in the deep voice of the four-time ex-consul.

"In the name of the Senate, the People, and the princeps senatus," Magnus said, "I order you to let them go in peace! There will be no more bloodshed this night. Go to your homes. Go to a tavern and drink to the memory of the most noble Severus Patronus. But do not seek vengeance now. In the morning, the consul provincae will call for the assembly of the Senate. And in the afternoon I swear to you that Metius, the consul, and I will go to the house of Cassianus Longinus. The consul's fascitors will arrest him if he does not respond to the summons as he has promised."

"Is Patronus truly dead?" someone from the middle of the crowd shouted.

Metius glanced at Aulan, who kneeled down again and placed his hand on his father's back. He could not feel a heartbeat, and he saw that his father's face was still, though still contorted with pain. He stood and nodded grimly.

The Falconian pushed his way forward and mounted the rostra's other steps with the anxious crowd's eyes upon him.

"Severus Patronus is dead," he told them.

The news was greeted with cries of anger and groans of dismay.

"What if Longinus isn't there when you come for him?" demanded Regulus angrily.

"Severus Regulus," Metius said, "if Longinus is not true to his word and does not submit himself to the verdict of the Senate, no power on this earth will save him. House Cassianus has but two legions, one retired. House Falconius has four, Valerius three. Your own House has two. If Longinus wants war, then by the Sanctiff and the Immaculate Heart of the City, I swear to you that we will give him war!"

SEVERA

THE day after the funeral, Patronus's oldest children gathered in the Quinctiline gardens behind the house. Thousands had come to honor the murdered prince of the Senate, but thousands more stayed home, or worse, walked about the Forum arm-in-arm and took turns reviling him and his supposed treachery. All three consuls and many foreign dignitaries were gracious enough to appear despite the controversy, but most of the patrician clausores and even a few dedicated auctores did not, so deep were feelings running throughout the Senate and the City alike concerning the shocking revelation of Severus Patronus's intended expansion of his clientele.

Some said Patronus intended to make himself king. Others asserted he was doing no more than breaking the half-barbarian princes of the provinces to civilized rule, a venator careful to maintain his whip hand over the wolves in his charge.

But to Severa, all that mattered was that it appeared increasingly clear that Cassianus Longinus would be facing a sympathetic audience in his trial before the Senate. If so, not even the fact that the prosecution was being brought by Pompilius Ferratus could guarantee that the Cassian would pay for her father's murder, given the widespread belief that his actions were justified by the threat to the city supposedly posed by her father.

Had he survived the assassination attempt, Severa thought bitterly, Father would have known how to turn the rumors around so that they would work in his favor. He would answer them in such a way that they would strengthen his position rather than weaken it. But there was nothing he could do to counteract the whispers, as venomous as the evil substance on the blade that killed him, now that Patronus was lying dead in his sarcophagus.

It was hard for her to know what emotion most powerfully filled her, her rage or her grief. Her mother grieved as befit a patrician widow, in noble silence, though her haunted eyes and increasingly drawn face betrayed her reluctance to eat more than the occasional morsel of food since her husband's death. Severilla didn't seem to truly understand that their father was gone forever. She still babbled nonsensically and never-endingly about her cats, but she did so in a subdued and intense way that told Severa her sister's innocence too had been slain by the poisoned blade wielded by the old clausor.

Her brothers were less possessed by grief than by an anger so intense it almost frightened her despite her own outrage. Regulus's ravings were no longer pompous and self-aggrandizing—they were seditious and alarm-ingly bloodthirsty. She was deeply grateful that her eldest brother was too young and of insufficient rank to inherit the reins of House Severus yet, as he left none of them any doubt that if matters were left in his hands, the Severan legions would already be marching upon every Cassian residence and stronghold in order to lay it waste.

Aulan's anger burned colder, though no less intensely. Having come so recently from the provinces, he was deeply concerned with the effect of their father's murder on the various barbarian kings who had placed their trust in him. Their pledges to a dead man were almost surely worthless now. Would they be willing to make new pledges to the new head of House Severus? Or would they use the turmoil in Amorr to follow the example set by the Cynothii and rise up in rebellion in order to cast off the imperial yoke? Aulan's musings, and his self-confessed inability to fully grasp his father's vision made Severa see that her father's murder was not only a tragedy for her family and her House, but for the Empire itself.

Tertius was, perhaps, the only one of the four of them whose mourn-ing for their father took an entirely pragmatic form. Despite being too

young for the cursus honorum, he seemed to understand, as their two
older brothers did not, that none of their opinions and plans would
amount to anything unless they were able to win the support of the
next head of House Severus. Whoever was chosen would only be head
suffectus, since Regulus had already been named the heir. But it would
be three years before her brother would be eligible for the Senate. While
there was no law requiring the head of a House Martial to be a senator,
the reality was that no major house could afford a leader who did not have
access to the city's center of power.

"Whoever we decide to throw our support behind, we have to be unified," her youngest brother asserted. Neither Aulan nor Regulus appeared
to be paying attention to him. "As Patronus's children, our opinion carries
a certain amount of weight within the family, so we have to be careful not
to squander it by dividing our voices."

"I'm the heir, everyone knows it," Regulus spat bitterly. "Father even
declared it in his will. So even if I can't be the formal head, I don't see
why the others shouldn't simply listen to me. After all, whoever is chosen
as suffectus is going to have to answer to me eventually. Everyone would
be smart to heed my opinion now!"

"A lot can happen in three years, Titus Severus," Aulan's voice was dry,
and Severa could tell he was seeking to restrain his own temper. "A week
ago, none of us would have imagined that Father would be gone. Tertius
is right. Before we concern ourselves with anything else, we have to be
sure whoever will stand in for Father can be trusted not to make a hash of
things."

"So we should support Uncle, I suppose?" Regulus shrugged. "He's
the most reasonable option."

Severa shook her head. Aulan grimaced, and Tertius openly laughed.
Regulus's machinations were invariably as clumsy as they were transparent. Not for the first time, she wondered how their subtle father had
ever imagined that his least intelligent and most self-serving son could
ever hope to serve adequately in his stead. Titus Severus Lucullus, the
younger brother of Severus Patronus, was a decent man, a paragon of

loyalty to House and Senate alike. But he was hopelessly susceptible to the suggestions of others, and his mind changed with every whisper into his ears.

"Regulus," Severa said, "you're forgetting that you won't be the only one with access to Uncle Lucullus, especially if he were ever—God forbid—to become head of the House. You have to be patient and give up the idea that you're going to be able to control anything now! You should be worrying about building up your clientele by convincing as many of Father's clients as you can that you are fit to be their patron. Otherwise they'll turn to Falconius Metius, one of the Crescentines, or perhaps even my father-in-law!"

"What do you know about it, little sister?" Regulus snorted contemptuously. "You would give me advice, when you've never even stood for election or held an office? Why is she even out here discussing this with us, Aulan? Go and play with Severilla and her cats, Severa, this is a matter for men."

Severa glanced at Tertius. He shook his head, and she understood that he was not backing Regulus but simply telling her to remain silent.

"Don't be ridiculous, Regulus." Aulan sighed. "She's right, and besides, we need her on board with us as well. Above all, we need to keep Valerius Magnus on our side, and she's our only connection to the man. It would be the easiest thing in the world for him to return to the auctores now that Father is gone. Their alliance was a purely personal one, and he obviously has no loyalty to our House. If we lose him, we not only lose the three Valerian legions, but we risk finding ourselves facing them!"

"It's not going to come to that," Regulus scoffed, but he didn't appear to be inclined to further argue Severa's right to involve herself in their deliberations. "Very well, so you don't think we should support Uncle Lucullus. What do you think, Tertius?"

Her younger brother blinked. He wasn't accustomed to either of his two older brothers asking for his opinion. "I think Aulan is probably right. Uncle is indecisive and isn't a leader. But Severus Pullus is."

"He's seventy years old!" Severa protested.

"Severus Pullus the younger," Tertius clarified. "He's never run for consul, but his father is the only Severan consul in the last twenty-five years besides Father. He was urban praetor, he served in Fulgetra like you, Aulan, and most importantly, he was the governor of Terracondus. So he's familiar with the provinces, which is something you seem to think is important right now."

"I knew Appius Severus was off somewhere governing, but I didn't realize it was Terracondus," mused Regulus. "He's got to be pretty rich, I imagine."

"He's probably the House's best bet for consul in the next year or two," Aulan said. "We're going to take a serious hit to our prestige in Father's absence, which means fewer clients, fewer votes in the Senate, and less influence. If Pullus lets it be known that he intends to run for consul next year, that would help considerably in restoring our losses, especially since it would bridge the gap between you and Father. I think you may be right, Tertius, but who else is there?"

Regulus shrugged. "Severus Structus was bending my ear at the baths after the funeral yesterday. He's a senator, and he's technically of pro-praetorial rank since he was appointed legate to Legio III after Menenius Lanatus was taken ill in the fourth Bithnyan campaign."

"He's a second cousin, right?"

"You sound less than enthused about him," Severa said.

"What is there to be enthused about? He held the command but did nothing with it. Never fought a single battle. Just sat on his fat arse and occupied Astacus while Valerius Magnus defeated both Bithnyan kings, one after the other, and brought back twenty thousand slaves with him for auction. House Valerius made a fortune, and Structus returned with nothing to show for it but a few idols and antiquities."

"Ugh," Aulan made a face. "Is there anyone else besides Uncle Lucullus, Structus, and the two Pulluses?"

"Not of praetorial rank," Tertius said, glancing down at the tablet he'd prepared. "There are three other senators, but they're mediocrities. The extent of Father's influence tended to blind everyone, including us, to the fact that House Severus has been devoid of any significant political talent for two generations now. It's up to you two—and you as well, Severa—to ensure the problem doesn't persist into a third one, especially now that we can't rely on Father anymore."

"What about you, Tertius?" Regulus said, looking down his nose at his younger brother. "Everyone says you're the smart one."

"Mostly because I am. But I'm also seventeen, and I can't even run for tribune for another two years. In the meantime, that leaves the two of you to prevent the damned clausores from destroying everything Father built in the Senate while I figure out how we avenge his murder. And you two have the harder job, because neither of you are in the Senate yet."

"You're going to kill Cassianus Longinus?" Severa stared at her younger brother. It wasn't all that long ago that he'd been battling trees with his wooden sword in this very garden, and now he was calmly telling them that he intended to seek revenge against the head of House Cassianus.

All three of her brothers stared back at her, each showing varying degrees of bemusement.

"Of course we're going to kill him," Tertius said, sounding a little surprised. "At least, we will if the corrupt old fools in the Senate don't execute Longinus, as he deserves. But leave that to me. Your job, Severa, is to see that Sextus Valerius becomes influential in House Valerius. We can't do anything about Corvus now, and Magnus will always be his own man, but it would be very useful if the Valerians were, if not friends, at least not outright enemies to us."

"He announced for tribune," she told her brother.

"I know. And he'll win. That's a given. But you'll need to keep him focused. He and Aulan have hit it off well enough to convince me he'll never be a willing politician."

"What's that supposed to mean?" Aulan demanded.

"It means you're a soldier," Tertius said, "and you'd rather carry out orders than give them. There's nothing wrong with that. It doesn't mean you can't be effective or influential in the Senate. Look at Corvus, for pity's sake! He was a thorn in Father's side from the moment he was summoned back to Amorr."

"Not unlike the thorn you're proving yourself to be in mine, little brother," Regulus said with a faint smile. "Although I'm not saying you're wrong. But look, I haven't just been sitting around weeping in my wine myself. At the funeral yesterday, I asked Metius and Magnus if they would be willing to meet me here this afternoon, and if I'm correct about what the sound of the front gate opening meant, they are here now. Since we're all agreed on what needs to be done, I say we meet them together.... Only let Aulan and I do the talking, Tertius, all right?"

"There is no point in letting them know about our secret weapon," Aulan said, swatting Tertius on his shoulder.

"It's not as if they're going to listen to me anyhow," her younger brother grudgingly allowed.

As it happened, both Falconius Metius and Valerius Magnus had arrived, along with Sextus Valerius. Severa blushed as he greeted her with a chaste kiss on her cheek. Despite the gravity of the situation, his proximity made her feel a little weak in the knees. It wasn't his first visit here since the murder. He'd actually stayed in one of the guest rooms that terrible night after rushing her all the way back to the Quinctiline from the Comitium. But she still wasn't comfortable with him touching her in front of her brothers, even if they didn't seem inclined to take offense.

The two senators insisted on paying their respects to her mother before meeting with her brothers, which gave Severa a little time alone with Sextus. She was a little disappointed when he didn't take advantage of the opportunity to kiss her more intimately, but she could tell by the somber look in his eyes that he had other concerns on his mind.

"What's wrong?" she asked, laying a hand on his forearm. "You don't seem very happy to see me."

He smiled wanly at her and shook his head. "You're more beautiful each time I lay eyes upon you, Severa. Black suits you. But the news from the north is as bad as we expected, and that's not even the worst of it. It appears that your father may have been more important than anyone understood."

"What do you mean?"

"It's not just the provinces that are up in arms against us. Two of the allies have risen, as well. My father learned this morning that the governor of Marruvium was driven out of the city two nights ago. And the five lords of the Quinqueterra murdered the quaestor who was there to collect the annual taxes. They returned him to the consul provincae in five pieces, accompanied by a letter signed by all five, disavowing the alliance with Amorr."

"God have mercy!" Severa was horrified. "In pieces? Oh, that poor man's family! What are we to do?"

"I don't know. The Forum is in an uproar and the Senate is divided. Everyone is terrified that the Marruvii and the Quinqueterrae won't be the only allied peoples to revolt against us. Half of our legions are filled with allies rather than true Amorrans, you know."

"Yes, I know," Severa said, thinking about the two Severan legions. Many of their legionaries, if not most of them, were from Salventum. But surely men sworn to serve House Severus would never raise their swords against the Senate and People! Or would they? Not two weeks ago, she would have been absolutely certain that no senator would ever raise a blade against the princeps senatus. It seemed as if all about her, the world was being submerged in a rising sea of blood and violence.

"Listen to me, Severa," Sextus said as he took both her hands in his. "We have to stay together in this, you and me, whatever may come. Severus and Valerius have been the two pillars of the city for four hundred years. You and me, our betrothal, is a symbol of the strength of Amorr united. And if we have to go to war against our allies as well as the rebel provinces, Amorr is going to need every last bit of that strength."

She looked up at him, surprised at his intensity. How strong he now appeared to be! It seemed to be some long distant past in which she'd looked over him, examined him, in this very garden, and seen the potential of the man hidden underneath an aristocratic wastrel. But she'd been right to perceive the Valerian steel hidden underneath the softness and weakness of the hedonist's mask that he wore as a habitual defense, and he'd proven it the awful night of her father's assassination.

"I am already yours," she told him sincerely. "And you are right: If there is to be war, then our two houses must stand together as one."

There was, however, at least one House Martial that, in the absence of her father, now mattered almost as much as both their houses combined, and its leader was walking down the steps toward them, followed by her brothers and father-in-law to be. With four legions at his disposal and enemies surrounding them in three directions, Falconius Metius was now both the leading auctor and the most important man in Amorr, the Sanctiff and the three consuls notwithstanding.

"I would apologize for having kept the two of you waiting, my lady Severa, but your fiancé does not appear to have been overly troubled by our absence."

The Falconian was a handsome man in his middle fifties, and while his shoulders were nearly as broad as Valerius Magnus's, he was lean where the other ex-consul was fat. He reminded Severa a little of her father, if her father had ever had a full head of hair shot through with grey on the sides and temples. It was in the way the two men carried themselves: Metius gave off the same sense of calm and self-assured superiority that had made it so easy for men to follow her father. She wondered if his sons took after him, or if, like Sextus and Aulan, they found life to be difficult in his shadow and sought to make their own way.

"I was telling her of this morning's news," Sextus replied, a little stiffly, provoking a smile from the older man.

"Valerians are such hopeless romantics." Regulus shook his head, and Severa had to bite her lip to keep from laughing at the look on her fiancé's face.

For all his easygoing manner, Sextus clearly did not like being teased in front of his father.

She went to his rescue by taking his arm and asking about her very real fears with concern in her voice that was only slightly exaggerated.

"Is it true? Are the allies truly going to go to war against us? Why would they ever do that?"

"Because with your father gone, they have no hope of being peaceably joined with us. Their philosophy would appear to be: If you can't join them, beat them." Magnus shook his head and looked at Metius. "Severus Patronus was a more farsighted man than I ever knew. He saw this coming, but we didn't believe him. How many times did I rally the Senate against him? Why didn't we listen?"

"You can't blame yourself," the Falconian replied. "I was his closest ally, and I didn't take his concerns about the provinces seriously, much less the allied cities. If I had, do you think I would have permitted Legio I to retire? And the Senate rejected the Lex Ferrata on its own, without your help."

"Thanks to my thrice-damned brother," growled Magnus. "But that's my own concern. What matters now is that our three houses reach an agreement that we can take to the Senate. This isn't a matter of auctores and clausores anymore—it's about the survival of the empire, if not the city herself. And that brings us to my question for you four Severans: Are you willing to set aside your desire for vengeance in the interest of Amorr?"

"Longinus unleashed forces he didn't understand when he slew your father," Metius hastened to explain before Severa or any of her brothers could respond angrily to Magnus's shocking suggestion. "Whatever the danger to Amorr he hoped to prevent by killing Patronus, and I will say that I don't believe that Severus Patronus ever had any intention of making himself a king, he brought about a force that is not only more dangerous but considerably more immediate."

"What does that matter?" Regulus's incredulous voice was very near to shouting. Severa didn't blame him. She wanted to shriek at Magnus herself. "He murdered a senator. He murdered the princeps senatus!"

"Yes, no one denies it, least of all Cassianus Longinus himself," Metius admitted. "He submitted to arrest at his home, just as he said he would. He's entirely willing to stand trial before the Senate. But as the head of House Cassianus, he has a pair of legions under his command, and until we learn which of the allies are going to remain loyal and which are not, we can't afford to spurn the use of any of the Cassianus legions."

"How do you know their legions will remain loyal?" Aulan asked. "Is there any news out of Aeternum? Most of the Cassian legionaries are Aeternii, aren't they?"

"We don't know anything yet," Magnus said. "We can't trust any legion or officer who isn't Amorran blood and Amorran bred until we find out who is going to take our side and who will side with the rebels. As much as it pains me to say it, I can't even be sure of my own House legions, since we draw from Vallyria just as your house draws from Salventum and the Cassians from Aeternum. Although Legio XVII and the City legion should be reliable."

"They were both raised in Amorr," Metius agreed. "The problem is that they were raised there only last year. Any of the veteran legions that turn will chew them up and spit out their bones without breaking a sweat."

Magnus nodded. "Tomorrow, I intend to ride west, to Vallyria. Legios VII and XV are both encamped there for the winter, and I expect they'll be much less likely to revolt if they have to revolt against their old general. Aulus Severus, if you're willing, I'd like you to come with me. I understand you've done well with the cavalry. I'll give you command of the combined horse since I expect the legions will be operating in unison for the initial campaign, regardless of where we're fighting."

"I'd be honored, of course," Aulan answered. Severa could see he was surprised and a little flattered at Magnus's unexpected offer. "But Falconius Buteo is expecting me to return to Fulgetra in the spring."

"Then we shall have to be certain that the new head of House Severus grants you permission to accept a commission with Legio XV. Have you given any thought to whom the four of you will support? I expect the opinion of Patronus's sons will be of some import, especially if that opinion is endorsed by House Falconius."

"It can't hurt if House Valerius also offers an alliance as well," Magnus said, "in keeping with the recent betrothal between our two houses."

Regulus and Aulan looked at each other, then at Tertius, who nodded. Severa had the uneasy feeling that it had not escaped either Magnus or Metius to whom the other two brothers had looked for approval.

"We thought to support Severus Pullus," Regulus said.

"The younger," Aulan added.

"He's the wise choice," Falconius said, nodding slowly. "But it would be a mistake to throw your initial support to him. If you'd take my advice, offer your collective endorsement to his father instead. He'll decline it, of course, because he's far too old to take the field, but he'll appreciate the gesture. Endorse him, and you endorse the son. You surprise me, though. I assumed you would back Severus Lucullus. He is your uncle, after all."

"He is," Aulan said. "Unfortunately, he's also a malleable fool, and Regulus prefers for House Severus to maintain some semblance of influence in the Senate by the time he comes of age."

Magnus chuckled. "Wise, very wise."

"So that's it?" Severa said, barely controlling her outrage. "We're just going to forget that House Cassianus murdered our father?" Sextus placed a hand on her arm, but she angrily shook it off. "I understand you don't want to lose their legions, but what's going to happen to Longinus? Isn't the Senate even going to try him?"

Metius looked at her pityingly. "It will… if anyone is willing to prosecute him. And as his most prominent ally, I am in a position to determine whether that will happen or not. The clausores won't prosecute. Their best advocates are lining up to defend him, and they have some excellent demagogues. It will take a Ferratus or a Caecilius to defeat them, especially given how highly charged the Senate is these days. Everyone is afraid of what is going to happen, so it's a bad time for a treason trial.

There are many who would say that it is Patronus who should be on trial instead."

"Treason? What does treason have to do with anything?" Severa protested. "He was murdered!"

"The clausores will make it about treason," Magnus said. "That is the defense, and attempting to argue otherwise serves no purpose, my dear. Longinus knows how to play the game, and he set out the ground rules. This is straightforward politics, and there is nothing clean or sensible about it. Justice doesn't enter into the equation, for all that we all appeal to it."

"It's no good, Severa," Tertius told her. "By now, hundreds have already died, maybe thousands. If we have to fight our own legions, tens of thousands will die. No one will care about the death of one man, no matter how important he was. What is the fate of one man when the empire itself may be in danger?"

Magnus stepped forward and placed his large, meaty hands on her shoulders. He smiled at her, a little sadly. "My dear daughter-to-be, I know very well what it is like to have a loved one slain unjustly, and by one who stands outside the law's ability to reach him. Rest assured, such crimes are not forgotten. There will be a reckoning one day."

"What is it you're asking us, my lord Falconius?" Regulus's voice lacked its usual stridency. He was a little intimidated by the two ex-consuls, Severa thought. "You want our blessing in letting Longinus walk free?"

"Think of it as a mere delay," Metius urged. "I promise you this: If Gaius Cassianus Longinus survives the war, I will personally prosecute him for the murder of Severus Patronus. Will that satisfy you?"

"You're that certain he's necessary if there is war?" Aulan asked.

"Do you think a fat old man like me would be riding north at this time of year if it wasn't?" Magnus snorted. "Aulan, if Quintus Falconius tells Longinus no one will prosecute tomorrow, he'll be off for Aeternum the next day. He's a murderer, but he's loyal to the city, and he's the best hope for keeping the Aeternii from joining with the Marruvii. If he can't stop Aeternum from rebelling, you may have your revenge sooner from them than you would from the Senate."

"I don't care how the bastard dies," Regulus announced. "Father trusted you both, and we'll do the same. As far as I'm concerned, you can tell the Cassian what you like so long as he stays away from the city and someone prosecutes him when this is all over."

"What about you, Aulan?" Metius asked.

Aulan shrugged. "I'll be in the north with Magnus. But I agree. Amorr's interest has to come first. We can sort this out after the war, assuming all of us survive it."

All eyes turned to Tertius, who was doing his best to look even younger than his years.

"Why are you looking at me, my lords? I'm not even old enough for the cursus honorum!"

The Falconian's eyes narrowed, although Severa thought she saw the side of his mouth twitch a little. "It's a little late to play the innocent now, Marcus Severus. Valerius Magnus and I may be doddering old men, but we are neither inobservant nor stupid. Do grant us the respect we are owed and refrain from insulting our intelligence by playing down your own."

"We ought to strangle the puppy now," Magnus grumbled. "No doubt we'd save our heirs a sight of trouble."

"No doubt. Well, Marcus Severus?" Metius asked Tertius. "Do you wish to maintain this charade, or will you swear, on the honor of House Severus, that you will not seek Longinus's death until I give you leave?"

Tertius glared at Metius. There was nothing insolent in it. Were it not for the forty-year age difference between them, one would have thought it was a contest of equals. Finally, he acceded.

"Very well. I swear, on the honor of House Severus, that I will not raise a hand against Cassianus Longinus until you give me leave, Falconius Metius. Unless, of course, events render you unable to do so."

Metius raised a hairy eyebrow at what could have been taken as an implied threat to him.

But Magnus only laughed and ruffled Tertius's hair. "You needn't show your teeth, puppy. Like it or not, we're all on the same side now."

Severa held her breath, hoping the two men would not turn their attention to her. She had no intention of swearing any such vow. Fortunately, feeling their mission accomplished, the ex-consuls instead began to make their farewells. Magnus bestowed a warm, fatherly kiss upon her before giving instructions to Aulan concerning their departure tomorrow, while a simple nod sufficed for Metius.

Then a terrible thought struck her and she turned to her betrothed.

"You're not going north with your father, are you?"

Sextus Valerius looked surprised at her question and shook his head. "I can't. With the elections in two weeks, I have to be here in order to stand for tribune. I'll probably spend most of that time canvassing. Metius says he'll help me since neither of our fathers are able to do it. But with my uncle standing for consul too, I don't think I'll be in much need of him to lean on anyone."

Severa didn't say anything, she just hugged him tightly in relief. It was bad enough that Aulan was riding headlong into danger, but he was a soldier and he was never happier than when he was off with the legions. But losing Sextus so soon after her father might have been more than she could bear.

"I'll come and see you tomorrow after they leave." He bent over and kissed her on the lips, sending a delicious shudder through her that she could feel from her shoulders to her knees. "Don't worry about Aulan: He can take care of himself. They won't be alone. They'll have a mounted squadron of House knights with them. Even if one of the legions has gone over to the rebels, they won't be caught off-guard."

He kissed her again then turned away from her.

She stood under the lemon tree and watched his tall, lean figure follow the other two men up the stairs, accompanied by Regulus and Aulan. Tertius did not go with them, but stood next to her, still cradling his tablet with the Severan names inscribed on it, his face an indecipherable mask.

THEUDERIC

THERE was something strange about the merchants and small groups of families traveling north along the Malkanway, Theuderic thought as he and Lady Everbright led the column that was the Savondese church embassy toward the great city of Amorr. The guards had protested his taking the lead, but on foot there was little they could do to avoid being outpaced by Theuderic on his horse, and they weren't about to leave either the archevêques or the silver behind.

Lithriel Everbright made for an incongruous sight: a tall, almost skeletal nun mounted astride a noble's warhorse. But none of the travelers appeared to take any notice of her. So little notice, in fact, that she had stopped bothering to throw her veil over her face when another group was seen on the horizon.

For one thing, there were an awful lot of such groups. They hadn't seen half as many people on the road the last time they'd ridden this way even though it had been at a time of year generally accounted more suitable for travel than now, the beginning of winter. They saw little snow this far south of the Souspleuvoir range, but the post-festival end of the year was not a favored time for travel throughout the empire.

And there was something else that struck Theuderic as odd, although he couldn't quite put his finger on what it was.

He pulled up his horse and waited for the guards at the fore of the column to reach him. "Guermont, is there anything that strikes you about these travelers we've been seeing?"

"They's a lot of them."

"Yes, yes, I know. But is there anything besides that?"

The guard scratched his head and looked puzzled. "Naught specially, 'cept of course that most of them ain't Amoorish. They's all from the outskirts of the empire, by the look of them."

Theuderic snapped his fingers. That was it! Few of the travelers had the distinctive, arrogant appearance of the true Amorran. Some had lighter hair or lighter skin, others were too hairy, or with features too soft and indistinct. He pointed to an approaching man driving a donkey cart, in which was sitting a fair-haired woman holding an infant.

"Guermont, you speak some Utruccan, do you not?"

"Aye, my lord comte."

"Then go and ask him what this is about. Find out why they are all leaving the city of Amorr. If there is something amiss there, I'd like to know before we stick our heads in the middle of it."

With what appeared to be some difficulty, Guermont managed to keep himself from saluting. He approached the donkey cart driver and conversed. Theuderic waited impatiently until he returned.

"Well?" he demanded.

"I ain't rightly sure, comte. He said something about one o' their big nobles, like, got hisself killed a week or so back by another noble. I don't know how or why, but somehow this made some o' the kings and princes out in the sticks real mad, so the Amoors been kicking all o' them out who ain't from the city, which I don't see is lahkly to help. But not all o' them, just some as are fixing to fight a war because they want to get conquered, and the Amoors won't do it. I don't know. It all sounds crazy to me, and he said it didn't make no sense to him neither."

"Does any of that to you make sense?" Lithriel asked him.

"It sounds to me as if they're having difficulties with their rustics again," Theuderic told her. "They lost a battle in Cynothicum this summer, so perhaps a few more principalities decided to throw off the imperial yoke. It doesn't sound like anything of much concern to us."

"Who will come to the waters? Who will receive new life?"

The Savondese column was traveling along the Malkanway, still three days north of Amorr. They'd unexpectedly encountered a crowd gathered near a ford across a river that paralleled the road about one hundred paces away. At first, Theuderic had thought they might be in for trouble, and while he wasn't worried about the men's ability to defend the silver, a general slaughter this close to Amorr would likely be frowned upon. But as he rode closer, with Lithriel on her mule beside him, he saw they had no need for concern.

Standing knee-deep in the river was a young monk with a stubbled head and a plain brown woolen tunic pushed up over his spindly thighs. He was slight and short, with a hunched back and a complexion that was worse than some Theuderic had seen before on poisoned men. Nevertheless, he held the crowd in thrall. Perhaps seventy folk—travelers, by the looks of them, and judging by the horses and wagons waiting all around—stood watching and listening.

The young man spread his arms to the people. "Come! Receive the forgiveness of the Immaculate. The water is cold—colder than sin! But sweet it is when your sins wash off you like dirt from the road. Who will come? Who will meet the Almighty?"

Lithriel's brow wrinkled with puzzlement as an old woman laid aside her outer garments and waded into the water to meet the man. "Are they so desperate for the baths?"

Theuderic had returned his attention to the head of their column, looking to make sure they hadn't stopped to gawk as well. "Hmm?"

"Those people in the river," she said, pointing with her chin. "Isn't it too cold for bathing?"

"Ah." He grinned. "No, my lady, it is not for a bath that these enter the water. It's not a literal cleansing of skin, anyway. Unless I miss my guess, that man is an itinerant monk of the Immaculate. He's preaching his religion's absolution by ablution, I believe. Baptismus, they call it. They think their god stands ready to forgive anyone his past crimes if they will avail themselves of the water."

"That water?" Lithriel looked incredulous as she looked over the brown, muddy water of the ford.

"It's not the specific water that matters. The water itself is symbolic. They feel that the real forgiveness is a matter between the believer and the Immaculate." He shrugged.

"Oh." Lithriel cocked her head to one side, fascinated by the way the man pushed the old woman under the slowly moving water. "But even if gods existed, how can crimes be forgiven by them when they are not the one wronged?"

"Ah, but our good monk here would counter that all wrongs are ultimately crimes against God, even if they victimize another man."

Surprisingly, she didn't look as confused. "That makes some sense, I suppose. The man who raped me and broke my magic would be executed in Merithaim for the crime of costing King Everbright a sorceress."

Theuderic cleared his throat and urged his horse on. They rode in silence as the woman came up again, spitting and off-balance, to the cheering of the onlookers. The joy on the woman's face stood in deep contrast to the blue of her lips brought on by the icy chill of the water.

"If it's symbolic," Lady Everbright asked a few moments later, "then why do it in the river at all?"

Theuderic grinned. "It would be more comfortable to do it in the baths, wouldn't it?"

Three days later, he was forced to reconsider his assumption that the expulsion of the Amorran rustics would not concern them.

They were stopped by the city guard at the bridge that crossed the river marking the outer boundary of the great city. It was still an hour's ride to the actual walls, but for all legal intents and purposes, they had reached Amorr. The guards were heavily armored but visibly nervous at the size of their contingent. Theuderic's troop outnumbered them nearly four to one. As they'd approached, he'd noticed a rider galloping off in haste across the bridge, and he surmised that reinforcements would soon be arriving.

"You cannot enter," said the guard with blue horsehair decorating his helmet, presumably the squad commander. He pointed to a written notice tacked onto the gate that blocked their way. "The city is closed to all foreigners by order of the Senate until further notice."

Theuderic spread his hands in disbelief. "This is a royal embassy from His Majesty the King of Savondir to the Most Holy and Sanctified Father! You cannot possibly expect me to believe that an order applying to foreign residents has any relevance to a royal embassy!"

"Believe it, Savonder. You ain't Amorran. You ain't an ally. You're a foreigner. You're all foreigners, and so the Senate order applies, you understand? I got nothing against you or your party, you see, but our orders is clear. You ain't coming in the city."

Theuderic nodded and decided to try a different tack. Sometimes even the most unlikely intellect would respond to sweet reason. "I understand, sir, and I am not unsympathetic with your position. But allow me to bring two things to your attention here. First, do you see the two elderly gentlemen on the mules toward the rear?"

The bridge commander allowed that he did, in fact, see the two men in question.

"While they are admittedly somewhat the worse for wear given the journey, they are not only men of God, they are archevêques of the Church. They have come here at the express invitation of the Most Holy and Purified Father. I suspect you would not want to defy His Holiness? Furthermore, this sister here, as you can see, is not actually a nun."

Lithriel, at his gesture, pushed back her veil.

The commander stepped backward in surprise.

"You're an elf!"

"You are observant, man." She stared down her long, slender nose at him, her eerie green eyes unblinking.

The Amorran looked thoughtful and just a little less pugnacious. "All right, I hear you, Savonder. What's the second thing?"

"I assume you are aware of the Sanctal Scot which is collected through-out the demesne of the Church by the various potentates on behalf of the Most Holy and Purified Father?"

"We call it the calx tax, but sure, I know what you mean."

"Now, do you see that wagon there?" Theuderic pointed. "And perhaps you recall that Savondir is a large and very wealthy kingdom?"

The commander looked from Theuderic to the wagon and back again. "You ain't… you ain't serious. That ain't all…? Not the whole wagon?"

"Please don't take my word for it. I suggest you have a look for yourself, Commander. Three hundred pounds of silver is a sight worth seeing, in my humble opinion."

Lithriel snorted beneath her veil but fortunately, held her tongue. The Amorran jerked his head toward the wagon, and one of his men followed him over to the wagon. Theuderic didn't dismount but urged his horse around so he could keep an eye on the two men. The six royal guards waited for him to nod his approval before they moved aside to permit the Amorrans access to the treasure.

With the practiced air of a man who'd searched many a cart for contraband before, the commander drew his knife and slashed through the rough canvas. Theuderic knew better than to protest. He simply watched in amused silence as the man realized that the chests under the canvas were locked. The Amorran's discomfiture was increased when the two archevêques, curious about what was delaying their entrance into the city, rode up on their mules and immediately began vigorously protesting this unseemly violation of Church property.

Theuderic dug into his pouch, found the key, and held it out before him.

The bridge commander, discovering that two outraged archevêques in full tongue were considerably more intimidating than the sight of two old

men on mules in the distance, was quick to seize upon the opportunity to
retreat from the prelates.

"You're not having us on about the silver, are you?"

"No, I am not. Nor about the archevêques either, as I believe you
have discovered, my good man. Or the lady elf. Now, am I correct in
assuming that you have no authority to let us pass?"

"You are correct, sir."

"The correct form of address is 'You are correct, my lord comte,' but
we shall let that pass. May I ask your name, Commander?"

"Paetinus Alvus, my lord, ah, my lord comte."

"Well, Alvus, I have a plan. Since I suspect you have no idea where to
even begin finding the individual with the necessary authority to permit
us to enter the city, and you probably have no more desire to watch over
thirty armed men than the archevêques and I have of sitting here for
the remainder of the afternoon staring at your lovely bridge, I suggest
a compromise. Why don't you and several of your men escort myself, the
archevêques, the nuns, and the silver to the Sanctal Palace, where you can
transfer the dilemma of this decision to a churchman of sufficient rank,
if not to the Sanctified Father himself? I will give you my word that my
men will wait here, more or less patiently, until they are given permission
to enter by someone whose orders will be accepted."

Alvus's face screwed up with concern. "I'm not sure…"

"The alternative, of course, is that I simply turn around and ride away
with the silver and a clear conscience. I have fulfilled my obligation in
delivering the scot to the city. If the Sanctified Father and the Church
won't accept this offering from His Majesty, well, I suspect I could find
some use for it."

"Of course they'll accept it!" Alvus looked alarmed. "You can't simply
ride off with it after coming all this way!"

"I don't see that you leave me any choice." Theuderic nodded to the
Amorran and began to back his horse toward where he would have room
to turn it around. "As much as I have enjoyed our little conversation,
Paetinus Alvus, I shall leave you to begin thinking about your explanation

to the Sanctified Father, or more likely, to the ever-curious Congregation for the Doctrine of the True Faith concerning where the Church's silver has gone and why you sent it away."

Alvus went pale at the mention of the holy inquisitors. Theuderic could almost see the calculations taking place inside the man's head. What was more likely to prove problematic for him: whomever was in charge of the city guards knowing that he'd let someone over the bridge, or the Church thinking he'd permitted a stranger to steal three hundred pounds of its silver?

"Fear not those who can kill the body, but rather those who can kill the soul." Theuderic helpfully reminded the Amorran of a heuristic he had always found considerably more poetic than applicable to his own life.

"Wait!" Alvus cried before Theuderic had even managed to turn his horse about. "I will bring you to the palace! If you'll only order your footmen to stay here until you send for them, I'll even see that they're given bread and cheese while they wait. But I'll have to accompany you alone. I've got the only horse."

"The archevêques and I should much appreciate your company, friend Alvus. I'm sure we need not fear being waylaid under your protection." Theuderic did not permit himself so much as a grin as he waved to the man driving the wagon, indicating that he should come forward. "And if you would arrange to see that my men are provided with a bit of wine as well, I don't believe it would be taken amiss."

Once broken, it seemed the Amorran dam gushed plentifully. After mounting his horse, Paetinus Alvus rode alongside him and showed no hesitation to answer his questions to the best of his ability.

It seemed that one of the leading lights of the empire's ruling council had been murdered by another council member, which would not have been of any great significance were it not for the fact that both men controlled massive family armies each comparable to the size of the king's royal forces. It was little wonder that the Amorran council had never evolved into a monarchy, not when its nobles were permitted to wield such power.

The new restrictions on foreigners were somehow a consequence of this murderous political struggle, which Theuderic was given to understand had been ongoing for more than a decade. The garbled version Guermont had received from the northbound traveler made a little more sense now, as it appeared that the murdered man had been a champion of giving imperial citizenship to the occupied provinces, a policy that looked to have died with him. His murder, and its subsequent justification by the council, had given violent offense to the nobles of the provinces, and many of them were now known or rumored to be in open revolt against the council, if not necessarily the empire itself.

It was all very complicated and legalistic, which was to say, characteristically Amorran, and Theuderic despaired of attempting to understand it well enough to explain it to the Haut Conseil when he returned in the spring. He decided to take an optimistic attitude toward the affair and assume it would sort itself out before his departure.

Recent events within the Church were rather easier to follow, at least to the extent they were explicable to anyone outside the internecine battles that took place within the hierarchy. The new Sanctiff was from one of the usual noble families, but he was younger than usual and, prior to his elevation to the Sacred College three years ago, had spent his archevêqueship in the provinces, thus rendering him somewhat of an enigma within the city. It was eminently clear that in Amorr, the difference between a man of the city and a man from anywhere else in the empire was nearly as vast as the difference between noble and commoner in Savondir.

Unlike the archevêques who now leaned in to hear the guard tell the tale, Theuderic had little interest in the man presently sitting on the Sanctal throne. He was rather more interested to hear of the murders that had helped put the young celestine on that throne. Mainly because murders by magic were nearly unheard of in Savondir, where its use was actively embraced. For anything of the sort to occur in a place so viciously anti-magic as Amorr was simply astonishing!

He was still marveling at the news of these peculiar and untimely killings when he saw they were approaching the city walls of Amorr. They stood some seventy piedz high, and while they didn't have the benefit of the mountainous terrain helping secure them, thanks to the Amorran legions scattered around the empire they were effectively as impregnable as the walls of Malkan. No enemy had ever forced them, and it seemed impossible to imagine that any ever would.

Nor had the Amorrans relaxed their guard over the centuries. Their reputation for rigid discipline appeared to be well-merited. Unlike the larger walled cities in Savondir, an undeveloped zone was strictly maintained, preventing the houses and other buildings of the exurbs through which they had ridden from piling up against the walls. It looked as if a spell had been cast recently, flattening everything in a concentric ring.

Only the bricked road continued past the invisible line of demarcation. The buildings and other detritus of civilization came to an abrupt end despite there being no marker that Theuderic could see. This grass-covered ring surrounding the walls was about four hundred piedz wide, and the children of the exurbs gamboled about it in the company of numerous goats and the occasional cow.

Alvus appeared to have taken a proprietary interest in them, and the Amorran officer called out aggressively to the guards at the open gate, telling them to fetch their captain. Theuderic didn't know if the gate commander was more impressed by the archevêques, the elf, or the fact that they were the invited guests of the Sanctiff, but after some brief, but animated wrangling between the two Amorran officers, Alvus proudly announced they would be permitted to enter the city proper and that a runner would be sent to the palace to warn the Church officials of their imminent arrival.

Lithriel had donned her veil again to avoid attracting unnecessary attention, but, once they followed the two mounted officers and entered the city itself, they quickly learned it wasn't necessary. The sights and sounds and press of the crowds were overwhelming, even to one accustomed to large cities such as Lutèce and Malkan. Amorr held more than twice the population of either of its rivals, and it seemed as if most of them were filling the streets and sidewalks today. Many of the residential buildings, which Alvus told him were incongruously called islands, were seven stories high. They appeared to be disturbingly ill-constructed too, as some of them visibly leaned over the streets they kept in shadow despite the clear skies and afternoon sun.

In such a place, even a single battlemage could wreak great devastation and remain undetected, Theuderic thought to himself. Surreptitiously transform just two or threescore stones at the ground level into their component sands, and you could kill ten thousand "island" dwellers in a matter of seconds, to say nothing of the hundreds more passing under the tilting buildings. The temptation to experiment with just one building whispered for a brief moment, but he reminded himself that he was now supposed to be a royal ambassador. Mass murder would hardly be diplomatic of him, even if no one suspected the truth.

Impeded by the crowds, they hadn't progressed far from the gate when blaring trumpets caused the street to clear as if by magic, and a small mounted squadron of gold-cloaked troops, followed by four squads of footmen in white armor, approached them. They did not look friendly. Theuderic glanced at Alvus and saw that the guard commander's eyes were wide with alarm, which did not inspire a great sense of confidence in his own heart.

"I assume the ones in white are the Sanctal guard. Am I correct, friend Alvus?"

"Mm-hmm," Alvus nodded.

"Then what is the meaning of the gold cloaks on the horsemen?"

"They are priests of the Order of St. Michael."

Michaelines. The mage-killers. Of course they were. Theuderic smiled ruefully. He couldn't help it. What were the odds? This sort of thing was exactly why he was convinced that even if there wasn't a God, there must be a Devil. And if he had observed anything over the years, it was that the prince of this world had a wickedly twisted sense of humor.

Fortunately, the Michaelines didn't appear to have any special means of detecting mages, as the priest-captain immediately took charge of them and ordered Alvus to return to his station without showing any indications that Theuderic was of any particular interest to him. Theuderic slipped Alvus a silver coin for his trouble as the pious wall commander received a parting blessing from Archevêque Nivelet. One never knew when it might come in handy to be on good terms with a guardsman.

But even if he wasn't hostile, the Michaeline captain was rather less friendly than Paetinus Alvus had been. He looked over both Theuderic and Lithriel with open suspicion, and Theuderic was reminded that these particular priests were not only the empire's witch-hunters, but were trained specifically to deal with orc shamen, elven sorcerers, and, as it happened, human mages like himself, on the field of battle.

He was very nearly certain the Amorran could not know that Lithriel had lost her magic or that he was more than a simple Savondese noble and king's ambassador, but from the way the Michaeline looked at them, he was clearly open to the possibility that either or both of them might be a practitioner of the forbidden. The priest-captain's suspicious glare made him very glad that he'd resisted the urge to experiment with the stability of the islands. Sometimes virtue truly was its own reward.

The Sanctiff's palace was constructed on the Inculpatine, the hill that marked the very center of the city. Built entirely of a white harabescato with only the faintest of light grey veining to the marble, it was a spectacular architectural achievement, particularly as Theuderic knew it had been constructed without the aid of magic or dwarves.

Guards wearing red cloaks over the same enameled armor as the footmen accompanying them took their horses and mules from them, at which point they had to climb the steps that led to the palace entrance. Neither Lithriel nor Nivelet had any trouble with them, but Vincenot was quickly exhausted, and Theuderic was forced to lend the elderly archevêque his arm for support.

The armored guards had unloaded the chests that contained the silver as well as those in which their clothes and personal belongings were stored from the donkey cart and were struggling up the steps behind them, two to each chest. The Michaeline priest-captain had offered to escort the cart around to the other side of the hill, but Theuderic had no intention of permitting the silver out of his sight until it was turned over to the Sanctified Father. If he and the elderly churchmen had to mount the stairs, then by God and His Vicar on Earth, their hosts would have to do so as well.

A small but impressive delegation of célestes and archevêques were waiting in the palace for them. Several of them appeared to know Nivelet and Vincenot, or at least knew of them, as the two archevêques were soon engaged in what appeared to be a warm and friendly conversation in the high Church Utruccan language that bore only a slight resemblance to the vulgar form that Theuderic spoke.

Vincenot informed Theuderic that they were fortunate indeed, as the sanctiff would grant them an audience that very evening, after which they were invited to a private dinner here in the palace given by His Eminence Petrus Clementus, a tall, white-bearded céleste whose episcopal cathedra of Mons Celsius was apparently of some renown, judging by the air with which the archevêque informed him of it.

"How very kind of the king-priest to permit you to give him tribute without first making you wait," Lithriel remarked irreverently. Fortunately, she had spoken in elvish.

"Some of these men are scholars, my lady. Perhaps the finest in the world outside of the Collegium. Don't assume none of them will understand your tongue."

"It's only been two years since they decided we weren't animals, my love."

"Pity, I might have been able to keep you in my room if they hadn't."

He winced as Lithriel's laugh sound drew the attention of the Church delegation.

A short, stout man wearing the céleste's light blue vestments walked over to them. He had bright, intelligent eyes. "Do excuse us, seigneur comte," he said in excellent Savondese. "Some of us have been corresponding with Archevêque Vincenot for thirty years, but this is the first time we have had the opportunity to meet with him. My lady Everbright, am I correct in assuming this is the human tongue with which you are most familiar?"

"I speak some, yes, sir priest."

"Then allow me to bid you and the Comte de Thôneaux welcome to Amorr and to the Aula Consecra. I am Céleste Praxidus Domenicus, of the cathedra of Sainte Marcellus, and it is my honor to host your mission to the Sanctified See. If you have any requirements or requests, you have only to ask me or one of my subordinates."

"Other than being shown to our chambers so that we can prepare for this evening," Theuderic said, "I have thirty men cooling their heels on the far side of the northern bridge, Your Eminence."

"Lodgings have already been prepared for them outside the walls, Comte, in Sainte Esquilinus. The messenger should have reached them by now, and they will likely dine long before you are able to do so. May I escort you to the rooms we have prepared for you now? I shall have the chests brought along immediately, of course."

Theuderic wasn't sure which was more impressive, the grand two-room suite he'd been given, which was large enough to sleep most of his thirty men, or the fact that his suite had direct access to the smaller, even more elaborately decorated chamber in which Lithriel had been installed. And he wasn't sure which was more alarming, the awareness that the Church already knew so much about him or that they couldn't be bothered to hide their knowledge from him. He was certain the arrival of the priests of St. Michael earlier had been no coincidence. If the Amorrans didn't know he was one of the King's Own, he would take bloody vows himself.

Unfortunately, there wasn't time to visit the baths, but the marvelous aqueduct system that brought water directly to the palace did allow him to at least sluice the dirt of the road from his face and hands. He even managed to shave himself. By rights, he should have had at least a manservant or two, but fifteen years of fighting in the field, mostly on the western borders, had left him too accustomed to solitude to welcome the intrusion of another. Perhaps more importantly, it would complicate things with Lithriel. The two of them were always happiest when they were alone together, and she had never expressed any desire for a lady-in-waiting. Elves, insofar as he could tell, didn't go in for such nonsense.

An hour later, Theuderic was escorted into the Sanctiff's throne room. It was built on a grander scale than anything the kings of Savondir had ever envisioned. There was a small army of white-armored guards, priests, novices, prelates, évêques, and archevêques in the domed chamber. The man himself wore a white robe embroidered with cloth-of-gold and wore a high, exotic headpiece in place of a crown. He sat upon the huge apostolic throne that was raised up on a platform that stood higher than a man's head.

Theuderic understood that the throne, the Sedes Ossus, was a holy icon of sorts, more like a veritable catalog of holy icons. But the effect of the various bones of which it was constructed and the four gold-plated skulls at its corners was rather gruesome, and almost barbaric. The simple, silver throne of the de Mirids was much more elegant and kingly in his eyes, despite being about one-quarter the size of the skeletal Amorran behemoth.

But he couldn't complain about their reception by the Sanctified Father. When he was summoned for the basiamanus and mounted the platform, he was surprised to see that His Sanctified Holiness Pelagianus was a handsome man not more than five years older than himself.

He looked at Theuderic with the piercing, intelligent eyes of the hunter, rather than the wise and gentle ones of the shepherd that his office tended to lead one to expect.

"You are the king's magus, my son."

Theuderic blinked, feeling as if he'd been unexpectedly stabbed in the stomach. He wasn't quite sure what to do, or if he was in danger, so he went with his instinct and dissembled. "I am the king's man, Sanctified Father. May I kiss the ring?"

The Sanctiff nodded impassively and extended his hand.

Theuderic quickly dropped to one knee and pressed it to his lips. He stood again and gestured to the chests which the Sanctiff's guardsmen were carting onto the platform behind him.

"Sanctified Father, please accept this gift from the first fruits of the bounty with which the Lord has blessed His Majesty the King of Savondir and his people, in the name of Our Most Immaculate and Holy Savior."

The Sanctiff nodded graciously and sketched a tree in blessing.

Theuderic was startled to see the three crossed lines of white light suddenly appear in the air between them, glowing softly without a hint of magic having been used to produce it. He did his best to hide his reaction, but not well enough, as a faintly sardonic smile appeared on the Sanctified Father's bearded face.

"Do convey our gratitude and our inestimable good will to His Most Constant Majesty. We are well aware that His Majesty, by the grace of God the King of Savondir, is a good and loyal son of the Church, and he is often in our thoughts and in our prayers." The Sanctiff's deep voice was clear and loud, carrying to the far ends of the chamber, but it dropped to a whisper as he addressed Theuderic personally. "There are powers well beyond the occult ones upon which you draw, my son. Seek them out, lest they destroy you unbeknownst. And remember, the light will always outlast the shadow."

And with that, the glowing light flared and disappeared. Theuderic understood the interview was over. He bowed low, in genuine respect for the man as well as the office, for he had the distinct sense he'd been told something of considerable import, even if he did not know what it was. Although he wasn't sure precisely what he believed, and he had never been purified, he found himself feeling strangely at peace simply from being in the presence of the Sanctified Father. It was absurd, he told himself. It made no sense at all, but he couldn't honestly deny the feeling.

The Sanctiff proceeded to give material evidence of his gratitude by summoning both Archvêque Nivelet and Archvêque Vincenot before him and elevating them to the Sacred College. Theuderic was almost as pleased as the two new célestes, and not only because the two primary goals of his embassy had already been fulfilled on his very first day in Amorr. In fact, His Majesty the King would have been satisfied with only one vote in the Sacred College. To receive a second without even needing to ask for it was a good sign of his favor with the Sanctified Father.

And, given the Sanctiff's relative youth, Savondir might well hope for a third, a fourth, and perhaps even a fifth before it met again. The Church would always be well beyond royal control, but at least His Most Constant Majesty might hope to gain some influence in the hierarchy, which would help considerably in maintaining his freedom of action with regards to vacant sees, difficult prelates, and fractious abbots in his realm.

Theuderic was waiting patiently for the newly named Céleste Vincenot to finish his conversation with the Sanctiff when he felt the first faint tendril of sorcery slithering through the air around him. With some difficulty, he controlled his instinctive reaction and sat motionless, staring fixedly at the three men on the platform as he summoned his powers to him and raised up the strongest shield he could improvise without a spell or a gesture.

He bowed his head and closed his eyes, as if in prayer, and gingerly began tracing the tendril back to its source. The sorcery was incredibly delicate, in fact, if he had not been in Amorr, in the Sanctal Palace itself, he probably would not have even noticed it. Here, though, surrounded by a vast magical void, even the most delicate magic was as easy to detect as someone snapping his fingers in a silent auditorium.

There was a strangeness to the sorcery that he could not identify, an alien sensation. It was not a mage from l'Académie, nor was it a shaman utilizing earth magic or blood magic—he would have recognized those. He was impressed with a definite sense of expertise, of an ease so effortless it almost smacked of carelessness. But who would dare to use magic so openly in Amorr? And what could the unknown sorcerer possibly be attempting to discover with his arts? Did the priests of St. Michael hold some sort of dispensation? Could it be that their famous talents were actually more esoteric than miraculous?

Perhaps it was only the elven ambassador keeping a watchful occult eye upon the imperial city. He assumed the elves would have sent more than one adept as part of their embassy to the Empire, as most of the royal family were supposed to be extraordinarily powerful sorcerers, and the ambassador would almost certainly be of the king's blood. And for all that the elves would have promised not to use their magic inside the city, even the Amorrans probably wouldn't have taken any such promise very seriously. So long as the elves didn't scare the children, horses, or priests with their dark and scandalous arts, he had no doubt that the magistrates of the city would studiously pretend not to see anything they didn't absolutely have to admit seeing.

Then he made his mistake. The faint sorcerous tendril was beginning to fade away, and in his eagerness to find the sorcerer on the other end of it, he attempted to catch hold of it.

The reaction was swift and violent. No sooner had he focused his concentration upon the barely perceptible magic than something very large and powerful seemed to swell before his mind, like a mighty sea monster rising up in front of a fisherman's ketch. He had the vague impression of an arrogant, inhuman mind holding him in contempt.

Then the sheer force that radiated out from it slammed into him, overwhelming his shields—and his senses.

He tried to scream, but the massive magical backlash rendered him mute and immobile. Just as everything faded into blessed black silence, he heard something speaking to him in a voice that lashed his consciousness with fire.

Leave, Magician. Go away. There is nothing for you here.

LODI

THE river was still moving quickly, as proved by the occasional branch that floated under the bridge at an alarming rate. But its dark surface was still unbroken as the first red-gold rays of the morning touched upon it. A few of the orcs were beginning to stir. Six of them were sleeping upon the bridge itself, and the rest were scattered haphazardly around the flickering remnants of a fire that had burned through the night. Fishbones and some larger bones that looked as if they had once belonged to a four-legged creature littered the vicinity, along with the other inevitable signs of orcish habitation. After three days, the stench was nearly strong enough to bring tears to Lodi's eyes, and he was hiding in the underbrush of the forest some thirty paces away.

There were still eighteen of them. Unfortunately, the plenitude of fish in the river prevented them from feeling any need to resort to cannibalism, which would have had the very useful consequence of reducing their numbers.

Lodi shifted his position uncomfortably, as the weight of the crossbow was starting to put his left forearm to sleep. He figured he and Thorald could both fire two bolts before the orcs would have any idea where they were, at which point the two dwarves would have to sprint for the bridge and cut their way through the survivors. The mer, assuming they showed up, might take down a few if they were so inclined, but it would be unwise to count on the watermen being able to do much more than provide a useful distraction, given their inability to fight on land.

One of the bigger orcs rose, emitted a thunderous fart, then looked around as it scratched itself. It kicked a nearby orc awake and pointed to the river. Grumbling, the smaller orc picked up one of the rude fishing rods that was lying near the bridge and staggered over to a pile of detritus that included several fishheads. After picking some flesh from one of the heads and impaling it on the hook, it trudged over to the riverbank and cast the line into the water. The bigger orc growled something at it, to which it appeared to take some offense. It turned its head and opened its mouth to reply.

Without even a ripple of warning, a mer rose up from the water and swept both legs out from under the orc with a thin wooden rod of some sort.

The orc shrieked, and the camp stirred to life.

With all eyes on the river, Lodi took advantage of the confusion to trigger the crossbow. The bolt smashed directly into the back of the bigger orc. It dropped instantly, but not a single one of the seventeen remaining orcs noticed, because the mer had raised its rod, which turned out to be a spear with a wickedly barbed head on it, and plunged it into the screaming orc's chest.

The orcs on the bridge and riverbank shouted and reached for their weapons, but the mer pulled its impaled and flailing victim into the rushing water, where it vanished, never to be seen again.

"Should I loose?" whispered Thorald as Lodi slipped another bolt into place and began cranking the windlass that drew the whipcord.

"No, just wait," he replied in a low voice. "But when you do, take the one with the bow on the north side of the bridge. Do you see him?"

"Yeah, I got him."

The orcs were distracted by the attack, but they weren't in complete disarray yet. Now they were all peering out over the water, with clubs and swords in hand. Four of them had bows, and it was those that most concerned Lodi now. The watery ambush had been effective, but he sincerely hoped it wasn't the mer's best—or only—shot.

It wasn't. Again without warning, the mer leaped from the water, but this time on the other side of the bridge. The orcs pointed and shouted, and three of those with bows loosed their arrows, but the mer was safely submerged again before they even struck the water.

The orcs were clearly frightened now, gabbling and shrieking at each other.

Three different mer surfaced on the south side of the bridge, and each hurled a spear at an orc on the riverbank. Two of the three hit went down screaming and wounded, the third simply collapsed, stone dead, with a spear jutting out both sides of its head. The orcs' fright turned into panic.

"Now!" hissed Lodi, and he loosed a bolt at one of the orcs on the bridge. It struck a little lower than he'd intended but pierced the orc through the neck, causing it to drop its bow and fall to its knees, scrabbling at the bolt. Thorald's shot was cleaner, as his bolt hit his target right in the heart and felled it where it stood.

Seven down, with four orcs already dead and a fifth that appeared to be mortally wounded. That was too much for the orcs. They began to flee away from the river in the direction of the forest.

One of them, a big naked brute with a broken lower tusk, came rushing directly toward them in its panic while Lodi and Thorald were still reloading their crossbows. Fortunately, it didn't see them or it would have caught them off-guard and helpless. Lodi smashed it across its flat-nosed face with the heavy crossbow, knocking it to the ground, then pounced on it and drove the bolt in his left hand into the monster's right eye socket.

The orc roared and threw him off before Lodi could pound it deeply enough to penetrate its feeble brain and kill it. But it had no stomach for continuing the battle, and it fled, bleeding, blinded, and shrieking, deeper into the trees.

"*Faenikh elvete!*" Lodi cursed, glaring at the crossbow's prod. He'd broken it on the orc's thick skull. He tossed the ruined weapon to the ground and pointed to the bridge. "Let's go, lad!"

He slipped his battleaxe from his shoulder and burst from the ground with a war cry that was answered by the high-pitched shrieks of the mer as they gleefully slapped their arms and tails against the surface of the water.

There were still two orcs on the bridge. One was cringing below the wooden sides in an attempt to hide from the screeching mer, and the other was attending to the one Lodi had shot through the throat. Although bows were within reach, neither of the orcs tried to reach them. Indeed, only the second one even rose to its feet and tried to defend itself.

But its crude wooden club was no match for mountain-forged dwarven steel. Two sweeps of Lodi's axe were enough to send the orc flying from the bridge, bleeding, to the waiting mer below.

The water fairly boiled as they swarmed upon it, tearing at the struggling orc with their thick, wicked teeth. Their murderous enthusiasm was truly frightening to see. Lodi almost felt sorry for the remaining *grønt* on the bridge, which screamed pitifully at him and bared its fangs despite the tears of terror running down its terrified green face.

Almost, but not quite. Unmoved by its unintelligible threats or pleas, Lodi lifted it up by its throat, then hurled it over the side and into the river where death waited below. Remembering his earlier promise, he flipped a gold coin in after it.

Lodi raised his axe in salute to the watermen, who were far too occupied with their bloody repast to pay the dwarves the least attention. He shrugged and beckoned for Thorald to follow him. Lodi stopped as soon as they'd crossed the bridge and began tearing dead branches from a dying old tree not far from the river.

"What are you doing?" Thorald asked. "Shouldn't we be moving on before those orcs find their stones and start chasing us? They've seen the two of us, and they can't be so stupid as to think the mer will come to our aid in the forest!"

"We have two choices, lad: Run, and hope we can outrun them, which we can't, or slow them down a bit. Quite a bit, considering how far south they'll have to go to find the next bridge. They damn sure aren't going to risk fording the river anywhere."

Thorald looked back at the deadly flowing water, and Lodi grinned to himself as the younger dwarf shivered. The blood was well downstream now and the mer had disappeared beneath the surface again, but he knew that Thorald would never look at the peaceful, undisturbed surface of a river again without wondering what lay beneath it.

The pile of branches was growing rapidly and had nearly reached their belts when Thorald suddenly seemed to grasp what Lodi was intending. "We're going to burn the bridge?"

"Why not? It's wood," Lodi answered. "But you've got a different job to do."

"What's that?"

Lodi pointed to the thick wooden supports that held the bridge fixed into the ground, then to Thorald's axe. "Unless you want to end up as stew, get chopping!"

Despite his youth, Thorald was still moaning about his aching arms and back on the morning of the third day after they'd crossed the bridge and left it a burned shambles behind them. It had cost them almost the entire morning to destroy it, but the party of orcs that showed up on the other river bank before Thorald had finished chopping through the wooden supports didn't dare to try to put out the flames that were greedily eating away at the beams suspended over the water. They cursed and jeered, and even loosed a few arrows that didn't come close to hitting either Lodi or Thorald, but they stayed on the far bank.

By the time the last remaining supports had finally snapped under the stress of holding the entire weight and the two-thirds of the structure collapsed, burning, into the rushing water, half of the orcs had already wandered away, and the rest had gathered in a circle watching two of their fellows roll around on the ground, snarling and snapping at each other.

The tactic appeared to have bought them the time they needed to make their escape, as they'd seen no sign of pursuit since they'd left the river behind them. Even so, Lodi kept them on the move from dawn until dusk, stopping to rest only when both of them were on the verge of collapsing. It was a brutal pace, and Lodi knew they couldn't maintain it much longer. But he was determined that they would get word of the imminent invasion to someone civilized, be it dwarf, man, or elf, before he would permit himself to relax. But civilization was nowhere to be found in the great forest of the Greenwaste. It had died there long ago with the fall of Glaislael.

"This is mad, Lodi. You're killing us!"

Thorald didn't sound petulant, merely resigned.

Lodi lay on his back next to the panting younger dwarf. His legs burned, and he dreaded the thought of looking at the bleeding mass that was the bottom of his feet. He hadn't felt worse since the time he'd been lying in a similar manner on the sands of the great Amorran stadium with tens of thousands of men watching him bleed to death.

"A little walking never hurt no one, lad."

Thorald snorted.

And in fairness, Lodi didn't believe his own words either.

MARCUS

THE men were beginning to break down. It was three weeks since they'd marched underground to escape the besieged cas-tra, and there had been three desertions yesterday. Another five, all from the same century, had vanished the day before. Nor was it merely their morale that was suffering. The wagons being drawn by the mule teams now contained more sick legionaries than supplies, which meant that they were not only going to have to find a way to restock before reaching the safety of Vallyrium but would probably also need to spend at least two days to allow the men to rest and recover their strength.

If the scouts' reports were correct, they would reach Solacte, the second-largest city of the Larinii, the day after tomorrow. Marcus toyed with the idea of pushing on until sunset and permitting an open camp, which in combination with an early start and a double-time march in the morning might allow them to reach it tomorrow evening, but after looking back at the long line of march, he resisted the foolish temptation. Too many men were already bowed and shuffling under the weight of their packs, and several centurions were shooting expectant looks at him, waiting for him to give the order to stop and begin constructing the castra in which they would spend the night.

He surveyed their surroundings with grim resignation. There was a hill ahead that would serve well enough, with plenty of trees nearby to log for the palisade. No source of water, which was a pity, but their canteens and casks were full of fresh water from the river they'd crossed in the morning. If they were marching along the roads, there would be stone castra waiting for them at the end of every day's march, but then, if he had been able to dare the roads, they would be nearly to Vallyrium by now.

Fortunately, the Cynothii appeared to have given up the pursuit after three days of losing ground to the Amorran double-time. As far as his scouts could tell, the Severan legion had simply taken over the empty castra they'd left behind at Gallidromum and had settled in for the winter there.

It was hard not to envy Falconius Buteo and his officers. They might be rebels and traitors, but while he was cold, lonely, and saddle-sore in the middle of nowhere, wondering how many men were thinking about deserting tonight, they were probably luxuriating in the small but comfortable Gallidromum baths or debauching themselves in its bordellos. He snorted in self-contempt. One little three-week winter march, and suddenly the fires of Hell looked warm and inviting.

"Centurion!" he waved the nearest officer over. "Do you see that hill? We'll stop and make camp there for the night."

"As you say, sir," the centurion said, his enthusiasm betraying his relief. No sooner had he bawled out the order than it was echoed down the cohorts, from century to century, and the line of weary men seemed to surge forward with the news.

Marcus reined his horse in and watched as the legionaries marched past him. They were tired, clearly, but still carried themselves with some semblance of pride. They might be retreating, they might be skulking shamefully over rough ground through Amorran lands, but they had not actually been beaten in battle.

As he expected, he soon heard the pounding of hoofbeats. He saw Gaius Trebonius and Lucius Dardanus, the former reguntur that he'd promoted to tribune, riding toward him. Trebonius didn't look happy.

"What's the trouble now?" Marcus asked.

"I was out patrolling with a squadron of knights this morning," Dardanus answered. "We went looking for the deserters and rode through three or four small villages as well as one reasonably sized town. I'm not sure what's going on, but something is stirring in these parts."

"What do you mean?" Marcus frowned. It didn't sound as if Dardanus was suggesting another legion was in the vicinity, but what else besides disease could threaten an Amorran legion, even weakened and low on supplies as XVII was?

"I realized it wasn't just the five men who deserted together that were from Larinum. The three yesterday, they were Larinii too!" Trebonius slapped his gloves against his horse's neck.

"What about it?" Marcus asked. "If men are going to desert, of course they're going to desert when they're near their homes and their people. That's hardly unexpected."

"No, but what is unexpected is that so many people would refuse to help us. At all." Dardanus looked as if he wanted to ride back and decimate the villagers. "It wasn't so much the refusal to help us find them, as the way they were looking at us. I'm telling you, Clericus, those shrieking goblins we faced up on the hill with Fortex looked sweet and loving by comparison. No matter where we rode, nearly every Larini we saw seemed full of hatred for us. I know it sounds strange, but it was almost as if they were on the edge of revolt!"

Marcus laughed. "The Larinii revolting against Amorr? No, that's not possible. They've been a loyal ally for four centuries! And there isn't even any cause for bad blood, not on either side. Perhaps another legion marched past here this fall, roughed up a few lads and raped a few ladies. They might have feared the same sort of treatment from us."

"It's more serious than that, Clericus," Trebonius said. "And no legion has been in these parts for the better part of five years, which is part of why you chose this route."

"True enough," Marcus admitted. "But it's one thing for a province like Cynothicum to take up arms—provincials always do that now and again. But the Larinii are Utruccans. They've been friends and allies of Amorr so long they're practically Amorran. Who knows, maybe some cretin of a quaestor enslaved one of their nobles and threw him into the games. Or maybe the Falconians raised their taxes too high."

"Come on, Clericus!" Trebonius shook his head. "Rustic people in backwater villages don't give a damn what happens to their nobles. And when haven't the allies been irritated about their taxes? Dardanus is a bright lad, and we should be more careful before we ride into some sort of trap when we reach Solacte."

"Lad? You're only two years older than me!" Dardanus protested, but was ignored by both of the other tribunes.

"We have no idea what could be waiting for us at Solacte," Trebonius said. "Give him a squadron, or maybe two just to be safe, and he can ride for Vallyrium tonight. If anything out of the ordinary is going on, we should be able to find out easily enough, and then you can decide if you want to go around the city or not."

"I don't see that we have a choice," Marcus said. "We have to resupply and give the men a chance to rest. Solacte is our best alternative regardless of what is happening in Vallyrium." Marcus pointed to the men marching past them. The winter-hardened ground had been torn up by the metal-studded sandals of the earlier centuries, making it even harder for those who followed to maintain their footing as they marched. They looked exhausted and miserable. "They're in no state to fight at the moment. We can't push them much farther."

"But even if you're determined to go to Vallyrium, don't you think we should see what we might find waiting for us there?" Trebonius protested.

"I'm not arguing with you, Trebonius," Marcus said. "It's a good idea. Dardanus, take Gavrus and his squadron with you. Proculus would be better, but Gavrus has a decent nose for a game too. Give him a small purse to lose, and he'll be able to tell you everything worth knowing inside a bell. Be careful and try to get back to me before noon the day after tomorrow. If there are even the smallest rumblings of rebellion, I want to hear about them."

"Aye, General," Dardanus tapped his chest with two fingers in a faint mockery of a salute and rode off to find the decurion.

Marcus and Trebonius watched him go, even as the first sound of axes began to ring in the direction of the hill upon which they would be staying tonight.

"You're too casual with us, Marcus Valerius," Trebonius commented. "Not just Lucius Dardanus and me, but with the centurions and decurions too."

"I'm a bloody tribune, not a legate or a real general. You know that. I know that. And the men know it too. I don't have any real authority from the Senate or even my uncle. All I have is my name. So they'll listen to me as long as what I'm telling them to do makes sense to them. Getting us out of Gallidromum might have bought me a little credibility, but that's gone now.

"They're cold, they're exhausted, and now they are beginning to wonder if I'm just a boy running scared. It's been too long. They've forgotten what a shock it was when Saturnius and the others were murdered and the Severans showed up in Cynothicum. All they know is that we should have been safely wintering a month ago, but instead they're following a young lunatic through the wilds of Larinum. It's more than they signed up for. We're just fortunate they're green enough that they don't know any better. A veteran legion would have mutinied a week ago."

Trebonius nodded. "I suppose we're lucky in that regard. Do you really think the Larinii might have rebelled against the Senate?"

"Who knows? Perhaps House Falconius just levied them again and they're sulking. But if Solacte hasn't rebelled yet, they probably will once they learn I'm not going to pay them more than a tenth of what we'll take to see us through the winter. I'll give them a draft they can draw against my House."

"It's not as if they're going to protest when you've got six thousand swords at your back." Trebonius grinned then looked skeptical. "We're not running out of coin already, are we? That can't possibly be right. What accounts have you been going over?"

"No, Cassabus has been keeping an eye on our funds. He says we've still got most of what Saturnius brought back from Amorr. But if I pay it out to the Solactae, I won't have enough to pay the men come spring. And if things back home are as unsettled as they appear to be, I don't think we can count on more coin being delivered. We're already pushing them hard enough, and we may have to push them a lot harder if the Utruccans have rebelled or if there are more rogue legions about. I'd rather not be forced to ask that of them when their pay is in arrears. My father always said that a legionary is never more loyal than when he's got fresh gold in his pocket."

"We could always sack a town or two, if they're truly in rebellion."

Marcus was surprised at his fellow tribune's casual suggestion. "We're not bandits, Gaius Trebonius! We'll pay for what we take. They'll just have to go to Amorr to get it."

Trebonius shrugged. "I'm just saying, if they're going to rebel, perhaps they should be taught a lesson, that's all. We are but the humble instruments of retribution."

"Whose, God's or the Senate's?"

"Does it matter?"

Marcus laughed. "I suppose not if you're on the receiving end of it. The problem is that if Larinum is up in arms, they may not be the only ones. For all we know, we might be the closest legion to Amorr, in which case we'd have to march all the way home instead of staying to winter in Vallyrium."

"What if Vallyrium rises too?"

Now there was an ugly thought. Marcus wished Trebonius hadn't voiced it, but he was right. Marcus might flatter himself to think that the Vallyrii would never rebel against House Valerius, but Larinum's ties to House Falconius were no less strong. He shrugged. They would find out soon enough when Dardanus returned. And besides, what were the chances of that with two legions wintering there?

They waited until the wagons carrying the supplies, the sick, and the wounded rumbled past, then they fell in with the squadron of knights bringing up the rear.

The decurion commanding the rearguard, an older knight named Arcadius, greeted them with the cheerful demeanor of a man who knew the end of the day's journey was nigh.

"Ho, tribunes! At last, we lay down our heavy burdens and rest?"

"I can't help but notice you're riding your horse, Arcadius," Marcus said. "He's the one who should be complaining, not you."

"Complaining? The men grumble and the centurions curse, but we of the equestrian class are far too noble to complain of our lot in life."

"Too well-mounted, I should think," Trebonius observed. "How many tried to fall behind?"

"Today? Twenty-eight collapsed on the march. Nine were malingerers. I gave them a dose of the *vitis*, and praise the Lord, were they not healed? The other nineteen were set upon the wagons. Winter ague, I think, not the flux."

Thank You, Immaculate Son, for small mercies, Marcus looked up at the sky. Were it the flux, he might as well set the men to digging graves as well as the ditches that were now being dug around what would be the perimeter of the night camp.

Somehow, no matter how deeply he read, the martial histories never seemed to talk much about the diseases that killed far more men than the battlefield ever did. During his first weeks in the legion, he'd idly wondered if he had what it took to succeed as an officer and commander, and he'd looked at the challenge as an intellectual one. Would he be able to master and stay on top of all the details, to make the right decisions, to recognize the moment of truth on the battlefield and arrange his forces in just the right way? He'd never realized how much more important it was to focus on keeping the men warm, fed, and well away from their own shit.

The true challenge was spiritual. Once, he had imagined there were right decisions and wrong decisions. Now that he was in command, he had been forced to accept the bitter truth that there were no right decisions—there were only consequences that were bad and consequences that were worse. It seemed that no matter what he decided, no matter what path he chose, men would die.

Even something so obviously right as the decision to retreat rather than submit to Falconius Buteo came with a heavy price. When they'd left Gallidromum in the middle of the night, they hadn't only left behind the merchants and whoremasters, who would be just as happy to serve Buteo's legionaries as they had served XVII. They'd also abandoned several hundred camp wives and scores of children, none of whom had any idea where their legionary "husbands" and fathers were now. No doubt some of the wives would find new men in the Severan legion, but those with children would likely be rather less inclined and less able to do so. The fate of the legion's camp followers was something he'd never given a thought to as a tribune, but in the last week alone more than twenty officers had raised the issue with him.

Trebonius and Arcadius were discussing whether it would be best to spend two or three days in Solacte, but Marcus paid them no mind. He was wondering how the men with women and children could let their dependents know where the legion would be when he himself didn't know.

The situation was ridiculous. It was absurd! How could he hope to make the right decisions, how could he even avoid the potentially disastrous ones, in the complete absence of information? He had written to both his father and Lady Shadowsong twice, and once to his uncle, sending the letters by hired rider both times they'd passed through a town large enough to maintain communications with the imperial city. But of course, any letters they had written him in return were hundreds of leagues behind him now, in Gallidromum.

As he rode through imaginary gates onto what would soon be the Via Principalis and into the marked outlines of the legion's fortress for the night, he was saluted by dozens of centurions, optios, decurions, and common soldiers.

It gave him no pleasure. Instead it made him realize, for the first time since he'd sworn the legionary's oath, that he probably should have taken vows instead.

The next day's march was equally long and perhaps even a little bit more miserable, as a clear winter sky caused the temperature to fall, and a faint dusting of snow fell throughout the morning. But the centurions reported no deserters, and the mood throughout the legion appeared to have improved considerably upon hearing that they would have at least two days' rest outside Solacte prior to the last push onto Montmila, the large fort in northern Vallyrium where he intended them to spend the remainder of the winter. The castra at Solacte was permanent, had higher stone walls than the one they'd left in Gallidromum, and, thanks to the thermal springs in the area, even featured its own baths.

He halted the march in the late afternoon again, but the ditches had barely been dug and the palisade was just rising when Trebonius drew his attention to a small body of their own horse riding toward them.

"Quintus Placidius Ulpius, Tribune," the knight saluted and identified himself after being permitted to address him, Trebonius, and Caius Proculus. "First Cavalry, Eighth Squadron. I bear grave news, sir. Larinum is in revolt against Amorr, as are Caelignus and Trivicum."

"Dammit, Ulpius," Proculus swore. "That can't be right!"

"Vallyrium too?" Marcus asked.

"Don't know, sir. The gates of Solacte are closed to us. The Solactae were already in arms when we arrived, and they were waiting for us. Between thirty and forty of them ambushed the tribune. My squadron and I were some distance behind, as we were separated when one of the horses startled and threw its rider, so they didn't see us. Lucius Dardanus didn't fight back. He ordered his men to stand down as soon as he saw they were surrounded by archers."

"What did the Solactae do to the men? Are they still alive?"

"They were unharmed the last I saw. Captured. The Solactae disarmed them and put their horses on leads but didn't bind their hands.

We followed them to within sight of the walls, but I didn't dare ride any closer. They're still in the city."

"How did you learn about the revolt and the other allies?" Trebonius asked.

"There are a number of farms and villages outside the walls. I thought you might like to know why the Solactae were so unaccountably hostile, so we captured a villager and interrogated him. It's mostly local rumors, so I don't know how reliable they are, but Larinum is definitely in arms. It seems a group of nobles in Falera is calling itself a Senate and has put out a call to raise three legions."

"What did you do with this villager?" Marcus asked.

"I released him. I thought he'd speak more truthfully if I promised we wouldn't harm him."

Proculus sighed theatrically, prompting a scornful glare from Trebonius.

Marcus shook his head at his senior centurion.

"No, he did well to spare the man, Proculus." Marcus nodded at Ulpius. "They have to know we're in the vicinity. This is too far off the beaten track for a squadron of legionary horse to be wandering about alone. Dardanus will have warned them we're right behind him anyway. Ulpius, well done. I commend your initiative and your mercy. Go and see to your horse. Proculus, will you find Cassabus and ask him to join us? I think we will be in need of his particular expertise for the morrow."

"You're going to take the city?" the centurion and the tribune exclaimed at the same time.

"In a manner of speaking." Marcus grinned at them. "You really need to read more Sextus Gaerus, Trebonius. It's not necessary to take a city so long as you convince those inside its walls that you can take it quickly if you want. If Dardanus and Gavrus had the good sense to tell their men to keep their mouths shut about our leaving the artillery back in Gallidromum, we won't have to waste another day here."

In the morning, a bleary-eyed Praefect Cassabus presented himself to Marcus at the daily pre-march convocation of the senior centurions and held up both hands.

"We've managed to build ten machines. Only one is operational, and I wouldn't count on it remaining that way for long. But they look convincing. Unless they can get a ballistarius within twenty paces to take a look at them, they'll put the fear of God into anyone inside those walls."

"Well done, Praefect. You and your men can sleep in the wagons on the march. Julianus, I want you to take ten squadrons from the First Cavalry and scare up as many cattle as you can find. Round up some dogs too. They'll make the driving that much easier. Bring them to the castra. According to the map it's west of the city, on the river."

"Do you want sheep as well?"

"Sure, but only enough to feed us while we stay in the castra. Say, five days' worth, in case this doesn't work and we have to storm the walls. Sheep are too slow, and I intend to set a good pace when we head south for Amorr. The men will be unhappy we're not stopping longer here, but at least we'll be on the roads from this point on."

"Be nice not to have to dig any more ditches or log trees for the rest of the way," Cassabus commented, yawning.

"Go get some sleep, Cassabus," Marcus ordered. "Everyone else, let's get moving. I want to be in Montmila within six days."

As the senior officers departed, Trebonius approached him with a smile on his face. "I didn't notice you telling Appius Julianus to pay for any of the cattle he scares up, Clericus. Or the dogs, for that matter. But why are you still concerned with resupplying if we're marching straight for Vallyrium? We've got more than enough for two weeks on hand."

"They chose war, did they not? We are but the humble tools of Senatorial retribution. If all it costs them is a few head of cattle, they'll be fortunate." Then Marcus sighed. "As for the supplies, Trebonius, we may be marching for Montmila, but who is to say we will be able to reach it if the Larinii are raising an army?"

They reached the outskirts of Solacte just before noon. Marcus considered the possibility of going straight to the castra and confronting the city authorities in the morning, but the capture of Dardanus, Gavrus, and the ten knights of his squadron all but forced his hand. He might not be able to take the city today, but, thanks to the ingenuity and hard work of Cassabus and the ballistarii, he was confident he could convince them to return his men and give them what they required. He didn't dare leave them behind for ransom later—rebels weren't known for respecting the traditional rules of war.

After sending two of the First Cavalry's five remaining squadrons to check on the state of the castra, he ordered Cassabus to be awakened and set to work.

The city cathedral rang two bells before the ten giant onagers were assembled, and Marcus imagined the third bell was approaching by the time they were moved into position in between the nine cohorts standing in their ranks facing the city gates some four hundred paces away.

There was frantic activity visible on the city walls, and he imagined there was probably a considerable amount of consternation among the Solactean leadership. He rather hoped they had chosen a king or elected a few consuls rather than a full city council, as it was always easier to deal with one or two men than a dozen.

"Is everything ready?" he asked Cassabus. The tall optio looked less than entirely refreshed after his morning nap in the supply wagons, but he nodded. "Very well, let us knock on the door, then."

Cassabus raised his hand and waited for an answering gesture from the crew of the oversized onager positioned directly before the gates. The praefect dropped his hand, and a moment later, there was a loud thumping sound, the big wooden machine bucked violently, and a large rock that had taken four men to load it in the onager's sling sailed through the air and smashed silently against the left gate, followed a moment later by a loud crack.

"That should get their attention, sir," the optio commented with satisfaction.

"Well done, Cassabus. Have them reload it just in case they've got any archers with twitchy fingers. Trebonius, you have the legion. Proculus, Commius, if you would join me."

"Sir," the four men barked in rough chorus.

They rode out slowly, with Commius serving as his draconarius and bearing the twin banners of Legio XVII and House Valerius. All three of them were wearing their helms and armor, more for effect than out of any expectation it would save them from arrows loosed by the archers they could see behind the merlons on the battlements above them. None of them appeared to have their bows nocked, which provided some relief. They halted fifty paces from the walls, close enough to see the large gouge Cassabus's doorknocking had torn out of the gate.

"I am Valerius Clericus, the commanding officer of Legio XVII," he called to the battlements. "In the name of the Senate and People of Amorr, I demand the return of the tribune Lucius Dardanus, the decurion Quintus Gavrus, and the ten knights who accompanied them!"

There was much stirring among the men on the walls and more than a little abuse was hurled at him, but no violence was offered.

Finally, a white head appeared in the gatehouse on the right side.

"I am called Opiter Florus Siculo. What do you want, Tribune?"

"Do you speak for the city?"

"I am the senator-in-chief, yes." His voice was on the querulous side, which made Marcus suspect he could be bullied. "How is it that you speak for the legion? You don't look old enough to shave, boy."

Or perhaps not. Marcus curbed his irritation provoked by the man's dismissive words and forced himself to remain calm. "There is no need to parley. I require the return of my men, their horses, and an amount of supplies. We intend you no harm. We are merely passing through. I intend to stay three days in the castra to the west, after which date we will move on."

"Throwing rocks at our gates is damned poor manners, boy."

"I merely wanted to ensure I had your attention, sir. And may I remind you that kidnapping a squadron of my horse is hardly the height of etiquette."

"Yes, well, we don't take kindly to Amorrans trespassing on our lands no more. So here is our proposal to you: Take your legion and go to Hell—or Amorr, whatever you prefer. And you can take your onagers and stick them up your arse!"

Marcus blinked, at a loss for words. He never seriously imagined the Solactae would turn him down. Quibble about the supplies, certainly, and he might have even been persuaded to pay for the supplies that he was taking, the wine, the flour, the salt, and so forth, but it made no sense to respond with such insolence to a man with siege engines and six thousand swords at his command. Was the man serious?

"Forgive me, Florus Siculo, but am I hearing you correctly? You do realize that I have ten onagers with which to knock down your walls and an entire legion to sack your city if need be, do you not?"

Siculo didn't respond himself; he didn't need to. A chorus of jeers and obscene invitations of varying degrees of crudeness and creativity rained down upon him, inundating him with insults. Clearly, the Solactae were unimpressed with his bluff. They might not know that only one of the ten onagers was capable of operation, but something had bolstered their confidence. Why were they so unconcerned?

"What do you think?" he asked the veteran decurion.

"They know we have to move on. They've had the lads for over a day now. They'll have talked. Everybody talks sooner or later. The Solactae know we didn't come all this way from Cynothicum in order to get bogged down in a siege here, especially if we're begging supplies. Those walls are thick enough to stand weeks of bombardment, and they're too high to storm easily."

Marcus nodded and called back to the walls. "Florus Siculo, I do not wish to be unreasonable! Return my men to me now and I will return tomorrow to discuss the supply issue."

"Reason with this, Amorran!"

A massive cheer went up as twelve pikes rose suddenly from the two nearest battlements. Upon each one was a head wearing an Amorran helm. Marcus was close enough to recognize the faces. Gavrus's eyes were closed but Dardanus seemed to be staring at him accusatorily. Sickened, he reeled in his saddle, badly enough that Proculus reached out to steady him. His vision went black, and for a moment, he was back standing on the platform, staring in horror at the bloody, headless body of his cousin.

"God, God, God," he whispered brokenly, despite himself staring at the lifeless faces of the men he had unknowingly sent to their deaths. "How can men do this? In what image of the devil are they made?"

"Steady on, Tribune." The centurion's calm tone more than his words were like a lifeline thrown to a drowning man. Marcus clung to it as he fought to master himself, to prevent his insides from turning themselves inside out and choke down the bitter gorge that rose and burned the back of his throat. "Steady on, General."

The Solactae were jeering him. Behind him, the realization of what was happening was just beginning to sweep through the legion, and soon the angry shouting became an indeterminate roar.

Marcus didn't know what to do. He didn't know what to say. He wanted to leap from his horse and clutch the insolent, elderly consul by the throat and squeeze until he turned black and his eyes popped from his head. But that was foolish.

Instead, he simply drew his sword, held it above his head, and waited until the taunts and howls from the Solactae died down as they grew curious about his reply.

"You shall have our response on the morrow," he shouted as calmly as he could manage, then sheathed his sword, spit on the grass and turned his horse around.

Caius Proculus and Servius Commius followed suit, and together, the three of them trotted back toward the legion in a somber silence that did nothing to disguise their mutual rage.

Behind them, twelve pairs of sightless eyes watched their retreat with the indifference of the dead.

SEVERA

SEVERA had not been so excited since the day she saw the gladiator wearing her token. But now she could show the world her delight, as there was no shame in taking pleasure in her handsome fiancé, who cut a very fine figure indeed in the unadorned white robes worn by the candidates for the various offices being presented to the voting tribes. Sextus was easily the most handsome of the fifty or so young men who were rivals for the twenty-four tribunates available, and she felt that even if he wasn't a Valerian endorsed by the heads of four of the most powerful Houses Martial, he would have commanded enough votes to win on the basis of his noble appearance alone.

If his speech had been nothing special, being full of the conventional platitudes and patriotic declarations, it was no worse than those of the other candidates. Indeed, the three years he had on most of them gave him an air of gravitas in comparison. There had been no jeering by the clausores or any of the common folk who sympathized with them, so it appeared her fear that Sextus might be harmed by his engagement to her, and therefore connected to her father's perceived betrayal, was groundless. Of course, it probably helped that he'd been nominated by his uncle, the consul suffectus, who was now seen as the city's great hope to quell the rising tide of rebellion outside its walls.

The tribal assembly was a massive affair, and the Forum was about three-quarters filled with the men gathered into their various tribes as well as the inevitable vendors and prostitutes looking to earn coin among the large annual gathering.

It was interesting to see the way in which the tribal divisions cut across the traditional house and class lines. With the exception of the three Houses Martial, Cassiana, Falconia, and Valeria, each of which served as their own tribe, a man's tribe didn't necessarily align with his House or his patronage. The Sabatina tribe to which most Severans belonged was easy to spot from her vantage point on the base of a statue on the west side of the square, as they were all wearing black in mourning for her father. Their gesture of respect touched her, and she bit her lip to distract herself before she started crying.

This was a day for celebration and joy, not grief, and she reminded herself of how proud her father would have been to see his future son-in-law standing astride the rostra in front of the assembled citizenry of the city, looking for all the world like a prince waiting to be publicly crowned heir to the throne.

"Do you see him?" Marcipor, her fiancé's golden-haired slave who was always underfoot, called up to her. "What is he doing?"

"Yes, yes. He's waving to people and talking to two of the other candidates."

"Amazing. Do you know, a week ago I'd have sworn we'd have to get him blind drunk to get him through this!"

She rolled her eyes at him and returned her attention to the platform. She didn't trust the beautiful slave and considered him to be a bad influence on Sextus, but she tolerated him for Sextus's sake. Though it was tempting to try convincing Sextus to get rid of the man, who was a notorious gambler and philanderer, her mother had advised her strongly against wasting her own influence on such trifling matters.

"Never attempt to convince a man of something he doesn't already think he believes," she'd told Severa. "When he is a man of influence, he won't have the time or inclination to run around carousing with slaves. But mind you don't let that slave compromise you either. You're quite right not to trust him. He knows very well how attractive he is, and he's not shy about using it either."

Marcipor was very good-looking, she supposed, especially if you didn't mind beards. She wondered idly what it would be like to kiss a man with a beard and grimaced at the uncomfortable prospect. It was just as well that she was immune to the slave's charms.

"Can you see who is voting first up there?" she asked.

"Not yet. The magistrate is still talking with the candidates."

The magistrate presiding was the outgoing urban praetor, a Viturius who was well past his year, being older than any of the consuls. It took him a long time to greet all of the fifty-some young men, but at last he turned his attention to the gathered tribes. But if his actions were deliberate and his shoulders were a little stooped with age, his lungs were in fine condition, because Severa could hear him clearly from where she was clinging to the oversized stone arm of someone the carvings identified as M. Fabius Pulvillus.

"Men of Amorr, you have heard from each of the candidates. The custodes will now present the lists of the men whose vote has been selected by their tribes, in the order that their name is drawn from the basket." He gestured to a slave who was carrying a small woven basket, and when the slave approached, he withdrew a small object from it. "Aniensis is the principium!"

A cheer went up from a small group of men belonging to the Aniensis tribe halfway back from the rostra. The other tribes applauded and made way for the proud custos as he marched toward the elderly praetor and handed him a wooden tablet. The magistrate peered at it, briefly consulted with the custos to clarify a name he could not distinguish, then read them aloud.

The third name on the list of twenty-four was Sextus Valerius. Severa shouted and shared a triumphant glance with Marcipor. One tribe and already one vote. That was a good omen: Sextus had told her that it was always lucky to be named by the first tribe to vote.

Tromentina was drawn next by the praetor, and they had Sextus listed fourth. He was also on the lists turned in by Tetius and Cassiana. A loud roar went up from the powerful tribe associated with the great House

Martial when the magistrate read the name Appius Cassianus Canina, which unsurprisingly headed their list. Menenia left Sextus off their list of names, but he was second on Papiria's, first on his maternal tribe of Romilia's, third on Falconia's, and fourth on Macea's. When Valeria's custos turned in his tablet, Sextus's name was met with a cheer to rival the one Cassianus Canina had received.

Even with less than half the tribal results in, it was obvious that Sextus would be elected one of the twenty-four. Indeed, his showing in the votes was so strong that the question now was whether he would be named first tribune! It seemed to be between Sextus and the younger Canina for whom would claim that honor.

Marcipor had disappeared, and she was not surprised to hear, upon his return, that he had gone to place a bet. The monetary stakes kept the crowd's level of interest high. The most common plebians, those without any political clout or even the least bit of interest in the Senatorial rivalries, alternately groaned and shouted with glee depending upon the order in which the most commonly heard names were read.

As pleased as Severa was for her husband-to-be, though, Severa felt bad for the young men who looked up in surprise on the rare instances when their names were called—and for those few who never heard their names at all. How cruel it was, she thought, for a father to insist upon his son's candidacy when he could not even deliver a single vote from his own tribe!

When the last tribe, Ramnes, turned in its list, only a very few of the most sober and keenly attentive were still keeping track. Fortunately, it did not take long for the three slaves who were acting as scribes to add up the results, so the crowd did not grow too restive before the list of winners was presented to the praetor. That magistrate, in keeping with the festive spirit that now pervaded the Forum, read the twenty-four names beginning with the winner who had received the least and lower-ranked votes.

It was a delight to see the reactions of some of the lesser candidates to their victories. Laughter filled the air when one unlikely winner, a thin young man with the decidedly unpatrician name of Hostus Herminius Tubertus, looked from side to side upon his name being called as the twenty-third tribune, as if there might be another Herminius in the contest. Another winner, from a lesser Falconian branch, finished fifteenth and fell to his knees sobbing in ecstatic disbelief. Others were not so fortunate, and as the names the praetor read out became more and more familiar to Severa, the faces of the likely losers grew longer and more grim.

Eventually, it came down to the last two: Sextus and Cassianus Canina. Severa frantically tried to recall how many times the Cassian, who was in his year, had finished above Sextus in the various lists. She thought the Cassian had finished first more often, but balancing that, he had failed to place in the top five as reliably.

"The second tribune," the praetor announced, "is Sextus Valerius. Elected first tribune, in his year, is Appius Cassianus Canina!"

The shouts and cheers from the crowd echoed off the buildings surrounding the Forum as the Cassians and Valerians alike celebrated their victories.

Severa was disappointed that Sextus hadn't finished first, but she was exceedingly proud of him. She watched him smile and congratulate the younger man with a hearty arm clasp then exchange words with his fellow victors and the disappointed losers alike. It was a signal victory for the clausores, which would have been a blow for her father, but anything else could not have been expected in light of the dreadful news from outside the walls. And it boded well for Sextus's uncle. To her surprise, that struck her as a very good thing. How ironic it was for a daughter of House Severus to anticipate the consular election of a Valerian with no little relief!

She climbed down from the statue and found Marcipor looking like a cat in the cow's milk, which she found a little suspicious.

"You didn't bet against Sextus winning first, did you?" she demanded accusatorily.

"No, I knew he'd be first three, but so did everyone else, so the odds weren't worth it. And it's always hard to say which of the best candidates will end up on top. With all the vote-swapping that takes place between the Houses, even the most obvious winners will sometimes fall a place or two. Second is a great finish for Sextus given that he was three years late entering his name. Magnus told him to be happy with anything better than sixth."

"So, what did you bet on, then?"

"Some fool gave me fifteen-to-one against Sextus finishing first on the Sabatina list. With all that's been happening the last few weeks, half the city has forgotten that you're engaged to marry him."

She burst out laughing. It was a rather clever bet on his part, for without taking her marriage into account, no one would have ever imagined that the tribe to which the Severans belonged would so heavily back a Valerian. Whoever took Marcipor's bet must have thought he was stealing from him.

"Let's go find Sextus," Severa said. "And then, as you're so newly wealthy, you can buy lunch for me and the new tribune. But I want to come back here for the consular vote."

"As my lady commands." He bowed deeply, and a just little mockingly, to her. Then his blue eyes, so like the sky, grew serious. "My lady Severa, I know you don't like me. But I beg you, after you are married, please don't make him send me away."

She didn't flinch from his accusation. "The problem, Marcipor, is that you think all women are stupid and too blinded by your beauty to see through your charm. I was taken in by a man like you once, and thankfully, my father forced me to see the truth."

"I don't think you are stupid, my lady."

She rolled her eyes. "Of course you do, Marcipor. How could you not? You've had slaves and patrician women alike eating out of your hand for years. Sextus says you've fathered more children than you have fingers and thumbs. And now you think to play the penitent with me, batting your eyes and beseeching me not to sell the little innocent orphan?"

His pretense of submission vanished. "So you intend to make him sell me." His voice was as cold as his eyes.

"No, not at all." It took more than a slave's anger to intimidate the daughter of Patronus Severus. "But if you ever attempt to seduce me, or any of my friends, or indeed, any other patrician woman, I will not only have you sold, I will first have you whipped and beaten so badly that your lovers will vomit to look upon you."

He frowned. "And what if a patrician woman pursues me?"

"Then you tell her no, Marcipor. No. I realize you may not have heard the word before, but I promise, most women understand what it means."

He favored her with the merest ghost of a smile. "I suspect my lady knows well how few patrician women are accustomed to hearing it."

"In such a case, come to me, Marcipor. If necessary, I will teach it to them. I will not pretend to like you, but we don't need to be enemies. If nothing else, I believe you are loyal to Sextus, and I am willing to put up with you on that basis, so long as you cease behaving like a bitch in heat around your betters."

"I can live with that," he said. "I don't like you either, my lady, but I think you may well be worthy of my master."

She snorted. "Of course I am. The only question there has ever been was if your master was worthy of me. Now, let us go find the new tribune and congratulate him."

Severa was not at all unhappy to discover that the speeches had been given and the voting was just about to begin by the time they returned. The eleven candidates for the three consulships stood shoulder to shoulder on the stage, awaiting the announcement of which tribe would begin the voting.

It had been difficult to pry Sextus from the clutches of the vast host of Valerians and other well-wishers, but with Marcipor's help she'd managed to extricate him and return to the Forum, which was much more crowded now, since the voting was taking place for the highest offices.

She was pleased to learn that one of her cousins had been elected to one of the twenty quaestorships. She didn't know Servius very well, as he was ten years older than her, but it was good to know that House Severus still commanded support among the tribes despite the unfair criticism of her father that was still on the lips of far too many Amorrans.

"Valeria is the principium," the praetor declared, brandishing the engraved stone he'd drawn from the basket. A hushed awe fell over the crowd despite the half-inebriated state of many of the voters. Surely this was a certain sign of the Almighty's hand at work! Marcipor wouldn't find anyone giving odds against Corvus, that much was certain. With the outcome pre-ordained, the Valerians went with a simple show of hands, and it wasn't long before their custos presented the three names to the elderly magistrate, whose voice was beginning to grow hoarse.

"For consul civitas, Tribe Valeria votes for Marcus Andronicus Declama. For consul provincae, Appius Appuleius Pansa. For consul aquilae, Sextus Valerius Corvus!"

As the three tribes cheered the entirely predictable vote, Severa looked at her fiancé, who was regarding his namesake with an odd expression that was almost regretful.

"What's the matter?" she asked. "Do you not want him to win?"

"It's not that. I'm not even angry with him. I know better than anyone what an ass Fortex could be. And I know it probably sounds awful to say it, but I have no doubt he had it coming. My uncle may be a hard man, but he's always been fair, and he never had anything against my brother. He wouldn't have executed Gaius Fortex if he hadn't given him cause."

"Then what's troubling you?"

He shrugged. "Corvus didn't think he'd ever be consul. He didn't want to be consul. He's nine years past his year, just like I'm three years past mine. And yet, there I was up there, all the same. Just like him— summoned by the tribes whether he wanted it or not."

She slipped her arms around him and pressed her face to his chest. Now she understood. He was seeing himself up there one day in his uncle's place, another reluctant consul raised up by a sense of duty and the voice of the People instead of his own ambition. And the grave responsibility of the magistracy lay much more heavily on those upon whom it was imposed than on those who sought it as a mere sign of their own glory.

The tribes were voting quickly now. Clustumina, Galeria, Quirina, Stellatina, and Voltinia all followed the Valerian lead. Only Amorres, Tromentina, and of course, Falconia, preferred Falconius Rullianus to Andronicus Declamas. The votes for the Provinces and Eagles were unanimous. The sun was just beginning to set when Declamas belatedly reached his majority, and the Viturian, now acting in a propraetorial capacity, announced the elections over after only nineteen of the twenty-six tribes had voted.

However, instead of announcing the three consuls for the new year, the propraetor looked to the side of the rostra, which was the signal for three squads of eight fascitors to march to the front of the platform. Severa, Sextus, and everyone else in the crowd fell silent upon seeing them, as each of the twenty-four men were carrying their axes unbound by their customary branches.

"We are at war," Sextus said, sliding his arm around her.

"I don't understand," Severa said, confused. "Aren't we always at war? My brothers have been away invading some province or breed land almost as long as I can remember!"

"No, the Senate permits the Houses Martial to use their allotted legions as the situation requires and as they see fit. Your House didn't care if our legions defeated the goblins or not, and your father would never have sent them to our assistance if we were losing. But formal war is something altogether different. I don't think there has been one in more than one hundred years. It means all the Houses are united, and that has to be a very bad sign."

The crowd, most of which was chattering about the uncovered axes, fell silent as the three newly elected consuls appeared again, each standing

in front of his fascitors. But instead of wearing the white robes they'd
been wearing before, under their purple capes of office, each of the three
men was wearing legionary armor. Corvus's was battered and dirty, while
Declama's was shiny enough to look brand new, but the effect was every
bit as grim as the consuls had intended.

"Men of Amorr," the propraetor cried out, "your new consuls will
address you now. I give you Marcus Andronicus Declama, consul civitas!"

"The new year is customarily a time of celebration and festivals."
Declama's voice was high-pitched, but the gravity of the occasion was
such that no one tittered. "That will not happen this year, for as you
have seen, we find ourselves facing imminent war. As consul civitas, I am
cancelling all public festivals and announcing three days of repentance
and contemplation, during which time I expect every man, woman, and
child to repent of their sins, to beg forgiveness of the Almighty God, and
to ask the intercession of the Immaculate Lord, the true King of this city,
to strengthen and sustain her."

The Forum buzzed with astonished discussion of what had provoked
these extreme measures. Declama nodded to Appuleius Pansa, the consul
provincae, who stepped forward.

"As consul provincae, I have nothing to say except to express my full
support for the actions of the consul civitas and to declare that we three
consuls have agreed that we shall henceforth speak with one voice, and
that any public statement made by one of us should be considered to have
made by all three of us, speaking in unison. With regards to the direction
of the anticipated war effort, the consul aquilae shall be the sole magister
militum, and the consul civitas and I will serve as his chief legates."

There was scattered applause, but the men of the tribes were too astonished and alarmed at the consul provincae's highly unusual announcement
to do anything but wonder what would come next.

Corvus stepped forward, and, as if to illustrate the truth of their
words, Declama and Pansa assumed parade-like military stances on either
side of him. His voice was strong and commanding as he addressed the
Forum in much the same manner as a general addressing his men.

"Men of Amorr, you have placed great trust in me and my colleagues in a most difficult time. Many of you already know of the Marruvian league, which our allies of the north and east have formed against us at Falera. What none of you yet know, and the reason for the extraordinary and precipitate actions my colleagues and I have taken, is that the other six Utruccan allies have joined together in a southern league, led by the Salventii. It is our belief that if we do not agree to their demands, these leagues will soon unite their forces and march upon Amorr in the spring."

The crowd erupted with cries of outrage, fear, and anger.

Severa could feel Sextus's tension, and it frightened her.

"I wonder if they're going to make him dictator," he whispered. "I hope not. My father would just love that. If Corvus is named dictator, I swear, Magnus may very well go to Salventum and volunteer to general for them."

God, what sort of family of madmen am I marrying into? She didn't know if she should laugh or cry at what Sextus was suggesting. And here she'd thought that being the daughter of the princeps senatus was difficult! Could she even marry Sextus if her father-in-law was leading rebel armies against Amorr? And as a leading military tribune, would Sextus even be in the city long enough to marry if war came?

"Men of Amorr," Corvus said, "it is the custom of the Senate to require three days of deliberation before a vote is taken on any suggested new law. Therefore, tomorrow when the Senate meets, I shall propose a reply by the Senate and People to the demands of these Utruccan leagues as well as the *Lex Valeria Corva*, which concerns how we intend to organize our legions and marshal our strength, assuming war with our former allies becomes unavoidable."

"Dictator, dictator!" The cry went up from various points around the Forum. "Corvus dictator!"

Severa felt Sextus wince, but his uncle was quick to nip the chant in the bud.

"You need no dictator, men of Amorr! Your laws are sound. Your walls are strong. Your will is certain. And your leaders are one! We stand at the crossroads. We must choose. Our erstwhile allies have made demands of us, men of Amorr, demands of you and of our sacred city. With insolence they demand their liberty. With threats they demand you grant them the very citizenship you possess. Shall we submit to their demands, men of Amorr? Shall we give them a voice in our governance? What say you?"

"No!" The very tiles beneath her feet seemed to shake with the thunder of the twenty-six tribes.

"Shall we answer them with words or shall we answer them with war? Tell me three times!"

"War! War! War!"

"Then so shall I advise the Senate tomorrow. Do not fear, men of Amorr. Some of us will bleed, and some of us will die, but as our forefathers defeated the Marruvii and the Salventii, so we shall defeat them once more!"

The crowd roared their approval of the three consuls standing together in their armor, displaying their united resolve and readiness to lead the city into war. Most of the members of the Senate who would be voting on the response to the allies were present in the crowd, shouting in enthusiastic chorus with the vulgar citizenry, so it was already clear that a Senatorial vote in favor of a belligerent reply was all but a certainty.

Sextus was not shouting, Severa saw. He was staring at his uncle in something akin to awe. She understood. All her life, she had found it almost impossible to balance her firsthand knowledge of her loving, if formidable, papa with the powerful, arrogant, and sometimes feared figure of the princeps senatus of whom she heard others speak. Sextus had certainly heard others talk about Corvus, the victorious general and battle-hardened leader of men, but this was probably the first time he had ever witnessed his uncle in this light.

Had Corvus ever been like Sextus? They had both been lost in the shadow of the same man—would the effort involved in stepping out of it and becoming his own man affect Sextus in the same way? Was the cost too great? She found it hard to picture her handsome, nonchalant fiancé executing anyone or standing before the Forum in battered armor, exhorting men to bloodshed and war. What would such a transformation do to their marriage? What grief would it bring her?

She shivered, even as the gathered voices of the angry men of Amorr crescendoed around her. To her, they sounded like wolves howling a fateful warning.

AULAN

THE Via Epra was a much more grim and depressing sight than it had been when Aulan and his men had ridden it toward the city only a month earlier. This time, they could seldom progress from one milestone to the next without encountering the huddled mass of a corpse, the well-stripped remnants of a cart, or a rudimentary memorial indicating a burial alongside the road.

The snow from the recent storm had already retreated to the distant heights, but fortunately the winter weather remained cold enough to prevent their journey from descending into a stinking miasma of rot and decay. If the remains of their passing were a reliable guide, the exodus of the provincials from Amorr had been a brutal one.

Aulan heard Magnus sigh as they passed yet another pair of unburied bodies, one of them tragically small. Against his expectations, he'd come to respect his father's old enemy and even understand why the man had been elected consul a remarkable four times, twice for the Eagles and twice for the Legions. The Valerian possessed a commanding presence that had won over Aulan's men almost from the moment he'd met them outside the outer walls, and the decisive manner with which he'd announced his intentions had made obedience seem the natural choice. Even when those intentions had turned out to be entirely different than Aulan was expecting.

"Legio VII is in the winter castra near Aviglianus. We'll see how matters stand with them, then continue north and round up Legio XV. It's a pity we can't be sure of XVII. No one knows where my blasted nephew has taken it."

"If Vallyria is in arms, do you think two legions will be enough to suppress it?" Aulan asked him as they left the bodies behind. At first, it had bothered Aulan to ride past the corpses of the poor unfortunates and leave them unburied, but he'd eventually gotten used to it.

"Suppress it?" Magnus laughed. He was a big-bellied man, and his laugh was as hearty as his appetite. "Don't be mistaken, Aulus Severus: Vallyria is already in revolt. And I don't intend to suppress it—I intend to lead it!"

Aulan wondered if he'd heard the ex-consul correctly. "Lead a revolt against the Senate and People?"

"Against who else? Everything changed when your father was murdered, Aulan. An amount of violence and so forth surrounding the elections is nothing new, of course, and senators have been passing laws to trip up their rivals and bringing petty prosecutions to force their enemies out of the game for centuries. But killing an ex-consul? Assassinating the princeps senatus in public at his own daughter's betrothal? This is not politics—it is monstrous."

"Then why do we not strike back in the same manner? How can we turn on the Senate and People?"

Magnus shook his head. "The Senate and People? What are they but the remnants of a mythical past? Your father was a great man. He was the first to see that change was upon us, and he did his best to bring it about peacefully. I wish to the Inviolate that I had seen what he saw sooner myself. I should have helped him, not led the fight against him! It is one of my great regrets that I did not come to see things his way until it was too late. Who knows? Perhaps together we might have averted this war. But he always knew that his efforts might fail, and so he also made alternative arrangements."

"Such as what?"

"Before the new year, your brother Regulus left to take control of Legio IV and Fulgetra, and he has done so as Dux Salventum. I am months, if not years, behind your father, and I'm not even certain I'll be able to take control of all three Valerian legions."

"Regulus is with our legions? That's where he's been?"

"That's where he is."

They rode in silence after that. Magnus had given him much upon which to think, and Aulan was wondering if he should believe the Valerian, or order his men to strike him down and ride with all due haste to the Senate instead.

He glanced at Lucarus. He was pretty sure that none of the men would protest if they were ordered to kill an ex-consul, as most of the knights in the squadron had about as much use for the Amorran Senate and its dignitaries as they did for the dead refugees on the side of the road. Even if they wouldn't accept such an order, it wouldn't occur to them to stand in his way.

Magnus noticed the look. "Before you do anything rash, Aulus Severus, I should very much encourage you to consider the matter more deeply. Think, lad! Why would I have asked for you, in particular, and why would your father have encouraged me to take you on as a tribune, if he was opposed to my plans?"

Aulan thought about it. "I don't know," he finally admitted. "Why?"

"These are treacherous times, lad. Civil wars are ugly. Brothers turn against brothers and sons against their fathers. But I suspect a son of House Severus is the very last man with whom the men of my House legions would conspire. I can trust you and your men in a way I won't be able to trust any of my other officers."

"That's a risky wager, old man." Aulan jerked his thumb back at Lucarus. "We're a long way from civilization. What is to prevent me from killing you now and bringing the Senate your head? Once he hears what you've done, your brother Corvus would probably pay your weight in gold for it."

"Not a damned thing, Aulus Severus, not a damned thing." Magnus surprised him by looking off into the distance and smiling. "I can't even tell you I would object, to be honest. You lost your father, true. But believe me when I tell you that there is nothing more dreadful than losing a son. The pain... a part of you dies with him. My wife... well, you're young, so that's of no concern to you. But nothing will bring Gaius Valerius back, and regardless of what you decide, someone is going to have to command those legions. And the Senatorial consensus seems to be that I have a knack for it."

For some reason, Magnus's fey words caused a lump to arise in Aulan's throat. He concealed it by hawking a few times and spitting. Then he looked over at the man and thumped his chest. "Speaking as one of your tribunes, my lord dux, I hope you are considerably more concerned with your men's lives than you are with your own."

Magnus smiled at that, but his eyes glistened with unshed tears. "I hope so too, lad. I hope so too."

The Old Man, as Aulan and the others had taken to calling him, was tough enough to allow them to keep a fast pace, so they reached Aviglianus only six days after leaving Amorr. That afternoon, bathed and slightly intoxicated thanks to the liberality of Magnus's purse, they came within sight of the castra where Legio VII was spending the winter.

That the legion was in revolt was not in question, as their armor aroused suspicion until Aulan convinced the suspicious bath attendants that they were cavalry from Legio VII on their way back from a scouting mission south. But it was still startling to see that the Amorran flag was missing from the gates of the castra. In its place was the white civic flag of Vallyria.

"That settles that," Magnus commented as they took in the sight of the gates. "It appears the noble Didius Scato has cast his lot in with the rebels. That is a relief."

"Why do you say that?"

"Because I should hate to lose his talents simply because he isn't a Vallyrian. There is a secret to being a successful stragister, Tribune, and that is to have good legates willing to execute your orders properly. Many a solid strategist has lost a battle or even a war due to inept or insubordinate tacticians."

"And you think he'll hand the command over to you?"

Magnus looked surprised, as if the thought of any other possibility had never occurred to him. "Of course he will! Why on Earth would he not?"

Aulan could think of a lot of reasons, most of them having to do with the idea that an army of rebel provincials would probably be disinclined to follow the orders of one of the most powerful members of the Senate against which they were rebelling. But then, it was also an army led by men with whom Magnus had fought and bled for years, if not decades. He gritted his teeth and decided to follow the Valerian's lead. Still, on the off-chance that the ex-consul might have gotten it wrong, he ordered Lucarus to keep the legionary standard stowed as they approached the southern gate.

The two pairs of guards manning scorpios mounted above the gate on either side stared down at them in a remarkably unfriendly manner. Aulan wouldn't have minded their apparent hostility so much were it not for the fact that one of the large bolt-heads was pointed in the general vicinity of his chest.

The watch officer, an optio who looked old enough to have retired five years ago, was staring too, but with an expression of disbelief.

"Lord Valerius, is that you?"

"I believe 'Who goes there?' is the appropriate question, Liberius Murillo. Have the centurions gotten slack in my absence?"

The optio grinned, clearly pleased at having been recognized. "As you like, my lord. Who goes there?"

"You know damn well who it is, Optio! No wonder you still haven't made centurion, you slack-witted bastard. Now go and tell Scato to get his ugly face out here post-haste!"

"At once, my lord!" The optio saluted, still grinning, and disappeared from the battlements.

A moment later, to Aulan's relief, the two scorpios swiveled forty-five degrees in opposite directions.

It wasn't long before the gates began to swing open, revealing a tall, cadaverous legate whose only sign of office was the crimson cape bound at his throat with a golden clasp. He was a man of about sixty. Had he carried a scythe in his hand, he could have easily passed for an incarnation of Death. Behind him tramped four contubernia, fully armored, who spread out behind him on both sides when he stopped in front of Magnus.

"My lord Valerius," the legate addressed Magnus in a neutral manner. "I am surprised to see you here."

Magnus grunted as he dismounted, a little heavily, and nodded. "Yes, I suppose you might be. This is my tribune, Aulus Severus Aulan. I see that you have made a few changes around here. Does that include your sworn allegiance to House Valerius?"

Scato raised his eyebrows at hearing the name Severus, but refrained from inquiring. "Tribune," he politely acknowledged Aulan before returning his attention to Magnus. "You pose an interesting question that inspires one of its own, my lord. Is House Valerius still beholden to the Senatus Populusque Amorrus, or does it stand with the people of Vallyria?"

Magnus nodded slowly and reached under his cloak, exposing a leather pouch suspended from his shoulder. From it, he withdrew a scroll and offered it to Scato. "This should answer your question for you, Legate."

The tall man looked suspiciously from Magnus to the scroll, then took it and unrolled it. He seemed to grasp the contents in a glance, as he rolled it up again and handed it back to Magnus almost immediately.

"All of them?" he asked a little incredulously.

"All of them," Magnus confirmed. "Barring the Faliscan cities. We should be able to announce a second league, in alliance with the Marruvian league, before the end of the month. The Quinqueterrans are still being difficult, but I expect they will fall in line as soon as Galabrus and Tarquinia publicly declare they are with us."

"My lord, I am astonished!" Scato shook his head. "Delighted, but mostly astonished. I will confess, I had some trepidations about the wisdom of facing you in the field. Is Corvus with us too?"

"No. I expect he'll be leading whatever forces remain to the Senate." Magnus smiled thinly. "We need not fear my little brother, however. He has his talents, but he has never been a match for me, in the field or anywhere else. In any event, he'll be occupied with raising new legions from the detritus of the city to replace those that have come over to us. The Senate will be in no position to take the offensive until the late spring at the absolute earliest. If we leave it up to Corvus, it will be a summer of battles."

"Very well, my lord." Scato reached up and unclasped his legate's cloak. "With your permission, Magnus, I will return Legio VII to your direct command and request that you release me from my vow of loyalty to your House."

For the first time, Magnus looked surprised, even a little dismayed. "You do not intend to join Corvus, Titus Didius?"

"No, my lord. Caelignus has risen and my place is there, with the city of my birth. The Caelignesi will need an experienced general, as I expect House Gaerus will side with the Senate. And my lord, I suggest I can serve you better—serve the Utruccan cause better—if you can operate in the confidence that your allies are competently led."

Scato was probably right, Aulan thought, not that Magnus was likely to need his advice. A big handicap faced by the newly allied cities was the fact that even in the legions where they made up most of the soldiery, the staff officers were largely Amorran. Unless the House that ruled over them also turned against the Senate, the legions they raised would not have experienced legates to general them. Aulan was no historian, but even he knew that in most battles, it wasn't usually the side with the larger numbers that won, but the side with the better generals.

"As you wish, Titus Didius." But Magnus rejected the cloak. "Keep it, and your helmet too. Tell the elders of Caelignus that if they won't accept you as their stragister militum and trust you with their legions, I'll gladly have you back and give you one of mine. And in my capacity as the head of House Valerius and Dux Vallyria, I release you from your vow."

The two men shook hands warmly, and if the Old Man was disappointed at losing one of his senior officers, Aulan thought he hid it manfully.

The Caelignian seemed relieved, so much so that he was almost babbling as he invited Magnus and his men to enter the castra while simultaneously providing the ex-consul with a status report.

"I think you'll find the men are in fine fettle, my lord, as I instructed the centurions to keep to the usual training schedule, with particular attention to the unit maneuvers. With such uncertainty, we can't be sure they won't have to go into battle sooner this spring than usual.

"The supply situation is excellent, and I've been in regular contact with Gerontius, as he's been wintering Legio XV in Montmila. However, I did receive a curious letter from him just two days ago, which may be good news. It seems Legio XVII has withdrawn from Cynothicum. They passed through Larinum, and I believe they are coming south to join us. That will put all three House legions at your disposal for the spring."

"Yes, you would think so," Magnus said, a little sourly. "Unfortunately, Marcus Saturnius is dead, and I've heard my nephew, the little priestling, is in command. He's a bright lad, so perhaps he caught wind of the general rebellion and had the good sense to retreat here before he got himself surrounded. On the other hand, if he's as stubborn and self-righteous as his father, we may have to give him a proper spanking before we can take the legion from him."

"Won't he just turn it over to you as the head of the House?" Aulan couldn't help asking.

Magnus snorted. "With Corvus in the field every year, that boy practically grew up in my domus. I'll be damned if he didn't read every bloody philosopher and sophist who ever came up with a way to prove a black cat was truly white. Don't be surprised if he talks me into handing over my legions to him and returning to the Senate to confess my sins and beg its pardon."

They reached the stables and Aulan was just dismounting when a centurion came jogging toward them.

He did a brief double-take upon seeing Magnus, but his attention was otherwise focused upon Scato. "Legate, a rider arrived from Montmila. The XVth came under attack by an elven sorcerer two days ago, and scouts from an unknown legion were seen in the area the following day."

Magnus groaned, but Scato slapped him on his beefy shoulder. "My lord Valerius, I cannot tell you how pleased I am to leave this matter in your very capable hands. I assume the unknown legion is XVII, though I confess I am at a loss to explain the elves."

"I wish I could say the same." Magnus all but growled. "I knew we should have left the damned boy safely in the clutches of the Church."

As the two generals followed the centurion back toward the forum, Aulan, forgotten and presumably dismissed, was accosted by Lucarus and the rest of his squadron.

"Sir, if'n ye don't think there'll be any need for us, the boys and me were thinking we'd wet the whistle."

Aulan rolled his eyes at the transparency of the decurion's request. The sizable town that had grown up over the years outside the legionary castra hadn't escaped his attention either. "Wet your whistle as you like, Lucarus. But don't you think the time would be better spent scouting the local talent and seeing if it was worthwhile wetting anything else?"

"Aye, sir. We would be glad of your company."

They were just on the verge of finishing their first round of ale at what, according to the crudely painted sign nailed to the doorframe, was the improbably named Caela Floralia when the legionary horns began blowing the assembly from the walls to the east.

Aulan looked at the three young women who were sitting in various degrees of *deshabille* on the other side of the dirt-floored chamber with no little regret, then sighed, drained his bowl, and pushed himself to his feet.

There was no rest for the wicked, he thought regretfully. But it struck him as deeply unfair that he should be deprived of rest and wickedness alike.

THEUDERIC

OW was he hungover without having engaged in any debauchery the previous evening? The painful mystery trampled its way through Theuderic's aching head like an iron-shod Amorran legion as he tried to figure out exactly where he was and why he felt as if a dwarf had beaten him about the head with a forge hammer. Had the debauchery been so epic that he simply couldn't remember it? Where was he?

Ah, yes. It was coming back to him now. He was in Amorr, and the day before, someone who was a damned sight more powerful than any of the vaunted Immortels of l'Académie had very nearly blown his mind inside out with the ease of an accomplished glass-blower. Were it not for his shields, which in retrospect now appeared rather feeble, he might well be a mindless, drooling creature of the sort one occasionally saw in the asylums.

He groaned, and in response, he heard Lithriel begin to move about in the attached chamber. Her footsteps made it sound as if the dwarf in his head had returned to his forge.

"What happened?" she asked him without prelude or the slightest indication of tender concern for his state.

Despite his throbbing head, her inhuman lack of sensitivity made him smile.

"I'm not entirely certain. But someone doesn't seem to like me very much."

Lithriel frowned. "You haven't been here long enough for it to be personal. I don't understand. One moment, you were sitting next to me. The next, you grabbed your head and collapsed. At first, I thought you might die, but the priests told me you were only sleeping."

"In a manner of speaking, I suppose." He winced as a jolt of pain stabbed through his brain. "Keep your voice down, my lady, if you please. I'm not sure what happened, but I can guess. Last night in the throne room I felt someone probing about me. Sorcerously. I followed the aura and tracked it back to something. I think it was inside the palace. But whatever it was, I'm fairly certain it isn't human.

"It was impossibly strong. Stronger than I had ever imagined. If I didn't know better, I'd say it was a sorcerer from the Collegium. Once it realized I was tracking it, it hit me hard. I think... I think it might have said something to me, but I can't remember now. The next thing I knew, I was waking up here."

She nodded grimly. "So, you think it struck you down. I did not think you would faint for no reason. I should have known it was something like this. Those chattering priests were convinced you were overcome due to your proximity to the holiness of the Sacred Father or some such nonsense."

"You didn't argue with them, did you?" He had a dreadful vision of his elven mistress blithely critiquing Immaculate theology in the sacred heart of Holy Mother Church.

She wrinkled her fine, narrow nose. "Of course not. What does it matter to me what nonsense they believe? But do you know, an évêque told me there are other elves in the city. I think we should go and speak with them first. They will have news, I have no doubt, and if anyone knows of this sorcerer who attacked you, it will be them."

"There are elves here in Amorr?" That was astonishing. He knew the previous Sanctiff had decided they were ensouled and thereby deemed worthy of civilization and salvation, but he found it hard to believe any of the *folk ancien* had been permitted entry, given the staunch Amorran hostility toward the arts. "Are they still here?"

"Yes, they're from Elebrion, and they're acting as some sort of visiting representative for the High King. The évêque said they were excluded from the Senate order to expel all the strangers here by the order of the consuls. They're on the west side of the city, though, and you don't look like you'll be able to walk so far."

"I'll be fine," he protested, but when he attempted to push himself upright, the sadistic dwarf in his head took severe exception and pain exploded just above his left eye. He cried out involuntarily and fell back onto the pillow.

"Sleep," Lithriel told him, lightly stroking his brow with her long, white fingers. "Just close your eyes and go back to sleep. We'll see how you feel when you wake, and perhaps we'll go and visit them later today."

Mercifully, the dwarf appeared to be content to bide his time so long as Theuderic held himself still and kept his eyes closed. After a while, once he'd stopped bracing himself against the next painful hammer blow, he managed to retreat into a restless, anxious dream in which the dwarf, beardless, big-nosed, and wearing a red cape, turned from his forge and drew from it a lithe, white figurine with long ears that vaguely resembled an elfess.

"The price of a whore," the dwarf demanded, waving it in his face, and Theuderic, inexplicably outraged, hurled fire at him, but as it struck him, it turned into a dagger and pierced the dwarf's throat. The figurine dropped from the dwarf's thick-fingered hands and fell to the floor, shattering into a thousand white little shards. And as the pieces melted away like ice on a hot stove, the blessedly insensate dark finally claimed him.

It was several hours later when they finally found themselves sitting in Lord Silvertree's luxurious dwelling, and Theuderic found it remarkable how Lithriel effaced herself in front of the high elf. It reminded him a little of the way a young noble from a backwater county had behaved upon his arrival at l'Académie. Elves, it seemed, were no more egalitarian than men. Still it was a little jarring to see her acting more humble and reserved than when he'd first met her in the company of dwarves, escaping from a whorehouse.

But Silvertree was certainly intimidating. He was more than a head taller than Theuderic, with skin that was whiter than marble and impossibly aristocratic features that made even Lithriel's look common by comparison. It was as if he'd found himself seated before a fallen angel that had not yet descended from Heaven.

The elf lord held his power tightly in check, but even so, Theuderic could sense the strength of his sorcerous potential. It didn't appear to be as overwhelming as the sorcerous power that had struck him down the night before, but he was sure it was considerably more than the best he could muster himself. And disturbingly, the elf did not appear to be at all pleased to see him in the company of an elfess who was no longer a maiden.

"So, a wood elf in Amorr," Silvertree commented in glacial tones. "And with a Man, no less. You must have been persuasive, magician, to be permitted entry into the city under the circumstances."

"I don't believe they know I am one of the King's Own, Lord Silvertree. As it happens, I am also one of His Majesty's vassals, being the lord of a small county in the Grand Duchy of Écarlate, and I am here representing the king in that capacity. The capacity involved bringing some three hundred pounds of silver to the Sanctified Father, as well as a pair of archevêques, for what I can only presume must be decorative purposes."

"Ah, that would explain why the gates were opened to you." Silvertree turned his attention to Lithriel. "And you, little one? What is your name? How come you to be accompanying a Savondese battlemage to Amorr, of all places?"

"I am called Lithriel. I was separated from my friends while riding in the forest one day and was captured by a human slaver who specialized in exotics. He sold me to a whoremaster in Malkan. I was rescued by a dwarf who was attempting to free several of his own race. Then the comte here saved me from being recaptured, and I chose to accompany him to Savondir."

"Rather than return to your own kind. I see. You were a sorceress once?"

"Once. No more," she said. Theuderic noted that she did not see fit to tell the high elf her family name or let him know she was cousin to the king of Merithaim.

"No, of course not. I see." The high elf showed no pity, but Theuderic thought he saw a flicker of some unidentifiable emotion flash in the strange green eyes. "And you have come to visit me for what purpose, my lady? I agreed to receive you because I found it marvelous that you should be here, but now that conundrum is solved. What can I do for you?"

"I'd thought to come here because it has been more than a year since I saw my own kind. And like you, I expect, the comte is supposed to gather information for his king, and I thought you might have some notion as to why the Amorrans have abruptly turned against foreigners. We saw many of them on the road as we rode south, and my thought was that you would have a much better understanding of events than the common traveller.

"But the main reason is that, yesterday evening, just after the comte had presented the king's silver to the high priest, he collapsed. When he woke this morning, he told me that he'd encountered the aura of a very powerful sorcerer who had struck him down. I was surprised, since I'd always been told there are no sorcerers in Amorr."

The high elf blinked once, and although his face didn't change expression, Theuderic had the distinct impression he was considerably more interested than he'd been a moment before.

"There are no sorcerers in Amorr, little one, save me and my colleague. And your companion here, of course. You said you were struck down, magician?"

"Yes, my lord. I felt someone spying on me. But when I attempted to determine who it was, I was too clumsy, and he noticed me. I say he noticed because it wasn't a woman, I'm sure of it. The next thing I knew, I awoke the next morning with the feeling that someone had tried to smash my head with a warhammer. The whole episode seemed extraordinary, since I too was under the impression that anyone with any training in the arts would not survive long here. My lady suggested we first come here and speak with you, if you would grant us an audience, and that seemed a wise course of action."

"We shall see. So it was a Man, or at least something male, at any rate. Did you notice anything else?"

"No," Theuderic shook his head. "Wait, yes, there was one thing. It was close, very close. In material terms. I'm convinced it was either in the palace or somewhere very nearby."

"Could it have been the Sanctiff himself? I have only seen him once, from afar, but he was only recently raised to the sanctal throne."

"No, absolutely not. I'd spoken with him and kissed his ring only a short while before. As far as I could tell, he has no magical capabilities at all."

"You are confident of your ability to notice such things?"

"I can sense yours, my lord, even though you keep it well-cloaked. You're very strong, and yet, I'm not sure even you are as powerful as whatever I encountered last night."

" 'Whatever'? It's fascinating you should say it that way. Wouldn't 'whomever' be the more natural term to use?"

Theuderic paused to think about it.

"It would," he admitted. "I suppose I don't truly think it was a man. I've known all the most powerful immortels at l'Académie, and none of them was anywhere nearly as strong as that thing in the palace."

The elf lord nodded. His face was still impassive, but he had abandoned all pretense at disinterest. "Yes, your academy magicians are poorly trained by our standards, and of course your lives are much too short to develop any real mastery, but even so, your powers are far from negligible. I wonder, was your *lamaranth* in place?"

"My what?"

"I think you would call them your shields."

"Yes, absolutely. He blew through them as if they weren't even there."

"I see. Then I believe your initial instinct was correct. What you encountered was no Man."

"In the Church?" Lithriel was skeptical. "Do you know what this creature might be, my lord?"

"Do I know?" Silvertree spread his hands and shrugged. "I cannot say that I am certain. But I have some very strong suspicions. Indeed, if what you say is true, I may have to give serious thought to returning to Elebrion myself. But first, I have a few more questions for your magician. Have you noticed any unusual upheaval in the north of late, either in Savondir proper or anywhere in the Seven Seats?"

"A year ago there was a rebellion in Montrove," Theuderic said. "The duc was killed and the city was sacked by the Red Prince. I was there, and I am confident it wasn't anything more than a discontented noble attempting to throw off his liege lord. Hardly the first time, and I can't imagine it will be the last. Although around the time we departed for here, the prince was sailing across the White Sea, as it seems the Dalarn have been all but wiped out in the Wolf Isles."

"Have they now?" The high elf's casual tone belied the sudden gleam of interest the news had sparked in his eyes. "And what nearly wiped them out? The demonspawn?"

"If by demonspawn, you mean the beasts they call aalvarg, yes. We call them ulfin. It seems they have all but destroyed the reavers. A pair of their young royals appeared before the king to beg his assistance in helping them drive back the monsters, which he granted."

"I shouldn't be at all surprised if the second one is behind those events. This bears a closer look. But where are the others? That is the question."

"The second what?" Lithriel asked before he could do the same.

"You think there are more of whatever this creature that attacked me is?"

Silvertree nodded. He rose gracefully from his seat and strode toward a table upon which were piled various old codices and capped cylinders containing scrolls. "About a month ago, two of the consuls visited me concerning some murders that took place within the palace. My companion and I were permitted to visit the chapel where the men died, and in the course of our investigation I observed the signs of a highly unusual sort of magic. It's not one with which you would have been familiar, as it has been some time since such spells were in use. Hundreds of years, to put it in perspective.

"Ah, there we are," he interrupted himself as he located the cylinder he wanted and unscrewed the brass cap. "As I told the consuls, the magic was distinctive. It's not a sorcery we elves have ever utilized, and it is well beyond the limits of Man's wizardry or the various primitive arts of the western races."

"What is it?" Lithriel asked.

"You could do worse than to view it as a perverted form of daemonology, which I believe your Savondese companion would customarily refer to as *diablerie*."

Theuderic considered himself more or less a prodigal son of the Church, the Sanctiff's blessing notwithstanding, but this shocked him more than just about anything had since his boyhood, when an elderly mage had first told him that he possessed a talent for the arts. "Are you saying there is a *diableriste* in the Coviria summoning demons—in the very bowels of the Church?"

"Oh, I'm afraid the situation is rather worse than that," Silvertree answered. "What I suspect is that there is not a diableriste but an actual immortal being residing within the bowels of Holy Mother Church. And I believe it intends to shape the Amorran Empire into a weapon capable of serving its purposes. And it would not surprise me in the slightest if it should turn out that there is another of its kind making use of the northern demonspawn for precisely the same reason."

Theuderic couldn't believe what he was hearing. "An immortal being? My lord, you elves are the closest things to immortal beings I've ever heard of, unless one counts dragons, I suppose. And I can't imagine you're suggesting that the Sanctiff is keeping a pet dragon in a giant cave underneath his palace."

Silvertree smiled thinly. "No, magician, I am not suggesting any such thing. Here," he said, extending the scroll he pulled from the cylinder. "Read this, and perhaps it will shed useful light on these matters. After my suspicions were aroused by the deaths in the chapel, I contacted an old friend of mine, the Magistras Daemonae at the Collegium. He has long been interested in these beings, for obvious reasons, and he sent me this document, which predates your calendar, as it was composed some three hundred years before the war with the Witchkings."

Lithriel glanced at Theuderic, and he nodded. They both knew he wouldn't be able to read such ancient elven writing. She took the proffered scroll from the high elf and perused it, clicking her tongue several times as she did so. Theuderic forced himself to wait patiently until she finally nodded and began translating it for him.

On the seventh day of the fourteenth month I reached Mount Arman and found that which I had sought. Upon the account of the king of Kir Kalithael, I spoke and conversed with the wondrous head of the divided man, who lived though he had been slain, and spoke though his head had been set upon a spear and his body given to the fire by the king of the men of the Cormazond.

Many prophecies did he speak unto the men who did not fear to approach him. Many oracles did he pronounce to all who listened. Many gifts did he promise to the man who would take his head down from the pike and give it to the fire, but none dared serve him in this manner for fear of the king of the men of the Cormazond. I climbed the mount in order to see what sort of man he was and what was the nature of this miracle that permitted him to see and speak although his head was cut from his body and his body was no more.

He told me of his kind, who are neither elves, nor men, nor angels, but a race that lived when the world was young. They were mighty and wise. They knew what was transacted in the heavens. They beheld the earth and understood what is there transacted, from its beginning to its end. They beheld summer and winter: perceiving that the whole earth is full of water; and that the cloud, the dew, and the rain refresh it. They considered and beheld every tree, how it appears to wither, and every leaf to fall off, except of fourteen trees, which are not deciduous; which wait from of old for the appearance of the new leaf, for two or three winters.

They saw that every work of the gods was invariable in the period of its appearance.

They considered the days of summer, that the sun is upon it at its very beginning; while the earth is scorched up with fervid heat, and the ground may not be walked upon in consequence of that heat. They considered the days of winter, which grow short with the retreat of the sun and witness the covering of the earth with ice and snow. They considered the days of spring, when the earth returns to life again and the trees put forth their green leaves, become covered, and produce fruit. They considered the days of autumn, when the earth brings forth her bounty and the harvests are collected against the barren season to come.

"Are you certain you have the right scroll?" Theuderic asked Silvertree.

"Indeed," the high elf replied, looking amused. "Be patient, magician. The depth of your understanding will not increase according to the speed with which your knowledge is acquired. I will admit our ancestors do often betray somewhat of a predilection for belaboring the obvious, but there is often method in their meanderings. My lady Everbright, do continue."

"Yes, my lord," she said absentmindedly, staring intently at the scroll. "But what does that word mean? Ah, pay no mind, I see it now."

It happened that his people looked upon the earth and saw that the sons of men had multiplied in those days, that daughters were born to the elves, elegant and beautiful, that in the forests and plains the generations of the orcs grew abundant, and that under the mountains the progeny of the dwarves swelled and became great in number. And they saw that even as the seasons proceeded from one to the next, one day they should have to make war upon the sons of men, the daughters of elves, the generations of orcs, and the progeny of dwarves, lest war be made upon them.

But they were mighty and they were wise and they were good, and their leader, Masyaza, said to them: we shall not stay and slay the sons of men and the daughters of elves, neither shall we remain and destroy the generations of orcs, the progeny of dwarves and the issue of goblins. I say we shall leave this world to walk the shadows and to build a new heaven and a new earth where we may live in peace, alone and unmolested. And their leader, Masyaza, said to them: I fear that you may perhaps be indisposed to the performance of this enterprise.

But they answered him and said: we all swear and bind ourselves by mutual execrations that we will not change our intention but execute our projected undertaking and walk the shadows with you.

Then their leader, Masyaza, said to them: how shall it be that we should leave this earth and build a new one if the sons of men and the daughters of elves will one day follow us? Then Qelbara, who was great among them and a keeper of the secrets, arose and vowed that he and twelve of his companions would not accompany Masyaza through the shadows but would remain behind to ensure that neither the sons of men, nor the daughters of elves, nor the generations of orcs, nor the progeny of dwarves would ever follow the path of their people. Masyaza acclaimed Qelbara, and the people acclaimed his companions, and those who were to stay behind were named the Watchers.

And the Watchers' names were Qelbara, Laesa, Zahamiseh, Arpho- qart, Herimon, Samsela, Samyaza, Merars, Vazeba, Amarazak,

Karanylas, Baatral, and Arazayel. Qelbara was their prefect and their chief.

The one with whom I spoke gave his name as Merars, one of the Watchers. He said the Watchers could take any form they wished, but that as their memories faded over the passing years, they found it more comforting to return again and again to the same form. They could not die, although they could be slain, and once their bodies returned to ashes and dust they would sleep for a time, then awake again, fully restored and in their original form, which he said is like unto a man or elf, only larger and more perfect. Again he begged me to take his head from the spear and give it to the fire, that he might be reborn again in time and avenge himself on the king of the people of the Cormazond or his descendants.

When I asked him how he had come to this pass, he told me that his fellow Watchers had gone mad and involved themselves with the various peoples of Thelenothas. Some of them had taken wives, each choosing for himself whom they began to approach, and with whom they cohabited. They taught these wives sorcery, incantations, and the dividing of roots and trees. And the women, conceiving, brought forth giants, and monsters, and great evils of every kind.

Others made themselves out as gods. Arazayel taught men to make swords, knives, shields, and breastplates, so that the race of men became warlike. Laesa taught our fathers the fabrication of mirrors, and the workmanship of bracelets and ornaments, the use of paint, the beautifying of the eyebrows, and all sorts of dyes, so that the elves changed and became beautiful, as if they were of the people who left the Watchers behind. Arphoqart taught the dwarves the use of stones of every valuable and select kind and how to delve deep beneath the ground for the metal rivers that flow through the roots of the mountains. And Amarazak taught the orcs that the life is in the blood.

"I believe I comprehend the gist of it," Theuderic broke in. He was never able to retain anything he learned by listening, but preferred reading things for himself, although that was hardly an option here. "You think this thing in the palace is one of these Watchers?"

"I think it is a very real possibility," Silvertree said. "And if that is the case, he will not be the only Watcher who has been roused to action by the present course of the moon and stars. That is why I am going to suggest that you both leave for the north as soon as you can. You must tell your king to prepare his realm for war on a scale that he has never before imagined. You may also assure him that, for as long as the situation persists, he need not waste his forces patrolling his borders against our kind. Before you go, I will prepare a letter to that effect."

"A letter?" Theuderic asked dubiously. "I can't imagine you're empowered to bind the high king in such a way."

"The gods themselves couldn't bind the high king even if they wished. I'm not promising anything. I'm merely suggesting that if your king sees fit to take the initiative, he will likely find King Mael unusually inclined to listen, given how I have been providing him with the same information I give to you now."

"I see. But I don't understand something. Just because we can't kill these creatures, at least not permanently, it doesn't mean they've got any interest in men or elves. If they've been around for thousands of years, they obviously haven't done us any real harm over all that time. Why are you suddenly so concerned about them now—because one of them might have killed a few célestes? The Church can always make more. The Sanctiff just named two new ones yesterday!"

"I think I may know why," Lithriel said, looking up from the scroll that she'd continued reading silently. "It says, 'All the earth has been corrupted by the effects of the teaching of Arazayel. To him therefore ascribe the whole crime, bind him hand and foot; cast him into darkness; and opening the desert which is in Dudael, cast him in there. Throw upon him hurled and pointed stones, covering him with darkness. But Arazayel learned of Qelbara's words, and with the aid of Amarazak he raised up a great and mighty army of orcs, with which he threw down Qelbara, he who had been the chief of the Watchers, and set up a mighty fortress, which he called Yhaddiloud, where he awaited the opening of the Door of Shadows.' That Door of Shadows must be some sort of portal to the new earth the leader of their people, Mazyeha or whatever his name was, led them."

"Masyaza," Silvertree corrected her. "That is indeed the crucial passage. As to the notion that the Watchers have done men and elves little harm over the ages, do allow me to disabuse you of that notion, magician. My researches have led me to conclude that one Watcher or another has been behind the irruption of the Witchkings five hundred years ago—and the great War of the Three Races that led to the destruction of the elven kingdoms of Arathaim and Falas five hundred years before that.

"Furthermore, I suspect your northern reavers would contest your assumption that no Watcher has done them harm, if I am correct concerning the remarkable rise of those you call ulfin. Neither of our races have ever feared war, but I believe several of the most terrible wars this world has known are the result of one or more Watchers attempting to take control of the gate that provides access to the various dimensional planes."

"You seem to know a lot about this," Theuderic said.

"I daresay I know more than any living being who is not a Watcher himself, save one. Few elves credit their existence, as there are hundreds if not thousands of references to other, equally outlandish beings to be found in the royal library in Elebrion. And you are likely the only man who has ever heard of them. When I was at the Collegium, I studied under Gilthalas and composed a paper on the topic. It's always been of interest to me. So when the opportunity to come to Amorr presented itself, I seized it."

"Why would a Watcher be in Amorr? Why not Savondir? Or the Wolf Isles, if you think a Watcher is behind the ulfin there?"

"Based on what Gilthalas and I have gleaned from oblique references and suggestive phrases in various old documents, there is a certain pattern I have observed in the past cycles of what I tend to think of as Watcher wars. The gate opens for a short period of time, more likely measured in weeks than months, and in a location that is not only unknown but is different than the previous occasions.

"However, the Watchers—at least, those interested—appear to have a good idea when it is going to appear. In preparation for its appearance, they raise armies by manipulating the lesser races, particularly the races of men and orcs, presumably because they are more numerous and warlike, then make use of these armies to gain control of the area in which the shadow door will appear. Or where it can be summoned, perhaps. We know very little of the door itself or the intentions of the various Watchers regarding it. We can only make reasonable assumptions based on the actions of those they are manipulating."

"Why do you suppose they don't make use of us?" Lithriel asked the high elf.

"Elves are too few, for one thing. We're too long-lived, for another. Five hundred years, give or take a half-century, appears to be the cycle, and while that's eight lifetimes for a man and twelve or fifteen for an orc, there are scores of elves who would live from one cycle to the next. So we're probably less susceptible to their manipulation. Although, who is to say they don't do so in more subtle fashion? In the end, it was the Collegium that put down the Witchkings, after all."

"When is this Door of Shadows going to open?" Theuderic asked. "Or appear, or be summonable? You obviously believe it's going to happen soon."

"From what I can see, the players are still selecting their pieces and moving them into position. If we look to what I believe to be the most recent example, it was seven years between when the Witchkings came to power and when they first began to spread across Wagria."

This, at least, was history with which every King's mage was familiar. "The first records in which the Witchkings appeared say they were a heretical death cult that appeared in the Margravate of Thauron twelve years before Thule Ahnenvater killed the margrave and crowned himself king."

"I did not know that," Silvertree mused. "I must confess, it never occurred to me that there might be useful documents in the possession of Men."

"Men can be useful for all sorts of things," Lithriel said, with a sur-reptitious wink at Theuderic. "Would you like me to see if they have any useful records that might reference either the Witchkings or the Watchers at l'Académie when we return?"

"Indeed. But I think you should consider returning considerably sooner than you have likely been intending. By which I mean that you should leave the city tonight. Do not even return to the Sanctiff's palace."

Theuderic stared at the high elf in amazement. He turned to Lithriel and saw that she too was nonplussed by Silvertree's unexpected suggestion. "I presume you have some reason for recommending such a drastic ac-tion," Theuderic asked. "Do you genuinely believe we might be in danger from the Watcher there, even if one is truly hidden within the curia? I can't imagine the Church itself wishes either the Lady Everbright or me any harm."

"I doubt the Church intends either of you any harm," the high elf said. "Even if they look upon your relationship with the lady elfess with little more approval than the high king would. But you are the only one who has detected magic where there should be none, and I doubt that after it has been given time to reflect upon the matter, it will hesitate to eliminate anyone who might threaten to expose it and upset its plans. Both you and the lady present a potential problem to it, since I am certain it knows nothing of the nature of elven sorcery and would therefore not be aware that you are no longer a sorceress, Lady Everbright.

"These beings are very cunning, adept at hiding themselves and their true intentions, and they are ruthless even by elven standards. No Watcher would hesitate to kill any number of lesser beings from the younger races rather than accept even a small risk of its plans being disrupted. And I fear your visit here may well have alarmed it, as where would one go to learn about them but to an elf?"

"I don't understand," Lithriel said. "How could we disrupt its plans?"

"By exposing it as a practitioner of the dark arts," Theuderic said before Silvertree could respond. "Which, here in Amorr, amounts to anything that even remotely smacks of magic or sorcery. But with all due respect, my lord Ambassador, this is all very farfetched. We don't even know if one of these things exists anymore, still less that it intends us any harm."

"That is true. We know nothing for certain. We merely have a few points of information from which the pattern is drawn, and perhaps it is the wrong one. But you may wish to keep in mind that one does not live five centuries without learning to keep an askance eye on everyone and devote a thought or two to their fouler possibilities. When dealing with men, I have learned to expect the worst, and I am very seldom disappointed."

"They surprise you sometimes," Lithriel said, flashing a rare smile at him. It was sweet, but it was like a dagger probing at the guilt and shame he carried deep within him. "But even if we were to heed your advice, how would you propose we leave the city tonight? All of our clothing and possessions are at the palace. Can you send for them?"

"And there is the matter of my men," Theuderic pointed out. "I can't simply abandon them here in Amorr without even telling them that I'm leaving."

"Where are they? Did they accompany you to the palace?"

"No, we had a troop escort of about thirty men-at-arms. They were forced to wait outside the outer wall, although I think they were permitted to stay in a barracks of some sort in that ring between the walls. I don't know where, although I recall someone told me it was near a church."

The high elf shook his head. "If you don't know where they are, there is nothing we can do. If it's possible, I will have my colleague see if he can find them after you've gone and let them know you've already left the city. If you wish, I can provide you with some writing materials, and you can leave them a message. But I don't think you need fear for them. They've done no wrong, and I expect they'll simply be ordered out of the city like any other group of foreigners."

"This is lunacy!" Theuderic slammed his fist down upon the arm of the chair in which he was seated. "I haven't agreed to go anywhere! Lithriel, we don't actually know that any Watcher even exists. For all I know, the Church could be keeping a pet elf somewhere in that vast mausoleum. Someone has to train the Michaelines, after all. And even if there was one of these immortal beings lurking in the bowels of the Coviria, we have no reason to assume that its presence is unknown to the Church hierarchy or to believe it intends us any harm at all! The fact that you've survived for five centuries doesn't mean that your paranoia is justified, my lord Ambassador. I simply must return to the palace."

The high elf spread his hands and shrugged. "You may well be correct. But if you do return to the palace today, I should still like to suggest that you leave Lady Lithriel here."

Lithriel made a face. "I don't know if that's necessary."

"No, that's not a bad idea," Theuderic said. "If I'm wrong and the Lord Ambassador is justified in his concerns, at least you'll not suffer for it. I'll have a better chance of escaping by myself too. It's not likely that they'd hold us in the same cell. And don't forget: I do have some protection by virtue of my being a representative of the king. You don't. My lord, could you get her out of the city, if need be?"

"Of course," Silvertree assured him.

Theuderic heard a noise from the corridor, and then the door opened into the sitting room in which they were seated.

It was the elf who had first greeted them at the door when they'd arrived, and although he looked as indifferent as ever, his words were alarming.

"There appear to be a large number of soldiers gathering outside the residence, Ambassador. Someone was knocking on the door, but I presumed we do not wish to permit them to enter, so I refrained from answering it. However, I expect it will not be long before they apply more vigorous measures."

Theuderic and Lithriel looked at each other in dismay.

Silvertree rose to his feet, though not hastily.

"What sort of soldiers, Miroglas?"

"Most are wearing white armor with red cloaks. I saw some wearing legionary-style armor with gold cloaks too."

"The Curian Guard and the Order of Saint Michael," Silvertree commented. "It appears I may have miscalculated how eager the Church is to retain your company, magician."

"Or the Watcher within it."

"As you say. Do you find yourself now more willing to credit my concerns?"

"Somewhat," Theuderic allowed. The presence of the Michaelines was particularly troubling. It indicated an expectation of resistance by someone with magical abilities. But was it his resistance or the high elf's that they were anticipating? "I will admit that the level of interest appears excessive."

"I suggest we see what they want. Miroglas, I assume you barred the door."

"Indeed, Lord Ambassador."

"Then let us go and see what the good priestlings have to say to us."

"Are you mad?" Theuderic protested. "You can't simply open the door and go out to them!"

"Whoever said anything of the kind?" The elf lord winked at Lithriel. "I had in mind we should address them from the roof. As for the door, I have already raised the wards. They will not be entering that way."

As he spoke, there was a loud explosion and a barely audible cry from the gathering crowd outside.

"You see? I imagine our visitors are already learning the foolishness of attempting to force the door. No doubt the windows will be next. Come, follow me, and let us learn the reason for this most undiplomatic intrusion."

FJOTRA

THE walk with Donzeau took considerably longer than Fjotra was expecting. Finally, they slowed. They neared a mansion with eight or nine young nobles lounging about the stairs that led to the front door, several of whom appeared to be drunk already. She assumed they had reached their destination. There were fewer catcalls than she expected, and none of the men grabbed at her or the other two girls despite the sudden and hungry interest with which they viewed them. The duc's companions were either uncommonly well-behaved, or as was more likely the case, aware of Donzeau's dangerous talents.

The troldmand led them through the sumptuous, high-ceilinged house without even glancing at the paintings and expensive furniture that filled it.

They found the duc upstairs, in the library, standing in front of a desk with his back to them and examining a painting of a man on a horse surrounded by a pack of dogs. The duc was taller than his brother the Red Prince had been. He had broader shoulders, but his build was slighter, and his black hair was cropped very short.

When he heard them enter the room and turned around toward her, Fjotra stifled her instinctive gasp. Prince Karl had been handsome, but his younger brother nearly took her breath away. His black eyes were like pools of dark radiance, drawing her in even as they threatened to burn the flesh from her bones. Unlike his brother, he wore no mustache, exposing a mouth that was arrogant to the point of cruelty. He would, she thought, more easily sneer or snarl than smile.

But she was wrong. He looked her over with indifference, then sniffed dismissively.

"Interesting. You are indeed a pretty thing, as savages go."

"I... my... th–thank you," she finally managed to stammer, not knowing what she should say. "I am sorry, I do not know how you are called."

"My name is Étienne-Henri, second in line to the throne of Savondir and the Seven Seats, the Duc de Chênevin. And soon, if you are amenable, your husband. Until then, you may address me as 'Your Royal Highness.'"

Her heart raced. What an impossible man! And yet, a girl who had fled from her homeland only one week hence could do considerably worse than to marry the heir to the throne of a king whose good will was vital to the survival of her people. In fact, any girl, any woman, could do considerably worse than to marry such a rich and powerful man. Such an attractive one too! But it was too much. And too fast.

"This is very soon, Your Royal Highness. I meet you only now. How can you want to marry me before you even introduce me?"

"That barbarian accent is downright charming on her, is it not, Guilhem?" The duc addressed the troldmand as if she was not even there, which bothered her until he flashed that brilliant smile at her again. "And I want to marry you—I am going to marry you—because I will be damned if I let my brother obtain a second crown through you. It is bad enough that he is the heir by virtue of having been born before me, but he has no more right to the Iles de Loup than any other man.

"So, today we shall be betrothed, and I congratulate you on your forethought in bringing along your attendants to share in our mutual joy. As for the actual marriage, that will take place as soon as my father's temper cools sufficiently to accept the fait accompli and recall that, regardless of which of his sons it may be, in either case there will be a de Mirid ruling over the Iles."

"But you know my brother will be heir after my father, not me," said Fjotra, a little suspiciously. Surely no man, not even a prince, would be so arrogant as to think he could deny her brother his birthright, not if he expected to survive a single night sleeping in her bed.

"Your father can't hold the Iles now. Can your brother win them back with nothing more than refugees in rags?" The prince raised a skeptical eyebrow and grinned. "You wear your doubts on your face, Your Highness. But I bear your brother no ill will, none at all. In fact, I have even gifted him his own comté, which will provide him with a secure income. It's not much but enough to allow him a place at court. When he is willing to cede his claim to the Iles in your favor, you and I shall raise an army and return to them as their king and queen."

"Why you think he do that?" she asked him. "Why he give you the crown of our father?"

"Because two bobs of silver in the hand are worth more than four ulfin-occupied islands in the north to a man without an army."

He had a point, particularly since this game of crowns and kings was foreign to the Dalarn anyhow. She and Brynjolf were aware they had to play at it, but they didn't understand it in the same way the nobles of Savondir did. The duc didn't realize it yet, but he had no real need to play that game himself since his brother was now dead. She didn't wish to tell him the terrible news, but she didn't see that she had any choice in the matter, as it appeared to be the only way to dissuade him from forcing her into a betrothal.

"Prince Étienne, I must say you, you do not need to marry me. You do not need to buy crown from my brother to be a king."

That perplexed him, as for the first time he did not appear to have a ready response. His eyes narrowed, with a predatory focus that made her shiver inside. "What do you mean?" he asked her, putting particular emphasis on the first word.

"I am sorry to say you, but your brother, Prince Karl, he is dead. He die eight days before. His body now go to Lutaisse, to your father."

The prince froze, struck dumb by her words. He stared at her without betraying any sign of grief or any other emotion beyond the sheer incredulity in his dark eyes. Then he did the very last thing she expected.

He grabbed her shoulders and kissed her. It was brutal. There was nothing loving or sensual about it, and yet the force of it all but made her knees buckle. She would have fallen, she thought, had he not gripped her so firmly.

"You are absolutely sure?" he demanded. "You swear this upon the name of every pagan god and demon you savages worship? Charles-Philippe is dead?"

"I swear, by Tordenfader and Dødsherre, by Hyppemoder and Skærmsøster, I was with him when he die. The ship bring him back, and Patrice take him right to Lutaisse as soon as ship land today."

He shook his head and leaned back upon the desk behind him, looking thoughtful. Then he flashed that beautiful smile at her and made her heart leap again, as if on command.

"That is the best news anyone has ever given me! My deepest and most heartfelt thanks, Fjotra Skulisdattir." He stepped forward to kiss her again, and this time she was ready. He crushed her lips with exuberance and her entire body responded as she pressed herself against him.

Svanhvit tried to protest, but the troldmand lifted a finger, and that was enough to dissuade her.

But when the duc stepped back, it was as if she was not even there. His eyes were not for her but were caught up in some distant vision somewhere beyond the ceiling at which he was staring in a sort of rapture. "You cannot know what this means," he said in a voice full of barely repressed exultation.

"I think it mean you do not need to marry me," she pointed out in an attempt to be helpful. She found his reaction more than a little alarming. What sort of man didn't even feel the smallest sense of loss at the death of his brother?

"Surely you jest," he said, returning his attention to her and smiling broadly as he squeezed both her hands. "I daresay I would be willing to marry the woman who brought me such news were she eighty years old, blind, and toothless! How did he die? In battle with the wolf-demons?"

She recounted an abbreviated story of that terrible night to him. She had just reached the part about when she'd noticed the second aalvarg, when two men burst into the library.

"My lord, we are under attack!"

The smile disappeared instantly from his face, and he pulled her to the side with surprising ease as Donzeau pushed Geirrid and Svanhvit toward her. "Attack? By whom?" the duc demanded.

"By me, myself, and I," announced a voice from behind the prince's men that sounded strangely familiar. "Tell your men to get out of my way, give me the girl, and get yourself to the royal palace with all due haste, Étienne-Henri. If you ride hard, you can still beat your brother's body there."

At a gesture from the duc, the two young nobles retreated, revealing the short, slender figure of the Comtesse de Domdidier's friend, the Comte de Saint-Agliè, standing in the doorway.

His pale face was slightly flushed, but his sword was still in its scabbard, so it appeared he must have men with him, following in his wake. He glanced at Fjotra, as if to confirm that she was actually there, then glared at the duc.

"The reaver maiden is not for you, Étienne. There are affairs of which you know nothing, and this is one of them. You needn't scheme and whisper in the ears of the royal conseilleurs anymore, or attempt to carve out a kingdom of your own. The realm will be yours, and likely sooner than you think!"

"This borders on treason, Saint-Agliè. And if you know my brother is dead, then surely you know that raising your sword against the heir to the crown is lèse majesté. As for my betrothed, I demand that you apologize for speaking of her in such a crude and vulgar manner. Do so again, and I shall have you whipped and paraded through the streets of Lutèce before being returned to your petty Écarlatean shithole."

The comte laughed, genuinely amused. "You have the makings of a proper monster in you, Étienne-Henri. Power will go to your head faster than champagne to a maiden's. And I see no priest here. She is not your betrothed, and she will never be!"

The duc glanced at her, and Fjotra, not knowing what to do or what was expected at her, simply stared at the two men, her mouth hanging open.

The duc seemed to take this as a sign of encouragement, because he flashed her a confident smile, then pointed at the comte.

"Courrat, Loys, do kill me this man."

The two young nobles obediently drew their swords and spread out as they approached Saint-Agliè. The comte didn't appear concerned, nor did he draw his own blade. Instead he spread his arms and bent his knees, keeping his eyes on both men as they came closer to him.

As one, they thrust, and it didn't seem possible that he could avoid either blade from where he was standing. But somehow, a moment later, there was a loud snap, he was unscathed, and the noble with the blond hair fell to the floor screaming with his arm broken.

Donzeau clapped slowly. The duc swore. He was angry, but he didn't move from the desk. Instead, he called out encouragement to his remaining champion. "Come now, Loys, mind his trickeries!"

The tall, dark-haired young noble slashed his sword down vertically to prevent the comte from either drawing his sword or ducking beneath another thrust, then he followed it with another diagonal slash that forced the comte to step backward, away from Courrat's sword now lying on the patterned rug that covered the wooden library floor.

But on his third slash, the comte hurled himself forward just as the blade swept down and crashed his body into the arm and shoulder of his attacker.

Loys stumbled backward before recovering his balance and his guard, but too late to stop the comte from smoothly stepping away and drawing his sword. Now the young noble was on the defense, and even to Fjotra's untrained eye, it was clear that the comte was the better bladesman by far. Loys was sweating, and his desperate eyes bulged with fear, as it was all he could do to fend off the comte's rapid thrusts and sweeping slashes that filled the air with the ringing clash of steel on steel. And when Loys finally managed a single hapless thrust of his own, the comte used it to expertly disarm him with a twist of his wrist, followed by a savage slash that opened up Loys's cheek.

The comte looked at the prince and smiled as he held the point of his sword to the throat of the young man. "What will it be, Étienne? Do I take your man's life or the reaver girl?"

"Neither," answered the prince, glancing at the last man still able to fight for him.

Faster than the eye could follow, there was a silver flash. The comte grunted and lurched to the left as Courrat's sword slammed into his right side. Geirrid screamed and Loys leaped backward, his breeches wet and his eyes wide with terror. At first, Fjotra thought Courrat had thrown the blade, but he was still down, being comforted by Svanhvit.

The prince only laughed. "Well done, Guilhem," the prince praised the troldmand, who was staring coolly at the mortally wounded comte as he tried to hold himself upright by clinging to a marble-topped dresser. "You see, my dear Saint-Agliè, there are also things of which you know nothing."

"You truly think I know nothing of his kind?" The comte's face was screwed up with pain as he supported himself with one arm on the dresser despite the sword that had pierced him all the way through. "Dear God, Étienne, what depths of foolishness have you gotten yourself into now?"

"How are you doing that!" The prince looked to his sorcerer in confusion. "Donzeau, how is he doing that? Shouldn't he be dying now?"

For the first time since she'd met him, Fjotra saw uncertainty on the face of the troldmand.

"One would certainly think so, your highness."

"Yes, well, I'm afraid that is not in the cards," the comte hissed. As the prince and everyone else watched in utter astonishment, he gritted his teeth, grasped the hilt in his right hand, and began pulling the bloody blade out of his body. He managed to pull it about halfway out before his arm had reached its full extent, and he groaned with what sounded more like exasperation than pain. "Fjotra, would you be so kind as to help me with this?"

"You're not a man!" Donzeau declared, his voice full of wonder. He raised his hand, and the sword slid itself the rest of the way out of the wound with a dreadful, sucking sound before falling with a dull thump to the carpeted floor. "You're not a man at all! What are you, my lord comte? Some sort of demon?"

"I should think you, of all men, would be aware that I am nothing of the sort, Guilhem Donzeau."

The pounding noise of a number of men rushing up the stairs precluded a response and was rapidly followed by a group of armed men in Saint-Agliè's black-and-green livery. Several of their swords were bloodied and two appeared to be wounded, but their concern was solely for their lord.

"You are injured, my lord!" exclaimed the leader, looking distressed.

"It's nothing, Arnaud," the comte assured him. "Merely an unfortunate misunderstanding."

"That must have been one hell of a misunderstanding!" Arnaud looked around the room, first at his master's torn and bloody chemise, then at Courrat's sword, blood-stained to the hilt, and finally, at its unfortunate owner and the unnatural shape of his arm. Then he did a double-take. "Sweet Lady of Sorrows, is that the Duc de Chênevin?"

"I fear so," admitted Saint-Agliè. "Now, if you will excuse me, Your Royal Highness, I believe my carriages are waiting, so I will be on my way to my castle. Arnaud, Sebastien, if you would be so kind as to escort the three ladies outside, I would appreciate it. Please be at ease, my lady Fjotra. Your very good friend the comtesse already awaits you there."

"How dare you take my betrothed from my very side?" the prince snarled. "What makes you think I won't expose you and have you hunted down like a dog, Saint-Agliè, or whatever you are?"

"Expose what?" The comte airily waved his bloody right hand. "Expose yourself as a lunatic? By all means, do the realm the inestimable service of convincing everyone that you are insane, preferably before you

succeed your father. Though I admit that 'King Étienne-Henri the Mad'
has a certain ring to it. But any sooner and you'll see the crown pass to
Comte d'Ainme instead. So have a care, my dear duc, and think before
you speak. There are those who are far more fearsome than me who shall
soon, very soon, stride openly across the world. Before them, kings and
empires will tremble. Count yourself fortunate indeed if I am the worst
creature you find yourself facing."

Fjotra thought of resisting the gentle pressure on her back, and she
looked to the duc for help. But he seemed to have forgotten her and was
staring at the creature that called himself Saint-Agliè with narrowed eyes
full of hate.

Better the devils you know, she thought. The comte and comtesse had
only ever sought to help her, whereas the Duc de Chênevin had ordered
her kidnapping and would have imposed himself on her had Saint-Agliè
not interceded.

And yet, she could not help herself. As the comte's man, Arnaud,
led her out of the library, she looked back again at the fierce young man
standing under the painting, his anger an almost visible aura radiating
outward from his body. Surely so handsome a man could not be either
monstrous or mad, she told herself.

And then a rebellious thought belatedly occurred to her: Who were
Saint-Agliè and Domdidier to tell a princess of reavers whom she could
and could not marry?

MARCUS

THE meeting of the senior officers that took place in Marcus's tent, after the first watch was underway, was unsurprisingly contentious. Marcus sat at his desk, upon which a map of Larinum was displayed, while the others paced about the command tent—with the exception of the exhausted Praefectus Ballistarius, who was slumped in a wooden chair. The dispute was centered around whether the affront to the legion, as well as the Senate and People, warranted the delay that would be required to sack Solacte. The two decurions, in company with Trebonius, were the most adamant about the need to mete out punishment to those who had slain their fellow knights, while the centurions were considerably more philosophical about their fallen comrades-in-arms.

"We cannot let these murders go unrevenged," argued Senarius Arvandus, first decurion of the First Cavalry. "Not only would it be a dereliction of our duty and an insult to their memories, but it would only encourage other cities in their mutiny. Consider how the Cynothi defeat of Andronicus Caudinus set the stage for rebellion to sweep across the provinces. Once word gets out that a city can thumb their noses in the face of an entire Amorran legion without consequence, whatever remaining allies we have will desert too."

"These aren't just legionaries, but knights," Trebonius pointed out. "Men from equestrian families, who are going to demand answers concerning the deaths of their sons. Clericus, do you seriously believe you can go to them in clean conscience and tell them that we didn't recover their bodies for decent burial, and worse, we didn't even attempt to call their murderers to justice?"

"It's war," Proculus growled. "It ain't just the infantry that dies. Knights die. Mules die. Children die. I got no disrespect for Gavrus or any of the other riders. Even the young lad, what was his name, Dardanus, he pulled his weight. But we lost more than twelve men just marching here. We'll be damn lucky if them twelve is all we lose afore we get to Montmila or wherever we're wintering."

"So you're advocating that we simply march on without so much as throwing another rock at their gates?" Arvandus was aghast. "Losing men to sickness is one thing. Disease and accidents happen, but enduring them doesn't lead to more of it. That's not the case here. We have to teach these murderous bastards a lesson no other city will forget!"

Proculus glared at the decurion. "I didn't say nothing about us not doing nothing! I just said that losing twelve men ain't so big a notion. Unless Cassabus can knock down those walls, storming them with ladders will cost us a sight more than twelve, I'll promise you that."

Marcus glanced at the praefect. Cassabus was leaning back in his chair, rubbing at his eyes. "What do you think?" Marcus asked the artillery officer.

"I think there is no way to be certain of taking the place in less than a month, unless you want to spend two or three centuries storming those walls. They're too high to climb easily and too thick to knock down in a reasonable time. It can be done, but it can't be done quickly."

"We don't have the time," Marcus said. "They will have sent riders to Falera and Fescennium, perhaps even to some of the Vallyrii and Caelignii cities as well. If the Larinii have been gathering their forces since the spring, we could find ourselves with an allied legion or two in between us and Montmila as soon as tomorrow. That would explain their insolence."

"So we should run again?" Trebonius spat. "Only this time, we're running from legions that may be entirely imaginary?"

"I didn't see you volunteering to stay behind," Marcus retorted. That made the other officers laugh and Trebonius raised his hand in rueful submission. "Arvandus," Marcus said, "what sort of lesson did you have in mind?"

"Blood for blood. We decimate them in reverse, ten for each of our murdered men!"

"Be a bit hard, I'd say, seeing how they's all on the other side o' those walls," drawled Marcellianus, centurion of the second cohort. "You got a plan to get them out?"

"We don't got to sack the damn city to teach every Utruccan who hears about it a good hard lesson," Proculus objected. "I'll wager Julianus seen plenty of folks about when he was out catching those cattle earlier. How many'd you get? I heard something like eight hundred head."

"Seven-sixty-two," Julianus said. "And one hundred seventy-eight sheep. Hope you got some lads who know how to drive them beasts, because most of my riders don't ever want to see a cow again unless it's butchered and served up as steak."

Marcellianus whistled. "Seven hundred? That should keep us in beef for a spell."

"Sixth cohort has two centuries designated pecuarii," Marcus said. "That doesn't mean the men can necessarily tell what end of the beast is which, though, so let the other centurions know that Nebridius can have any of their men who is experienced with cattle at his sole discretion, so long as he gives them one of his own as a replacement. Temporary transfers, of course, to return to their original units once we reach Amorr and the men transferred out can be trained properly."

"Let's get back to the lesson we intend to teach the good people of Solacte," Trebonius said impatiently. Marcus saw his fellow tribune was taking the death of Dardanus very hard. "Proculus, unless I failed to understand you correctly, you were suggesting that Julianus could round up the requisite one hundred twenty locals to slaughter tomorrow. Can you do it, decurion?"

Julianus shrugged. "If that's what the tribune decides he wants. You want men, women, or sweet innocent little babies for your blood offering, Clericus?"

"It don't really matter," Proculus said indifferently. "The more important question is if you want to impale them, behead them, cut their throats, or crucify them."

"Forget crucifixion," Cassabus declared. "It's too much work, and they'd take too long to die. But if we're not going to use those fake onagers, we can just build a pyre and burn them all on it."

"There ain't no need for theatrics," Marcellianus said. "Just kill 'em where you find 'em and leave them lay. The Solactae'll figure it who did it and why soon enough.

"Now just hold on here, gentlemen!" Marcus broke into the macabre discussion. "We're not crucifying or burning anyone. I haven't even said we're going to kill anyone. But even if it's only to keep our options open and let them know we are serious, let's round up the hundred twenty, boys and young men between the ages of ten and twenty, assuming you can find enough of them. A lot of them may have already flocked to their standards now that the revolt is open. If not, girls of the same age will do. My thought is that we probably can trade them for the remains of our men and an amount of supplies."

Trebonus looked betrayed. "How is that teaching them or anyone else a lesson?" The other officers looked at each other, not so much in mutiny as in disbelief. "Attack our soldiers with impunity and we very well might... demand lunch and an apology?"

"The demonstration of power need not necessarily involve its actual exercise," Marcus said, feeling even as the words left his mouth that this was an argument that left much to be desired.

"It's not about power, Valerius—it's about revenge and retribution!" Trebonius nearly shouted. "You're not bloody Corvus, you know. Killing a few enemies of the Senate and People for their acknowledged crimes isn't at all like executing your nephew. You didn't hesitate to kill goblins in battle, so why would you hesitate now?"

"Thinking before one acts is not hesitation, Trebonius!" Marcus quelled his instinctive rage at the unfair mention of his father. "Shall I throw caution to the winds and order the storming of the walls? No,

Cassabus knows better and can advise otherwise. But who is there to tell me of all the possible long-term consequences of slaughtering more than one hundred innocent young Larinii and making a public spectacle of it in the process? Can you? Can anyone?"

"There are no innocent Larinii," Julianus said. "They broke the alliance, they chose war. Even the youngest child among them is guilty of war against the Senate and People."

"You're not trained as a sophist, Julianus, so don't try to play philosopher with me," Marcus replied scornfully. "I think we have discussed the matter sufficiently for tonight. Round up the young men, ten dozen of them, and leave it to me to decide what will be done. We will meet here again at sunrise, and I'll give everyone their orders then. In the meantime, unless anyone has any further questions, you are all dismissed."

Each officer saluted crisply enough, although the praefect equitatus was visibly angry and the two centurions seemed less than entirely pleased with the lack of definite resolution. But it couldn't be helped. No doubt his father would have ordered the deaths of everyone in Solacte, figured out a way to infiltrate the city's walls, then avenged the legion upon their bodies to the admiration and applause of his senior officers. But, as Trebonius had pointed out, he wasn't Corvus.

The centurions and decurions left the tent, but Gaius Trebonius turned back and approached him. "Permission to speak, General?" he asked with mock propriety.

"Shut up, Trebonius. I know you think I'm flirting with disaster. What's on your mind?"

"I want to know what is holding you back from doing what needs to be done. Because whatever it is, it had better be pretty damned important if you're willing to risk losing the men over it."

"I know, I know. They think I'm a coward because we've been doing nothing but run instead of standing and fighting."

"They don't think you're a coward. They know better. The decurions haven't forgotten how you led the charge down the hill to rescue Fortex and break the wolfriders."

"I didn't lead it," Marcus corrected him.

"Led it, ordered it—it doesn't matter. That's not the point. The point is that they don't think you're a coward. They think you're soft. They think you're afraid to make the hard calls because you're too young and inexperienced. Too romantic."

Marcus shook his head. "That's not it at all."

"Then what is it?"

"It's that I'm truly not sure what is the right thing to do here. Trebonius, I've read all sorts of philosophers and theologians. I've read Oxonus. I've read Tullius. I've read the Testaments and the Apostolics. And you know, none of them directly address the sort of situation I'm facing here.

"Do you truly think I'm afraid to tell Proculus to butcher all those Larinii? Nothing would be easier. I could give the order tonight, ride for Amorr tomorrow, and they'd celebrate me in the city for it without me having to watch a moment of it. And even if I were to ignore the moral aspects, who is to say that slaughtering our own allies won't inflame what is already a dangerous situation?"

"You need to forget Oxonus and the Testamenti and turn to your Frontinus," Trebonius said. "I think it's to your credit that the moral aspects matter to you, it truly is. But there is a reason most of our generals haven't been scholars for over four hundred years of empire, Marcus Valerius. Your primary concern has to be the morale and well-being of the men, not the morality of your orders. You're their general, not their priest. And if you don't permit them to avenge their comrades, you're going to risk losing them."

Marcus nodded. "You may well be right. I'll think on it. Tell Father Gennadius I'd like to see him, if he is amenable."

Trebonius saluted and left.

Marcus folded his hands and rested his chin on them. In all the lessons he'd learned, in all the lectures he'd heard, in all the books and scrolls he'd read, nothing had prepared him for this. He knew his duty to his men. If he could not save their comrades, he must avenge them and demand ten lives for every Amorran soldier slain.

But did he not also have a duty to the Immaculate Son of God? Was it not to glorify Him by his every thought, word, and deed? How could the murder—he chose the word deliberately, so that he might not give himself the excuse of evading what he was contemplating—how could the murder of young men and women who had never raised their fists, let alone their swords, against Amorr be to the glory of God? How could hands stained red with blood be Immaculate?

He rose from his chair and went in search of the scroll Trebonius had recommended. Perhaps the answer would be found in Frontinus. Where are you, Sextus Gaerus? Then he spotted the scroll that had once belonged to Marcus Saturnius. *There you are.* He ran his finger over the sections that seemed as if they might be relevant. *On Distracting The Attention Of The Enemy. On Quelling A Mutiny Of Soldiers.* He hoped he wouldn't ever need that one. *On Creating Panic In The Enemy's Ranks. On Ambushes. On Letting The Enemy Escape Lest He Renew The Battle In Desperation. On Restoring Morale By Firmness. On Bringing The War To A Close After A Successful Engagement.*

On Creating Panic seemed potentially relevant. He moved to the place and read. *The Faliscans and Tarquinians disguised a number of men as priests and had them hold torches and snakes in front of them, like Furies. Thus they threw the army of the Amorrans into panic.*

Perhaps not. That was useless, as was the rest of the section. It seemed hard to imagine such a childish tactic working, although perhaps by "priests" Frontinus actually meant "mages." He wondered if it was really the crude tactic described or if, like the good son of the Church that he was, Sextus Gaerus had shown delicacy in the portrayal of an enemy's use of magic. He spread out more of the scroll, and his eye fell upon *On Bringing The War To A Close.*

I. Cassanius Inregillensis, having met the elves on their way from Kir Donas to Glaislael under the command of Prince Seabringer, defeated them and threw the Seabringer's head into the elven king's camp. As a result, the king was overwhelmed with grief and the army gave up hope of receiving reinforcements.

II. When Lucius Comminus was besieging Thursia, he fastened on spears the heads of Thursian generals who had been slain in battle, and exhibited them to the besieged inhabitants, thus breaking their stubborn resistance.

III. Arminghast Fourfinger, leader of the mountain orcs, likewise fastened on spears the heads of those he had slain, and ordered them to be brought up to the fortifications of the enemy.

IV. When Domitius Corbulus was besieging Burgruneaux and the Tarcondii seemed likely to make an obstinate defense, Corbulus executed Vadandus, one of the nobles he had captured, shot his head out of a ballista, and sent it flying within the fortifications of the enemy. It happened to fall in the midst of a council which the barbarians were holding at that very moment, and the sight of it (as though it were some portent) so filled them with consternation that they made haste to surrender.

It appeared someone in Solacte has been reading Frontinus, he murmured to himself. Only he couldn't see that exhibiting poor Dardanus's head had filled him or anyone else with the desire to surrender. But answering terror with considerably more terror would appear to be the tactic in order here. He rolled the scroll up again as a small man with a shaven head wearing a simple black robe pushed aside the tent flap.

"By your leave, my lord Tribune?"

"Please, Father Gennadius, do come in."

The little priest had been with the legion since its formation and was a favorite with the men and officers alike. He took the chair that Marcus indicated. He was popular with the soldiery because his weekly sermons were short and pithy. The men said that the priest who had been travelling with Legio VII for more than twenty years could go two bells without ever once appearing to pause for breath, and regularly did so. But

Father Gennadius was also popular with the officers because he handed out relatively light penances for sexual peccadilloes, which kept the men coming back for confession. If he wasn't the fine scholar that Marcus's longtime tutor, Father Aurelius, was, Gennadius was a font of calm and sensible wisdom, and Marcus always enjoyed talking with him.

"Gaius Trebonius seemed less than pleased with you, Clericus. There was a disagreement? The deaths of Lucius Dardanus, Quintus Gavrus, and the other knights trouble you?"

"In a manner of speaking," Marcus admitted. "Father, can one repent and confess a sin prior to committing it?"

"I should not think so. To repent is to abjure the sin, to cast its impurity forth from the soul it stains and henceforth resist its temptation. If one commits the sin after its confession, then one has not truly repented and therefore merits no forgiveness from that false repentance, either before or after the act."

Surprised, Marcus raised his eyebrows at the priest's answer. "You're saying the act then becomes unforgivable? That seems excessive."

"Not at all. Only that to commit the sin following the confession is to render it void, as if the confession had never happened. Repentance must come after the fact if it is to be considered even potentially genuine. Is there a particular sin you are contemplating, my son?"

"I'm not even sure if it is a sin, Father. Or rather, it strikes me as a sin, but then, it also strikes me as my duty, and shirking my duty would also be a sin. So, it would appear I'm damned either way."

"In a manner of speaking," the priest said with a faint smile. "But let us not resort to cheap theatrics. It is my duty to see that you are not damned at all, Marcus Valerius. So tell me your dilemma, if you can."

Marcus laid out the facts for the priest. It came as a relief to honestly admit his concerns without the need to fear if doing so would cause Father Gennadius to think less of him as a man or a commander. The priest was technically under Marcus's orders so long as he was attached to the legion, but Marcus couldn't imagine actually trying to give him one, and he had no doubt that the little man wouldn't hesitate to disobey him if he saw fit to do so.

"If I have understood you correctly," the priest began when Marcus had finished, "you feel that your duty as the general of the legion conflicts with your duty as one who attempts to walk in the sanctified footsteps of the Immaculate. Neither Oxonus nor Tullius can help you here, as both the Larinii and the Solactae have given you sufficient *jus ad bellum* with their abrogation of the alliance and the murder of your men.

"The real question is one of *jus in bello,* but I agree with you that the Tullian dictate concerning the imperative to spare those who have not been bloodthirsty and barbarous in their warfare is a collective one. He refers to tribes, cities, and peoples, not individuals. As to whether this is a war for survival or supremacy, I should say that while it is too soon to say, I incline toward the latter. The Larinii and the Cynothii may wish to throw off the Amorran yoke, but they have shown no sign they wish to march on Amorr, much less destroy it."

"This is all beside the point," Marcus complained. "My concern is for my officers and my men. How can I lead them if they do not respect me as their general?"

"I wonder how you can think to lead them if you are determined to follow their opinion? But no, that is unfair. My son, there is no conflict. There is no dilemma at all, except in your own mind. That is the essential problem you face. Nor is this chiefly a military matter, or even a moral issue, at least not the one you wrongly believe it to be."

"What are you talking about? Of course it's neither one nor the other—it is both!"

"I fear you have not properly considered the logic, Clericus. Let us assume that your officers are correct and it is to the genuine military advantage of Amorr to slaughter the young Larinii who have neither killed your men nor taken up arms. This despite your feeling that it would be more in accordance with God's will to spare them. This puts you in a difficult situation because you have a solemn and sworn duty to serve

Amorr to the best of your abilities and yet you are also a child of the Immaculate and are sworn in your soul to obey Him."

"That is so," Marcus allowed, unsure where the priest was going with this.

"Is whatever is of military advantage to Amorr the sole factor that one who serves the Senate and People must take into account?"

"No, of course not. It's one of a number of factors."

"Therefore it is not intrinsically dispositive. Military victories are to be desired, certainly, and they may even be absolutely vital in certain circumstances, as one cannot serve that which is nonexistent. But that is not the case now. Amorr will not be destroyed regardless of what you do here. Its survival is not currently hanging in the balance. Now, are the Senate and People dedicated to any purpose beyond the continued survival and prosperity of the city?"

"To serve God as their true king...."

"Precisely. It seems to me then that your choice is between serving God as a follower of the Immaculate or serving God as a tribune elected by the tribes and sworn to the service of the Senate and People. Your concerns about what your men and your officers might think is merely a matter of pride, Marcus Valerius, which I have observed that the members of your House tend to possess in some quantity. You already know what to do, but you simply wish to find a way to rationalize your natural desire so as to have your men think well of you."

Marcus stared at Father Gennadius in shock. He felt as if one of his family's loyal dogs had turned on him and bitten him to the bone. Here he was asking the seemingly inoffensive little man to give him counsel about a difficult situation, and somehow the priest had turned it into an accusation of his personal failings! He felt his temper rising, and it was only with the utmost difficulty that he managed to prevent himself from shouting at the man.

"You are wrong," he stated calmly. "I would take no pride in killing the young ones."

Father Gennadius smiled. "Of course not, Clericus. Their deaths would be merely the means, not the end. The pride that blinds you to your duty to God and Amorr alike is rooted in your desire to be seen as a general worthy of the traditions of your house, victorious and beloved by his loyal men. Fortunately, you are either too sensible or too well-schooled in strategy to be entirely ruled by your pride, or I have no doubt you would attempt to besiege Solacte while fighting off all the rebel legions that come to break the siege."

The justice of the priest's statement forced Marcus to swallow the first two or three retorts that occurred to him. He had, in fact, spent some time flirting with the idea of feigning a march south, then doubling back and storming the city at night, gambling that any significant rebel forces would either be committed elsewhere or too slow to respond to the city's original summons. He'd even discovered a more outrageous idea in Longinus, when Sextus Gaerus described the way Antiochus had taken Suenda by intercepting a supply train, killing its teamsters, and replacing them with his soldiers to get them inside the gates. Intercepting an entire legion or two, however, struck him as overly ambitious.

"So your advice is to simply march on and leave the Solactae unmolested?" He tried to keep the irritation out of his voice and was not entirely successful.

"My advice is for you to pray and be honest with yourself." Father Gennadius rose from his chair and took one of Marcus's hands in his own. "You find yourself facing pressures that no young man your age is expected to face, Marcus Valerius. Have courage and give more credence to the still small voice you hear in your heart than to the roaring of your centurions or the whispers of your soldiers. And whatever you decide, know that God is not only watching—He is with you."

Marcus nodded. "Thank you for the counsel, Father."

"At your service, General." The priest smiled, bowed, and departed.

Well, that was rather less than helpful, Marcus thought. He was unimpressed by the priestly logic. During his time preparing for the priesthood, he had known men who could utilize the dialectic as if it were a musical instrument, blowing whatever tune they chose. Cassius Clodius, in particular, could probably find a way to prove that burning the Larini youth as a sacrifice to the devil was a divine mandate and make it sound not only convincing, but conclusive. And yet, Father Gennadius had reminded him of one thing that he had failed to consider.

No man, still less a general, could ever hope to lead by following.

The cathedral tower was ringing out terce as the First Cavalry and the first and third cohorts emerged from the morning fog and approached the gates of Solacte. The prisoners marched alongside the two centuries assigned to guard duty, many of them stumbling and crying from fear and a lack of sleep the night before. The centurion commanding the century from the fourth assigned to watch the gates over the night saluted Marcus wearily as he and his men were dismissed and began the trek toward the warmth and safety of the castra.

Trebonius was back at the camp making preparations for their planned departure the following day, but Father Gennadius had insisted upon accompanying them, though it was unclear what he hoped to accomplish in the morning after their conversation the previous evening.

But to Marcus's surprise, the priest did not say anything upon being greeted by the sight of the young men and women standing with their wrists bound, each of them held leashed by a legionary. He simply nodded calmly to Proculus, Arvandus, and Marcus before clumsily mounting his mule and falling in at the end of the line of march. And if the father wondered about the empty mule-drawn cart or the twelve sheep that followed behind, driven by two legionaries from the sixth and a dog, he kept his questions to himself.

They were greeted by the grim sight of the twelve heads still protruding from the gate towers. Marcus nodded to Proculus, and at a gesture from the centurion, a pair of drums began to boom with a slow, ominous beat that would be heard throughout the city before them.

Once more, Marcus rode out in the company of a centurion and a decurion. But this time they were followed by the two centuries accompanying the prisoners. Before he reached his intended mark, signs of activity could be seen all along the walls and in the battlements as well.

Proculus held up a fist, and the drums picked up their pace, then fell silent when he dropped his arm. That was Marcus's cue.

"People of Solacte, I have returned as promised. With me, I have brought one hundred and twenty young men and women from the villages and farms that surround this city, ten for each of my men whose bodies you have defiled. By the laws of war and the laws of the Senate of Amorr, your rightful rulers, I declare their lives forfeit. However, as Tullius writes, 'It is sufficient that the aggressor should be brought to repent of his wrongdoing, in order that he may not repeat the offence and that others may be deterred from doing wrong.' I therefore summon your senator-in-chief, Opiter Florus Siculo, to answer for the crimes of your city."

He counted to one hundred. Meanwhile there were no shortage of jeers and insults shouted from the walls. But Siculo did not appear.

Marcus sighed and raised his hand. As the drums again began to thunder, a legionary frog-marched a struggling young man to the fore and forced him to his knees and placed his gladius at the man's naked throat. After taking a deep breath, Marcus lowered his arm, the drums stopped, and the legionary drove his sword into the kneeling man's throat, then jerked it left and right before drawing it forth again, bloody with the now-dying man's lifesblood.

Angry cries rained down upon him, but Marcus only nodded to acknowledge the killer's salute before the legionary withdrew. He waited a little while, listening to their rage and their hate, before he raised his voice again.

"I summon your senator-in-chief, Opiter Florus Siculo, to answer for the crimes of your city."

But still, Siculo refused to show himself. Marcus counted to one hundred again, praying now for the soul of the young man killed and for the next ones in line. Then he raised his hand again. The grim play was reenacted, and soon there were two lifeless bodies lying face down in pools of bright crimson blood on the snow-dusted brown grass of the field.

"I summon your senator-in-chief, Opiter Florus Siculo, to answer for the crimes of your city," he shouted again.

Still nothing. The sequence repeated itself. There were four bodies on the ground before the gates parted and began to slowly separate. They opened enough to permit a party of three men to emerge before closing again as Siculo and two elderly companions, both shorter and fatter than the senator, approached the three Amorrans.

"Butchering our neighbors' children isn't going to cause us to bend the knee again, boy," Siculo, who up close was younger than his white hair had seemed to suggest from afar, fairly spat at Marcus.

"I didn't imagine it would," Marcus agreed. "I am requesting your repentance and your submission, but I don't expect to receive it... yet. All that I am demanding today is the return of my men's remains so that they may receive proper burial."

The Solactean frowned and pursed his lips in what looked like suspicion, but Marcus suspected it masked relief.

"Just their bodies?"

"And their heads, of course."

"Yes, yes, naturally. And then you will release your prisoners, alive and unharmed, and agree to leave our lands?"

Marcus smiled coldly. "I will release my prisoners, alive and unharmed. I will not agree to anything else. As it happens, I do not mind telling you that I still intend to depart the castra in two days regardless of your decision."

"And yet you won't agree to something you say you intend to do? You can't murder all of these men and women over such a small matter,

Tribune. You know perfectly well that your men were soldiers. These are innocent people taken from their homes!"

"I would have to agree… if you had killed them in battle, Consul. But they would not have laid down their arms had they imagined they would be butchered and their bodies defiled."

The Solactean looked down at the bloody ground for a moment. "Tribune, you cannot know what it is like for a people to have been under the Amorran heel for centuries. Yesterday, when you were at the gates with your siege engines, well, emotions ran high. Killing your soldiers may have been a mistake. It was not necessary."

"No, it was not. In fact, it was a foolish provocation, and it will not be forgotten. Let us be honest with one another, Consul. If I had the time, I would sack your city, raze its walls, and sell your people into slavery as an example to the other cities across Utrucca. But I do not. I do, however, have the time to kill every last one of these young rebels, and you know I am perfectly within my rights to do so. If you value dead men's bones more than the lives of your neighbors' children, you have only to say the word, and I will supply you all the bones you could ever desire."

"I see." The older man seemed to squint a little as he peered closely into Marcus's eyes. "You understand I cannot promise you anything, Tribune. Only the Council has the authority to make this decision. I am but one of twelve. I will take them your offer, and I will advise them to accept it. Will you consent to wait until tomorrow for our answer?"

Marcus shook his head. "I will give you until sext. Before the bells stop ringing, the next will die."

The older man nodded slowly. "Very well, Tribune. You will have our answer before then." Without another word, he turned and began walking quickly back toward the gates, which opened just wide enough to receive him and his two companions.

"Ten silvers they take it," Proculus said as soon as the Solactae were out of earshot.

"Five against your ten they don't," Arvandus answered. "These people were dumb enough to capture Dardanus and his men in the first place, then kill them with an entire legion on their doorstep. What did they think would happen, that we'd run away scared?"

"Done," Proculus accepted the odds. "Tribune, they could be a while yammering at each other. Do we really have to wait out here like this? This horse is giving me a right pain in my arse."

"No, we don't. Tell the men to stand at ease. Let their prisoners sit if they want. If the Solactae have come to their senses, they'll accept our offer. If they're determined to be unreasonable, it doesn't matter what we do, they'll turn down whatever we offer simply because we're offering it."

As they cantered back toward the warmth of the fires the centurions had ordered built near the wagon, Marcus saw Father Gennadius blessing a kneeling legionary, and he wondered how many penances he would have to accept before again receiving one himself. But there was nothing to do now but wait and see if his strategy had been effective. So instead of staring impotently at the city's walls, he urged his horse in the direction of the priest.

"Greetings, Father," he said respectfully.

"Tribune," the priest said in a conspicuously neutral tone. "I see you reached your decision, although I have to admit I am a little disappointed. I hope you will be moved to discuss it with me one day in the future."

Marcus smiled. He was aware that the priest was referring, circumspectly, to an eventual confession. He also knew he had nothing to confess, although Father Gennadius had no way of knowing that. The priest had seen what everyone else saw—a soldier, a blade, and the death of an innocent man. But eyes can be deceived, and no one but God can truly see whether a soul is innocent or not!

"That seems unlikely, Father. You appear to be operating under a misapprehension."

The priest looked up at him with a skeptical expression and pointed toward the field, where the two centuries were still standing with their captives, at the bodies of the two fallen Larinii. "Sin is not a question of quantity, Marcus Valerius. A man is a murderer whether he kills one innocent or one thousand."

"And I have killed none." An impromptu cheer went up around him, and Marcus looked over his left shoulder to see what had provoked such an enthusiastic response from his men. Nothing seemed to be happening, and he squinted at the distant walls in bewilderment. Then the slight motion caught his eye, and he realized that the pikes upon which rested the heads of his men were disappearing one by one into the tower. He smiled with satisfaction.

"I don't understand," Father Gennadius said, looking from Marcus to the city walls, then back again.

"Last night, the night patrol encountered scouts from the first Larini army that's coming this way from Fescennium, Father. The decurion managed to capture a few of them for interrogation, and when Arvandus reported to me this morning, I realized I might have an additional use for them."

"So the two men that were killed...."

"Were not the young Larinii that Julianus rounded up. They were enemy combatants captured in war. Now, I know their blood is on my hands, but it is legitimate, and I suspect there will be a lot more of it by the time this is over and done. I prayed about it, as you suggested, and not an hour after that, Arvandus came to tell me that his men had captured the six scouts."

"There are a lot more than six men and women still out there on that field, Marcus Valerius."

"And none of them need die. Unless I miss my guess, the Solactae are about to return Dardanus and the others to us. As soon as their bones are safely stowed in that wagon, we'll march the captives back to the castra and leave them there when we depart this afternoon. The rest of the legion will be ready to march by the time we return."

"We're leaving today? I thought we were going to stay here for two more days."

"So did I." Marcus shrugged. "There are ten thousand armed Larinii marching this way and those are only the ones of which we know. I don't plan to be here when they arrive. Trebonius and the others can grumble all they like, but it's not their decision. The first priority is to get to Montmila and see how much of Vallyria is still loyal to its House, if not Amorr. What we learn there will determine our next march."

The priest turned back to look at the prisoners shivering miserably on the snowy field. Behind them, the twelve gruesome standards had disappeared from the wall tower. "Tell me truthfully, Marcus: What would you have done if the Solactae hadn't given in and agreed to return the remains? Would you still have spared the young ones?"

Marcus shook his head and smiled. "I believe I've confessed to enough sins that I needn't admit any hypothetical ones, Father. Let us just be grateful that the cup was taken from me."

THEUDERIC

LORD Silvertree smiled at Lithriel and Theuderic, but it was a cruel and arrogant smile, the smile of a wolf that finds itself cornered by rabbits. "I have heard so much about the unusual abilities of these Michaelines—how fortuitous it is to have the chance to test them for myself! Had I only known the occasion would present itself, I would have devised a number of experiments. But, even as it stands, this is an opportunity that shouldn't be missed."

Theuderic rolled his eyes. "You may be more capable of defending yourself than we are, but I don't think it would be wise to to fight the Amorrans in Amorr. It won't be long before you'll find yourself fending off half the Order of Saint Michael." The high elf appeared to be listening, so Theuderic continued. "You suggested before that we leave. Why don't we do that? I have some money with me, as well as my sword. Are there any of your possessions at the palace that you simply can't abandon, Lithriel?"

The elfess shrugged. "Just some clothes. But you can always buy me more." Then, to his surprise, she asked about the two nuns with whom they'd come to the city. "Do you think the Watcher will revenge himself upon the other Savondese who came with us?"

Silvertree laughed. "It's highly unlikely. Insofar as I understand their peculiar perspective, doing so would be akin to revenging oneself upon a pile of rocks. No, little cousin, your acquaintances should be in no danger once the two of you depart."

"Well, what do you think, my lord comte?" Lithriel asked him. "Do we run, or do we take our chances and return to the palace? And if we run, how do you propose to help us escape, Lord Silvertree, since our horses are at the palace stables and I saw no sign of any stables here on the premises when we arrived."

Theuderic smiled at his lady elf. "One of my favorite things about being a royal mage is that we have been given a standing order to preserve ourselves for further service to his majesty at all costs. If there is reason to believe the danger is real, and I suppose there is, then I have a solemn duty to take every measure to preserve *mon vraiment peu de derrière*. To say nothing of the aesthetic responsibility to preserve your much more beautiful specimen, my lady."

"So chivalrous." She smiled at him, and he had the sense that, had Silvertree not been there, she would have stuck out her tongue. No, he thought with a mild frisson of pleasure, more likely waggled the specimen referenced. "So, we run!"

"Only because duty demands it," he said. "Naturally. Now, about those horses that apparently don't exist? It would be a shame for you to sneak us out of here, Lord Silvertree, only to see us caught before we reach the outer wall."

"You won't be sneaking out, nor need you worry about either the inner or the outer walls," the high elf responded. "I chose this manor for a very specific reason. Not only is it right on the inner wall, but it also has excellent access to the roof via a staircase. This evening, once darkness falls, your transportation will arrive. It seems you are not alone in your affection for the race of man, Lady Lithriel, as one of the high king's household has struck up a peculiar friendship with a consul's son. She is coming here tonight at my request, as a favor to the consul."

"I'm surprised the high king permits any such friendship."

"He doesn't know about it. And anyway, it is not a friendship of the sort the two of you appear to enjoy. The Lady Shadowsong knows Mael would have both their heads before permitting anything of the sort."

"I don't understand," Theuderic was puzzled. "How is this Shadowsinger going to get us out of Amorr?"

"Shadow*song,* my dear magician. And she's going to get you out the same way she's going to arrive: on the back of her warhawk."

"You're jesting!" Theuderic looked at Lithriel, who shook her head. "You're not jesting? We're actually going to fly over the walls?"

"It's that or dig under them, and dwarves are rather hard to come by in these parts. She'll fly you out to a place I have prepared against the need for our own retreat. Then she will leave you there, and in the morning, you can walk due east to the nearest town. It will take some time to get there, as it will probably be close to noon by the time you arrive, but you'll be able to acquire horses there and you won't need fear anyone pursuing you."

Theuderic felt a little ill. It was bad enough that they weren't going to have the chance to go back to the palace for their things, or even rest after their long journey south. He'd anticipated several months of relaxing, being able to share his bed with Lithriel on a regular basis, and perhaps even indulging in the famously decadent Amorran baths before having to travel all the way back to Savondir again in the spring.

The idea of an immediate return in the middle of winter was horrific enough without the thought of having to actually fly through the air, on what would have to be the most precarious of mounts. He'd heard of the elven warhawks before, certainly. That was why he'd pursued the spell used to tame them. But he'd never truly laid eyes upon one. Did they have saddles of some sort? They must have. But what if one fell off?

"You can't simply start throwing fire in their midst to see if they can stop it." Theuderic didn't have much sympathy for the Amorrans, but he knew enough about elven inhumanity from the last year with Lithriel to realize that the high elf was likely capable of slaughtering every human in the near vicinity out of simple curiosity. "You'll burn down the bloody city! Half these buildings are about one brick away from collapsing already!"

"Would you rather I permitted them to remove you from my protection? They have no quarrel with me, magician. And it is going to be some time before nightfall."

"No, of course not."

"Very well then." Silvertree pointed at the books and scrolls scattered around the table. "Miroglas, please see that all of the various codices and documents are safely stowed for travel, then bring them to the roof. And lay out our travelling clothes as well, since we should depart tonight. I intend to go above myself now, and then we shall see if we cannot arrange to disperse our unwanted visitors."

He indicated that Lithriel and Theuderic should follow, then he led them to a circular staircase that culminated in a door that opened out onto the roof.

The sunlight was dazzling as there were only a few clouds interspersed throughout the blue sky, and while the wall blocked the view to the west, the view of the city to the other side was nothing short of spectacular. The Sanctiff's palace, rising on its hill in the center of the city, could be seen in all its alabaster splendor, almost blinding as it reflected the bright rays of the sun. There were many other wonderful buildings throughout the city, built of the fine white marbles that were quarried to the south, but none of them were quite as splendid as the one that held a dark cancer at its heart.

Below, the Curian guards were easy to see in their distinctive red cloaks. There appeared to be twenty or thirty of them, including one with a tall horsehair plume that Theuderic guessed denoted their captain.

It was even easier to spot the Michaelines, all five of whom were gathered in a circle on their knees and appeared to be engaged in either prayer or some ritual of their order. Wondering how their famous anti-magic worked, if it indeed was not some sort of Amorran sham, Theuderic summoned his power and caused flames to erupt from his outstretched fingers before banishing them again a moment later. He shrugged, feeling perversely disappointed by the ease with which he'd done so. Whatever the Michaelines were doing, it didn't seem to interfere with his magic in the slightest.

"You can't feel anything?" The high elf had noticed his little experiment.

"No, nothing at all. I can't imagine you'll have any problem casting whatever you like upon them. May I ask what sort of spell you have in mind?"

"I don't know if I can answer that question in your tongue. But wait and see what happens, then perhaps you can explain it to me."

But before the high elf could do anything, the captain of the Curian Guard spotted them atop the roof and first waved to get their attention, then cupped his hands around his mouth to call up to them. "Greetings, my lord ambassador. I trust you will forgive our indiscretion in visiting you in such numbers."

The high elf placed his hands on his hips and affected an indignant pose. "Who are you and why in the name of all that is clean and purified are you surrounding this embassy? Must I remind you that, for all intents and purposes, by treaty between consul and high king and by Amorran law, this residence is to be considered Elebrion itself? You, sir captain, are very nearly engaging in what could be considered an act of war and an offense against the high king himself!"

"I am aware of that, and I sincerely apologize for any offense or inconvenience we have caused," the guard captain shouted insincerely. "Allow me to introduce myself. I am called Nonus Sulpicius Deodatus, and I am captain of the third Curian century. May I enter the residence so that we may discuss this matter in a less public fashion?"

It was little wonder that the captain of the church troops didn't wish to continue the shouted conversation, Theuderic thought. The mere presence of the troops had been enough to attract a crowd, and now that their captain was shouting at one of the only elves—in fact, now one of the only foreigners—in the city, more and more people were beginning to stick their heads out of windows or join the crowd that was aimlessly milling around the soldiers. But not very closely, as many of the Amorrans appeared to be aware that the elven ambassador was a sorcerer and none of them looked as though they wanted to get too close to his most obvious targets.

"Let your deeds be done under the clean light of the sun, Sulpicius Deodatus, and you need fear no evil of man or beast," Silvertree answered the captain. "Is it not written? Now, state your business or begone. I have neither the patience nor the inclination to give an audience to those who arrive at my doorstep in the company of armed men."

Theuderic could clearly see the expression on the captain's face, and he didn't appear to be the least bit surprised or frustrated at the elf's recalcitrance. "I have been ordered to escort your recent visitors, who are guests of the Sanctiff himself and under his protection, back to the palace. I am here in force because there is reason to believe they may be in danger, and the Most Holy and Sanctified Father wishes to assure himself of their safety. My orders were given by the Sanctified Father himself, who also wishes you and your colleague to come to the palace as well."

"If my guests are in danger, I assure you, Captain, I can guarantee their safety. They need fear no injury here in the elven residence. But I have had many visitors. Which of them concern you?"

"The Comte de Thôneaux and his paramour. Unless I miss my guess, he is the man standing beside you."

"I am not inclined to play puzzle games, Captain. Now, lest I be forced to encourage your departure, I suggest you return to your master and inform him that my guests are beyond his reach and will be staying with me for as long as they wish. Nor do I, or any of my staff, intend to accompany you anywhere!"

There was a long moment of silence. Theuderic could see that most of the crowd, which now amounted to more than three or four hundred people, were staring at the captain, waiting for his reaction.

Deodatus puffed out his cheeks, looked down at his feet, then finally shook his head before addressing the three of them on the rooftop again.

"This isn't a game, my lord ambassador. I regret to inform you that if you and your visitors will not come with me, I shall be forced to enter your residence with or without your permission, as your appearance before the Sanctified Father is not a request. My orders are clear on this matter, and before you attempt to characterize this unfortunate intrusion as an act of war, let me remind you that I am in the service of the Church, not the Senate or the People."

"The offense to his Illustrious Majesty is the same, Captain, whether you do it in the name of your god or your government. But as you will, enter by force if you can. If you wish to do so, you will have to do it over my objections."

Sorcerous wards suddenly swelled to life, and the crowd gasped as, even in the daylight, the eldritch gleam of them could be seen by the naked eye. It wasn't so much the power involved that was astonishing to Theuderic as the intricate skill they revealed. There were delicate layers upon layers, illusions piled upon magical reality, but very material traps that would kill as surely as any sword. It was like looking upon a deadly war machine that was made miraculously from the most expensive lace.

The elven wards were impossible, and yet they surrounded him to the right and the left, above and below, and shielded him on every side. It was a tremendous working that would have taken every Immortel of l'Académie their cumulative lifetimes to construct, and weeks to enact, but Silvertree had erected it in a matter of seconds. Theuderic would have bet his life that it would kill every guardsman it didn't send fleeing in fear as soon as the captain triggered the first one.

The people surrounding the soldiers in the street saw them. They were meant to be seen, to be feared. All of them, excepting only a few young boys and three or four of the most intrepid observers, drew away from the guardsmen for fear of what the captain's attempt to enter the residence might unleash. The soldiers saw them too, and they began to exchange nervous glances at each other, looking as if they wished to join the crowd and put some distance between themselves and their foolhardy officer.

Only Deodatus and the Michaelines appeared to be unconcerned. One of the warrior-priests rose to his feet and conferred briefly with the captain before stepping forward and raising one hand toward the building as if in blessing.

And then, as quickly as they had risen the wards disappeared.

Theuderic staggered. He felt as if the air had suddenly grown heavy and thick, falling like a weight upon his shoulders. He tried the same spell he'd used just a little while before, but this time, the fire did not come to him. It was as if they were fish that found themselves caught in a huge invisible net, tumbling helplessly and inexplicably unable to swim away. He could barely hear the astonished cries of the crowd as they reacted to the unexpected vanishing of the elven spells.

He heard Silvertree saying something in a shocked and angry voice, and he guessed the high elf was cursing in his native tongue. "You can feel it too, magician?"

Theuderic nodded, unable to speak. The sensation wasn't painful, but it felt distressingly like being pinned under a heavy wool blanket, running out of air as the heat rapidly rose around you. The harder he tried to call upon his power, the more the stifling, heavy weight seemed to press upon him. He wondered if the elf had it worse, or if his greater power allowed him to resist the priestly anti-magic more strongly.

"What can I do, my lord?" Lithriel rushed to the high elf's side and was helping him stand.

"I can't maintain them," Silvertree gasped. "I never thought... Bessarias once said... it is too much!"

He doubled over, and a severe coughing fit racked him.

Theuderic winced and wouldn't have been surprised to see blood on his lips when it ended.

"Let it go," he urged the elf. "Are you still trying to hold up the wards?"

The elf nodded, his face uncharacteristically suffused with red and twisted with the strain of his effort.

"Let it go! You have to drop them! The more you fight it, the more the spell grips you tighter."

"Not a spell," the elf hissed. "Not possible!"

"Please, my lord, do as he says," Lithriel begged. "If you die, the wards will fall anyway and then your king will remain in ignorance of what these strange priests can do."

Pride warred with duty in the ambassador's strange green eyes, until finally he sank to his knees and lowered his head.

Barely a moment later, the terrible pressure disappeared so unexpectedly that Theuderic nearly lost his balance. Overcome with relief, he could do little more than place his hands on his knees and breathe deeply, a little of his strength returning to him with every breath he took.

"I see you have lowered your wards, my lord ambassador," the captain called up to the high elf. "Will you now permit us entry, or will you come out to us?"

Silvertree looked at him, and Theuderic swallowed. They both knew there wasn't anything more they could do.

"I'll go out," Theuderic said. "Without magic, we can't hold them off. They're too many, and they can easily send for more. Perhaps they'll be content to take me first and come back later for you and the others."

"They won't accept that. We can try to delay them, of course, but I doubt we will be able to put them off until nightfall."

"There's no point," Theuderic said regretfully. "If they'd come late in the day perhaps it would be worth trying, but even if we destroyed the roof access, they'd have ladders here before the next bell. Or maybe even ballistae, depending upon how much we irritated them. Who would have known those damned priests could play such a trick?"

He walked to the edge of the roof and looked down. Hundreds of expectant faces looked back at him, but only one was of any real import.

"The Comte de Thôneaux, I presume?" the guard captain said. Theuderic noted with reluctant approval that the man was too professional to allow any hint of sarcasm or irritation to be heard in his voice. "If you would be so kind as to descend, my lord, it will be my privilege to escort you, your companions, and the elven ambassador to the palace."

"We shall be with you shortly, Captain," Theuderic said. It was pointless to resist. He couldn't help but feel how ridiculous it was that, after surviving more than one dangerous infiltration into enemy lands, usually on his own, it might be an open and well-escorted royal embassy that would prove to be his ultimate undoing.

CORVUS

C ORVUS had never seriously thought he would ever become consul himself, though the thought of what it would be like occasionally crossed his mind. Especially after the first time Magnus had been elected consul civitas. Magnus always wore the title lightly, as if it were merely another honor he'd accrued and not a responsibility. And his brother not only enjoyed being consul, he was good at it too, or he would not have been elected with such ease each of the three subsequent times he'd stood for the office.

He, on the other hand, was beginning to wonder if he would ever be regarded as anything but a complete failure. In his defense, he supposed it was probably a lot easier to serve as the consul aquilae if you knew how many of your legions would acknowledge your orders—and that none of them happened to be engaged in open rebellion against the Senate. He looked down at the map on his desk, and the little pieces of wood that served to represent Amorr's legions, both loyal and disloyal, then at the numbers on the waxed tablet representing their respective numbers.

He sighed, wishing that circumstances were different and that he could talk to his brother about the daunting challenges he now faced. Especially since, as head of House Valerius, it was Magnus, not Corvus, who was formally responsible for the legions that Corvus had been commanding for the last year. But Magnus barely even knew the generals, let alone the tribunes, of the three legions. He hadn't shown much interest in them since his second term as consul aquilae five years ago. And, except for approving the necessary funds, he hadn't even had any involvement in the formation of the House's newest legion.

The thought of Legio XVII reminded him of its present commander, and he reached out again for the much-creased letter from Marcus. It was short, and the news it contained was almost uniformly bad, but he took comfort in the certain knowledge that his younger son was well. But the death of Marcus Saturnius was a tremendous blow, both to him and to Amorr, particularly at this dangerous juncture. Losing Saturnius now felt like losing his right arm. It was so rare to have a subordinate who was both supremely competent and completely trustworthy, and the fact that the groundwork for his assassination had been planned nearly a year in advance was chilling. Combined with the death of Corvinus, about whom he could still barely permit himself to think, it was very nearly more than he could bear.

He knew that as a tribune, Marcus had likely been targeted for assassination too, but he refused to permit the thought to cross his mind. There were always risks to an officer, although they usually came more in the form of disease and enemy artillery than daggers in the night.

So many deaths and in such a short time! It seemed almost as if God had withdrawn His protection from His own consecrated city and thrown Amorr to the wolves of chaos. But then, Corvus had been spared and his son had been spared. Perhaps they had been spared for a reason. He desperately wished he could travel to Vallyrium and relieve Marcus of a command for which he was not nearly ready, but he was honor-bound to stand for consul in a week's time. The assassination of Severus Patronus, combined with rumors about the rebellion growing throughout the empire, had thrown the entire city into a state of chaos, and his allies in the Senate strongly felt that as proper consul, Corvus would serve as an important stabilizing force in helping restore a sense of order.

And there was no question that one was needed. He felt a little guilty about the consular order he and Torquatus had jointly issued three days after Severus's death, forcing all non-citizens to leave the city within three days on pain of having their wealth seized and being forcibly expelled, but there was no question it had been necessary.

The People had reacted to the news of Patronus's plans to enlarge his clientele with no less rage and considerably more violence than the Senate had, and more than two hundred, most of them provincials, had died in the various riots and massacres that had begun the night of his funeral. Even with the full support of the Sanctiff and the military orders, Torquatus simply didn't have enough armed men to quell the rising tide of violence.

It was a real shock to learn how many foreigners had settled in Amorr over the years. Nearly one in twelve of the city's residents had been non-citizens, and it had been difficult to watch the long line of merchants and laborers, many of them accompanied by wives and children, trudging reluctantly toward the city gates and the long roads that would lead them away from the only home that many of them had ever known. How many of them would die on those harsh, wintry roads, or be waylaid and lose everything to bandits en route to the ancestral lands where they rightly belonged? Far fewer than would die before the fury of the People died down, especially if any of the rebellious provinces followed through on their threat to march on Amorr.

He and Torquatus both knew that, if a provincial army managed to fight its way past whatever legions remained loyal, it would take a miracle to save even a tenth of the resident provincials from the outraged wrath of a frightened People.

They had done what they could to protect the expelled, of course. The entire body of the Redeemed, some two-hundred strong, reinforced by the Petrines and the Jeremiads, were given the task of patrolling the four major roads leading out from the city. On his own authority, Torquatus had given all three groups the right of high justice for the duration of the expulsions, permitting the execution on the spot of anyone caught molesting an expelled traveler, and they had already received reports of twenty such executions.

But Corvus was under no illusion that they were doing more than putting a dent in the number of predations taking place up and down the roads, and they simply couldn't afford to devote any more mounted soldiers to the patrols, not with the city in such an unsettled state. And, he reminded himself, there had been only two more mid-sized riots and one massacre of about twenty Trivici merchants after the announcement of the expulsions. Deprived of its natural focal point, the lethal anger of the city had rapidly dissipated and been replaced by simple fear.

Both consuls well understood that, for a city, the fear of the people was the glowing coals of their fury, and any sufficiently strong rumors arriving on the wind could easily stoke those embers into another raging fire.

Corvus returned his attention to the map. There were twenty-four legions nominally under his command, twenty-seven if the three retired ones were counted. That meant somewhere between one hundred forty-four thousand and one hundred sixty-two thousand soldiers to be accounted for. Of them, he could be certain of less than thirty thousand. Another twenty thousand were very likely to remain loyal.

He'd gone over the makeup of each legion with a member of the House Martial that supposedly controlled it. Any legion with more than six in ten Amorrans, he'd counted as likely loyal. Those with more than eight in ten citizens, he assumed would be fully trustworthy. He was a little ashamed to realize that only one of the three Valerian legions qualified as likely to be loyal by that metric. But House Valerius had always relied heavily on the broad-shouldered Vallyrian peasantry to man their legions, and they'd never been given cause to regret it.

We should have seen this day coming, he berated himself and his ancestors alike. Only one true city legion? How did we ever think one would be enough? We were too proud, too jealous of our prerogatives, too fearful of our rivals, and most of all, too concerned of giving the Senate the ability to make war on its own behalf. But how was it any wiser to hand even greater power over to the very people we ruled?

Severus Patronus had been right to worry about the fate of the empire, he realized. The man's diagnosis had been correct, even if his prescription was as dangerous as it was self-serving.

"What's wrong, my love?" Romilia was standing in the doorway. "You are shaking your head."

"Am I?" He hadn't noticed. "Nothing. Or rather, everything, but nothing new. I'm finding myself tempted to resign from the Senate and leave this mess up to Declama and Pansa. How am I supposed to plan a war when I don't know which are my soldiers and which belong to the enemy? And when I don't know what allies will remain loyal and which have already raised their banners against us?"

"You can't resign!" She sounded genuinely distressed. "You're twice the general of any of them. Three times!"

"No, I suppose I can't." He sighed. "I never thought I'd be facing a challenge of this magnitude, and I certainly never thought I'd be doing so without the help of either Magnus or Marcus Saturnius. I can't believe he's gone."

She nodded, her lips pressed firmly together. It would not have escaped her that their only remaining son might well have died in the attack that had killed his general and most of the legion's officers. They still didn't know how Marcus had escaped the fate of the others, but as far as Romilia was concerned, it was only by the grace of God, and Corvus had heard her murmuring prayers of heartfelt thanksgiving throughout the day ever since Marcus's letter had arrived.

At least the prayers were better than the sobbing that too often filled her nights of late. He knew she blamed herself for the fact that Corvinus had been in the city, no matter how many times he assured her that was not the case.

"I'm going to go to Marcus as soon as I can, my dear. In the meantime, he should be safer than you or me. Even with my fascitors and the house-hold guards, we don't have six thousand battle-tested men surrounding us on every side at all times."

"Saturnius had six thousand men around him, and it wasn't enough to save him."

It was hard to argue with that, so Corvus didn't try. "Marcus said he found the assassins. They were led by a centurion who had been planted in the legion when it was formed."

"Maybe there are more."

"We're not discussing this again, Romilia. There is nothing I can do about it now." He tried to keep the irritation out of his voice but didn't entirely succeed. "*Romilia!*"

It was too late. She had already turned her back on him and left the room.

What did she want from him? He couldn't bring Corvinus back to life. He couldn't even bring Marcus back to Amorr. It wasn't possible to be everywhere at once, and although he didn't trust his son's ability to lead his legion into battle yet, he was confident that Marcus was fully up to the task of weeding out potential traitors, especially given that he would know his life depended on it. Corvus had found that the threat of death tended to inspire one with a tremendous ability to focus on vital issues.

He returned to the legionary figures he'd scratched into the waxed tablet. Word should come soon from Falconius Aquila and Cassianus Longinus. As for the provinces, depending upon how many of them actually went to war, as opposed to simply declaring independence and hoping Amorr would be too busy to chastise them, his current estimate was that the provinces could be expected to raise around three hundred thousand troops. However, the number they could reasonably bring against Amorr was likely less than one third of that. They simply didn't have the necessary foodstuffs, equipment, and transportation to project force that far.

His real concern was the allies. They were closer, they were better trained, and they were properly equipped. Man for man, they were not only as good as any Amorran legionary, they knew it too. His generals wouldn't be able to make use of the psychological advantage Amorr habitually enjoyed when suppressing a rebel province or warring against the undisciplined orcs and goblins.

Somehow, he had to figure out how many of the eighteen allies would turn against them. Riders had been sent to sixteen of them, excluding only the two they already knew to be disloyal: Marruvium and the Quinqueterra. He felt certain Vallyrium would not turn against either House Valerius or the Senate, and he found it hard to imagine that Larinum, Amorr's richest and most populous ally, would seek to throw off the governance of House Falconius. So the west would likely hold. He was less certain about the northern, eastern, and southern allies.

Regardless, it was clear that he needed to raise at least four new legions in Amorr itself, plus an additional four from whatever allies proved to be loyal. It would take time to raise and train them, but then, the rebels would not be able to gather their forces and reach Amorr before summer at the soonest. And if he could convince the Senate to permit the use of slaves, perhaps with the promise of manumission and citizenship at the end of their twenty-year service, he could raise yet another four legions within the city itself.

It was Ianuarius. The twelve new legions would need to be raised and equipped by the Ides of Aprilis if they were to receive a full month of training before the traditional campaigning season began with the Nones of Maius. It wouldn't be nearly as much as they needed, of course, but at least a solid month would permit them to take the field as a reserve for the more experienced legions.

Twelve legions. Ten Houses Martial. And under the circumstances, he couldn't start raising any of the allied legions until he learned which allies could be trusted to contribute them. One legion per House Martial would not only avoid disturbing the uneasy balance of power between the Houses, it would be a more practical objective as well. He nodded with satisfaction and returned to the text of what he intended to be his first act as elected consul—the submission to the Senate of a law entitled Lex Valeria Corva, which would require each House Martial to raise a new legion, and in doing so, permit them to enlist those slaves who were willing to take the eagle.

There would be opposition to the use of slaves, of that he had no doubt, but he was equally certain that the Senate's terror of the coming spring would allow the law to triumph in the end. So long as the use of slave legionaries was limited to the ten new legions, he didn't see it creating any serious problem beyond the precedent it was establishing. But surely future senators would understand this was strictly an emergency measure, to which the Senate was resorting only due to the extreme danger to the city.

He was wrestling with the question of whether there should be a specific ban on masters forcing slaves to enlist or if the language suggesting voluntary enlistment was strong enough when Romilia returned. He knew at once that something was wrong, as she looked neither hostile nor apologetic as she told him that a runner had come and insisted his news was urgent. But the way in which she squeezed his hand as he quickly made his way to the front entrance let him know that bygones would be bygones soon enough.

He didn't recognize the young man at the door, but a glance at the guard was enough to inform him that his visitor had been searched and was unarmed. And he could see by the lad's red face and the sweat that dripped down from his hairline despite the cold Ianuarian air that the youth had been running hard. He steeled himself to hear the bad news. Saints and sinners, was there no end to it? Who had been murdered now?

"My lord consul?" The lad bowed hastily. "My lord, I am sorry to disturb you, but you must come at once! There is a large body of Church soldiers surrounding the elven embassy and demanding entrance!"

Corvus breathed a sigh of relief. At least it wasn't another riot or massacre. Whatever outbreak of episcopal nonsense had produced this minor diplomatic outrage would be much easier to stop and set right than trying to talk sense into a fear-maddened mob.

"Then upon their heads be it. Lord Silvertree is perfectly capable of taking care of himself. At worst, a few of the fools will end up with singed fingers, or find themselves set alight."

"They brought Michaelines with them, Lord Consul!"

"Did they now?" Hmm, that was indeed troubling. It indicated a suspicious degree of purpose and greater influence within the Coviria than he'd initially assumed. "Has the ambassador addressed the soldiers?"

"No, Lord Consul. When I left, he had not yet showed himself to the crowd."

"Yes, of course, I imagine this would have drawn a crowd. How many?"

"Five hundred, maybe six hundred, Lord Consul."

Corvus uttered a short series of mildly blasphemous expostulations about the Church hierarchy, its policy concerning magic, and the Order of St. Michael, drawing a smile from the nearest guard. It would also almost certainly draw a penance from whatever priest heard his next confession.

"Why did you come to me with this? This is an affair for the consul civitas. It hardly concerns the legions!"

"I'm sorry, my lord, but I couldn't find Manlius Torquatus at his residence or at the baths. I thought it would be wiser to call upon you rather than the consul provincae."

"I can't argue with you there. All right, you did well to come here. Don't mind me biting your head off."

"No, Lord Consul." The lad bowed deeply, looking rather as if he wished he had gone to Fulvius Paetinus instead.

"Damn it all, as if we didn't have enough on our hands," Corvus muttered to himself as Nicenus joined in the doorway. "Nicenus, give this young man 10 sesterces, will you? Then find Caius Vecellius and tell him that he and his men need to be armed and axed immediately. We're off for the Volsian Gate, and we need to hurry."

Leaving the young man to the majordomus, Corvus ran back into the domus. "Romilia? Where did I put my armor?"

"It's hung up on its stand in the bedroom," she called back. "Your sword is in the chest behind it. What's going on? Why do you need your armor?"

"It seems some damned fool of an archbishop has decided this is the perfect opportunity to take exception to the two bloody elves in our midst." He began slipping on the stained leather vest he wore under his lorica. "Half the empire is baring their teeth at us, so naturally the Most Holy Mother Church is beside herself with worry about the danger posed by one wretched elven sorcerer. Well, if this doesn't convince the high and mighty elf lord that he's wasting his time on us idiot mortals and ought to take the first ship back to Kir Donas, I don't know what will."

Romilia entered the room. "Will you please bring your guards with you?"

"There is no need. Vecellius and his men will do. This sort of thing requires a show of authority, not force, and I don't have enough guards to manage a show of force anyhow."

Her face darkened, but this time she managed to hold her tongue. "Just be careful, love. Promise me you'll be careful."

He leaned forward to kiss her, hard, then drew the segmented armor over his head. "I'm a Valerian, Romilia. We're dashing and handsome and brave, and we don't have the sense to be careful. You know it, that's why you married me."

"Oh, shut up, you idiot!" She rolled her eyes and reached into the chest. "Here's your helmet, not that you've got any brains for it to protect. Will you be home for dinner?"

"I don't see why not. This won't take long."

She put on a brave face and did her best to smile. "Try not to get too upset with anyone and ruin your appetite."

He nodded and kissed her again, knowing that she'd probably spend the next few hours alternating between praying for him and lamenting the day she'd met him.

Caius Vecellius and his seven men were already waiting for him by the time he left the house. They were staying in the servants's wing, which was severely overcrowded now. Now that he was consul, he would have to give serious thought to buying a larger domus, which he couldn't really afford. Normally, one of the benefits of a consulship was the easy credit that was extended in the knowledge of the post-consular governorship to come.

But, he realized, that might not be the case anymore, given the present circumstances.

They half-ran, half-walked in legionary double-time, and Corvus was breathing very hard indeed by the time they reached the quarter in which the elven embassy was located. He must have spent too much time on horseback on the last campaign, he thought to himself in between painful gasps for air. What a ridiculous sight he would make, arriving on the scene looking like some sort of bloated, panting, red-faced parody of a general come straight from the theatre.

"St... stop," he wheezed with some difficulty. "We... should... we should walk... from here."

"Do you want some water?" Vecellius asked him in an irritatingly unlabored voice.

"No," he said instinctively. "No, wait—give me that!"

He need not have feared looking undignified and unsuitable for his office. Were it not for the branch-wrapped axes he and his personal guard wore, which caused the crowd to part as if by magic before them, no one would have even noticed him.

There might have been five hundred people gathered when the young man had come for him, but there were at least a thousand now, and it seemed as if all of them were trying to talk at once. He had known battlefields that were quieter and less stressful. It was little wonder that soldiers ordered to play urban guard so readily resorted to massacre. The mere press of the many bodies pushing up against them made him want to draw his sword and lay about him simply to create some space, and no one was even paying them any attention, much less shouting or throwing things at them.

"Where shall we go, consul?" Vecellius shouted at him.

"That way!" He pointed in the direction of the ambassador's residence.

It took them some time to work their way through the boisterous crowd, but when Corvus caught sight of red cloaks and white armor, he knew they had arrived in time.

"There, there," he directed his fascitors. Once they were close enough, he pushed past Vecellius and grabbed the arm of one of the Curian guardsmen.

The guard raised his armored elbow and nearly smashed him in the face with it before seeing the purple consul's cloak and recoiling so violently that one might have thought Corvus had struck him.

"My Lord Consul," he stammered, his face almost as pale as his armor as he awkwardly tried to bow despite the pressure of the crowd around them. "I'm so sorry, I did not know!"

"Never mind that," Corvus waved away the near laesa maiestas. "Where is your captain? What is his name?"

"Sulpicius Deodatus, Lord Consul. He's over there, but you probably can't see him past all the others. I'll take you to him."

But it wasn't only Deodatus to whom he was led. Standing in front of the guard captain, bound in silver chains wrapped around their wrists and with their arms held fast by a pair of Michaelines, were the elven ambassador and a Savondese nobleman. Behind them, if he was not mistaken, was a tall, beautiful woman who looked very much like a female elf, which a moment ago he would have thought impossible. Lord Silvertree looked shaken, the Savondese resigned, and the elfess's ethereal beauty was contorted into a mask of inhuman rage as she railed at Deodatus in a completely incomprehensible farrago of Elven and Savondese.

Corvus stepped in front of the guard captain and leaned down so he was nearly nose to nose with the man. "What in the clean and consecrated name of Amorr do you think you are doing here, Captain?" He laid a particular stress on the man's rank.

"Who are you?" the captain snarled back, unintimidated. Then he took in the legate's helm, the purple cloak, and the axe-bearing men standing behind Corvus. "My Lord Consul! I do apologize. I had no idea!"

"I asked you a question, Captain!" Corvus had no intention of letting Deodatus off as easily as his subordinate. He addressed the captain in much the same voice he reserved for chewing out arrogant young tribunes for the first time. "What demon, what devil, what complete and utter madness could possibly possess you to arrest a credentialed plenipotentiary representing the High King of Elebrion? Do you have even the faintest, most fractional idea of what you have done here? Does Amorr have so few enemies now that you think we should war against the elves too?"

The guard captain was made of strong stuff, Corvus had to admit. Although his eyes were wide and he too had blanched at the realization he was facing one of the three most powerful men in all the empire, he did not back down.

"My Lord Consul, forgive me, but I am only following my orders. The Sanctiff requires the two elves and the sorcerer to come before him. It is not for me to decide—I merely obey."

Corvus folded his arms. "Very well, I understand and will not hold you responsible for obeying them. Now, Sulpicius Deodatus, I am giving you a new order. Tell your men to release your prisoners to my custody. Then return to the White Palace, and inform the Sanctiff that, while I am second to none in my respect and regard for Holy Mother Church, his jurisdiction does not extend to the embassies of foreign powers or their representatives who are not baptized members of the Church." Corvus glanced at Lord Silvertree, whose equanimity had returned and was watching the exchange with what looked to be some amusement. "Lord Silvertree, am I correct in assuming you have not been baptized or received the Holy Sacraments?"

"I regret to say that I have not," said the elf without so much as cracking a smile.

"You see, Captain? Now, release your prisoners, and I shall do you the good service of forgetting that you ever did anything so asinine as to attack a foreign embassy and molest the person of the ambassador!"

"My Lord Consul…" Deodatus looked at his feet, took a deep breath, and then stared directly into Corvus's face. "I cannot accept that order, my lord. I am sorry. I am not a legionary. I am an officer in the Curian Guard, and my commander-in-chief is the Sanctified Father."

Dammit, dammit, dammit! Corvus hadn't thought that the young fool—and the captain couldn't have been more than halfway into his twenties—would be stupid enough to try to pull rank on him. Had he done anything else, they might have worked out some sort of arrangement, however transparent. But now, with such a public audience, he had no choice but to face him down. His only hope was that if he spelled everything out clearly enough for the thick-headed young officer, Deodatus would grasp the lifeline Corvus was throwing him.

"You are an Amorran citizen, are you not?"

"Yes, my lord consul."

"Then let me be absolutely certain about this, Captain Sulpicius. You are an Amorran citizen who has received a lawful order from the Consul Aquilae Suffectus in a time of war, and you are declaring that you will not accept that order. Do I have that correctly?"

The captain swallowed hard, then looked back at his men. The sight of them, some thirty strong, seemed to stiffen his spine. "I would accept it if I could, my lord consul. But I cannot."

"I'm sorry to hear that, Captain." He glanced back at Caius Vecellius, who was watching the exchange without any visible emotion. "You heard the man, did you not, Vecellius?"

"Yes, my lord consul. I most certainly did." The head fascitor pointed to the guard captain. "Seize that man in the name of the Senate and People!"

His men were quick to obey. Deodatus was so taken aback that he didn't offer even a token resistance, nor did any of his men, who fell back before the potent symbols of consular authority. In a matter of moments, Deodatus had been forced to his knees by four of the fascitors, one behind him, two on either side, and the fourth holding his head down and pulling it forward by his ears, exposing his unarmored neck. Another of the fascitors, with the forearms and biceps of a blacksmith, had already stripped the branches from his axe.

Screams of horror and wordless protests erupted from the crowd, but no one, not even one of the Curian guards, dared to step forward and interfere. The axe rose quickly and fell even faster. Deodatus was dead without offering so much as a word in his own defense.

"So die the enemies of Amorr!" called out Vecellius.

"So die the enemies of Amorr!" shouted back the fascitors in ritual response, along with the few members of the crowd who were not shocked into silence.

Corvus put his hands on his hips and struck what he thought of as his lordly general's pose, ignoring what he suspected were some stray flecks of Deodatus's blood on his face. His fascitors abandoned the body and fell in behind him as he stood before the captives and the warrior-priests still holding them. All of them were stained with the blood of the guard captain. Silvertree was wearing an uncharacteristically pained expression, but Corvus assumed the elf was more upset about his ruined silks than the sudden death of his late captor.

"Is there anyone else here who intends to interfere with a consul engaged in the affairs of the city?" Corvus asked the crowd. No one answered him, and if the Michaelines did not look cowed, neither did they appear defiant. "Release these men!"

"At once, Lord Consul," the warrior-priest to the left of Silvertree said. He nodded to the priests holding the Savondese man, and after some fumbling with the iron locks holding the chains, both man and elf were released. "May we have the lord consul's permission to withdraw?"

"Granted," Corvus answered with a slight nod. He had fought with too many of these warrior-priests' brothers to treat their order with any disrespect. "Please convey my regards to Grand Master Arnaudus and let him know I am at his disposal if he would question me on this matter."

"Thank you, Lord Consul. I will do so." Visibly relieved, the Michaeline banged his chest in a military salute that Corvus promptly returned, then he led his brothers in the direction of their priory near Saint Marcellus cathedral.

That left the Curian guardsmen, who were standing in shocked silence, waiting for him to address them. Instead, he simply stood there, staring at them in contemptuous silence. Finally, one of them, bolder than the rest, cleared his throat nervously and approached him.

"My lord consul, may we have your leave to take the captain's body and return to the palace?"

"You may. But first, I would have you clear the streets of the crowd your captain's reckless antics have attracted."

"As you command, Lord Consul!" The guardsman saluted.

But this time Corvus didn't deign to return it. Instead, he went to Silvertree and his two companions, who were talking quietly among themselves.

The nonplussed guard hesitated for a moment, then began bawling out orders to his fellow guardsmen, who were soon pushing against the nearest of the bystanders and shouting at them, telling everyone to return to their homes.

"I am deeply sorry for this, Ambassador," Corvus said to the high elf. "I don't know how this happened, but you can rest assured that I will look into it immediately and see that all of the responsible parties are held accountable and make any restitution necessary."

"I fear that may well be beyond your power, my lord consul," Lord Silvertree said grimly. "If you recall our conversation upon your previous visit, there is some reason to believe that the murderer of the celestines is also behind this attempt to eliminate anyone with sufficient familiarity with the esoteric arts to reveal his presence."

Corvus tilted his head. "You think the Sanctiff did not order those men to come here? You think this 'murderer of the celestines' did so? Or that the Sanctiff himself is possessed by this creature?"

"I do not know," Silvertree said. "But I am coming to suspect that there is a master of sorcery somewhere inside the Sanctal Palace. I have some reason to believe he may even be stronger than I am."

"That would mean he's not human, then, would it not?" Corvus turned to the female elf. She was simply remarkable and, despite the situation, he found it hard to take his eyes off her. "Who is she? Another sorceress?"

"No, she is merely a Merithaimi elf under the protection of the Comte de Thôneaux. I'm expecting your son's elven friend to arrive tonight, and I plan to send them away with her."

Corvus blinked at the unexpected news. "Lady Shadowsong is coming here? Tonight? The elf to whom my son is always writing?"

"The same," Silvertree confirmed. "I will take the opportunity to give her your letter to Marcus. Do you have any further message for him? This may be the last opportunity, as I think it unlikely that she will be able to return here."

Corvus sighed unhappily. "Well, I..." There was so much more he wanted to tell Marcus, but everything was so fluid that he was reluctant to give him any further instructions. "I suppose... tell him he is to trust no one—no Amorran, ally, or provincial—until he hears from me. Tell him to trust his intuition and his training."

"I will see that he is so informed. Do I correctly glean from your message that you have received some unwanted news? Is it something you feel able to share?"

"You'll find out soon enough, I expect. It's not just the provinces any longer. Two of the allied peoples are in revolt, and there may well be more. It's an unprecedented situation. If you can arrange to leave soon as well, I recommend you do so. I'm going to be fully occupied with raising the new legions, so I may not be in a position to intercede if this powerful creature you say is living in the Coviria makes a second attempt on you."

"My companion and I will depart tonight," the elf assured him. "I have already made the arrangements. There is no need for you to offer us an escort. I will assure the High King of your good offices, so you need not concern yourself about this unfortunate affair. I am afraid you face some very serious challenges, Valerius Corvus, and not all of them will come from outside the walls."

"I appreciate your warning, Ambassador. Were it not for you, we would have no idea there was anything amiss inside the Coviria. Apart from the dead bodies, that is."

The elf showed his white teeth in an uncharacteristic smile. "They do tend to be informative, do they not—bodies? Be very careful, Lord Consul. It is never wise to stand between a sorcerer and his aim."

"Says the sorcerer." Corvus laughed. "May God bring you safely to Elebrion, Ambassador. I wish we could have hosted you longer, but for your sake, I'm glad to hear you are leaving now."

There was a commotion behind him, and Corvus turned around to see what was the matter. He saw a slave he vaguely recognized as belonging to Manlius Torquatus speaking to Caius Vecellius. Corvus closed his eyes, knowing that whatever the news was, it was unlikely to be good. He gestured at the head fascitor, who immediately came over to him.

"Well?" he demanded. "What is it now?"

Vecellius glanced at the high elf, then back at him, and shrugged. "The north."

"The allies? Which ones. We already knew about the Marruvii."

"All of them."

"What? That's not possible!"

"Torquatus's man says a rider arrived from Falera. Marruvium, Aeternum, Caelignus, Larinum, Silarea and Telinus have declared their independence from the Empire. Yesterday they formed a league vowing mutual defense against any Amorran attempts to force them back into the fold."

Corvus's heart sank. Even if all the provinces rebelled at once, they were too diverse and geographically separated to successfully join together. Many of them would have difficulties even speaking to one another. But among all the allied peoples, there were only the Utruccan and Faliscan tongues dividing them, and every city was filled with men who spoke both. Corvus himself was fluent in Utruccan, thanks to his childhood summers in Vallyrium.

The six allies not only shared a common language, but had literally hundreds of years of experience cooperating with one another, even if it was usually in pursuit of Amorran interests. Larinum posed a particular threat, as it was not only the wealthiest ally, but also the traditional stronghold of House Falconius. It contributed at least ten of the twenty-five thousand who presently served in the four Falconian legions.

He took a deep breath and reminded himself that there were thirteen more allies who might still be loyal. And a league with defensive intent might pose a threat to Amorr's empire, even to her long-term wealth, but not to the survival of the city herself—and right now that had to be his primary concern.

"Are you sure you don't wish to flee with us?" Silvertree said lightly, though Corvus suspected the elf understood the implications of Torquatus's news as well as he did.

"I don't suppose there is any chance of convincing your high king that it would be in his interest to send an army to aid us?"

"None whatsoever, I am afraid. But allow me to leave you with this thought: If our surmised killer in the Coviria was expecting to utilize Amorr's might in pursuit of his interests, the actions of these rebellious tribes will vex him severely. You may find him a powerful ally rather than the enemy you naturally assume him to be."

Corvus nodded. Ally with a non-human sorcerer of incredible power who killed priests. Why not? At this point, it seemed anything was possible. He was already attempting to update his estimates on the legions in his mind, but there would be time for that later. "Fare you well, Ambassador."

"And you, Consul."

Corvus turned his back on the high elf and what would soon cease to be the elven embassy, and he found himself walking through the blood of the man whose execution he had ordered. Was he cursed to always find himself surrounded by death and wading through gore, until his own time came?

If so, so be it. If the Almighty had turned his face from Amorr, Corvus would fail no matter how many legions he managed to raise from the fallow ground of an Amorran people enervated by wealth and power. And if God were on his side, then he would triumph even if every last province and ally raised their hands against their rightful master.

But was God on his side? That, he feared, was a question that could be answered only after the fact.

There was but one way to find out.

FJOTRA

I F the comtesse's mansion had not changed at all, it seemed nearly everything else had. Before, she was treated like a nonentity, a pet of the comtesse's a little less important than one of the small tri-colored dogs who were given their run of the place and occasionally stole into Fjotra's bed at night. Now, it seemed that everyone knew who she was, and even high-born guests customarily addressed her as "Princess" and "Your Highness" without any of the amusement that Prince Karl had always shown.

It was the Red Prince's death, the Comte de Saint-Agliè had finally explained to her on their third day back in Lutèce, as well as the arrival of the ships in Portblanc and her brother's presence at the court, that had made the difference.

Following his injury, Brynjolf had been given an apartment in the palace in which to recover. But even after he was healthy and hale again, he'd chosen to stay there instead of returning to the mansion on the hill. Far from being displeased, however, Roheis was delighted, as she told Fjotra with some enthusiasm how "the Reaver Prince" had become bosom companions with the Duc de Chênevin, Prince Karl's younger brother, and until a few weeks ago, the second in line to the throne.

Unfortunately, Brynjolf was not in Lutèce upon her return, as he had been invited to spend the Hivernalia at the prince's winter court being held at his castle, Montégut, a twelve-day ride away. But the comtesse assured her that the king would have already sent for Étienne-Henri, and that

Brynjolf would surely be among the party returning with him to witness his crowning as the Red Prince and heir.

Roheis, Fjotra realized, had been told nothing by the comte of the prince's attempt to marry her by force. Unsure if she would be believed, Fjotra, too, held her tongue.

More importantly, Roheis also assured her that the king did not blame her or her people for the death of his eldest son and that her fears it might cause the king to change his mind about giving her people land in which to settle and accepting them as his subjects were unfounded. Fjotra slept considerably better at night now that she knew the women and children in Portblanc would not be forced to return across the White Sea, for that way lay certain death. If only her father and mother would make the crossing safely. Every night she, Svanhvit, and Geirrid went out to the garden and made blood offerings to the sea gods at the little saltwater shrine she had created out of what had been a bird bath.

Fjotra found it hard to understand the comtesse's reaction, or rather, lack of one, to her lover's death. It wasn't as if Roheis was in denial over it, as she spoke openly about it, mostly in connection with the various ramifications that had resulted from it. Had she ever cared about Prince Karl at all? It didn't seem possible. Fjotra had been there when the Comte de Saint-Agliè delivered the news, as it had been literally the first thing he'd told her when they'd arrived at her home not long after sunset.

But Roheis hadn't screamed, fainted, wept, or reacted in any of the hundred ways Fjotra had imagined during the course of their carriage ride from Portblanc. She had merely blinked once, with her perfect porcelain face betraying no sign of grief or even surprise in the shadows of the torchlight. Then she'd nodded and coolly invited them to come inside. And in the days and weeks that followed, though she'd dutifully worn mourning like the rest of the nobility, Fjotra had never once seen the comtesse show a hint of genuine sorrow.

She was sitting in front of the fire with a blanket wrapped around her shoulders against the winter chill, lost in her idle dreams about what might have been, when she heard a familiar voice behind her.

"Fjotra, is that really you?"

She looked back over her shoulder, then cast the blanket aside and leaped to her feet. It was Brynjolf!

"You're back!" she cried happily and ran to embrace him. "Your wound, are you well? It's so good to see you!"

He grinned roguishly, looking very handsome. Except for his height and fair hair that was tied neatly back with a black ribbon, he was also looking more like a southern noble than a northern reaver. "Never better! I was off hunting orcs with Étienne, Hugues, Thierry, and a few others when the dreadful news arrived. We left at once, of course, and we rode so hard I think we must have made record time."

"You didn't come straight here, did you?" He looked too clean and well-kempt to have spent the last week on the road.

"No, of course not! Étienne had to go directly to the palace, naturally, so I went with him and changed my clothes there before coming here. The king was kind enough to give me an apartment, and since I thought it was best to stay near the court as a representative of sorts until Father arrives, I've been staying there."

"Yes, the comtesse told me." Fjotra frowned. Her brother had never been the deepest of thinkers, but she would have thought that even he would have realized he was essentially a prisoner of the crown, held hostage against the very sort of outcome that had come to pass. "I have something for you. Let me go get it."

She went to her room and retrieved their father's sword, which she brought to Brynjolf. She held it out in both hands before her in its black leather scabbard. "He wanted you to have this in case he and Mother can't escape the castle before the aalvarg break through and Raknarborg falls."

"Is it that bad?"

"The castle is under siege by three different armies of the beasts. They all tried to storm the walls the night before my ship sailed. The attack went on most of the night, and I was told we lost nearly two hundred dead and wounded. There are thousands of them, Brynjolf, tens of thousands, and the Skullbreaker is in no shape to fight. His arm was torn up by an aalvarg same night another one killed Prince Karl.

"But they can be beaten. Earlier that day, Prince Karl rode out with the Strongbow and killed four or five hundred of them in an ambush. That's how they got inside to attack Father and the prince—the mages wanted two captives for questioning, but both of them turned out to be sigskifting."

Her brother nodded absently. He had drawn the sword from its scabbard and was admiring the intricate runes etched into the blade. "Are they all like that?"

"Patrice—the king's mage who came back with the prince—doesn't think so."

"He doesn't think so? They'll have to do better than that!"

"They will. I was with them at the ambush. They're very clever. I think if we had them on our side before, the aalvarg might not have defeated us so easily. Father says they used their shapechanging to get into our villages at night, and that's why we could never stand against them."

"That does make sense." He slammed the sword back into the scabbard. "Well, I must return to the palace." By the way, Étienne wants you at the ceremony to see him crowned as the heir. He's made some noises about marrying you once the king takes Father as his vassal and claims sovereignty over the Isles. If I understand correctly, there are some counties and principalities between Écarlate and Méridiony that have been in escheat to the crown for decades that may be given to Father to serve as his duchy. It's far from the sea, but then, I suppose the great lords of the Haut Conseil want to avoid subjecting us to any temptation to return to the old ways."

Fjotra nodded. Father wouldn't like it, he might even see it as an insult, but he could hardly blame the king or his councilors for preferring to keep the descendants of the men who had harried their coasts for centuries well away from the shores of the sea they once ruled. It would be hard and humiliating to live as the grain farmers and pig-keepers their fathers despised, but it was better than the alternative. And how could he refuse the granting of free lands?

"Wait, before you go. What's he like, your friend?"

"Who, Étienne?" Brynjolf laughed. "So you like him too! He's a prince of the blood, so he's arrogant and he is always accustomed to get his own way. But he's quick to laugh and he's brave and generous too, almost to a fault. He even gave me a small seigneurie in his demesne of Chênevin, a place called Fronmorat. I have arms now!"

"Really? What are they?"

"A white castle on a field of blue."

"I can't wait to see them. The duc, what do you think of him?"

"Well, he's neither so tall as his brother was nor so brawny. But he's smarter. Not even the sharpest fool in the court can better flay a man with his tongue—and he does it with a smile."

"So he is not kind?"

"No, kindness is not the first word that leaps to your mind with Étienne. And yet, he has been very good to me when he had no reason to be. When some courtiers affected to make sport of my accent, he silenced them by mocking their own errors in speech."

"Your Savoner is better now?"

"You should say 'Savonnaise,' dear little sister," he said in a surprisingly fluid demonstration of his improvement in the southern tongue. "I need more words, but I'm beginning to understand how it goes together."

"Brynjolf, that's amazing!" His Dalarn accent was still very strong, but the words flowed smoothly and without awkward pauses. She clapped her hands, impressed and a little envious. "If your prince is such a good teacher, perhaps he will help me learn to speak it better too."

"I have no doubt. But remember, Sister, if the king decides you two are to marry, this won't be a love match, even though he likes you well. It's an alliance. And for the sake of our people, you'll have to stand by him even if he beats you and mounts every lady-in-waiting and page boy in the palace."

"I know." She nodded grimly. Even when she'd thought that Prince Karl might be her husband, she knew she might have to accept living in the shadow of the comtesse if he chose to continue his affair with Roheis. But no Dalarn girl grew up with any illusions of male faithfulness, not when every village had its share of sea wives acquired on past reavings. "If he's even half the man his brother was, he will treat me well."

"Don't say that around him," Brynjolf cautioned her. "I don't know why, but I think he truly hated Charles-Phillippe."

Fjotra shrugged. "Brothers will be brothers. They say the Blacktooth hated the Skullbreaker more than the aalvarg when they were younger too. Eiríkr Ulfsson used to say that if it weren't for the coming of the aalvarg, one of them would have killed the other."

"I don't think it was ever that bad with Étienne. I'm just saying you need to be careful about praising Charles-Phillippe around Étienne or any of his friends. Don't say anything at all about him if you don't have to." He shook the scabbarded sword in his left hand and embraced her with his right arm. "Thanks for bringing me Father's sword, Fjotra. I'll give it back to the Skullbreaker when he crosses the sea." He paused and raised an eyebrow. "Any message for the prince?"

Fjotra blushed. "Just tell His Royal Highness that I am mindful of him, and I am eager to visit the land that was his gracious gift to you."

It was just after breakfast several days later and Geirrid and Svanhvit were preparing Fjotra's hair for the memorial tournament being given by the king in honor of his late son later that day when Roheis, accompanied by the Comte de Saint-Agliè, entered her room.

The news was bad, she knew it immediately from the carefully veiled look in the comtesse's usually expressive eyes. She tried not to let her fear of the troldmand show.

"What happen?" she asked, wincing as Svanhvit tugged a little energetically at one of her braids.

"We need to speak to you alone," the comte answered. "If you please."

Fjotra glanced at her two friends and indicated the door. They obeyed as quickly as if they were genuine ladies-in-waiting, even remembering to offer half-curtsies to the two nobles as they exited the room. One of them quietly closed the door behind them.

"The ships should come back from Raknarborg two days past," Fjotra said, feeling as if her heart was skipping a beat. "Did they sink?"

"No, they all safely reached Portblanc not long ago." The comte looked closely at her and raised his chin. He was such a little bantam cock that it was almost possible to forget how dangerous he was. How inhuman he was. "Fjotra, you do understand that I have certain talents, do you not?"

"You're a troldmand. A mage like the King's Own. You know I know."

"That's not strictly true, I'm afraid, but it's close enough. The reason I remind you is because I need you to understand that I have certain means of communicating with various other individuals, one of whom was on a ship that anchored in the harbor less than one bell ago."

Fjotra thought of the far-seeing that the battlemages had made from water. "Portblanc is a long way away from here. What you know came from no rider."

"That is true. And soon everyone will know what we know. But for reasons that will soon become clear to you, we had to speak to you first. I am sorry to tell you this, Fjotra, but Raknarborg is fallen."

A shock ran through her. Too soon—it had fallen too soon! Her first thoughts were of her parents. Were they on the last ships or not?

"When the four ships finished the last crossing and came in sight of your land, they saw black smoke filling the sky and only two towers where there should have been three. They approached as close to the docks as the commodore dared but had to retreat when stones were thrown at them. Ulfin were seen manning the catapults."

Fjotra closed her eyes and bit her lip.

The comtesse put her arms around her. "I'm so sorry, my dear."

She knew that hundreds of the men who had remained to hold the fortress until the final evacuation was complete were probably dead now. Her father and mother might well be among them. She couldn't imagine the Skullbreaker boarding a ship before every last man had boarded first. Nor could she imagine her mother boarding without him. Her eyes welled up with tears. She'd known this was a possibility from the night the Skullbreaker had sent her away with his sword. But with each successful transportation of women and children, then fighting men, her hope had been born again.

The comtesse's arms tightened around her, and Fjotra was tempted to release her grief and sob into the woman's breast.

But that would not do. Not now, not when she and her brother might be the last hope of preserving her people and keeping them alive.

It dawned on her that this was probably not even the important news that Roheis and de Saint-Agliè needed to discuss with her. Otherwise Roheis would have come alone. She supposed it must be something that they had previously expected to discuss with her father.

"You want... wanted to talk to the Skullbreaker I think. But now, you must talk to me and my brother instead."

"We don't want to, my dear," the comtesse said. "I would much rather permit you to grieve in peace for your parents. Unfortunately, sometimes events cannot wait for us to be ready for them. Now, Fjotra, you have to understand that what I am going to tell you could make a lot of very powerful people at court extremely unhappy. Unhappy with you and unhappy with me. So, I have to ask you to promise to keep this to yourself. You can't talk about it with Svanhvit or Geirrid, and I'm not even sure you should discuss it with Brynjolf. Do you promise? This is a very delicate affair, and it will not do for it to come to light before its time."

Fjotra felt a little bewildered, but if she trusted anyone in Savonne, it was the comtesse.

"Yes, I promise."

"Do you swear to hold your tongue, by all your gods and by the honor of your father and your brother?"

She was frightened, but what could be worse than what she'd already heard? "Yes, I will never tell anyone what you tell me. Not even my brother. I swear. You have been so good to us, I would never see you harm."

The comtesse kissed her. "That's a good girl. You did the right thing, my dear."

"I did?"

"Indubitably," the comte answered. "Now Fjotra, I know you believe the king is going to allow your people to settle here in Savondir. And not without reason. I suppose the king himself probably believes that. But it is not going to happen, at least not as you and your brother envisioned."

She narrowed her eyes distrustfully. She and Brynjolf had been given assurances, repeatedly, that so long as their people swore to serve the king loyally and well, they would be permitted refuge here in the south. But was now the time when she would discover that the copious volume of words produced by the southerners was good for nothing?

"You see, too many of the nobles of the north hate and fear the reavers. The Haut Conseil knows this and has to respect their feelings. Before, when the expedition to rescue your people was underway, they did not dare to speak out against the settlement because they were aware of Prince Charles-Phillippe's ambitions to claim the Iles de Loup for the crown, and they knew they could not openly oppose him. But now Charles-Phillippe is dead, and his brother has little interest in the Isles and none in your people. In fact, Étienne-Henri even encourages their opposition and offers them support. He seeks to win the nobles' favor, and one way he can do so at no cost to himself is to indulge their fears of the Dalarn."

"I don't understand. Why the new prince make friend with my brother if he hate us Dalarn? Why he give land and name? Why he try to betroth me?"

"No, my dear, he doesn't care enough about you to hate you. You already know why he wanted you as his wife—he wanted the Isles. That's why he lost interest in you the very moment he learned that Charles-Phillippe had died. Brynjolf is nothing more than an amusing new toy for the prince," Roheis explained. "To have a barbarian in his entourage, a fearsome reaver from the legends of old… it shocks the court, you see? It offends the old and the unfashionable, and it lets him impress the younger nobles with his daring. But think on this, my dear: Where did he give your brother his land? To whom is Brynjolf sworn?"

"I don't know."

"No, you don't, so you cannot understand the significance. Now, do you remember when I told you that the wars I fight are different than those fought by your father and brother? This is one of those wars. Battles at court are more complicated than those contested honestly in the field. Swords don't lie, but tongues often do. Do you recall your brother's new title?"

"He's now viscomte of somewhere, I don't remember."

"Fronmorat," the comte answered. "Fronmorat is a small comté in the prince's demesne of Chênevin. It's only two or three days' journey from my own lands as well as the lands the Haut Conseil intends for the king to give your people. They make it sound generous, but instead of a single duchy near the sea, where your people could prosper and grow powerful, the haut seigneurs will divide them and scatter them among the Écarlatans in five or six different comtes. They will do so in the hopes that, in another three generations, all that remains of your people will be the occasional fair-haired, blue-eyed child. And that will destroy your people as completely as the ulfin wanted, albeit in an indirect and more sophisticated manner."

"Suppose you are telling me truth." Fjotra didn't know if what Saint-Agliè described was actually what the king had been planning to offer her father, but she knew that neither she nor Brynjolf would have ever noticed the fatal poison in the proffered bait. "What would you have us do, refuse the lands? I not see how we could. Where do we go? Even without the last ships, there must be twelve thousand Dalarn living outside of Portblanc now, and they live on the king's goodwill. If he will not feed them, they will starve!"

"I very much doubt the king is foolish enough to refuse to fill the bellies of ten thousand desperate and hungry reavers. What they are not given, he knows they will take. Even the Haut Conseil knows that. But Fjotra, do you understand why those lands are at the king's disposal to give?"

"Are not all lands in Savonne for him to give? He is the king!"

The comte rolled his eyes. "Ah, the joys of barbarism. No, the king is neither a god nor a tribal chief, my lady. Since I can't possibly supply the knowledge you lack of five hundred years of law and civilization now, you'll just have to accept that the reason they are in his possession is because his grandfather stole them from the nobles of Écarlate when he defeated their king. A few of those noble families were permitted to retain their ancestral lands. My lady Desmargoteau here is one example. Her Domdidier is a small comté in vassal to the Grand-Duc. My own comté of Saint-Agliè is another."

"I don't see how this matters. You do not want my people to take the land the king give because his father's father steal them?"

"No, my dear, of course we want you to take the lands," Roheis assured her. "It was the Grand-Duc himself who suggested the Écarlatean lands to the other seigneurs on the Haut Conseil, once he understood they wanted to divide the Dalarn and keep them from the sea. And he did so because we want you and your brother to swear to be loyal to the Grand-Duc as his vassals, and we want your people to join us when he declares himself King of Écarlate and rises against the de Mirid crown."

It was too much to follow. The strangeness of this place, the death of Prince Karl, and now possibly her parents, was hard to accept. And now, instead of finding the hoped-for refuge in the south, there was more war and death on the horizon. What had she done, what had her people done, to make the gods hate them so? It was as if a curse was following them, so that not even crossing the sea would permit them to find peace. Were they being punished for the reaving of their forefathers? Was this retribution for the bloodshed and fear her people had visited on generation after generation of dwellers on the sea coasts?

"Fjotra, what's wrong?" The comtesse crouched down before her and held her hands. "Your people will have their place! The women and children, they will be safe from the battles."

That made Fjotra laugh. She pulled a hand free to wipe away her tears. "My lady comtesse, you not know war like me. You can make no promise so. War touch everyone. Even the little children die. Comte, why you think you can win against the king? I know from Prince Karl that another duc try last year."

"An astute question, my lady. The reasons are four. First, we will not be alone. The Seven Seats will also rise, because the Vagran nobility cannot stomach the notion of Étienne-Henri as king. He is an insolent wretch with no concern for the crown, the kingdom, or anything beyond his appetites. Second, the royal academy of king's mages have not been so weak in many years. Many of the Immortels are aged, and ten of its strongest mages died in a sorcerous experiment earlier this year. Moreover, some of the mages are sympathetic to the Écarlatean cause.

"Third, two hundred men-at-arms died in the suppression of Montrove and another five hundred are believed to have fallen at Raknarborg, at least forty of them knights. And fourth, because there are two thousand four hundred seventy-five more or less healthy Dalarn men of fighting age presently in the camps outside Portblanc."

"But why should they fight for you against the king who promises them land?"

"Not for us—with us! Consider where they will be, my lady. They will be surrounded by rebels on every side, so they must either fight for us or against us. Neither the Grand-Duc nor the king will permit you neutrality. And what else can such men do? What else do reavers know? Will they fish the mountains or drag their nets across the valleys? Will they harry our villages and then attempt to flee on foot? No, they must learn how to work the land, and who better to teach them how to do so than the very folk who have worked those lands for centuries?

"You and your people need us as badly as we need you, Fjotra. And, unlike the Haut Conseil, the Grand-Duc does not fear your people. He will not divide you among the comtes to have your blood watered down but will give you portions of his own lands, tying your little comtes together into one sustainable principality that will permit you to remain one people, together. And he will swear to protect you as your liege lord."

"He will pay our men to fight?"

The comte nodded. "Naturally. He will pay one silver coin plus mercenary wages to each man who fights, plus one gold coin to you and your brother for every ten, as well as enough grain to supply the women and children until the return of your men. He'll also give you four hundred cows, five hundred pigs, a thousand sheep, and a quantity of laying chickens to distribute among your people as you see fit."

"What if the king will give us more?"

The comte shook his head and chuckled. "He won't. I am certain he won't because most of what he will promise you will be coming from the Grand-Duc's lands, not the royal treasury. Oh, he'll promise to pay for the grain and the animals, to be sure, but it will just be more debt to be added on top of what is already owed. But you need not take my word for it, nor must you decide tonight. You thought the king would give you lands by the sea, did you not?"

"The Red Prince say that to me, yes. He think it too."

"Then it will not be hard for you to discern the truth. If the king stands by his promise to your people and makes Brynjolf a duc of a fief on the coast, you may forget everything we have said to you. I only ask that you keep your word to remain silent. On the other hand, if the king divides your people and proposes to send them south into Chênevin, Méridiony, and Écarlate, then you will know that we spoke the truth."

Fjotra nodded. And it was true that Brynjolf's lands, wherever they were, were in the south. And the comte was correct to ask what else the Dalarn men could do. In fact, she was certain that, if she asked them if they preferred to work the land or war against the Savoner king, nearly all of them would choose the latter. They were a people of war. Most of them had never known anything else. It would take many years before they could become a people of peace.

Fjotra met his cold and strangely remote eyes without flinching. She knew he was perfectly capable of ordering her killed in order to prevent her from telling anyone in the court about the Grand-Duc's rebellious intentions. But then, she assumed the Écarlatans must have begun their preparations long ago and made their decision to rise almost as soon as news of the Red Prince's death had arrived. They might well be ready already, and were merely delaying the rebellion in the hopes of enlarging their forces first.

And so she lied.

"I will not open you, Comte." She frowned, irritated that she didn't know the word. "*Svigte*, to make known, you know, to the king."

"Betray?" suggested the comtesse.

"Yes! Betray. I will not betray you, either of you. The king, he is generous. Prince Karl, he was a good man. I like him. But what you give us, you give us life for all the people. If you do not help, the ships do not come. If you do not help, we die. We Dalarn do not forget this. As the comtesse tell me and Brynjolf when we bring your letter, now I say to you: We help if we can."

The comte looked at the comtesse, who looked at him expectantly. "I think that is a satisfactory response for the time being. The Comte de Aumont will meet you in Portblanc. He is the son of the Grand-Duc. You can trust him as you would trust me or the comtesse, this I assure you."

Fjotra allowed him to kiss her hand as he bowed and departed the room.

The comtesse breathed a loud sigh of relief.

"Well, that's done with. I'm so relieved you answered as you did, my darling. I told him you were not to be touched, but he doesn't always listen to me. But you realize that Brynjolf may think differently than you do? His affections for the prince are genuine. De Chênevin has not bought them."

"Brynjolf do not think different than me. He do not think at all. He will do as I say."

The comtesse stroked her hair. "Are you sure you still wish to attend the tournament? In light of the news from across the sea, I am sure it will offend no one if you stay home in mourning."

Fjotra nodded. "Yes, I not wish to go out, if His Majesty take no offense."

"Of course not," the comtesse reassured her. "Is there anything I can do for you? You understand that I must attend myself, of course, although you know my heart grieves for your loss."

"I do. I thank you, Lady Roheis." She smiled, letting her genuine sorrow hide her secret intent. "You are so kind, my lady comtesse, and I know you have preparations you should be making. So I ask you send in Svanhvit and Geirrid and not to worry for me until the morning. I must tell them of Raknarborg. They had kin there too."

Lady Roheis held her close for a moment then kissed her cheek. "You chose well, Fjotra. I knew you would. If you want anything tonight, call for Maronne, and she will bring it to you. I will not return until late tonight. Grieve in peace with your friends today, and we will speak more in the morning." She exited the room, trailing her sweet perfume.

Moments later, Svanhvit and Geirrid rushed back into the room.

"What's the matter?"

"Has the castle fallen?"

"Shut the door!" Fjotra wiped her eyes and pulled them both closely to her. She kept her voice low and her eye on the door, knowing that any careless slip at this point would kill them all. "We are leaving here tonight. The comtesse and Saint-Agliè are lying to us. Once they leave for the tournament, we are going to leave as if for a picnic. Pack two baskets, but we must put everything we don't want to leave behind in them."

"But is Raknarborg fallen or not?" Geirrid said. The tears in Fjotra's eyes hadn't escaped her attention.

"I don't know. I'm not sure. He said it had, but he lied about the duc, so he may be lying about that too. The important thing is that we have to leave here before they send us south to Écarlate."

"How do you know he's lying?"

Fjotra shook her head in disgust. "He tried to make me think Étienne only wanted the Isles, not me. As if a woman cannot see how a man looks at her. He says Étienne is a monster, but he is the one who is not even a man! He is a liar. He only wants Dalarn bodies to throw against the king."

"Where are we going to go? Portblanc?"

"No, the royal castle." When her two friends looked at her, surprised, she smiled, her face full of Dalarn determination. "We are going to Étienne-Henri. He said he wanted to betroth me quickly—I intend to hold him to his word."

THEUDERIC

THIS far south, the winter sun did not set so early, Theuderic noted, not for the first time, as he wrapped himself tighter in his wool cloak against the cold evening breeze. But now that he was waiting for darkness to cover their escape from this imperial madhouse of a city, it seemed as if night would never fall. He looked down on the narrow, shadowed streets of Amorr and watched the incessant movements of its people with the suspicion of a recently clawed man regarding a slumbering cat in his arms. Everything appeared to be peaceful, but he knew how deceptive such appearances could be, and how rapidly apparent safety could be transformed into danger.

"How much longer, do you think?" he asked Lord Silvertree's companion, Miroglas, who had just brought up a sixth chest to accompany the five that were already arranged side by side on the rooftop of the soon-to-be abandoned residence. Another two were set apart from those six. Those were full of clothes and books that the elven ambassador had given to Lithriel and him for their own journey.

The high elf looked up at the purpling sky. "Not long now. Sometime soon after the next bell, I should think. Shadowsong won't wait for the stars to come out fully before departing, and it's not a long flight. It's a pity there aren't more clouds this evening or she could have departed soon after twilight. But the Amorrans have too many archers and scorpios on the walls to risk it."

"Who is she, this Lady Shadowsong?"

"I don't know," Miroglas admitted. "An elfess with some connection to one of the Amorran noble families, whatever that might be."

"Is that common?"

"Not in the slightest. I'm mildly curious about her myself. If I recall correctly, it had something to do with the Amorran embassy that led to the current rapprochement. I expect Morvas knows all about it. He has rather more interest in Men than me. I intend no offense, of course."

"Not at all. Morvas?"

"Lord Silvertree," the elf explained.

As if summoned, the ambassador himself stepped up upon the roof, followed by a seemingly overburdened Lithriel with her arms full of blankets.

"Do you have any coin?" Lord Silvertree asked Theuderic bluntly.

"Not much, I'm afraid. I was planning to draw on the king's draft with the Farsingers. But I suppose we could stop in Malkan, or preferably, an Utruccan city, and do it there."

"Take this instead." The high elf handed him a sizable pouch, which, judging by its weight, consisted mostly of gold.

"Thank you, Lord Silvertree." Theuderic paused, wondering if he should simply accept the gift and keep his mouth shut. But he couldn't resist the temptation. "If you don't mind my asking, why are you willing to help us?"

The high elf smiled a little bitterly. "Events often mock our intentions, Magus. I came here thinking to reward the Church and Empire for the wisdom their leaders showed in embracing elvenkind. We elves have made many mistakes, and we have dwindled as a consequence of them. We have but three kingdoms where there once were seven. Increasingly we find ourselves supplanted, not only by Man, but by Orc and Dwarf and even Troll. So it was good to find some token of friendship with men. But it seems I was too late, and already the corruption is at the heart of Amorr. I would have you warn your king, and especially your college of mages, of the danger."

"You have put the codices in the chests we are to take with us?"

"Even so. There were certain works that I cannot give you, but I have given you what the Collegium can spare. At least your realm will not be entirely blind as events unfold. But be warned: If your kingdom is as influential as it seems, it is likely that a Watcher is already ensconced within it. They are drawn to power, and they always use others to exert their will."

Theuderic smiled wryly. He wondered how the proud immortels of l'Académie would react to learning that they were merely the pale shadows of true immortal powers. It would certainly be amusing to see how quickly the news would wipe the arrogance off Grandmagicien D'Arseille's face.

"I see two, no three hawks approaching!" Lithriel cried, pointing toward the north.

Theuderic peered into the night sky, but even his mage's vision could not match the keen eyes of an elf. He started as a piercing whistle nearly deafened his left ear. He looked over and saw Miroglas lowering his hands from his mouth.

"Was that really necessary?" he asked, wincing and thumbing his ear.

"She doesn't know exactly where we are," Miroglas said. "Well, now she does. Here they come! Step back. And you might want to hold onto something—three of them can generate a veritable wind, and it's a long way down to the street."

Theuderic felt a little cowardly retreating from a bird. But when he saw all three elves get down on one knee, he quickly followed suit. Moments later, he was glad he had.

Three giant warhawks backflapped their wings at the last moment as they came in for their landing. The force of the breeze they stirred up nearly caused him to fall over.

The hawks were huge beasts, nearly twice as large as he imagined, with bright, intelligent eyes and beaks that were easily capable of snapping off a man's head. His eyes widened and he wondered whether sneaking out through the inner and outer walls, then spending a month trying to evade Amorran patrols, bandits, and desperate refugees on the winter roads would actually be any worse than coming within reach of those vicious, curved beaks. To say nothing of soaring high above the earth on one of their backs.

Only the middle warhawk bore a rider: a surprisingly short elf with a reddened, runny nose and bright red cheeks. She wore a strange leather armor that covered her from her fingers to her toes.

"Lady Caitlys Shadowsong," Silvertree said to her, "what an honor to finally meet you."

"The privilege is mine, Lord Morvas Silvertree. I'm so pleased I could be of assistance to you and your companions." Caitlys turned to the larger riderless warhawk beside her and stroked the back of its head. "What a beautiful bird you have, Lord Silvertree! My own Vengirasse had the devil's own time keeping pace with him, so eager was he once your summons arrived."

The elf smiled at the compliment to his hawk, which he was stroking just under the huge, saucepan eye. His bird was rather striking in comparison with the others. It had a golden ruff and white streaks on its wings that distinguished it from the drab dark brown on light brown pattern on the feathers of the other two. Theuderic shook his head, thinking about the size of a writing quill constructed on the scale to make use of the massive feathers.

"Lady Shadowsong," Lithriel said, "I am Lady Lithriel Everbright. And this is my companion: Theuderic de Merovech, the Comte de Thôneaux. I thank you so much, Lady Shadowsong, for helping us leave this accursed city. Lord Silvertree tells us there is great evil here."

In her flight gear, Lady Shadowsong looked less like a lady than Lord Silvertree had in his robes. She frowned. "You're a sorcerer, aren't you?" she observed, sniffing and rubbing at her nose with her sleeve.

"That too, my lady," Theuderic admitted. "We ask only that you take us past the walls, and preferably leave us where we can purchase horses for our journey north, if it would not be too much of an imposition."

"Oh, we can do better than that, I think. Lord Silvertree, you said you had some letters for Marcus?"

The high elf nodded, bent down, and handed her a leather satchel.

Shadowsong turned back to Theuderic. "I've got to find my... well, my young Amorran friend. These letters are for him. Apparently he is marching his legion down into Vallyrium, so I'm going to fly north and west. You will both accompany me. That might take you a little farther west than you were intending, but it should put you considerably closer to your destination. And I imagine I can convince him to give you a pair of horses, as I understand he has several hundred of them."

Theuderic raised his eyebrows. Had the young Amorran officer seduced the elfess? Well done, lad, he thought. No, he must not have actually followed through, not if the elfess was still flying her warhawk. If she was still a sorceress, she was still a virgin. Still, it wasn't just any man who could manage to befriend a beautiful high elf.

He decided to accept the high elf's offer. If her young Amorran friend had his own legion, and Theuderic saw no reason to assume the elfess was lying, he could hire a small escort from the army of camp followers that accompanied every legion.

"We should be most pleased to accept, Lady Shadowsong," Theuderic told her.

The high elf looked from him to Lithriel. "So you answer for both?" she commented. "By 'companions' do you mean to say 'lovers'?"

"Ah, well," Theuderic mumbled, looking to Lithriel.

"Yes," Lithriel said, ignoring him.

"Now that is interesting," Lady Shadowsong said. "Lithriel, I think we must speak more of this later. But for now, both of you must call me Caitlys, as we shall be in rather close quarters on Vengirasse's back where it would be absurd to observe the formalities."

Theuderic hadn't realized before then that all three of them, plus their chests, would be riding one bird. But of course, since Silvertree's bird and the warhawk would be used to bear the Ambassador and his colleague from the city. He glanced up at the big bird, wondering if it was big enough.

"Are those your chests?" Caitlys asked.

"Yes, my lady."

"Good, give me a hand with them, Miroglas. And then, with the Lord Ambassador's permission, we will be underway. Considering what Marcus has told me of this place, I don't wish to stay here one moment longer than necessary."

As soon as the chests were stowed in the thick-roped netting that was cleverly attached to the huge leather saddle that was strapped to the hawk's back, Theuderic found himself climbing up the swaying corded ladder that hung down from the saddle's horn.

The bird's head swung around, and he nearly fell off in panic. But it didn't try to bite him with its wicked beak, which looked as if it could take off his arm. It merely considered him with what he hoped was idle curiosity and not irritation or hunger.

The saddle was an impressive construction made out of several thick layers of leather. It was divided into three sections, so each rider essentially had his own saddle, complete with a horn. Three thick straps were firmly affixed to each horn. These, he learned, as Lithriel adroitly wrapped them around his belt and tied them off, were designed to prevent him from falling to his death. Two straps held him securely fore, and the third one held him aft.

He was given the rear seat, partly because Caitlys was interested in talking to Lithriel, but mostly, he suspected, because she didn't want him pawing and clawing at her in terror or shrieking in her ears throughout the flight.

As he and Lithriel wrapped themselves in the blankets they'd been provided, he saw that Silvertree and Miroglas had both changed into their own flight leathers, which apparently had been stowed on the back of their birds. Thusly armored against the frigid air of the winter sky, the two high elves were carefully arranging their chests in the saddle netting. That done, they began tying the saddle lashes to the rings sewn into the waist of their leathers, firmly attaching themselves to their saddles.

Silvertree gave the lashes a few firm tugs then raised a hand in a manner that was both benediction and farewell.

"The best of fortune to you all," he called out to them. "Good luck finding your Valerian, Lady Shadowsong. Lady Everbright, you shall be welcome should you ever choose to visit Elebrion. And Magus, do try not to fall off!"

That caused the other elves, including Lithriel, to laugh, which only served to underline his theory that elven humor was not merely inhuman but downright ghastly. The Lady Shadowsong—or Caitlys, he reminded himself—said something in Elvish too rapid for him to follow, and the two high elves responded similarly.

"Are you ready?" Lithriel called over her shoulder.

No, sweet heavens, no, he thought to himself. Are you mad? Never in ten thousand years! But instead of shrieking like a coward, he heard himself grandiosely quoting a half-remembered poem:

"When winter's winds their quarrels try, let us contend them for the sky."

He suddenly found himself wishing that he had taken any of the many opportunities to repent of his many sins, or at least confess a few of them, when he had been travelling with the archevêques. Then again, the Sanctiff himself had blessed him—surely that had to count for something! He was still in the middle of a silent but complicated bargain with God that involved both proposing marriage to Lithriel and limiting his use of sorcery to express orders given by the king or the appropriate haut conseilleur, when Vengirasse gave out a great shrieking cry and leaped into the night air.

How he managed to avoid shrieking himself as the bird beat its wings against the cold, heavy air, he would never know. The sudden ascent felt like being rowed along a river, if every stroke of the oars thrust you backward with the force of a lance striking your breastplate, then was interrupted in regular intervals by the empty-bellied sensation of plunging to your doom.

The violence of the bird's motion as it struggled to rise into the sky first left him with the distinct impression that he was about to tumble backward over and off the bird's feathery arse. And then they were all falling downwards together. For all its noble efforts, efforts that Theuderic saluted with all that was in his well-stained soul, the laboring hawk couldn't seem to gain any height.

Just as he was about to shout into Lithriel's ear and ask her if they should jettison some or all of the chests that were weighing the bird down, everything went silent. It was as if he was not flying on an oversized bird's back anymore but floating on top of a cloud. He felt a relief that was so powerful it nearly caused him to wet himself—followed by a wild, unreasoning panic. Were they falling? Had the bird given up? Was this what death was like?

"You can open your eyes now, my lord," Lithriel told him. "Look at the fires of the city, how large it is!"

He started to protest but, realizing how foolish that would be, looked down instead.

The sight of the city below was astounding. They were soaring high over the center of Amorr—about a mille above it, if his eyes could be trusted, and the view was simply spectacular. He could see hundreds of fires, from small ones in pairs indicating torch-lit paths to various clusters of larger ones that indicated group gatherings in places like the Forum and the palestras outside the baths. Between the light given by the fires and the stars above, he could just make out the two vast oblongs of the inner and outer walls. Below them to the left, the large white edifice of the Sanctal Palace thrust upwards from the Inculpatine like a challenge raised against the dark of the night.

"We're flying south first," Caitlys shouted back at them. "I doubt anyone was watching us, but it can't hurt to lay a false trail. And I wanted to see the city. I've never seen it before."

"Where are the other two?" Theuderic looked around but couldn't see them. "Did they go north?"

"No, I expect Morvas had much the same notion." Caitlys pointed down, ahead of them and to the right. "They can fly faster and maneuver more easily, so they can risk flying lower. Do you see them there?"

Lacking the sharp eyes of the elves, Theuderic couldn't make them out at first. But then one of them flew over a large white-roofed building, and he saw the unmistakable shape of the warhawk, its wings outstretched, before it disappeared into the darkness again a moment later. He thought it must be Miroglas, since he didn't see any of the white markings indicating the other elf's bird, but the sight was too brief for him to be certain.

"Is it dangerous, flying that low?"

"Only during the day," Lithriel said. "At night, no one but other elves can see well enough for archers to be a danger, and they're not low enough to risk running into anything. But flying through the mountains at night is a very good way to kill yourself and your hawk."

"We won't be doing any of that, I hope."

"How fast do you think we can fly? The mountains are at least a week's flying north of here, and I believe her Amorran friend is well south of them."

Theuderic nodded and returned his attention to the city below them. It was truly a beautiful sight, almost worth the stark terror required to see it from this altitude. During the day, one would be able to see for leagues in every direction. What the king would not give to have such scouts at his disposal!

Now he truly regretted the failure of the dragonspell. Before, he had only imagined what the power of flight could do, but now he clearly saw how no walled city, not Amorr and not even Malkan, would be able to resist an army that could enter it at any place, at any time, as easily as if they were strolling through the gates.

And whereas a warhawk carried only three riders and could be brought down by an arrow, a dragon could carry thirty, and it would regard anything but a war machine's bolt as no more than a pinprick. If they could be taught to breathe fire on command, even a small squadron of trained dragons would make for an invincible weapon.

One that might even prove effective against immortals such as the one presently hidden in Amorr.

With the exception of the cold, which, in addition to burning his face, was now beginning to cause his fingers and his toes to grow numb, he was starting to feel almost comfortable when the southern walls came into view and the sky suddenly seemed to whirl around him.

He shouted in alarm and for a moment lost his balance as well as his grip on the pommel. But just as he felt that he was sliding off the left side of the saddle, the lashes held him tight. Then Vengirasse was back flying on a smooth and level path, his wings beating powerfully as they headed north.

"Are you all right?" Lithriel leaned back against him and looked up. "I thought I heard you cry out."

"It must have been the wind," he lied easily. He leaned up and kissed her forehead. "But if you don't mind, my love, would you please ask the Lady Shadowsong if she would be so kind as to warn us before her damnable bird changes course again?"

Theuderic arranged the kindling in the middle of some deadwood he'd collected the night before, then he snapped his fingers. It obediently burst into flames. That useful little trick made the King's Own tremendously popular on the borders, even if it had occasionally made him feel as if he was little more than a walking tinder box during his stint with the royal rangers. They'd even called him Torche, although the nickname was spoken with considerably more respect after he'd burned to death a troublesome orc-shaman they'd been hunting for weeks with a pair of well-aimed fireballs.

He heard a noise from the snow-covered lean-to in which the three of them had slept the previous night, and it occurred to him that even if he was still spending his nights without a proper bed or even a roof, his life had improved considerably from the times he'd shared a tent with five of the king's rangers. Unfortunately, the presence of Lady Shadowsong inhibited intimacy with Lithriel as effectively as Sieur Osmont, Sieur Gautier, and the archevêques had on their journey south.

As if summoned by his thoughts, the Lady Shadowsong's face, which had improved considerably in his estimation now that it wasn't chilled, wind-burned, and leaking from the nose, appeared at the entrance as she held out a handful of leaves of indeterminate origin to him.

"I see you've got the fire going. Will you make us some tea, Magus?"

He nodded and took the leaves from her, whereupon she promptly returned to her blankets. Lithriel, he assumed, was still sleeping, as she harbored an intense dislike for rising with the sun. It was a habit that proved useful when he wanted to get things done without being forced to hear her opinion on the matter. Such as which particular strips of meat he should cut from the deer that Vengirasse had left hanging gutted and half-eaten on a tree about thirty paces away at some point during the night. Theuderic found he had come to rather appreciate the warhawk's bloody version of manna from Heaven.

Either the bird wasn't naturally possessive of its kills or it had been trained otherwise, as it raised no fuss when Theuderic wrestled the deer off the branch upon which it was suspended then bent over it and carved away enough meat to supply the three of them with their next three meals. But the scent of blood did draw the hawk's interest, and it bobbed its man-sized head up-and-down until Theuderic tossed it a hunk of raw venison, which it caught and swallowed in a single gulp.

"We'd make a good team, you and me, noble Vengirasse. However, speaking of breakfast… I don't suppose there is any chance you also lay eggs?"

The hawk stared at him, its huge eyes expressionless. Then it spread its wings and leapt into the air, just about scaring Theuderic witless. For a moment he'd thought it had taken offense and was leaping at him. The creature couldn't possibly have understood him!

Fortunately, he managed to quell the lightning spell he'd inadvertently begun to cast. Still, little sparks of electricity danced and leaped on the end of his fingertips for a short while, numbing them as the energy of the interrupted spell dissipated. He breathed a sigh of relief, as he really didn't relish the notion of trying to explain to an elven sorceress why he'd blasted her little pet. And it would have truly been a shame to harm such a magnificent beast, which looked all the more spectacular as it majestically rose into the dawn-red sky.

So there were no eggs to be had, but at least there was a surfeit of fresh meat to fry in the high elf's battered brass pan. Once the water was boiling, he called out to the two elfesses and was surprised to see Lithriel crawling out of the lean-to behind Lady Shadowsong, yawning and rubbing her eyes.

"You're awake," he commented blandly.

"Tea," she mumbled. "Caitlys promised *khairithal*. Haven't had it in years."

"Is that what this is?" He examined the cup in his hands, which happened to be one of the two cups in Lady Shadowsong's pack, then handed it to her.

Lithriel sniffed at the steam trailing up from it, then inhaled deeply and held it in her hands as if it were some sort of steaming treasure.

"Oh, that's tremendous," she all but moaned. "I almost don't want to drink it. Such a magical moment should never end."

Theuderic laughed at her. It smelled like burning cat fur. "I'll leave the two of you alone." He turned his attention to the meat, which was very nearly seared to a sufficiency.

Lady Shadowsong contributed some biscuits from her pack before pouring her own tea, and soon the three of them were breaking their fast and discussing the day's flight. It had been four days since leaving Amorr, and still there was no sign of the Valerian legion she was seeking. For that matter, there hadn't been any sign of any legion.

"I think we've gone too far north and not enough west," the high elfess declared. "We should fly due west today."

"No, we haven't flown far enough north," Theuderic said. "Based on what you told us from his last letter, your Valerian was planning on staying just south of the mountains then approaching Amorr from the northwest.

I think west-northwest is the furthest south we could possibly encounter him today. Amorrans never stray far from their roads."

"He's going to go through Vallyrium first, though, and you're forgetting that is further to the east. There are roads there too, I'm sure." Lady Shadowsong screwed up her face in a manner that would have looked ridiculous if he didn't know she was deep in thought. "We can try west northwest, though. If we can't find him today or tomorrow, I'm afraid we're going to have to assume his plans were interrupted somehow."

"It would take a hell of an interruption to disrupt the plans of a man with six thousand Amorran legionaries behind him."

"That's what is beginning to concern me," Lady Shadowsong said. "Lithriel, what do you think?"

"I think," his lover said, proffering her empty cup, "that I shall have more tea."

The sun had fully risen by the time they were in the air again, and Theuderic congratulated himself for the relative equanimity with which he had borne this latest launch into the sky. What had previously been an endless period of mute and petrified terror was now little more than a few short moments of white-knuckled worry as the great bird fought the wind for altitude.

He didn't think he'd ever get used to the dreadful, lurching sensation of falling during the up-stroke, when the hawk's wings folded in and lifted in preparation for the next mighty thrust upward, but he was now able to endure the feeling without the need to close his eyes or do more than silently recite the occasional Rosarian mystery.

Whoever shall have a true devotion for the rosary shall not die without the sacraments of the Church. It was a comforting thought, even for so consistent a sinner as himself. He wasn't even sure that a sorcerer could possess true devotion, especially one who lacked so much as an actual bead-chain, but he was confident that the company of a pair of pagan elfesses put him about as far from the Church sacraments as he could get without actually taking part in a cannibalistic goblin rite celebrating of one of their demon-gods.

They flew in silence for several hours. Theuderic, frozen nearly solid despite being wrapped in two heavy blankets, was just about to suggest they stop for food and some much-needed thawing, when Lithriel called out.

"Look there." Lithriel pointed at something on their right. "Look at that big square thing. It looks like a city, but I don't think it is."

"That's the legion!" Lady Shadowsong said enthusiastically. "Marcus told me about their camps. They're always built in squares like that."

She didn't seem to give Vengirasse any command, but a moment later the hawk banked its massive wings, and they inscribed a gentle curve in the sky that ended with them heading due north in the direction of the encampment that Theuderic still couldn't see.

Soon, however, even his human eyes could make out what was clearly a fortified army camp. It was rigorously laid out in simple and straight lines, with two pathways bisecting the walled square. A large stream flowed past it to the east, while a chaotic collection of tents, carts, and temporary wooden structures seemed to grow out from it in a sort of architectural tumor to the west. Several moving rectangles on the west side proved to be formations of soldiers going through exercises, and while the legion's camp was relatively peaceful, the area given over to the camp followers teemed with activity.

"Don't go any lower," Theuderic suddenly called out to Lady Shadowsong. "In fact, I strongly suggest we do not land here."

Vengirasse dutifully changed the angle of his wings at his rider's command and they began to climb toward the clouds again.

"What's wrong?" Lithriel asked.

"Something isn't right. Look at those walls, how thick they are. They're made of either brick or stone. Caitlys told us her friend was on the march. That down there is an army that hasn't been marching anywhere. That's an army that's been wintering there for weeks, perhaps even months. And those two flags," he said, pointing. "Does either of them look like an imperial flag to you?"

One flag was maroon and grey. The other was white with a large red V on it as well as some other detail he couldn't make out. Neither was the familiar flag of Amorr: red with the three ubiquitous letters, S P A, sewn in gold upon it.

"How many legions in this area can there be? And who else besides the empire has legions?" Lady Shadowsong scoffed at his concerns as they circled high above the camp. "Anyhow, the Amorrans have permanent camps like this constructed all across Utrucca, Falisca, and the provinces. I must have seen thirty empty ones along the way. They march from one to the next whenever they can. Two of the last three letters I received from Marcus were written from this sort of camp. They usually build them close to towns and cities when they can, so I'll bet there is a good-sized village within a bell's ride upstream from here."

"All right, then look outside the camp." Theuderic pointed out to the mass of human activity below. "How do you explain all of those people?"

"They're called 'camp followers' for a reason, magus," the elfess said disdainfully. "I shouldn't think the concept was beyond you. But if you like, we can make a low pass before landing. That should attract sufficient attention for the guards to inform an officer or two."

"That seems a reasonable precaution," Theuderic said.

The elfess directed the warhawk on a descending path that would take them directly along the west wall.

Truth be told, Theuderic was more than ready to land, but he had the sneaking suspicion that landing in the middle of the legion's camp would be a remarkably terrible idea for two elves and a royal battlemage. Even if there weren't any of the cursed priests of Saint Michael about, he doubted Lady Shadowsong's ability to hold off dozens of iron bolts shot by the huge crossbow-like machines he saw were mounted on the walls. He counted twenty of them, five on each wall section. Although only four of them were presently manned, he anticipated the rest of them could be in short order.

They were perhaps four hundred paces away and thirty paces above the top of the walls when one of the guards above the northern gate spotted them. Theuderic could see him calling another guard's attention and pointing directly at them, following which the second guard drew a horn from his belt and blew five short notes.

This created a veritable upheaval within and without the camp, and it rather humorously reminded Theuderic of the frantic activity that usually follows the overturning of an anthill. But the sight of men in armor rushing toward the deadly bolt throwers reminded him that, even if these were the right Amorrans, they could not know the warhawk's riders intended them no harm. So, despite the cold, he slid the blankets down and slipped off his cream-colored shirt. Vengirasse sailed past the southern end of the camp and began to flap his wings to gain altitude for a return pass, turning eastward in order to make it even closer to the western wall.

"What are you doing?" Lithriel sensed his activity and tried to turn and see why he was moving about the bird's back.

"They don't know who we are, so we need to tell them we want to parley. Tell Caitlys we can't even think of landing if they don't wave a white flag back at us."

"What are those men with the upside-down horns on their heads?" Lady Shadowsong called back at him, ignoring his suggestion.

"Centurions. There's an officer, right there!" Theuderic pointed to a large, thick-waisted man who had just come out of a large tent near the middle of the camp. Several centurions and men with plumed helmets gathered around him. "Is that your friend?"

"No, he's much too old and fat. Marcus is younger, younger than you."

"And he commands a legion?" Theuderic found that hard to believe.

"Maybe that's not the commander," Lithriel suggested, even as the large man pointed up at them, and the group of men around him abruptly dispersed, shouting orders and running for the wall. "Or maybe it is. Look out!"

Theuderic had learned enough about Lady Shadowsong's approach to flying to grab the saddle horn with both hands and lean forward as far as he could into Lithriel. That cost him his shirt—it went fluttering away—but it kept him from testing the strength of the saddle straps again as Vengirasse tucked his wings, rolled left, and dove toward the ground.

Someone fired a bolt from the wall. It probably would have missed them anyhow, but the warhawk's move caused it to pass well over and behind them. Vengirasse leveled out and beat its wings to pick up speed as it flashed over wide-eyed children, screaming horses, and open-mouthed women in the tent city below.

It was a cunning move on the high elf's part, as the imperials on the wall couldn't fire more bolts without putting their camp followers at risk. Unfortunately, the legionary commander was entirely willing to do just that, as four more bolts fired in near-chorus, one of which passed just over their heads.

Screams and shrieks erupted below them as the bolts landing unexpectedly in the midst of the camp followers set off panic in the civilian population. The artillerymen on the west wall were reloading their bolt-throwers, but it was the five on the northern wall that were the most threatening, and Theuderic could see they were already rotating their loaded machines toward Vengirasse's flight path.

"Distract them!" Lady Shadowsong shouted. Her eyes were locked on the bolt-throwing crews, trying to anticipate the moment to slow Vengirasse. They were too near to the ground for diving and picking up speed to be an option. "Now, Magus!"

His training took over. Without thinking, Theuderic raised his arms, and two massive bolts of lightning arced instantly from his hands to the first bolt-thrower.

There was a deafening thunderclap, followed by screams and the sound of bodies and large pieces of wood and stone striking the ground within and without the wall. Two bolts flew well in front of them, loosed reflexively by their crews. The crew of the closest surviving bolt-thrower held their fire, but the noise of the explosion caused them to dive behind the wall's low parapet.

"Straight on," Theuderic shouted. "Straight on, and stay low! We're clear to the north." He cast a different spell, this one aimed more judiciously this time. A single fireball struck the second bolt-thrower and set it alight before its crew could man it again. The last bolt-thrower on the northern wall loosed its bolt in response, but it was too far to the east to be dangerous and amounted to little more than a last defiant gesture as the warhawk bore its riders safely away.

Lady Shadowsong looked back and said something in Elvish, then shook her head. They continued flying north, slowly rising higher, until even Lithriel's keen eyes couldn't see the legionary fortress anymore. Then the hawk curved to the east and flew that way until they passed over a series of well-forested hills and landed despite Theuderic's protests that the imperial cavalry might already be riding in pursuit of them.

"Don't be absurd, Magus." Lady Shadowsong leaped down from the great bird and massaged her legs. "First, they'd ride due north because that's the way we flew away. Second, they have no way of tracking us around to here. Third, they're not about to chase what they must think to be elven magisters. And fourth, Magus, are you trying to start a war between Elebrion and the empire? What could you possibly have been thinking?"

"You said to stop them," Theuderic found himself protesting.

"I said to *distract* them, not attack them!"

"Yes, well, that's how a battlemage distracts people. Besides, I told you they might not be your boy's legion!" he shouted back at her. "They had us bracketed! Those bolt-throwers are accurate enough to skewer a man at two hundred paces and that first volley nearly spitted your bird like a chicken! If I hadn't done something, we'd all be dead!"

Lithriel put her hand on the high elf's shoulder. "He's right, Caitlys. But you needn't worry. If Lord Silvertree is to be believed, the imperials have sufficient problems nearer to hand. Those will occupy them nicely. I hardly think they're likely to go to all the trouble of trying to start another war with King Mael over the crew of a single war machine."

The high elf made a face then shrugged. "Better them than us, I suppose. It will be interesting trying to explain this to Marcus. But if these people are so hostile and frightened of magic that they'll attack a warhawk on sight, how am I supposed to reach him? For all we know, that was his legion, and now we're flying away from them. I suppose I could go back. Land out of sight and walk to the camp. But that might be even more dangerous. Imagine if we had landed there...."

Lithriel looked to Theuderic as if expecting him to do something. What was he supposed to say? Of course it would have been disastrous to land in the middle of a bloody Amorran legion, but it wasn't as if they'd been stupid enough to do it. Then he realized how sore and tired he was after only three days of flying—the Lady Shadowsong had been flying for more than three weeks.

"Don't worry, my lady," he told her. "If you happen to have something that might serve as a dart or an arrow, I think I can arrange to get a message directly to your friend without putting anyone at risk."

"You can't use magic, you know," she cautioned him. "Marcus is most particular about that."

"There is no need for even the smallest sorcery." He smiled. "But I'm afraid it will require finding the legion first. The correct one, this time."

CORVUS

THE Sanctal Palace cast long shadows over the great hill upon which it stood and onto the plaza below. Corvus and his fascitors strode into the crowds in the plaza, which were considerably more orderly than the mob surrounding the elven embassy had been, but they were very nearly as numerous. Monks from the various orders wandered about, awestruck to find themselves in the vicinity of the holy site. Priests closer to the bottom of the holy hierarchy than the top strolled about arm in arm, discussing theology. And the common people pushed and shoved to get closer to the fountain at the center of the square, the water from which was said to have been blessed by Sanctus Petrus and was known to possess miraculously curative powers.

But all of them, clerics and common citizens alike, hastened to get out of the way of Caius Vecellius and his axe bearers with unusual alacrity. Corvus wondered if it was possible that news of the impromptu execution of the Church guardsman had already reached the crowds here. It seemed unlikely. But then, it was said that bad news flew faster than the crows who bore it.

He had his answer soon enough, as the coldly glaring stares of the guards at the foot of the steps at the bottom of the hill told him they were still respectful of his office though clearly not of the man who held it. It was apparent that they knew very well what he had done, and they did not approve. Even so, they made no move to intercept his progress, which was a relief. The very last thing the city needed right now was a power struggle between the government authority and its religious counterpart.

"We may be wise to be a little circumspect in our actions," Corvus said to Vecellius as they began to mount the marble steps that would lead them directly to the entrance. "One more beheading, and they'll be calling me Carnifex instead of Corvus."

"Men have borne worse," the unflappable captain replied. "Any citizen who fails to respect consular imperium deserves to die. For stupidity, if nothing else. Are you well, my lord consul? Your breathing is a little labored."

Corvus stifled a groan as they continued to mount the steps. One tended to forget how heavy one's armor could be when one was accustomed to one's mount doing most of the work of carting it about. He wasn't merely breathing hard—his legs were downright burning by the time they reached the top of the stairs and the path to the palace's great double-doors, which were standing open.

To Corvus, the opening looked more like a monstrous maw than an indication that they were welcome in the heart of the Church. Of course, only he knew the secret of what might be waiting for them inside. He still found the elf's tale to be fantastical, but then, the Scriptures were full of wonders that no Amorran had ever seen. His own son had claimed to see things on his trip to Elebrion in which Corvus still couldn't honestly say he believed. It was said that God worked in mysterious ways, so who was to say that men understood the works of the devil any better?

A bishop in gleaming white ecclesiastical attire greeted him at the head of a group of white-armored guards. "My lord consul, I am Father Sebastius. The Sanctified Father asked me to await your arrival. If you will be so kind as to accompany me, he will receive you in the Apostular."

Corvus nodded, noting the double bars on the symbols stitched onto the priest's mitre. Not a bishop, but an archbishop then. And, unlike the guards at the stair, the archbishop didn't seem to consider anything amiss about a consular visit. But it was interesting, if not entirely unsurprising, to learn that his visit was anticipated. "Thank you, Excellency."

Again he was led through the maze of colorful patterns cast on the floor by the plated windows, past paintings and statues of incalculable value, each created by the past masters of their day. But the holy awe that had struck him so powerfully before was now gone, replaced by a burning anger that this holiest of Man's holies had been desecrated, not by the spiritual powers of the air, but by a much more earthly and material evil.

For the first time, he truly understood what was meant by the concept of righteous wrath. The anger that filled him was not his own, he was merely its vessel. All his fear and all his worries for his family, for his House, and for his city were like logs thrown on a mighty bonfire, consumed by his fury that not only Holy Mother Church but the Sanctal Office itself had been corrupted by an inhuman invader.

Ecclesiasticals of every rank bowed respectfully as he and the archbishop passed. Corvus ignored them all. Some were offended by the slight. Others, perhaps more perceptive, were only troubled. They knew it was never a sign of Heaven's favor when armed men with faces like thunder strode purposefully through God's temple. Particularly on those occasions when such men were followed by other men bearing fasces and axes.

When they reached the heart of the palace, Sebastius stopped at the closed doors behind which the great throne room lay. He gestured toward the fascitors with an expression of mild regret on his face.

"His Holiness has instructed that only the lord consul may enter into his presence today."

Caius Vecellius quickly looked to Corvus, who shook his head. There was no point in protesting the matter. In the unlikely event that the Sanctified Father, or whatever it was that possessed him, intended to start a war with the Senate by murdering him, eight men armed with axes could hardly hope to defend him from the hundreds of Church guards, the brutal ex-gladiators of the Redeemed and the priests of the various military orders, throughout the vast palace. If he was expected, then the creature wanted something from him.

And he had a pretty good idea he knew what it was.

"Relax, Captain. I very much doubt I'm in danger of anything but a lengthy penance."

Vecellius nodded, but he didn't look happy. Corvus didn't know what the captain had gleaned from the various conversations he'd overheard during the past few days, but he seemed to be aware that something well out of the ordinary was taking place. The archbishop smiled, nodded to Vecellius, then indicated that the doors should be opened.

For the third time since he'd come back to Amorr, Corvus walked down the long, carpeted aisle toward the spectacular Sedes Ossus. This time, the throne of bones was alone on the dais except for the red-robed figure enthroned upon it. It was a magnificent sight in the dim torchlight that lit the room, although from a distance, the red of the Sanctal robe made it look as if the throne preserved not only the bones and gilt skulls of the apostles but also their blood and gory viscera. Behind him, there was a dull boom as the doors closed, but Corvus didn't break his stride, determined to cloak his fear in his rage as he stalked toward the seated man.

The Sanctiff hadn't moved or shown any reaction to his approach, and for a moment Corvus wondered if he might be sleeping or perhaps even dead. Then he lifted his head, and Corvus recognized the bearded face of the man he'd acclaimed himself in this very room.

His Sanctified Holiness Pelagianus, formerly Giovannus Falconius Valens, did not look well. His face was white and drawn, his dark eyes were haunted, and there were lines etched deeply into his face despite his relative youth. What struck Corvus most, however, was the way the Sanctified Father flinched as Corvus mounted the three stairs that led up to the platform upon which the precious relic of relics was set.

The four grinning skulls on the throne were more welcoming than the one that flesh still covered, if tightly. But, being a dutiful son of the Church, Corvus fell to one knee and kissed the carved gold ring that was held out to him by Pelagianus's long-fingered, almost skeletal hand. The metal was surprisingly cold on his lips, and he jerked back then looked up and was startled to see that the Sanctiff's eyes were no longer haunted, but were staring at him in an almost inquisitive manner.

"Rise, my son," Pelagianus said in a quavering voice that matched his sickly, almost withered appearance. Surely this could not be the immortal monster of whom the elves spoke with equal measures of respect and fear.

"Your Holiness, are you well?" Corvus asked, confused and almost more dismayed at finding this shrunken wreck of a man than the ancient and powerful creature he'd been expecting to confront.

The Sanctiff started to respond, but then he cried out like a child and raised his hands over his face. He began gibbering fearfully as if terrified by Corvus's mere presence.

Or, Corvus thought as his blood ran cold, by someone behind him.

He straightened his back and turned deliberately around. He was not entirely surprised to see a figure standing in the middle of the carpeted aisle down which he had just walked a moment ago. It was the archbishop, Sebastius.

Despite the mitre he wore, he was neither tall nor imposing, but there was something intimidating in the way he slowly walked toward Corvus. In contrast to the friendly, welcoming smile he'd worn earlier, the side of his mouth was twisted in a contemptuous smirk. His white vestments stood out against the rich red carpet of the throne room. It gave Corvus the impression of a bone jutting out of a river of blood.

So here was the answer.

Corvus walked slowly down from the dais, resisting the temptation to reach for his sword hilt. The elves said such creatures couldn't be killed. But he found that hard to believe. After all, elves were said to be immortal too, and yet they died as easily as anything else a man could swing a sword at. "Who are you, and what have you done to the Sanctified Father?"

"Sextus Valerius Corvus," the archbishop replied in a voice that seemed oddly deeper than before. "Permit me to congratulate you on your election as Consul Aquilae. I am told it was by near-historic margins."

"Thank you," Corvus said. "You have me at a disadvantage, Excellency. How shall I address you? I doubt your true name is Sebastius."

"My name is not relevant. And it would take you a lifetime of study to begin to understand the advantage I have over you, my lord consul.

But I mean you no harm, Corvus. In fact, I have been waiting for you. I have need of you."

Corvus nodded. As for what it told him, he wasn't surprised. Any creature, however powerful, that preferred to operate by stealth would naturally be loathe to engage in a direct confrontation that would bring the wrath of the Senate down upon it. And if it wanted him dead, he'd already be dead. He decided to test its willingness to cooperate. "Release His Holiness. Then I'll speak with you."

"Very well." The thing called Sebastius gestured with its left hand. "You may go, Valens."

Corvus looked over his shoulder.

The Sanctiff seemed to roll off the apostolic throne. Hunched over in his finery like a beggar trying to stay warm, he scurried down the steps and off into the deep shadows of the chamber. His movements were barely human. It almost looked as if he had been reduced to the state of a mindless, frightened animal.

"Thank you," Corvus said. "Is that how you treat every man who cooperates with you?"

"It is how I treat those who play me false. He thought to use me to serve his ambition." It chuckled softly. "I see you are not entirely without fear, Lord Consul, and yet you master it well. Yes, I think we can be of use to each other, Valerius Corvus. I believe you are the one I seek."

"Ah, but do I have need of you?"

This time, the creature actually laughed out loud. "My dear lord consul, your empire is crumbling! Your city is on the edge of panic, your allies have abandoned you, your enemies outnumber you, your own brother has turned against you... and you ask me if you need me?"

"I didn't say I lacked problems. I merely wondered what, if anything, you could possibly do to help me with them. I can't see that you have served the Sanctified Father well."

"I do not serve."

"We all serve someone," Corvus said with a contemptuous smile. "In one way or another. Even your kind has its purpose."

The creature smiled, exposing teeth that were whole and strangely unstained, as pearlescent as a child's milk teeth. Corvus remembered the elves telling him the creatures could remake themselves even when dismembered and burned, and he wondered how long ago this thing had become Father Sebastius. Months ago? Decades ago?

"Don't you wish to know what I want from you?"

Corvus shook his head. "I already know. I'm a general and the consul of the legions. You're a creature who skulks in darkness and wears a false face. You want me to fight your battles for you. What else could you possibly want?"

It glared at him, anger flashing across its nondescript face. For all its age, it did not appear to have much self-control. He supposed it was not accustomed to being spoken to in such a manner. "Yes," it admitted reluctantly. "I do. But don't be fooled, Lord Consul, and don't presume to judge me. I am far older than you would believe. I have raised armies and led them to victories greater than any you could even conceive."

"But you don't have the time to raise one now, do you?" Corvus broke in. When it remained silent, confirming his conclusion, he continued. "Are you the one behind all this? Behind the rebellions in the provinces and the allied leagues?"

"I had nothing to do with them. Indeed, I wish for you to quell them with all haste."

"So do I. What is in it for you?"

"I need a strong and united empire, led by a skilled and charismatic leader. I need an army of five hundred thousand, with which I can defeat the armies my brothers are raising even as we speak. I need Amorr hale and whole. And I need you, Valerius Corvus."

"Amorr doesn't have an army of five hundred thousand. I wish it did."

"I can give you one. With my help, the people will flock to your standards. The opposition will lay down their arms and join you; those who don't, you will crush yourself."

"How can you help…?" Corvus's voice trailed off. His eyes narrowed. "You are saying there is another one of your kind involved with the revolts?"

"It seems likely. Amorr is the great power on Selenoth. Perhaps all the unrest here is simple human intransigence, but I sense a familiar hand behind it. I thought to use the Church because it was less obvious than the Senate, but it seems one of my brothers has been subtler still."

Corvus nodded. It seemed he had found the chapel killer. But was this its true body, or was it a spirit possessing the body of the real Sebastius? "Why?" he asked. "Why Amorr? Why use the Church, the Senate, or the allied cities?"

"Because the moons and the stars are coming into alignment, and when the Gate of Shadows opens, I must be the one to control it!"

"What is this gate?"

"Everything! It is the only way out of this dreadful shadow! I was foolish and afraid, and I stayed behind. But it was a mistake, a mistake for which I have been paying for aeons! You cannot imagine, Corvus. Suppose everyone you knew left you, abandoned you, and you knew there was only one way to see them again. Would you not sacrifice the world, would you not sacrifice a thousand worlds, to see them again?"

Corvus nodded pensively. He could understand, perhaps even sympathize a little. What would he not give to have Corvinus back? What would he not give to see his son again, as a boy or as a man, to put his arms around Corvinus's shoulders and embrace him? Anything. Anything at all… except for Valeria, Valerilla, Marcus, Romilia, or the grandchildren.

Or his honor.

Or his God.

"Why were you afraid? Weren't you more afraid to be alone?"

The creature looked pensive. "I don't know," it admitted. "Even ageless ones fear the unknown, maybe more than most. I thought the others were fools. I thought it was like jumping off a cliff without looking down to see if there was water or rocks below."

"And now?"

"There were always rumors about the Gate of Shadows opening every once in a great while, rumors that someone came back. That was when the wars started. Some of those who stayed behind said they'd promised to keep it shut. Others of us wanted to use it to leave here. Then, when something else came through, something that didn't come from here, we all knew there were other shadows, other worlds."

"Something else?"

Sebastius gestured to indicate the great chamber surrounding them.

"You don't mean… the Immaculate?"

"I don't know if he was what he claimed or not. I myself have been worshipped as a god more times than I can count. I didn't even hear about him until a century after his death. But I heard enough to know that he wasn't one of us and he wasn't one of you. That was when I knew that it was safe to go through the Gate, that there is water, not rocks, waiting below."

For the first time, Corvus truly felt in awe of the creature that stood before him. To think it had been walking the earth at the same time as the Son of God! And there were others of its kind, perhaps even others who had seen the Immaculate, had spoken to Him! Still, Corvus was almost tempted to agree to its wishes, if only to have the chance to inquire of its fellows.

It seemed to sense this, because it spread its hands and implored him.

"Will you not help me, Corvus? I don't ask more than you can give. It is only one campaign, one glorious campaign. When it is over and I am gone through the Shadowgate, Amorr will be master of all Selenoth. And you will be the master of the world! Serve me in this, only for a little while, and I will give you everything you've ever dreamed, everything you've ever wanted!"

Corvus thought for a moment. It could give him many things, that much was true. It could give him victory, power, and glory. But not everything. It could not give him what he wanted most. No one could.

"No." He said it with an amount of regret, but he said it firmly nonetheless.

A look of confusion crossed the immortal's incongruously young face. "What do you mean, no?"

"I mean this." Corvus drew his sword and lunged.

The thing didn't have time to react. Before it had even begun to raise its arms to defend itself, Corvus's sword was buried to the hilt in its chest.

It staggered backward, and Corvus let go of his weapon. So the elves were wrong, and he was right: Immortal didn't necessarily mean unkillable.

He was bitterly disappointed when the creature regained its balance and stared reproachfully at him, with its hands on its hips and his sword sticking out of its chest. It shook its head, more in sadness than anger. It placed a hand on either side of the hilt and pushed the sword out of its chest with a loud sucking sound. The bloody sword dropped to the floor, though the carpet masked the noise when it struck.

"What did you do that for?"

Corvus shrugged. "I had to try."

"No, you didn't! You stupid, foolish worm, that hurt! Why?"

"I serve the Almighty God. I serve Amorr. I don't serve you. I won't serve you."

He faced the ancient thing calmly despite the fear that clutched at his heart. Now he didn't even have his sword. He would not die less courageously than Fortex had, of that he was determined. He only wished that he'd been able to kiss Romilia one last time, to give Valerilla one last hug, to give Marcus one final piece of advice. But then, Corvinus was waiting. He had no fears of what lay on the other side.

To his surprise, Sebastius didn't strike him down. "You must serve me, Corvus. I require your service. I can force you to bend the knee, you must know that!"

"How? By killing everyone I love? By slaying my entire House?"

"Do you think I can't?"

Corvus could still see the wound from which the blood had spilled, though no more blood was seeping out of it. It was a strangely fascinating sight.

"No, I think you don't know House Valerius. Do you think any of us would choose to save ourselves at the cost of tens of thousands, no, more like hundreds of thousands, of Amorran lives?" He reconsidered. "Well, Magnus might."

It pointed its finger at Corvus and fairly shrieked at him. "Death will avail you nothing, Sextus Valerius Corvus! If you will not serve me, I will flay you with fire from inside your bowels. I will rape your wife. I will slaughter and devour your children. And then I will go to Manlius Torquatus and make him the same offer I made you. The world, or blood, death, and fire. And if he refuses me, I will go to your brother. Either Amorr will serve me or Amorr will die such a death that it will make kings and emperors shudder on their thrones for a thousand years!"

Corvus took a deep breath and prepared to die. But there was movement from behind the creature, and he heard someone—the Sanctiff!—shouting out something that sounded far too aggressive to be a blessing or a prayer.

The creature whipped its head around, and they both stared at the unexpected sight of Valens stumbling toward them with a torch in one hand and a small bowl in the other.

"*Exorcizamus te!*" he cried. "*Omnis immundus spiritus, omnis satanica potestas, omnis incursio infernalis adversarii, omnis legio, omnis congregatio et secta diabolica, in nomine et virtute Domini Nostri Immaculati!*" The Sanctiff hurled the contents of the bowl at the thing in the bloody bishop's robes.

It was oil, presumably holy oil, but it had precisely no effect at all. Nor did the exorcism, as there was no demon here to exorcise.

Sebastius simply raised its hand, and Valens collapsed, howling wordlessly like a burning animal, dropping the torch onto the carpet.

Corvus bound forward to pick up his sword. He swung it with both hands like an axe at the immortal's neck. It struck true. Not a clean decapitation but a deep gash. Sebastius screamed in pain and fell to all fours.

Corvus hacked ruthlessly at it, ignoring the screams and the spattering blood. He struck again and again and again, until he finally beheaded the thing. The head rolled across the carpet like a distended ball. Without pausing, he did the same to its legs and its arms.

Not until the creature was fully dismembered and silent, hewed into six separate pieces, did Corvus stop and wipe the blood from his face. He was out of breath, and his arms ached.

Abruptly, the Sanctiff stopped screaming. Corvus was just stepping over one of the legs to see if Valens was still alive when he saw the eyes on the severed head open.

Dammit, sooner than I expected.

He could hear the pounding on the doors from outside the chambers. Vecellius and his men had surely heard the screams. It seemed the creature was still able to hold the doors shut with sorcery, and they were thick enough that his guards' axes would take a little time to break through it. They would not arrive soon enough to help him.

"You can't kill me, you fool!"

"I know." Corvus reached down to feel the Sanctiff's throat, then rapidly drew his hand away. The Sanctified Father was definitely dead, though his skin was literally burning hot. At least it had been fast, Corvus told himself. *Requiescat*, and all that.

"Then why did you do that? You know what I'm going to do!" Its voice was high-pitched, as if the pain had driven it half-mad.

"No, I don't think you will." Corvus reached over and picked up the torch, which had already set a bit of the carpet on fire, and touched it to the bloody cloth covering the two limbs he could reach. Despite the blood, the flames began to lick at the remnants of the robe almost immediately. "You said the moons are nearly in alignment and the gate will open soon. I have no doubt that you can recover from being burned to ashes, but I suspect you can't do it soon enough to win over the Senate and drag the People to the slaughter before the gate shuts again."

"Do you think I will not kill you now?" the head spat, its face contorted with rage.

"I had been hoping otherwise," Corvus admitted as he methodically set the other two limbs and the torso alight. "But you will not enter the Shadowgate! You and I will burn here."

It screamed something in a wordless language.

Corvus was ready for the pain. The ancient sorcery erupted inside him with what felt like the fury of a thousand suns. And yet Corvus smiled grimly as he pressed the flames against the screaming face of the immortal and saw the oil ignite and its hair begin to burn. He was the Consul Aquilae, the consul of the legions, he reminded himself. He was Valerius Victus.

If this was his last battle, he would not lose it!

Forgive me, Fortex, he thought as the sorcerous fire consumed his insides and agony dimmed his eyes. I love you, Romilia. Romilia. Romi....

THEUDERIC

THE last vestiges of blue were about to disappear from the increasingly red-purple sky as Vengirasse circled over the encamped legion for the third time. This one was no permanent castra, Theuderic observed, because in the place of stone walls there was a simple wooden palisade. The earth inside the palisade was still covered with winter-brown grass that had not yet been worn away to dirt and dust.

Furthermore, there were no camp followers at all, and the castra was full of the sort of activity that behooved an army that had only recently finished marching. Stablehands were feeding and brushing horses, there were hundreds of small fires over which men were huddled, obviously preparing food, and there were a number of small groups filling casks in a nearby stream or bringing deadwood back to the rudimentary fortress.

"This must be it." He withdrew the makeshift spear he'd made the previous day. "Are you finished yet?"

"What do you think?" Caitlys asked Lithriel. "That hill over there? There is enough open space to land safely.

"Yes," his lover answered. "It's nearly due south, and it's not too far from the camp, so long as he rides."

Caitlys nodded and returned to her writing, which, judging by the elven cursing that accompanied it, was somewhat trickier a few hundred paces up in the air than it was on the ground. "Here," she said finally, passing a scroll back to him. "Be sure to affix it tightly enough that it doesn't fall off when you throw."

Theuderic focused on passing the strips of cloth he'd cut off one of the chemises Lord Silvertree had given him through the two holes he'd worked through the scroll with his knife. He tied it off with a moon knot, affixing it securely to the peeled, knobby shaft, then hefted it in his right arm. The wind of their flight didn't tear the scroll away, so he assumed it would hold long enough for their purposes.

"What if this doesn't work?" Caitlys asked.

"Of course it will work," Lithriel said. "Even if it doesn't, they don't have any bolt-throwers assembled. So we can come back and try again, if need be."

"Just take us down and head for that big tent in the middle of the camp," Theuderic ordered. Caitlys's increasing moodiness was beginning to get on his nerves. The closer they got to finding her damned Amorran, the more strangely she behaved.

The great warhawk stooped so gracefully that Theuderic didn't even feel it in his belly this time. But the green mass of the trees below rapidly came to dominate his vision as they rushed toward the ground. The sensation of speed replaced the peaceful sense of soaring.

He focused on the large tan square of the command tent, ignoring the shouts and cries and pointing fingers of the legionaries as they approached. When the tent loomed large, he hurled his crude spear directly toward the grassy ground in front of it, hoping to avoid hitting the two guards who were standing oblivious to their danger just outside the entrance.

"Dammit!"

"What?" cried both elfesses in unison.

"It broke!" Theuderic looked back and saw that the speed with which they were flying, combined with the pull of the ground, had caused the uneven shaft to shatter. Where was the message cloth? He couldn't see. But he could see five or six legionary archers rushing down the path between some smaller tents behind them. Two of them were already raising their bows.

"Shall we circle around again?" Caitlys asked.

"No!" he shouted. "And fly lower!"

For the second time in three days, shafts flew over their heads. Fortunately, they were much smaller this time, and wooden, but they gave Theuderic shivers all the same. What was wrong with these Amorrans—and from whence sprang this damnable instinct to turn everything that flew over their heads into a pincushion?

They landed on the hilltop, mercifully unpricked. Theuderic went through his now-accustomed routine of massaging his thighs and trying to walk some feeling back into his legs, then he tore down a few of the more dead-looking branches from the nearest tree and started a fire the easy way. The wood popped and steamed and gave off a bitter odor, but it was warm and after spending most of the day high in the sky being frozen by the winter winds, that was all that mattered.

The two elves, with their long, sensitive ears, heard the horses long before he did. Seeing their reaction, Theuderic grabbed a pack full of dried meat with one hand, Lithriel's arm with the other, and dragged her into the woods. If things went horribly wrong, perhaps he could ambush the unsuspecting Amorrans, or at least remain free to steal a pair of horses and continue their journey north. Lithriel protested instinctively, but she gave way when Caitlys saw what he was doing and nodded her approval. She would meet the soldiers alone.

Three horsemen entered the clearing. The one in the middle, presumably Caitlys's friend, wore a plumed helm. The horses were visibly nervous upon seeing the massive hawk on the hilltop. They snorted and struggled against their riders' attempts to control them.

The tall young officer didn't hesitate to dismount and hand his reins to his companion on the left. He walked quickly toward Lady Shadowsong.

She looked uncharacteristically unsure of herself, facing him with her arms folded and her chin lifted defiantly. She raised a hand in greeting.

He ignored that completely. Instead, he strode forward, took her face in his hands, and kissed her passionately.

"Oh, look at them." Lithriel sighed happily. "Isn't that sweet?"

Sweet or not, the sight made Theuderic happy too. He vastly preferred Amorrans who welcomed them with kisses to those who made concerted attempts to kill them. It made for a distinct improvement, in his considered opinion. "It is indeed. Of course, he might not be so enthusiastic once she tells him the tidings we bring."

While the other Amorran officers were markedly less pleased to be hosting two elves and a Savondese nobleman, they were most appreciative of the information concerning the legion they'd tangled with to the south. And several of them became downright friendly when Theuderic suggested how they might use Vengirasse to quickly and easily seize the castra and force the surrender of Legio XV's disloyal general. It seemed that they were able to identify the legion's commanding officer based on the description that Lithriel provided. He was, it turned out, a provincial from the Utruccan city of Silarea.

Theuderic thought Caitlys's friend—the young general, Valerius Clericus—was a little optimistic in assuming that the other legion's soldiers would so readily transfer their loyalties to him on the basis of his family name, but then, he didn't pretend to know much about Amorran politics or the rivalries of its Houses. He had far more confidence in the idea that the men of the rebel legion would rather surrender than be slaughtered in their tents by their fellows.

That was why he was now sailing through the darkness below Caitlys Shadowsong and her hawk, with an improvised leather harness attached to the strap that held Vengirasse's saddle serving as the only thing between him and a short but fatal fall to earth.

Three centurions dangled alongside and behind him. They were tied in pairs with two on the left side of the giant bird and two on the other. They were, if possible, even unhappier than he was, as he could hear their pained grunts and stifled curses over the rush of the night wind. In addition to the helpless feeling of being hung down over the ground, the straps from the heavy packs on their backs pressed their armor uncomfortably hard against the shoulders. Theuderic, listening to them, was happy he was laden with neither armor nor pack, but only a large leather pouch containing torches and some flints and steel, which were entirely superfluous for a battlemage.

The Amorrans believed he was the Lady Shadowsong's personal guard, hence the necessity of his involvement. They didn't know he was a mage, but that didn't prevent him from using his magesight. His night vision was not as keen as either of the two elves', but it was considerably better than the near-blindness of the Amorrans in the dark. Also, he had a feeling that his esoteric abilities might be useful in a pinch.

Valerius Clericus had made it abundantly clear to Caitlys that she could not, even on pain of death, reveal her sorcerous talents unless she wanted to risk being immediately murdered by his men. But of course, the young general hadn't said anything to Theuderic, not realizing that he too was a trained mage. So Theuderic was relatively confident that, in all the confusion and darkness, the ignorant Amorrans wouldn't recognize anything short of explosive pyrotechnics as being magical in source.

The basic concept was simple. Two cohorts were to take positions about two hundred paces from the north and south gates, respectively, of the permanent castra they had visited so briefly before. Once the pair of guards who walked a torchlit patrol on the battlements between the northeast corner of the wall and the north gate turned toward the gate, Caitlys would drop them down silently behind the guards, where Theuderic and the three centurions would ambush them, then take out the two guards and the guard captain at the gate. Everything depended upon this, so if they failed, the attack would be called off, and the waiting cohorts would melt away into the night.

It was a low-risk, high-reward plan, and Theuderic would have thoroughly approved of it were he not one of the four men who would find themselves behind in the midst of a roused and vengeful Amorran legion if anything went awry.

He felt himself swinging to one side as Vengirasse flew over the southern cohort and made a gentle, semicircular turn. The heavy whoosh-

whoosh as the bird flapped its wings to pick up speed sounded almost deafening in his ears and he marveled that the guards on the wall couldn't hear it. He looked down as the bird stopped beating its wings and began to make another turn and saw the northern cohort was in place as well. His heart began beating faster as the warhawk glided lower and lower in haunting silence toward the dark mass of the castra's thick walls. Where were the guards? As he withdrew a knife from its scabbard on his belt, he picked out the torch, which was near the northeast corner. But which way was it moving?

As the wall rushed toward him, he saw with some relief that the torch was moving back toward the center, toward the gate. One moment they were twenty paces above the ground, and the next they were right above the bricks of the battlements. There was a sudden pressure on his chest, and his legs swung forward as if he was on a swing as Vengirasse, on command, raised its wings and beat them backward, slowing itself so that it was nearly suspended.

This was the moment! Theuderic slashed at the rope holding him aloft, once, twice. On the third attempt, he fell to the bricks, landing on his cloth-wrapped forearms and knees. That cushioned most of the blow, but it stung nevertheless. He heard a painful grunt as one of the centurions landed a moment later behind him.

"One," he heard Nebridius, the centurion in command, whisper. The other two responded in kind, followed by Theuderic. "Savonder, with me. Marinus, Lucilius, other side. No signal. Just take the second man when you hear me take the first."

Theuderic crouched low by the centurion's side, watching as the guards turned leisurely around and the torch came closer. And closer.

In a moment, the small circle of illumination would fall upon them where they crouched in the shadows of the crenellations, and they would have only a split second to silence the men before they could cry out. Unless, of course, fate happened to be on their side. And by fate, Theuderic meant himself.

A small gesture loosed the spell he'd prepared earlier, and a sudden gust of wind blew the torch out. The two Amorrans stopped, afraid of a misstep in the darkness with their night eyes ruined by the flame.

"What happened?" the second guard asked.

"Damn thing blew out," the one with the torch said.

But that was all he said as Nebridius was quick to recognize the opportunity and take full advantage of it. He pounced in the darkness like an owl on a rat and killed the man, stabbing him in the throat and easing his body to the bricks without making a sound. The other two centurions were just a little louder, but nearly as quick in killing the other guard.

"Get that damn thing lit!" Nebridius ordered.

Theuderic fumbled for the torch, found it, then called fire to light the torch again, pretending to strike a nonexistent flint. Once lit, he stood up and began walking slowly away from the gate, as if he were the guard on patrol. By the time he reached the northeast corner, checked to confirm the presence of a bolt-thrower, and walked back to the gate, the three centurions had slain the two additional guards as well as their captain.

Instead of opening the gate, however, they slipped off their packs and removed the weighted rope ladders inside. They anchored the ladders to the battlements and threw the ropes down the outside of the wall.

"Walk down to the other corner and back," Nebridius whispered to Theuderic. "Walk slow. Lucilius, go with him."

Theuderic nodded. Overhead, a large shadow briefly blocked out the stars as the warhawk ghosted silently over them and toward the waiting cohort. He couldn't see Caitlys, but he waved to her all the same, knowing that her elven eyes would permit her to recognize him.

Those giant hawks were remarkably useful for a broad range of applications, he mused, wondering if it might be worthwhile to try the binding spell on another species more amenable to magical influence than dragons. Or perhaps they could begin breeding their own warhawks.

The century assigned to lead the assault was already clambering up the ladders when he and Lucilius returned to the gate, and they continued their slow, measured stroll as the armored legionaries, led by a conturbium of archers, passed them and quietly made their way along the wall toward the guards on the southern gate, taking possession of each mounted bolt thrower as they did so. To Theuderic's surprise, the young Amorran commander climbed the rope ladder himself, and both Nebridius and Lucilius beamed with pride as he clapped them on the back in a quiet gesture of approval.

A loud caw ripped across the sky and was followed by four short blasts on a horn. In answer, over one hundred torches were rapidly lit and held up by men standing upon the walls.

Thousands of men began to emerge from their tents, nearly all of them naked or nearly so. As they did, a flaming arrow buried itself in the ground, and both the northern and southern gates burst open, revealing multiple columns of fully armored legionaries holding shields and pila at the ready. Along the battlements, the scorpios had been lifted from their emplacements, turned about, and pointed down into the camp.

The young Amorran stood before two draconarii, one holding the black banner of Legio XVII, the other holding the red banner of Amorr. "In the name of House Valerius," he shouted, "I call the legate Lucius Gerontius to answer for his treason against the Senate and People."

Gerontius, wearing no more than a wool tunic and pantalons, had stumbled out from the large wooden structure near the Forum that had been built in the location where the command tents were usually erected. He was a big man, with a quantity of fat layered over a considerable quantity of muscle. Even without any badge of office, he radiated power and authority.

"What madness is this?" Gerontius's deep voice made that of the Valerian's sound like a pubescent boy's. "Who are you, Tribune, to call me to anything? Get down off my walls and explain what this is all about before I send my men up there to drag you down and give you a whipping!"

"I am Marcus Valerius Clericus, and I am the senior commanding officer of Legio XVII! I see no banner bearing the SPA on these walls, legate. Are you still loyal to Amorr, Gerontius? Do you still honor your vows to serve my House?"

The legate looked around at the centurions who had rushed to his side. They all stared at him expectantly, but none of them dared to speak. Finally, he cleared his throat. "Ah, Clericus. You are Corvus's son, of course. Yes, you know well I honor my vows to your noble House!"

"Excellent," Clericus called down to him. "Then order your men back to their tents and turn yourself over to Centurion Proculus, at the Praetorian Gate, in the name of House Valerius!"

The legate spread his hands. "Come now, Clericus, this must be a tremendous misunderstanding. It is a mistake! Come down from there and let us discuss this like civilized men, commander to commander. We should not bark at each other like dogs in front of our men."

Theuderic was standing close enough to the young Amorran to hear him swear under his breath. "I see that you did not answer my question about your loyalty to the Senate and People, Gerontius. Mark this. I do not discuss anything with traitors. Cassabus?"

"Sir?" called back a voice from the darkness nearby.

"If you please."

A deafening crack nearly sent Theuderic jumping off the wall. The noise was followed by a violent clattering sound as the bolt thrower hurled its bolt toward its target below. At such a close range, the war machine could hardly miss. The heavy bolt hit the legate squarely in the center of his chest, hurling him backward and pinning him to the ground with his arms and legs splayed. The spray of blood that erupted from his pulverized chest covered him from head to knees. It was obvious to everyone that he had been instantly killed.

"So dies Gerontius the traitor and the enemy of Amorr!" the Valerian shouted. "Men of Legio XV, are you traitors too?"

"No," a few hundred men shouted.

"Men of Legio XV, are you enemies of Amorr?"

"No!" several thousand more answered this time.

"Men of Legio XV, are you enemies of House Valerius?"

"No!"

"I am glad to hear it. Return to your tents now. Your centurions will have orders for you in the morning." The young commander pointed to the center of the fortress, where the two roads that bisected it met. "In the meantime, I want the Primus Pilus and the senior centurions from each cohort to meet me and my officers in the Forum. Do you hear me, Legio XV?"

"Ave!" nearly every single one of the six thousand men of Legio XV answered, followed by the meaty sound of hundreds of fists striking bare chests.

As Valerius Clericus and his officers went down the stairs that led from the battlements to the ground, Theuderic saw the great warhawk landing in the darkness outside the walls, well beyond the limits of any man without magesight. Caitlys gestured at him—angrily, he thought— which mystified him in light of how everything seemed to have gone much better than planned. He too walked down the stairs, then past the century at the gate and out into the night.

"What were you thinking, you idiot!" Caitlys snarled at him so ferociously he thought she was going to hit him. "I saw you snuff out that torch!"

"What torch?" he feigned innocence. "I did nothing of the sort. I think it was the wind from your bird's passing, actually. Most fortuitous."

She stared at him in the starlight, as if by sheer force of will she could lay bare his guilt. Then she shrugged and unfurled a rope ladder. "If you want to return to the encampment, get on. Unless, of course, you prefer a legion of Amorrans to the Lady Everbright."

He laughed and clambered atop the resting hawk. By now, he was able to find the saddle straps and tie himself on without even looking, although he still tested the leather with a few firm tugs before telling the elfess he was ready. She urged the giant beast into the night sky without so much as a word of warning to him, but for some reason he found the violent jerks to be a little less terrifying when it was hard to see exactly how high above the ground they were.

Vengirasse had barely reached his cruising altitude when Caitlys leaned back toward him. "Magus?" she called.

"Yes?"

"Are you firmly secured?"

"Yeah, of course…." An evil thought occurred to him. He felt about his waist and realized that somehow, all three straps had come undone. He grabbed tightly to the pommel, knowing it was futile if Vengirasse tilted too far to one side or the other, dropped suddenly, or even made a tight turn.

"Is something wrong?" Caitlys laughed, a slightly lower version of Lithriel's high-pitched elven cackle that made his skin crawl, and she caused the hawk to bank to the left.

Theuderic could feel his body sliding slowly, oh so slowly, off the saddle, and he leaned the other way to compensate. "Well, now that you happen to ask…"

"Do I have your attention?" she asked.

"Absolutely," he avowed with utter conviction.

"Good," she said, and to his relief the bird leveled out its flight again. "Let us be clear about two things, little magus. First, if you ever insult me by attempting to hoodwink me in such a painfully transparent manner again, I will feed your liver and eyeballs to Vengirasse. They are a particular favorite of his. Second, if you ever disobey me or Marcus Valerius again, particularly with regards to the use of sorcery or sorcerous items, I will have Vengirasse take you in his claws and drop you from such heights that you will run out of breath with which to scream before you strike the ground. I will not find myself burning on a pyre because a stupid human magus can't keep his magic under control!"

Theuderic sat silent and motionless behind the high elfess. Then, in a very humble and respectful voice, he asked for her permission to retie the straps that held him to the saddle. She didn't answer, but a moment later, the leather started moving rapidly of its own accord, like small constrictors seizing their prey. It was only then that he realized his pantalons were soaked with urine.

THE CROWS

E YEPOPPER followed twenty or thirty of his fellow crows as they rode the north wind and cawed excitedly back and forth. Death was in the air.

It was in the scent left behind by the huge masses of men below. It was in the shape of the formations being formed on opposite sides of the valley. It was in the massive black murder of crows that was continuing to grow like a thundercloud in the skies over the armies. And it was in the cruelty of the ravens that swept back and forth over the coming battlefield like a giant demon's hand enacting a curse upon the earthbound race of Man.

Soon they would feast. Soon, but not yet.

Eyepopper let out a loud, raucous caw, and with it, inadvertently defecated without even realizing he had done so. He beat his wings to catch up with the others, heading south.

Centurion Bauto was less than entirely pleased as he looked up the hill at the waiting enemy forces.

Where had the younger Marcus Valerius come by a second legion? And how was it that Magnus hadn't heard about it? Winter was no time to be campaigning. The only thing that had convinced Bauto and his fellow centurions that leaving the castra at Aviglianus and marching north was worthwhile was the wily old ex-consul's assurance that they would surprise his nephew—and his one legion—if they did so. Bauto figured Magnus was right and a winter attack was the last thing the half-trained men of Legio XVII and their inexperienced commander would expect. So how was it that they'd been intercepted by not one, but two, legions three days south of Montmila, two legions that were now looking down on them, well-rested, as Bauto and his men trudged up the snow-slick hill?

As far as he could tell, the younger Marcus Valerius had played the elder one by leading his uncle to believe their lines would meet halfway. Bauto's century, the third of the fifth cohort, was at the front, between the fourth century on their right and the cavalry guarding the legion's left flank, and they found themselves facing an alarmingly long uphill march into battle, now that the legions opposing them had suddenly come to a halt. Somehow, despite having two legions to his uncle's one, the younger Valerian had stolen a march on them and reached the valley first in order to seize the higher ground to the east.

Then, to top it all off, his draconarii had sounded the advance early this morning, triggering Legio VII's own advance in response, as per the norm. But no sooner had they begun to move forward, expecting to meet their opposing numbers in the middle of the valley, than the two loyalist legions had unexpectedly halted in their tracks, holding their ground and forcing Bauto and the rest of Legio VII to come to them. It was a long and difficult slog uphill over ground that was slick and white with the morning frost, and with their position already fixed, the loyalist legions would be able to bring their war machines to bear on the men of Legio VII as they struggled toward the waiting enemy, while the Vallyrian rebels would have to move their scorpios and ballistae forward before being able to return what was sure to be a hailstorm of rocks and other missiles.

This wasn't right! It should be them up there on that hill, watching as the enemy exhausted themselves and waiting to kill them. One of the reasons he and the other officers had been supremely confident taking the field this morning despite being outnumbered was their uniform belief that Magnus was worth at least two legions on his own. But it had been years since he'd won his last battle. Was it possible the genius was gone? Or worse, had passed on to his brother's son? The boy's father, Corvus, until his return to Amorr and elevation to the consulate their stragister militum, had been no slouch as a general, and there had been tribunes with less impressive military lineages who had led their legions to victory in the past.

Bauto shrugged. As far as he knew, this was all some trick Magnus was playing on his nephew. He'd lived through too many battles to worry about the outcome this early in the proceedings. And as a centurion, he had too much on his mind to worry about things that weren't his responsibility. He didn't have the luxury of fear, not with eighty men to keep in line.

"Get a move on," Bauto shouted at his grumbling, stumbling men, several of whom were dragging their feet and threatening to turn their orderly formation, ten wide and eight deep, into a ragged mess. They were all veterans, some with nearly twenty years to their name, and they saw the developing danger as readily as he did. "Form up, you worms. Keep the bloody line straight!"

After an exhausting slog that, thanks to the poor footing, took longer than it should have, they were coming into range of the loyalist war machines. Bauto was taking a deep breath, just about to order his men to raise their shields and brace themselves for incoming fire, when the horns from the rear unexpectedly sounded a halt.

He shouted at his signifer, who planted the century's standard and fumbled for his horn before repeating the call, and the Third finally came to a stop, more or less in line with the rest of the cohort to their left. The cavalry was less precise, as usual, but the knights gradually got their horses reined in despite many a tossed tail or snorting protest.

Now what in the frozen hells was going on now? He hoped to God they weren't about to be ordered to retreat, as the enemy horse was looming to their left, and retreating would be an open invitation to ride right over them. Even the cavalry screening their flank wouldn't be much use, as the loyalists had three times more horse than Legio VII did, and most of it seemed to be stationed right in front of them.

"See if anyone in the Fourth knows what's going on," he told his optio, Sextus Phobus, who saluted and headed off toward the next century at a jog. Then he felt something strike his left shoulder with a dull, plopping sound. With the sour cynicism of the true veteran, Bauto looked down expecting to see an arrow sticking out or perhaps something even worse. But it was nothing, merely a dollop of white slime decorating his well-polished armor, and he looked up to see the culprits had already passed by well overhead. Bird shit, of all things.

The men nearby laughed, but he knew better than to chastise them. One of the first things a centurion learned was that chickenshit was for the castra, not the battlefield.

"Hey, that's good luck, sir," one of them called.

"Come here, Leporius, and I'll rub some of that luck off on you!" he called back, to the delight of the others nearby. His men were cold, wet, bored, and on edge, a potentially lethal combination. Fortunately, the aerial assault kept them amused for a while, and Phobus returned before their discipline began to crack.

He told Bauto of the modified plan of attack.

"Magnus saw they weren't coming off the hill, so he wanted to give us a breather before we make the push. We're to go at them fast and hard. As soon as the horns sound the charge, shields up and double-time."

Bauto nodded. He didn't like it, as they'd have to climb more than two hundred paces under fire. But this rest should let them get there with enough energy to engage the enemy's front lines. And then the battle would truly begin. He sent Phobus to spread the word down the line, then he gave the new instructions to the century's signifer himself.

His wind was coming back and his calves and lower back had ceased to burn, so he considered the rest to have negated the larger part of the younger Valerian's discreditable tactic. But even if Magnus had swiftly countered the other's move, Bauto knew he wasn't the only centurion who found it worrisome that the other side's young general had been able to get a leg up on the old fox twice.

The horn sounded, and the Third's signifer repeated it, blowing double-time before the last note had finished. They were on the move, quickly now, and as Bauto expected, they'd barely taken four steps before the enemy's artillery loosed for the first time.

"Shields!" he shouted even though the front line was already a wall of black steel. Not that steel would do much to protect the men against the big wooden bolts fired by the scorpios or the huge rocks flung by the ballistae. "Move it, move it! Keep it moving!"

They were close enough that he could hear the creaking of wood and the snapping of the tormenta as the loyalist artillery fired over one hundred bolts into their lines. He winced as the unmistakable sound of the big wooden bolts slamming into metal, flesh, and bone was followed immediately by the screams of men in pain, but the screams were all to his right, and a quick glance along the line showed that none of his own men had been hit. Even so, their movement faltered.

So he joined his voice to the chorus of centurions urging their centuries on.

"Don't stop! If you stop, you die! Forward! Faster, now, faster!"

Now the ballistae loosed, but again, the enemy was targeting the centuries to their right, mostly those in the center of the advancing legion. Aware that they were unscathed, the men of the Third didn't slow this time, and they began to edge in front of the rest of the legionary line. Bauto was just about to rein them in when he saw the archers slipping forward between the enemy principes and begin forming a screen in front of them. He waited until the archers were bringing up their bows, then shouted a reminder to his men.

"Shields up! Keep moving! Shields up, damn you!"

He raised his own shield just in time, as he felt a sharp blow, heard a dull thud, and then saw the shattered remnants of the arrow shaft under his feet. He heard someone curse behind him, but he didn't spare them a look, as he could see that their tight formation had largely defeated the missile attack.

The archers rained down five more volleys upon them as they continued to grimly march up the hill, until some unheard command was given, and the screen dissolved, the archers disappearing back into the enemy lines like water being drained from the bottom of a bowl. The Third gave out a ragged cheer, but it was short-lived as they saw the first row of the enemy infantry begin to raise their spears in preparation for the casting of the heavy pilum.

They were close enough to the enemy lines now that Bauto could easily read the numbers of the cohort and century painted onto their shields. To his surprise, they were the first of the second cohort, by tradition one of the weaker cohorts. Better yet, they were the green youths of Legio XVII, soldiers of the new legion whose battle experience was scanty and most likely limited to a few minor encounters with goblins.

The sight was an encouraging one, and he knew his hard-bitten veterans, most of whom bore scars from more than two dozen battles, would feel the same. But that didn't mean the boys weren't properly trained, and from their uphill position, they could throw their spears sooner and with more force than Bauto's men could.

The opposing centurion, his bright armor and transverse crest easily spotted, shouted, and the front two lines stepped forward, brought up their arms, and hurled their pila in one massive volley.

Unlike the earlier attacks by the ballistarii and the archers, this one hammered directly into the Third, and the heavy spears drove through shields and armor alike. Of the ten men in the front of the line, four went down, and a fifth was left open and vulnerable as the pilum's spearhead fouled his shield, forcing him to drop it.

"Second rank, move up! Fill in the gaps!" Bauto was beginning to sweat now with his exertions, and the battle was heating up too. He'd felt the wind as one pilum in the first volley had passed just over his left shoulder and another one in the second had struck the ground right at his feet, nearly impaling his right foot. But now it was time to give the enemy century a taste of their own medicine. "Pila ready, throw on my command!"

He didn't carry a pilum himself, but he withdrew a verutum from its slot inside his concave shield and raised it high. He glanced across to see that the men had their pila up over their shoulders, then he shouted as he threw his little javelin at the enemy, knowing it was unlikely to do more than bounce off a legionary's helmet or shield.

But the seventy-some pila that followed it were another matter entirely, and he could see the front ranks of the enemy century stagger and gaps opened up in the black-faceted face of the shield wall as wounded men fell back and others, their shields encumbered by as many as four pila in one case, were forced to cast them to the ground.

Now was the moment to charge. A scant distance now separated the two lines, and Bauto drew his sword. He had just raised it and turned to the left in order to tell the signifer to sound the charge when something struck him in the side, under his right arm. It didn't hurt, but he grunted as the force of the impact caused him to twist and stumble. A heavy weight on his right side somehow interfered with his balance, and he fell to the cold, hard ground, still wet from the half-melted frost.

"Sir? Sir!"

He saw Phobus's face leaning in toward his own and saw the man's mouth moving, but he couldn't seem to make sense of what the optio was saying. The charge, Bauto tried to tell his subordinate. Order the charge! You have to tell the men to charge now! But the optio didn't seem to understand him. He had turned his face away from Bauto and was shouting something toward the men behind them.

Then something seemed to pull Phobus, and the Third, and the very battlefield itself away from Bauto, like a curtain being rapidly raised at the theatre. Bauto struggled, reaching out, trying to grab his optio and make sure Phobus understood what the men needed to do. But Bauto couldn't reach him, and as the sounds of battle, all the clashing of metal and the shouting of men, subsided into darkness, the centurion was still trying to comprehend why the optio hadn't heard him.

Paccius Vintius raised his fist in triumph when he saw the centurion abruptly whirl about and fall. It was glorious to see that Vintius had felled the man with his pilum. Indeed, it was still sticking out of his side as he lay on the ground.

"Did you see that?" he asked Orfitus, standing three paces to his left. "Did you see that? I got the centurion!"

"Sure you did," Orfitus replied laconically. "Yeah, and I think I got bloody Magnus with mine. Better get your sword out, though. Here they come!"

It was an intimidating sight. The enemy legion looked considerably more dangerous now that they were only a few armslengths away than they had when they were struggling up the frost-slicked slope earlier in the morning.

For the first time since he'd kissed the eagle, Vintius wondered if he'd made the right decision in joining the legion. He hadn't minded the training last summer. It had been hard and repetitive, but it had also been easier and more interesting than working in the fields had ever been. And the pay was good too, so good that he'd had to work on developing new vices just to spend it all. He'd also learned, much to his delight, that women liked soldiers, so much so that sometimes you didn't even have to pay for it. That had never happened to him back on the farm.

On the other hand, on the farm, no one had ever come running toward him with a sword in his hand and a look of raw hatred on his scarred face.

The worst that had ever happened there was the time Pacuvio, the butcher's son, had knocked him down for trying to talk Pacuvio's sister into showing him her fica. It was the great regret of his life that he had never succeeded in laying eyes upon that wonder. Sometimes, when he lay with one of the camp whores, especially one with long black hair, he closed his eyes and pretended it was her.

Whang! The heavy clash of a sword against his shield brought him brutally back to the battlefield.

He was startled to see that the rebel legionary was practically an old man, with deep lines carved into his face by nothing worse than age. He wasn't a feeble old man, though, as another crashing blow upon his shield half-deadened his arm.

Vintius was confused for a moment, wondering why the rebel wasn't thrusting his sword as they'd all been trained, until he realized that the rebel wasn't attempting to stab him, but was instead trying to beat his shield aside. He tried a thrust of his own, but it was too slow and cautious, and his opponent blocked it easily with his own sword before hammering Vintius's shield again, half-knocking it aside.

Vintius stabbed at the man's angry brown eyes and was rewarded with a flinch. It was a small victory, but it gave him confidence that he could survive this fight, that he could survive the battle.

Then the man ducked behind his shield and ran right at Vintius, smashing violently into him, shield to shield. The force of the blow sent Vintius reeling backward, where he was caught by the legionary waiting to take his place should he fall. His opponent couldn't follow up his advantage, however, as a man in the third rank jabbed his pilum out and struck the rebel squarely on the shield, pushing him back and giving Vintius time to get his balance again.

Truly frightened now, Vintius shouted as he ran at his opponent and bashed at the other's shield. He could see irritation in the man's eyes and he stabbed at them, forcing the other to jerk his head sideways to avoid the jab. But the movement caused the man to shift his shield to the right, just enough to expose his left side.

Vintius saw the opening. With a third thrust he managed to stab the man's hip just under the mail that covered his torso. It wasn't a deep cut, but he could feel that it went to the bone, and he heard the main cry out in pain. When he pulled back his sword for another thrust, its tip was red with blood.

But before he could follow up the attack with another one, his opponent had fallen back within the ranks of the enemy lines and was replaced by another man, this one younger but equally hard-eyed and at least a head taller.

"Got lucky, did you, puppy?" his new opponent spat contemptuously at him, blocking his first thrust without even taking his eyes away from Vintius's face. He was a big man, and his neck was thick and muscular like a bear's. He blocked the second and third thrust just as easily, not even making an attempt to strike back. Then a fourth, followed by a fifth. "That's it, puppy! Get it all out!"

Vintius was panting now, and despite the hours at the training block, his shoulders and forearms were starting to burn. Holding up his shield was an increasing struggle, and the point of his sword was now dropping toward the ground. Fear swelled inside him as his new opponent bared his teeth in a confident smile, as he realized that the man was about to move to the attack.

Where was the horn? Wasn't it time for the first rotation yet? Desperate to buy himself time, he summoned what felt like his last reserves of strength and leaped at the big rebel, bringing his sword down in a powerful arc to smash the man's shield aside.

Only it wasn't there. Instead, pain exploded in his chest as the man's sword punched through the meticulously polished scales of his armor, which protected him about as well as an insect's carapace from a man's iron-shod boot.

Vintius dropped his shield and tried to pull back, but the weight of his body held him suspended on the killing steel that ran through his body. He shrieked and tried to cry for help from Orfitus, but little more than blood came out of his mouth. Then, the ground was rushing up at him as the sword abruptly vanished from his chest, leaving only the terrible pain behind.

"Didn't nobody ever tell you not to lead with your rear, puppy?" he heard an amused voice call from the sky. It sounded very far away.

He lay motionless on the ground, his lifesblood leaking into the sodden earth also watered by his tears. Why didn't I stay on the farm? he wondered as the pain in his chest gradually faded. It wasn't such a bad life, in the end. His last thought was the bitter regret that he'd never even dared to try kissing Pacuvio's sister.

Manlius pulled out his sword from the stricken boy's torso and laughed at his dying opponent. A simple sidestep, and the lad had all but impaled himself on Manlius's sword. He didn't bother to finish the boy off. He had killed enough men and orcs over the years to know a mortal wound when he felt one. Instead, he looked left and right, seeing if he could sneak in a strike to help one of his line mates before he took on his next opponent.

These brats from Legio XVII were greener than an apple in spring, and he could see that two or three more had already fallen to the more experienced swords of the Third. No wonder Magnus had simply flung them forward despite their inferior ground and without care for their lack of numbers. This was like killing kittens.

But even kittens had claws. The centurion—that was just bad luck. He hoped Musius Bauto wasn't too badly hurt. Manlius hadn't actually seen Bauto go down, but since it was the voice of Phobus, the optio, bawling out orders and encouragement now, it appeared that the word the centurion had been wounded by an arrow was legitimate.

No opportunities presented themselves, so Manlius took note of the young legionary who came forward to fill the gap in the line left by his idiot predecessor. Manlius doubted he'd be so fortunate as to find his second opponent as readily accommodating as the first, but again he waited patiently, letting the other man uselessly expend his energy by banging on Manlius's shield to no avail.

It was almost too easy. He watched as the other's shield dropped lower by a finger or two with each exchange, and he kept an eye on the sword that came back lower with each futile thrust and jab. Soon enough, the opening for which he'd been waiting appeared. He stepped into a half-hearted thrust and blocked it aggressively with his shield then slashed at the other's eyes over the man's lowered shield. His opponent had no choice but to reel backward and to his left to avoid the flashing blade, leaving him off-balance and vulnerable to Manlius's next move.

Manlius put his shoulder behind his shield and smashed his full weight into the reeling man, who went down onto his left side as his sword went flying out of reach. Manlius continued charging forward until he was crouching over the prone man, but he held his shield up high to block both the thrusting pilum and the downward stroke of a sword from the ranks behind his fallen foe.

Even as he blocked their attempts to defend their companion, he was stabbing downward, once, twice, three times. Once, his sword met armor and slid off it into the ground, but the other two attempts met with flesh that gave way before it. Without looking to see how badly he'd wounded the man, he leaped back into the lines before the legionaries on his left and right could cut him off from the rest of the Third.

Manlius was breathing hard, but he wasn't the least bit tired. He felt more alive than ever as he saw four pairs of hands reach out from the ranks behind to drag his wounded foe off toward the rear, leaving a nice, wide trail of blood behind him. Six-to-one that man would die before the end of the day, Manlius thought, satisfied. With that much blood, at least one of his blows must have struck something vital. Two up, two down. He could do this all day. All bloody day!

He stared with no little amusement at his third opponent, who still had his pilum and appeared to be intent upon using it instead of his sword, poking it out in a manner that betrayed his panic. Manlius could see the fear in the young man's green eyes, and he laughed out loud, which seemed to further frighten the boy.

"Didn't anyone teach you anything?" he marveled, shaking his head, as the head of the spear licked out at him and back again like a large, black snake's tongue.

The boy dropped his shield and jabbed the pilum toward him again.

Tiring of the game, Manlius grabbed the spear by the shank and jerked it past his left side. As he expected, the terrified youth instinctively clung to his weapon and was pulled forward by it, thus allowing Manlius to drive his sword right into his face, above his helmet's cheekpad and through his left eye, killing him instantly. He had to push the dead man off his blade with his foot, which he did before picking up his shield again and stepping back into the line.

Three up, three down. Manlius was beginning to think that actual kittens might put up more of a fight than this piss-poor excuse for an Amorran legion.

He flicked his blade at the next man to step forward, sprinkling his face with the blood of his predecessor.

"Do you renounce the devil and all his works, little one?" Manlius mocked his next victim. "Best do so now, since you'll be seeing him soon enough!"

Then an unseen fist smashed into his throat. Manlius stumbled backward, his eyes bulging in disbelief. He hadn't even seen his opponent move! What had happened?

He tried to bring up his shield, but his strength was suddenly sapped by some mysterious force, and he couldn't even seem to move.

What was going on? A fiery hand gripped his throat, burning him even as it mercilessly choked him. He tried to call out to his fellows, but only blood came out of his mouth. His mind screamed the furious curses that his voice could not. He took one last defiant step toward the enemy, then toppled over onto his face.

"Now there was a throw!" Parthender complimented Orodes as they saw the big legionary, his larynx crushed by the perfectly placed stone, crash to the ground like a felled tree. "The damned fool never knew what hit him."

"Rest in peace." Orodes lifted a hand in blessing the man he'd just slain. Then he shook a finger at his friend. "Don't mock the dead. One day, we too will be in their number. And we may hope that he is not damned, but rather is now at peace in the bosom of the Inviolate. It is not for us to judge."

Parthender sighed as he began slowly whirling his sling behind him. "Can't you, for once, just be happy killing somebody who needed killing?"

"Never." Orodes shook his head and withdrew another lead bullet from his pouch. He ran his thumb over the sigil carved in the side, as was his habit. "We diminish ourselves, even as we exalt those we kill."

There was a soft snap as Parthender released his bullet, which disappeared into the mass of the enemy legion without any noticeable effect. "Then I suppose you're pretty damned diminished by now, Orodes! For someone who says he regrets killing, you're rather good at it."

"God would not give us gifts He did not intend for us to use," Orodes observed, scanning the slope below for a likely target. "If we are to praise Him in all things, how shall I not praise Him even as I slay the children of His Creation? In any event, we should be grateful. Think of how our forefathers would envy us!"

"That one, there, the signifer. He's a ways off—think you can hit him?"

Orodes put a hand over his eyes against the sun, peered in the direction Parthender was pointing, and continued as if he had not been interrupted. "Our ancestors fought the empire with great bravery and died. And here we find ourselves, after eight generations under the imperial heel, eight generations filled with countless prayers for deliverance, watching Amorrans kill one another and being paid well to kill more of them ourselves. Are we not blessed?"

"I've never been able to tell if you're a philosopher or a lunatic." Parthender followed the path of the shot as it flew toward the Amorran holding the third century's banner.

"You can, however, tell that that one is fortunate," Orodes said, chuckling, as the banner wavered below, its bearer lurching to one side after having been struck, more or less harmlessly, on the side of the helmet. "God has spared him for now, so who am I to object?"

Parthender didn't reply. His head exploded in an obscene splatter of red mist as a rock significantly larger than the pellets they'd been hurling at the legionaries below sent his headless body flopping to the ground, then crushed Orodes's right arm, shoulder, and hip as it bounced.

As rapidly as it had come, the boulder departed, continuing on its bloody path through the crowd of Balerans behind them.

Stunned by the awesome violence of the unexpected assault, Orodes lay on his back, staring up at the lightly clouded sky in mute astonishment. It took him a few moments to realize what had happened, and when he did, he began to laugh at the foolish arrogance of Man, of which he knew he was the first and foremost example.

He raised his head long enough to see the red ruin of his friend lying nearby, then he looked down at his own mangled body. Poor Parthender. At least it had been quick for him. Orodes felt he would not have minded missing out on the pain that now threatened to transform him from a rational being into a mindless, screaming animal. But at least death would come soon, judging by the quantity of blood that was seeping out onto the ground.

More importantly, soon he would finally have all the answers that had so long eluded him. Forgive me, Inviolate Lord, he begged, for I have sinned against You, and to You I commend my tattered, blackened, prideful, blood-stained soul, in the name of Your Most Holy and Immaculate Son.

I praise you in all things, Lord, even this, my final hour. *Nunc dimittis servum tuum, Domine, secundum verbum tuum in pace.*

The Baleran died, still staring open-eyed at the sky, with the edges of his mouth turned up in a faintly ironic smile.

Clodius Secundus winced as Fuscus, his optio, put his hands on his hips and shook his head in disgust. The stone his crew had just loosed went bouncing wildly among a group of slingers, a full ten degrees away from where he'd told them to throw it.

"Sordes, Secundus," Fuscus said. "What in the stinking sulfurous smoke of Satan's fartbiscuit was that? You do know what 'cavalry' means, right? You know, the plummy arses who sits on the little horsies? The bastards that's riding this way now?"

"Yes, sir!"

"Then throw the damn rocks at them!" Fuscus screamed at him. "Magnus don't care about no pebble throwers. We got to thin out that horse before they run over our bleeding flank!"

The optio pointed, and Secundus could see that the loyalist horse had engaged their own cavalry and was steadily driving it back. In addition to having the advantage of the slope, they outnumbered the legion's horse by a significant margin, although the veteran knights of Legio VII seemed to be successfully executing a fighting retreat. Even if they weren't losing many riders as they withdrew from the battle, they were on the verge of leaving their infantry completely exposed to the enemy cavalry.

"We'll do better this time, sir. We were, uh, just trying to avoid our own horse."

Fuscus nodded angrily and stalked away to shout at another onager crew. Secundus turned to his two fellow crew members and shrugged. This particular machine had been a nightmare ever since they'd been assigned to it. But there was nothing to be done, so they put their shoulders to it and muscled it to a position where it was aiming just a little east of where the cavalry battle was most fiercely raging.

"Do you see that decurion?" Secundus pointed to one of the enemy knights who could just barely be distinguished from the others by his plumed helm. "We'll use him as our reference. If the left beam is warped, that might explain why we're dropping the rocks so far to the right of where we want them. Maybe we just have to compensate for it."

Together, they took another rock from the pile of eight remaining ones and loaded the big leather pouch. Fuscus inserted the pin to secure the arm, and the other two ballistarii winched it down, grunting as the twisted ropes were strained by the tremendous tension. Secundus nodded when the arm was down far enough and twirled his hammer. He eyed the decurion again, just to be sure of himself, and was raising his arm to drive the pin out and let the onager kick when the hidden fault in the wooden beam gave way.

The onager didn't kick so much as erupt. The wood splintered, the ropes snapped, and the rock simply dropped onto the ground with a dull thud.

Secundus screamed and clutched at his abdomen where a thick block of oak had gone all the way through him and poked out his back like a large, bloody wart.

"Am I going to die? Am I going to be all right?" He begged the optio to reassure him. "Please, I don't want to die! I didn't do anything wrong! I swear, it just went to pieces!"

Fuscus sighed and shook his head. "Bloody hell, Clodius, only you could get yourself wounded so bad when you're perfectly safe at the rear. Now shut up, knock off with the crying, and let's get you comfortable. We'll get a medicus over here to take that out, and you'll be fine. You'll be fine!"

Fuscus was lying. The optio was a mean, hard-hearted man. He'd seen scores of men under his command die. Clodius Secundus wasn't the first, and he wouldn't be the last.

Even so, Fuscus crouched down beside the stricken ballistarius and continued to talk with him until the unlucky young man finally stopped his pathetic crying. Then he reached out and gently closed the eyes on the tear-stained face before standing up and turning to the tribune that Magnus had sent to keep an eye on the right flank as it came under pressure from the enemy cavalry.

"Tell Magnus I'll want to know who sold us the beams for these onagers. We've got a big bone to pick with the thieving bastard."

The battle was proceeding beautifully according to plan, insofar as Nobilianus could see. The infantry was in a good position on the slope and holding strong despite the best efforts of the rebel legion to dislodge them. Now Legio XV's cavalry wing had finally been unleashed, and they were driving back the rebel horse with ease.

Magnus's knights were still holding their formation, retreating before each charge, only to regroup as soon as the tribune commanding the wing called them to heel. But the rebels lost a few more knights with each pass, riders they could not afford to lose, and as the wagons of the rebel baggage train came within sight, Nobilianus sensed that one more charge would break them.

He glanced back at his squadron, which had the honor of serving as spearhead to the three-hundred-strong wedge of the united cavalry wing. They were in good order, having lost only two men in the initial encounter. Unfortunately, one of them had been Carus, who'd taken a lance through the leg, leaving him with only one junior decurion. But, perhaps because they were fighting fellow Amorrans, his knights had so far been inclined to keep their customary freelancing to a minimum. Only a few of them still had their spears, but their swords would be sufficient.

The only question, to his mind, was whether they would be ordered to attack the baggage train or the left flank of the enemy foot. He hoped for the former, as there would be considerably more loot to be had from the train than from the pathetic corpses of the commoners.

The horn blew. Nobilianus drew his sword again and called out to his squadron.

"Wedge on me! This time they run! For Amorr and Vallyria!"

"Amorr and Vallyria!" the knights shouted back.

The charge began, slowly as it always did, with the horses trotting, then cantering, and then, to his savage satisfaction, he saw the enemy horse turn tail and flee instead of riding forth to meet them.

Seeing them turn, Nobilianus kicked Phasmatis into a full gallop. He could hear the thunder of the twenty-seven horses behind him as his men did the same. He was close enough now to see the faces of the rebel knights, white with fear as they lashed their horses, desperate to escape the field of battle.

"We have them!" he turned his head and shouted gleefully to no one in particular. The entire world was shaking and thundering, a glorious chaos of wind and the excited fever of the hunt, as he chased the fleeing rebels. He might have been alone instead of at the fore of some three hundred horse, or the lead hound in a pack chasing a terrified fox. And he was gaining on them!

At first, he thought his horse was simply faster. Then he realized the enemy was slowing, though he couldn't imagine why. As he galloped closer and closer to them, he could see they were forming into columns even as they continued to flee. What could possibly be the sense of that? The answer struck him just as the last line of the enemy horse broke apart, revealing the menacing, well-spaced lines of at least three centuries of infantry. The retreating horse disappeared down the columns opened for them like water running out a sieve.

No sooner had the last horse galloped through the gaps than the lines began to close, with each spearman in the second rank stepping forward and to the right to block the way forward.

Magnus had played them, Nobilianus realized with horror, and played them badly. With the charge already at full speed and the squadron wedge following upon his heels, there was no way to avoid crashing into the deadly forest of pila planted in the ground and waiting for them. Trying to stop would be futile and almost surely more fatal than trying to break through, so he aimed at a gap slightly to his left that a legionary had failed to fill, urged Phasmatis on with his heels, and prayed that the horse wouldn't shy from the spear wall.

"Amorr!"

He crashed into the enemy lines, slashing blindly to his left and to his right with his sword. Spearheads jabbed up toward him as he rode past, licking up past his face and then down again like lethal dragons' tongues. But aside from one that bounced off his shield, he was miraculously unharmed.

Somehow, he was very nearly through the infantry line! Then Phasmatis screamed and shuddered as one spear plunged into his breast, followed rapidly by two more in his right side. The mortally wounded horse twisted and tumbled, sending Nobilianus flying head over heels beyond the enemy's rear. He slammed onto the ground, fortunately on his back rather than his neck, but the force of the impact took his breath away.

The decurion lay there for a moment, heaving madly as he struggled for air, then rolled to his stomach and began to push himself up. He had just enough air to scream as the metal tip of the lance held by the enemy rider, now galloping back toward the melee, penetrated his mouth and punched through the back of his skull. His neck snapped and his body flopped over like a rag doll as his killer galloped past him, cursing and trying to free his fouled lance.

Aulan dragged the body of the dead decurion for some distance before concluding that his lance was hopelessly stuck. "Hey, you!" he shouted at a nearby legionary who was watching him with bemusement. "Make yourself useful!"

The soldier obediently jogged over, and with a little effort, managed to pull the lance free from the corpse. "Mind if I, uh, you know?" The gold ring on the dead man's finger clearly hadn't escaped his attention.

Aulan laughed and shook his head. "Not often you get to loot a decurion, eh? He's yours, but if he's got any papers on him, give them to your centurion."

"Yes, sir," the man saluted energetically. "Thank you, sir!"

Aulan acknowledged him with an indifferent nod and looked past the killing ground, where the three centuries of the first cohort were busy slaughtering the greater part of the younger Valerian's cavalry, which was now caught in his uncle's lethal trap. It was brutal butchery.

Several of his own squadrons were already chasing the few horsemen who'd somehow avoided the trap back up the hill, but Magnus had more in mind than the mere destruction of the enemy cavalry. Aulan waved to his draconarius, who blew the signal to gather on the banner, then had him follow at a slow trot around the infantry and up the slope. It wasn't long before the senior decurions were gathered around him, breathless and excited by how well the plan had worked.

"Well done, gentlemen. We've got a free hand now," Aulan observed. "So let's make the most of it and see what Legio XV is made of. Nothing much, I expect. We'll ride wide and hit them in the side. Give them room to run, though—they're more useful to us spooked than dead."

The infantry lines were still fully engaged when they reached the heights. They'd come under attack by some slingers but were taking no serious casualties as the ballistarii covering their movement from below soon had the slingers disrupted and retreating out of range in disarray. But whereas their own infantry managed a smooth rotation, Legio XV made a shambles of theirs as the rear ranks were more occupied with watching the approach of Aulan's wing than following their centurions' directions.

Aulan raised his hand, and the squadrons began to form up in three large wedges around him, as they'd previously arranged. He laughed as he saw the enemy flank start turning haphazardly before any signal was given. Their discipline was breaking down. He closed his hand, and in response, the knights began clashing their mailed fists on their shields and chanting.

"Magnus! Magnus! Magnus!"

He waited a moment, letting the terror build in the enemy formation, already under heavy pressure from the veteran infantry at their front. The infantry, sensing weakness, took up the chant and redoubled their efforts. The front line began to buckle.

That was the moment Aulan was waiting for. He whistled at his draconarius, who promptly sounded the charge. One hundred twenty knights roared in response, and the three wedges, each led by a much-decorated decurion, hurled themselves toward the enemy's right flank.

Fifty paces separated the points of the wedge from the enemy. Forty. Thirty. At twenty, Legio XV broke, the first of more than four thousand legionaries began to turn their backs to their attackers, and for the first time in history, a Valerian legion began to flee the field.

Victory! Aulan would have given much to see that clever bastard Clericus's face right now, realizing that he'd been outsmarted and outgeneraled by his uncle. But he made do with driving his lance into the back of a retreating legionary. He hoped that somewhere, somehow, his father was watching Valerians kill Valerians, and laughing.

As the battle raged up the hill, the bodies of men and horses below were forgotten.

But not by everyone.

Eyepopper came in steeply and landed awkwardly on a horse, from which he was promptly driven by a protesting raven half again his size.

He cawed in futile defiance, then hopped onto the chest of a man whose head was hanging awkwardly to the side, partially obscuring one eye.

Eyepopper turned his own head to the side, wondering how he might get at it, then he pecked eagerly at the more accessible orb. It burst open with the usual pop, and Eyepopper cheerfully began his much-anticipated repast with no small degree of relish.

MARCUS

FIVE days had passed since his unexpected defeat at the hands of Magnus. Five days and four mostly sleepless nights since his legion had retreated in shock and dismay from the battlefield to the legionary fortress at Montmila.

During the days, Marcus was too busy giving orders and keeping up a brave face for his men to dwell upon what had happened, though it nearly killed him to look them in the eyes.

He had failed them. All of them. He had failed the living, the wounded, and worst of all, the dead. Their fears that his youth and inexperience would let them down had come to pass, and at the very worst possible time. He knew that if he let them see weakness, if he let them see his remorse, he would lose them entirely. So he smiled, and nodded, and slapped them on the back. And he never showed them any sign of the doubts that filled his heart.

It was the nights he dreaded most. No sooner was he alone than he relived the battle and his preparations at least twenty times each night. There had been so many mistakes, but which one was the crucial one? Should he have ordered his horse not to pursue? He knew from personal experience how futile such orders could be when every knight was sure the enemy was ready to run. Had it been a mistake to reinforce Legio XV's knights with an entire wing from Legio XVII?

He'd had the numbers! He'd grabbed the better ground! He'd made the enemy come to him! He'd done everything right—everything except win.

One hundred fifty horse to his four hundred fifty, and they'd still destroyed two-thirds of his knights and driven his infantry from the field. How was that even possible? Was Magnus a genius? A wizard? He'd grown up in the man's house, he'd studied most of the man's battles, and yet he still couldn't figure out how his uncle could possibly have won the day with all the odds stacked against him. If he hadn't been there and witnessed it, he would not have believed it possible.

With the exception of the First Knights, who'd died on his shattered right flank, Legio XVII's losses hadn't actually been terribly severe. Most of the casualties were taken by Legio XV before they broke and ran, and before their senior centurions betrayed him by surrendering to his uncle the day after the battle.

At that single stroke, his fighting forces had gone from ten thousand to four thousand, while Magnus's had grown to the point that he now had more than three men for Marcus's two. And despite Legio XVII's successful retreat to Montmila, it was only a matter of time before he would have to decide whether to surrender it or order the men to take the field again despite being outnumbered and demoralized.

He stared down at the crumpled letter from Magnus, and unable to help himself, began reading it again. It was a portrait in magnanimity, carefully composed to spare his feelings and flatter whatever might remain of his pretensions. But his uncle's iron fist was there, unmistakably, with no pretensions of concealing it beneath the fine velvet glove.

To M. Valerius Clericus, tribunus militum, legatus locum Legio XVII

Montmila (Ianuarius)

My dear nephew and namesake, I hope you will allow me to congratulate you on your remarkable performance in admirably filling in for the late Marcus Saturnius as legatus locum tenens for Legio XVII. I know you well, Marcus, and I know how the sting of this defeat will be painful to you. But it is no hollow compliment when I tell you that I would count this among the foremost of my victories were it not for it having been won against my own House and my own legions. Your strategy was decisive, your tactics were sound, and even in defeat, your leadership was magnificent. Far more experienced generals than you have failed to execute such a well-disciplined fighting withdrawal from the battlefield.

But, as you have now learned, the wisdom of age and the lessons of experience will trump even the most gifted young mind. So I call upon you to heed that wisdom, to listen to the voice of that experience, and come to me. I do not ask you or your men to lay down your arms, as I will have need of them, come spring. I do not have so many officers of skill and experience at my disposal that I would spurn your services, nor will I hold against you what might be seen by some as a rebellion against the rightful Lord of your House. I am aware that you were only seeking to continue to serve Amorr and honor your tribune's oath to the best of your understanding and ability.

Your ability, as I always believed it would be, has proved prodigious. However, your understanding of the complicated and unprecedented situation that has arisen in Amorr, in Vallyria, and in the allied cities is understandably deficient. I shall, of course, be pleased to fully apprise you of it upon your arrival, but suffice it to say that the Amorr of the Senate and People we knew and served is no more.

While the empire and its trappings still exist in superficial form, there is no life in them. Not only are the imperial provinces in revolt, but after years of having their demands for full imperial citizenship rejected, in no small part due to me and my party, the Utruccan allies have formally rejected Senatorial rule and formed an independent league that dwarfs Amorr in manpower and geography alike. Vallyria is of course among them. So, as Dux Vallyria, it now falls to me to lead our House legions on behalf of the Vallyrian people and their ruling council.

You know the motto of our mutual House: Our House is Amorr. But what you must understand this means is that our allegiance must be to

House Valerius, not to what is the now-shattered empire of Amorr. It is our House that is Amorr, not Amorr that is our House! Marcus, I call upon you to be faithful to your House, to be true to your ancestors, and to be honest with yourself. You are House Valerius first and foremost, and therefore I expect you to surrender Legio XVII to me within seven days of receiving this letter.

In other news, Sextus sends you his greetings and his best regards. He was betrothed to Severa, the daughter of A. Severus Patronus, at the winter festival, and by this time will have been elected tribunus militum as well. So, as you see, much has changed, and it is becumbent upon us to ride the waves of those changes to the benefit of our House and the people of Vallyria.

I pray you will come to me soon, lest I be forced to come to you.

M. V. Magnus

At Aviglianus

"Send in the tribune who brought the letter," Marcus called out to the guards standing at the door of the chambers he'd taken in the luxurious praetorium.

The blood that had stained the marble floors outside where its previous inhabitant had fallen was gone, and Marcus wondered how long it would be before his own was spilled if he did not submit to his uncle.

They couldn't hope to hold the fortress against the veteran engineers of the other legions, and they couldn't retreat back into Larinum. And even if he could somehow manage to find a way past Magnus and his two legions, there was no chance that the Senate would permit him to retain the legion. It might not even allow him to turn its men over to his father. With Houses Martial turning against the Senate, the unthinkable had suddenly become reality. Everything was in a state of madness.

If he could be certain that Corvus would be retained as consul aquilae and given command of the Senatorial forces, trying to slip past Magnus might be worth the risk. But it was just as likely that Magnus's betrayal would cause the Senate to turn against his father and arrest him, perhaps even execute him. If what Magnus was saying about the allied league were true, the Senate would never permit his father to go into exile, for fear he would return at the head of an allied army.

"Tribune Aulus Severus Aulan from Legio VII," one of the two guards accompanying his uncle's messenger announced.

Marcus waved them off, and they left the two tribunes, one sitting, one standing, to examine the Severan tribune they'd escorted in. Marcus was thinking that, while the Severan was neither particularly tall nor handsome, he did carry himself well, with the self-confidence of an experienced decurion well-accustomed to victory.

"I understand congratulations are in order, Tribune." Marcus tapped the letter. "My uncle tells me that your sister is to marry my cousin."

"Yes, I stood with Sextus at the betrothal. They make a handsome pair. Unfortunately, it was a less than joyous occasion."

"Why is that?"

"Because my father was murdered immediately after the betrothal. By Cassianus Longinus." The Severan smiled bitterly. "I imagine you can understand how that might have put a slight damper on the celebrations."

"Yes, of course!" Marcus was shocked. "Severus Patronus is dead? Are you certain it was Longinus?"

"The entire city is certain it was Longinus. He was standing on the Comitium, holding up his blood-stained hands for all to see."

"I don't know what to say. I am very sorry for your loss, Tribune. I knew nothing of this."

"No, I understand. And I, in turn, must offer condolences for yours. Your brother Corvinus is dead."

Marcus shook his head, not sure that he'd heard the other correctly. "What?"

"He chose a bad time to visit the city. There has been considerable unrest there. Riots. It seems he was caught up in one."

"No," Marcus protested. "That's not possible. He is a farmer. He almost never visits Amorr! Are you certain it was Servius Valerius, the son of Corvus, and not some other Valerian?"

"I'm afraid so. I'm quite certain of it."

Everything seemed to flicker. For a moment, Marcus was too shocked to speak. Then he shook his head and firmly set the dreadful news aside. Of course Corvinus wasn't dead. What would a Severan and a rebel know about his brother, anyhow? Surely Magnus would have mentioned it in the letter... No, he had no time to think about this now.

"Be that as it may," he said coldly, "I need you to tell me why you are here."

Severus Aulan pointed to the letter. "Magnus did not send me to be a bearer of bad tidings, Valerius Clericus. Your uncle knows you've been parading around the provinces for months. He is aware you don't know anything about what's been happening in the city. Everything has changed. Death stalks the city like the plague. No one is safe. The Sanctified Father is dead, celestines have been murdered in heart of the Sanctal Palace, senators are slaughtered in public, and half the lords of the Houses Martial have abandoned the city to take command of their legions. It's not so much a civil war as simple chaos. No one knows who will stand with the Senate and who will stand with the leagues."

"Leagues?"

Marcus was still having trouble focusing on what the tribune was telling him. How could his big brother be dead? He was a farmer, for God's sake! Farmers don't die in city riots! It was absurd. He shook his head again. He'd think about it later. This was too important, he couldn't afford to miss anything.

"Yes, plural. The allied cities have formed two leagues, and they have made common cause against the Senate and People. Marruvium leads the north and east, Salventum the south and west." He shrugged. "My father was trying to prevent all of this, but your father and the clausores first blocked him in the Senate, then killed him for fear he'd ultimately find a way to succeed. They brought this on themselves."

"My father blocked him? But Magnus was the first man among the clausores, not my father."

"Your uncle had a change of heart. I expect you know why. Your father stepped in to replace him in the Senate upon his return to the city. His political skills were rather a surprise to everyone, especially my father."

Marcus thought about Fortex and the look of abject astonishment on his face when the unexpected death sentence had been pronounced. "Yes," he said slowly. "Yes, I think I do know why."

The Severan nodded sympathetically. "Look, Valerian, you really don't have a choice. You know Magnus will beat you again, whether you stay here or you come out to meet him. What you don't know is that the two legions raised by the Larinii are on the march. They'll be here within a week. They're blocking your line of retreat, so running isn't an option. Magnus doesn't want you to throw away your men's lives, and if you're half the man Magnus is, you won't do it."

"You sound almost as if you admire him. That sounds strange, coming from the mouth of a Severan."

Severus Aulan laughed, a little self-consciously. "Yes, well, I suppose you recall the cavalry that broke your right flank?"

"I do." He could hardly forget it. He saw it every night in his dreams.

"I was leading it, but the plan was all Magnus's. The false retreat, the hidden infantry, and the way Legio XV crumbled. Everything went exactly as he said it would. I've been in the legions for six years, and I've never seen anything like it. The only thing that surprised him was how you got there first and stole the high ground. How did you manage that, anyhow?"

Marcus wasn't about to tell the Severan about his elven eyes in the sky.

"You really expect me to surrender, don't you?"

"Magnus says you're not entirely stupid." The Severan shrugged. "So does Sextus. So I'm confused that you're even hesitating. It seems to me you'd have to be entirely stupid to fail to see it's your best option."

"Sextus Valerius, tribunus militum." Marcus rolled his eyes. "God help the poor legate to whom he's assigned."

"I like Sextus. He's a good lad."

"You don't know him like I do." Marcus was still trying to picture his shamelessly hedonistic cousin in a tribune's helm. "All right, Tribune. You're correct that I have no choice. You may return to Magnus and tell him I will leave here in two days. If, for some reason I have not arrived in Aviglianus within the seven days he demands, then he may come here to take possession of the legion from my second-in-command, Gaius Trebonius, in person. Trebonius will have orders to give the command to him."

The Severan bowed in graceful acknowledgement of Marcus's submission. "I will do so. It would be helpful if you would put that in writing, Commander."

Marcus smiled grimly. "Tribune will do. It appears my command pro tems is at an end. You are dismissed, Tribune."

The Severan started to turn around to depart, then hesitated, and turned back to face Marcus. "Look, Valerian, you cannot come to Aviglianus. Send the other tribune, what was his name, Trebonius? You'd better send him instead."

"Why?" Marcus frowned. "Won't Magnus be less likely to fear a trap if I appear before him myself?"

The Severan shook his head slowly. "No, Valerian, he doesn't fear any trap. You cannot come, because if you do, your uncle will kill you."

Marcus stared at the other tribune. He saw no dissembling in the man's aristocratic face, only a mild sort of pity in his eyes. And a cold fury began to rise in his own breast, as he thought he realized what the Severan was telling him without actually making the accusation explicit.

It was Magnus who had killed Corvinus, no doubt in revenge for Fortex's death. And Marcus knew Magnus well enough to be certain that merely trading a son for a son would not be enough for his vengeful uncle.

"Come away with me," Caitlys urged three days later.

Night had fallen, she was finally back from her daily reconnaissance flight, and she was not pleased to hear of Marcus's decision to surrender the legion to Magnus. She and Marcus stood in the command tent, along with the Savondese man, Theuderic, and the other elf, Lady Everbright.

Caitlys demanded Marcus's attention. "What is this war to you? You don't even know what the sides are, still less which side you favor!"

The Savondese man laughed. "Daddy on one side, uncle on the other, and little boy blue blood caught in the middle. Now there's an argument for monarchy and hereditary rule!"

"Shut up, Theuderic," Marcus said sourly. He found the man's nonchalant sarcasm irritating in the extreme. He wished he could spare Caitlys long enough to have her carry the man back to Savondir. "Was Severus Aulan telling the truth about the Larini forces?"

"He was," Theuderic nodded and poured himself a liberal portion of the red Galabrian that the late commander had left behind. "Two armies, two camps, each about six days' march from here. I'd say three thousand in the one, six thousand in the other."

The uneven division was potentially intriguing, offering as it did a very faint ray of hope. "How far away from each other are they?"

"Not far enough," Theuderic answered readily, dashing his hopes. He saluted Marcus with his brimming goblet. "The same thought occurred to me, but they're too close together. Maybe three, four hours apart at most. And they're in close contact. We saw riders passing back and forth between the two camps all afternoon."

"They wouldn't have to hold us long before Magnus would be on our tail."

The Savondese laughed at the absurd notion of trying to attack the two Larini armies with two enemy legions at his rear.

Marcus growled under his breath. "Well, it wasn't much of a chance, but it seems even that door is shut as well. Caitlys, you know I can't simply fly off with you. How can I surrender my men to Magnus without surrendering myself as well?"

"Why not?" the elfess demanded. "How do you know this uncle will not kill you? An elf would say anything, promise anything, to get you in his power. How do you know he does not seek your blood in payment for your cousin's?"

"Because Magnus isn't an elf," Marcus wearily lied. He hadn't told her about Severus Aulan's warning. "My blood won't bring my cousin back to him. Look, I don't want to take sides in this war anymore than you do, especially when I could easily find myself on the wrong one. But unless your bird can fly four thousand men and their supplies away from here in less than three days, I can't think of any honorable alternative."

Caitlys, still clad in her flying leathers, glared at him unhappily. Lithriel was silent, as she had been throughout.

Only Theuderic was in a conversational mood, wandering about the chamber as he sipped at his wine, admiring the thick carpets and bright mosaics that decorated the walls.

"Given how you officers live, Clericus, I can't see why you're agonizing over this affair. Join your uncle, and then if you happen to find yourself on the wrong side, by which of course I mean the losing one, then what is to prevent you from switching yet again? There's no newly converted adherent to the cause so welcome as the one who brings an army with him. At any rate, all of this is only a sideshow anyhow. We are but the playthings of the gods. And when those bastards war, kings and empires fall."

Marcus was still attempting to sort out Theuderic's cynical meanderings when a guard entered the chamber and stood stiffly at attention. "What is it?"

"A visitor seeks an audience with you, General. A dwarf, General."

The two elves looked at each other, then at Marcus.

Theuderic laughed, a little too loudly. "Quite the menagerie you're assembling here, General."

"Does this dwarf have an orange beard that is…" Marcus gestured at his chin. "Sort of short and not entirely dwarf-like?"

"Indeed, General." The guard's face remained impassive, and yet somehow managed to convey his surprise. "Shall I send him in to you?"

"Yes, yes, absolutely," Marcus said. A moment later, he was on his feet, warmly greeting the dwarf who had briefly been his slave. "Lodi son of Dunmorin! What in the name of Iron Mountain brings you here?"

The dwarf was wider than Marcus remembered, and he wore what would have passed for a respectable beard on a human face, but it was short enough to qualify as clean-shaven for a dwarf. He looked exhausted, and the lines on his face were deeper than the last time Marcus had seen him, almost two years ago. But those dark brown eyes still sparkled with pleasure.

"I been hearing you got yesself an army, boy, but I didn't believe it. Figured it were a different Valerius. They just hand these things out to yez Amorrans?"

They embraced briefly but warmly, and Marcus couldn't help but notice that the dwarf had not bathed in what must have been a very long time. He could also feel that, beneath the weather-stained cloak, Lodi was wearing heavy chain armor.

"It suddenly strikes me that you may not be visiting for the sheer pleasure of seeing me."

"No, but I'm damn glad to see ye, lad. Damn glad!" The dwarf wrinkled his nose and glared at the elves. "I sees you picked up some bad habits in Elebrion."

"You've met the Princess Shadowsong, of course," Marcus said, stifling a smile at the disdainful way both elfesses were looking down their elegant noses at the dwarf. "But allow me to present to you the Lady Lithriel Everbright of the Greenwood, and her companion–"

"I knows the other elf and the mage. Ran into them in Malkan. The Golden Rose, as I recall. Killed a man there. What the hell is they doing here with ye?"

Marcus stared at the dwarf, then looked over at Theuderic, who had turned white and was very uncharacteristically tongue-tied. The Savondese man looked to the ceiling and shook his head, then met his eyes and shrugged helplessly.

"A mage? Is that true?" Marcus took a step toward the Savondese nobleman and put his hand to his sword hilt. "You're not truly a mage, are you?"

"Marcus!" Caitlys protested, but he waved her off, waiting to hear what Theuderic had to say.

"I do indeed have the honor to be one of the King's Own," Theuderic admitted. "Truly. Though rest assured that no one has lied to you. As it happens, I am also the Comte de Thôneaux."

"Do you have any idea what would happen to you if anyone outside this room knew what you are, you cursed fool?" Marcus was nearly as frightened as he was furious. The senior centurions had already made it clear that neither they nor the men approved of his unorthodox auxiliaries. If they learned that Marcus had not only been relying upon elves but upon a Savondese mage as well, they might not merely mutiny, they very well might burn him with the magician.

"I imagine much the same thing that would happen to me," Caitlys answered, placing a slender hand on Marcus's armored forearm. "Control yourself, my dear. He hasn't been doing anything he shouldn't. Much of anything. I've kept a close watch on him."

"You knew, as well?"

Caitlys rolled her eyes.

"Of course I knew!"

Marcus didn't know if he felt more foolish or betrayed. "Why does everyone seem to know more about what is going on than I do? Why does even Lodi know him? Why didn't you tell me?"

"Marcus," Lodi's gruff voice broke in. "I knows the Savoner and the other elf because we was all in Malkan at the same time last winter." The dwarf glanced at Theuderic, then back to Marcus. "Lad, there's an army of orcs hereabouts. It's real big, they got some otherworld muscle behind it, and it's coming this way."

An army of orcs? Invading the lands of men? Marcus wouldn't have thought it possible a moment ago. But Lodi was right: The news was perhaps the only thing that could have convinced him to put the question of the mage to the side, at least for the moment. "How big is 'real big'?"

"Real damn big. We counted roundabout two hunnert thousand. Me and one of the lads was hunting in the mountains out east, and we come across them on the way back. Don't know if they's intending to go after the elves or strike north toward Savonne, or even maybe have another go at Iron Mountain, but I thought someone in the Man lands better know. You was the only one I knowed would listen to me, so we comes and found ye. I tried telling a few folks, but they just looked at me like I had two heads."

No wonder. Two hundred thousand. They probably thought he was mad. Two hundred thousand orcs! Marcus struggled to grasp the concept. There had never been an army so large, not in all the histories he'd ever read. The largest army Amorr had ever put into the field at one time was fifty thousand strong—eight legions plus auxiliaries. With an army four times that size, the logistics would be absolutely impossible.

"You're certain of this? You said 'we' were in the mountains. Who is we? And did you see them yourself, with your own eyes? What do you mean that you came across them?"

"I saw them, lad." The dwarf snorted. "Me. My own eyes. And ye knows I can count better'n ye. What I means by 'coming across them' is that I saw them and the demon altar they was summoning Gor Gor on. This ain't a raid or the usual campaign, lad. They's up to something, and it's something big. I was with another dwarf—a young lad, but real smart. We split up so he could warn the king. If he made it, the elves already know."

"Well, this would appear to add an interesting complication to the situation," Theuderic said brightly. The mage was obviously happy to no longer be the subject under discussion.

"Shut up, Northman," Marcus snapped. "I still might burn you."

"Marcus," Caitlys said, "I think there is something you need to know about."

Marcus slammed his steel gauntlet against his desktop, disturbing two stacks of folios and startling everyone. "Oh, and what else have you been keeping from me? Do you know what—I don't care! What's next, you're going to tell me that Lodi is actually your husband? That the mage here is really a toad? No! I don't care! All of you can go to the bloody devil as far as I'm concerned!"

He stomped out of the room and headed for the stairs that would lead him to the roof. He needed to get away from them, from the guards, from the men, from the centurions, from everyone who needed something from him, even if it was only a decision. Two guards who had been standing outside his chamber whirled around at the sound of his approach, but he waved them off, and they obediently returned to their stations.

A mage? A mage! How could Caitlys have thought to hide that from him? What could she have been thinking? God, he'd known there was something off about Theuderic. He'd never liked the man, but he'd also never imagined that the irritating Savonner could be a sorcerer.

The trapdoor opened easily, and he clambered up the ladder into the cold night air with more than a little relief. There seemed to be as many fires stretching out in the darkness of the castra below him as there were stars above him. So many fires. It seemed impossible to believe that he was looking out over a defeated army, over a legion that had no choice but to surrender.

Caitlys's betrayal hurt him, and the thought of surrendering to Magnus frightened him, but it was the knowledge of his failure that rankled at him. It was like a cancer in his stomach eating away at him, at his pride, at his very sense of himself.

Pride. That was his problem. That was his sin. Wasn't that what Father Gennadius had told him at Solacte? It was his pride that had been the source of his downfall. He'd wanted to prove himself better than Magnus, greater than the great. And why? For what purpose? He'd been seeking his own glory, not Amorr's, not House Valerius's, and most certainly not God's.

Magnus was in rebellion, to be sure, and the attempt to stamp out that rebellion had surely been Marcus's duty. But if he were honest with himself, brutally honest, the real reason he'd been so eager to meet his uncle on the battlefield was to show him up. To show him who the better Valerian strategist was. He shook his head. It was nothing more or less than simple pride.

He sighed and sat down on the edge of the flat roof and let his legs dangle over the side. He looked up at the sky. It was a clear night with nary a cloud obscuring the stars or either of the moons. Arbhadis was high in the sky to the north, large and luminous, while Ustruel lurked, low, red, and crescent-shaped to the southwest.

"Forgive me, Heavenly Father." He placed his face in his hands. "Forgive me my pride, my arrogance, and my forgetfulness. Please don't forget me as I was forgetting You. Give me wisdom, give me knowledge. Show me the way, Dominus—tell me what I am to do! You saved me from the killers at Gallidromum. You saved me from the false priests in Elebrion. So You must have some purpose for me! I will do it, even if that means going to Magnus and to my death. Only show me what it is! Send me a sign! Send me an answer!"

When he looked up again, the stars were still motionless, as indifferent to his fate as they had been before. The moons took no notice of him. They had their own troubles as they floated through the vast and mighty sea of darkness in the sky. No epiphany awaited him in the stars.

Nor was there a divine message to be seen in the fires below. Circles of men surrounded them, men who were laughing, drinking, talking, joking, complaining, and doing all the things that men do—except for one. Not a single one of them was wrestling with his fate, come the morrow. That burden fell to him and to him alone, and he wondered if ambition was a curse or just a form of madness.

"What are you doing?"

Marcus jerked upright and very nearly fell from the rooftop. Two slender arms encircled his shoulders from behind, and he smelled the sweet, intoxicating scent of the elven sorceress as she pressed her cheek against his.

For a moment, he let himself relax and sink back into Caitlys's embrace, forgetting his anger, forgetting his desperation, forgetting his unanswered prayers. And for just a moment, he even allowed himself to forget about the thousands of men in his charge.

He hoped she would not ask him to flee with her again, because he was not sure he could resist the temptation now.

No, he told himself, he would not run. That was the easy path. To humble himself before Magnus, to sacrifice himself for his men if his uncle demanded it—that was the harder path. That was the right way.

Gently, he removed her long, white fingers from about his wrist and kissed them before extricating himself from her arms. It would not do for them to be seen together in such intimacy. Already there had been far too many close calls with Trebonius, the senior centurions, and more than a few of his guards. But it was hard, so hard, to refrain from clasping her to him and crushing his lips against hers whenever they found themselves alone.

"I should have told you about the Savonder," she told him as he rose to his feet to face her. "I'm sorry. I thought he'd be gone immediately and it wouldn't matter."

He nodded. It hardly seemed to matter even now. By this time tomorrow evening, the mage would be gone and Caitlys with him. When would he see her again? This might be their last night, their last chance. And yet, it could never be. No matter what they might feel for each other, they could never live and love as one. She would not give up her magic, nor would he pollute the sacred temple of his body by taking her unwed. And when he was dying of old age, she would still look like a maiden untouched.

No, he told himself firmly, she would still be a maiden untouched. She was not for him. He sadly ran his finger over one pointed ear, then the other. It was an impossible dream. Even so, when she looked at him with her inhuman green eyes, he wanted nothing more than to ask her to call her hawk to them so they could fly off into the darkness together.

Then an idea struck him. He stepped back from her and began to pace on the rooftop, causing her to stare at him, mystified.

Darkness was an escape. Darkness. But the night sky was not the only darkness on the earth. The siege at Gallidromum. In the sky or in the earth, safety lay in darkness. He thought back to his readings of Longinus. It wasn't merely the battlefield victors that the great strategist celebrated, but also those cunning generals who slipped their armies from the hangman's noose, who saved them to fight another day.

Example after example filled his mind. The bullocks with their flaming horns. The stranded gallies. The false reinforcements. The scattered gold. None of those brilliant stratagems would help him now, but he didn't need them—he had his own.

Or at least he might, if he could make proper use of what the mage had dismissively labeled his menagerie. But he would need them all, even the king's mage, if what he had in mind was going to work. Still, there was a chance. He reminded himself that, if it was going to be victorious again, the first thing a defeated army had to do was to survive and remain intact.

Suddenly filled with hope, even if it was one last roll with the bones loaded against him, he seized Caitlys and kissed her. She melted into him, and for a moment, it seemed as if nothing could ever stand between them. And then, it was over. He released her and stepped back, smiling at her sweetly confused expression.

"I can't come away with you, Lady Shadowsong. But if you will fly north with the mage, I think perhaps I may be able to arrange to meet you there."

She regarded him suspiciously. "What is your idea?"

He laid it out for her, the plan becoming even more clear in the telling.

Then, as awareness dawned on her face, Caitlys returned his smile. "I'd still rather you came away with me, but I think we should be able to convince all the necessary parties. Will you come down from the roof, or shall I fetch the dwarf to come up here?"

"I will go down. But give me a little while to think on this more. There are still some details that demand consideration."

"Of course. I will find him. Your quarters?"

Marcus nodded, and she came close, kissed him lightly on the lips, then turned to go below.

He stared in mute appreciation at her slender back until she vanished from sight, then he turned back toward the sky. The two moons seemed to represent the two armies, his and Magnus's. The dull red-horned beast was stalking the defenseless silver orb as it fled into the safety of the distant darkness. To the north. To the dark. To the deep.

He bowed his head in grateful humility. He knew this inspiration was not his own—it was an answer to his prayers. It seemed that, even for the haughty, whom God hates, and even for the proud, whom He holds in His divine contempt, salvation might be found.

AULAN

M Y bloody nephew should have gotten here by now!" Magnus
slapped his desk, glaring at Aulan and two of the other
tribunes he'd summoned to his office as he ate his lunch.

The headquarters building at Aviglianus was a basic brick-and-mortar
construction and far from the most luxurious that Aulan had ever seen,
but it wasn't a bad place to spend the winter. A roaring fire kept the room
warm enough that all of three of them had taken off their heavy wool
cloaks.

"If he's coming at all," Magnus said. "Haven't the patrols reported
anything?"

"I'm afraid not, General," Tarrisinus Opilian said. He was the tribune
commanding the Fourth Knights, which mostly consisted of the few surviving knights from the newly disloyal Legio XV.

"Our patrols have been on the thin side," Aulan said. "We don't have
enough horses or riders to cover much ground, and it's been too cold this
week to permit them to stay out overnight on wide patrol. We might well
have missed a small party."

Magnus folded his arms, his heavy features clouded with suspicion.
"This morning was the seventh day, was it not? I told him to be here in
seven days, did I not? Aulus Severus, you were clear about my requirements?"

"I was." Aulan did not bother to remind Magnus that Magnus had
spelled them out himself in his letter. The Duke of Vallyria, as Magnus
preferred to style himself now that he was the unquestioned master of the

region with three legions answering to him, was not at his most rational. "It is possible, Magnus, that your nephew met with ill fortune en route. It is winter, after all, and it's not impossible that he could've been lost in that storm we had two days ago if it caught him on the road."

"I'm a lucky man, Aulus Severus, but I'm not that lucky," Magnus said. "I can't believe that little bastard is actually going to force me to march both legions north in the dead of winter and dig him out of Montmila. The Larinii probably have him invested already, but they have no engineers. When was the last time we heard from them?"

"Three days ago, before the storm," the third tribune, Cunctor, said. He was a big, stolid fellow and utterly devoid of imagination. "They were a day away, according to their consul."

"Their consul!" Magnus snorted. "They demand their freedom, and the first thing they do as free men is start aping their former masters. Well, I'm not going to uproot my men until I know it's necessary. Maybe the sight of the Larinii will be enough to bring that priestling to his senses. He should have stayed a priest. He'll wish he had by the time I'm done with him!"

The other two tribunes laughed.

Aulan didn't. He knew personally that Magnus wasn't speaking in jest. Magnus had already killed one nephew, and he obviously had no intention of leaving the other one alive. Aulan wondered if the task would fall to him again, and he shrugged. He'd rather not. But then, orders were orders. He had been with the legions too long to feel regret in carrying them out, no matter what they were. Best to get it over with as soon as possible. He cleared his throat.

"What is it, Aulus Severus?"

"Sir, the weather is clear enough now, and it doesn't look like snowing again soon. With your leave, I'll take a squadron and see if I can intercept either your nephew or any Larini messengers. If not, I'll ride to Montmila and see what's causing the delay. Your nephew said that, if he didn't arrive on the appointed day, we should speak with the other tribune, Trebonius."

Magnus nodded but made a sour face.

"Yes, in light of the circumstances, that would be for the best. It's just a pity it's necessary. Keep an eye on the skies. I don't have so many knights that I can afford to lose another squadron. Will Trebonius know you?"

"Yes, we've met."

"Good, good." Magnus looked halfway cheerful for the first time since the sun had risen with no sign of riders on the northern horizon. "Can you leave today?"

"I hope to be out the gates before the next bell. It's early enough to catch the men I want to take before they start drinking." He saluted, and threw his cloak back around his shoulders, and left the headquarters.

He stood for a moment out in the cold before going in search of Lucarus and his squadron. He grinned at the thought of the look that would cross the decurion's face when Aulan told him he'd be spending the next few nights freezing his arse on the road instead of keeping warm in the plump arms of the centurion's widow he'd been comforting since the internecine battle.

That would teach the bastard not to clean him out of a month's pay at dice again.

The icy roads turned what should have been a three-day journey into four, but it was otherwise uneventful. Aulan had been somewhat warmed throughout the long days by Lucarus's bitter complaints. The decurion was worried that the centurion's widow would be married again by the time they returned next week. Life might be hard for the women who followed the legions, but a strong, good-natured woman who could sew and launder and keep a man warm at night seldom lacked a husband for long.

They saw neither Larinii nor any sign of Legio XVII on the road, not even a messenger. Lucarus's theory was that the storm had inspired everyone to sit tight for fear of another one, which was precisely what he felt they should have been doing themselves. But the weather held, and it was early afternoon on the fourth day since they'd departed when they caught their first sight of the thick stone walls of the castra off in the distance.

But even so far away, both Aulan and Lucarus could tell that something was wrong. They reined in their horses and stared at the distant compound.

For one thing, there was relatively little activity outside the fort. They hadn't seen a single patrol throughout the morning, which was inexplicable since, even with its losses, Legio XVII still had more cavalry than the average legion. There was also not much in the way of a camp following. There were a score of wagons on the castra's western side and a few small, ramshackle constructions, but it was more reminiscent of a little crossroads village than the sort of movable city the legions inevitably attracted.

But the smoke from hundreds of fires rose from inside the walls, so it was clear that the barracks were still inhabited.

"Do you think maybe he took his horsemen and ran?" Aulan asked Lucarus. It made sense. Marcus Valerius couldn't easily outmarch the Larini armies with the entire legion, but it would have been simple for him to avoid them on horseback. And while twenty or so squadrons of knights might be an insignificant force in ordinary times, it would be more than enough for the tribune to set himself up as a warlord of substance in these more troubled circumstances.

"Only one way to find out, sir."

Aulan nodded. The decurion was right. They continued riding toward the castra, and the men, seeing ahead of them the promise of warm billets and a roof over their heads, picked up their pace.

They had nearly reached the gate when Aulan had his answer. There were two banners erected over what was the Porta Principalis Dextra on the east-facing fort. They were blue, not red, and they bore the he-goat sable passant of Larinum.

"Do you see that, sir?" one of the knights pointed to the Larini banners.

He did. Aulan didn't bother responding. He was too busy wondering, if their Larini allies were camping here in Montmila, then where in the world was Legio XVII?

A bell later, Aulan was considerably warmer though no better informed as to the whereabouts of the missing legion. He was seated in the legate's quarters, sitting across the desk from Florus Siculo and Corippus Nolens, who commanded the two armies of Larinum.

Nolens seemed to defer to the Solactean, even though, as far as Aulan could tell, the elderly man had no military experience at all. Neither of them appeared to be particularly inclined to be helpful. He wondered if he should have worn something less identifiably Amorran than his tribune's cloak.

A map and a sealed scroll lay on the desk. Aulan drew two lines on the former with his finger from Solacte and Fescennium to Montmila, indicating the twin Larini lines of march.

"So you arrived here a week ago, and they were gone? You didn't even send out patrols to find them, or let us know they'd run away? They could be anywhere by now."

"Do you think us fools, Tribune?" Siculo was irritated. "Of course we sent out patrols. Two came back without finding any sign of them. Two didn't come back at all. The two we sent north, toward Gorignia. We couldn't risk losing any more riders."

Nolens waved a dismissive hand. "They've obviously marched north, but where can they go? The goblin lands? They haven't entered Larinum, or we would already know. They can't winter in Gorignia either—the Gorignii have raised ten thousand men, and we sent riders to both Acerrae and Berdicum. We warned them to keep an eye on their castras and to let us know if a legion tries to settle on their lands."

"Have you heard back from either city?"

"No one has seen them near Acerrae. We won't hear from Berdicum until tomorrow at the soonest." Siculo shook his head.

"And you didn't send one to us?"

"The weather was bad, and then, we thought we might as well wait to hear from Berdicum first. We were expecting to send him tomorrow or shortly thereafter. Besides, they weren't marching your way."

Aulan sighed, disgusted but not surprised. It was always difficult dealing with auxiliaries and provincials, and clearly it wasn't going to get any easier now that the empire was devouring itself.

"Tell Magnus we'll keep him informed as soon as we figure out where they've gone," Siculo said. "But he needn't be in a hurry to hunt his nephew down."

"No? And why not."

"He can just let General Winter do the work for him. They cleaned out everything and took it with them, including the hundreds of cattle they stole from Solacte. Unless they're going to winter near Berdicum, they'll be sleeping in their tents without much in the way of supplies. By spring, they'll be sick and hungry, and willing to surrender without a fight."

Siculo pushed the scroll across the desk.

Aulan picked it up and saw that it bore the seal of House Valerius, as well as "M.V. Magnus" written on it in black ink.

"You can give that to him too," Siculo said. "We found it in here, on this very desk." The elderly man raised an eyebrow as Aulan cracked the seal open and began to unroll it. "It is to Magnus!"

"I know," Aulan said absently as he read its contents.

To M. Valerius Magnus

Aviglianus (Ianuarius)

*By the time you read this, I will have gone where you cannot follow.
But know that I rebuke your actions, as they are not worthy of our
House or your late son's memory. Fortex would be ashamed of you.
Nor will I surrender a loyal Amorran legion to your command. I urge
you to repent of your rebellion, go to Amorr, and make amends with
the Senate and with my father, who by now will have been elected
Consul in his own right.*

*You defeated me once. Do not think you will do so again. And if
you are not reconciled with those whose faith in you has been so sorely
abused by the time we meet again, then rest assured I will show you
precisely the same mercy you intended to show me.*

M. Valerius Clericus, tribunus militum, legatus Legio XVII

At Montmila

Aulan leaned back in his chair and stared at the mosaic on the wall
behind Siculo's head, ignoring the anticipatory looks the two Larini leaders were giving him. Magnus was not going to be happy with this. Not
at all. And where could the younger Valerian go that his elder could not
follow? It made no sense! An entire legion could not simply disappear.
He must be headed for the goblin lands, gambling that Magnus wouldn't
dare to follow him there, not with a massive civil war in the offing.

He shrugged. At least the tribune had not betrayed Aulan's indiscretion in warning him about Magnus's intentions. No good deed goes
unpunished, it was said. Aulan had regretted that warning almost as soon
as it left his mouth. It could even be that his foolish words had influenced
the younger Valerian's decision to run, which would make this debacle his
fault. But whether the blame lay with him or not, there was absolutely
nothing he could do about it now. Then a thought struck him and he
laughed.

"What is it?" demanded Siculo.

"What's in the letter?" the other Larini asked.

"Oh, nothing of much interest to anyone outside of House Valerius," Aulan lied easily. "It just struck me that, if Magnus's nephew ever learns to fight as well as he runs, we may all be in for one devil of a time."

SEVERA

AMORR grieved. It grieved for the Sanctified Father, the second to die in less than six months. It grieved for the Consul Aquilae, the second to die in a year. It grieved for the devastation wrought by the mysterious fire at the Holy Palace, even as they marveled at the miraculous salvation of the Sedes Ossus. Somehow the throne of bones had remained immaculate and untouched by the flames. But most of all, the people of Amorr grieved for the loss of their empire.

It seemed as if God had abandoned them. Every day seemed to bring worse news than the next. Severa had finally asked Sextus to stop telling her of the latest uprising, the most recent defeat, the most unthinkable betrayal. There were too many of them. Had the whole world gone mad?

Falconius Aquila had returned to Amorr with only two legions, since Legios V and IX had joined with the rebels in Larinum. House Cassianus's two legions remained loyal, but Longinus was defeated outside of Aeternum by a Marruvian army led by Herius Obsidius that outnumbered him three-to-one.

Fear and grief filled the city. But it wasn't until rumors began circulating that Sextus's own father, four times consul and acclaimed Magnus by the will of the People and the vote of the Senate, had turned traitor and was openly ruling over Vallyria and Larinum, that Severa truly understood what it meant to feel despair.

"It can't be true," she told herself as she sat and stared in her mirror. "Magnus would never do that. Aulan is one of his senior tribunes! He would never let Magnus turn traitor!"

Her reflection didn't speak. It stared at her, unconvinced.

She reminded herself how easily the crowd got things wrong. Even now that Cassianus Longinus's fears had been proven correct, there were still some who believed that he was right, that her father could have been a traitor too.

"My lady?" She hadn't noticed Quinta Jul enter the room. "Sextus Valerius is here."

"He is?" Severa leaped to her feet and straightened her gown. "Am I presentable?"

The servant woman reached out and brushed a few stray hairs out of her face. "Always, my lady."

She ran from the room and down the stairs.

Sextus was standing at the foot of the stairs, wearing his full tribune's armor, with his helm under his arm. He was as handsome as ever, although these days, on the rare evenings when he was able to visit her, he was usually exhausted. It seemed the centurions training the thousands of new recruits, both voluntary and conscripted, were nearly as hard on the new officers as they were on the former slaves. Today, his eyes didn't light up when he saw her. Instead, he flushed and looked away, as if he was ashamed of her.

She stopped on the landing above him. Something was wrong. She could see it in his face. Something was dreadfully wrong.

"Sextus, what is it?"

He looked up at her. His lips were tightly pressed together. He looked almost in pain.

"What is it?" she repeated.

"Can we step outside, my lady?"

My lady? He was never so formal with her. Her heart was racing, and she was too upset to say anything, so she only nodded and allowed him to hold the door open for her.

They walked in silence along the brick path toward the hill that led down to the city. Sextus didn't offer her his arm or attempt to take her hand. Only when they reached the wooden benches that offered a grand view of the Sanctal Palace, still sitting proudly atop its own hill in the distance, did he turn to her and gesture toward one of the benches.

"Will you sit down?"

It was right here that her father had waited for her in the darkness, she thought. *That night, my life changed. Is my life about to change again now?*

She sat down. She waited.

He wasn't looking at her. Instead, he was staring at the city, the frightened, desperate, grieving city.

"I wish to release you, my lady Severa," he said, still looking away.

"Release me? From what?" She was so confused by how strangely he was acting that she didn't even understand what he was saying. "What is wrong, Sextus?"

He finally looked at her, and she saw he was silently crying, tears tricking slowly down his cheeks. She wanted to go to him, to hold him and wipe his tears away, but something in his eyes held her back. Pain? Fear?

He cleared his throat and raised his chin, and this time he looked her directly in the eyes. "I wish to release you from our betrothal, my lady Severa."

She stared at him in disbelief. "But... but why?"

"Because the daughter of Aulus Severus Patronus cannot marry a traitor's son."

"No!" The cry ripped itself from her throat. She jumped to her feet and pushed him hard, with both hands, in the stomach. The breastplate was hard and cold beneath her hands. She pushed him again, almost hitting him, and he did not resist her. "No!"

"Severa," he protested, and now she could hear the shame and despair in his voice. "It's true. The whispers, the rumors, they're all true! Father betrayed the Senate and People! He's calling himself the Duke of Vallyria or some other nonsense like that. He even fought a battle against Marcus and won!"

"Marcus?" She had no idea Andronicus Aquila had even left the city. "I thought he was your legate?"

"Not Marcus Aquila—my cousin Marcus. The tribune. The cousin I got Marcipor from."

"Oh, of course." She paused, still confused. "Your cousin has an army?"

"Yes. Well, he had one, I guess, until my father's legion beat his. But that's not the point!"

"So what is the point?"

He glared at her, infuriated. "The point is that you can't marry me! My father's a cursed traitor. So I'm releasing you. I'm breaking the betrothal!"

She breathed a sigh of relief. God, he was such an idiot. Noble, of course, and she admired his determination to do the right thing by her, but an idiot nonetheless.

"You're doing nothing of the kind, Sextus Valerius," she told him in a tone that brooked no argument.

"I'm not?" He stared at her, confused.

"Of course not. Sextus, everything is falling apart. The empire, the Houses, the Church, everything. My father was murdered. Your father is a traitor, and only God knows what happened to your uncle. No one's heard from him since the fire. Maybe he and the Sanctiff were murdered too. In three months, both of those damned rebel leagues could be at our walls, and you're going to have to fight them."

He eyed her warily. "I don't understand how that is supposed to make me feel any better."

"It's not, you idiot! It's supposed to remind you that all we have is each other!" She glared at him. "Sextus, do you love me?"

"Well, yes," he said.

"Are you going to betray the Senate and People? Are you thinking of running off to join Magnus?"

"Hell no! I'll kill him myself if I get the chance."

"Good." She pulled him down to her and kissed him, hard, on the lips. "Then it's settled."

He pulled back, looking alarmed. "What's settled?"

"We're getting married next week."

He sputtered. "But that's... I mean, if I... Severa, we can't do that!"

"Don't be absurd. Of course we can." She pointed back to the city. "Amorr needs some good news. Do you remember what you told me the war declaration meant? It meant the Houses are united. So it must be. You and me, Sextus. House Valerius and House Severus. United."

She looked up at him expectantly.

He was staring out over the city again, but the pain and the shame were gone. Then he turned back to her and smiled.

"I'm sorry. You're right, of course. I don't know what I was thinking."

She kissed him again. "I do. I think it was extremely brave and noble and self-sacrificing of you. And I don't ever want to hear anything like that again."

He pressed her close to him, crushing her against his inflexible breastplate. And yet, for the first time since she'd seen him standing before the stairs, she felt she could breathe again.

Quinta Jul watched with amusement as her beautiful young charge gamefully but incompetently attempted to put together a meal for her betrothed. She took pleasure in the mutual affection between Severa and Sextus. Young love was so clumsy, and yet that very clumsiness was part of its charm. Finally, she shooed Severa out of the kitchen with two goblets of wine and took over the task of slicing up some bread and cheese for the tall Valerian.

"Quinta!" Severa called from the nearest triclinium.

"Yes, love?" she called back.

"Sextus likes grapes. Green ones. Do we have any?"

"If we do, I'll bring them."

A sharp pain unexpectedly struck her hand. For a moment, Quinta Jul thought she'd been bitten by one of Regulus's hounds that lounged about the residence. Then she looked down and realized she'd accidentally cut off the tip of her left index finger.

How annoying. She picked it up and regarded it thoughtfully for a moment.

Dust and water. That was all they really were, in the end. As short-lived as flies. And yet, endlessly intriguing nevertheless. That was what her brothers so often failed to see, why they so often found themselves beheaded or dismembered or burned to ashes blown on the wind.

She wondered if the brother she'd been hunting all these years had been the consul or His Holiness. Probably the latter, she reflected, though the former would have been more apropos. She would have to watch for his reappearance, of course, but in the meantime, there were others she must find. They were not in Amorr, but then, the Empire was not the only power on Selenoth.

She slipped the fingertip into a pocket in her dress. The finger had already stopped bleeding, but she would have to be careful to hide it from sight for the next few hours, she realized.

Until it grew back again.

THEUDERIC

IT was springtime in southwestern Savondir. The rain had stopped three days ago and the morning sun was dawning over the hills of Bassas Vidence, a bucolic place Theuderic had never thought to see, much less visit in the august company with whom he now rode. Beside him, on a delicate grey mare, was the royal chancelier. Ahead of them both, riding a giant roan stallion that dwarfed both du Moulin's mare and his own gelding, was de Beaumille, the elderly Maréchal de Savonne. The two members of the Haut Conseil were accompanied by an honor guard of sixty royal men-at-arms, led by Sieur Janequin de Recheusoir. The grandmagicien had also graciously permitted four of Theuderic's colleagues from l'Académie to accompany the expedition. They were all inexperienced young battlemages, but under the circumstances, Theuderic considered they were potentially worth more than all the fighting men combined.

And neither the men-at-arms nor the battlemages were as important as the twenty wagons full of barrels containing meat, flour, and wine that followed them.

The winter had passed pleasantly enough once he was able to explain to the royal council why he was back in Lutèce nearly five months before his return was expected. However, any suspicions about his unlikely story disappeared once word of the violent convulsions of the Amorran Empire began to make its way north and rumors of a vast army of orcs began to frighten peasants and nobles alike living on the edge of the great forest of the Grimmwalde. Lithriel was gone now, having departed with Caitlys to be sure the dwarf's warning had been taken seriously in both Merithaim and Elebrion. But he had reason to hope that she would be back soon, although he was more certain that Lady Shadowsong would return.

Which, from the point of view of l'Académie, would arguably be preferable. The immortels were still attempting to refine the elven bird spell, but still hadn't managed to make it work yet on so much as a little lizard. It would be years, he guessed, before anyone was bold enough, or stupid enough, to try it on another dragon. And when they did, Theuderic was determined to be as far away as possible.

"I couldn't help but notice that your long absence prevented you from being with your colleagues when they swore their vows of loyalty to the new heir to the throne," du Moulin remarked, as innocently as if he were merely commenting on the weather.

"Alas, I was otherwise occupied," Theuderic felt rather like a mouse being stalked by a cat. "No doubt I shall have to rectify that upon my return to Lutèce. I am, of course, a loyal subject of His Royal Majesty and delight in the happy news of His Royal Highness's recent betrothal."

"Are not we all?" The chancelier cleared his throat. "Naturally, the Maréchal and I both bitterly regret the manner with which our responsibilities similarly stood in the way of our being able to do the same."

Theuderic's eyebrows seemed to rise of their own accord, and he couldn't resist glancing at du Moulin, whose expression didn't betray the least sign of a guilty conscience. Then again, from what Theuderic had observed in working for the man, he didn't appear to have a conscience at all. Still, it was good to know he was not the only one with doubts about Étienne-Henri's fitness for the throne.

"I trust the Haut Conseil always has the interests of crown and throne close to its collective heart."

A flicker of a smile barely appeared on du Moulin's lips before it vanished. "Well spoken, Sieur Theuderic. We do indeed."

The crown and the throne, thought Theuderic. Which was not necessarily the king who wore the one and sat upon the other. "I am, of course, always delighted to be of service to the council."

"I rejoice to hear it." The chancelier adroitly changed the subject. "I can't help but notice, Sieur Theuderic, that there does not appear to be anyone, let alone an invading army, anywhere in the vicinity. Are you certain we are in the location appointed?"

"I think so. We must be close."

Theuderic looked around the empty field, which was bordered by budding trees to the east and a gentle, tree-covered hill to the south. As far as he could tell, they were approaching the location the dwarf had showed him three months ago. Indeed, the Lady Shadowsong's hawk had landed on that very hill. He recognized a large rock about fifty paces away that might serve as a marker, but unfortunately, Lodi hadn't told him exactly where the entrance was.

He pulled on his horse's reins and called to the Maréchal. "Monseigneur, I believe we're here." He very much hoped he had gotten it right. Otherwise he was going to look a dreadful fool before his four fellow mages, to say nothing of the two royal councilors. Then the ground began rumbling, as if the earth was quaking, and the horses flattened their ears and began to step nervously about.

He grinned at du Moulin. "Have I ever failed you, Monseigneur Chancelier?"

"Not yet, Magicien."

There was a dull roar and the front side of the hill abruptly collapsed, causing the horses to shy. A large cloud of dust and debris billowed out toward them like a dirty brown cloud. It dissipated before it reached them and revealed a brick arch over a packed dirt ramp, from which two heavily armored dwarves were marching out. They were followed by ten more dwarves, then another ten, who spread out on either side of the hill and the opening that gaped like an open wound. Then a pair of taller figures strode out into the light, and they held their hands over their eyes to shield them from the brightness of the spring morning sun. They both wore tribunes' helms.

Theuderic dismounted, followed by the two royal councilors, and the three of them walked toward the two Amorrans. Both young men were as white as slugs and their faces were thin and drawn, as if they had not eaten well for months. Which, Theuderic considered, was very probably the case. But they were smiling as triumphantly as if they had won a great battle.

"Chancelier, Lord Maréchal, it gives me great pleasure to introduce to you the Tribunes Clericus and Trebonius, both formerly of Amorr." Behind the two young officers, armored men were spilling out of the hill like ants when an anthill is disturbed. "And with them, the four thousand armed fighting men of Legio XVII!"

Valerius Clericus greeted him with the forearm grasp of the soldier rather than with a bow or the handclasp of civilized men. The gesture secretly flattered Theuderic.

"I never thought I'd be so happy to see a sorcerer's face," the tribune told him, still squinting against the sun.

"It is a handsome one, isn't it?" Theuderic said, stroking his neatly-trimmed beard with his free hand. "Trebonius, I trust you enjoyed your stroll?"

"Next time, you walk and I'll take the bird," the young Amorran said with a scowl. But he grinned as he clasped Theuderic's arm.

Then the lord maréchal stepped forward and looked from one tribune to the other. He was old enough to be their grandfather. "Welcome to the Kingdom of Savondir, my lords. We have food and wine for your men, though you will have to provide your own accommodations. I am impressed. Never in all my years have I heard of an army marching six hundred miles below the ground."

Or in such good order, Theuderic thought, as the Amorrans continued to come up out of the earth and fall into formations worthy of any parade ground, despite their filthy appearance.

Their discipline didn't appear to escape the maréchal's attention. "I have heard that the legionaries of Amorr are unmatched in all Selenoth when it comes to killing, though I regret to say I have never had the privilege to witness them demonstrate their excellence in the art of war."

Valerius Clericus bowed respectfully to the old general. "If you'll give us a few days to recover and point us in the right direction, my Lord Maréchal, I should be glad to arrange a demonstration. I am given to understand you may have a few orcs that require killing in the near future."

"I fear that is indeed the case," du Moulin said. "Here in Savondir, we appear to have rather a lot of killing that needs doing." He coughed delicately.

"As it happens, not all of it necessarily involves orcs."

closing time

APPENDIX

A S is surely obvious throughout the text, the Amorran names are based on historical Roman ones, which can be more than a little confusing. This is because aristocratic Roman names during the Republic customarily consisted of three or more parts, the tria nomina of praenomen, nomen, and cognomen. Additional cognomina, or agnomina, were sometimes added as well. There were a severely limited number of praenomina used, which is why they were usually abbreviated in writing as follows:

A.	Aulus		N.	Numerius
App.	Appius		P.	Publius
C.	Caius		P'.	Postumus
D.	Decimus		Q.	Quintus
C.	Gaius		S.	Spurius
Cn.	Gnaeus		Ser.	Servius
L.	Lucius		Sex.	Sextus
M.	Marcus or Marcius		T.	Titus
M'.	Manius		V.	Vitius
Mam.	Mamercus		Vo.	Vopiscus

Number-based names such as Primus and Secundus were indicated by a number, I. for Primus, II. for Secundus and so forth. As time went by, the system became more lax; in *A Throne of Bones*, the traditional naming conventions are mostly preserved by the patrician class while the names of the plebians, the allies, and the provincials tend to indicate the decreasing influence of the convention the further one goes from the city of Amorr.

As confusing as the Amorran names may be, they could have been considerably worse. For example, M. Livius Drusus, the tribune of the plebs upon whom the figure of A. Severus Patronus is very loosely based, and whose assassination set off what is known as the Social War of 91 BC, was the son of M. Livius Drusus and the father of M. Livius Drusus Claudianus. Claudianus was adopted from the Claudius family; had M. Livius Drusus the younger a son by birth, it is quite possible that he, too, would have been named M. Livius Drusus. Throughout the book, considerable liberties were taken with assigning different, (and in some cases, unlikely), praenomina to various nomina and cognomina in order to reduce the problem of sons, fathers, and grandfathers all having exactly the same three names.

The Ecclesiastical Hierarchy

The Sanctiff

His Sanctified Holiness Charity IV, the 44th Sanctiff of Amorr, formerly Quintus Flavius Ahenobarbus

The Sacred College of Celestines:

His Eminence Giovannus Falconius Valens

His Eminence Gennarus Vestinae

His Eminence Baccius Antonius

His Eminence Paulus Masella

His Eminence Ildebrando Ortognan

His Eminence Mam. Severus Furius

His Eminence Cn. Attilius Bulbus

His Eminence T. Falconius Tigradae

His Eminence Sex. Aemilianus Damasus

His Eminence Carvilius Noctua

His Eminence App. Gennarus Vestinae

His Eminence Petrus Clementus, a celestine of the cathedra of Mons Celsius

His Eminence Praxidus Domenicus, a celestine of the cathedra of Saint Marcellus

The Episcopate:

His Excellency Laris Sebastius, a bishop and candidate for an archbishopric

His Excellency Nivelet, a Savondese archbishop

His Excellency Vincenot, a Savondese archbishop

The Curian Guard and the Military Orders:

Nonus Sulpicius Deodatus, captain of the third century

Arnaudus, Grand Master of the Order of St. Michael

THE LEGIONS

LEGIO XVII, A VALERIAN HOUSE LEGION

M. SATURNIUS, Legate

THE SENIOR OFFICERS:

A. CRESCENTIUS, Tribune Laticlavius

SEX. CASTORIUS SPINA, Praefectus

G. VALERIUS FORTEX, Tribune

L. VOLUSENUS, Tribune

G. MARCIUS, Tribune

G. TREBONIUS, Tribune

M. VALERIUS CLERICUS, Tribune

CN. JUNIUS HONORATUS, primus pilus, first centurion of the
first cohort

T. FALCONIUS, pilus prior, first centurion of the second cohort

V. SINTAS TERTIUS, pilus prior, first centurion of the third cohort

C. PROCULUS senior centurion of the second cohort

THE JUNIOR OFFICERS:

SENARIUS ARVANDUS, decurion of the first squadron, first knights

APP. JULIANUS, decurion of the first squadron, second knights

Q. GAVRUS, second decurion of the fourth squadron, second knights

BARBATUS, a decurion

ARCADIUS, a decurion

T. CASSABUS, optio, senior ballistarius

CLAUDIUS DIDIUS, first centurion of the eighth cohort

HOSIDOS, a centurion

NEBRIDIUS, a centurion

MARINUS, a centurion

LUCILIUS, a centurion

THE KNIGHTS:

L. DARDANUS, reguntur, second knights

CLAUDIUS HORTENSIS, a knight of the fifth decuria of the second knights

L. ORISSIS, a knight of the fifth decuria of the second knights

LEPORIUS, a knight of the fifth decuria of the second knights

SER. COMMIUS, a draconarius

N. AEMELIUS PETRUS, a knight

Q. PLACIDIUS ULPIUS, a knight of the eighth squadron of the first knights

THE LEGIONARIES:

LABECULUS, a scout

FABERUS, scout

SEDARIUS, a medicus

CN. SEXTIUS BAIULUS, a legionary

CORANDER, a Baleran slinger

QUINCE DE SORRENGIS, a legionary

SEBELON, a legionary

NARBONIO, a legionary of the first cohort

FATHER GENNADIUS, priest of the legion

JERON, a stable slave

DECCUS, a stable slave

LEGIO VII, A VALERIAN HOUSE LEGION

T. DIDIUS SCATO, Legate

THE OFFICERS AND LEGIONARIES:

CN. LUCRETIUS SICULUS, a tribune

LIBERIUS MURILLO, an optio

MUSIUS BAUTO, a centurion

SEX. PHOBUS, an optio

LEPORIUS, a legionary

MANLIUS, a legionary

FUSCUS, an optio ballistarius

CLODIUS SECUNDUS, a ballistarius

LEGIO XV, A VALERIAN HOUSE LEGION

L. GERONTIUS, Legate

THE OFFICERS AND LEGIONARIES:

TARRISINUS OPILIAN, a tribune

CUNCTOR, a tribune

NOBILIANUS, a decurion

CARUS, a decurion

PACCIUS VINTIUS, a legionary

ORFITUS, a legionary

LEPORIUS, a legionary

PARTHENDER, an auxiliary slinger

ORODES, an auxiliary slinger

LEGIO III, A SEVERAN HOUSE LEGION, ALSO KNOWN AS FULGETRA

II. FALCONIUS BUTEO, Legate

THE SENIOR OFFICERS:

APP. MALLICUS, Tribune Laticlavius

A. SEVERUS AULAN, Tribune

LEGIONARIES AND AUXILIARIES:

KING LADISMAS, the rebel king of the Cynothii

VESTREMER, a Cynothi auxiliary captain

P. TERENTIUS, a knight and draconarius

RUFUS, a knight

LUCARUS, a decurion

The Patricians

House Valerius

M. Valerius Magnus, Senator, Ex-Consul (4x)

His family:

Julia, his wife,
G. Valerius Fortex, a tribune of Legio XVII
Sex. Valerius, his son

His household:

Galerus, the majordomus
Clodipor, a messenger slave
Dompor, a slave scholar
Lazapor, a slave scholar

Sex. Valerius Corvus, Senator, Stragister Militum, Dux Ducis Bello, Consul Suffectus Aquilae

His family:

Romilia, his wife
Ser. Valerius Corvinus, his son
Valerina, his daughter
Valerilla, his daughter
    G. Decius Mus, her husband, curule aedile
    Gaius Decius, her son
    Decia, her daughter
M. Valerius Clericus, his son, a tribune of Legio XVII
    Father Aurelius, his tutor

His household:

Nicenus, the majordomus
Caius Vecellius, the captain of fascitors

HOUSE SEVERUS

A. SEVERUS PATRONUS, Princeps Senatus, Senator and auctare

HIS FAMILY:

DECIA, his wife

T. SEVERUS REGULUS, his son

    VOLSILLA, his wife

A. SEVERUS AULAN, his son, a tribune of Legio III Fulgetra

M. SEVERUS TERTIUS, his son

SEVERA, his daughter

SEVERILLA, his daughter

HIS HOUSEHOLD:

DELMATIPOR, the majordomus of House Severus

HIMCRIUS, a guard

APIDAMUS, a guard

MARSUPOR, Marcius's body slave

VERAPORA, Severa's body slave

QUINTA JUL, Severa's body slave

EUDISS, a slave from Illyris Baara

D. AULAPOR, a slave

DOMITIUS, a guard

POMPONIA, a lady-in-waiting, daughter of Pomponius Mathus

T. SEVERUS LUCULLUS, Brother of A. Severus Patronus, Senator

    T. SEVERUS SEPTIMUS, his son

    A. SEVERUS SERENUS, his son

    M. SEVERUS GALLUS, his son

APP. SEVERUS PULLUS, Senator, urban praetor, provincial
    governor

    APP. SEVERUS PULLUS, his father, ex-consul

S. SEVERUS STRUCTUS, Senator, propraetor

OTHER PATRICIANS

THE GENERALS:

L. ANDRONICUS CAUDINUS, Consul Aquilae, Legate of Legio XIV, killed in Cynothicum

L. GERONTIUS, Legate of Legio XV

II. FALCONIUS BUTEO, Legate of Legio III Fulgetra

Q. MARTELLUS DURUS, Legate of the Legio Civitas

L. FAVRONIUS, Legate of the Legio Provincia

THE SENATORS:

T. MANLIUS TORQUATUS, the Consul Civitas

M. FULVIUS PAETINAS, the Consul Provincae

M. CARVILIUS MAXIMUS, an ex-consul and clausor

L. POMPILIUS FERRATUS, a senator, author of Lex Ferrata Aucta

Q. FALCONIUS METIUS, Head of House Falconius and auctare

Q. FALCONIUS RULLIANUS, senator and consular candidate

M. ANDRONICUS AQUILA, Head of House Andronicus, ex-consul, and clausor

M. ANDRONICUS DECLAMA, senator and consular candidate

V. CRESCENTIUS RUFINUS, an ex-consul and auctare

P. LICINIUS DIVES, wealthy senator

P. DECIUS MUS, ex-consul Provincae, father-in-law to Valerilla

G. CASSIANUS LONGINUS, Head of House Cassianus, ex-consul, and clausor

LUCRETIUS CAECILIUS, Head of House Lucretius, ex-consul, and clausor

L. GAERUS TILLIUS, military commander of House Gaerus and clausor

GAERUS ALBINUS, his father, Head of House Gaerus

A. LAELIUS FLAMININUS, senator and clausor

APP. APPULEIUS PANSA, senator and consular candidate

Q. CURIUS, a senator and clausor

OTHERS:

Q. FALCONIUS, a friend of M. Severus

G. MAECENAS, a patrician

CAERA, a daughter of House Caerus

FALCONILLA, a daughter of House Falconius

FALCONATERA, daughter of G. Falconius Aterus, friend of Severa, also
known as Tera

Q. FABRICIUS, son of G. Fabricius Luscinus, ex-consul

Q. SABENUS, neighbor to S. Valerius Corvus

N. VOLSIUS, a candidate for quaestor

LUCRETIUS PONTICUS, a friend of Corvinus

RUBELLIUS DRUSUS, a friend of Corvinus

CN. PALFURIUS, a candidate for aedile

GAERUS BALBUS, a candidate for aedile

APP. CASSIANUS CANINA, candidate for tribune

SEX. GAERUS FRONTINUS, a deceased author of military history

THE COMMON PEOPLE

THE PLEBIANS OF AMORR:

SILICUS CLUSIUS, a gladiator of the Blues, a dimachaerus

CALADAS THE THRAEX, a gladiator of the Reds

SER BORGULUS THE BUNNYSLAYER, a gladiator of the Greens, a dwarf

SER SNOTSHAFTER RABBITSBANE, a gladiator of the Greens, a goblin

CN. RABIRIUS, a poet

MONTANUS, a gladiator of the Reds, a retiarius

PULLUS MUCRO, Weaponsmaster of the Blues

M. LADRUS, scribe for the Blues

LAEVIUS, a poet, author of the Amorriad

OPIMIUS, an equestrian and friend of Corvinus

PAETINUS ALVUS, a city guard commander

HOSTUS HERMINIUS TUBERTUS, a candidate for tribune

THE PEOPLE OF THE PROVINCES AND ALLIED CITIES:

CLAUTUS, a merchant of Medonis

IDEMETA VENFICA, the witch woman of Seijiss

BERROGA, a messenger to Legio III

OPELIUS MACRINUS, a representative of the prince of Oscium

KING SYRMIS I, SON OF HALOS, king of Thursia

OPITER FLORUS SICULO, senator-in-chief of Solacte

CORIPPUS NOLENS, a Larinian general

HERIUS OBSIDIUS, a Marruvian general

THE KINGDOM OF SAVONDIR AND THE SEVEN SEATS

HIS ROYAL MAJESTY LOUIS-CHARLES DE MIRID, the Fourteenth of His Line

HIS FAMILY:

HER ROYAL MAJESTY INGEBORG, his wife, the queen.

CHARLES-PHILLIPE, his son, the Red Prince and Duc de Lutèce, also known as PRINCE KARL

ÉTIENNE HENRI, his son, the Duc de Chênevin

GUILHEM DONZEAU, his wizard

COURRAT, a courtier

LOYS, a courtier

JEAN-MICHEL, his son, the Comte d'Ainme

FRANÇOIS DE SAINTONGE, his son, the Comte de Belfrellieu

THE HAUT CONSEIL:

PIERRE-GASTON BONPENSIER, Archbishop du Royaume

HENRI DE RICHETTE, Bishop de Châlaons

JACQUE-RENE D'ARSEILLE, Grandmagicien, l'Académie des Sage Arts

Seigneur Antoine de Beaumille, Maréchal de Savonne

Seigneur François du Moulin, Chancelier

The Peers of the Realm:

Philippe-Charles de Mirid, his brother, Duke de Savonne

Renauld de Montbélial, Duc de Méridiony

Lothar D'Aulon, Grand Duc d'Écarlate

Chlodos D'Aulon, Comte de Aumont, his son

L'Académie des Sage Arts:

Sieur Theuderic de Merovech, an Académie battlemage, also
    Comte de Thôneaux, also known as Nicolas du Mere

Seigneur Narcisse de Segraise, an immortel

Seigneur Josce-Robinet, an immortel

Seigneur Gabrien de la Poterrie, an immortel

Laurent, an Académie mage

Charles-François, a mage

Tycelin, a mage

Patrice de Foix, a battlemage

Blais Blancas, a battlemage

The nobles and people of Savondir:

Sieur Theuderic de Merovech, the Comte de Thôneaux

Sieur Charibert, a knight, guardian of the Duc de Montrove

Huruat, the Lord Admiral

Lady Roheis Desmargoteau, the Comtesse de Domdidier, widow
    of the former Duke D'Aubonne

Henriot, a servant

Amelot, a lady-in-waiting

Maronne, a lady-in-waiting

SEIGNEUR CLOTHAR SAINT-SAVEUER, the Comte de Saint-Agliè

    ARNAUD, his man

    SEBASTIEN, his man

SIEUR OSMONT, a church knight

SIEUR GAUTIER, a church knight

SIEUR MICHEL DE PLATINS, a knight

GERARD DE COUCY, Comte de Montbrelloz, captain of cavalry

GUERMONT, a guard

JOSSON, a street thug

SIEUR JANEQUIN DE RECHEUSOIR, a knight

THE DALARN CLANS

SKULI SKULLBREAKER, Chief of the Fifteen Clans, called the Reaver King

HIS FAMILY:

    INGEBORG, his wife

    BRYNJOLF, his son

    FJOTRA, his daughter

        GEIRRID, a friend and lady-in-waiting

        SVANHVIT, a friend and lady-in-waiting

THE PEOPLE:

    STEINTHOR STRONGBOW, a Dalarn warleader

    GLAMMAD, a Dalarn warrior

    ASMUND HAIRY-ARSE, a Dalarn warrior

    NERI, a Dalarn rider

    GRENJAR, a freed thrall

THE OTHER RACES OF SELENOTH

THE DWARVES:

LODI SON OF DUNMORIN, a dwarf and former Amorran slave-gladiator

THORALD, a dwarf

THE ELVES:

LADY LITHRIEL EVERBRIGHT, a wood elf, ex-sorceress, and cousin to the King of Merithaim

LADY CAITLYS SHADOWSONG, a high elf, sorceress, and niece to the High King of Elebrion

LORD MORVAS SILVERTREE, a high elf, ambassador to the Senate and People of Amorr

MIROGLAS, companion to the elven ambassador

BESSARIAS, Magistras of the Collegium Occludum

AMITLYA, sorceress and Magistras of the Collegium Occludum

GALAMIRAS, Magistras of the Collegium Occludum

GILTHALAS, Magistras Daemonae of the Collegium Occludum

THE GOBLINS:

MEERFIN SHISTGURBLE, Third Assistant Frogcatcher and conscript in the Eight Goblin Auxiliary Foot of Zorn Narvog

GROONUL POISONSPEAR, Master Frog Hunter

WOBBRAN TWICE-BITTEN, Stoneholder

BARKMOSS, a goblin of the Aeglu tribe

OTHERS:

ASLAUGHYRNA, a drake

VERMILIGNUM, a demon

VENGIRASSE, a warhawk